PRAISE FOR M. M. KAYE'S

TRADE WIND

"TRADE WIND . . . IS A SOPHISTICATED TREAT
FOR THOSE TRADITIONAL READERS WHO FA-
VOR GOOD WRITING, SUBTLE CHARACTER
DEVELOPMENT, CLEVER PLOTTING."

—*Washington Post Book World*

The new bestseller that's "filled with excitement—
revolution, natural disasters, epidemics—and drenched
in the sensuous, lush beauty of Zanzibar . . . the best
by far of M. M. Kaye's works."

—*Chattanooga Times*

"Mollie Kaye is a storyteller of impressive flair. She
brings us, subtly interfused, the beauty and barbari-
ty of Zanzibar, characters of real substance, and a
story mighty hard to put down."

—*Publishers Weekly*

"Meticulously researched and liberally drenched in
romance . . . exciting . . . reading."

—*Des Moines Register*

A LITERARY GUILD FEATURED ALTERNATE
A DOUBLEDAY BOOK CLUB ALTERNATE

Trade Wind

M. M. KAYE

BANTAM BOOKS
TORONTO · NEW YORK · LONDON · SYDNEY

TRADE WIND

*A Bantam Book / published by arrangement with
St. Martin's Press*

PRINTING HISTORY

St. Martin's edition published July 1981
4 printings through August 1981
*A Featured Alternate Selection of Literary Guild, February 1982
and a Selection of Doubleday Book Club, March 1982*
Bantam edition / July 1982

ISBN 9-553-20901-9

Published simultaneously in the United States and Canada

*Bantam Books are published by Bantam Books, Inc. Its trade-
mark, consisting of the words "Bantam Books" and the por-
trayal of a rooster, is Registered in U.S. Patent and Trademark
Office and in other countries. Marca Registrada. Bantam
Books, Inc., 666 Fifth Avenue, New York, New York 10103.*

PRINTED IN THE UNITED STATES OF AMERICA

0 9 8 7

For
Goff, Carolyn and Nicola
with love.

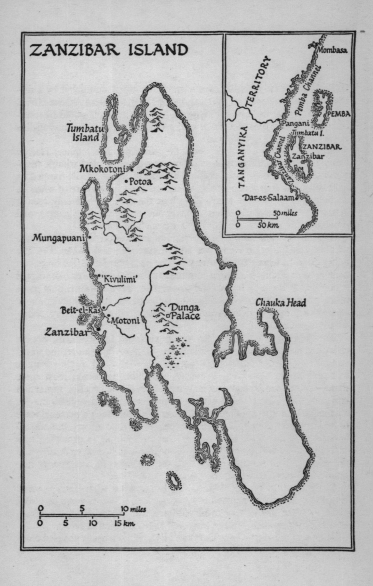

ZANZIBAR ISLAND

Tumbatu
Island

Mkokotoni

Potoa

Mungapuani

'Kivulimi'

Beit-el-Ras

Motoni

Zanzibar

Dunga
Palace

Chauka Head

0   5   10 miles
0   5   10   15 km

TANGANYIKA TERRITORY

Mombasa

Pemba Channel

PEMBA

Pangani

Tumbatu I.

ZANZIBAR

Zanzibar

Zanzibar Channel

Dar-es-Salaam

0   50 miles
0   50 km

I

In view of the far-reaching effects that a few words mumbled by a disreputable old Irishwoman were to have on the life of Hero Athena Hollis, only child of Barclay Hollis of Boston, Massachusetts, it would be interesting to know to what degree, if any, pre-natal influence was responsible for her character and opinions.

Heredity clearly had a finger in the pie, since her mother, Harriet Crayne Hollis, had always been a fervent supporter of charitable institutions, crusades and causes. A fact that Barclay, unexpectedly trapped by a classic profile and a pair of blue eyes, had been fully aware of when he became a suitor for her hand, though at the time he had only seen it as the sign of a sweetly compassionate and truly womanly nature, and proof that his Harriet's beauty was far from skin deep.

What he had not bargained for was finding himself married to a wife who expected him to share her enthusiasm for good works. But the honeymoon had been barely over when he discovered that his bride, not content with adding her name to numerous subscription lists, conceived it her duty to serve on boards and committees, write and distribute pamphlets protesting injustices and urging reforms, and campaign vigorously against such evils as drink, child labour, prostitution and slavery. Particularly slavery . . .

Barclay, an indolent and peace-loving man with a fondness for horses, chess and the classics, had never suffered from any urge to set the world and his neighbours' affairs to rights, and he considered that his Harriet was carrying things too far. Naturally any thinking person must agree that the world was (and always had been) over-full of cruelty, oppression and injustice. But it was surely both unnecessary and unfeminine for Harriet to take it so passionately to heart and make such a personal issue of it? He was, in consequence, doubly delighted when his wife announced herself pregnant, since he imagined that in addition to providing him with an heir to inherit the broad acres of Hollis Hill, maternal cares and the setting up of a nursery would divert her interests and energy into quieter and more domestic channels.

A large, healthy family, decided Barclay, was just what Hatty needed: handsome, intelligent sons who would share his own interest in Greek mythology and the raising of blood stock, and pretty, lively daughters who would keep their mother busy and fully occupied at home.

But it had not worked out like that. His wife's too easily aroused emotions, and a few lines of print on a crumpled sheet of newspaper, had put an end to that dream – and to Harriet.

The instrument of fate had been a parcel containing a knitted shawl and a pretty silver rattle, sent in anticipation of the coming event by an erst-while school-friend who had married a planter in Georgia. A sheet of newspaper had been used as an additional protection for the rattle, and on it a single paragraph, printed in bold type, had had the misfortune to catch the expectant mother's eye:

To be sold. A negro woman and four children. The woman 23 years of age, of good character, a good cook and washer. The children are very likely from 6 years down to 1½. Can be sold separately or together, to suit purchaser.

The advertisement was only one of many. But to Harriet, always a passionate opponent of slavery and herself shortly to become a mother, the callous inhumanity of that concluding sentence was like a blow in the face. *Can be sold separately or together, to suit purchaser . . .*

She had paled alarmingly and cried in a high, strangled voice: 'But surely they cannot take her children from her? Not her *own* children? They have no right! It is vile – horrible! It should be stopped! . . . Oh God why doesn't someone put a stop to it?'

Dropping the crumpled sheet of newspaper as if had been some loath-some insect, she had favoured her husband with a hysterical denunciation of the whole hideous institution of slavery, and ended by snatching up shawl, rattle and paper and flinging them violently on to the fire, where the paper, bursting into flames, created a sudden draught that sucked one of the wide muslin sleeves of Harriet's négligé into the blaze. The filmy material had flared up as if soaked in oil, and though Barclay had leapt at her and crushed out the flames with his bare hands, she had been so badly burned that the pain and shock had brought on a premature and protracted labour, and a day and a half later her daughter had been born, and Harriet herself had died.

Barclay had not married again. He had been thirty-nine when he had offered for Harriet, and his brief experience of matrimony had been enough to convince him that he was not cut out to be a family man.

Having shocked his relatives by insisting on having his daughter christ-ened 'Hero Athena' (the latter name, to make matters worse, being be-stowed in honour of a favourite mare rather than the Goddess of Wisdom), he had then touched and surprised them by declining his sister Lucy's generous offer to bring up the motherless infant among her own large and thriving family. Though if the truth were known, his refusal of Lucy's offer had not been prompted by any excess of parental feeling for the tiny, squalling hideosity in the lace-draped cot, but by the fact that Lucy too was addicted to good works. In her case, foreign missions.

Barclay felt that he had had quite enough of that sort of thing, and he had no intention of allowing his daughter to follow in her mother's footsteps and become an active and vocal supporter of Causes. In his opinion, a woman's place was in the home and not on a public platform. And had it not been for the fact that some few years later he had elected to visit a sick friend on the same evening that his daughter's governess, Miss Penbury, had promised to deliver her contribution to Lucy's latest Sale of Work, it is quite possible that Hero Athena would have obliged him in this. Though one cannot of course be sure, since she was, after all, Harriet Crayne's child. But in the event the temporary absence of Mr Hollis left the way clear for a certain Biddy Jason to pay a surreptitious call at Hollis Hill – something that would never have been allowed to happen if the master of the house had been at home!

It was said of the Widow Jason that she was the seventh daughter of the seventh son of that Bridey Clooney of Tyrone who had been famed as a Wise Woman and burned as a Witch. And it may even have been true. Certainly there were plenty of folk in Boston who were willing to believe it, and to believe too that old Mrs Jason had the Second Sight and could foretell the future: among them Mrs Cobb, the cook at Hollis Hill.

Mrs Cobb had sent word to the seeress that the coast was clear, and she was engaged in having her fortune told, in return for a packet of snuff and two ounces of China tea, when her master's daughter, six-year-old Hero Hollis, sidled into the kitchen.

By rights, Hero should have been in the nursery. But her governess would not be back for another hour, her Papa was out and she was bored with sewing the singularly dull sampler that Miss Penbury had given her to keep her occupied. She was also accustomed to doing what she pleased, so she folded up the sampler and went downstairs in search of cookies and crystallized sugar.

The lamps had not yet been lit and the hall was in darkness, but Hero could hear voices from the kitchen, while a warm gleam of light showed that the door at the far end of the long stone-flagged passage had been left ajar. She tiptoed towards it very quietly, and easing her small body through the narrow gap, stood listening in the shadow of the big dresser: enthralled by the sight of the strange, witchlike old crone in the old-fashioned tall-crowned hat, and the sound of a muttering voice that spoke of unexpected meetings, dark men and journeys over water, and warned Mrs Cobb to beware of a fair woman who boded no good.

'That'll be Alice Tilberry from the Stonehavens' place,' said Mrs Cobb, breathing heavily with excitement. 'If I ever catch the hussy . . .! Go on, tell me more.'

'There's no more,' said Biddy Jason, pushing the plump palm away.

'An' I'll thank you for the tay and the snuff. Though I'm thinking it's the master of the house should be getting me thanks, for well I know you niver paid for either!'

Hero had made no sound, and Mrs Cobb, owl-eyed and absorbed, had not seen her. But perhaps Biddy Jason was in truth the granddaughter of a witch, for though she had been sitting with her back to the door she appeared to know that Hero was there, and now, unexpectedly, she turned her head and spoke over her shoulder: 'And what is ut that you're wish-ful for, ye young spalpeen? Come away out now, and let owld Biddy get a sight av ye. My, my! 'tis a big colleen you are, and a rare pretty one too.'

The ancient creature cackled with laughter and beckoned with a gnarled and crooked finger, and Hero moved out of the shadows into the lamp-light: a small girl in a red velveteen dress, ruffled pantalettes and pina-fore, with a mop of unruly chestnut-coloured curls inadequately confined by a ribboned snood.

'Who are you?' enquired Hero, interested. 'What were you talking about?'

'Nothing to do with you, miss!' scolded Mrs Cobb. 'Just you get right back to the nursery this minute. You've no business to be creepin' about down here, giving folks a start. Go on now, or we'll be havin' that govern-ess of yours down looking for you.'

'Miss Penbury's taken a parcel over to Aunt Lucy's house, and it's cold in the nursery. What were you doing?'

'Jus' readin' av her palm I was.'

'Her palm?'

'Her hand, child. Sure an' it's all there for them that can see it. What ye'll be and what'll happen to you. Yes, yes, it's all there. Your fortune writ plain.'

Hero stared down at her own small palm and could see nothing in it except lines, and an ink stain that she had tried to remove with spit but that was still clearly visible. 'What's a fortune?' she enquired.

'The things that'll happen to you when you've grown up. The good luck an' the bad.'

'But Mrs Cobb is grown up already,' protested Hero indignantly. 'She's old! so how can she have a fortune?'

'That's enough,' said Mrs Cobb sharply. 'You'll get along out of my kitchen. Hurry now!'

But Hero was not afraid of Mrs Cobb. And nor, it seemed, was the Widow Jason, who laughed until her little eyes disappeared into folds of yellow wrinkles: 'Ah, sure now, there's always somethin' ahead of folks they don't know about, no matter how old they get. Like what'll happen to 'em tomorrow, or the next day. Or next week. Always somethin' they don't know.'

'Do *you* know, then?' demanded Hero, her eyes as round as dollars.

Biddy Jason's eyes were small and black, and despite her age very bright and observant. They reappeared now from among the wrinkles and stared into Hero's grey ones, and presently she looked away again and said in a harsh whisper, and almost as though she were talking to herself rather than to the child: 'Not always . . . No, not always. There's times it seems I do, and times I don't. But when I don't I just tells the fools what they're wishful to hear, an' that's just as good for 'em – or better!'

She gave another shrill cackle of laughter and stretching out a claw-like hand, gathered up the two small packets that Mrs Cobb had laid on the table, and stowed them away in the recesses of her rusty garments: 'I'll be goin' on me way now. 'Tis a cold night and a dark one, an' there'll be rain before long. Good day to ye, Missis Cobb.'

She rose stiffly, and Hero took another step forward and said breathlessly: 'Would you know about me? What will happen when I grow up, I mean? Do you think you could read my – my what you called it?'

She held out her hand for inspection as she had seen Mrs Cobb do, but old Biddy Jason shook her head and said sourly: 'Tell ye for free? Now how would I be getting me living if I were to tell folk their fortunes for naught? Things ye want ye have to pay for. You should be knowing that.'

'I'd ask Papa,' said Hero breathlessly. 'He'd pay you. I know he would.'

'You'll do no such thing!' intervened Mrs Cobb, understandably agitated. 'I'll not have you worritin' your Pa with such stuff, and that I tell you. Now be a good girl and quit bothering and I'll give you a sugar lump.'

'I don't want a sugar lump,' said Hero obstinately. 'I want to have my fortune told.' Suddenly, it had become important to her.

'What would you want your fortune told for?' snapped Mrs Cobb. 'You heard Mrs Jason say it was all lies, didn't you? Now be a good girl.'

But Hero was not paying attention to her. She was busy searching in the pocket of her pinafore, and now she found what she was looking for: a cheap gilt brooch that had come out of a Christmas cracker and that for months past had been one of her most cherished possessions. Even now, looking at it, she hesitated. It was such a pretty thing! But curiosity, that fatal and ineradicable legacy from Eve, was too strong for her, and she held it out and said huskily: 'I don't have any money, but you can have this. You could sell it, couldn't you? It's – it's gold!'

'*That?*' scoffed Biddy Jason. She glanced scornfully at the little trinket and then at the child's anxious face. But if she had meant to laugh, she did not. She was greedy and sly and undoubtedly dishonest and it was difficult to imagine that she had ever been young. But now some long-buried memory from her own far-off and forgotten childhood stirred to life in her, and for a moment she saw the cheap trinket as Hero saw it. An object of glittering beauty and incalculable value. *Gold . . .*!

Looked at in that light the brooch represented a magnificent fee, and one relatively far greater than the small packets of tea, snuff and sugar, or the rarer dimes and quarters, that were normally paid her in return for mumbling the time-worn and time-hallowed clichés and clap-trap that credulous women never seemed to grow tired of hearing. She reached out and took the little piece of gilded tin, and surprised herself by saying: 'Yes, that'll do. Give me your hand, child. No, not the left one: that one'll only be showin' what you could do and not what ye will. It's the other one that counts——'

She took the small pink palm between her ancient, claw-like hands, and peering at it intently was silent for so long that Hero began to get restless and to wonder anxiously if there was, after all, nothing to tell about. Perhaps, unlike Mrs Cobb, she was to have no Fortune? She could hear Mrs Cobb's stay-bones creaking to the rhythm of her heavy, indignant breathing, and presently the kettle on the hob began to sing softly to itself and the ticking of the kitchen clock became loud and intrusive, hurrying towards the moment when Miss Penbury would return from Aunt Lucy's and she, Hero, would be ordered back to the nursery.

Biddy Jason spoke at last, but in an entirely different voice from the one she had used when she had told Mrs Cobb about the fair-haired woman who boded no good. She spoke in a hoarse, low sing-song, barely above a whisper: 'There's sun in your hand, and wind and salt water. And rain . . . warm rain and an island full of black men . . .'

The wrinkled face dropped to within an inch of Hero's palm, and the whispering voice became almost inaudible: 'Ye'll sail half way round the world to meet the work that is waiting for ye to do and the one who'll help ye to do it . . . Ye'll have a hand in helpin' a power o' folk to die and a sight more to live, an' ye'll get hard words for the one and no thanks for the other. Ye'll lay your hand on gold past counting, but no good will ye get of it. And all your life ye'll do what you have to do. Ye'll make your own bed . . . an' ye'll lie on it . . .'

The hoarse murmur died into silence and the old woman released Hero's hand and backed away, shaking her head as though to free it from something, and looking dazed and stupid. The little brooch fell to the floor and Hero picked it up and held it out to her, but she pushed it away muttering: 'Keep it, child. 'Tis no manner av use to me. No use . . . wind and salt water and trees like broomsticks – and brown men and black a' dyin'. Dyin' in the sun and the rain . . .'

She stumbled towards the door, hugging her rusty black shawl about her shoulders and mumbling something about 'dogs and dead men', and then the kitchen door shut behind her and Mrs Cobb said loudly and angrily: 'There now! – didn't I tell you it 'ud all be lies? Black men and trees like broomsticks, indeed! Stuffin' your head up with such nonsense. What your Pa 'ud say——'

She crossed quickly to the dresser, and lifting down the big blue and white crock where the sugar was kept, fumbled in it for the largest lump she could find. 'Here you are, you just suck that and keep your little mouth shut.' Her voice took on a wheedling tone: 'She's a wicked old woman, that one, and I wouldn't have let her put a foot inside my kitchen only she came begging to the door and I hadn't the heart to turn the poor creature away: not without giving her a scraping of tea and a sit by the fire for the sake o' Christian charity. But your Pa wouldn't like it, and that's a fact, so you be a good girl and don't go tattling to him and gettin' me in trouble. Just you forget it, see?'

But Hero had never forgotten it.

Sun and wind and salt water, and an island full of black men . . .

'Are there really trees like broomsticks?' she enquired of her father next day.

'Like broomsticks? Do you mean palm trees?' Barclay smiled indulgently at his spoilt only child: 'Who's been telling you about palm trees?'

'No one. I just wondered. Where do they grow?'

'Any place where it's hot enough to suit them. They like plenty of sun. Places like Florida and Louisiana and the West Indies. And India and Africa.'

'Not in Boston?'

'No, not in Boston. Look, I'll show you.'

Barclay laid aside Plutarch's *Life of Lycurgus*, and taking her over to the low table by the library windows showed her the big softly-coloured globe that stood on it, pointing out the poles and the oceans, the cold countries and the hot: 'This one is Africa, where the negroes come from. Zulus and Hottentots and men who are seven feet tall and pygmies who are no higher than your knee.'

'Negroes?' Hero's face fell. 'You mean people like Washington Judd and Sary Boker?'

'That's right.'

'But they came from Mississippi,' said Hero disgustedly. 'I know they did, 'cos Sary told me so herself, and Mrs Cobb says they're just runaway niggers an' one day they'll be cotched and taken back to their master who'll whale the livin' daylights out of them an' serve them right. What are livin' daylights, Pa?'

'Mrs Cobb is an old——' began Barclay hastily, and turned the word into a cough. 'Well, maybe they did come from Mississippi, but their parents and their grandparents came from Africa.'

'Why did they? Didn't they like it there?'

'I guess they liked it all right. But slaves were needed to work the plantations, so people caught the poor creatures and shipped them over here to be sold for good money to the planters. And now their children and their children's children are born as slaves and have no country of their own.'

'Then why don't they go back?'

'Because that would take ships and money and a lot of other things they haven't got. Freedom, for one. Besides, how would they know where to go back to? Africa's a pretty big country you know, Hero.'

'How big?'

'Oh – bigger than America. And a lot wilder. They have lions and giraffes and elephants there, and apes and ivory, and – "*men whose heads do grow beneath their shoulders*".'

'Like this——?' enquired Hero, hunching her small shoulders up to her ears and dropping her chin into the front of her starched pinafore.

'Maybe. Nobody really knows very much about the middle of Africa yet. But people are finding out, and any day now a white man may climb the Mountains of the Moon or find King Solomon's mines.'

'Is Africa an island, Papa?'

'No, it's a continent.' Barclay picked up a pencil and using it as a pointer said: 'Look – these little bits round the edge are islands. That big one is Madagascar and these are the Comoro Islands. And this is Zanzibar, where the clove trees grow, and all kinds of other spices that Mrs Cobb puts in your Christmas cake.'

Hero bent to stare at the minute speck as though searching for those spices, and presently she laid a small possessive finger on it and said firmly: 'Then I shall choose that one, because it has a nice name and I should like my island to have a nice name.'

'Zanzibar? Yes, it is a pretty name. A singing name. But what's all this about your island?'

'When I'm grown up I'm going to go there.'

'Are you, my daughter? What for?'

'To – to do something,' said Hero vaguely.

'Going to pick yourself a pocket-full of cloves, eh, Hero?'

Hero considered the question gravely. 'No, I don't think so. I don't think it's *that* kind of work. I think,' she said making up her mind, 'that I shall do something very good and useful. And very clever.'

'Oh, you will, will you? You sure sound very certain about it, daughter.

Let's hope you ain't going to take after your——' he checked himself abruptly. Had he really been about to say 'your mother?' If so, he changed it, for after a brief pause he said instead, and with unnecessary heat, '– your Aunt Lucy. I don't want you to grow up into a strong-minded little busybody. Or a prig. I don't think I could stand it.'

'What's a prig, Papa?'

'You are, when you talk like that!' said Barclay irritably. 'I suppose that prissy, feather-headed milk-sop of a Penbury woman has been reading you improving books and filling your head with a lot of clap-trap about Good Works being the only thing worth doing. I might have known it from the way she dresses and the fact that your Aunt Lucy approves of her!'

He paused to cast a mental eye over Miss Penbury and his sister Lucy, and suffered a sharp spasm of sheer panic. Lucy had approved of his marriage to Harriet, and Harriet herself would undoubtedly have approved of Miss Penbury . . .

He said violently, and as though he were defying them all: 'I'm damned if I'm going to have 'em turn you into a priggish little do-gooder! I'll get you another governess. A pretty one with a sense of humour, who'll know how to keep you in order – which is more than Miss Penbury does! It looks to me as if I can't do it soon enough.'

But of course he had done nothing of the sort. It had been too much trouble and Barclay Hollis was an easy-going man who preferred to avoid trouble – and anything else that might interfere with his reading and riding and the pleasant placid routine of his life. Agnes Penbury stayed, and Hero grew up spoilt, strong-minded and undeniably priggish. And still firmly convinced that she would one day set sail for Zanzibar, though anyone less self-willed would have abandoned such an idea in her early teens: if only because of her father's strongly expressed detestation of what he called 'traipsing around' (a term that apparently included everything from foreign travel to a journey involving more than a single night away from Hollis Hill).

In later years it had taken all her powers of persuasion to coax him into travelling as far as Washington in order to stay with a Crayne cousin whose husband was a well-known Senator, and when, while there, they had received a pressing invitation to visit relatives in South Carolina, Barclay – who could on occasions be every bit as obstinate as his daughter – had flatly refused to move a step further, so that in the end Hero had gone without him.

'I guess you get it from your Mama's side of the family,' sighed Barclay resignedly; 'all the Craynes have been great ones for moving around. You look a lot like your Ma, and maybe if she'd lived she'd have come to be a gadabout too. She wasn't as big as you . . . You know, you ought to have been a boy, Hero. Mother Nature sure changed her mind about you at the last minute, and that's a fact!'

He had sighed again as he said it, and Hero had wondered for the first time if her father regretted her sex and would have preferred a boy, and if that might not have been in his mind when he had named her 'Hero' instead of calling her Harriet after her mother? He had certainly never made any attempt to bring her up as a 'womanly woman', but in defiance of the Craynes and his sister Lucy had permitted her to learn to shoot and ride, to read before she could write and write before she could sew. The remainder of her education, however, had been left to Miss Penbury, and he had done nothing to correct some of the opinions that his daughter acquired at second-hand from her governess and her Aunt Lucy; or from sundry works of fiction obtained from the shelves of the 'Ladies' Lending Library'.

It had been a popular novel by Mrs Harriet Beecher Stowe, read in 1852 at the impressionable age of fourteen, that had convinced Hero that the world was a hotbed of injustice, cruelty and squalor, and that something should be done about it at once. *Uncle Tom's Cabin* had succeeded in making yet another convert to the cause of Anti-Slavery, and Miss Penbury, in the process of continuing the good work, had escorted her young charge to a lecture on the 'Evils of the Slave Trade', given by a local parson who had quoted the words of Lord Palmerston:

'If all the crimes which the human race has committed from creation down to the present day were added together in one vast aggregate, they would scarcely equal, I am sure they would not exceed, the amount of guilt that has been incurred by mankind in connection with the diabolical Slave Trade.'

But whatever she might think of slave trading, that visit to South Carolina had served to modify Hero's view on slave owners, for the Langly family's slaves had been as healthy, happy and as well-cared-for a community as anyone could wish to see, and neither Gaylord Langly nor his overseer even remotely resembled Simon Legree. Clarissa Hollis Langly, having been born and raised in Massachusetts, disapproved in principle of slavery, but confessed herself unable to see any way out of it:

'It is as though we were caught in a trap,' she explained to Hero. 'Our entire economy is bound up with slavery, and if we were to free the negroes we should not only ruin ourselves but them as well, since without slave labour the South could not last a day. We would all go bankrupt, and then who would feed the negroes? or clothe them or give them work? Not the Northern Abolitionists, for all their pious talk! I can see no way out: though it is at times a sad weight on my conscience.'

16

Mrs Langly applied salve to her conscience by taking a fervent interest in foreign missions, in the belief that if there was nothing that could be done towards freeing the enslaved negroes of America, at least there was much that could be done towards improving the lot of coloured races overseas. She lent her young cousin a number of pamphlets that vividly described the horrors of life in Africa and Asia, with the result that Hero's sympathies had been widened to include 'Our Poor Heathen Sisters' whose status in harems and zenanas appeared to be quite as bad as that of any slave.

Brooding upon the fate of these unhappy women, it had seemed to Hero cruelly unfair that while she herself enjoyed the full benefits of freedom in a civilized and prosperous country, hapless millions in Eastern lands were doomed to live and die in unrelieved misery for lack of a little enlightenment – a crumb from the Rich Man's table. There were even times when she could almost imagine that those anonymous, suffering millions were calling to her: the sequestered women in harems and seraglios, the slaves in the black holds of dhows and the disease-ridden poor . . . 'Come over into Macedonia and help us' . . . !

'I must learn something about nursing,' decided Hero. And to the dismay of her father and the strongly expressed disapproval of her relations she had actually done so. Going three days a week to a local Charity Hospital whose staff had been only too glad to accept the services of an unpaid voluntary assistant, and whose head doctor had informed her disgruntled parent that his daughter was not only a born nurse, but a credit to her sex: 'We get a heap of rough characters in our wards, Mr Hollis,' said the doctor, 'but you ought to see the way their eyes light up when your girl comes in. She seems to be able to comfort them; and to give them confidence that they'll get well, which is half the battle. They just about worship her. Even the worst of them!'

But Barclay was not to be placated by such praise, and he continued to regard Hero's visits to the hospital with a baffled mixture of disbelief and aversion. 'If I'd known what bees you were going to bring back in your bonnet, damned if I'd ever have let you go traipsing around in Carolina with those Langlys!' he observed sourly.

He was not to know that the shorter stay in Washington was to have a far greater effect on his daughter's future than all Clarissa Langly's pamphlets. The reason being that the Crayne cousins in the capital had entertained lavishly for their guests, and since their friends were largely drawn from Government circles, Hero had been able to hold forth on her favourite topics (slavery and the sad state of that infamous centre of the trade, Zanzibar) to a wide variety of disconcerted Senators and Congressmen. So that when, a few months afterwards, hearing that her Uncle

17

Nathaniel had been appointed American Consul in Zanzibar, his brother Barclay had declared it to be an odd coincidence and his niece had seen it as the finger of fate, neither had been right. For in point of fact a solid hour of Hero's conversation during an evening party at Cousin Louella's house, had caused the name of 'Hollis' to become so inextricably linked with Zanzibar in the mind of one influential guest, that the appointment had been more in the nature of a reflex action.

Uncle Nathaniel had not been pleased, but he was too conscientious a man to contest the posting; and Hero Athena, sublimely unaware of being in any way responsible, had been torn between awe and envy. It was unbelievable! Zanzibar – her chosen island! . . . and Aunt Abby and Cousin Cressy would be going with him; and Clayton too. If only . . . If only . . .!

But there had never been any question of her accompanying them. And in any case, relations between the two families had recently become strained, owing to Barclay having taken a sudden and violent dislike to his brother's step-son, Clayton Mayo.

Long ago, on the occasion of his daughter's christening, Barclay had hotly defended his choice of names for the motherless infant: 'Just you wait!' he had retorted to the shocked chorus of disapproval: 'She'll have them swimming the Hellespont in droves one of these days. She's going to be a beauty, is my girl. You'll see!'

Well, he had been right in the last of those predictions, because Hero had certainly grown up to be a beauty. But a beauty without an ounce of coquetry or feminine allure. 'The best lookin' gal in Boston,' as her cousin Hartley Crayne had been heard to remark, 'and the biggest goddamned bore!' By the time she celebrated her twentieth birthday – and according to the standards of the day was in grave danger of being classed as an Old Maid – there had still been no sign of any Leander: unless her Uncle Nathaniel's handsome step-son, Clayton Mayo, could be regarded as a possible swimmer of the Hellespont. Numerous young men had looked and admired. But only from a distance, for a closer acquaintance had invariably resulted in disappointment and a hasty retreat; the young sparks of Boston preferring dimpled and sweetly feminine charmers to Grecian goddesses who looked them squarely in the eye, had no patience with coyness, swooning or the vapours, and considered flirting vulgar.

Clayton Mayo had proved to be the solitary exception. But Barclay, in his daughter's opinion, had been impossible about Clay!

Hero was well aware that her father (when he took the trouble to think about it!) was worried by the lack of suitors for her hand. Yet he had been extravagantly annoyed by young Mr Mayo's attentions to her, and greatly relieved when Clayton had agreed to accompany his step-father to Zanzibar in the semi-official capacity of confidential secretary.

Hero had not seen Clayton again, but in a letter smuggled to her by a sympathetic housemaid he had promised to 'prove by his constancy the enduring nature of his regard', and to return one day, having made his fortune, and formally request her hand in marriage. Which, though gratifying, was hardly romantic. But then it had not been a particularly romantic affair.

Clay had only kissed her once – and then on the cheek, because realizing his intention she had suddenly taken fright and turned her head away at the last moment. And after he had sailed and the strife and agitation had had time to subside, she was inclined to think that perhaps everything had turned out for the best, because until her father had interfered she had not been in the least certain about her feeling for Clay.

Then, little more than a year later, Barclay died very suddenly from a heart attack, and after that there was nothing to keep his daughter in Boston or prevent her from setting out in search of her destiny. Nothing but an unbearably empty house, for even Miss Penbury had long since retired to a cottage in Pennsylvania. Hero Athena Hollis was free to do what she liked and go where she wished, and when Aunt Abby's letter arrived urging her to visit them in Zanzibar, she had accepted thankfully and without hesitation. And without pausing to remember that old Biddy Jason, who had spoken of sun and salt water and an island full of black men, had also said: 'Things you want, you have to pay for.' Whether Clayton was one of those things remained to be seen.

There had, of course, been difficulties. Cousin Josiah Crayne, who as Chairman and co-owner of the Crayne Line Clippers might have been expected to help, had been deeply shocked. It was unthinkable that any young woman of his family (Hero must not forget that her own dear mother had been a Crayne!) should even contemplate a voyage to such an outlandish spot – and without so much as a maid or a chaperone to accompany her! He would have nothing to do with it, and he had taken the opportunity to read her a blunt lecture to the effect that people who felt called upon to do good to others had much better make a start in their own back-yard rather than in someone else's. She would find, said Cousin Josiah, plenty of scope for her charitable instincts right here in Massachusetts.

He had not been the only one to express disapproval. Numerous other relatives and connections had not hesitated to add their own strictures, but neither lectures nor family disapproval had altered Hero's decision: for save in the matter of Clayton she had always had her own way and got what she wanted, and now she wanted to go to Zanzibar. Not only as an escape from grief or to see Clay again, but because she was firmly convinced (or, as Josiah Crayne observed tartly, had convinced herself), that

Providence intended her to go. She had always known that there was work there for her to do. And in the event there was no one with the authority to stop her, since in addition to being in sole possession of a considerable fortune, she had now turned twenty-one and was her own mistress.

Cousin Josiah gave up the unequal struggle and arranged a passage for her on one of his own clippers. And since he had also managed to placate family opinion by conjuring up a chaperone for her in the person of the captain's wife, in the spring of 1859 Hero at last set sail for Zanzibar.

2

''Ere she comes, sir!'

The *Daffodil*'s coxswain spoke in a hoarse whisper, as though he were afraid that even in that surf-loud, murmurous night, any more audible sound might carry to the deck of the distant ship that was slowly emerging from among the trees and the tall coral rocks that masked the entrance to a small, hidden bay.

Few were aware of the existence of that bay. And those few used it exclusively for unlawful purposes. It did not appear on the official maps of the East African coast or figure on any Admiralty chart, and Lieutenant Larrimore, in command of Her Britannic Majesty's steam sloop, *Daffodil*, had frequently passed within half a mile of it without even suspecting that what appeared to be part of the mainland was, in reality, a high, narrow reef of wind-worn coral, topped by a tangle of palms and tropical vegetation, and concealing a small, deep bay capable of sheltering half a dozen sea-going dhows.

Daniel Larrimore knew the coastal waters between Lourenço Marques and Mogadishu well, for he had spent the best part of the last five years assisting in the thankless task of suppressing the East African slave trade: that traffic having greatly increased of late as the trade shrank on the West Coast, where stricter surveillance and the strengthening of the West African and Cape Squadrons had combined to make slaving an increasingly dangerous and unprofitable venture. Although he had on occasion heard rumours of a hidden bay, he had never been able to confirm them, and as recently as a week ago would have been inclined to dismiss them as fables. On the previous Thursday, however, while his ship was engaged in taking on water and supplies of fresh food at Zanzibar, one of the negro slaves whom the Arab contractor employed to carry baskets of fruit and vegetables on board had plucked furtively at his sleeve and whispered a highly interesting piece of information . . .

The hidden harbour, it appeared, was no myth, but a secure and secret haven known to certain of the Arab slave traders, where they could embark slaves in safety, take refuge from storms and doldrums, and lie concealed when naval vessels were known to be on the prowl. Moreover, a notorious English-owned schooner, loaded with illegal cargo, would be leaving it at nightfall the following Tuesday, bound for an unknown destination.

The information had been both detailed and circumstantial, but the negro could not be persuaded to tell how he had come by it, and when pressed had become frightened and stupid, and backing away, muttered that he did not understand the white man's talk.

Lieutenant Larrimore had been of two minds whether to believe him or not. Yet the story not only confirmed those earlier rumours, but explained how certain ships, sighted and pursued towards sundown, had managed to escape in the darkness when their sailing speeds were certainly not superior to his own. At least there could be no harm in acting upon the information; and the *Daffodil* had raised steam and left Zanzibar on the following day, heading northwards; her commanding officer having announced his intention of visiting Mombasa.

Once out of sight of the island, however, he had altered course, and turning south crept down the coast as close to the shore as reefs would permit. And now, late on the Tuesday evening, his ship lay in wait; lights darkened and full steam up, keeping watch on the barely visible break in the long, uneven line of coral cliffs and dark jungle, and rocking idly to the slow-breathing swell that broke lazily and monotonously against the darkened shore.

There had been little wind that day, or for many days; but an hour ago a breeze had arisen with the rising moon, and now it blew strongly off the land, dispersing at last the stinging, singing cloud of mosquitoes that had been plaguing the watchers, and bringing with it the taint of an odour; rancid, sickly, and entirely horrible.

''*Strewth!*' muttered the coxswain, grimacing with disgust: 'Stinks like a floating sewer, don't she? Must 'av a full load on board this trip; and 'arf of 'em dead already, I'd say. You'd think them dhows would 'av more sense than to kill off their own goods, wouldn't yer?'

'This one isn't a dhow,' said Lieutenant Larrimore grimly. 'If my information is correct, it's a bird of a very different feather. Look——'

The slave ship had edged forward into the unseen passage, and now the moonlight caught her full on and she was no longer a shadowy and unidentifiable shape, but a thing of silver, picking her way cautiously through the narrow channel under jib and foresail, and sounding as she went.

'Schooner!' exclaimed the coxswain. 'I believe it's – no, it couldn't be ... By goles, sir, I believe it is! Look at the cut of 'er jib – if that 'aint the *Virago*, I'm a Dutchman!'

'So that negro was right,' said the Lieutenant between his teeth. 'It *is* Frost – we've got him at last, and red-handed.'

He whirled round and yelled: 'Up anchor! Headsails out! Full speed ahead!'

The anchor came up with a rattle that drowned the slow crash and mumble of the surf, furled sails blossomed white in the moonlight, and smoke and sparks lit the blue of the night as the paddles threshed and turned.

The schooner had seen them, but too late. She was too nearly free of the channel to check or turn, and there was nothing for it but to crowd on sail and go forward; and winning clear of the shoals she came about and fled before the strengthening wind, heeling to larboard with the long wake of foam streaming out behind her like a shimmering path across the dancing sea.

Colours broke from her masthead and fluttered in the breeze, but by the light of the half moon it was difficult to make out what they were, until a midshipman staring through a telescope announced: 'American, sir. She's hoisted the stars-and-stripes.'

'Has she, by God,' snarled the Lieutenant. 'That trick may work with the West Coast Squadron, but it won't with me. There's nothing American about that bastard except his blasted impertinence. Put a shot across him, Bates.'

'Ay, ay, sir.'

There was a flash and a boom, and the shot passed over the schooner's masthead and plunged into the sea beyond.

'They're lightening ship, sir.'

The fleeing shape ahead of them was flinging everything movable overboard. Spars, casks and timber flashed briefly in the moonlight and bobbed away in the creaming wake, and as the breeze freshened the tiny dark figures of her crew could be seen throwing water on her straining canvas and scrambling from one side to the other to trim the ship.

Even in those light airs she was faster than Lieutenant Larrimore had thought possible, and it was obvious that she was being handled in a masterly manner. He began to realize that even with the advantage of steam in his favour she might draw away from him if the breeze continued to strengthen, for he could not keep up the chase for long – the Admiralty being notoriously parsimonious in the matter of fuel, his supply of coal was far from adequate.

'Come on! come on, blast you!' muttered the Lieutenant, apparently urging the threshing paddles to greater speed: 'We can't let that chousing scug get away from us this time. God damn this wind! If only . . .' He turned abruptly to snap out an order to the coxswain demanding another knot from the engine room. Two, if possible.

But half an hour later the schooner was not only still ahead of him, but appeared to be increasing her lead. And though the *Daffodil*'s guns had scored several hits, a cross swell combined with the uncertain light had not been conducive to good shooting, and none of them had served to slow the slaver's pace.

Lieutenant Larrimore, fuming, was recklessly ordering the fires to be stoked to danger point, when a lucky shot cut away the schooner's steering sails. She yawed and lost way, and five minutes later another shot ripped through her mainsail and the taut canvas split and fell idle. The crippled ship hauled down her colours and hove to – though only backing her fore topsail, and leaving her fore and aft sails still set.

The Lieutenant, observing this last, remarked grimly that Rory Frost must think he was born yesterday.

'If he imagines that he can trick me into lowering a boat, and then pile on sail and run for it while we're getting back on board again, he's much mistaken.'

He picked up a speaking trumpet and yelled through it:

'Lower your sails at once, and come aboard!'

The breeze distorted the reply so that the words were unintelligible, but the coxswain, who was peering through a telescope, ripped out a sudden oath, and said: 'It 'aint the *Virago*, sir. Same build, but she's a shade sharper forrard, an' she 'aint got the port'oles.'

'Nonsense! There isn't another ship in these waters that—— Here, give me that.'

He snatched the telescope and peered through it at the drifting moonlit ship with the torn mainsail, and then put it down again and said heavily: '*Damn and blast!*'

'Probably a genuine Yankee after all,' said the Assistant-Surgeon apprehensively. 'If she is, we're for it.'

'Hell to that! she's a slaver – you can smell her,' snapped Lieutenant Larrimore. 'I'm going aboard.'

He picked up the trumpet again, and shouted through it, and this time the reply was audible:

'*No understand Inglese!*'

'That's a relief. Try him with French,' suggested the surgeon.

The Lieutenant's French, however, produced no result, and losing patience he issued a curt order to the gun's crew to fire at the slaver's jib halyard block and to continue doing so until it was cut away.

'Good shooting,' commended Lieutenant Larrimore, watching the halyard block come rattling down. 'Lower a boat. I'm going over.'

'You cannot board me!' yelled a bearded man in a peaked cap, whose suit may have once been white, but which even by moonlight showed blotched and stained with dirt and sweat of many seasons. 'It is illegal! I am *Americano*! I report you to your Consul! I make much trouble for you!'

He appeared to have learned to speak English with remarkable rapidity. 'You can report me to the Archangel Gabriel if you wish,' retorted the Lieutenant, and scrambled aboard.

Five years in the East African Squadron should have inured Daniel Larrimore to horrors, but he had never got used to the sight and stench of human suffering, and each time he witnessed it, it seemed to him like the first time – and the worst. Mr Wilson, the coxswain, a hearty, grizzled mariner newly out from home, took one look at the schooner's crowded and filthy deck and was instantly and violently sick, while the Assistant-Surgeon turned an unhealthy green and found himself feeling oddly faint as the intolerable stench took him by the throat.

The ship was crammed with naked slaves: their emaciated black bodies patched with festering sores, their ankles and wrists chafed and bleeding from heavy iron fetters or gangrenous from ropes that had been tied so tightly that they had eaten into the dark flesh. The schooner's hatchways had been secured by iron crossbars, and pressed against them from below were the heads of men, women and children who had been packed into the hot, dark, airless space as though they had been bales of cloth; crouching ankle deep in their own filth, unable to move and barely able to breathe, and chained together so that the starving, dying, tortured living were still manacled to the decomposing bodies of the fortunate dead.

Apart from the crew there were three hundred captive negroes on the schooner, and of these eighteen were found to be dead, while a dozen more lay on the deck, huddled together at the foot of the foremast and dying of disease and starvation.

'Bring 'em up,' ordered Dan Larrimore, his voice as hard and expressionless as his rigid face. He stood back while they were drawn up through the small hatches to collapse on to the deck where some lay still and moaned, while others crawled feebly to the scuppers and licked the salt water with tongues that were blackened and swollen from thirst.

More than half of the captives were children. Boys and girls whose ages ranged from eight to fourteen years, who had been captured by men of their own race to be sold into slavery for a handful of china beads or a cheap knife. Young and defenceless creatures who had committed no crime against humanity, but who represented a fat profit in counted coin, and whose hands were needed for planting, tending and picking the sugar-cane and cotton on rich plantations on the other side of the world. In Cuba and Brazil, the West Indies and the Southern States of America.

'And we dare to call ourselves Christians!' thought Dan Larrimore bitterly. 'We have the infernal impudence to send out missions to the heathen and preach sanctimonious sermons from our pulpits. And half

Spain and Portugal and South America light candles to the saints and burn incense and go to Confession, and can hardly move for priests and churches and statues of the Virgin. It's enough to make one vomit . . .'

A dazed, emaciated negress stumbled towards the rail, holding in her arms the body of a child whose skull had been crushed, and seeing that the ugly wound was fresh and bleeding, Dan said sharply: 'How did that happen?'

The woman shook her head dumbly, and he repeated the question in her own tongue.

'My son cried when your ship came near,' said the woman in a parched whisper, 'and the overseer feared that you might hear and struck him with an iron bar.'

She turned away from him, and leaning over the rail dropped the little body into the sea. And before he could stop her, or even realize what she was about, she climbed onto the rail and leapt in after it.

Her head surfaced only once, and as it did so a black, triangular fin sliced through the water. There was a swirl and a splash and the sea was stained with something that would have been red by daylight but that by moonlight showed only as a spreading patch of oily darkness. Then the shark sank out of sight, and the woman with it. Presently other bodies were sent to join them as the dead were separated from the living and flung overboard, and the scavengers of the deep tore them in pieces and dragged them under, and the waves washed the sea clean again.

The slaver's boats were lowered, and her hapless cargo – dazed, apathetic and convinced that they were merely falling from the clutches of one set of brutal captors into the hands of another and possibly worse one – were transferred to the *Daffodil* to the accompaniment of hysterical threats from their late owner.

The schooner's Captain stormed and raged, calling down curses upon the collective heads of the entire British Navy, and shouting that his name was Peter Fenner, and that he was an American citizen and Perfidious Albion would be made to pay dearly for having fired upon him. But his log had been written in Spanish, his flag lockers proved to contain the flags of a dozen different nations, and his papers gave his name as Pedro Fernandez and his 'Country of residence' as Cuba.

'What do you propose to do with him?' demanded the Assistant-Surgeon, gulping brandy from a bottle that he had found in the Captain's cabin – for he, like the coxswain, was new to the realities of slave trading. 'If we take him back to Zanzibar they'll only keep him there for a month or so, and then ship him off to some place like Lourenço Marques where he'll be treated like a prodigal son and allowed to get off scot free. And we haven't enough coal to take him to the Cape.'

'I know. That's why we're going to leave him here.'

The slaver's Captain, smiling broadly, spoke insolently over his shoulder, and in Spanish, to his first mate:

'You see, Sanchez? They can do nothing. They dare not hold us, and when they have gone we shall go back and pick up more slaves, and these pigs will not even know. *Por Dios!* What fools are these English!'

Lieutenant Larrimore returned the smile, though less pleasantly, and remarked in the same language: 'But not too foolish to speak Spanish – which is unfortunate for you Señor *Perro* (dog) is it not?'

He turned back to the Assistant-Surgeon and continued as though there had been no interruption:

'We're well clear of the land and the wind seems to be dying down again, so I shall sink his boats and confiscate his canvas. We'll let him keep some food and water – about the same amount, and in the same proportion, that he seems to have considered sufficient for those poor devils. Agreed?'

'Agreed!' said the Assistant-Surgeon briskly. 'I shall enjoy seeing to it.'

They finished the brandy and returned to the deck, where the boarding party unbent all the sails and removed every shred of canvas ('Nothing to stop them using their bedding to rig up a jib,' suggested the Lieutenant unkindly), unreeved all the rigging, threw guns, bunting, and every movable object overboard, let go both anchors to the limit of their chains, and dealt drastically with both food and water.

'And you can thank us,' said Lieutenant Larrimore in conclusion, 'for leaving you a compass.'

He climbed over the side and was rowed back to the *Daffodil* in the first pale light of dawn: unaware that behind him a dhow that had also been lurking in the hidden bay, and that had left it as soon as the chase had moved far enough out to sea, had slipped away unseen and set her course due south for a rendezvous that was no more than a pin-point on a well-thumbed chart.

3

Captain Thaddaeus Fullbright of the *Norah Crayne*, ninety-eight days out from Boston, glanced at the barometer for the fourth time in ten minutes, and frowned. The sea was as flat and as motionless as it had been for the past three weeks, but the glass continued to fall, and although it was midday the sun was still veiled by a hot, tarnished haze that was neither fog nor cloud.

It was an ugly and unseasonable haze, and it disturbed Captain Fullbright, for this was normally the season of swift passages; of roaring blue seas and scudding cloud shadows. But ever since they had rounded the Cape they had met with nothing but this unnatural calm and these rusty, hazy days. The *Norah Crayne* had idled up the coast of Africa, often making less than a knot, and now it began to look as though they would be lucky if they made land in another ten days.

'If at all!' muttered Captain Fullbright. And was startled to discover that he had spoken the words aloud.

It was a measure of his anxiety that he could even entertain such a thought, let alone put it into words, and it occurred to him that at this rate he would soon be emulating Tod MacKechnie, that maundering old Scotsman back in Durban who had discoursed so depressingly on death and the Judgements of Jehovah.

'*Bah!*' said Captain Fullbright, addressing himself impartially to the barometer and the shade of the absent MacKechnie. He turned his back abruptly upon both, and staring out at the flat leagues of tarnished silver, wondered pessimistically what further mischances might lie in wait before he saw Boston harbour again.

It had been a bad voyage so far, and he regretted this as much for his wife's sake as his own, for it was not often that Amelia was permitted to accompany him. The owners had never previously encouraged it, and she would not have been here now if a cousin of the Craynes' had not happened to be the only lady among a long list of male passengers, and Josiah Crayne, being strongly opposed to Miss Hollis travelling unchaperoned, had not personally requested Amelia's presence.

Mr Crane would have done better, thought Captain Thaddaeus wryly, to prevent his young cousin from sailing at all. But then Miss Hollis appeared to be a headstrong young woman who was obviously accustomed to having her own way, and Josiah Crayne had probably found it less fatiguing to let her have it than to attempt to argue with her. It was also possible that he was not altogether sorry to be temporarily rid of her!

Captain Fullbright grinned to himself; and immediately suffered a twinge of remorse. It was plumb ungrateful of him to criticize a girl who had heroically conquered her own nausea, and reversing their roles, nursed her chaperone through several bad bouts of seasickness. His poor Amelia – she had been so delighted at the prospect of accompanying him on this voyage, but he feared that it was proving a sad disappointment to her, for it had been an ill-fated trip from the start. The weather had been stormy and inclement, and at Bermuda one of the cabin stewards had been left behind in hospital with broken ribs. A deckhand had been swept overboard and drowned off the Cape Verde Islands, and another died from an outbreak of malignant fever in the Gulf of Guinea. And now the Trades had failed!

'It's a gey ill year,' Mr MacKechnie the ship-chandler had said in his dockside office in Durban as he checked the list of stores that the Captain was buying: 'Aye, a verra ill year! I doot but it'll be the waurk o' the Lorrd as a punishment on the sinfu' worrld for the continuin' evil o' slavery. First 'twas the rains failed and then 'twas the winds. And now there's a tale that awa' back in the bad lands there's a pestilence broke out that's killin' off the tribes like a black frost'll kill the greenfly, until soon there'll be naebody left alive in Africa, and a' the great land will be as empty as the back o' me hand! 'Tis the Judgement o' the Lorrd, and if ye are a wise mon, Mr Fullbright, ye'll keep awa' frae the coast this trup.'

Captain Thaddaeus had been moved to retort that if the Lord intended to deal out punishment for the evils of slavery, it was surely illogical that He should vent His wrath upon the Africans, who were the hapless victims and chief sufferers from the trade, instead of upon the Europeans who had reaped much profit from it.

'Europeans, did ye say?' enquired Mr MacKechnie, wagging his white head and looking at the Captain with bleary, near-sighted eyes that yet retained a disconcerting gleam of northern shrewdness. 'But is it no a fact that in the last twa years nae less than five-and-twenty slave ships ha' been built and fitted out in the porrt o' New York alone? Or that your ain nation is fallin' apart and dividin' and quarrellin' on account o' this verra question o' slavery? It's my opeenion there are few worse evils than bad blood between brithers, an' maybe ye'll find that the Judgements o' Jehovah ha' fallen upon those that profited by the black trade, ta'gither wi' those who engaged in it. Aye! an' a' those that did little tae prevent it or put it doon! As fer the puir benighted heathen themselves, 'twas more often than not their ain blood and kin that caught them and drove them like kine and sold the puir deevils into slavery – thae Judases!

I'm a God-fearing mon, and I've nae doot but it's their ain evil murderin' ways that have tried the patience o' the Almighty, and that He has sent a pestilence to wipe them frae the face o' the earth as a punishment on the evil-doers, and a mair mairciful release for the innocent than slow death in the bight o' a slave ship. *Imphmn!'*

After which weighty pronouncement the God-fearing man had attempted to cheat Captain Fullbright in the matter of ships stores and fresh vegetables. But although he had not succeeded in this, for some unaccountable reason his senile croakings had lingered uncomfortably in the Captain's mind, nagging at him with the persistence of circling flies, until he was almost tempted to believe that the hot, miasmic haze that lay along the sullen sea and obscured the horizon was an emanation of the pestilence that old Tod MacKechnie had spoken of; creeping down from the vast unknown hinterland of Africa to still the Trade Winds and calm the ocean, and visit the judgement of an angered Jehovah upon erring mankind.

Such an idea was fanciful to the point of absurdity, and he was ashamed of entertaining it. But all the same he kept well away from the coast. And continued to regret that he had brought his wife with him, for Amelia was far from strong, and the breathless heat was causing her almost as much discomfort as the Atlantic storms had done. He should have had more sense than to allow Josiah Crane and his spoilt, obstinate, self-willed chit of a niece to——

A shadow fell across the threshold of the chartroom, and Captain Fullbright looked up to see the chit in question framed in the open doorway. A tall young woman in her early twenties, dressed in the unrelieved black of deep mourning, and wearing her thick, chestnut-brown hair in a severe chignon whose weight tilted her firm chin and gave an added stateliness to a naturally upright carriage.

Thaddaeus Fullbright did not approve of passengers in the charthouse, but Miss Hollis was a privileged person for more reasons than one. Apart from being a Crayne on her mother's side and travelling under the care and chaperonage of his own wife, her personal appearance was such as to assure her of privileges that plainer and less well-favoured women might sigh for in vain. Though it held little or no appeal for Captain Fullbright, whose taste ran to smaller, softer and more yielding damsels.

The 'New Woman', of whom Miss Hollis was an outstanding example, frankly terrified him. And certainly there was nothing small, soft or yielding about the youthful Juno who stood looking in at the door of the chartroom. But despite his prejudices the Captain could appreciate good looks when he saw them, and there was no denying that Miss Hollis was a remarkably handsome young woman.

Not even the unwieldy fashions of the day could disguise the excellence of her figure, while the sombre mourning hue of her dress merely served to accentuate an admirable complexion that had frequently, and with justice, been compared to magnolia petals. Her eyes alone would have given a plain girl pretensions to beauty, for they were large and grey, black-lashed and wide set. Unfortunately, they were also disconcertingly direct, and apt to flash in a manner that had intimidated many a young man who had been temporarily attracted by her looks; and possibly by her fortune.

Captain Fullbright studied his intrusive passenger with a wary eye and said: 'Yes, Miss Hollis? Anything I can do for you?'

Miss Hollis frowned and said with a touch of impatience in her voice: 'You can stop calling me Miss Hollis for a start, Captain Thaddaeus. After all, it's not as though I were one of your ordinary passengers. I'm being looked after by your wife, and I don't call her "Mrs Fullbright". And nor does she call me "Miss Hollis". If Amelia can call me "Hero", so can you.'

Captain Thaddaeus smiled and the lines of strain eased about his eyes and mouth. He said dryly: 'Can't say as I've noticed her calling you "Hero" much. Seems to me it's more often "dear" or "honey".'

Miss Hollis laughed, and looked the prettier for it. 'Yes, indeed. Do you know, your wife is the first person who ever called me "honey"? Papa never called me by pet names. I was always "Hero" to him. He said it was a beautiful name: and it is, I guess. But ... sometimes I missed the pet names.'

Her face was suddenly as wistful as her voice, and she gave a sharp sigh, and then remembering what it was that she had come to ask him, said more briskly: 'Captain Thaddaeus, how much longer is this going to last? This weather, I mean? We don't seem to be moving at all. Mr Stoddart says he does not believe we have advanced more than a mile these last two days, and that at this rate we shall not reach Zanzibar within the month.'

'Maybe not,' agreed Captain Fullbright placidly. 'But there ain't nothing we can do about it, that's for sure. Unless Mr Stoddart cares to try a bit of rowing! You tell him that he'll soon get all the movement he wants. And maybe a sight more.'

'Why do you say that?' asked Hero, interested. 'Do you mean we shall have a wind soon?'

'I wouldn't be surprised. Glass is falling.'

'But you said that yesterday, and it's still as calm as a duckpond.'

'And the glass is still falling. There's dirty weather brewing, and I don't like it. I'll sure be mighty glad to see Zanzibar, and that's a fact.'

'Yes, indeed!' agreed Hero warmly. 'It's the one place I have always meant to see, ever since my father showed it to me on a globe when I was quite young – five or six . . .'

She turned to look out across the hot, sun-baked deck and the motionless shadows of the mast and the standing rigging, and thought of that long ago day. And of other things too: the lamplit kitchen at Hollis Hill with its dark, beamed ceiling and rows of copper pans, and the whispering voice of old Biddy Jason who had told her her fortune.

For years Hero had believed whole-heartedly in those mysterious predictions; though once free of the schoolroom she had pretended to laugh at them. Yet now they were actually coming true! Or had she herself made them come true because of what old Biddy had told her? It was a debatable point. But at least one thing was certain. Here she was, sailing half way round the world to an island full of black men, where there must be plenty of work for her to do: and Clayton Mayo to help her do it!

She turned impulsively to the Captain: 'You've been to Zanzibar several times, Captain Thaddaeus. What is it like? Will you tell me about it, please?'

'Well, now: it's no more'n half the size of Long Island – around fifty miles long by ten wide, I'd say – and it lies near enough to the mainland for folk in the city to see the hills of Africa on a clear day. Its nearest neighbour is an island called Pemba which is even smaller and a heap wilder, and——'

Hero shook her head and said: 'No, those are not at *all* the sort of things I want to hear about. I want to know what it's like.'

Captain Fullbright replied unhelpfully that she'd soon be finding that out for herself and, for his part, he preferred to let people get their own impressions instead of handing them his spectacles to look through. But Miss Hollis was not to be fobbed off so easily, and seating herself with some deliberation, she announced calmly that in *her* opinion looking through other people's spectacles could be very instructive, since it would often show one a viewpoint that was totally different to one's own: 'And I find it interesting to know how other people see things. You have to know, if you're going to do any good in this world.'

Captain Fullbright raised a pair of bushy eyebrows and looked faintly surprised: 'Good? What sort of good?'

'Helping people. Setting things to rights.'

'*Humph*. What sort o' things?'

Miss Hollis sketched a small impatient gesture: 'Slavery. Ignorance. Dirt and disease. I don't believe in sitting around with folded hands and saying "The Lord's Will be done," when there are so many things being done that cannot possibly be the Lord's Will. One should start right in and do something about it.'

Captain Fullbright observed dryly that he could see that she was going to have plenty to keep her occupied in Zanzibar.

'I know it,' agreed Hero calmly: 'That is largely why I made up my mind that I must go there at once. You see, there was nothing for me to do at Hollis Hill. And I wanted to get right away from Boston – the house seemed so empty after Papa died, and I couldn't bear . . .'

Her crisp, confident voice wavered unexpectedly, and she did not complete the sentence but said hurriedly: 'Besides Cressy – my cousin Cressida – particularly wished me to come. We have always been great friends and she was lonely in Zanzibar; and it seems that the climate does not suit Aunt Abby. So I felt that since they both needed me, it was my duty to——' She paused briefly, as though examining this statement, and then said a shade ruefully: 'No, I am not being quite honest. It was very pleasant to feel really needed.'

Captain Fullbright's lips twitched and he remarked in a deceptively innocent voice that he seemed to remember hearing something about someone else needing her. Maybe Mr Clayton Mayo?

Miss Hollis blushed, and Captain Fullbright, who had not believed her to be capable of such a thing, was mildly astonished. The rush of bright colour suited her, and he thought idly that she should do it more often.

'You've been talking to Amelia!' accused Miss Hollis.

'Sure. It's usual, 'twixt husbands and wives,' admitted Captain Thaddaeus with his slow smile. 'But I weren't aware that there was any secret about it. Your cousin, Mr Josiah Crayne, told me that it was kind of understood in the family that you were planning on becoming Mrs Clayton Mayo, and that was why he'd allowed you to sail.'

'Indeed?' said Hero haughtily. 'Well, he is wrong. As it happens, I have not yet made up my mind about Mr Mayo. I have always esteemed him, and I know that Aunt Abby and Uncle Nat hoped that we should marry some day. But Papa took against him. Not that I should have allowed such a thing to over-influence me had I been convinced that we should suit, but I do feel very strongly that marriage is not an estate to be entered into on the basis of mere pleasure in another's society, and that one should look for more than that.'

'Oh . . . er . . . sure. Sure,' agreed Captain Fullbright, disconcerted and more than a little shocked by the unmaidenly frankness with which Miss Hollis was prepared to discuss such delicate matters as marriage and affairs of the heart. Surely a certain show of coyness – something more in keeping with that blush – would have been more fitting?

But Miss Hollis, though she might not be able to control her blushes,

33

obviously had no patience with coyness, for she proceeded to tell him that she already knew Mr Mayo to be serious-minded and eager to do good, because they had enjoyed many talks together and found themselves to be in complete agreement on a wide variety of subjects. And that he had also proved himself to be truly honourable by steadfastly refusing to countenance any suggestion that they should elope.

'Whose suggestion?' enquired Captain Thaddaeus, interested.

'Mine, I regret to say,' admitted Miss Hollis with a disarming twinkle. 'Though I guess I only made it in the heat of the moment, because I was exceedingly annoyed with Papa, and I don't believe I would ever have carried it out. But Clay – I mean Mr Mayo – would not hear of it, and though my cousin Arabella Strong said that it was only because he knew quite well that Papa had threatened to cut me off with a quarter if I married against his wishes, I had enough sense to realize that Bella had a fondness for Clay herself and was only speaking out of jealousy. He is very handsome, you know.'

Captain Fullbright controlled his features with difficulty, and said gravely: 'So now that you are rich and independent you're hurrying right out to your handsome sweetheart, with the Craynes' approval, to be married in white satin and a wedding veil and live happily ever after. That it?'

'No-o . . . not exactly. I am going out to see for myself what may be done to put a stop to the disgraceful traffic in slaves that is carried on in Zanzibar. And while I am there I shall also be able to renew my acquaintance with Mr Mayo before deciding whether we could make a success of marriage. We have not seen each other for nearly two years you see, and he may well have changed.'

'And you too, I guess.'

'I never change,' asserted Miss Hollis confidently. 'But from all I have heard and read, the tropics are apt to have a deteriorating effect on men who are compelled to live there.'

'On their health, certainly.'

'Oh, and on their characters too, I assure you! That is why I felt I must see for myself. And even if it should turn out that Clay and I do not suit, I shall not have wasted my time, since quite apart from the slaves there must be so many things crying out to be changed in Zanzibar that I shall find plenty to do. I have been studying Arabic and Swahili for some months now, and though I am afraid that my vocabulary is still very small, I am told that I speak both languages passably well.'

She leaned forward to lay a hand on the Captain's sleeve, and said coaxingly: 'So now won't you please tell me something about the Island?'

'Why don't you go ask that young Mossoo Jooles?' retorted the Captain gruffly. 'Reckon he'll be pleased enough to tell you anything you want to know. His Pa's French Consul in Zanzibar, so he's lived there; which is more'n I have!'

'Yes. He told me so,' said Hero. 'But then he also told me that the Island was "A paradise on earth, colourful and exotic, and of a beauty inconceivable. A page," he says, "from the Arabian Nights!"'

Captain Fullbright, amused at the quotation and the expressive look that accompanied it, laughed heartily and remarked that all Frenchmen – and for that matter most foreigners – only said what they felt a lady would wish to hear. 'Did he tell you anything else about it?'

'Indeed yes: a great deal. He told me that he is convinced that the British intend to annex the Island, together with Pemba and the Sultanates' dependencies on the mainland.'

'Did he, now! Waal, ma'am, I guess that's something I wouldn't know a thing about. How d'you reckon they'll set about it? – or hain't he told you that?'

Apparently he had, and Miss Hollis (never one to shirk instructing the ignorant), explained that it was really very simple; and quite infamous! The British, it seemed, were supporting a puppet-ruler – a most weak and vicious man, who besides encouraging slavery and wasting the revenues on riotous living, had no real claim to the throne, since he was merely a younger son of the late Sultan. The rival claimant, according to the French Consul's son, was not only infinitely better fitted to rule, but possessed the respect and loyalty of nine-tenths of the local population together with the support of every thinking foreigner in Zanzibar with the exception of the British, who recognizing that his strength of character might be a bar to their schemes for colonial expansion, preferred to have a more malleable tool as a ruler. Had the Captain ever heard of anything more shameful? Of course she herself, as a good Republican, could not approve of kings in any form. But then nor could she tolerate injustice.

Indignation brought a flush to Miss Hollis's classic features, and her eyes sparkled in a manner that Captain Fullbright considered magnificent, though hardly alluring. He shrugged non-committally and remarked that in his opinion all power-politics were apt to be a dirty business, and though he did not hold any brief for the British, he doubted if any Frenchman could be regarded as neutral or unbiased in the matter of the East African territories. Or Zanzibar either!

'Are you suggesting that the *French* might wish to annex the Island?' exclaimed Hero, shocked. 'But that is absurd!'

'Nothin' absurd about it that I can see ma'am – Miss Hero. All these Europeans are colonialists. Six of one and half-a-dozen of the other. And not a pin to choose between them.'

'There I *cannot* agree with you! The French have always hated tyrants and upheld the cause of Freedom and Equality. Well, anyway, ever since the Revolution. And look at the way that Lafayette ... I admit they *have* colonized, but——'

'But the fact is that as a good American you're for the French and agin' the British. Which I'll allow is fair enough, for it's a thing we'd most of us agree on. But it don't necessarily make for fair judgement if you're prejudiced in favour of one party before you start!'

'I would never,' Hero assured him emphatically, 'permit personal prejudice to blind me to facts.'

The Captain, finding himself in deep waters, observed with another shrug that speaking for himself he was not particularly interested in the internal affairs of Zanzibar, which were, he thanked the Lord, none of his business. An observation that scandalized Hero, who informed him roundly that Christian people should always be interested in matters that affected public welfare anywhere in the world, and that responsibility towards one's fellow men should not be limited only to those of one's own race and colour.

'Oh – sure,' said the Captain woodenly, his face expressionless and his sympathies veering strongly to the side of the volatile, quarrelsome and happily heathen population of Zanzibar, who did not know what was coming to them. 'Well ma'am, you'll soon be able to talk it all over with your uncle and give him your views. I guess his opinions are likely to be worth more than mine – or that young Mossoo's either, with his 'Paradise on Earth' and Arabian Nights twaddle. *Paradise* indeed! Maybe there's some who can see it that way, but to my mind it's no more'n a cross between a cess-pit and a pest-house.'

He had spoken with intentional brutality, but if he had expected to shake Miss Hollis, he failed to do so. Far from being disconcerted she appeared only too willing to accept his unfavourable opinion of Zanzibar, informing him with the greatest cordiality that she had always suspected that a deal too much of what was said and written about the glories of Eastern lands and tropical islands was grossly misleading, since it stood to reason that places where there was so great a degree of heat and such a low level of living and morality could not possibly be other than squalid.

'I reckon it's squalid, all right,' agreed Captain Thaddaeus. 'I've read that you can smell the scent of cloves and spices far out to sea, but all I've ever smelt is the stench of drains and garbage – and worse things! A filthier town I've yet to see, and in my opinion it's no place for a lady. It ain't any wonder your aunt is feeling poorly. She'd no right to send for you, and that's a fact.'

'Oh, nonsense, Captain Thaddaeus. My cousin Cressy hasn't taken any harm, and she's four years younger than I am. And what's more, she too thinks that Zanzibar is a lovely and romantic spot! She wrote and told me so.'

'Maybe she's in love. I've heard tell that falling in love is a great thing for putting rose-coloured spectacles on folk.'

'In *love*? Why, who could she possibly be in love with? There isn't anyone——'

'There are men even in Zanzibar, ma'am – Miss Hero. That Frenchman's on his way back there, and there's a fairish big white community. Consular officials, British Navy men, business men, blackguards——'

'*Blackguards*? What sort of blackguards?' enquired Hero, intrigued.

'Adventurers. Black sheep. Runagates. Varmints like "Roaring Rory".'

'Who is he? – a pirate? He certainly should be with a name like that!'

'Wouldn't put it past him,' said Captain Fullbright. 'He's an Englishman, and a mighty ornery one by all accounts. What they'd call a "remittance-man", I guess. If there's anything plumb discreditable going on, from black-birding to gun-running, drug-smuggling, kidnapping or murder, you can bet your last dime that Rory Frost's mixed up in it. Young Dan Larrimore, he's been laying for him for the past two years, but he ain't caught him out yet. All he needs is the proof, and he'll sure get it one day. He's the persevarin' kind, is Dan.'

'And who is Dan?'

'Hain't your cousin Cressy ever made no mention of him? Well, now! An' here was I thinkin' that maybe he was responsible for those rose-coloured spectacles. Lieutenant Larrimore is a Limey who commands a little toy gunboat in the name of Queen Victoria, and it's his painful duty to put down the slave trading in these waters – or try to. He don't do too badly, considering all things, but he ain't caught up with Rory Frost yet, and I figure he'd just about give his eye-teeth to do it. Thought he had him once, too – came bang up to Rory in a light wind off Pemba, with the corpse of a nigger floatin' peaceful in his wake. Dan knew well enough what *that* meant – there was slaves on board and a dead one had just been pitched over the side. He thought he'd cotched him red-handed, but when he yells to him to heave-to, the *Virago* cracks on sail and——'

'The what?'

'The *Virago*: Frost's ship. He named her, so he should know. Steers wild, they say – like her master.'

'And what happened then? Did he get away?'

'Nope. On account of that gunboat has steam, so in the end it over-hauls her. But when they board her there's narry a smell of a slave. And though Dan Larrimore searches her from stem to stern, not so much as a lick of evidence does he find, and Rory he sticks to it that he knows nothing about any corpse and that it must a' been some poor nigger who falls off a passing dhow. He apologizes for not heaving-to when requested; explainin' that he was below having a bite to eat at the time and that his crew had mistook the gunboat for a French slaver. Dan, he was hopping mad, but there weren't nothing he could do about it. Not even when he hears later that while Rory is drawing him off on this wild goose-chase, an Arab slaver pal of his is running a cargo-load of slaves out of Zanzibar and getting them clean away.'

'You mean he did that on purpose? That it was all a trick, just to . . .?' Hero turned quite white and her jaw set in a manner that recalled her grandfather, Caleb Crayne, when that gentleman was in one of his rages. She said furiously: 'Men like that ought to be hanged!'

'Daresay he will be one day. Born to it, I'd say. And Dan Larrimore would sure like to have the hanging of him. Can't say as I blame him. Myself, I don't normally take to the British, but the Lieutenant is a good man, and I'm for him.'

'And you think Cressy is, too?'

'For Dan Larrimore? *Waall* . . . I guess she wouldn't be the first one, for there's no denying he's a well set-up man. But I was only guessin' when I said that about your cousin. It's getting on for a year since I was last in Zanzibar, and the two of them were only just getting acquainted then; though anyone could see she liked his looks. It was you telling me how she'd said the Island was romantic that give me the idea that maybe something had come of it. On the other hand, Dan ain't by no means the only man in Zanzibar, and I've heard tell that your Aunt Abby and her daughter are well liked by the Sultan's family. Some of those Arab princes are right handsome men.'

'*Handsome?* You mean *black* men? – Africans? Are you suggesting that Cressy——' Hero's face was rigid with affront.

'Arabs, ma'am! Arabs! They're neither black nor African, and many of 'em are as near fair-complexioned as I am: no more than a trifle sun-burned you'd say. The Sultan's family were Kings of Oman, and they're a sight prouder of their lineage than your cousin Josiah is of being a Crayne – which you'll allow is plenty! The men are a fine-looking lot. And I've heard tell that some of the palace ladies are as pretty as pictures; though that's a thing I couldn't swear to, for they're kept shut away in the women's quarters, poor critters. It must be real interesting for them to meet ladies like your Aunt Abby and your cousin Cressy, who can go about anywhere they fancy and not worry about it.'

'Yes indeed,' agreed Hero warmly, her interest instantly diverted: 'I shall have to see what I can do for the poor creatures. Perhaps I can arrange to give them classes in cooking and needlework, and teach them how to read and write? It must be terrible to be ignorant and unlettered, and to live little better than prisoners – treated as mere chattels of the male. That is something that will *have* to be changed.'

Captain Fullbright opened his mouth to remonstrate and then closed it again without speaking. It occurred to him that Miss Hollis was due for several surprises on her arrival at Zanzibar. And also that it was strange to find a young woman so physically and materially well-endowed, obsessed by a zeal for reform. One would have expected her to be more interested, at her age, in balls and *beaux* than in Good Works and the welfare of coloured races in out-of-the-way and insalubrious portions of the globe. There certainly was no accounting for tastes! She had, he decided, missed her vocation, for she would have made an admirable schoolmarm of the stricter sort. And might yet become one! since from his brief acquaintance with Clayton Mayo (and judging from rumour and hearsay) he could not visualize that handsome, ebullient gentleman being seriously attracted to such an outspoken and probably frigid young woman. Miss Hollis's views on marriage were enough to chill the most ardent suitor, and he felt sorry for her husband – if she should ever acquire one, which he doubted.

'Handsome is as handsome does,' mused Captain Thaddaeus, scratching thoughtfully at his grizzled beard. Though of course there was always her fortune to be considered, and he supposed she might yet be married for that. A bleak enough prospect for any girl, but perhaps no more than this one deserved. What Amelia could see in her he did not know.

4

Miss Hollis rose with a rustle of black poplin, and straightening the sombre folds above the modest hoops of her crinoline, dabbed the sweat from her brow with a cambric handkerchief.

The few unruly tendrils of chestnut hair that had escaped from the strict confines of her chignon clung damply to the white column of her neck, and she was uncomfortably aware that there were other damp patches under the arms and between the shoulder blades of her tight-fitting, high-cut bodice.

'Is it always as hot and unpleasant as this in the Indian Ocean?' she demanded with a tinge of despair.

'Not when the Trades are blowing,' said Captain Fullbright. 'Which I reckon they'll do soon enough. Why don't you go below and change into something cooler? You must have gotten yourself a muslin dress among all that gear. Something lighter coloured and looser than those things you're wearing.'

'Yes, of course I have. But they are for when I am out of mourning. I could not wear them yet. Not for another six months at least. It would not be respectful to Papa. And besides, some people might think that I did not – that I had not——'

Her voice failed her and suddenly there were tears in her eyes. She blinked them away and blew her nose, and said apologetically: 'I'm sorry. That was foolish of me. But I do miss him so. You see, I – we were such friends.'

Captain Fullbright was surprised and touched. Yes, there was something lovable there after all; and maybe Clayton Mayo had found it. He said gruffly: 'All the more reason ma'am – Miss Hero – why you should act in a way that would have pleased him. And I don't reckon your Pa would have wished you to bundle yourself up in that smothering black stuff. Not in this kind of weather. It's plumb unhealthy and I've been meaning to speak to Mrs Fullbright about it. Your Pa would have wanted you to keep yourself in good health, and you won't do that for long if you rig yourself up in such gear as that.'

Hero smiled faintly, but shook her head. 'You are very kind, but I would not care to discard my mourning for any such trivial reason. Consideration for one's personal comfort should not come first. Besides, I cannot believe that this weather can last much longer. Surely we shall find a wind soon?'

'Like I've told you – a sight sooner than we'd wish, if the glass is anything to go by,' said the Captain grimly.

He mopped his neck with a bandana handkerchief and escorted Miss Hollis out on to the deck, noting as they went the curious paleness of their shadows and the bubbling pitch between the deck seams, and wishing yet again that Amelia was not on board. Or Miss Hero Hollis either!

The heat in the tiny charthouse had been oppressive, but out on the open deck it was almost unbearable, and Hero paused in a patch of shade, and leaning on the rail looked enviously down at the cool depths below, where the weed of the long voyage stirred and waved like meadow grass.

Apart from the gentle rhythmic snoring of a fellow passenger who lay asleep in a long cane chair under the awning, and a subdued murmur of voices from forward of the weather deck, where the cook's mate and a cabin boy were fishing hopefully for basking shark, the normal shipboard noises had dwindled to no more than a drowsy creaking of the blocks as the *Norah Crayne* moved lazily to the slow, glassy swell.

A trickle of sweat crawled down between Hero's shoulder blades, and suddenly the clogging, sleepy silence of the afternoon seemed curiously sinister; as though the heat and the haze and the stillness had combined to bring Time to a standstill, and left the *Norah Crayne* suspended in some strange, aimless vacuum between reality and Cloud-cuckoo-land. Doomed to drift until her timbers rotted and her sails fell to dust, and she sank and was lost . . .

Hero shivered, and was aroused from this unpleasant reverie by footsteps and the cheerful, prosaic voice of the first mate, Mr Marrowby, who stopped beside her to remark affably that it was sticky hot, but that it would be a mighty lot cooler before nightfall.

'Do you really mean that?' asked Hero doubtfully. 'I confess it always seems to me to be even hotter at night.'

'Ah, but there's a wind on its way; and it's my guess she'll blow rough.'

'That's what Captain Fullbright says. But I don't see any signs of it yet.'

'You can smell it, though. And see over there——'

He pointed a blunt forefinger, and turning to peer out across the silky, shimmering waste, Hero saw what seemed to be a stain far out on the colourless ocean.

'Is that wind?'

'A breath of it. But there'll be a sight more behind it.'

Captain Fullbright, returning from the forward deck, joined them at the rail, and Mr Marrowby wetted a finger and raising it said: 'She freshens, sir.'

The stain on the water flitted towards them, ruffling the glassy surface into a myriad shivering ripples, and a faint breath of air shivered the sails and rattled the top hamper. For the first time in several days the *Norah Crayne* answered to her helm, and they could feel life flow through her as she woke from her long drowsing and thrust forward, the sea gurgling softly under her cut-water.

The boy at the masthead called: '*Deck ahoy! Sail, sir——*'

'Where away?' bellowed Mr Marrowby.

'*Over the starboard bow, sir. Headed north.*'

Mr Marrowby put his spy-glass to his eye and presently announced that it was a relief to raise another sail again, since speaking for himself he found this idling on an empty sea kind of lonesome.

'What kind of ship? I can't see anything,' said Hero, shading her eyes with her hand.

'Three-masted schooner. But you won't see far in this haze. There, I've lost her now. She was a fairish way out; and moving, which means she's caught the wind. We'll be getting it soon, and then it'll blow this haze clear and we'll be on our way again.'

Even as he spoke, another and stronger cat's-paw of wind ruffled across the water; and all at once the drowsy lethargy of the last two weeks was over, and Hero found herself standing alone while orders rattled and canvas filled to the breeze, and a white lace of foam spun out from the cut-water. The breathless heat of the afternoon gave place to a salty, refreshing coolness that was a deep relief after the sweltering temperature of the past days and the airless torment of the long nights, and they were moving again. They were on their way, and Life and Adventure, the Island of Zanzibar, Destiny and Clayton Mayo, lay ahead.

But by six bells the wind had strengthened ominously, and two hours later it was blowing in savage gusts and the sea was white with foam.

Below decks the cabins were still uncomfortably hot, for with every porthole closed and secured, the wind could not reach them: only the noise and the shuddering lift and plunge as the *Norah Crayne*, making up for lost time, raced northward under every stitch of canvas she could carry, reeling to the lash of the gale and the surge of the furious sea.

Captain Fullbright's frail little wife had taken to her bunk over two hours ago, and now she lay clutching a bottle of smelling salts and apologizing incoherently to her charge: 'I feel downright ashamed of myself,' whispered Amelia. 'It's just plain degrading . . . a sailor's wife! Mr Fullbright used to tell me that I would grow out of it and find what he calls my "sea-legs". But I never have. Such a bad example to you, honey. Are you *sure* you feel all right?'

'I feel fine, thank you,' said Hero buoyantly. 'Now that we are moving again I can put up with anything. It was that dreadful, aimless drifting that I found so exasperating. Don't you *detest* doing nothing and getting nowhere?'

'I can't say that I do, dear. But then I guess I'm not an energetic person, and maybe it's just as well that we are not all alike. It would be so dull. Oh . . . oh mercy! . . .'

Mrs Fullbright shut her eyes briefly as the ship gave a particularly malignant roll, and Hero said consolingly: 'I read somewhere that some famous Admiral – Nelson I think – never cured himself of being seasick, so I don't see that you need worry. Do you think you could manage a cold drink if I fetched you one? Some lemon water?'

Amelia Fullbright shuddered and closed her eyes again. 'No thank you, honey. Just sit and talk to me. I like to hear you talk. It takes my mind off this horrible rolling and pitching.'

'What would you like me to talk about?'

'Yourself. Your young man.'

'He's not mine yet,' Hero assured her hastily.

'But I feel sure he will be. He sounds very charming; and so suitable in every way. Though I could wish he were not quite so closely related. A first cousin——!'

'But he isn't, you know. In fact, he is no blood relation at all. Clay is Aunt Abby's son by her first marriage, and his father's name wasn't Mayo, but something long and unpronounceable that he changed to Mayo because two of the syllables sounded like that, and it saved time – his own father had emigrated from Hungary and his mother was Polish. I believe she was very beautiful, and they say Clay gets his looks from her; though Aunt Abby must have been pretty too when she was young. Clay was only six months old when his father died, and Papa once told me that it was a mercy that he did, because it seems that he was addicted to drink and gambling, and in the end some dreadful woman shot him in a Dance Hall – *imagine*! It must have been terrible for Aunt Abby, but fortunately she met Uncle Nathaniel about five years later, and married him. Though Cressy – that's my cousin Cressida – wasn't born until nearly six years after that. Yet in spite of everything, I think Aunt Abby always loved Clay best. Which is odd, don't you think? I mean, when his father had treated her so badly, and Cressy was Uncle Nat's child?'

Amelia smiled faintly and said: 'With some women, I guess it has to be a man.'

'But Cressy is so pretty; and she is the baby of the family.'

'I'm sure your uncle loves her best.'

'Yes, that's true. Cressy can do anything with Uncle Nat. He did not at all want to take her to Zanzibar, because he was afraid that the climate would not suit her and that she would catch some dreadful disease, or die of heatstroke or sunstroke or something; and Aunt Abby too. He meant to leave them both behind, but Cressy teased him into taking them. She is very young. And very sentimental and romantic.'

'And Mr Mayo? Is he romantic too? I hope he does not take after his father!'

'Oh, no!' said Hero, shocked. 'Not in the least, I assure you. In character he is wholly from Aunt Abby's side of the family, and *her* father was a deacon. His appearance may be romantic, but he is really a most sensible person and not at all frivolous like Cressy. He is much older than her, of course. Cressy is only seventeen – no, she must be almost eighteen by now! But Clay is twenty-nine.'

'High time he was married,' commented Amelia drowsily. 'I hope you do not mean to keep him waiting much longer, honey, or he will be so difficult . . . for a young wife.'

Her lashes fluttered and closed and she did not speak again, and presently Hero became aware that she had fallen asleep.

The cabin rocked and swung and tilted, lifted up and up, creaking and shuddering, and sank again with appalling swiftness to the accompaniment of a crescendo of noise in which it was impossible to separate the sound of falling furniture from the crash of cataracts of water sweeping across the reeling deck. But except for the heat Hero was aware of no discomfort, and she was gratified to find that the frenzied motion of the ship was, if not precisely pleasant, at least greatly to be preferred to the sluggish inactivity of the past ten days. She had already taken the precaution of removing anything movable to a safe place, and as Mrs Fullbright continued to sleep and there seemed to be little chance of obtaining a hot meal while the *Norah Crayne* flung herself to and fro in this abandoned manner, Hero made her way to the saloon where she collected a handful of ship's biscuits and retired with them to her own berth to copy her chaperone's excellent example.

The night that followed had been anything but peaceful, for the *Norah Crayne*, her masts bare and her stay raised for a storm spanker to keep her head up and the wind and the sea on her bow, plunged and reared like an unbroken colt on a lead rein, and when she fell off, her bows swooped down into a cross sea, and with nothing to lift her the ocean leapt aboard and raged boiling along her decks.

Dawn broke grey and reluctant through heavy black clouds and furious rain, and thunder rolled across the tossing desolation while lightning flashed and the gale screamed in the rigging. The rain and spray between them had reduced visibility to a matter of yards, and the sea had combed the clipper's decks of anything movable. Her boats were gone and their davits had been smashed to matchwood, but still the storm showed no signs of abating, and Captain Fullbright kept the pumps going and wondered how far his ship had drifted off course.

The *Norah Crayne*'s passengers, with one exception, had remained prudently in their berths. The exception being Miss Hollis, who had not only managed to dress herself (no mean feat in that rolling, pitching pandemonium), but had actually made her way to the saloon where she had drunk a pannikin of cold coffee and eaten a hearty meal consisting of salt beef, pickles and biscuits. After which, on finding that there was still no assistance that she could render to Amelia, she had returned for a time to her own cabin. But it had been far too dark to read or sew (even if the violent motion of the ship had not precluded either occupation) and there had been nothing to do but lie and look up at the ceiling, or endure with closed eyes the unpleasant sensation of being lifted up for dizzying, interminable moments of time, only to be dropped again with a long jarring rush that seemed as though it must end with the entire vessel being engulfed and dragged under by the enormous seas.

Hero had always thought of herself as being sensible and level-headed; but the gloom and the incessant creaking, grinding, deafening tumult, and above all those terrible downward swoops into unseen gulfs, began to tell on her nerves, and presently the uncomfortable thought crept into her mind that the narrow, high-sided berth in which she lay bore a depressing resemblance to a coffin.

She had heard stories of ships that had vanished in storms and never been heard of again, and once, when she was a little girl, one of her Crayne cousins had told her how, when on a voyage to Rio de Janeiro, he had seen a great ship under full topsails slide into a long watery hollow and disappear – run under in a wild waste of ocean. If a similar fate should overtake the *Norah Crayne*, she would know nothing about it until the cabin door burst in and the black water swirled up to the ceiling. She would not even be able to get out of her berth, but would be trapped there and drowned, and the whole, desperate, straining ship would become one vast wooden tomb, sinking slowly down through leagues of cold darkness until it came to rest at last on the quiet ooze of the sea floor.

Perhaps the frenzied motion of the ship was making her a little light-headed, for her imagination suddenly presented her with a vivid and startlingly unpleasant picture of great eels and octopuses slithering down the wrecked companion-ways and through the cabin doors to batten on the bodies of the drowned, while sharks swam hungrily past the blind portholes and between the tangled rigging outside . . .

Hero dismissed the horrid fancy with an effort; angry with herself for entertaining such absurd notions and beginning to wonder if it had been really wise to eat salt beef and pickles for breakfast. For there was no disguising the fact that she was not feeling at all well, and it could not possibly be seasickness, because Mr Marrowby had told her that once she had got her 'sea-legs' she would never need to suffer from such a thing again. And she was sure she had acquired those weeks ago. But either Mr Marrowby was wrong or else the heat had had a deleterious effect upon the beef, for she was certainly feeling distinctly queasy.

The cabin tilted at an acute angle as the ship struggled up the long slope of a watery mountain, and as it reached the top grey daylight peered through the porthole and the rain and spray hissed against the glass as the *Norah Crayne* balanced briefly on an even keel. Then the bows crashed down and they were falling again, rushing downward into darkness with the seas roaring up and over the glass; down and down until it seemed impossible that they could ever rise again; to bring up with a shock and a jar and a savage roll, as the dead weight of hundreds of tons of water swept across the deck, and the *Norah Crayne* struggled upwards once more; sluggish, dizzy and punch-drunk, but still gallantly fighting back.

'I can't stand this!' said Hero, speaking aloud into the stifling, heavy darkness: 'If I stay down here I shall only be sick, and I will *not* be sick. I will not!'

She crawled out of her bunk, and groping for her shoes in the grey gloom, put them on and left the cabin. It was not an easy matter to remain upright, and she was bruised and giddy by the time she reached the door at the top of the saloon companion-way. The bolts were stiff, and when she had drawn them it was a hard struggle to force the door open, for the wind was leaning against it at gale force. But with the aid of a momentary lull she managed it at last, and was out in the open – breathless and instantly soaked and realizing too late the incredible folly of her behaviour.

She must, she decided, have been sick or mad or both to venture up on deck in a storm of such magnitude, and the sooner she returned to the safety of her cabin the better. But that was easier thought of than done, for the door had slammed shut behind her and once again the wind was holding it closed. Hero discovered to her horror that she could neither get a satisfactory grip on the wet handle nor pull on it, for the gale forced her hard against the dripping panels and drove the breath from her body. Pressed against the closed door and struggling to breathe, she was aware for the first time of panic, for although the morning was far advanced and she knew it must be close on noon, the day still seemed almost as dark as the night had been; and seen from the open deck the storm appeared infinitely worse and far more terrifying than anything her imagination had pictured for her.

Enormous iron-grey hills of water, foam-streaked and furious, reared up against the black storm-clouds and the jagged lightning, and tossed the helpless ship to and fro; playing with it as though it were a wounded mouse in the grip of a gigantic cat. The helmsman, lashed to the wheel, fought grimly to keep her head to the wind; but the gale was a living thing, lifting the labouring ship, dropping it, flinging it aside and snatching it up again.

Hero released one shaking hand and attempted to clear her eyes of the rain and spray that slashed across the deck, and as she did so a boiling cauldron of foam sprang over the bow, and catching her about the knees, broke her loosened hold on the door handle and swept her away to bring her up with bruising abruptness against the side of the charthouse. Her skirts clung to her in drenched folds while her abundant hair, whipped from its chignon, streamed out on the wind like long ribbons of wet brown seaweed. She was aware of a heavy body blundering against her; of wet oilskins and a furious, incredulous face. A hand gripped her arm and fragmentary words reached her above the howling of the gale:

'What in thunder . . . doing up here? This ain't passenger's weather! . . . Get out of it! Get below! Get . . .' The wind tore the words away and a crash of thunder drowned them.

Once again the greyness was ripped by a livid blaze of lightning, and she heard the man shriek '*Christ!*' And saw in the same instant what he had seen——

There was another ship out there, bearing down on them. A schooner in irons, broached to and unable to get her bows back in the teeth of the wind; her foremast gone and her rat-lines trailing. A thing as deadly as a charging tiger or a hidden reef.

The hand that gripped Hero's arm released its hold and its owner raced towards the wheel, and shouldering the spray-blinded helmsman to one side, wrenched the spokes hard over. But Hero could not look away. She could only watch the schooner plunge towards them, knowing that this was death. In a moment – in less than a moment – it would strike, and there would be a rending crash of timber and the crack of falling masts, and then the sea would boil over the wreckage and suck it under, and no one would ever know what had happened. She would not have to make up her mind about Clay after all. Or about anything else. There was no time – no time——

The *Norah Crayne*, answering to her helm, fell off to starboard into the trough of a cross sea, and a long grey cliff of water lifted out of the storm and fell upon her, racing across the tilted deck, waist high and ruthless. It whirled Hero's wet skirts about her knees, and knocking her down, carried her with it as though she had weighed no more than a shuttlecock. She snatched wildly at a stanchion and missed; saw for a brief, terrifying moment that there were no rails left at the far edge of the steeply sloping deck and nothing to hold on to. And then she was rolled over and over, blind and deaf, and tilted overboard in a cataract of boiling foam.

No one had ever taught her to swim, and it would have made no difference if they had, since no swimmer could have fought that furious sea. A mountain of water dragged her under and threw her up again, and for an instant rain and spray lashed at her face. But before she could do more than gasp for air she was down again, choking and struggling. A second wave caught her and swung her up and threw her into something that tangled about her arms and her helpless body, and she grasped frantically at it and felt rope between her numbed fingers.

For a period of time that seemed endless, but which could not have lasted for more than a few minutes at the most, she clung there, fighting to keep her head above the angry sea, and gulping alternate air and water as the waves dragged her down and tossed her up again. And then at last the rope drew taut and she was being drawn up, hauled in hand over hand as though she had been a mackerel on a line, to be dragged bruised and bleeding and three parts drowned on to a tilting deck that was mercifully solid.

Hands caught her wrists and ankles, and among a medley of voices that yelled above the gale she caught an odd and entirely incredible sound. Laughter . . .

Someone was shouting with laughter, and someone else – or perhaps it was the same person? – said: 'A mermaid, by God!' And laughed again.

And then suddenly they were all slipping and sliding along the deck in another swirling fury of foam, and the whole wild, wet, horrible world turned black, as Miss Hero Athena Hollis lost consciousness for the first time in her life.

5

There was a weight pressing down upon her back. Pressing down and lifting again and then descending once more. Her hands were strained uncomfortably behind her and were being roughly and rhythmically thrust outwards and brought back again, and altogether she had never felt so sore and sick and uncomfortable in all her short and pampered life. Not even when Barclay's groom, Jud Hinkley, had been teaching her to ride, and she had been thrown from the back of a bolting horse on to hard and sun-baked ground . . .

Somewhere quite close to her someone was making a hideous groaning noise as though they were in pain, and it was several minutes before she realized that it was she herself who was responsible for this abominable sound.

She struggled feebly and attempted to turn over, and in immediate response to that movement the hands that gripped her wrists relaxed. The man who had been kneeling above her and applying a rough and ready form of artificial respiration turned her on her back, and she found herself looking up into the face of a complete stranger.

During the nine long weeks of the voyage Hero had come to know every member of the *Norah Crayne*'s crew, at least by sight, but this was someone she had never seen before. A fair-haired man with a thin, deeply sunburned face, a cleft chin and a pair of remarkably pale eyes.

Hero passed her tongue over her swollen lips and tasted a saltness that was not of the sea, but blood welling from a cut on her lower lip. She grimaced weakly and attempted to sit up, but finding the effort beyond her strength, forced her voice to a croaking whisper:

'Where is . . . Captain Fullbright?'

'Captain who?'

It was, she thought vaguely, an educated voice. Then he *must* be a passenger. She could not understand it. Unless—— For a brief, ridiculous moment it crossed her mind that she might be dead and the fair-haired man the soul of some drowned sailor sent to set her on her way. But if she were dead she would surely not be in such pain, and it was an undeniable fact that every single part of her body was bruised and aching.

She could feel the warm, steady trickle of blood from her cut lip and from another cut on her temple, and there seemed to be a haze before her eyes; a haze full of odd, dancing lights. Her gaze moved slowly from the man's face, and she saw that she was lying on the floor of a strange cabin, though it still pitched and rolled as dizzily as her own had done. A passenger's cabin.

She said in the same husky whisper: 'Why haven't I . . . seen . . . you . . . before?'

The stranger laughed and said: 'No reason why you should, is there?'

A faint flicker of indignation arose in Miss Hollis, and she said more strongly: 'You were the one who was laughing. Why did you laugh? It was not at all funny.'

The man laughed again with regrettable heartlessness, and said: 'Perhaps not to you. But it isn't every day we hook a mermaid.'

His voice was curiously clipped, while at the same time possessing a faint suggestion of a drawl. An English voice, thought Hero dizzily. *Why, I believe he's English!*

The man came to his feet, and bending down lifted her as easily and carelessly as though she had been a side of bacon, and deposited her in a large leather-covered chair that seemed to be screwed to the cabin floor. Standing over her he looked very tall. Taller than Captain Fullbright – or Clay.

He said: 'You're an exceedingly lucky young woman. You ought by rights to be drowned, and but for a miracle you would have been. However, I suppose the same could be said for all of us. That was the closest I've ever been to the next world, which is saying a good deal. Here, you'd better take a drink of this to replace some of the water we've tilted out of you.'

He reached for a tin pannikin that stood in a wooden holder against the wall, filled it from a silver flask, and finding that her hands were too bruised and nerveless to take it, held it to her mouth while she drank.

The fiery liquid burned Hero's throat and brought a stab of agonizing pain to her cut lip, but though she coughed and choked and managed to swallow a reasonable quantity of it and was grateful for the glow of warmth it brought to her cold stomach. But the relief was only temporary, for presently she began to shiver violently and found that she had to clench her teeth to prevent them from chattering. She wished that she could lie down somewhere – anywhere. On the floor if necessary, but preferably in her own berth. If only she could contrive to get back to her cabin and out of these dreadful sodden clothes she could crawl into her berth and go to sleep. But there was something that must be said first, and she frowned in an effort to concentrate, and forcing the words between her chattering teeth said: 'D–did you . . . w–was it you who p–pulled me out?'

'Among others.'

'T–then I have to t–thank you for s–saving my life. I am t–truly grateful.'

The tall man grinned and said: 'It's your guardian angel you should thank, my girl. I didn't arrange to snarl you up in that mass of torn rigging, and it was that and nothing else that saved your life. We only had to haul you in. And by the look of you we gave you a pretty rough time in the process!'

Hero attempted to return his smile, but found that her mouth was so cut and swollen that the effort was too painful, and abandoning it she asked instead for Mrs Fullbright: 'If she is n-not too ill I w-would like to see her, please. A-at once. And if you w-would be so k-kind as to ask the Captain to come here——'

'He's here,' said the tall man briefly. 'I'm the Captain. You're on the wrong ship, young woman. No Mrs Fullbrights here. In fact no other woman of any sort, which is a piece of bad luck for you. Or good luck, whichever way you choose to look at it.'

He grinned at Hero, who said incredulously: 'It isn't true. It can't be. This is the *Norah*——'

She stopped suddenly, and her right eye – the other had made contact with a bollard and was already too swollen to see out of – widened in horror. 'Why – it must have been *your* ship that ran us down. *This* ship!'

'You mean who just missed running you down. That's right. Though I have to admit that it was no thanks to us that we are not all providing food for the fishes at this moment. That helmsman of yours is a hell of a smart seaman, and I'd like to meet him. He snatched his ship out of the way as neatly as be damned, with less than an inch to spare and without so much as scraping our paint. Here's to him!'

He drained the pannikin, and setting it down, turned his attention to more practical matters: 'I must get back on deck and you'd better get out of those clothes and between blankets. Think you can manage it?'

'I – I'll try,' shuddered Hero.

The man laughed again, and said: 'You won't find it too difficult, for you left half your clothes on a broken spar, and we cut your laces. You'd better take over my bunk: it doesn't look as though I shall be needing it for some considerable time – if ever!'

He jerked his chin in the direction of the narrow berth that occupied one wall of the cabin, and picking up a dripping oilskin, shrugged himself into it and went away; moving as easily as though the ship had been drifting in a flat calm instead of lurching violently to a howling hurricane.

The door closed behind him and presently Hero dragged herself painfully out of the chair and discovered that the stranger had spoken no more than the truth on the subject of her clothes, for her dress was in shreds. The bodice hung loose to the waist with every button gone, and the laces of her stays had been cut. Even so it required prodigious efforts to remove the tattered remains, and it was probably the brandy more than mere will-power that lent her the strength to do it, and, when the last sodden garment had fallen to the floor, to stagger across to the bunk and crawl under the blankets.

She did not know how long she slept, but when she eventually awoke it was to find that someone had lit a curious oriental lamp of pierced bronze that swooped and swayed to the motion of the ship, throwing a scatter of dancing stars across the walls of the darkened cabin. Watching them, she had fallen asleep again, and then later on someone had lifted her head and given her water to drink. There had been a time, too, when the sun had been shining. But on each occasion she had fallen asleep again almost immediately, and when at last she awoke to full consciousness the lamp had again been lit.

The same small gold spatters of light that she remembered seeing before were once again dancing across the walls and ceiling. But this time they moved to the measure of a slow and stately saraband, and no longer in the frenzied tarantella of the previous night.

Hero lay still and watched them, and presently became aware that she could only see out of one eye. Touching the other one gingerly she found that it was not only swollen but exceedingly sore, and the discovery effectually banished the last traces of drowsiness and jolted her into full consciousness of where she was and how she had come there.

Her first instinctive feeling was one of profound gratitude for being alive, and for several minutes it was enough to think only of that and to be thankful, since it was indeed, as the blond stranger had said, a miracle that she had survived: a chance in a million! And then she remembered Amelia Fullbright and Captain Thaddaeus, imagining her to be dead. Oh, poor Amelia! she would take it dreadfully to heart. But how surprised and delighted she would be when Hero reappeared safe and sound. Perhaps the *Norah Crayne* was already standing by, waiting until she awoke, for the gale appeared to have blown itself out at last and by now it might be possible to launch a boat. She must get up at once!

It was at this point that Miss Hollis made the unpleasant discovery that the slightest movement was not only extremely painful but very nearly impossible. She appeared to have scraped an astonishing amount of skin off herself, and every inch of her body was stiff and bruised from the savage battering it had received as she had been dragged on board.

It took a considerable effort of will to pull herself out of the berth and across the room, but she set her teeth and managed it at last, though the effort brought cold beads of sweat to her forehead and made her gasp with pain. There was a tin basin, and a can of fresh water – stale and tepid but still drinkable – among other necessary amenities in a dark little closet that adjoined the cabin, and Hero drank long and thirstily and was uncritical of the taste.

There were none of her own garments in the cabin, but there was an assortment of male attire in a wall cupboard, and she pulled out a shirt at random and had barely managed to slip it on when the cabin door opened cautiously and a grizzled head peered round the corner:

'Ah! So you're up,' it announced in a tone of satisfaction. 'I suspicioned you might be. Been in 'arf a dozen times, I 'ave, just to take a look. I reckoned you'd be wantin' yer vittles soon's yer woke.'

The door opened wider to admit a spry little man with a broken nose in the middle of a face that was as brown and wrinkled as a walnut shell and entirely surrounded by grey whiskers. He sprang agilely on to the only chair, and turning up the wick in the bronze lamp said happily: 'There now! That's better, ain't it? Now we can see wot we're at.'

Miss Hollis, adequately concealed by white cambric as far as the knee but painfully conscious of a lavish display of bare leg and ankle below it, retreated hurriedly back to the bunk; a proceeding which her elderly visitor regarded with a tolerant and entirely understanding eye:

'You don't 'ave to worry, miss,' he assured her. 'I'm a married man I am – five times over and two of 'em legal. Yore safe with Batty Potter, for I seen too many wimmin to get a'sizzlin' over 'em at my time of life. Which is why the Captain 'e says ter me, "You better do nursemaid, Batty," 'e says, "for by this-an'-by-that, you're the only respectable member of me ole crew!" Which was right 'andsome of 'im when you come to think of it. So 'ere I be, and werry much at your service, miss. What'll it be? Some nice fried pancakes and a cuppa coffee?'

Hero said cautiously: 'That sounds very nice, Mr – er – Potter. But I would like my clothes first, please. As soon as they are dry.'

'They're dry all right,' nodded the only respectable member of the crew, 'though a bit wore-out like. But I'm doing me best with them, an' you shall 'ave them back as soon as I can get 'em to 'ang together. 'Ere's your supper.'

At any other time Hero would undoubtedly have rejected the meal as uneatable, since the pancakes turned out to be flat cakes of unleavened bread, imbued with curious Eastern spices and fried in clarified butter, while the coffee was black and very sweet and thick with grounds. But by now she was feeling far too hungry to be critical, and Mr Potter, removing the denuded tray, remarked approvingly that he liked to see a wench that could do justice to her vittles, and at this rate they would soon have her on her feet again.

He had forgotten to turn down the lamp when he left, or perhaps it had simply not occurred to him to do so, and sitting propped up against her pillows Hero at last had time to take stock of her surroundings.

She was occupying a cabin that was not in the least like any of those on the *Norah Crayne*, for it was neither as large as her own comfortable one nor as well equipped as the Fullbrights', and there was no comparable display of polished mahogany, bright chintz or gleaming brasswork. The furniture consisted of a single chair, a wire-fronted bookcase, a large built-in desk flanked by wall-cupboards, a chest and a wash-hand stand. The berth filled a recess facing two doors, one of which opened on to the small closet that combined the function of washroom and privy, and the other on to a companion-way that led up to the open deck. The cabin boasted two portholes, but no ornaments (unless the intricately wrought Moorish lamp and a fine Persian carpet that covered the floor could be counted as such), and except for the books, whose titles it was impossible to decipher at that range, it gave no indication as to the character or tastes of the owner.

Hero found herself wondering about the Captain. She had not met many Englishmen before, for Barclay, that normally peaceable man, had unaccountably taken exception to the policy of the British Navy, when on anti-slavery patrol, of stopping any ship suspected of being a slaver. It being his considered opinion that no damn' Britisher had any right to search an American ship, not even if it were crammed from top to bottom with slaves and could be winded five miles off!

'What we do with our own ships is our own damn' business,' Barclay had said, 'and we'll sort it out ourselves.' He had ceased to invite English visitors to Hollis Hill, and thereafter the few English women whom Hero had met had been teachers of music or deportment – stiff, bony spinsters, or faded widows living sadly in the past. They had not impressed her, and her history books had given her a profound distrust of their nation. But the ship she was now on was presumably British (if the accent of her Captain and the dropped aitches of Mr Batty Potter were anything to go by), and since she owed her life to them, she must show a proper degree of gratitude. Though recalling the Captain's pale eyes and misplaced sense of humour, she was not sure that this would prove too easy.

It occurred to her that she had read somewhere that exceptionally light-coloured eyes were a sign of a deceitful, untrustworthy and cruel nature, and she wondered if this were really so. Clayton's eyes for instance, though not precisely dark, were the grey of slate or storm-clouds. But the English Captain's were as pale as snow water – and as cold. Decidedly *not* a person to be trusted.

The slow swing and sway of the fretted light across the wall of the cabin had failed to make her drowsy again, and she had passed an uncomfort-

able night and been relieved when the sun rose and morning brought Mr
Potter knocking at the door with a breakfast tray, a pile of clothing and a
can of hot water:

'You'll be needing a wash,' announced Mr Potter. 'And 'ere's your
duds. I done a right pretty job on them, though I says it meself. But if
you were to ask me, I'd say you'd be better off in bed for another day or
two. That peeper of yours is terrible swole, and you don't look too good
to me. If I was you I'd rest meself – stay on me back.'

Hero thanked him gratefully for the return of her clothes, but assured
him that she felt quite well enough to get up, and asked him if he would
add to his kindness by telling his Captain that she would like to have a
few words with him in half an hour's time.

'Well – I *could*, o' course,' admitted Mr Potter. 'But I ain't so sure as
'e'll be able to spare you the time. 'E's got a mort of work on 'is 'ands,
what with one thing and another.'

'Tell him that it's urgent,' said Hero with decision.

Mr Potter shrugged, and having deposited a neatly folded pile of clothing on the end of the bunk, departed again; leaving her to wash and dress
herself and eat a frugal breakfast.

She was surprised to discover that he had indeed made a good job of
her torn garments, though being unable to match the buttons that had
been wrenched from her basque he had substituted a colourful and varie-
gated assortment that had evidently been selected at random from a well-
stocked button box. But the pile did not include either slippers or stock-
ings, and Hero realized with dismay that she must have lost the former
and torn the latter to shreds, and would have to return to the *Norah
Crayne* barefoot.

Dressing herself had proved a considerable ordeal; less on account of
her bruised body than because of her stiff and painfully lacerated hands.
But Miss Hollis was both stubborn and courageous, and wrestling grimly
with tapes, buttons and fastenings, she had managed it at last. There
remained only the tangled mass of chestnut hair that fell below her waist
and defied all her efforts to reduce it to even a semblance of order, and
searching for a comb she opened the nearest cupboard – to be confronted
by a strange, blotched and distorted face that made her jerk back with a
gasp of alarm.

It took her a full ten seconds to realize that she was looking at her
own face, reflected in a small square of looking-glass above an empty
shelf. And when she did so she could only stare at herself in frozen un-
belief, for though it had been impossible not to be aware of the extent of
her injuries, nothing had prepared her for that staggering display of
bruises, or for the fact that a cut lip and a swollen jaw could present such

an outrageous effect of depravity when allied to an unkempt mop of salt-stiffened and medusa-like hair. To make matters worse her once sober mourning dress of sedate black poplin, with its modest neckline and buttoned basque, now looked quite as disreputable as her battered face and tangled hair. The cheap, gaudy and ill-assorted buttons lent it an appearance of gipsy-like vulgarity, and she looked like – like some drunken, brawling drab off the street. A harpy. A harridan!

She was still staring at her reflection in horrified revulsion when a knock on the door reminded her that Mr Potter might be able to procure arnica, cold compresses and a set of plain buttons, and she turned hastily to bid him come in. But this time it was not Mr Potter, but the rightful owner of the cabin.

He stood in the open doorway with the sun shining down on his blond head, and surveying his guest, broke suddenly and outrageously into a roar of laughter. Thereby instantly and permanently dissipating any feelings of gratitude that she might have felt towards him.

'I am glad, sir,' pronounced Miss Hollis, quivering with affront, 'that the sight of my injuries and my unfortunate state should afford you so much amusement. May I hope that when you have laughed your fill you will perhaps feel able to offer me some assistance?'

Her words acted as a check to his laughter but failed to take the amusement from his face, and he bowed and said: 'My apologies. It was unkind of me to laugh, but I couldn't help it. It's that eye. It makes you look like some disorderly Billingsgate doxy who has been involved in a drunken brawl. Does it hurt very badly?'

'Strangely enough, it does! And if there is such a thing as a doctor on your ship, I should be glad of his services.'

'We don't carry one, I'm afraid. I do most of the doctoring around here; though I admit my qualifications are hardly impressive. I once worked for six months in an apothecary's shop in my early youth, and studied oriental medicine at Aleppo for an even shorter period of time. But I can probably do something about that eye.'

He called up the companion-way in a language that was unfamiliar to Hero, and turning back to her, said: 'I was told you wanted to see me urgently. Was it about your eye?'

'No, it was not. I wished to know how soon you would be able to transfer me back on to the *Norah Crayne*.'

'Your ship? So that's who she was – I didn't have time to recognize her. She's calling at Zanzibar this trip, I believe.'

'She is. And if you will signal her to stand by, Captain Fullbright will send a boat for me. It should be quite easy to do so now that the sea has gone down.'

'Oh, quite easy – if she were anywhere in sight, which she is not. But you don't need to worry. I'll be able to put you ashore at Zanzibar myself, eventually.'

'*Eventually?* But I wish to get there immediately!' Hero's voice lost its note of dignity and became agitated. 'Surely you must understand that I cannot allow Captain Fullbright to reach Zanzibar ahead of me? Why, if that were to happen Clay would – I mean, my uncle and aunt would imagine that I had been drowned, and I could not think of subjecting them to such a dreadful shock. We must overtake the *Norah Crayne* at once!'

'Not a chance,' said the Captain callously. 'Even allowing for her having been blown off course she'll raise the island inside three days with this wind. But I'm afraid I have business in these waters, and owing to that storm I may not get there myself until somewhere around the end of the month. I'm sorry, but there it is. Business before pleasure.'

Hero said, aghast: 'But – but today is only the *eighteenth*!'

'Nineteenth. You've missed one.'

'You mean I may have to stay on this ship for another ten days? But I can't! I won't. This is *ridiculous*! You must see——'

She checked herself with an effort, aware that it was she who was being ridiculous, and struggling to regain her composure said stiffly: 'I must apologize. What I should have said was that I fully realize how inconvenient it may be for you to proceed direct to Zanzibar, but I will see to it that you are not the loser. You can be sure that any financial loss you may incur will be made good, either by myself or by my relations.'

'I doubt it,' said the Englishman, and laughed again as though at some private joke. 'Not on this occasion, at all events. I admit it's bad luck on your relations, but I expect they'll survive the shock. And you can always console yourself with the thought of how delighted they will be to have you restored to them, alive and well.'

Hero's chin lifted dangerously and once again she had to struggle against a rising anger; but she contrived to suppress it and say civilly enough: 'I guess you think I cannot carry out such a promise, but I can. My uncle, Mr Hollis, is the American Consul in Zanzibar, and my cousin Josiah Crayne owns the Crayne Line Clippers; which should serve to convince you that you will lose nothing by conveying me to Zanzibar with the least possible delay.'

'Well, well!' grinned the Captain. 'So you're Miss Hollis, are you? I can't say your uncle is a personal friend of mine, but at least we know each other by sight. I heard that he had a niece coming out to visit him, though I didn't imagine I'd ever meet her.'

'Then you will——?' began Hero, but was interrupted by the arrival of a tall Arab wearing a white cotton *kanzu* and carrying a copper bowl and some lengths of clean linen. The bowl proved to contain a curious aromatic mixture that looked as though it were made of crushed herbs, and further conversation was abandoned while the Captain ladled a quantity of it on to a folded square of linen, applied it to Miss Hollis's eye, and tied it in place with another strip of material.

'How does that feel?'

'Better, I think,' said Hero doubtfully. 'Except that you've tied my hair into it.'

'It was difficult not to. I'll have to lend you a comb and a brush. Or better still, a pair of shears. Now let's have a look at your hands.'

He examined her scraped knuckles and blistered palms, and said: 'They'll heal clean in a day or two; salt water is a great purifier. I'll tell Batty to give you some ointment for those knuckles. And find you a comb.'

He turned away with the obvious intention of leaving the cabin, but Hero was not so easily put off. She said quickly: 'That is very kind of you; a comb will be most welcome. But about that other matter we were discussing: is it settled that we make immediately for Zanzibar?'

The Englishman paused and looked back at her over his shoulder with complete disinterest. 'No, Miss Hollis. It is not. I am sorry to disoblige a lady, but I'm afraid it is not possible for me to abandon my present plans in order to speed your restoration to the bosom of your family. And in any case I couldn't get you there in time to prevent Captain Fullbright breaking the sad news of your tragic end, so a few more days of mourning are not going to hurt them.'

'But I have just told you that you will be paid for your trouble, and I can assure you that I am not in the habit of making promises that I cannot keep.'

'And neither am I in the habit of altering my plans, Miss Hollis.'

'Except, I suppose,' retorted Hero, exasperated, 'to suit yourself.'

'Of course: and on this occasion it does not happen to suit me. But you may rest assured that we shall do our best to make your stay on board comfortable, and if it's any consolation to you, the delay will at least give your looks a chance to improve before we reach Zanzibar. For if your loving relatives were to see you at this moment the odds are that they wouldn't even recognize you – much less own you!'

He grinned unfeelingly and departed, shutting the cabin door behind him and leaving his involuntary guest a prey to unprofitable emotions; not the least of which was wounded vanity.

Even her detractors could never have accused Hero Hollis of being vain of her looks. But she had become accustomed to hearing herself referred to as a 'beauty', a 'goddess', or a 'damned handsome young woman', and until this morning had seen nothing in her looking-glass to contradict any of these statements. It was somehow deeply humiliating to discover that in the eyes of this obstructive and unsympathetic Englishman she must appear not only unsightly but positively grotesque. And the fact that he looked upon this as a matter for jest added a final touch of indignity to the whole undignified and deplorable situation.

Hero could only regret that she had been led to thank the man for saving her life, because now that she came to think of it she was not at all sure that the dreadful episode of her fall from the deck of the *Norah Crayne* – not to mention her present predicament and her damaged looks – could not be written down to his account. It was his inability to handle his ship in a storm that had resulted in the *Norah Crayne* being forced into a cross sea, and but for that she, Hero, would never have been swept overboard, or sustained these disfiguring injuries. Therefore the very *least* he could do to atone for all this was to take her to Zanzibar without delay. What did his own selfish private concerns matter when compared with the grief and despair that Aunt Abby and Cressy would be enduring? The anguish of poor Clayton, who would think her lost for ever, and the remorse of Amelia Fullbright? The thought that their sufferings were now to be unnecessarily prolonged, and by the very man whose criminal lack of seamanship had caused them, was insupportable.

'There y'are, miss,' said Mr Potter, breaking in upon her angry musing. He deposited a brush and comb, the promised ointment and a pair of scissors on the desk, and remarked affably that if there was anything else she fancied she had only to give a shout and Jumah would attend to it: 'You just tell 'im what you wants, for 'e speaks the King's English as good as I does, and I can't come 'opping in and out meself. It's still all 'ands to make-and-mend, for the pore ole bitch got a fair batterin' in that storm.'

'The poor old . . .?'

'The ship. The *Virago*. Fair catched it, she did. Foremast gone, spars broke, 'atches stove in——'

'The *Virago*?' For some reason the name seemed vaguely familiar, and Hero was wondering where she had heard it before, when a snatch of conversation returned to her: '*He named her, so he should know.*' Captain Fullbright had said that. But . . .

'That's right,' said Mr Potter. 'Rum name for a ship, I'll allow. She were the *Valerian* once; built special for one of them Bristol Nabobs who 'ad a fancy to go cruising to the gorjus East – 'ence them pretty little port'oles, and such. But Captain Rory changes 'er name to the *Virago*, which 'e claims is a durned sight more suited to 'er nasty cantankerous ways. Of course 'e were only 'aving 'is little joke, but I'm not saying 'e wasn't right at that, for there's times she can act as spiteful as a dockside drab. Look at the way she cuts up two days ago? Mules weren't in it! Fair got the bit between 'er teeth she did, and——'

Hero said sharply: 'Captain *who*? What did you say his name was?'

'The skipper? Captain Rory – Captain H'Emory Frost. An 'oly terror, and don't you let no one tell you different! But there's times when the old *Virago* 'as come near beating him. Two of a kind, they are. Why, once when we was off Ras-al-Had——'

But Hero was not listening to him. She was recalling with cold horror several things that Captain Fullbright had said about the owner of the *Virago*. Adventurer . . . black sheep . . . blackguard. '*If there's anything discreditable going on, you can bet your last dime that Rory Frost's mixed up in it . . .*' And now she, Hero Hollis, niece of the American Consul in Zanzibar, was actually on this ruffian's ship and in his clutches!

It was an appalling situation. And even as she contemplated it, a further and far more horrifying thought occurred to her: Captain Fullbright had also mentioned piracy and kidnapping. Supposing that this Captain Frost, having realized who she was, had decided to hold her for ransom? Could *that* be why he had refused to pursue the *Norah Crayne* or to set out at once for Zanzibar?

The plot of several popular novels, borrowed in recent years from the Ladies' Lending Library, flashed through Hero's mind and added considerably to her disquiet. Those pale eyes – how right she had been to distrust them! Yes, undoubtedly that must be what he planned to do . . . hold her to ransom. Why, she must seem like manna from Heaven to him! How *could* she have been so foolish as to tell him who she was before asking his name? For now that he knew (she had insisted on his knowing!) that she was both rich and influential, it followed that if even half the things that Captain Fullbright had said of him were true, he could not be expected to miss such a golden opportunity.

It's my own fault! thought Hero frantically: *I ought to have thought . . . Why didn't I think? Why didn't I ask for his name?*

She could only put it down to the shock of those terrifying minutes in the sea and the injuries she had received while being dragged on board. But whatever the reason, the fact remained that until this moment the identity of her rescuer and the name of his ship had not seemed to her of the least importance.

6

The week that followed seemed endless to Hero, for even with her limited knowledge of the sea it soon became clear to her that the *Virago* was merely idling to and fro.

The Trade Wind was blowing strongly, and had they taken advantage of it they could surely have made Zanzibar in a matter of hours; or a day and a night at most. The fact that they did not do so lent weight to her suspicion that Captain Emory Frost was playing a deep game that involved threats and ransom money, and though she refrained from accusing him of it to his face, she was secretly convinced that he must be waiting for the reply to some message he had sent to her Uncle Nathaniel.

It may have been the effect of those hard, light-coloured eyes that prevented her from taxing him with it, for Miss Hollis had never been noted for guarding her tongue and was normally outspoken to a fault. But there was something about Emory Frost, quite apart from his reputation as sketched for her by Captain Fullbright, that suggested that he would be an ill man to cross swords with, and Hero curbed her impatience and concealed both her anger and her alarm. And was chafed by the necessity for doing so.

Her lacerated hands, as Captain Frost had predicted, had healed remarkably quickly, and her bruised eye and jaw soon regained their normal proportions, though they and numerous other contusions (the majority mercifully concealed) remained shockingly discoloured. But her hair had proved a major disaster, for, impeded by stiff and exceedingly painful fingers, she had found it impossible to drag a comb through that heavy, matted mass, and losing all patience with it, she had thrust the shears into Mr Potter's reluctant hands and commanded him to cut it off. The result of this impetuous action had been unhappy to say the least of it, for she had emerged from the operation looking, as Captain Frost had been ungallant enough to remark, 'like a cross between a deck-swab and a sea urchin'.

'Why didn't you get me to do it?' he enquired, surveying the wreckage with considerable amusement. 'Uncle Batty may be an admirable lady's maid, but he's no barber.'

'Is Mr Potter your uncle?' asked Hero, momentarily diverted from the ruin of those magnificent chestnut tresses.

'Only by adoption. We've been together for a long time. I made his acquaintance a good many years ago when he was a very well known character in certain parts of London. Here, give me those shears——'

He had actually succeeded in trimming the ragged crop into some sort of order, and had told her that she would be well advised to keep it that way during her stay in the East, for although it might make her look like a cabin-boy in skirts, she would find it a deal cooler and more comfortable than a chignon. An observation that did nothing to console her for the sight of herself in the looking-glass.

Hero had always despised tears, but gazing at her reflection she had come perilously near to shedding them. What was Clayton going to think of her altered looks? Would he even recognize her? She could only hope that he would not, and she turned her back on the glass and thereafter avoided looking at herself, even though Mr Potter made her a black velvet patch to wear over her discoloured eye and assured her earnestly that she 'didn't look 'arf bad'.

Mr Potter was a friendly soul, and it was not long before Hero found herself being regaled with the saga of his by no means blameless past.

His name, it appeared, was neither Batty nor Potter. But having been born out of wedlock in an attic above a pottery shop in Battersea (a borough, Hero gathered, of the City of London), and in his prime earned the proud sobriquet of 'The Battersea Cat' owing to a talent for breaking and entering through top-storey windows, he had adopted both. It was during this period of his fame that he had acquired the first of his two legal wives, and all might have gone well with the marriage had he not contracted a second and bigamous one with a widow in Houndsditch, and the rightful Mrs Potter discovered the fact. Inflamed by equal parts of gin and jealousy she had 'squeaked beef' on Batty to the 'Peelers'. With the result that three nights later he had been caught red-handed, sliding down a drainpipe with his pockets full of stolen property, and spent the next five years at Her Britannic Majesty's expense.

'It was when I come out,' confided Batty, recalling those distant days in a tone of nostalgic affection, 'that I marries me second – me first 'aving snuffed it while I was doin' time, and the widder 'aving taken up with a bruiser. But Aggie she turns out to be a proper shrew; which just shows 'ow you can be took in by a petticoat.'

Advancing years and several more spells in Her Majesty's prisons had impaired his agility but done nothing, it seemed, to improve his morals, for he had apparently been engaged in burgling Captain Frost's bedroom when the Captain had awakened and caught him at it:

'To tell you the truth,' admitted Batty with disarming candour, 'I'd seen 'im come 'ome and I would a' laid me 'and to it that 'e were drunk as a lord, or I wouldn't 'ave tried it! I didn't know then that 'e can 'old more liquor than 'arf a dozen Irish lightermen and still keep 'is wits about 'im. Sorted me out proper 'e did, and was all for turning me over to the Peelers. But 'e give me a swig of booze first, out of the kindness of 'is 'eart, and we gets to chewing the rag all friendly-like, and in the end 'e says "Well, come to think of it," 'e says, "I'm agin' the law meself, so why should I 'elp the barstards" (beggin' your pardon, miss) "to fill their jails?" 'e says. You see, 'e was in a bit of trouble 'imself – 'adn't seen 'is relations for a matter of years, and being 'ard pressed 'ad looked 'em up to ask for a loan, but all 'is uncle gives 'im is a bed for the night providin' 'e gets out the werry next day and don't come back! So we prigs anything we can lay our 'ands on, and skips out smart, and in the morning we ships for the gorjus East.'

'Prigs——?'

'Nabs. Snitches. Re-moves.'

'You mean *steals*? Are you telling me,' demanded Hero, horrified, 'that you – that Mr Frost actually assisted you to rob his uncle's house?'

'That's right,' confirmed Batty, pleased at what he obviously took to be commendation. 'Not bad pickings, neither. All the spoons solid silver, and an 'andful of joolry and two 'undred and seven-five golden guineas in a safe wot a child could 'ave broke into with a bent pin. Set us up proper it did. That were nigh on fifteen years ago, or maybe a little more, and we been together ever since. Up and down, 'ere and there—— and I can't say as I've ever regretted it. Though there 'as been times when I'd 'ave give a lot to see ole London town again ... *Tch, tch!*'

Mr Potter drifted off into reverie, his bright, observant eyes misting with tender memories as he remembered London fogs and London river, and the sights and smells of home.

Hero shrewdly suspected that Mr Potter's apparent predilection for her society disguised some ulterior motive. The most likely, in her opinion, being that Captain Frost had given orders that she was to be kept occupied and under observation so that she should see nothing he did not wish her to see. Nevertheless, she was grateful for the old man's company, since Mr Potter, as might have been expected, knew (or professed to know) a great deal about Zanzibar, and would entertain her for hours on end with fantastic stories of the island. Tall tales of witchcraft and black magic. Of sacred drums, and a disastrous drought brought about by the spells of a local chieftain who had quarrelled with the late Sultan and built himself a palace that was haunted by the ghosts of murdered slaves: 'The Mwenyi Mkuu builds 'em inter the walls alive, t'bring good luck,' explained Batty. 'And kills a sight more so's to mix the lime wiv their blood, see.'

'Oh no!' shuddered Hero, appalled. 'I don't believe it. That can't be true!'

'True as I'm sitting 'ere. Arsk anyone!'

Hero had asked Captain Frost, who shrugged and said that he wouldn't be surprised.

'But surely you can't believe that they'd *really* do such a thing? In this century?'

'Why not? The Mwenyi Mkuu were famous witch doctors, and that's the way their minds would work. Life is cheap to the Africans, and murder is their favourite sport. I'm quite willing to believe that there are any number of bodies built into the walls of Dunga Palace.'

'But why didn't the Sultan stop it?'

'Seyyid Saïd? He may have made himself Sultan of Zanzibar, but the Mwenyi Mkuu were there a long while before he was. And besides, I don't suppose he wanted to risk another three-year drought. Didn't Batty tell you about that?'

'Yes, but . . . It couldn't possibly have happened! *You* must know that. Or if it did, it was only a coincidence.'

'A very convenient one.'

Miss Hollis decided that the Captain was amusing himself at her expense, and observed tartly that she supposed he also believed that absurd story of Batty's about the Sacred Drums of Zanzibar?

'Which story?'

'Is there more than one?'

'Half a dozen, I should say. Which one has Batty been regaling you with?'

'He says that the priests of the Mwenyi – whatever the name is – keep them hidden away in a secret place near Dunga, and that the drums beat of their own accord if any disaster threatens the island.'

'So I've heard.'

'And you believe that?'

Captain Frost laughed. 'I never believe anything I haven't seen or heard myself. And as I don't recall being present during a disaster or just before one, perhaps that accounts for my not hearing them.'

'*All* superstitions,' announced Miss Hollis loftily, 'are a bar to education and progress, and should be eradicated.'

'It depends on what you mean by superstition.'

'Why, believing in things that are not true, of course!'

'But then what is truth? That, my self-opinionated child, is the great question. Is it what you believe? Or what I believe? Or what the Mwenyi Mkuu believe?'

'I am *not* self-opinionated – or your child!' flared Miss Hollis, temporarily abandoning the abstract for the personal. 'And you cannot argue in favour of superstition.'

'I'm not arguing. You are—— and since we are on the subject, what about that gold and those islands full of black men that I heard you telling Batty about on the after-hatch this morning? If that's not superstition, I don't know what is!'

'That's different,' said Hero, blushing hotly. 'That was only . . .'

'You mean you don't believe a word of it?'

'Yes—— No! I mean . . .' She realized that he was laughing at her, and turning on her heel left him without deigning to complete the sentence.

He really was an infuriating person, and her dislike of him had been sharply exacerbated by the discovery that the flyleaves of several of his books bore an engraved coat-of-arms that was undoubtedly his own, since below each one, written in faded ink and an unformed childish hand, ran the inscription: *Emory Tyson Frost, Lyndon Gables, Kent. Anno Domini 1839.* The motto they incorporated, *'I Tayke Wat I Wyll',* seemed singularly appropriate, but the books themselves were an oddly assorted collection. Not in the least what she would have expected to find in the possession of a slave trader, since they included such items as biographies and military campaigns, the Greek and Latin classics, three different translations of the *Odyssey* and two of the *Iliad*. The Koran, the Talmud, the Apocrypha, the *Analects of Confucius, Biographia Juridica* and *The Admiralty Manual* shared a shelf with *The Travels of Marco Polo*, Malory's *Morte d'Arthur, Don Quixote* and *Lavengro*, while a book on metallurgy and three on medicine, together with the *Principles and Practices of Modern Artillery*, provided strange company for the collected works of Shakespeare and the novels of Walter Scott. There were also at least half a dozen volumes of poetry, and when Hero had removed one of these at random it had fallen open at a page marked by a frayed strip of ribbon, on lines that had instantly captured her attention and her imagination:

> With a host of furious fancies
> Whereof I am commander,
> With a burning spear and a horse of air
> To the wilderness I wander.
> By a knight of ghosts and shadows
> I summoned am to tourney
> Ten leagues beyond the wide world's end.
> Methinks it is no journey.

The lines held a music and a magic that Hero had never encountered in the sedate volumes of selected verse that had hitherto come her way, and she turned the pages slowly, and yet more slowly: *'Go and catch a*

65

falling star,' ... *'Tell me where all past years are,'* ... *'Teach me to hear mermaids singing'* ...

The Elizabethan poets had not figured on the shelves of Barclay's library, but judging from the well-thumbed pages of this salt-stained, leather-bound book, they were familiar companions of Emory Tyson Frost's, and the discovery angered Hero even more than the sight of that coat-of-arms had done.

It would, she thought, have been possible (though difficult) to find excuses for a man handicapped by poverty, ignorance and low beginnings. But there was something not only indefensible, but downright *indecent* in the fact that a person possessing the advantages of birth and education could stoop to such an infamous and revolting method of earning a livelihood. Captain Frost was not only a disgrace to his own nation, but to the whole of the civilized West!

All the same, she could not believe that on this voyage, at least, the *Virago* was engaged in slaving, for she had read a great many tracts on the subject of the slave trade, and few had failed to mention that a slave ship could be winded from a considerable distance owing to the stench of unwashed and overcrowded humanity, packed below decks into dark and insanitary holds. But there was certainly no insalubrious smell about the *Virago*. Only such normal shipboard odours as tar and salt water – if one excepted the exotic and unfamiliar ones of Eastern cookery – and this despite the fact that the crew, with the sole exception of Mr Potter, consisted of a motley collection of coloured cut-throats ranging from Africans to men from Malabar and Macao, with the position of first mate being filled by a tall, hatchet-faced Arab who went by the name of Ralub and was accorded the title of 'Hajji' on the strength of having made the pilgrimage to Mecca.

The business of the ship was largely conducted in Arabic, with a smattering of assorted dialects thrown in for good measure, but the precise nature of that business still remained to be verified, and Hero had finally discarded caution in favour of direct attack:

'Just what do you and your men do?' she enquired of the Captain.

'Trade,' replied Captain Frost briefly.

'In what?'

'Anything that seems likely to make a profit.'

'Does that include slaves?'

Captain Frost gave her an oblique look and grinned. 'Certainly; on occasions. Though if you are wondering if I have any on board at the moment, the answer is "No".'

Hero drew a deep breath and said carefully: 'I would not wish to be rude to someone to whom I must owe a debt of gratitude for saving——'

'I shouldn't let that worry you,' interrupted the Captain cheerfully. 'No one risked a thing in hauling you aboard, and it was probably as much our fault as yours that you got washed off your ship.'

'I am well aware of that!'

'Oh you are, are you? Then in that case you need not hesitate to be as outspoken as you please. Do you disapprove of slavers?'

'*Disapprove*,' said Hero with emphasis, 'is hardly the word I should have chosen. "Detest" is a better one. Or "despise". To traffic in human beings, and batten on the misery of our fellow creatures, must surely be the most detestable and despicable trade in the whole history of mankind . . .'

This being a subject on which she felt fully qualified to speak, she had spoken on it at length; giving him her views on the indefensible iniquity of the entire system and ending by telling him, in detail, just what she thought of white men who engaged in it for sordid profit. He might not like it, but it would do him no harm to be told it to his face, and there was always a chance that it might bring him to see the error of his ways.

Captain Frost leant against the rail and listened with an expression of polite interest, and when she had finished, said affably:

'Ah well, it doesn't look as though there will be much more of it now that Cass is no longer Secretary in Washington. Without him, your countrymen may even get around to joining the British in putting it down, instead of doing their damnedest to keep it going. The bottom's going to drop out of the trade, and detestable and despicable characters like myself will have to start looking around for other ways of making easy money.'

Hero's face paled with anger and she said hotly: 'I don't know how you *dare* to say such a thing! We have *never* attempted to keep it going! Just because General Cass would not permit you to stop and search our ships——'

Captain Frost laughed and raised a protesting hand: 'Come, come, Miss Hollis. You wrong me. I assure you I should never dream of stopping or searching anyone else's ship. The boot, alas, is on the other foot. Her Britannic Majesty's Navy, who appear to have taken upon themselves the sole responsibility of putting down the trade, have been stopping and searching peaceful and harmless people like myself for the past fifty years or more. But owing to the howls of rage and fury raised by your freedom-loving nation, they are still not permitted to stop and search any ship flying an American flag. With the pleasing result that every slaver, whatever his nationality, immediately hoists the stars-and-stripes if sighted and challenged. I confess to having done so myself before now. And why not? It has often proved most useful.'

'*Why not?* Why, I have never heard of anything so – so——' Words appeared to fail Miss Hollis.

Her indignation evidently amused the Captain, for he laughed and said: 'My good child, like everyone else I am in this for money. And if your nation chooses to take up the attitude that it is an insult to her flag to have a suspected slaver flying it stopped and searched by the Royal Navy, then she must be prepared to put up with the alternative insult of finding that flag used by less favoured nations as a cover to every variety of illegal transaction. She can't have it both ways. General Cass, with his Anglophobia and his rooted conviction that Her Majesty's Navy are using the cloak of Philanthropy to disguise a plot aimed at interrupting the trade of all other nations, has proved a godsend to all hard-working slavers, and we are duly grateful to him. I can only regret that I, personally, have not been able to derive more profit from your country's patriotic attitude on this issue. But alas, the naval gentleman who esteems it his duty to put down slave trading in these waters knows the *Virago* only too well, and I doubt if half-a-dozen American flags would stop him from boarding me if he thought he could catch me out with a cargo of black ivory aboard.'

'I don't believe it!' said Hero furiously. 'I do not believe *one word* of it!'

'Ah, but then you don't know Dan Larrimore,' said Captain Frost, wilfully misunderstanding her.

'I didn't mean that. I mean I don't believe that we . . . that America . . . Well, maybe some of the Southern States, but we in the North——'

She stopped abruptly, checked by the uncomfortable recollection of a speech that she had heard delivered at an Abolitionist Rally in Boston not so long ago. '*The Southern States,*' the speaker had asserted, '*may provide the market. But we cannot absolve ourselves on that account, for it is notorious that the real traffickers in flesh and blood are the citizens of our Northern States. It is in Yankee ships, floated by Yankee capital, commanded by Yankee skippers and sailing forth on their abominable errands with the connivance of bribed Yankee authorities, that the work of the Devil is carried out!*'

Hero had been disposed to think that the Reverend gentleman had been exaggerating. But a doubt remained, and encountering Captain Frost's derisive gaze she said defiantly: 'I guess every country has its share of rascals and – and blackguards; and it is well known that England instituted the slave trade and built the fortunes of half-a-dozen of her most flourishing ports on the sufferings of millions of unfortunate negroes. But at least we in the North mean to see that slavery is outlawed, and I assure you that we shall do it!'

'I'm afraid so. It'll probably go on in the East for another century or so, but as far as the West is concerned the game is very nearly played out.'

'*Game?*' said Hero in incredulous distaste. 'How can you possibly call anything so hideously cruel a "game" – or even attempt to defend it?'

'I'm not defending it. Only making money out of it.'

'Out of death and suffering?'

'Oh, I don't think so: if you are suggesting that I am one of those sub-human fools whose idiot greed prompts them to thrust four hundred slaves into accommodation which is only fit for less than half that number of hogs. Personally, I've never lost a slave yet from an avoidable cause, and the trade would have lasted profitably for many more years, and without earning itself such a bad name, if others had had as much sense. But unfortunately there will always be a few greedy *cretins* who can be counted upon to ruin any really lucrative dodge.'

'And that is how you think of it—— as a "lucrative dodge"? Have you no – no *compassion?*'

'No, I don't think so. Compassion is an expensive luxury and one I can't afford. And as far as I can remember no one ever had any for me.'

'I can't believe that. *Someone* must have been kind to you – fond of you. Forgiven you things. Your mother——'

'She ran away with a dancing master when I was six.'

'Oh . . . Well then, your father.'

'If this is an attempt to coax me into telling you the sad story of my life,' said Captain Frost with a grin, 'I feel it is only fair to warn you that you would find it intolerably dull.'

Miss Hollis regarded him with undisguised loathing, and having coldly informed him that she had already heard more than enough about him and was profoundly uninterested in his past, retired to her cabin in considerable dudgeon: firmly resolving to avoid his company for the remainder of her stay in his ship, and on no account to ask him any further questions.

She had not, however, been able to keep either of these admirable resolutions, for three nights later, aroused by the sound of a boat being lowered over the side, she had left her berth to investigate, and been startled to find that someone had not only blocked her view from both portholes by hanging heavy strips of coconut matting from the deck above, but had also bolted her cabin door from the outside.

Tugging at the handle in the hot darkness she became aware that the *Virago* was no longer moving, and that it was the unaccustomed silence that had made those other noises so clearly audible. Yet she could not believe that they were near land, for there was no sound of surf. The matting rasped against the side of the ship as the schooner rolled sleepily to the swell, and from behind it came a soft splash of oars that retreated until Hero could no longer hear them, and after a long interval returned again. A boat bumped alongside, and presently there were other noises; a murmur of voices and a familiar laugh. The squeak and whine of the windlass, and once again a boat pulling away . . .

Something was either being taken off the ship or on to it, and quite suddenly Hero was sure that she knew what it was. They were taking on slaves! This, then, was what Captain Frost and his venal crew had been waiting for. A rendezvous with some sinister Arab dhow, presumably delayed by the storm (which would account for the loitering of the past week!) A dhow which was at that very moment engaged in transferring a human cargo to the dark hold of the *Virago*.

For a wild moment anger and shock almost betrayed her into hammering on the door and screaming to be let out, but the futility and foolishness of such an action came home to her in time. If the men out there were engaged in some ugly transaction that they did not wish her to witness, no one would come. Or if anyone did, it might well be the worse for her. For the moment, at least, there was nothing that she could do; – except register a solemn vow that as soon as she won free from this infamous ship she would do everything in her power to see that its owner was brought to justice and made to pay for his crimes.

'And I'll do it, too!' Hero promised herself in a passionate whisper. She would find an opportunity the very next day to see for herself what cargo had been taken aboard, and if it proved to be what she suspected, she would tell Uncle Nat, who could be counted upon to inform the proper authority: presumably this British naval Lieutenant that Captain Fullbright had spoken of – Daniel Larrimore, who would 'like to have the hanging of Rory Frost'.

She slept badly, and awakened late to find the cabin full of sunshine and a sea breeze billowing the curtains as the *Virago* raced before the wind with all sails set. The matting that had covered the portholes had vanished, and when she tried the cabin door she found that it was no longer secured. But her breakfast that morning had included ripe figs and a fresh paw-paw, neither of which had figured on the menu before or would have kept for any length of time on board, and though Jumah, the Captain's personal servant, spoke tolerable English and was fond of airing it, when she enquired where the fresh fruit had come from he affected not to understand her and replied affably in Arabic. Batty Potter having proved equally unhelpful, Hero had broken her resolution not to ask any further questions or enter into conversation with the *Virago*'s infamous owner.

'The fruit?' said Captain Frost, in no way disconcerted by her query:

'I hope there was nothing wrong with it? It came off a coastal dhow that we stopped to speak to last night. We lowered a boat and took on some supplies. I'm surprised we didn't wake you.'

There was a faintly satirical note in his voice and a distinct glint of amusement in his regard, and Hero was seized with the uncomfortable suspicion that he was not only well aware that she had been awakened, but also that she had attempted to push the matting away from the port-hole and had tried the handle of the door.

She said in a carefully controlled voice: 'You did. But when I wished to come up on deck to see why we had stopped, I found that I was unable to do so because someone had locked the door.'

'Indeed? You should have called out,' said Captain Frost blandly. 'Or perhaps you did so, and no one heard you?'

'You know very well that I did not,' retorted Hero crossly, 'and that if I had, no one would have come. In fact I wouldn't be a mite surprised if it was you yourself who locked me in!'

'It was. It seemed to me a wise precaution, and I see that my fore-thought was fully justified. It would not have done at all for you to have been seen on deck last night.'

'Because I might have seen something that you wished to conceal?'

'Not at all. Merely because the – er – gentlemen I happened to be meeting would not have understood your presence aboard my ship. They might have taken it amiss, and so I preferred that they should be kept in ignorance. There are a good many rough characters in this part of the world, Miss Hollis, and it does not pay to take chances with them.'

'Thank you. I will remember that,' said Hero meaningly. And was both disconcerted and unreasonably annoyed when Captain Frost laughed. The Captain, she considered, laughed a great deal too much and always at the wrong things. But he was to disconcert her to an even greater extent in the next few seconds:

'That eye of yours seems to be improving,' observed the Captain, looking her over critically. 'In fact, with a little luck, your relatives may even be able to recognize you when we land.'

'You mean – you mean we really *are* going to Zanzibar?' demanded Hero breathlessly.

'Of course we are. Did you think I had kidnapped you?'

It was so exactly what she had thought that an uncontrollable wave of colour rose from the base of her throat to the roots of her cropped hair, temporarily dimming the rainbow hues that still surrounded her left eye and drawing another shout of laughter from the Captain.

'By God, you did! Well I'll be damned! Hi – Batty, d'ye hear that? Our super-cargo thought we were kidnapping her. It's not such a bad idea, now I come to think of it. How much do you suppose they'd pay to get her back?'

Mr Potter, who with the aid of a pockmarked Arab named Hadir was busy laying a much-mended sail over most of the after-deck, made a rudely derisive noise, and the Captain grinned and said regretfully: 'The trouble is, of course, that no one is ever going to believe we've got you unless we actually produce you, so I'm afraid it wouldn't work. You see, Miss Hollis, you're dead: lost overboard and drowned in mid-ocean. And as everyone must know that by now, anyone who might be interested enough to pay up would think we were spinning a very tall yarn if we said we'd got you. They'd want to see you before they parted with a dollar; and at pretty close quarters too, since no one is going to recognize you at long distance at the moment – not with that hair-cut and the state your face is in. No, it's a pity, but I'm afraid that as a money-making proposition you're no use to us. And just to reassure you, for anything in the nature of my personal pleasures I only kidnap pretty women.'

He slapped Miss Hollis encouragingly upon the shoulder in a manner that he might have employed towards a twelve-year-old schoolboy, and remarked unforgivably that he could only hope that her relatives would be pleased to have her back.

'Why should you suppose they might not be?' snapped Hero, betrayed into rudeness. (*Pretty women*, indeed!)

'Well, it depends on how much they think of you, doesn't it? The majority of my relations, for instance, would be profoundly relieved if they heard that I'd been drowned at sea, and no bells would be rung if they subsequently discovered the report to be exaggerated.'

'I cannot say I am altogether surprised,' said Hero. 'I guess if I had a nephew who repaid my hospitality by stealing my property while staying as a guest in my house, I should not feel any too kindly towards him either.'

If she had expected the Captain to be abashed she was much mistaken, for he only laughed and said: 'I see Batty's been telling tales out of school. No, I don't suppose my uncle was any too pleased about that. But then I wasn't either. In fact the whole thing was a grave disappointment, for I'd always thought the old skinflint kept a really tidy sum in that safe, and though the amount we got out of it was not to be sneezed at, it wasn't a fraction of what I reckoned he owed me. As for my aunt's diamonds, they turned out to be very second-rate stuff and we got little more than a hundred guineas for the lot.'

'You would appear,' said Hero frostily, 'to consider theft amusing. Possibly that is an English viewpoint.'

'I wouldn't be surprised. The English have always been great ones at grabbing everything they can lay hands on and then piously pretending that they only did it for the previous owner's good. A hypocritical lot.'

Hero's jaw dropped in an inelegant manner and she stared at him, momentarily rendered speechless.

'Now why are you looking at me like that? Surely it's a well-known fact?'

'But I thought you were English.'

'Whatever gave you that idea?'

'Your voice . . . the way you talk . . . those books. The—— What are you, then?'

'Myself.'

'Do you mean,' said Hero, bewildered, 'that you do not know who your parents were?'

'Oh, they were English. English of the English! The Frosts were probably sitting smugly in Kent when the Romans came, and they were certainly there when the Normans landed. But that doesn't mean the country has to own me, or that I have to owe it anything.'

'Patriotism——' began Hero, but was not permitted to continue.

'Patriotism be damned. That whole concept is merely a combination of self-interest and sentimentality. You're an American, aren't you?'

'And proud of it!'

'Why? The herd instinct? *We mustangs are a far better lot than those vulgar pit-ponies or any horse that ever came from out of Arabia, while as for those impossible African zebras——! That sort of thing?'

'Not at all. One's ancestors——'

'A man is not responsible for his ancestors, so why should he accept credit or shoulder blame for anything they did? Or, for that matter, be judged in advance by the fact that he happens to have been born on one side or another of some imaginary line? It's an archaic and dangerous idea and it's quite time it became outmoded, since it leads to a deal of trouble. People are people; black, white, yellow or brown. You either like someone or you don't, and the bit of earth they were born on shouldn't have anything to do with it or be allowed to influence your judgement in any way. Yet it does. You, for instance – You haven't even laid eyes on Zanzibar, but I'm willing to bet that you've already made up your mind that its people are a poor ignorant lot of heathens who are probably dishonest and certainly dirty, and all in crying need of the civilizing influence of the wonderful white man. Am I right?'

'No. Yes—— But then one knows . . .'

'I can see I am. And almost every white man in the island would agree with you, though there isn't one of them who cares a snap of the fingers for the place or its people. They are only there for what they can get out of it for themselves or their firms or their countries. Yet the place that they regard as little better than a cess-pit was old Sultan Saïd's idea of an earthly paradise. He fell in love with it at first sight and resented every minute he had to spend away from it; and he died trying to get back to it . . . and made very sure he would be buried there.'

The mockery had suddenly vanished from the Captain's voice and been replaced by an odd note of regret – or could it have been affection? – that made Hero say curiously: 'Did you know him?'

'Yes. I had the luck to do him a good turn once, and he never forgot it. He was an amazing man, and a great one; though he should have known better than to make treaties with Western nations. There are a good many Europeans in Zanzibar now; merchants and consuls and consular staffs of half-a-dozen different nations. Every last one of them as convinced as you are that the native population can only derive benefit from contact with their superior civilizations, and must inevitably regard them with envy and admiration.'

'But they – the Westerners – *are* bringing them the benefits of civilization,' insisted Hero. 'Even if only by example.'

'You think so? But they are not there as missionaries. They are there for profit. And in pursuit of that noble aim they intrigue against each other with Machiavellian zeal and viciousness, while at the same time uniting to describe the natives as backward and immoral savages. Old Sultan Saïd didn't know what he was letting himself in for when he started signing treaties with European nations!'

Hero's reading had not included much information on the score of Europeans in the Sultan's territory or the reasons for their presence there, but remembering what young Jules Dubail had told her, she said on impulse: 'I understand that the present Sultan, Majid-bin – er – something, is not the eldest son?'

'Majid-bin-Saïd? No. But he's the eldest surviving son of those who were born in Zanzibar. And he won't survive much longer if he doesn't wake up and start cutting a few of his relatives' throats in the near future! Which I'm afraid he won't do, because he's an amiable and easy-going creature – more's the pity.'

Hero frowned and remarked with considerable acerbity that she wished he would stop saying things that he could not possibly mean.

'But I do mean it. Life is a great deal harsher in the East than you would seem to imagine, and those who want to keep their thrones have to kill or be killed. The history of Majid's family is one long murder; and to be easy-going and incapable of knifing a rival is a great disability in Arab eyes, let me tell you! According to their reckoning, if you haven't enough spirit to kill a man who stands in the way of something you want, then you don't deserve to get it. They didn't call old Sultan Saïd the "Lion of Oman" for nothing.'

He laughed at Hero's disapproving face, and said: 'Do you know, you look exactly like a governess. Or a parson about to preach a sermon on Hell Fire. I'm afraid Eastern ideas are likely to come as a shock to you.'

'It is not *Eastern* ideas that shock me,' said Hero with emphasis. 'I am naturally aware that untutored heathens are bound to hold different views from us on the subject of morality. But I cannot say the same when such views are apparently endorsed by white men.'

'Men are much the same, you know, whatever the colour of their skins. There may be more excuse for the behaviour of "untutored heathens", but that's the best you can say about it. The new Sultan is not a bad little man in many ways, and personally, I like him. But he's weak, and that spells trouble: specially when your silly little cousin and her friends start mixing themselves up in palace politics.'

'What do you mean? What can you possibly know about my cousin or her friends?' demanded Hero, outraged.

'Only what everyone else knows. It's a small island, and you'll soon find that everyone there knows everyone else's business. Your uncle is an easy-going man, but he ought to wake up to the fact that his daughter is dabbling her pretty little fingers in a keg of gunpowder.'

'I cannot help thinking,' remarked Hero in a deliberately dulcet tone, 'that my uncle, as Consul, must know a great deal more about the internal affairs of the Island than you imagine. And though I do not suppose that he could teach you anything about slave trading – and whatever else you do – I feel sure that he knows quite as much about his business as you know about yours.'

'I doubt it,' said the Captain, unabashed. 'I've drifted around this part of the world for a good many years now, and I've precious few illusions about it. But your good uncle still cherishes a sight too many. Though I imagine even he must have lost one or two during the last year!'

'Are you personally acquainted with my uncle?' enquired Hero.

'My *dear* Miss Hollis – what a question! To be plain with you, he is going to be far from pleased at having his beloved niece restored to him by an untouchable like myself, because it'll mean that he might even have to consider nodding to me in the street by way of thanks.'

'My uncle,' said Hero in an arctic voice, 'will never permit his personal opinions to affect either his gratitude or his manners. He will naturally be greatly indebted to you for your part in rescuing me, and I am sure you will be suitably thanked and rewarded.'

'In cash?' enquired the Captain, amused. 'I wonder what he'll think you're worth? Or are you imagining that he would go so far as to be seen calling at my house in order to express his gratitude in person?'

'That would be the *least* he could do,' said Hero with emphasis.

'My poor innocent! He wouldn't dream of doing such a thing. And neither will he permit you to do so. I shall be lucky if I get so much as a verbal message of thanks, and even that is going to stick in his gullet like a fishbone.'

'Nonsense,' said Hero tartly. 'He might not wish to call upon you – which you will allow me to say is a thing I can fully understand – but you can take my word for it that he will. Not only from gratitude, but from mere courtesy. And if he could not get there himself, he'd send Clayton – er – Mr Mayo, or even myself, to do so in his stead. We are not barbarians.'

'Poor Miss Hollis! So you really think that your relatives would permit you to call at my house even on such an errand, do you? If I know anything about your uncle he'd see me jailed first – and to hell with courtesy and gratitude! Of course, you can always try your hand at getting him to put his gratitude in writing, though I doubt if you'll succeed. It might come in quite handy as a testimonial; and with the world getting so damned moral I may even find myself having to earn an honest living one of these days.'

'I shouldn't think that you would know how to,' snapped Hero, unable to resist the retort.

'Possibly not.' He grinned at her and enquired unexpectedly if she were possessed of independent means, or had she to rely upon her relatives to support her?

'Because,' explained the Captain kindly, 'the only thing I can think of that might sweeten the prospect of taking on a homely-looking wife with a critical disposition, a quick temper and an acid tongue, would be a large private fortune. So I hope for Mr Mayo's sake that you have one. That is, if there is any truth in the Island rumour that you are on your way out to this outlandish spot to marry him, which I begin to doubt.'

Hero opened her mouth to retort in kind and then closed it. It had obviously been a grave mistake to engage Captain Frost in conversation, since it had merely encouraged him to be impertinent. And there being no possible reply that a lady could make to such insufferable observations, she could only turn her back on him and feign an interest in the activities of Mr Potter and Hadir until he left. She heard him laugh and walk away, but did not turn her head; continuing to stare woodenly at Mr Potter who was crooning a tuneless ditty about someone called 'me bonnie brown Bess', and staining his sail an unpleasing shade of brown with the aid of a mop and a bucketful of evil-smelling dye.

Batty's proceedings seemed, in Hero's jaundiced view, both messy and useless, and she was about to say as much when it occurred to her that the expanse of wet canvas sealed off the hatch more efficiently – and a great deal less obviously – than any number of bolts; and that as long as it remained there it was going to be impossible for her to discover what lay below it in the hold. Which was a disturbing thought: but not so disturbing as the two that followed close on its heels.

That strong-smelling dye—— Could it be being used to disguise another smell? . . . the stench of shuddering, sweating, unwashed captives, jammed together in the airless dark? And was Batty Potter's tuneless humming as innocent as it appeared, or was he doing it deliberately, to drown any untoward sounds from below?

She said breathlessly, aware that her voice was not quite steady: 'Why are you doing that, Mr Potter?'

Batty looked up, blinking in the harsh sunlight: 'Eh? Oh, paintin' this 'ere sail d'you mean? Well it's gettin' old, and this 'ere muck sorter keeps it from rottin'. Pre-serves it, as-yer-might-say. We does it sometimes on our spare canvas. Never know when we might need an extra sail or two. Don't let it get on your 'ands, miss . . . *"so I plugs 'im through 'is gizzard with me bonnie Brown Bess . . ."* '

Hero abandoned the indirect approach and said flatly: 'Are there negroes down there in the hold, Mr Potter?'

'Not at this time of day, miss. They'll be cooking their prog forrard about now. 'Cept for young M'bula, 'oo's scrubbing out the scuppers.'

'You know quite well that I was not referring to the crew. I mean slaves. Are there any slaves down there?'

'Now, what ever give you that idea?' wondered Batty, his brown be-whiskered face a picture of innocent reproof. 'Why, 'aven't you 'eard that black-birdin' is illegal outside of 'Is 'Ighness the Sultan's own territories? Slaves——! Whatever next? Not that the old 'arridan 'asn't carried 'er wack of black ivory in 'er day, but that's all over now. We gone 'onest, we 'ave.'

'Then what is it that you are carrying?'

'Cargo, missie. Just cargo.'

'What *sort* of cargo?' persisted Hero.

'A little of this and a little of that. Ivory – the white kind – and rhino 'orns and some bits and bobs; clock-work toys and the like wot the Sultan fancies, and a sophy and a set of chairs for 'is Palace. Nothing that would interest you, miss. And anyways, they're all done up in packing cases so there ain't nothin' to see. So now, if you'll excuse me, miss, I shall 'av to be getting on with me work . . . *"And that's the end of 'im, as any cove'll guess, for she ain't a one t'miss, is me bonnie Brown Bess!"* '

The canvas had remained there all day, and on the following morning another had replaced it and been similarly treated. The schooner reeked with the smell of Batty's dye, and although Hero had been unable to detect any suspicious noises, she was still convinced that his reason for staining those sails had nothing whatever to do with preserving them.

In which she was right. Though the reason was not what she had supposed.

7

It was her last night on board the *Virago*, and once again, but this time quite openly, she had been locked into her cabin.

'Captain's orders,' said Batty, in answer to Hero's heated demand for explanations. And added reprovingly that 'them that didn't ask questions wouldn't be told no lies,' and that she should stop worrying and get her beauty sleep, because they expected to fetch Zanzibar by morning.

They had evidently 'fetched' something a good deal earlier than that, for lying awake in the hot darkness Hero heard the rattle of the anchor chain and a sound that she had heard before, and recognized: a boat was being lowered and rowed away. But this time the *Virago* must be close to land, because she could also hear the murmur of surf breaking on a shelving beach.

Once again, as on that other night, both portholes had been blocked, and the little cabin was pitch dark and insufferably hot. But although the thick curtains of coir matting effectively prevented the entry of either light or air, they seemed powerless to keep out the hordes of mosquitoes whose shrill, droning song was maddeningly audible above the coming and going of men on deck, the sound of surf and the splash of retreating oars. Hero slapped futilely at them, and eventually crawled out of her berth, and having found the matches, lit a tallow candle and splashed water over her face and down Captain Frost's shirt that was still doing duty as a nightgown.

Thus cooled, her energy and her curiosity revived, and she remembered the shears with which Batty had chopped off her hair, and which she had seen him put away in a drawer of the desk. They were still there; large and heavy and surprisingly sharp. Hero looked thoughtfully at them, and then at the thick matting that screened the portholes.

Ten minutes later, after a hard struggle, she had succeeded in cutting a ragged slit in the matting and was peering cautiously through it, having first taken the precaution of blowing out the candle. They were riding at anchor near a dark shore that seemed to be thickly wooded, and Hero could make out the white line of surf on a little curving bay, and the ragged shapes of tall coral rocks that formed a natural breakwater on either side of it.

The breeze that blew gently off the land and cooled her hot face smelled deliciously of cloves – a strange, heady fragrance to find on the warm night air. There were other scents too; scents that were less familiar and that she could not place, since she had never known flowers that smelt as strong or as sweet. The odour of salt water and wet sand mingled pleasantly with them, and to the right and left of the bay she could see the tall, graceful heads of innumerable palms, swaying to the night breeze.

The moon had not yet risen but the sky was ablaze with stars, and as Hero's eyes became accustomed to the uncertain light she saw that there was a house standing among the trees above the bay. A tall, white, flat-roofed house, protected from seaward by what appeared to be a massive, crenellated wall. It was clearly visible in the bright starlight, but either the occupants were asleep or else it was closed and empty, for no gleam of light showed from any window or from among the massed trees or on the surrounding wall. There were, however, men on the curving beach beyond the phosphorescent surf; half-a-dozen dark figures that were barely discernible against the pale expanse of sand, and who seemed to be engaged in either loading or unloading a boat that had been pulled up on the beach. After a time they thrust it off again, and Hero watched it being rowed back to the ship, and when it had passed out of her line of vision heard it bump alongside, fended off by hands and oars.

It was only then that she became aware that there could be no lights on the *Virago* and that even the riding light had been extinguished, for the water below her reflected only stars and shadows. The schooner must have crept in close to the land in the dark hour before moonrise, with every light extinguished and (why had she not thought of that before?) using the sails that Batty Potter had carefully darkened with a pail of brown dye so that they would be difficult to discern by night and the uncertain starlight, either against the dark sea or the darker land.

The voices and footsteps began again, accompanied by thuds and dragging sounds, and ten minutes later the boat came into view once more, pulling for the shore and riding low in the water as though it was heavily laden. They were not taking on cargo this time, but landing it. And whatever it was, it was certainly not slaves; though Hero had little doubt that it was the same cargo that had been transferred to the *Virago* in mid-ocean two nights ago.

She watched the boat reach the shore, and saw the dark, unidentifiable figures unload it and carry what appeared to be long and apparently heavy bundles across the white sand of the beach towards the rocks and the shadow of that high curtain wall. And quite suddenly a thought struck her that for a horrible moment seemed to check the beating of her heart. *Bodies!* Was that what they were carrying? Had there, after all, been slaves on board the *Virago*, and were the crew now getting rid of those who had died in the airless hold – burying black corpses somewhere in the tree-filled garden of that shuttered house, where the graves would not be found and no one would ever know?

It was a full five minutes before sanity and commonsense told her that Captain Frost was not the man to waste time and effort digging graves for bodies that could be far more effectively disposed of by simply throwing them into the sea. But could those oblong bundles possibly be living people, and was she watching some gruesome method of smuggling human wares into the island?

Hero was aware that any British or British-Indian subject caught trading in or owning slaves was liable to a very heavy fine or imprisonment, though by the terms of what she could only consider to be a callous and scandalous treaty, the Sultan and his subjects were still permitted to continue the practice within the strict limits of His Highness's territorial possessions. Yet in this respect Captain Frost, whatever his assertions to the contrary, would presumably count as a British subject, and could therefore be visited with the full penalties of the law if convicted of slaving – which could account for the secrecy with which this particular cargo was being landed.

Straining her eyes in the bright starlight, she tried to gauge the size and length of those bundles. But though she was unable to arrive at any reliable estimate, the casualness with which they were being handled did not support the theory that they contained living people, since no human freight could have escaped injury from being tilted out so roughly onto the sandy shore. Unless of course the Captain's men simply did not care?

Once again the boat returned, riding high and light, and this time Hero could hear it being drawn up and swung aboard, and shortly afterwards there came the squeak of the windlass and the rattle of the chain as the anchor was weighed. Water gurgled under the prow and the dark outlines of the land began to slide away as though the shore and not the ship was moving, and presently the *Virago*'s bows swung seaward and there was no more land, but only the wide expanse of ocean.

Hero turned from the portholes and groped her way back to the bunk to sit cross-legged in the darkness, slapping absent-mindedly at the mosquitoes and brooding on Captain Frost's sinister and secretive behaviour, and she was still meditating this vexed problem when the matting was drawn up and out of sight, and once again the sea breeze blew through the cabin and she could see the stars and the night sky. They were heading south, and it occurred to her then that they must have by-passed Zanzibar and 'fetched' the Sultan's neighbouring island of Pemba, and were now going back on their tracks and in the right direction after all. Comforted by this thought, and by the fact that the cool current of air had at last dispersed the mosquitoes, she fell asleep at last: and woke to find Jumah knocking at her door with a breakfast tray and the news that they would reach Zanzibar harbour within the hour.

A glance through the porthole disclosed that they were already in sight of the Island, and Hero scalded her tongue gulping hot coffee, ate half a banana, and having washed hurriedly and dressed in frantic haste, picked up the brush and comb and went to the looking-glass; to be confronted by a reflection that reduced her to tears for the first time since Barclay had died . . .

'Oh *no*!' wailed Hero, speaking aloud into the silent cabin. '*Oh, no!*'

She did not hear the knock on the door or know that it had opened, and only realized that someone had entered the cabin when a hand gripped her shoulder and swung her round, and she found herself looking with streaming eyes at a tear-blurred vision of the *Virago*'s Captain.

'*Go away!*' said Hero furiously.

Captain Frost made no attempt to do so. He shook her instead and enquired impatiently if she had hurt herself.

'No, I haven't!' wept Hero. 'C-can't you *see* I haven't? – go away!'

Captain Frost relaxed his grip on her shoulder and producing a handkerchief, attempted to staunch the flow and spoke in a voice that despite its peremptoriness was a good deal pleasanter than any she had heard him use before: 'My good girl, you can't be shedding all those tears for nothing. What's the matter?'

'Mosquitoes – Clay . . . I look *hideous*!' sobbed Hero incoherently.

She snatched the handkerchief from him and burying her face in it spoke in a muffled wail: 'As if it wasn't bad enough already! Just *look* what those horrible insects have done to my face. I m-might as well have m-measles. And if you *dare* laugh, I'll – I'll——'

Captain Frost pushed the handkerchief aside and taking her chin in his hand turned her face to the light. It was indeed a sorry sight, for in addition to tear-stains and the fading but still evident blemishes incurred in the course of her rescue, there were now a liberal sprinkling of angry-looking mosquito bites. But though his lips twitched he did not laugh. Instead, and entirely unexpectedly, he bent his head and kissed her.

It was a fleeting and completely sexless gesture that held no more emotional content than a pat bestowed by an adult on a weeping child. But no man had ever done such a thing to Hero Hollis before. Barclay had not been a demonstrative man and his only daughter had not been at all the kind of little girl who invited caresses: there had never been anything sweet or winsome about his Hero, and on the rare occasions that he had kissed her it had been on the cheek or the forehead. Even Clayton had never achieved more than that, but Emory Frost had kissed her casually on the lips, and to Hero the brief caress was more shocking than a blow.

She wrenched herself free and stepped back swiftly, one hand to her mouth and her eyes wide and horrified. But Captain Frost appeared entirely unaware of her perturbation. He said encouragingly: 'Don't worry, it doesn't look any worse than freckles, and they won't last. In any case, your relatives are going to be so pleased to find that you are alive that they won't care about anything else. And neither will Clayton Mayo if he really means to marry you. Does he?'

The sudden change of subject disconcerted Hero, and she scrubbed her eyes with the crumpled handkerchief, and having blown her nose, said with quivering hostility: 'I cannot see that it is any affair of yours, and I might with more justification ask you what you were doing last night. I know you were landing something.'

'Was I? What makes you think so?'

'Because I've got ears,' retorted Hero. '*And* eyes.'

'And also a pair of scissors,' grinned Captain Frost, not a whit disconcerted. 'I admit I'd forgotten the scissors until I saw the gash you'd made in that piece of matting.'

'*Were* you smuggling slaves?'

'What a persistent young woman you are! No, I was not.'

'I didn't think you were, but ... Where were we last night? Was that Pemba or Africa?'

Captain Frost shrugged and said: 'You'll have to ask Hajji Ralub. He's our navigator.'

'You must know perfectly well where we——' began Hero hotly, and then realizing the futility of such a conversation, abandoned the subject and said instead: 'What did you come in here to see me about?'

'Nothing. I merely wanted a clean shirt to land in, and they happen to be in that cupboard. Do you mind if I get one?'

He did not wait for her permission, but walked past her, selected a shirt and left: leaving Hero still clutching his crumpled handkerchief in one hand and staring after him with compressed lips.

After a moment or two she raised the handkerchief and rubbed it back and forth across her mouth, her gaze still on the closed door, and then suddenly realizing what she held, dropped it quickly and ran to the basin where she scrubbed her lips with soap as though they had been in contact with something unclean. The narrow oblong of cheap looking-glass that hung above it reflected her reddened eyes and tear-stained cheeks, and she splashed her face again and again with the tepid, soapy water, and having dried it, turned away from the glass without a second look, and went up on to the deck with a laggard step and none of the happy anticipation that she had once imagined herself feeling at the sight of Zanzibar. But the scene that met her eyes was enchanting enough to banish the deepest despondency, and forgetting both her recent humiliation and her lost good looks, she ran to the rail to take her first look at the lovely island.

The morning sun was shining on a coast that was more beautiful than anything she had ever visualized, and looking at it she could well believe the tale Captain Frost had told her of the Arab Sultan who had fallen in love with Zanzibar. It was not surprising that a man born and bred among the harsh, sun-baked sands of Arabia should have been caught by the beauty of this green and gracious island and left his heart, and at the last his body, on that lovely shore. The young Frenchman, Jules Dubail, had been right when he had described it as a 'Paradise on earth, colourful and exotic and of a beauty inconceivable'. And so had those long-ago Arabs who had named it *'Zayn za'l barr'* – *'Fair is this land'*.

The schooner was moving gently along the inside of a long coral reef that protected the coast from the worst of the monsoon storms, and the water between ship and shore was glass-clear and streaked with every imaginable colour from amethyst to veridian: clear blue where the sand lay fathoms deep below the slow shadows of the sails, and milky jade where the shoals neared the surface. A line of foam creamed on a long beach of dazzling white sand fringed by shallow coral cliffs and sand dunes sculptured by the Trade Winds, and behind these arose stately ranks of coconut palms and the dense, metallic green of innumerable trees.

There seemed to be no hard lines in the island, and no mountains. Only gently swelling hills, curving bays and beaches, and the rounded greenery of massed foliage. The warm breezes smelled of flowers and cloves and the rustling fronds of the palms waved and swayed in unison, as though they had been some graceful Eastern *corps-de-ballet* performing an ancient and traditional dance of welcome. And gazing at that lovely shore, Hero was no longer surprised that Cressy had written so ecstatically of Zanzibar. For a moment she felt tempted to fall into similar raptures, but a recollection of the heat and mosquitoes of the previous night, together with the fact that this was one of the greatest centres of the slave trade, restored her sense of proportion and reminded her in time of the danger of judging by appearances. The island might seem on the surface to be a paradise, but she must be prepared to find it far otherwise and not permit any hazy and deceptive veil of romance to blind her to its harsher aspects.

'Well, miss, 'ow do you like the look of it?' enquired Batty Potter, pausing beside her. 'Nice little place, ain't it?'

'It *looks* very pretty,' agreed Hero cautiously.

'It do – if you likes palm trees and such. Some does and some don't.'

Batty sighed deeply and spat a dark stream of tobacco juice into the pellucid water as the *Virago*, rounding a rocky point, brought into view a business-like steam-sloop that flew the white ensign of the Royal Navy and lay half a mile ahead, slantwise across the narrow channel that divided the reef from the palm-fringed shore.

A peremptory signal fluttered from the sloop's yards, and Captain Frost, joining Hero at the rail, said: 'Ah! I thought so. Here's the Reception Committee. That's the *Daffodil*, and here comes Dan. Hi, Ralub! heave to. Look lively there!'

The *Virago*'s crew leapt into activity and the schooner lost way and glided gently forwards, the glassy water clucking and chuckling along her salt-caked and sun-blistered sides until the splash of the heavy sea anchor brought her to a stop a bare hundred yards from the waiting sloop.

Captain Frost shaded his eyes against the sun-glare and watched while a small white-painted boat was lowered and rowed briskly towards them, its bow occupied by a man who signalled authoritatively with an uplifted arm.

'Going to let 'im come aboard?' enquired Batty with mild interest.

'Why not? Lower a ladder for 'em and roll out the red carpet, Batty. What have we got to worry about?'

'You're right, there. Narry a thing! Wonder if 'e nabbed Fernandez? You might ask 'im while 'e's over.'

'If he didn't it's high time he went home and took up farming. We practically handed him the bastard in wrapping paper and blue ribbons. He'll have got him all right. Suliman said he was smack on his tail and going so hard that he swears he could have sailed half-a-dozen dhows out in his wake without being seen – let alone one! Very pretty shooting, Uncle. Two beautiful birds with one stone. Stand by: here he comes——'

The jolly-boat closed in, shipping its oars, and a man wearing the uniform of a British naval officer swung himself up the swaying rope ladder and came over the side.

He was a slight man, and not much above medium height; but with a personality that made itself instantly felt and had the effect of convincing others that he was considerably taller than his inches warranted. Dark hair and a deeply sunburnt face combined to make him look as swarthy as an Arab, but the square cut of his features and a pair of startlingly blue eyes were unmistakably and uncompromisingly Anglo-Saxon.

'Well, well!' said Captain Frost cordially. 'If it isn't Danny-boy! Nice of you to call on us, Dan. To what do we owe this signal honour?'

The slight suggestion of a drawl in Captain Frost's voice was suddenly more than a suggestion and nicely calculated to annoy; but Lieutenant Daniel Larrimore had learned many lessons in a hard school, and one of them was when and when not to lose his temper. A muscle twitched at the corner of his jaw, but he spoke politely and without heat: 'Good morning, Frost. I want to take a look at your cargo. That is, if you have no objection?'

'If I had, it wouldn't make any difference, would it?'

'Not in the least. But I'd prefer to do it without interference from your crew, so just call them off will you. And you can tell Ralub to stop fingering his knife in that offensive manner and stay away from that hatch.'

'Give me one good reason why I should, Dan?'

Lieutenant Larrimore jerked his thumb over his shoulder in the direction of the sloop and said briefly: 'I've got both guns trained on you, and I can blow you to matchwood.'

'So I see. But haven't you forgotten something?'

'Not if you mean that I myself might get damaged in the process, so don't bank on them not opening fire on that account. They've got their orders and somehow I don't feel that you'd get much satisfaction out of the mere fact that you might be taking me to Hell with you.'

Captain Frost laughed with genuine amusement. 'You're right, Dan. You know damn' well I wouldn't! – though I've no doubt at all that you'd be prepared to go there yourself as long as I accompanied you. But this time I've got you checkmated. You can't loose off either one of your little popguns at me today, Lieutenant, because I happen to have a very valuable hostage on board. You've probably never met a mermaid before, but here's one we caught in a gale off the Comoros. Allow me to introduce you . . .'

He turned to Hero and made her a formal bow: 'Miss Hollis, may I present Lieutenant Daniel Larrimore of Her Majesty's Navy? He's quite human when you get to know him. Miss Hollis, Dan, is a niece of the American Consul and first cousin to Miss Cressida.'

Lieutenant Larrimore stared at Hero, his eyes a blue blaze in his brown face, and stupefaction and disbelief showing plainly in his tight mouth and startled brows.

Captain Frost watched him take in the enormity of that cropped hair, black eye and much-mended salt-stained dress, and was interested to see that despite these handicaps his cabin-passenger managed to retain an air of distinction and a certain youthful dignity that belied her raffish appearance. She was, he thought, a tiresome girl, but a courageous one; and he found himself wondering just how many young women in her position, fancying themselves to be held for ransom on board a slaver, would have had the courage to lecture their captor on the iniquities of his trading activities. The reflection amused him and he grinned to himself, and Lieutenant Larrimore, catching sight of that grin, said angrily:

'But that's impossible! Miss Hollis was coming out on the *Norah Crayne*.' He turned sharply on the *Virago*'s Captain: 'Is this another of your damned tricks, Frost? Because if so——'

'You still couldn't fire on my ship,' observed Captain Frost pleasantly: 'Not while I've got a lady on board, even if she wasn't Miss Hollis. Which she is. She fell overboard from the *Norah Crayne* just short of the Comoros, and we fished her out in a mess of torn rigging. If you'd been back to harbour you'd have heard all about it.'

'Is this true?' demanded the Lieutenant, swinging round to address Miss Hollis.

'Quite true. I'm Hero Hollis, and I – I guess everyone must think I am dead.'

Lieutenant Larrimore, recovering his manners, bowed briefly and said that he was more than pleased to meet her: adding that as the *Norah Crayne* had reportedly arrived a week ago, he presumed that her aunt and cousin would have heard the news, and that he could well imagine the blow it must have dealt them. They would be overjoyed to see her.

'But not in small pieces,' pointed out Captain Frost affably. 'So what about those guns of yours, Dan? Don't you think you'd better call it quits and transfer Miss Hollis to the *Daffodil* so that you can restore her to the bosom of her family without further delay?'

'It will give me great pleasure to do so,' said Lieutenant Larrimore: 'Just as soon as I have satisfied myself as to your cargo. But I am not moving off this ship until I have done that, and I am sure you ll perceive the advantages of allowing it to be done peaceably.'

'Why, certainly, if you're set on it. But I warn you, you're going to be bitterly disappointed, Danny. You ought to know by now that there is no green in my eye.'

He turned to address his impassive crew in Arabic, and three of them moved forward to open the hatches while half-a-dozen British sailors from the jolly-boat clambered briskly on board.

Hero did not accompany the search-party below, for although she had once wished quite as urgently as the naval Lieutenant to see what the *Virago* was carrying in her hold, she was certain that it was no longer there. It had been landed somewhere else late last night, and if the present cargo contained any trace of contraband, or even evidence that any such thing had been carried, she would be very much surprised. She therefore stayed where she was, looking out at the lovely shore and the jewel-coloured water.

Presumably the town and harbour could not be far distant, for among the trees on a low promontory a mile or so ahead she could catch a glimpse of white-walled houses: and though the breeze that blew towards her was still perfumed with flowers and the scent of cloves, it also carried a faint but unmistakable effluvia of ill-kept drains and sewage. Hero's nostrils wrinkled in distaste. It was only what she had expected, but it was unpleasant to be reminded so soon that the beauty of the Island was only skin-deep. She could hear crates being shifted and opened below, and was seized with sudden impatience. Surely that Larrimore man should have enough sense to know that he was merely wasting his time and providing a great deal of amusement for the *Virago*'s insufferable Captain? The cases he was opening would be found to contain the items that Batty had listed for her. Ivory and rhino horns, clocks, furniture and fripperies for the Sultan of Zanzibar. And nothing else!

A clatter of boots on the deck heralded the return of the search-party, and she turned to see Captain Frost looking relaxed and bored, the naval Lieutenant expressionless, Batty aggrieved and the Arab, Ralub, amused.

'You can take that grin off your face, Hajji,' snapped Lieutenant Larrimore, beating the dust off his uniform. 'I know damned well that you've been up to no good, and one of these days I'll catch you out at it and get the whole bloody lot of you thrown in jail. That'll teach you bastards to laugh on the other side of your faces!'

He became aware of Miss Hollis, whose presence on board had obviously slipped his mind, and apologized in some confusion for his language.

'It doesn't matter,' said Hero tonelessly. 'May we please go now?'

'Yes, of course. I'm sorry to have kept you waiting. Isn't there anything you want to take with you?'

'I'm afraid Miss Hollis neglected to bring a valise with her,' said Captain Frost blandly: 'But she's welcome to take anything she wants from my inadequate wardrobe.'

The Lieutenant raised his brows and said coldly: 'I only wished to make certain that Miss Hollis had not left anything behind on this ship.'

'Only her reputation,' murmured Captain Frost gently.

'Why, you unspeakable——!' The Lieutenant's hands clenched suddenly into a pair of formidable fists, and Captain Frost side-stepped neatly and raised a deprecatory hand:

'Now, now, Dan! I'm surprised at you – brawling in front of a lady! Where are your manners? Or your brains, if it comes to that. I am merely saying aloud what the entire European community in Zanzibar will soon be whispering behind its collective hand. That is, unless we take steps to prevent it.'

'What do you mean? What steps? I don't see how——'

'Neither do I,' intervened Hero with asperity. 'I have never heard such nonsense in my life. I would like you to know, sir, that my reputation is not such a poor thing that it can be damaged by my being in your company.'

'You don't know Zanzibar,' said the Captain with a laugh. 'Or, for that matter, *my* reputation. But Danny does, don't you Dan?'

He cocked an amused eye at the Lieutenant's rigid face, and turned back to Hero: 'In the circumstances, Miss Hollis, I think it would save your uncle and aunt, if not yourself, a deal of embarrassment if people were allowed to suppose that you had been found clinging to some piece of wreckage – a spar, perhaps? – and been picked up by the gallant crew of Her Majesty's sloop, *Daffodil*, who were providentially patrolling in the vicinity. I can answer for my men keeping their mouths shut, and I have no doubt that Lieutenant Larrimore can promise the same for his. What do you say, Dan?'

The Lieutenant was forestalled by Miss Hollis, who said flatly: 'Thank you. But I do not believe that any dissimulation is necessary. My uncle and aunt will naturally accept my word that you and your crew have behaved with complete propriety towards me, and I assure you that I am entirely uninterested in what anyone else may choose to think of me. Shall we go, Lieutenant?'

But the Lieutenant did not move. The anger in his pleasant face had faded and been replaced by doubt, and he pushed up his peaked cap with one hand and looked from the Captain to Hero, and back again, and at last said slowly: 'I am obliged to you, Frost. It seems that I was mistaken in supposing that you retained none of the instincts of a gentleman.'

'You flatter me,' grinned Captain Frost.

'I'm sure I do. And I am equally sure that you have some excellent and entirely un-altruistic motive for advancing this suggestion. But for Miss Hollis's sake I am prepared to accept it at its face value.'

He turned abruptly to Hero and said: 'I think it very likely, ma'am, that Mr Frost is in the right of it. If you will forgive me for speaking plainly, his reputation and that of his ship are such that your relatives could not welcome your name being mentioned in connection with either of them, and I think it would be advisable if you consulted your uncle before committing yourself to any statement. He may well agree with Mr Frost's view, for small communities are apt to indulge in gossip to a greater extent than large ones, and as you are a stranger in Zanzibar, little will be known of you, while a great deal is known of Frost – and none of it to his credit.'

Captain Frost bowed gravely, and the Lieutenant's voice took on a harder edge as he said curtly: 'That is why, ma'am, I imagine your uncle may well prefer it to be given out that you have spent the last ten days on my sloop rather than on the *Virago* and in the company of her Captain.'

'Exactly,' agreed Captain Frost cordially. 'One cannot, in short, touch pitch without being defiled, and I'm afraid that in the opinion of the European community of our insalubrious city I am pitch personified.'

Hero frowned, shrugged, and capitulated without further argument; since if the truth were known she was not indifferent to the advantages of arriving in Zanzibar under the protection of the British Navy rather than being handed ashore by a notorious slave trader with an unsavoury reputation. To be bracketed in the public mind with such a person could not add to her consequence in the island or increase the credit of her uncle the Consul, so it seemed best, in the circumstances, to fall in with Captain Frost's unexpectedly chivalrous suggestion. She therefore thanked him for his services with a greater degree of graciousness than she would otherwise have shown towards him, and accepting Lieutenant Larrimore's proffered hand, went over the side to be rowed across to the *Daffodil* by six deeply interested bluejackets of Her Majesty's Navy.

8

The sloop rounded a green headland and Lieutenant Daniel Larrimore, who had been endeavouring to make polite conversation and tactfully avoid any direct question for the last quarter of an hour, turned to his passenger and enquired abruptly: 'You say you were on the *Virago* for ten days, Miss Hollis. Were they carrying slaves?'

'Not that I know of. And I cannot help thinking that I would have known if they had been.'

'You would indeed,' said the Lieutenant grimly. 'From the smell if nothing else. It's not a thing that anyone could overlook; which is why I had to make that abortive search this morning. I found no trace of it, but all the same I'll lay any money that Rory Frost was up to some roguery, and I'd give a lot to know what it was.'

Hero opened her mouth to tell him of the ship they had met in mid-ocean and the mysterious transactions of the previous night, but she shut it again without speaking. Not because she held any brief for Captain Frost and his disreputable crew, but because it occurred to her that it was a poor return for the surprisingly magnanimous gesture that had resulted in her transfer to the *Daffodil*, to betray their proceedings to the Lieutenant without giving the matter some further thought.

She was not even certain that the British Navy had any legal right to exercise authority in these waters; though a glance at the Lieutenant's square jaw and determined features was enough to convince her that such an argument, even if valid, would not weigh with him for an instant. Legally or not, his countrymen had arrogated to themselves the right to police the seas that linked them to their Empire, and to put down the slave trade. And Lieutenant Larrimore would conceive it his duty to carry out that policy at whatever cost.

But that was no reason, decided Hero, why she should confide in him. Uncle Nat was the proper person to tell these things to, and he would know what to do about it. Besides, at the moment there were other things to occupy her attention, for the *Daffodil* was passing between a sprinkling of little rocky islets, and ahead of her lay the harbour and the capital city of Zanzibar: a white town of tall, flat-topped Eastern houses, an ancient fort and a confusion of shipping – sails, hulls, masts, and spars duplicating themselves in the opal-tinted water, with among them, dwarfing them all, the familiar shape of the *Norah Crayne*.

'I'm glad for your sake, that she hasn't sailed yet,' commented Lieutenant Larrimore as the *Daffodil* dropped anchor: 'You would not have wished her to leave again without hearing the good news.'

He handed Hero into the jolly-boat once more, and two minutes later she was being rowed briskly across the dancing water on the last lap of a journey that had started long ago in the lamplit kitchen at Hollis Hill, when an aged Irish crone had told a six-year-old child her fortune . . .

Viewed from a distance, with a mile of blue water separating the ship from the shore, the Arab town of Zanzibar had looked colourful and romantic and not unlike some Eastern Venice. But a closer acquaintance with it not only robbed it of all charm, but confirmed Miss Hollis's worst fears as to the state of sanitation prevailing among backward and un-enlightened races.

The white coraline houses stood crowded together, covering a tri-angular spit of land which the sea, flowing at high tide into a creek to one side of it, daily transformed for a few hours into an island. There was no pier, and the long, sandy foreshore that separated the houses from the harbour was apparently used not only as a landing stage, but as the repo-sitory of every form of filth and refuse that the inhabitants thought fit to throw out of their courtyards and kitchens. The stench that arose from it made Hero bitterly regret discarding Captain Frost's handkerchief, and she covered her nose with her hands. And would have shut her eyes, ex-cept that sheer horror prevented her from doing so. For there was not only garbage on the beach, but worse things. Dead and bloated things that were being torn by lean, scavenging dogs and fought over by raucous clouds of gulls and crows.

'But – but those are bodies!' gasped Hero. 'Corpses!'

Lieutenant Larrimore followed the direction of her gaze and said un-emotionally: 'Yes. I'm afraid you'll see a good many more of those before you are through: though it's a deal better now than it was in the old Sul-tan's time.'

Hero swallowed convulsively and turned from the appalling sight, her face white with shock and horror. 'But why don't they bury them?'

'Bury slaves? They wouldn't consider it worth the trouble.'

'*Slaves?* But do they – are they——?'

'This is where the Arab slavers land their cargoes. They ship them from the Sultan's ports on the mainland, crammed into dhows without food or water; and if the winds fail and the passage is a slow one, over half of them die before they get here. When the dhows are unloaded the dead are merely thrown out onto the beach or into the harbour for the dogs and fishes to dispose of.'

'But it's horrible!' whispered Hero. 'It's – it's *inhuman*. Why is it allowed?'

'It's improving. A few years ago they used to throw out the ones who were not yet dead but seemed unlikely to survive. They'd leave them on the beach to see if they'd recover, or to die slowly if they didn't. But Colonel Edwards managed to put a stop to that.'

'I didn't mean that,' said Hero. 'I meant all of it. Slavery. Why don't the foreign consuls do something about it?'

She received no answer, for the simple reason that she had lost the attention of her audience. The sight of the landing steps had deflected the Lieutenant's thoughts onto other and more personal problems, and he was thinking of her cousin Cressida and wondering, with a mixture of hope and apprehension, how Cressy would receive him? Their last meeting had been a distinctly stormy one, and he had been obliged to sail before he had a chance to see her again and put things right: an omission that had been preying on his mind ever since.

Daniel Larrimore had been on slave patrol for some little time before he first met Cressida Hollis. And taking into account that his duties were confined to a part of the globe where personable, white and unattached young ladies were rarer than blackberries in June (and also that the very nature of those duties brought him into contact with worse things than the average human is capable of imagining) it is not surprising that he saw Cressy as a being from another world – a sweeter, cleaner world that was a million miles removed from the savagery and squalor to which he had become accustomed.

There was very little that Dan did not know by now about the uglier aspects of the slave trade: or of Zanzibar either. He had seen for himself, while on a brief visit to the interior, one of the slave routes that wound across Africa. A trail that had been clearly marked by hordes of vultures perched among the flat-topped thorn trees, and the bleached bones and rotting corpses of innumerable captives who had been unable to stagger any further and been left to die where they fell. He knew, too, that this was only one of many such trails along which the African and Arab traders drove their human wares with whips and clubs towards the sea, where those who survived the journey were subjected to worse torments in the airless bowels of a slave ship. In Zanzibar itself he had seen a dhow land twenty-two emaciated skeletons out of a cargo that ten days before had numbered two hundred and forty able-bodied negroes – and on that occasion even the Sultan's Government had jibbed at the prospect of two hundred and eighteen corpses littering the foreshore, and the slaver had reluctantly stood out to sea and dumped its dead overboard into deep water: from whence the tide had returned many of them during the next few days.

It had not been many months after this episode, and while it was still raw in his memory, that the Hollises had arrived in the island, and Lieutenant Larrimore, accompanying Colonel Edwards to a formal call on the new American Consul, had met the Consul's daughter. And straightway lost his heart . . .

She was seventeen and as pretty as a spray of apple blossom: 'A sight for sore eyes' indeed – and Dan's had been sore for too long. Everything about her enchanted him: her gaiety, her impulsiveness, her enjoyment of all that was strange and new, her obvious love for her father and her pretty, coaxing way with him. Even her youthful silliness, which in another girl he would probably have thought tiresome, merely made him feel fondly indulgent and increased his desire to protect her: from which it may be seen that Dan, like Captain Fullbright, did not demand brains and force of character in a woman, but preferred sweetness and charm; qualities that Cressy possessed in abundance.

Yet in spite of the fact that the object of his devotion showed every sign of reciprocating his feeling for her, his wooing had not gone smoothly. Partly because his visits to Zanzibar were erratic and never long enough for him to make the headway he could have wished with her parents, let alone with Cressy, and partly because her half-brother, Clayton Mayo, had unaccountably taken a dislike to him and gone out of his way to see that Dan's visits to the Consulate were as short (and as well chaperoned!) as possible – though fortunately Mayo, being a popular young man, was often out, and left to herself Cressy's mother was far from strict. Dan was at a loss to know what he could have said or done to arouse Mayo's hostility, and it still puzzled him. It could not, surely, be because of his nationality, for Mayo was on excellent terms with the rest of the British community. Perhaps it was only because he did not consider a mere naval lieutenant a good enough match for his pretty sister? In which case . . .

The jolly-boat passed under the tall, carved poop of a dhow and the beach was hidden from them, though the stench remained heavy on the hot air and followed them to where a flight of stone steps rose up from the oily water.

'I'm afraid you'll find the smell a bit overpowering in the daytime,' apologized the Lieutenant, who had obviously got used to it, 'but it's not too bad at night when the wind blows off the land. They're an insanitary lot, and as long as their houses are clean they don't seem to care what state the streets get into – or the beaches either. But it'll be a lot better once the monsoon breaks and the rains clean the place up a bit.'

He handed Hero on to the slippery, weed-grown steps and hurried her up through a narrow street where the gutters ran with filth, and veiled and shrouded women and a motley, idling crowd of black, brown, yellow and coffee-coloured men stared at her curiously.

'Why do they all look so different?' enquired Hero, gazing back with equal interest: 'From each other, I mean?'

'They are different. The people here come from a dozen different places. Madagascar, the Comoro Islands, India, Africa, Arabia, Goa – even China. It's the last great slaving centre in the East, and thousands of slaves pass through the Zanzibar Customs House every year. In fact here are some now on their way to the slave market.'

He drew her back against the wall as a file of negroes stumbled past them through the narrow crowded street, roped together and under the charge of a stout Arab trader and half-a-dozen swaggering African retainers who were armed with whips and staves. Fear and starvation had given them a dazed and uncomprehending look that verged on idiocy, and Hero stared at them in white-faced horror: realizing for the second time that morning the enormous difference that lay between reading about something and actually seeing it with one's own eyes.

She said in a high, choking voice: 'Why do you allow it? Why don't you do something? Why don't you do something *now*?'

The Lieutenant turned to look at her, his brow wrinkled in a frown. 'Didn't your relations tell you about this? I know it's upsetting, the first time you see it, but——'

'*You'll get used to it!* Don't say it! Don't! I shall never get used to it – *never*! Those poor creatures. Half of them are children. You've *got* to do something! You stopped the *Virago* to look for slaves, didn't you? Then why don't you arrest that man there and take his slaves away? Now, at once?'

'Because he's not a British subject and so there's nothing I can do about it,' said Lieutenant Larrimore curtly. He took her arm and began to urge her along the street.

'But you could buy them . . . *I* could buy them. Yes, that's what I'll do! I can buy them myself and set them free.'

'To starve?' enquired the Lieutenant dryly. 'How are they going to live?'

'My uncle would employ them at the Consulate. He could find work for them, I'm sure. He would if I asked him to.'

'I doubt it. The consulates are over-staffed already, and it would create a deal of trouble among your uncle's other servants. He wouldn't have quarters for them for one thing, and for another they would have to be fed and clothed as well as housed, and it would take a long time to train them to do even the simplest tasks.'

'But we could surely find *someone* who would be glad of their help and would be kind to them?'

'If they are bought by any of the local Arabs they will be treated kindly enough,' the Lieutenant assured her. 'The Koran forbids the ill-treatment of slaves, and any who are bought here and remain on the island will be lucky. It's the ones who don't get sold and are shipped off somewhere else whom you can be sorry for. Even if you did start buying them, you could only buy the smallest fraction of the number that pass through here yearly, and you wouldn't know what to do with them when you'd got them.'

'I could hire a boat and send them back to – to wherever they came from. Some of them, anyway. The ones that no one else wanted to buy.'

'The chances are that they haven't any homes left to go to and would be caught and sold again inside a week. What's more, you'd only be suspected of making money out of it, because not one of the locals would believe you were being altruistic. You can't afford that. Or rather, your uncle can't. It would not only be misunderstood, but if it once got about that you were prepared to buy slaves, for whatever reason, half the rascals in the town would bring you their oldest and most useless slaves in order to avoid having to care for them themselves. And it would be your uncle and not you who would have to shoulder that problem. I'm afraid that as his niece and house-guest you are hardly a private individual, and that sort of thing could make things very difficult for him – officially.'

Hero jerked her arm away and quickened her steps as though she could by doing so escape from the cold-hearted common sense of those arguments. But she knew that he was right. To buy and free a few slaves, even a few hundred slaves, would not help. And this – this hideous cruelty – was something that men like Captain Frost were responsible for. She had been sailing with a slaver . . . on a slave ship! That was suddenly something as dreadful to contemplate as the sight of those dazed, starving captives had been.

She did not notice that they had reached a quieter and more open part of the town until, turning a corner they came upon palms and green grass and a frangipani tree whose white, waxy blossoms smelt piercingly sweet after the fetid atmosphere they had left behind them. The tree threw sharp black shadows across the front of a tall white house from the roof of which a flag bearing the familiar stars-and-stripes snapped briskly in the wind, and Lieutenant Larrimore said briefly: 'This is the American Consulate. Your uncle's house.'

Aunt Abigail Hollis had been sitting on a sofa in the drawing-room; clad in deep mourning and engaged in consoling Mrs Fullbright, who was still tearfully blaming herself for the seasickness that had prevented her from taking proper care of her charge. Neither lady had at first recognized Hero, and when they had at last done so, Amelia Fullbright had swooned and Aunt Abby given way to strong hysterics.

Lieutenant Larrimore, dismayed by this display of feminine sensibility, left hastily in search of Mr Hollis, leaving Hero to contend single-handed with the situation. And Cressy and her father, arriving upon the scene simultaneously and from opposite directions, found bedlam reigning and someone who appeared to be a complete stranger slapping Amelia Fullbright's hands while exhorting Aunt Abby to stop screaming and fetch the hartshorn.

'*Hero!*' shrieked Cressy, turning alarmingly pale and showing every sign of following her mother's example: 'It isn't – it can't be. I don't believe it! Whatever *have* you been . . . Hero!'

'Yes, it's me,' said Miss Hollis in ungrammatical agitation. 'And don't you dare start screaming, Cressy. Go get some water . . . for pity's sake *do* something! Uncle Nat – oh, thank goodness you've come. Help me lift her.'

The next few minutes were fully occupied by restoring Mrs Fullbright and quieting Mrs Hollis, and after a further and confused interval of tears, kisses, laughter and embraces, a servant was sent running down to the harbour to fetch Captain Thaddaeus and another to find Mr Clayton Mayo, who was thought to be at the French Consulate.

'I just can't believe it,' wept Mrs Fullbright, keeping tight hold of Hero's hand: 'If you *knew* what agonies of remorse I have suffered. I don't know how I survived it. I felt like I'd absolutely *die* when Thaddaeus told me the dreadful, dreadful news – *Drowned!*'

'We held a memorial service,' sobbed Aunt Abby, clasping the other hand. 'Oh, if only I could feel sure that this isn't a dream and that I shall wake up and find it isn't true!'

'Your hair——' gasped Cressy between tears and laughter. 'Hero *why*? Oh honey, your poor face . . . You look as though you had been in a battle. Does it hurt real bad? Weren't you *terrified*? How did it happen? And to think that it was Dan – I mean the *Daffodil* – that found you.'

'It wasn't. Well, not exactly . . .' Miss Hollis hesitated and looking at her uncle took a deep breath and said resolutely: 'I think, Uncle Nat, that I had better tell you at once that I was picked up by a ship called the *Virago*.'

'The *Virago*?' exclaimed the Consul sharply, 'you mean that blackguardly slave ship? But I thought——'

He swung round to glare at Lieutenant Larrimore who shrugged and said resignedly: 'Yes, I'm afraid that is so, sir. It was Frost's ship that picked up your niece when she fell overboard, and the reason that she came ashore in my charge was because I had occasion to stop and search the *Virago* this morning off Chuaka Head, and discovered your niece to be on board. We decided . . . that is, Frost suggested . . . that in view of his – er – reputation in these parts, it might save Miss Hollis embarrassment if we let it be supposed that she had been found clinging to a spar and been picked up by my ship.'

'He did, did he?' growled the Consul. 'Then I guess he must have a few good feelings left, after all. I'm obliged to him. But it won't work out: his men are bound to chatter.'

'It is plain that you do not know Rory Frost, sir,' said the Lieutenant wryly. 'Those men of his are closer than oysters when it suits them.'

'And your own, Lieutenant?'

'I will answer for mine, sir. I have explained the situation to them and they will not talk. The only thing that worries me is why Frost should have suggested such a thing in the first place, for it's not like him.'

Hero shook out her crushed skirts and said crisply: 'There I cannot agree with you. I imagine that it is his own reputation that he is concerned about and not mine at all. It stands to reason that men engaged in illegal traffics can have little reason to trust each other, and I daresay if it were known that the Consul's niece had occupied a cabin on the *Virago* for ten days, and then been returned in safety to her uncle, some of Captain Frost's more dubious associates might suspect him of playing a double game. For myself, however, I am quite prepared to tell the truth, be- cause——'

An agitated outcry from her aunt interrupted her: 'Oh, no dear! On *no* account! You cannot *possibly* know that man's reputation. I do not mean just slaves. He is a *shocking* libertine. Why, there was Mrs Hallam who . . . and an unfortunate girl from Mozambique (a missionary's daughter, too! quite dreadful) and that Frenchwoman, what was her name? who ran away from her husband and then tried to poison herself when he took up with a half-caste dancer from Mombasa, and——'

'Mrs Hollis!' bellowed the Consul, scandalized.

'Oh goodness! . . . of course . . . I-I guess one shouldn't mention such creatures. But when one *knows*—— Well, you can see what people would say if it were known that Hero had spent ten days in his company. It would not do at all. People are so – so . . .'

Aunt Abby broke off with a fluttering, helpless gesture of her small plump hands, and her husband said impatiently: 'Yes, yes, we all fully understand the situation and if we are to accept this version – and I reckon we should – we had better agree on what is supposed to have occurred.' He turned to glare at the Lieutenant and added: '*You're* the one who'll have to think up the answers to that!'

'I know, sir,' concurred the Lieutenant without enthusiasm, 'and all I can suggest is that we say that her recollection of the whole affair is extremely vague, but that she must have remained afloat with the aid of some piece of wreckage for several hours until a providential wave flung her aboard my ship, and that owing to shock, exposure and severe bruising she was unable to answer questions for several days. That will account for the delay in bringing her to Zanzibar, and should serve to satisfy the curious.'

'Yes, indeed,' agreed Aunt Abby. 'One does not like to tell deliberate falsehoods, but right now I can't help feeling that we are justified in – in——'

'In telling deliberate falsehoods,' said Hero bleakly. 'I guess so. And now, please, if you will show me to my room, Aunt, I will see if I cannot do something towards improving my appearance.'

Escorted by all three ladies, none of whom felt able to let her out of their sight, she was swept up to a cool white bedroom that looked out upon a garden full of flowers and trees, where there was the luxury of unlimited fresh water to wash in. But it was disconcerting to discover that her uncle having decided that her luggage had better be returned to Boston, her trunks were still on board the *Norah Crayne*; for barely ten minutes later Clayton had arrived, breathless from running, and hammered impatiently on the door demanding to see her immediately. This being out of the question until she had something better to wear than that dreadful dress, he had been forced to kick his heels downstairs while Mrs Fullbright left to arrange for the trunks to be sent from the ship, and Cressy helped her cousin out of the much mended black poplin, poured hot water and demanded answers to an endless stream of excited questions.

The luggage had arrived within the hour, but it was midday before Hero descended to the drawing-room. And though a careful application of calamine lotion had been unable to do more than minimize the spotted effect produced by a dozen mosquito bites and tone down that distressing bruised eye and jaw, a very creditable transformation had been wrought. Freshly ironed folds of black sarsenet spread demurely over a crinoline whose hoops, though moderate, served to emphasize the slenderness of Hero's waist while drawing attention to her admirable proportions, and her short-cropped hair, newly washed and freed from the stickiness of salt water and the sweat of the hot nights, curled about her head in a childish manner that was reminiscent of the style made fashionable earlier in the century by such beauties as Madame Récamier and the Lady Caroline Lamb.

The effect of those curls was undeniably frivolous and Hero regretted the dignity of that heavy chignon. But studying herself in the glass she was not too dissatisfied with her appearance, and had been able to go down to meet Clayton feeling slightly more like the stately Miss Hollis who had embarked on the *Norah Crayne*, and less like the bedraggled castaway who had arrived that morning on a ship with a reputation, like that of her Captain, that did not bear investigation.

9

Clayton had not been alone, and Hero could only feel thankful for it, since she was a little uncertain as to how she should greet him. Their last meeting had been an emotional one and she was not entirely sure what she had said, or how far she had committed herself. But fortunately Aunt Abby and Uncle Nat, Cressy, Amelia and Lieutenant Larrimore had all been in the drawing-room; together with Captain Fullbright, who had leapt forward to wring her hand and offer gruff but heart-felt congratulations.

Hero replied to him politely but at random, for looking past his shoulder at Clayton, she was startled by the expression on that handsome, Byronic face.

Clay was standing stock still, staring at her with an unflattering mixture of shock, dismay and outraged incredulity, and it was instantly obvious that owing to the general turmoil no one had remembered to warn him that his love was not in her customary looks. Hero's heart sank while the colour rose painfully to her cheeks, but he recovered himself almost immediately and came quickly to meet her, both hands outstretched:

'*Hero* – Oh, my dear!'

He brushed past Captain Fullbright, brusquely interrupting the older man's congratulations, and grasping her hands lifted them and kissed them passionately: 'I can't believe it!' said Clay emotionally: 'We had given up all hope. They told us that there was no chance of your surviving in such a sea, and I thought I should go out of my mind!'

Hero looked down at his bent head and then above it at the other faces in the green-shuttered, white-walled room. At Uncle Nathaniel blowing his nose to disguise his feelings, Captain and Mrs Fullbright radiating relief, Cressy and Aunt Abby smiling with wet eyes and Lieutenant Larrimore looking carefully at nothing. There was something in the Englishman's expression – something that she had no time to define – that deepened the hot colour in her face and made her suddenly aware of embarrassment and a new and entirely unfamiliar feeling of panic.

She had always hated to be touched and Clay knew it. But she could not snatch her hands away, because that would only wound him. It was her own fault for meeting him like this – in public and under the watching eyes of strangers. She should have seen him at once and alone, and not kept him waiting, for naturally he would be shocked at the change in her appearance, and it was only the effect of that shock that was driving him to behave in so emotional and possessive a manner in front of all these people. But they were not betrothed. Or were they? Clay ought not . . .

Hero glanced again at Lieutenant Larrimore, but the Englishman was no longer looking at nothing. He was looking at Cressy, and that carefully blank expression that had so disconcerted her had gone from his face. She could not even remember why it should have disturbed her, and when Clayton lifted his head and smiled at her she thought, as she had thought so often before in the days when he had been courting her, *How handsome he is!*

It was going to be very pleasant after all – beginning all over again and getting to know each other once more as two quite different people: older and more adult people. Relief welled up in her, and with it a heady feeling of excitement; and forgetting the barely healed cut on her lip she laughed aloud and gaily. And instantly regretted doing so, for it had been exceedingly painful – and not only to herself. The smile vanished from Clayton's face and he dropped her hands and stepped back as swiftly as though she had struck him. But having started to laugh she found that she could not stop, and she clapped her hands over her mouth as much to stifle her unfortunate mirth as to protect her lip from splitting again.

Everything had gone awry, and this was not in the least how she had visualized her arrival in Zanzibar and her meeting with Clayton. She had thought and dreamt and planned for it so long, but now Clay's hurt, shocked face and Aunt Abby's horrified one, the unmistakable embarrassment of the naval Lieutenant and all the alarming and improbable happenings of the past ten days and the last four hours suddenly and for no reason at all struck her as wildly funny, and she laughed and gasped and laughed again, and could not stop.

'She's hysterical,' cried Aunt Abby agitatedly. 'Hero honey, now *do* stop. Cressy – the hartshorn! Now, now, dear, we all understand how you feel. Clay, fetch a glass of water – and my smelling salts! It's just nerves.'

'No, it's not,' gasped Hero, subsiding on to the sofa. 'Oh mercy! now I've split my lip again. Clay, *do* stop looking like that. I know it isn't funny, but if only you could have seen your face when you saw me! You looked so h-horrified. And so s-shocked when I laughed. I didn't mean to laugh, but I couldn't help it because suddenly it all seemed so absurd . . . all of you d-dressed in deep m-mourning and holding a m-memorial service for me, and then seeing me walk in alive and looking like a – a disorderly Billingsgate doxy!'

Lieutenant Larrimore was betrayed into a grin, and Aunt Abby, who had never heard of Billingsgate and certainly never met a doxy, said: 'Really, Hero! I cannot think where you can have picked up such a dreadful expression!'

'From Captain F-Frost,' giggled Hero, staunching a trickle of blood from her lip with a vast bandana handkerchief gallantly proffered by Thaddaeus Fullbright.

'*Frost?*' exclaimed Clayton, thunderstruck. 'Did you say Frost?'

'He s-said that was what I looked like, and as soon as I s-saw your face I knew he had been right. I guess I should have w-worn a b-bonnet and veil, and b-broken it to you gently. I'm so sorry, Clay. I wasn't laughing at you. Truly I was not. It's just that it was so funny. *Do* I look like a disorderly doxy?'

A chorus of indignant protests answered her, and Captain Fullbright observed heartily that she looked just about wonderful to him: 'A sight for sore eyes, ma'am. And I know Mrs Fullbright, who has been blaming herself for it all, will agree with me. It is a miracle that you're alive, and what are a few cuts and bruises against that? They'll heal soon enough and you won't be a mite the worse. And now, if you ladies will excuse us, Mrs Fullbright and I'll be getting back to the ship. We sail tomorrow morning on the tide.'

Lieutenant Larrimore recollected urgent business at the British Consulate and left with them; though reluctantly and with a glance at Cressy that immediately recalled to Hero's mind the comments that Captain Thaddaeus had once made on the score of Cressy's interest in the Englishman. But either the Captain had been mistaken or else the boot was on the other foot, for Cressy had shown only the barest civility towards the Lieutenant, and her acknowledgement of his farewells as he took his leave was noticeably cold and distant.

The door had barely shut behind him when Clayton turned swiftly on Hero and said in a hard grating voice that she had never heard him use before: 'What was that about Frost? Where did you meet the man? How did he come to say such an outrageous thing to you?'

'What outrageous thing?' said Hero, bewildered.

'You said five minutes ago that he had described you as a – as a disorderly doxy,' said Clayton angrily, 'and I should like to know how in tarnation he had the opportunity to do so?'

'Why, on the *Virago*, of course. Didn't they tell you?'

Aunt Abby said faintly: 'It was Captain Frost who rescued her, Clay dear, not——'

'*Frost!* But she arrived here with Larrimore. It was Larrimore who brought her back. She was on the *Daffodil*. Joe Lynch told me – he saw them arrive. He was——'

Hero said: 'Lieutenant Larrimore took me off Captain Frost's ship this morning and brought me ashore. But it was the crew of the *Virago* who picked me up during the storm.'

'That goddamned blackguard!' said Clayton furiously. 'Do you mean to tell me that you have spent the last ten days in his company?'

'I have spent them on his *ship*,' corrected Hero sharply.

'It's the same thing! God Almighty——'

'There is no need to blaspheme, dear,' intervened Aunt Abby reprovingly. 'I guess we all know it was unfortunate, but as Captain Frost has kindly agreed to its being put about that dear Hero was picked up by the *Daffodil* (which you must admit is *most* considerate of him) no one but ourselves need ever know. And in any case, there is nothing we can do about it now.'

'Except,' said Hero, unaccountably annoyed and looking challengingly at her relatives, 'to take the first opportunity of thanking him for being the means of saving my life and for conveying me to Zanzibar.'

The Consul looked a little taken aback, but said readily enough: 'Why, sure we'll do that. We're all mighty glad to have you back, Hero. But I won't disguise from you that I would rather you'd been picked up by almost anyone else. Frost's got a bad reputation in this town, and it's blamed awkward that in my position I should be under any obligation to him. I can only hope that he does not presume upon it.'

'He will,' said Clayton bitterly, 'you can bet your last dime on that. I wouldn't have had this happen for worlds . . . Frost, of all people! Why couldn't it have been Larrimore? Or almost anyone else? Even the dirtiest Arab dhow would have been preferable to the *Virago*.'

'What nonsense, Clay dear,' said his mother chidingly. 'As if it mattered who it was. The only thing that matters is that dear Hero is safe, and if the good Lord permitted that man to be His instrument in saving her from a watery grave, I'm sure we have no right to cavil at it.'

But here neither her son nor her husband were in agreement with her. Both appeared to think that it was the Devil rather than the Deity who had been responsible for selecting Emory Frost as the instrument in question, and Hero would undoubtedly have agreed with them had it not occurred to her that they were giving far more attention to deploring the identity of her rescuer than to rejoicing in her rescue. Piqued by this, she was moved to defend him. With the unfortunate result that in less than two minutes she found herself involved in a heated quarrel with Mr Clayton Mayo.

Clayton had been cruelly hurt by having his emotional welcome greeted by an outburst of laughter, and now he chose to take her defence of Captain Frost as a direct affront to himself and an indication of worse things. It being well known, asserted Clay, white-lipped with anger, that Rory Frost was not only a criminal, but a debauched *roué* with whom no woman was safe. To be associated in any way with such a man was tantamount to being ruined, and he had not expected her to enjoy the process.

'Of course I didn't enjoy it!' retorted Hero, stung by the injustice of the attack. 'It was exceedingly unpleasant and most humiliating, and——' She caught sight of her aunt's horrified countenance and her uncle's dropped jaw and realized too late the interpretation that could be put upon those words.

Hero Hollis was neither slow-witted nor ignorant of the facts of life. But she was, in many ways, remarkably innocent, and the fact that she might have been 'ruined' by Captain Frost, in the sense that Clay had used that word, had never once occurred to her. It did now, with all the force and outrage of a blow between the eyes, and she stared at Clayton with a face that was quite as horrified as Aunt Abby's.

'Hero, honey!' moaned Aunt Abby. 'Really, Clay, you should not even *suggest* such things!'

'Yes, he should,' said Hero clearly. 'Go on, Clay. I am interested. We are all interested in just exactly what you mean by that. How am I "ruined"? In what way? Are you suggesting that this man Frost made improper advances to me?'

'*Hero!*' – this time it was a shriek as Aunt Abby reached wildly for her vinaigrette – 'how can you say such a thing? Cressy, go to your room at once. Oh, this is terrible. Clayton——'

'Please be quiet, Aunt Abby. I wish to hear what Clay has to say, and I would prefer him to say it now and before witnesses. Am I supposed to have been ravished?'

'Hero——! You ought not to *know* about such things! Cressy, didn't I tell you to leave the room? Oh mercy, where are the smelling salts?'

No one paid any attention to the afflicted lady. Her husband pursed his lips and stood looking thoughtfully at his angry niece, and Cressy moved no further than the sofa.

Clayton said: 'I happen to know the man. *And* his reputation.'

'But it seems that you do not know me,' said Hero, 'or *my* reputation. If you did, you would not dare to suggest such a thing.'

'Hell! I am not suggesting it. I am only telling you that no one outside ourselves is likely to believe that you spent over a week alone with that man without——' He was interrupted:

'*Alone?*' blazed Hero. 'I was not alone! The ship was crammed with people – dozens of other people. Black and brown and white ones.'

'*Men!*'

'What else do you expect? That Captain Frost ships a female crew? How many women are there on that British Navy ship? Of course they were all men! But that doesn't mean . . . Why, he hardly looked at me.

105

Or spoke to me. I might have been a – a vegetable for all he cared. He wasn't in the least bit interested in me, and if you had a mite of sense you'd know why!'

'I can see why,' said Clay unkindly.

'Yes, I know you can. You made that perfectly clear to me the moment I came into this room. And let me tell you I looked a good deal worse than this a week ago! No one – not even a m-monster – would have wished to make advances to someone with a black eye and a cut mouth and——' Hero caught her breath on something suspiciously like a sob, and recovering herself, said defiantly: 'He was extremely kind!'

'Was he, indeed! I thought you just told us that you were uncomfortable and humiliated.'

'So I was. But not half as uncomfortable and humiliated as I am right now!'

'I'm glad to hear it,' said Clay shortly. 'It shows you have some sense of proportion.'

Hero made an unintelligible sound that was strongly reminiscent of an indignant kitten, and whirling round, fled from the room, followed precipitately by the sympathetic Cressy.

'*Now* look what you've done,' said Aunt Abby accusingly. 'Really Clay, it is too bad of you. You *cannot* believe that Hero . . . that Captain Frost . . . Though of course you are quite right as to her reputation. People are always *so* unkind and only too ready to believe the worst. But then no one will know of it, so nothing will be said. I guess you'd better go right upstairs and apologize: go on. Best do it now.'

Her son took an angry turn about the room, his handsome face set in a scowl and his hands deep in his pockets, and presently he said sulkily: 'If it should get out, no one could be blamed for thinking the worst. The man's a notorious lecher.'

'*Clay!*'

'Oh, Mama darling, don't play prunes-and-prisms. You've heard all the scandal about him and you know as well as I do that there are only two places where he feels truly at home: in a brawl or a brothel! It makes me madder than fire to think of him laying his filthy hands on Hero and . . . Why, I'd almost rather she had been drowned!'

'How can you, Clay? I can't and won't believe that he did anything of the sort. Oh, this is all too dreadful . . . and just when I was so happy!' Aunt Abby dissolved into tears and following her niece's example, hastily left the room.

The door banged behind her, and Clay said sullenly: 'Well, maybe I'm wrong. But I don't have to like her being on his ship, even if it's true that he never laid a finger on her.'

'Of course it's true.' His step-father's voice was curt and edged with impatience. 'Goddammit you've only got to look at the girl! You showed plainly enough what you thought of her when she walked in just now – and that in spite of knowing that she's a fine, handsome young woman when she isn't looking like a – a – whatever it was that man said she looked like. Ten to one he put her down as a plain piece and not worth wasting his time on. Besides, he'd know she was my niece and entitled to proper respect, and in the circumstances he wouldn't have dared treat her roughly.'

'Oh, wouldn't he!' scoffed Clayton. 'That's all you know about it, sir. He wouldn't care a curse about that, though I guess you're right about the rest of it. Frost wouldn't be interested in a plain woman.'

'You seem,' said his step-father disapprovingly, 'to know a damn' sight too much about this unsavoury slaver. I didn't know you were that well acquainted.'

'I'm not. It's just that . . . . well, I guess it's because I get about a good bit more than you do, so I hear more gossip – and there's always been plenty of talk about him. As to his slaving activities, Larrimore and the British Navy have been laying for him for years. Not that they'll ever get him. He's a darned sight too well in with the natives around here, and he's got the Sultan in his pocket.'

'I know. It's downright disgraceful, but there isn't much we can do about it. Majid is a weak no-good, and in some ways it's almost a pity that the younger brother didn't succeed. Bargash has got twice as much guts, and if his father had been as shrewd a man as they like to make out he'd have realized it and left the throne to him.'

'Maybe he'll get it yet; and a heap sooner than we think.'

The Consul looked at his step-son sharply. 'What makes you say that?'

Clayton flushed and turned away to stare out at the hot, tree-shaded garden. 'Nothing. It's like I said: there's always talk, and Majid is not too popular with the Palace crowd and his royal relations. Most of them seem to think as you do, that the Heir-Apparent is the better man and ought to have been Sultan.'

'So I gather. And I can't say I'm surprised, for the Arabs don't fancy weak rulers. But if young Majid carries on as he's doing right now, that brother of his'll certainly get the throne soon enough, for it'll take a cast-iron constitution to stand up to the shenanigans that go on up at the Palace, and anyone can see Majid ain't got one.'

Clayton gave a short laugh: 'Maybe not. But will Bargash be content to wait for dead men's shoes?'

'He hasn't any alternative. Twenty years ago, or maybe even ten, he could have stuck a knife into his brother and no one would have raised a finger. But times have changed, and this ain't Muscat. Besides, the British are here.'

'The British! That prosy old bore George Edwards and one ten-cent sloop with Dan Larrimore in charge! And I'd like to know what good Larrimore does – apart from hanging round this house whenever he's in port and making sheep's eyes at Cressy.'

Nathaniel Hollis pulled his lip and regarded his step-son with a shrewd and ruminative eye. He was fond of Clay in a detached and un-emotional way, but unlike Abby he had never been blind to the boy's defects. There were times when he wondered if he ought to have been firmer with him; taken more interest in his education and upbringing and the forming of his character; put down his foot and stopped Abigail's slavish spoiling of her son. But that would have meant fighting Abby, and Nathaniel, like his brother Barclay, was too easy-going a man to face such a prospect. Besides, he had always felt a certain diffidence in taking a strong line with another man's son.

He said now: 'I wouldn't underrate the British if I were you, Clay. George Edwards may be a prosy old bore and not overburdened with brains, but he's got plenty of influence around here. Anyways, it's not what he is that counts, but what he stands for. Behind him there's an autocratic old matriarch who wears the crown of England, and behind *her* the whole weight of the British Empire. And neither of 'em are what you might call negligible. As for young Dan Larrimore, I reckon he's a lot smarter than you think. It can't be an easy job, trying to put down slaving in these waters: not when every man jack of 'em around here are up to their necks in it and can't see a thing wrong with it. Why, even the slaves themselves aren't all that grateful for being freed. With no one to feed 'em and look after 'em, or to keep them busy and out of mischief, they were most of 'em a heap better off before; and they know it. And so does Dan! In his line of work it's all kicks and no ha'pence.'

'I hope, sir,' said Clay with a trace of acid, 'that your preference for him isn't going to make you encourage him in his pursuit of my sister?'

A suggestion of a twinkle lighted the Consul's sleepy grey eyes, and he said: ''Far as I can see, he doesn't seem to need much encouragement. But I don't think you need worry. Cressy may have been a mite interested in him once, but that's only natural when you consider that until recently he was just about the only eligible young man around the place.'

'Eligible!' snorted Clayton with scorn.

'Well, let's say "good-looking", if you like it better that way. But I didn't see her throw him so much as a kind word last time he put in here, and she didn't seem any too pleased to see him today either. Though I'll allow that isn't always a good sign where women are concerned! Seems to me she's cooled off him since that young Italian sprig began to pay her attention; he certainly seems to have been around here a lot. And your friend Joe Lynch, too. I reckon they don't come to see me – or your mother, either! When you get around to marrying, don't raise daughters, Clay. They're quite a problem.'

'It begins to look as though my problem will be getting married at all,' said Clayton morosely.

'You mean to Hero?'

'Who else? I thought it was all fixed up, but now . . . Oh heck, I suppose I shouldn't have spoken as I did, but it kind of jolted me – hearing that it was Frost who'd picked her up. And then her laughing at me and defending that skunk. I guess I lost my temper and spoke out of turn. But darn it, it was only natural to suppose that a man like that would go the whole way – or try to. It wouldn't have been her fault if he had, and no one could have blamed her. But I suppose if she says that nothing happened——'

'You can take it that nothing did,' finished his step-father firmly. 'She's always been a truthful girl, Hero. A durned sight too truthful for comfort at times! I know your Ma is set on the match, but I wouldn't have thought you and she would suit, Clay. Always surprised me that you should have taken to her. Not your kind, I'd have said. Too damned hard to handle; which was Barclay's fault . . . he gave her her head too much.'

'I can handle her,' said Clayton shortly.

'Maybe you can. I certainly hope so, if you intend to marry her. But if you do, I guess you'd better start by making your apologies. The poor girl's had a rough time of it. Losing her Pa, setting off alone from the opposite side of the world, nearly drowned, rescued by a rascally slaver, face bashed about and her looks lost. And what does she get when she fetches up here? A tirade on the subject of her lost reputation instead of the open arms and tears of joy she had every right to expect from you. You know, Clay, your trouble is that you don't look before you leap. Or if you do, you sure don't look long enough!'

Mr Nathaniel Hollis pulled his lip again, nodded sagely at his step-son and returned to his study without waiting to see if his advice was followed or not.

10

Hero slammed the bedroom door behind her with such violence that the key leapt from the lock and slid away across the polished floor. But before she had time to do more than stoop and retrieve it, the door opened and shut again, and Cressy was there; breathless and sympathetic:

'Oh, Hero darling, *don't* cry! Please don't cry. I'm sure it's all a mistake. I'm sure Clay didn't mean to offend you.'

'I'm not crying,' raged Hero, flinging herself face downwards on the bed and burying her face in the pillow. 'And he did mean it!'

She wished Cressy would go away. Or that she herself could go away. Everything had turned out wrong and she ought never to have come out here. They had been right after all – Cousin Josiah, Aunt Lucy Strong, Miss Penbury and all those elderly and disapproving Craynes who had shaken their heads over her and prophesied disaster. They had warned her that she would live to regret such rash and headstrong behaviour, and she had refused to listen to them because she had wanted to travel and to see the world. To see Zanzibar. To see Clayton . . .

How *could* Clay have brought himself to speak to her like that? How could he! Hero struck her pillow with a clenched fist and became aware that the door must have opened once more, for her aunt's voice, tearful but authoritative, was saying: 'Run away, Cressy. I'm sure dear Hero does not want to speak to you just at present. Leave her alone, there's a good girl.'

Cressy withdrew reluctantly and Hero sat up, feeling a little ashamed of herself, and avoiding her aunt's anxious gaze, went to the wash-hand-stand to dip her handkerchief into the rose-painted ewer and mop at her angry eyes and flushed cheeks. Aunt Abby said coaxingly: 'You must try and make allowances for Clay, honey. He has been distracted with grief. You can't know what a shock it was to all of us when the ship arrived and they told us that you had been drowned. Specially to Clay. He is so devoted to you, dear. He loves you so much. You do know that, don't you?'

'No, I don't!' said Hero tremulously. 'Not if he can accuse me of . . . How *could* he say such things? If that's what he thinks of me——!'

'But honey,' quavered Aunt Abby, unaware of paraphrasing words that were being spoken at that precise moment by her son, 'he did not mean that it was *your* fault. He would know you could not prevent . . . prevent anything.'

'Oh, couldn't I!' retorted Hero, her eyes flashing. 'As it happens, there was nothing to prevent. But if there had been, I would certainly have prevented it!'

Aunt Abby flushed and said hurriedly: 'You cannot possibly know what you are talking about, honey. As an unmarried girl there are things that you do not at all understand – which Clay would have realized if only he had given himself time to think. I guess it was your defending this man Frost that upset him. Though I can fully understand your attitude. Naturally, you feel grateful to the man; and for my part I am quite prepared to believe that he behaved with the *utmost* propriety towards you.'

'Then you are wrong, Aunt, because he did nothing of the sort. He was rude and insufferable, and he had the impertinence to treat me as though I were ten years old and – and of no importance at all.'

The indignation in her niece's voice brought a sudden and unexpected smile to lighten Aunt Abby's troubled face, and she said with a quiver of amusement: 'Did he indeed, dear? Well, at least that was preferable to being made an object of gallantry.'

'Gallantry? I don't believe that man knows the meaning of the word!'

'I did not mean *that* kind of gallantry,' reproved Aunt Abby. 'I meant – well, just supposing he had attempted to kiss you?'

'He did kiss me,' said Hero shortly.

'Oh, *no*!' gasped Aunt Abby in quite another voice.

'But not in the least in the way you imagine,' finished Hero bitterly. 'He was certainly not being gallant, and he did not consider me in the least degree attractive. I believe it was merely because he felt sorry for me.'

'Oh mercy!' moaned Aunt Abby, groping helplessly round in search of the hartshorn. 'Yes, I'm sure he was. But I do *trust* that you will not repeat that sort of thing to Clay. About being kissed, I mean. Or to anyone else. You should never have allowed such a thing. People would not believe . . . I mean, they would think . . .'

'The worst, of course. You do not have to tell me that, Aunt Abby. Possibly I should feel flattered that you and Clay appear so ready to believe that my charms must have impelled Captain Frost to make an assault on my virtue. But the truth of the matter is that he did not consider that I had any charms at all, and he was not in the least interested in either me or my virtue. He thought I was a nuisance. And I was! I got in his way.'

Hero returned to sit on the edge of her bed, and jerking the wet handkerchief between her hands, said: 'He was engaged upon some business that he did not wish me to know about, and he was not at all pleased to have me on his ship, let me tell you, Aunt! He even locked me in the cabin twice, in case I should see something that he did not wish seen.'

'Locked you in?' demanded Aunt Abby, affronted. 'How exceedingly impertinent! What can he have been doing?'

'I wish I knew. I think he was smuggling something – slaves or opium or contraband of some kind. I wouldn't put anything past him. And I must say, Aunt Abby, that I cannot help agreeing with Clay that I would rather anyone had rescued me than that – that *slaver*! It is too humiliating to have to be grateful to a common criminal: and for something that would never have come about if he had known how to handle his ship.'

Hero brooded darkly for a moment or two, then her brow cleared, and rising abruptly she embraced her aunt with a fervour that set that afflicted lady's cap askew, and said remorsefully: 'No, that's not quite true. It was my fault too, and I am only making excuses for myself. I should never have ventured on deck in such weather, and I am excessively sorry, Aunt. I have caused you all such a great deal of trouble and behaved very badly, and I don't suppose Clay meant to be insulting. He merely lost his temper – as I did, too. Let us forget all about that, and be truly thankful instead of engaging in arguments and quarrels.'

Aunt Abby heaved a sigh of relief, and returning her niece's embrace with equal fervour, said warmly: 'That's my sweet, sensible child. Clay shall apologize, and then we need not mention the matter again. And I think, honey, it would be an excellent thing if you were to keep within doors and in seclusion for at least a week, to give those cuts and bruises time to heal before you meet any of our community here. We will get Doctor Kealey to see what he can do for you, and in the meantime we can give out that you are in need of rest and quiet; which is a thing that will be *quite* understood by everyone. Perhaps if we applied a little witch-hazel?' ...

Aunt Abby hurried away to look into the matter of salves and lotions, but no sooner had she departed than the door opened again without ceremony to admit her daughter.

'Hero, did you really mean it?' demanded Cressy in a voice breathless with excitement and awe. 'Did Rory Frost *really* kiss you?'

'Cressy, you've been listening at doors,' accused Hero. 'It's too bad of you and I shall tell your Mama.'

'You wouldn't be so mean,' said Cressy confidently. 'Not when you must know that I could not resist it. You can have no idea how tiresome it is always being told to leave the room as soon as anyone mentions anything in the least interesting. After all, it is not as though I were a child. Why, Mama was already married to Clay's father by the time she was my age; yet I once heard her telling Olivia Credwell that a young girl should not only be innocent, but in some matters entirely ignorant. Such flummery! I do not agree at all that one should be ignorant, so of course I have no choice but to listen at doors. You must see that.'

'It's underhand,' said Hero severely.

'But it's sensible. And anyway, if I hadn't listened I wouldn't have heard about Captain Frost kissing you. I *had* so hoped that you would decide to marry Clay, but now I suppose you will have to marry him instead.'

'Marry who?' demanded Hero, bewildered.

'Rory Frost, of course.'

'Marry that – that *pirate*! Whatever for? What on earth are you talking about, Cressy?'

'But Hero, if he kissed you . . .'

'If you imagine that a girl has to marry any man who kisses her, then all I can say is that you have not listened at enough doors!' retorted Hero with vigour.

Cressy threw a quick look over her shoulder, and lowering her voice to a whisper said: 'But supposing you have a baby?'

Her cousin sat down abruptly upon the ottoman and burst out laughing, and Cressy, looking mortally offended said: 'I don't see anything to laugh at. *Everyone* knows that you don't have to be married to have a baby and that it's the kissing that counts.'

'Cressy darling,' besought Hero, recovering her breath, 'do take that expression off your face. You look just like Clay did when I laughed in the drawing-room, and I am not making fun of you any more than I was of him. But don't you ever use your eyes? I mean, animals and things? Of course you don't have a baby just because you kiss someone. Why, even Clay kissed me once, and you must surely have been kissed under the mistletoe a dozen times.'

'Oh, *that*!' said Cressy, subsiding on to the far end of the ottoman. 'That's quite different. Just boys pecking at your cheek with everyone looking on and laughing. I'm sure that being kissed by a man when you are all alone with him must be *quite* different.'

'Not all that different,' admitted Hero, trying to recall what she had felt on the only occasion when Clayton had kissed her. It certainly had not been the thrilling and heart-stopping affair that she had once imagined it must be, and honesty compelled her to admit that Captain Frost's insultingly casual caress had been infinitely more disturbing. The reflection did nothing to soothe her, and glancing at her cousin's pretty, eager face she said a shade tartly: 'I expect you'll find out one day. Hasn't Lieutenant Larrimore tried to kiss you yet?'

A bright wave of colour flooded up to burn Cressy's cheeks, and she said stiffly: 'Certainly not! And he is never likely to.'

'Isn't he? Then I have been misled, for Captain Fullbright told me that he fancied you had a fondness for the Lieutenant.'

'Captain Fullbright,' said Cressy with dignity, 'should mind his own business. No, I do not have a fondness for Lieutenant Larrimore. I mean, he does not have a fondness for me. I mean, he – we . . . Oh, Hero, it is all so difficult! You don't *know* what I have been through.'

She cast herself into her cousin's arms, and Hero sighed, and heroically abandoning her own problems in favour of Cressy's, said encouragingly: 'Tell me about it.'

'It's Dan,' said Cressy, sitting up and speaking the name with a gasp of relief as though she had been waiting for this moment. As indeed she had, since the subject was not one that she felt herself able to discuss with her Mama, while Clay, when appealed to, had been most unsympathetic and effectively put a stop to further confidences. True, there remained her friends Olivia Credwell and Thérèse Tissot. But though she admired them both excessively they were not only married but a great deal older than herself: as well as being indirectly responsible (though they were unaware of this) for her present unhappy situation. It was therefore an inexpressible comfort to have someone nearer her own age to confide in.

'You mean Lieutenant Larrimore,' prompted Hero helpfully.

'Yes. You see he . . . we . . . well, I *did* like him, Hero. I mean I do like him. And I'm sure he likes me, although he has never actually said anything, you know. But he used to call a great deal whenever his ship was in port, and——' Cressy paused uncertainly, her brow puckered and her red lips drooping like a sad baby's.

'Have you quarrelled?' asked Hero.

'In – in a way. He told me that I should not call on the Sultan's sisters so often, and I said that I should do so as often as I chose, and that he had no right to criticize or to try to dictate to me. And he hasn't any right! So then he said that it was because he did not like to see me becoming involved in anything unpleasant, and that if I did not know what I was doing, then Olivia and Thérèse ought to.'

'And what were you doing?' enquired Hero, interested.

'Nothing,' said Cressy, 'nothing at all!' And added defiantly: 'Though I do not mind telling you, Hero, that if there was anything I could do, I would do it. You see, it is like this . . .'

Judging from Cressy's somewhat incoherent account, it had been Madame Tissot, the wife of a French merchant, and her friend Mrs Credwell, the widowed sister of Mr Hubert Platt of the British East

African Coastal Trading Company, who had introduced Cressy and her Mama to the Sultan's young half-sister, Salmé. The Seyyida Salmé, explained Cressy, was a daughter of the late Sultan, Seyyid Saïd, by a Circassian concubine, and unlike a good many of the older and more conservative ladies of the ruling house of Zanzibar, she was not only deeply curious about European women, but eager to meet them. Salmé had been shy but friendly, and it was through her that Cressy had met others of the royal ladies, and in company with Madame Tissot and Mrs Credwell, had ended by becoming an enthusiastic supporter of the present Sultan's younger brother and Heir-Apparent, Seyyid Bargash-bin-Saïd.

'Not that I have ever met him,' confided Cressy, 'because he has never called upon his sisters when I have been there – you have no idea how strict Arab women are about men visiting them. Far stricter than we are. They make the most ridiculous fuss about it, even though some of them are terribly fat and old and one cannot imagine any man being in the *least* interested. Though to hear them talk you'd think that they were all as beautiful as the day and that all men were monsters. Some of them are of course: as beautiful as the day, I mean. Like Salmé's half-sister, Cholé. Cholé's mother was a Circassian slave-girl too, and she is simply lovely; you've no idea, Hero. Like an *Arabian Nights'* Princess. And then there's Méjé – she's another sister . . .'

It was obvious that the sentimental and romantic Cressy had fallen completely under the spell of the Sultan's charming half-sisters, despite the fact that they were apparently engaged in plotting to depose their brother Majid and seat the Heir-Apparent in his place. 'You see, Bargash would make a much better Sultan than Majid,' explained Cressy earnestly. 'Even Papa says so.'

'You mean Uncle Nat knows all about this?' demanded Hero, startled.

'Oh no, indeed not. But I have heard him say a hundred times that Majid is weak and dissolute and quite unfitted to rule. And everyone knows that Prince Bargash is not at all like that: one has only to look at him. I saw him once at a big reception at the Palace, and he is really very handsome. Dark of course, but not nearly as dark as you would think. Lots of them are not. Cholé and Salmé are quite fair, and I know you'll just love them, Hero. They are so charming and graceful and . . . But Dan – I mean Lieutenant Larrimore – said that it was a great mistake to see so much of them, because they were playing with fire and that I was too young to understand what was going on. He said he was only warning me for my own good and – and then we quarrelled, and in the end he walked out of the house and his ship sailed the next day, so I didn't see him again.'

'But you saw him only this morning,' Hero pointed out.

'Not to talk to. And he only gave me the *stiffest* bow when he saw me – as though I was some old dowd like Mrs Kealey. So of course I was stiff too and wouldn't look at him. But if he had a spark of – of feeling, he would apologize and beg my pardon.'

'You ought to know by now that the English never apologize,' said Hero crisply, 'because they are always quite sure that they are in the right. And if I were you, Cressy, I would not have anything more to do with him. Why, there are thousands of American boys – millions of them – who are much better looking and far nicer than Lieutenant Larrimore.'

'Not in Zanzibar,' said Cressy sadly.

She brooded for a silent minute, her white forehead puckered in a frown, and then said resentfully: 'They are all on the side of the Sultan, of course. The English, I mean. That stuffy old Colonel Edwards, and the Kealeys and the Platts. Olivia is the only one who is not, because she has a great deal of character and sensibility. But all the rest of them are for Majid just because he is older than Bargash, and because he's *there* and the English don't like things changed unless it's they who change them. They haven't any imagination, and they don't care a bit that Majid is no good at all while the Prince could be counted on to bring about sadly needed reforms.'

Hero herself had set out for Zanzibar with reform in mind, and she had not forgotten what Jules Dubail had said on the subject of the present Sultan. Nevertheless she could not refrain from pointing out that history had shown all royal and hereditary rulers to be narrow-minded tyrants, so how could anyone be sure that this younger brother, once he was in power, would prove any better than the older one?

'Because his sisters say so,' retorted Cressy, firing up. 'And they would know, just as I would know about Clay. I guess girls always know about their brothers. They say that Majid is no good and that all he wants to do is drink and spend money, and – and have orgies and things with people like Rory Frost. Papa says that Captain Frost is hand-in-glove with him and forever at the Palace, and that Colonel Edwards ought to put a stop to it. But I don't suppose he will, because of Captain Frost being an Englishman too. I *told* you the English were all on the Sultan's side. Even Dan is, and that's why he doesn't want me to see so much of the Princesses. He's just taking sides like the rest of them!'

'He wouldn't take Captain Frost's side,' said Hero thoughtfully. 'He doesn't like him any more than Uncle Nat and Clay do. In fact, a good deal less.'

'I know. He says Rory Frost is a disgrace to the nation. But wouldn't you think that would show him how *dreadful* the Sultan is? – having a man like that for a friend? But it doesn't. He's as bad as Colonel Edwards and I'd like to know who told him that I'd been seeing the Princesses; and what business it is of his anyway ... I won't be spied on and told what I should do and what I shouldn't. If Papa doesn't object, I don't see why Dan——'

Cressy stopped and bit her lip, and after a fractional pause said carefully: 'I don't mean that Papa knows what we talk about, but he does not mind my calling at Beit-el-Tani. Grown-ups,' added Cressy (who despite her recent assertion that she was no longer a child, still thought of her elders in that schoolroom term), 'have to be so careful about that sort of thing, and Papa would only say that it was none of my business. Which is not really true, because *I* think that – that helping the populace should be everyone's business, don't you?'

'Certainly,' agreed Hero emphatically: unaware that the warmth of her agreement sprang not so much from zeal to assist 'the populace', as from the fact that she was instantly sure that any boon companion of Captain Frost's was, *ipso facto*, a thoroughly bad character and quite unfitted to remain in a position of authority.

Had it not been for the introduction of Captain Frost's name, Hero might well have been inclined to treat her cousin's confidences as trifling, and to regard Cressy's fervent championship of a dusky princeling who desired to usurp his brother's throne as a matter for amusement. But the mention of the English slaver had put quite a different light on the affair, for it succeeded in arousing both her hostility and her own crusading instincts.

Could this, she wondered, be the work that Providence intended her to do? If so, then even that terrifying fall from the deck of the *Norah Crayne* had its place in the scheme of things, since but for that she would have known little (and that only by hearsay) of Emory Tyson Frost and the *Virago*. But because she knew him, she also knew that if he were hand-in-glove with Sultan Majid it was for no good purpose, and that the sooner such an unholy alliance was broken up the better.

No doubt 'Roaring Rory' acted as a jackal to the Sultan; smuggling slaves either to or from the island for their mutual profit. In which case it was not surprising that Lieutenant Larrimore had so far failed to lay him by the heels, since such a partnership would be difficult to defeat. With the Sultan's resources placed at his disposal and the Sultan's police force – if any – turning a blind or at best an unhelpful eye, it was no wonder that the *Virago*'s insolent Captain continued to flourish like the green bay tree of the Bible and to avoid all attempts to bring him to book. But if this Prince Bargash, who aspired to the throne, disapproved of his dissolute brother, it followed that he must also disapprove quite as strongly of his brother's dissolute friends. Which meant that the downfall of the

Sultan would automatically entail the downfall of Captain Emory Frost...

'*I am* not *ungrateful*,' Hero assured her conscience, '*but one must be just*.' Unprincipled scoundrels such as Captain Frost were a disgrace to the white races, a menace to society and an ugly example to the unenlightened Heathen who were – Heaven and Hero Hollis knew – quite bad enough on their own without any Western encouragement. She might not be able to release slaves, but at least she could strike a blow against the whole detestable system by helping to rid the island of one self-confessed slaver. And if this entailed espousing the cause of Prince Bagash and assisting to depose Sultan Majid, she was perfectly ready to do so, since it was only too clear that the 'populace' would be greatly benefited by the removal of the present ruler and his renegade friend from any position of authority.

'But are you quite sure,' demanded Hero, struck by a sudden and unpleasant thought, 'that they do not intend to do the Sultan any harm? They are not planning his assassination or anything like that? – you know what Orientals are capable of.'

'Good gracious, no!' said Cressy, scandalized: 'Why, he's their *brother*. Or at least, their half-brother. I believe they all had different mothers, though Sultan Saïd was their father. Harems, you know. And – and mistresses and things.' Cressy blushed, and added hurriedly: 'They wouldn't dream of harming him. They only wish to depose him, and then, when Bargash is Sultan, Majid can retire with a pension to somewhere on the mainland like Dar-es-Salaam, where he has been wasting a lot of money building himself a new palace.'

The artlessness of this pronouncement was lost upon Hero, who in common with her cousin knew little or nothing of the history of the Seyyids of Muscat and Oman (or indeed of any Eastern rulers) and had by now quite forgotten Captain Frost's assertion that fratricide, and worse, spattered the pages of such chronicles with ugly scarlet stains. Cressy's statement sounded entirely reasonable to her and she had no hesitation in accepting it. The Sultan's sisters were clearly working for Justice and the Common Good, and therefore merited her support, and all that remained was to make certain that their brother Bargash was truly fitted to rule.

Any other young woman might have been expected, on such a day, to brush aside political problems in favour of more personal ones. But Hero Athena Hollis was made of sterner stuff, and moreover she conceived herself to have a Mission. The strange, high-roomed Arab house, the cruel, beautiful, horrifying Island, her fantastic rescue from death and Clayton's recent unpardonable observations, all faded into insignificance when compared with the prospect of striking a blow against the detestable institution of slavery. *'I always knew that there would be something for me to do in Zanzibar,'* thought Hero with a deep sense of gratitude and fulfilment.

She had entirely forgotten about Clayton, and it was Cressy who heard the knock on the door and answered it.

'No, of course you can't come in, Clay,' protested Cressy, every bit as shocked at the prospect of a gentleman entering a lady's bedroom as any ornament of the harem would have been under similar circumstances. 'Yes, I'll tell her.'

She closed the door firmly, and turned to whisper that it was Clay and what should she tell him? 'He says he wants to see you. I guess it's to apologize.'

'Tell him that I'll be down in five minutes,' said Hero.

It was, in point of fact, nearer twenty. But the delay had at least given Clayton more time in which to prepare his excuses and put his apologies into an acceptable form, and all might have been well had he not finished by saying that in proof of his repentance he had asked to be associated with the message of gratitude from his step-father that was being conveyed by a trusted member of the Consul's Arab staff to Captain Frost's house in the city:

'Though I can tell you it went against the grain to do it,' admitted Clayton frankly. 'However, as he seems to have treated you with tolerable civility, I felt it was the least I could do.'

His words awoke a disturbing echo of something that Hero herself had recently said to Captain Frost, and troubled by it she said anxiously: 'But surely Uncle Nat means to call upon him personally to tell him how grateful I – we are? When you consider what we owe him, to send only a letter——'

'A message,' corrected Clayton. 'I'm sorry, Hero, but I guess you still don't understand the difficulties of our situation. I know that you'll think us hard and ungrateful, but we have to think not only of you but of our official position here. We have agreed that although it may seem discourteous, we cannot allow a man who is known to be an unscrupulous lawbreaker to get his hands on something that he might one day make use of to press some fancied claim upon you.'

'But he does have a claim on me, Clay. I owe him——'

'You owe him nothing,' interrupted Clayton sharply. 'Captain Fullbright made that quite clear when he told us that Frost's vessel was completely out of control and that it was only luck and the mercy of God that saved the *Norah Crayne* from being rammed and sunk, or overwhelmed by a cross sea. And you yourself told us that if a wave hadn't carried you on to the *Virago*'s rat-lines you couldn't have avoided being drowned. It was Frost himself who was responsible for you being swept into the sea, and Providence and not Frost who saved you. And if he'd had the smallest consideration for our feelings, he would have brought you to Zanzibar immediately and saved us days of unnecessary grief and mental suffering. I reckon he hasn't put himself out in any way, and I for one find his callous display of dilatoriness unforgivable.'

'Yes, I – I know all that,' said Hero unhappily. 'And to tell the truth, Clay, I agree with you. But all the same he *was* instrumental, under Providence, in saving my life, and we cannot overlook that however much we may dislike it. Besides, as you have just pointed out, he could have made himself exceedingly unpleasant to me had he wished.'

'If he'd attempted anything of the sort he would have paid heavily for it,' retorted Clayton hotly. 'No, Hero. It's generous of you to feel grateful to this man when he has done little or nothing to deserve it, and knowing you as I do, I feel sure that you've already said all that is necessary to him in the way of thanks. But if any of us were to be seen calling at his house, particularly when it is not known that you were on his ship, it would cause a great deal of comment. And one cannot,' added Clayton, clinching the matter, 'touch pitch without being defiled.'

It was unfortunate that he should have elected to repeat an adage that Captain Frost had himself quoted earlier in the day, since it recalled to Hero's mind a good deal more that the Captain had said. She had already decided that for its own good the Island must be rid of this man, but the reflection that he had forecast the reactions of her relatives with regrettable accuracy and could now not only say '*I told you so*', but convict her, with them, of lack of courtesy, was not to be borne. It became, in that instant, a point of honour that he should be personally and properly thanked.

But it was a point that Clayton refused to see, and Uncle Nathaniel and Aunt Abigail, entering the drawing-room some five minutes later, had taken his part:

'The man Frost,' said Uncle Nathaniel, summing up, 'is, as you have already been told, just a low-down rascal, and I guess every Consul in the place has had to fight against his pernicious influence with the Sultan. I'm telling you straight, Hero, that even sending along Selim with a message of thanks went mighty hard against the grain, yet I did it – for precisely the reason that you keep urging on me. Because I will not give a white-trash slaver any excuse to accuse me of discourtesy. But I'm not going to meet him or have him enter this house, or allow any relative of mine to put a foot inside his. Nor will I, by putting my thanks on paper, provide him with written proof that you have spent ten days unchaperoned on board his ship, which he might well use one day to blackmail you with. You will have no more to do with him, and that's an order!'

'But Uncle Nat——'

'That's enough, Hero. Now let's go eat, and forget about all this.'

11

There had been a great many callers at the Consulate on the day of the *Norah Crayne*'s departure, for the dramatic story of young Miss Hollis's return from the dead had spread rapidly, and the European community, who barely a week ago had left cards of condolence, were now hastening to present their congratulations and meet the heroine of the drama. But Aunt Abby had no intention of presenting her niece until those disfiguring bruises had faded, and she had been adamant. Dear Hero, she informed them, was still feeling very shaken, and Dr Kealey had advised that she should rest as much as possible, and on no account be permitted to discuss her terrifying ordeal, since to do so would only distress her and retard her recovery.

The callers had had to be content with a colourless account of the rescue, in which the *Daffodil* played substitute for the *Virago*, and when Dr Kealey, the Medical Officer attached to the British Consulate, had been interrogated by half-a-dozen interested matrons, he had been unable to add anything to the story.

Lieutenant Larrimore had proved equally uncommunicative (though in his case reticence had been misconstrued as modesty), while as for Hero herself, she possessed sufficient vanity to fall in with her aunt's wishes and remain *incommunicado* until the interest died down and her bruises with it. This might entail several days of enforced seclusion, but would at least give her plenty of time in which to find some way of escaping unobserved from the Consulate in order to pay a courtesy call upon Captain Emory Frost. For if the Consul imagined that subject to be closed, he did not know his niece! Hero had no intention of being dictated to on a matter that she conceived to be a personal point of honour, and she had made up her mind that if neither Clayton nor Uncle Nat would oblige her by squaring her account with the *Virago*'s Captain, she must do so herself.

It had been easy enough to decide on such an action, but putting it into practice had proved unexpectedly difficult, for when she suggested taking a short walk in the evening – bonneted, veiled and unaccompanied so that no one need suspect who she was – she had received a horrified refusal from her aunt. Never, positively *never*! was she to go out alone. She must remember that this was the East and not America, and that many of the natives here were quite uncivilized. Anything might happen. Why, even well-bred Arab women never dreamed of going out by day, and those of the poorer classes kept their faces covered when in the streets.

Uncle Nathaniel had endorsed these strictures: adding that apart from the impropriety of such an action, there were grave risks attached to walking alone in Zanzibar city, for the late Sultan had signed a treaty that had led to the freeing of a considerable number of slaves, with results that had not been visualized by the well-meaning Western philanthropists whose efforts had brought it about. The freed slaves had been turned adrift by men who could not afford to pay them wages as well as keep, and now the town was awash with homeless negroes, unemployed and rapidly becoming unemployable, whose only means of livelihood was begging or theft.

'Mind you, I'm not defending the old system,' said Uncle Nat. 'There can be no defence of slavery. But people should have been able to figure out a less cruel way of ending it. I sometimes feel it's a pity that some of those talkative and charitable folk back home can't come out here and see what their abstract philanthropy has led to.'

'But it is a beginning,' urged Hero, 'and surely that's better than nothing? Though I do think that the owners should have been forced to keep them.'

'As slaves?'

'No, of course not. As properly paid servants.'

'Can't have it both ways,' said Uncle Nat, snipping off the end of a fresh cigar. 'Folk in this part of the world can't see anything wrong in slavery. I guess it's been going on ever since the sons of Noah divided up the world after the Flood, and by now it seems as natural to them as breathing. They just can't understand why anyone should want to stop it, and the Sultan himself couldn't make them free their slaves and at the same time house and feed them.'

'But if there was work for them before,' persisted Hero, 'it must still need doing, and people would surely pay to have it done?'

'It's not as simple as that. When it was only a matter of feeding and housing his labour, a man could afford to keep a large number of slaves: they added to his prestige and he very seldom overworked them or turned them off in their old age. But as soon as he had to pay them he found that five hired hands, working for a wage, could easily do what twenty-five slaves had previously parcelled out between them. That's why only the strongest and best get hired now, while the rest are turned off – and turned out. They are becoming a mighty serious problem, and no one is really safe on the streets: certainly not a lone white woman walking round town unattended!'

This was a situation that had never even occurred to Hero. And the obstacle it presented was not the only one, for the Arabic and Swahili of which she had been so proud turned out to be largely unintelligible to her uncle's servants. They listened to her with polite, expectant smiles and nodded their heads (which she had at first taken for assent, not realizing that in general it signified the reverse), and it was soon clear that the languages she had so painstakingly acquired in Boston differed as widely from the real thing as Miss Penbury's French differed from that spoken by Monsieur Jules Dubail.

Without a working knowledge of one of the local tongues, and some knowledge of the town, Hero did not see how she was to find her way to Captain Frost's house. But these last two problems were speedily solved, for Aunt Abby had engaged a personal maid for her, Fattûma, who not only spoke and understood English, but was familiar with every street, lane and alleyway in the city.

Questioned by her new mistress, Fattûma assured Hero that the house occupied by the Captain and several members of the *Virago*'s crew was well known and lay in one of the quieter streets near the edge of the town, less than a quarter of a mile from the Consulate. It was known locally as 'The Dolphins' House' – taking its name from a frieze of those creatures carved above the door – and could be easily identified because it faced an ancient graveyard; a small private burial ground, much overgrown by trees, where half-a-dozen broken tombstones were said to mark the graves of a Portuguese Admiral and his Arab wives.

The only question that remained was how to get there, and though this should have been the easiest part of it, it proved the hardest. For though the European community in Zanzibar made it a custom to stroll or ride upon the open *maidan* in the cool of the evening, Aunt Abby was certainly not going to permit her niece to join such promenades until the damage to her looks had been repaired, and Hero found herself virtually a prisoner, with her walks restricted to the Consulate garden. A situation that in the circumstances she found distinctly frustrating.

The garden was not a large one, but it was cool and shady. A stone-flagged terrace, on to which the doors and french windows of the ground-floor rooms opened, was made colourful by jars filled with flowering shrubs, and a short flight of steps led down from it to a formal pattern of little paths bisecting the equally formal flowerbeds which centred on a small pool sprinkled with lily-pads. Frangipani and jasmine scented the air, there were pomegranates, jacarandas, a palm and a feathery pepper tree, and, at the far end of the garden, a cluster of orange trees that concealed a thatched summer-house, a litter of flower-pots and watering-cans, and a small iron-barred door that was used only by the gardeners and the night-watchman.

An old, high and solid wall enclosed the whole, and from the far side of it rose the noise and clamour of Zanzibar: the cries of coconut-sellers and vendors of fruit and water, the creak of *homali* carts, the shrill voices of children, a babel of tongues gossiping, quarrelling, cursing, laughing; the twang of zithers and the thump of drums, the braying of donkeys and the bark of pariah dogs. But inside the wall the scent of flowers and the green shade of trees gave an illusion of quiet, and it was as though the garden was some small enclosed backwater beside a rushing river.

At any other time such an atmosphere might have seemed soothing and pleasant to Hero. But now she found it exasperating to stroll gently along garden paths when she wished to go out into the city and look for a house with dolphins carved above its door. She was unused to being thwarted, and the whole situation had begun to irk her abominably, because she could not feel free to embark upon any campaign against slave trading in Zanzibar until she had paid her promised debt to one shameless trader. Once that was done and the slate clean, she need have no qualms about doing all that was possible to have him outlawed from the Island. But until then she felt as though her hands were tied, and she she did not relish the feeling. There *must* be some way of getting out of the house unseen and without her relations.

Three days later, in the dullest hour of the day, a solution to that problem suddenly presented itself . . .

The long hot gap between noon and the hour when the air cooled toward sundown was occupied by a siesta: a custom which appeared common to all Zanzibar, and seemed a scandalous waste of time to Miss Hollis, who could not understand how white people could let themselves become so sunk in sloth as to sleep away the greater part of each day. On this afternoon, as usual, the voices and the busy clatter of the morning had died down to a drowsy murmur no louder than the sound of distant surf, and even the crows and the pariah dogs appeared to have fallen asleep. And once again a suffocating feeling of frustration pressed upon Hero like a tangible weight: the whole situation was ridiculous, and in her present position she was not much better off than those unfortunate Arab women who lived penned up in harems and were only allowed out cloaked and veiled and——

Why, that's it! thought Hero. *Of course that's it! Why ever didn't I think of it before?*

She sprang up from the bed, and in the next instant was across the room and ringing the small brass hand bell for Fattûma.

That same evening Uncle Nat and Clayton were engaged to visit an influential landowner who lived some few miles outside the city on the east coast of the island. As his estate could be reached more easily by sea they were taking a boat, and it had been decided that Aunt Abby, Hero and Cressy should accompany them for the sail: the ladies to remain on board during the call, which might be expected to last for at least an hour. It was to have been Hero's first outing, and she regretted having to miss it, but the opportunity it offered her was far too good to be wasted.

She consoled herself with the reflection that duty should come before pleasure, and when Cressy came to rouse her from the afternoon siesta she pleaded a headache and urged that the expedition should not be cancelled on her account, but that she might be left to sleep. Fattûma, said Hero, would look after her, and there was not the least need for either Aunt Abby or Cressy to remain in the house. In fact if they meant to forgo their evening outing on her behalf they would only succeed in making her feel sadly upset.

It was this last observation that had persuaded them to leave her, and the rest had been simple. Ten minutes after their departure Hero was safely in the summer-house and being robed by the resourceful Fattûma in a *schele*, the street garb of an Arab woman. A shapeless black garment that covered her from head to foot and left only a narrow, heavily fringed slit for her eyes.

Worn over her own dress it proved stiflingly hot, but she could not very well appear before Captain Frost in her petticoat. It was bad enough to have to remove her hoops, for she would naturally have preferred to look dignified and well dressed on such an occasion. But that could not be helped, and Hero Athena had never been one to cry over spilt milk or allow trifles to obstruct her. If this was the only way in which she could pay a personal call upon Captain Frost to thank him – and thereby prove him wrong – then it would have to be taken.

She removed her shoes, and exchanging them for a pair of heelless curl-toed slippers that Fattûma had provided, shuffled after her maid through the grass and the fallen leaves to the door in the garden wall. The hinges squeaked as Fattûma eased it open, but there was no one at hand to hear or see the two women slip out into the hot dust of a narrow, evil-smelling lane, closing the door cautiously behind them.

The air inside the garden had been sweet with the scent of flowering trees and cool from the newly watered earth, but once outside, the heat and stench of the city met them like a waft from a burning rubbish dump. Fattûma glanced anxiously about her, but except for a gaunt pariah dog nosing at a litter of decaying refuse the lane was deserted, and she turned down it and led the way at a brisk pace for some fifty yards to where a sharp turn brought them into a busy street full of cobblers' shops.

If Hero had had any qualms as to the efficiency of her disguise they were soon proved groundless, for no one paid the least attention to her. No heads turned, and it was plain that shuffling, shrouded women were a common sight in Zanzibar. But she was not tempted to linger and look about her. She could see nothing in the least attractive in these narrow odiferous streets or in the colourful crowds that filled them, and as she picked her way between the dirt and garbage and past the loitering, chattering citizens, her only emotions were disgust and indignation.

It was a crying disgrace that the public should be permitted to throw their refuse into the streets – and with no proper gutters, and flies everywhere! What were the foreign community thinking of to allow it? Surely *they* must be able to see, even if the unenlightened heathen could not, that such a degree of filth could only lead to disease and epidemics? Why did they not bring pressure to bear on the Sultan's Government, and see to it that half these squalid houses were pulled down and the tortuously narrow streets widened? It was their plain duty to do so, and she would speak to Uncle Nat about it. '*Romantic Island*' indeed! What was romantic about dirt and ignorance? It was all very well for writers of fiction, or unthinking little sentimentalists like Cressy, to pronounce palm trees and unhygienic Eastern towns 'picturesque' and 'romantic', but anyone who could describe Zanzibar city as either must be lacking both eyes and a sense of smell!

Hero had been too occupied in looking where she stepped to pay much attention to where she was going, but now at last they had left the shops behind them and were in a quieter part of the town where the old Arab houses, three and four storeys high, towered up on either side of streets so narrow that friends living opposite each other must surely have been able to lean from their windows and touch hands above the heads of the passers-by.

The sun had long since left these man-made canyons, but the heat still lingered in them, and high overhead innumerable wooden shutters, closed throughout the hot day, were being thrown open to catch the first cool of the evening. From somewhere on the far side of the houses came a dry rustle of coconut palms in the sea wind and the sound of waves on an unseen beach, and presently the road bent and widened, and Hero could smell salt water.

A single dark patch of greenery broke the line of close-packed houses: rain trees, a flamboyant, a frangipani white with blossom, and a tangle of weeds and creepers fenced in by what had once been iron railings. There was a rusty wrought-iron gate in the railing, flanked by crumbling stone pillars carved with the arms of Portugal; and behind it, among the shadows and the encroaching creepers, half-a-dozen weather-worn tombstones lifted their heads through the weeds.

It was the little graveyard that Fattûma had spoken of, and facing it stood an old, pink-washed Arab house, four storeys high and boasting an imposing door studded with the big conical bronze nail-heads that were a relic of the long-ago days when Arabs of the coast protected their doors from the assaults of war elephants. A frieze of carved dolphins gambolled above it, and the door itself stood wide, showing an open courtyard in which a fountain played and idling men lolled and chattered.

Hero recognized several members of the *Virago*'s crew, unfamiliar in their shore-going splendour of flowing white robes, gorgeously embroidered waistcloths and freshly laundered turbans; and looking upward she saw that the house stood four-square about the courtyard, rising up in tiers of shaded verandahs. The sound of women's voices and the tinkle of a mandolin drifting down from them suggested that not only privileged members of Captain Frost's crew, but their families as well occupied quarters in the big rambling house, and in response to a call by the elderly doorkeeper a small stout negress trotted out and looked at the visitors enquiringly.

Hero turned to Fattûma and said: 'Tell them what I am here for, and ask this woman if there is a looking-glass anywhere. And a room where I can take these things off and make myself tidy.'

The little negress smiled widely and led the way up a curving flight of stairs to a long verandah, and through a curtained archway into a room furnished with Persian rugs, small inlaid tables, a pair of richly carved brass-bound chests and orange lilies in glazed earthenware pots. A vast looking-glass in an ornate gilded frame covered most of one wall, and although it was stained and spotted from the heat of many summers and the damp of many monsoons, the dim, silvery image that it reflected was still clear enough to show Hero that a short walk in a *schele* was not calculated to improve any lady's appearance.

Her hair clung to her forehead in damp tendrils and her dress was not only shockingly creased but stuck moistly to her back, while as for the curling toes of those Eastern slippers, they were as incongruous as jackboots at a ball. She should have thought to bring her own shoes with her – and a comb. But it was no good regretting that now. She would just have to face Captain Frost as she was and since he had never seen her looking anything but dishevelled he was not likely to find fault with her present appearance.

Hero brushed the sweat from her forehead and shook out her crumpled skirts, and telling Fattûma to wait there for her, returned to the verandah and followed the fat little negress up yet another flight of stairs, along another verandah, and finally into a long, high-ceilinged room where a line of arched windows looked out above the tops of palm trees and casuarinas onto the open sea.

The room was furnished in much the same fashion as the one she had just left, but contained in addition several divans, a great many flat, silk-covered cushions, a white cockatoo with a sulphur-yellow crest, and a dark-eyed, golden-skinned woman who wore a loose green tunic, full trousers of lilac-coloured silk, a spangled head veil and a great deal of silver jewellery. There was also a child, similarly dressed and apparently about three or four years of age, and Hero checked uncertainly, realizing that she had been brought in error to the women's quarters and that this must be the family of Hajji Ralub or some other member of the *Virago*'s crew.

It had obviously never occurred to the negress, or to Fattûma either, that she could possibly wish to be ushered, unveiled and unattended, into the presence of a man. The woman appeared equally disconcerted, and the child abandoned its pursuit of a small Persian kitten to stare at the visitor in wide-eyed interest.

Hero said hastily, and in English: 'I am afraid there has been a mistake, Mrs – er – is it Ralub?'

She turned enquiringly to the negress who nodded vigorously and said something that Hero took, correctly, to mean that the Hajji was from home, and the woman moved forward doubtfully and said in halting English:

'You – you wish – to speak with me?'

Her voice was soft and hesitant and as charming as her face, and for the first time in her life Hero was conscious of feeling clumsy and over-sized. The pretty creature was so small and slim, and so delicately formed! As exquisite as a portrait of a Sultan's favourite painted on ivory.

'No. That is . . . It was Captain Frost I really wished to see, but I am afraid my maid misunderstood. I am so sorry.'

'There is no sorrow. He will come soon. You will wait – perhaps?'

She gestured gracefully towards a cushioned divan, inviting her un-expected guest to be seated, and turned to give a brief order to the negress, who scurried away and returned almost immediately accompanied by two women carrying a selection of refreshments that included glasses of sherbet, assorted sweetmeats and coffee in tiny cups of egg-shell china enclosed in filigree holders.

Hero accepted the coffee and instantly wished that she had taken sherbet instead, for the coffee was sickly sweet and so full of grounds that she found some difficulty in swallowing it without choking. The sweet-meats looked to be equally exotic and she refused them with what she hoped was a polite smile, and cautiously nibbled a blanched almond while her hostess saw the trays conveniently disposed on various tables and dismissed the servants with a wave of her hand. The curtain fell behind them and Hero, searching for conversation, said: 'You speak very good English.'

The woman smiled and made a pretty, deprecating gesture: 'No, no. Amrah speak well. Not me.'

'Amrah?'

'My daughter. I am Zorah.'

'Mama,' said the child firmly, removing its finger from its mouth and pointing.

The woman smiled and said something in murmured Arabic that Hero did not catch, and the child came forward and made a solemn little obeisance. It did not look like the child of such a mother, for its rose-petal skin was almost as fair as Hero's own and the dark eyes and curly hair were brown rather than black. It might almost have been a European child in fancy dress, and for a moment Hero wondered if the negress had misinterpreted her question, and it was not Hajji Ralub but the bigamous Mr Potter who was the head of this particular family. But that was surely impossible! Batty was elderly and grey-headed, and this woman was so young and so lovely—— And yet, *Arabs!* ... Hero remembered being told that the late Sultan had had children born to him long after he had become a grandfather.

She returned the child's bow with suitable gravity and said: 'So you speak English, Amrah? That's very clever of you.'

'Yes,' agreed the child complacently. 'What's your name?'

'Hero. Hero Hollis.'

'That ain't a proper name.'

'It's mine,' Hero assured her. 'It's a Greek name.'

'Are you a Greek lady?'

'No, I'm an American.'

'What's a Na'merican?'

The woman, Zorah, intervened with a gentle reproof, but was ignored: 'Where's Na'merica?' demanded Amrah.

'It's a big country a long way away across the sea.'

'How long 'way?'

'Oh – miles and miles. Hundreds of miles. On the other side of the world.'

'Did you come in a ship, n'see sharks n'whales n'a mermaid?'

'Sharks and whales, yes. But no mermaids. Have *you* ever seen a mermaid?'

The child shook her head, and coming a little closer to Hero lowered her voice and said confidentially: 'I thought I done once, but Unker Batty said it were only a fish.'

'That's the trouble with mermaids,' agreed Hero gravely.

Amrah took another step forward and looked up into Hero's face, studying her with earnest intentness and frowning a little. 'I like you,' she announced abruptly.

The candid tribute brought a surprised flush to Hero's cheeks and she was astonished to find herself feeling as gratified as though she had been given an unexpected and delightful present. It was not that she was unused to compliments, but she had never before received one quite like this. She had not had much to do with young children, and had never been able to gush over them in the pretty feminine manner that was fashionable among her contemporaries. And yet this small sturdy person in fancy-dress had disarmed her with three short words. Feeling warmed and foolishly flattered, she blushed and smiled, and said: 'Thank you. I like you too.'

She held out her hand a little diffidently, and her youthful admirer took it confidently and said: 'Why's your hair all short n' funny?'

'*Amrah!*' deprecated her mother softly, but Hero only laughed and said: 'Because it got into such a bad tangle that I had it all cut off.'

'How did it got a bad tangle?'

'Well, it's a long story——'

But it was a story that was to remain untold, for quick footsteps sounded in the verandah outside, the curtain was brushed aside, and Hero turned – the child's hand still in hers – and for a moment imagined herself to be facing a stranger.

Captain Frost's shore-going clothes, like those of his crew, were very different from the salt-stained and workmanlike attire he had worn on the *Virago*. They were not even of European manufacture or design, but consisted of a long white robe sashed about the waist with scarlet, under a loose coat of some dark material that was decorated and bordered with elaborate embroidery in gold and silver thread. Except that his head was uncovered he might have been blood-brother to any of the better dressed Arabs that Hero had passed in the streets, for taken in conjunction with that Eastern attire even his sun-bleached blondness and the colour of his eyes suggested an Albino rather than a European.

The momentary surprise on his face changed to the more familiar look of amusement, and he bowed and said formally: 'This is a most un-expected pleasure, Miss Hollis.'

His voice contained no trace of sarcasm, but his expression failed to match it, and Hero resisted an impulse to reply sharply. She said instead, and with equal formality: 'I have only called, sir, to bring you my aunt's and uncle's thanks, and my own, for all you did for me in the matter of my rescue, and for bringing me safely to Zanzibar. We are most grateful.'

Captain Frost remained in the doorway and regarded her steadily for a full half minute. Then he bowed again, with *empressement*, the laughter back in his eyes: 'It was a privilege, Miss Hollis. Is your aunt here with you? Or did Mr Mayo accompany you? Surely you did not come alone?'

Hero was angrily conscious of her rising colour, but she managed to say composedly enough: 'No; one of the house servants accompanied me, for my aunt was unfortunately unable to come this evening, and my uncle and Mr Mayo have an official appointment that could not be cancelled. But as I did not wish to delay any longer in calling upon you to express my – our – thanks, I decided not to wait. You cannot be surprised to see me, since I told you that I intended to call.'

'So you did,' grinned Captain Frost. 'No, I am not surprised to see you. And may I say that you relieve me, Miss Hollis? I had put you down as incurably truthful, but I should be surprised indeed to discover that your uncle and aunt, or Mr Clayton Mayo either, knew anything of your intention or have the least idea where you are at this moment.'

'My aunt and uncle,' said Hero frigidly, 'are well aware what they owe you, but it happens that they – they——'

'Were unfortunately unable to spare the time to accompany you this evening,' finished Captain Frost glibly. 'I quite understand. All the same, now that you have discharged your errand I do not think that you should waste any time in returning to the Consulate. This is not Boston, and your visit here might give rise to the sort of comment that I am sure your relations would not approve of. They should have considered that before sending you to convey their thanks.'

Miss Hollis raised her brows and took the wind out of his sails by remarking sweetly: 'Oh, but surely you must realize that after spending well over a week in your company I have no reputation left to lose, and may therefore do as I choose?'

'Vixen!' commented the Captain appreciatively. 'And after all the care we took to provide for your comfort – not to mention protecting your morals.'

'If by that you mean locking me up so that I might not see what you were doing, I imagine it was your own safety and not my morals that you were concerned to protect,' retorted Miss Hollis with asperity. She rose, the child still holding on to her hand, and giving her crushed skirts a little shake, said casually: 'Just what cargo *were* you carrying on the *Virago*?'

'Still inquisitive, Miss Hollis?'

'Still interested, Captain Frost.'

The Captain laughed and said lightly: 'Obviously it was nothing illegal, or else our enthusiastic young naval friend would have been onto it in a trice. He has the most suspicious nature I have ever had the misfortune to encounter, and he is quite as inquisitive as you are.'

'I guess he knows you too well,' observed Hero pleasantly. 'And I was not, as you are well aware, referring to the cargo that Lieutenant Larrimore had occasion to inspect, but to that portion of it which you landed somewhere else on the previous night. I admit to being still interested in that, for if it were not slaves I cannot understand why you should be so excessively secretive about it.'

Captain Frost said dryly: 'There are other commodities besides slaves which the authorities take an undue interest in, Miss Hollis. Arms, for instance.'

'Arms? Do you mean firearms? – muskets? But what for? I mean—— So *that* was what you were carrying!'

'I did not say so.'

'But you were,' said Hero with conviction, recalling the shape of those heavy bundles that had so unpleasantly suggested dead bodies. 'Of course they were muskets! But why should anyone want so many? Or did you want them for yourself?'

'For myself?' The idea seemed to amuse Captain Frost and he laughed again. 'Good God, no! I'm a peaceable man who detests loud noises and martial attitudes. But that doesn't mean that I'm not prepared to sell such things to anyone who is foolish enough to want them and prepared to offer me a good enough price. Trade's trade, and it's all in the way of business. You know, I hate to hurry you, Miss Hollis, but hadn't you better be getting back before your relatives return from their evening sail and start asking where you are?'

'How did you know they——' began Hero; and bit her lip, angry with herself for the slip. Captain Frost's burst of laughter was hatefully familiar, and she drew herself up and said coldly: 'Pray do not worry yourself on my account. I had no intention of making a long call and have been most hospitably entertained by these ladies.'

She bowed graciously in the direction of Zorah, and then turned to the child who still stood beside her, and said: 'Goodbye, Amrah. I have to go now.'

The small fingers tugged at her hand demandingly. 'Will you come back?'

'To see you? That would be very nice, but I think it would be even nicer if you would come and see me. We must try and arrange it sometime.'

'You will forget.'

'No, I won't,' promised Hero. She shook hands gravely, exchanged another smiling bow with the child's mother, and went out under the curtain that Captain Frost was holding aside for her.

He dropped it into place behind her and she turned with a stiff, social smile and held out her hand: 'Goodbye, Captain Frost. You need not trouble to come down with me. In fact I would far rather you did not. Fattûma will be waiting for me and we can find our own way out.'

Captain Frost ignored the proffered hand. 'I'm sure you can, Madame Mermaid, but you will perhaps allow me to see you as far as the stairs.'

He fell into step beside her as the stout little negress, who had been squatting patiently in the verandah, rose to her feet and scuttled away to call Fattûma. Hero glanced down at the deep well of the courtyard and observed conversationally: 'What a very large house this is when one sees it from the inside. It does not look nearly so big from the street. Whose is that enchanting child?'

'Mine,' said Captain Frost.

'Yours? But——'

The full meaning of that casually spoken monosyllable suddenly dawned on Hero, and she stopped on a gasp and turned swiftly to face him: '*Yours?* You mean—— But you never told me you were married?'

'I'm not.'

'But then——' Hero checked herself again, and observing her scarlet cheeks and the appalled comprehension in her eyes Captain Frost laughed and said: 'There is no need for you to look so shocked. It's an old established custom in the East. And a most convenient one for those who like myself are really bachelors at heart. I paid a few shillings and a bolt of striped calico for Zorah twelve years ago, and it was the best bargain I ever made.'

'You *bought* her?'

'Off a rascally negro slave dealer in Lagos, who was preparing to ship the child aboard a slaver bound for Charlestown and the North American plantations. God knows where he picked her up – somewhere a good deal further north, I'd say, for she spoke Arabic and had only a few words of the coast dialect. It was a sentimental gesture on my part, but one I have never regretted. Though I'm bound to say——'

But Hero did not wait to hear any more. Gathering up her skirts in both hands she ran from him down the long length of the verandah and took the shallow stone steps of the staircase two at a time. Fattûma was waiting for her in the courtyard, and oblivious of a dozen curious onlookers she snatched at the crumpled *schele*, and pulling it on, dragged the fringed head-covering into place and hurried through the open doorway and out into the quiet street as though she were escaping from the plague.

The sky above the high, flat rooftops had turned from pale blue to an even paler green, and now that the air had grown perceptibly cooler there seemed to be more people abroad in the main streets of the city. But Hero,

134

hurrying away from the shameful house that she had entered so carelessly, had no attention to spare for the jostling crowds or the beauties of nature.

How right Uncle Nat and Clay had been to forbid her to go there! She should have listened to them instead of being so foolishly stubborn. They had repeatedly warned her that Captain Frost's reputation precluded any gentleman, let alone any lady, from having dealings with him (or indeed being seen speaking to him), and striven to impress upon her that even a verbal message of thanks to such a man was a concession. Yet instead of listening to them she had actually called on a man who kept a mistress. A *coloured* mistress! A creature whom he had bought off an African slave-dealer for a handful of silver and a bolt of cheap cloth, and raised in his house until she was old enough to share his bed and bear him a half-caste bastard.

How many other native doxies did he keep hidden away in those curtained, sandalwood-scented rooms? – and how many more casually fathered brats whose veins mingled his Anglo-Saxon blood with the dark strains of Africa and Asia?

Hero had always prided herself on being a modern, forward-looking and outspoken girl with no nonsense about her, but her views on such dark matters as mistresses and miscegenation had been largely gathered from half-hints on the part of her Aunt Lucy and certain shocking confidences whispered by Clarissa Langly, and despite her boasted emancipation she was every bit as capable of being shocked by the visual evidence of such things as the primmest and most prudish of Victorian virgins.

It was true that history books and novels frequently made reference to mistresses and 'kept women', and that some of the more colourful examples – such as Madame de Pompadour and Nell Gwynne – could even be mentioned in polite society. But it had never dawned on Hero that anyone she was actually acquainted with could keep such creatures. Or that she herself would ever speak to one. That child——! No wonder it had seemed so un-Eastern! The cleft chin and the straight line of the eyebrows should have told her at once who its father was; – and would certainly have done so had it even entered her head that Captain Frost, in addition to his other sins, could sink to such depths of depravity.

Recalling the voices and laughter and the strains of the mandolin that had drifted down from the upper verandahs of The Dolphins' House, she visualized a harem of coloured concubines scheming and intriguing for the favours of that gun-running slave trader, and bearing him a succession of mulatto brats who could not fail to provide the native population of Zanzibar with a visual commentary on the depths to which white races and Western men could sink. '*It's an old established custom in the East, and a most convenient one . . .*' How dared he!

All the inborn Puritanism that Hero had inherited from her New England ancestors and her Scottish great-grandmother flared into life, burning in her with a violent sense of outrage that far transcended her previous anger and indignation on the score of Captain Frost's dealings in slavery and smuggling. She felt as though she had touched something unclean and must wash it off her with hot water and a scrubbing brush to rid herself of its slime. And she did, in fact, do exactly that as soon as she was safely back in the Consulate: to the consternation of Fattûma and the water-boy, who had been kept busy toiling up and down the back staircase with steaming cans to fill the tin tub that stood in Hero's stone tiled bathroom.

No other visitor had ever demanded so much hot water at a time of year when the rising temperature called for tepid baths, palm-leaf fans and cold drinks, and Fattûma was of the opinion that her mistress must be suffering from some illness of the brain that necessitated drawing away the blood from the head. But an energetic session with carbolic soap and a scrubbing brush had left Hero with a self-righteous feeling of having symbolically cleansed herself of defilement, and by the time the Consul and his family returned from their evening expedition she had decided to put the whole distasteful episode out of her mind.

There were, she considered, other and more important things to think of: Clayton, for one. And her visit to The Dolphins' House had not been wasted, for in addition to discharging her debt it had served to confirm her in the opinion that Jules Dubail, Cressy's two married friends, and the Sultan's sisters, were undoubtedly right. The present ruler of Zanzibar must certainly be deposed, and the sooner the better, since no friend and ally of Emory Frost's could be other than corrupt, and therefore quite unfitted to hold any position of authority.

12

'What do you yourself think of him, Uncle Nat?' asked Hero; still bent on discovering whether Bargash possessed the right qualifications to succeed Majid, but using an oblique approach to disguise her objective.

'The Sultan? *Waall* . . .' Uncle Nathaniel leaned back in his chair and considered the question.

They were seated, all five of them, on the terrace in front of the drawing-room windows, sipping coffee while an enormous yellow moon rose above the jacarandas and the orange trees, and Aunt Abby plied a large palm-leaf fan to keep the mosquitoes at bay.

'I guess he's not much worse than the rest of these Eastern potentates,' said Uncle Nat. 'But then I'm happy to say I haven't met too many of 'em.'

Five hot, idle days had passed since the evening that Hero had paid her ill-advised call upon Emory Frost, and when not engaged in listening to Cressy's confidences she had, in spite of herself, spent an undue proportion of them in brooding upon the infamous conduct of that slave-trading libertine. But though time had done little towards lessening her indignation, it had undoubtedly done a great deal towards improving her looks, and seen now by the pale light of the rising moon and the warm, reflected glow from the lamplit drawing-room, her face no longer displayed any trace of swelling or bruises. All that remained of the injuries that had so disfigured her were a small scar on her lower lip and that short-cropped hair, and Clayton Mayo, studying her over the rim of his coffee cup, came to the conclusion that both improved her.

That scar, for instance, had the odd effect of making her lips look less severe and more . . . Clay groped for a word and was astonished when his mind presented him with 'kissable', because it was a term he had certainly never thought of applying to them before. As for that shorn head, though he had thought it a disaster when he had first seen it, there was no denying that the crop of childish, chestnut curls served to soften a certain austerity that had made the perfection of Hero's features a cold rather than an alluring thing. They made her look younger and gentler . . . more like a charming Botticelli angel than a forbidding marble goddess from Ancient Greece.

Yes, she was certainly a good looking girl, mused Clay, and might even, some day, be a pretty one. Which to his way of thinking was a deal better than being merely beautiful. If only she were not so set on her own opinions . . . so inflexible in her views and her virtue and her condemnation of the faults of others . . . Contemplating Hero's unconscious profile, he found himself wondering if a taste of rough treatment, adversity and harsh experience might not exercise the same beneficent effect upon her character as those wild minutes in a stormy sea had exercised upon her looks. It was an interesting idea and he toyed with it, withdrawing his attention from his step-father, who was still pursuing the subject of the Sultan:

'I've been told,' said the Consul, 'that his father was a great man. Well, maybe he was. But if so, this son certainly ain't inherited any of his old man's grit and gumption. Majid just lolls around in the Palace and lets the rest of the Island go govern itself.'

'Then why don't you do something about deposing him?' enquired Hero.

'Nothing I could do,' said Uncle Nat. 'And it's no business of mine, either. I reckon if his subjects like it that way, well, that's the way they like it. *We* don't own the place – thank the Lord!'

'But surely we have a certain moral responsibility?' argued Hero.

'Moral nothing! The only reason we're here is because there's a whole heap of our whalers in these waters, and our responsibility is to look after our own interests and lend a hand to any of our nationals who may be in need of help. We aren't out for grabbing bits of Africa like all these Britishers and Dutchmen, and it's none of our business if the people around here choose to put up with a hereditary ruler who's got nothing to recommend him 'cept that he's the son of his father.'

'But he's not even the oldest son, Uncle Nat.'

'That's so. But the old man's will divided up his Kingdom, and the oldest son, Thuwani, has gotten Muscat and Oman for his share – and would have grabbed Zanzibar too if it hadn't been for the British being none too happy about having their sea-way to India cluttered up with the war fleets of a couple of squabbling Sultans! Their Navy turned big brother Thuwani's ships back home, and I don't imagine he'll try *that* again.'

'But there are other brothers.'

'Sure. The Heir-Apparent, for one. *He* tried to jump his brother's claim too, just as soon as his old man died. But Majid outsmarted him, and young Bargash has been biting his nails and biding his time ever since.'

'Do you think Bargash would have made a better Sultan?' enquired Hero in a deceptively innocent voice.

Mr Hollis, deceived by the tone, treated the question as purely academic and only put to him out of idle curiosity, and said with a chuckle:

'Bound to, I'd say! He couldn't be worse, that's for sure. What these Zanzibaries need right now is someone who is tough enough to make 'em toe the line whether they like it or not. They'll respect a man who can do that – and despise one who can't!'

Cressy, who had been listening to the conversation with considerable interest, intervened to say: 'They certainly despise Majid, Pa, I can tell you that! And *everyone* says that Prince Bargash would have made a much better Sultan.'

'Do they, Puss? First I've heard of it. Unless you mean those little Arab lady-friends of yours up at Beit-el-Tani. I understand that several of them think that the wrong brother got the throne, and I daresay they'd be quite ready to push him off it. They're a queer lot, these orientals – no family feeling when it comes to wanting something the other fellow's got. They'll plot against each other and plan the death or downfall of their kin without a twinge of conscience or batting an eyelid. Cain and Abel . . . Cain and Abel.'

He turned back to Hero and added confidentially: 'Cressy's gotten mighty friendly with some of the Sultan's sisters. Seems to spend half her time with them – when she isn't over at the Platts' or the Tissots'. She's learning to speak Arabic too. Just like she's one of the natives. I tell her she'd better take over my job.'

Cressy blushed and disclaimed, and her mother remarked plaintively that she could not understand how her daughter could continue to be so interested in those girls at Beit-el-Tani Palace. They might be Princesses, but it stood to reason that they couldn't be anything but downright dull; living as they did in harems, poor creatures, quite divorced from the outside world and never being permitted any freedom or allowed to meet any men.

'But Mama, they meet dozens of men,' protested Cressy. 'All their brothers and husbands and sons and uncles and—— You've no idea how many men they are allowed to meet! Of course Cholé and Salmé aren't married yet, so they haven't any husbands or sons. But they have a great deal more freedom than you'd think. They go riding and sailing, and pay visits to their friends and go on picnics. Why, they aren't *nearly* as dull as we are! We just sit about all day with the shutters closed, and sleep in the afternoon and go for a walk or a drive in the evening, and sometimes take dinner with Colonel Edwards or the Dubails or——'

'Or go riding and sailing, and visit our friends and go on picnics,' teased Clayton. 'Not to mention flirting with gallant young Frenchmen and humourless Englishmen.'

'Clay, how can you! And he's not humourless, and I don't flirt.'

'Don't you, Cress? Then I'd like to know what it is that you've been doing with that tedious Lieutenant if it isn't flirting. As to his sense of humour, he wouldn't see a joke if he met one in the road!'

Cressy sprang to her feet in an indignant whirl of blue muslin flounces and retreated precipitately indoors, and her mother said reprovingly: 'Now that's really too bad of you Clay, when you know how much she dislikes being teased on such matters.'

'She used not to object to being quizzed on her conquests. In fact she used to take it as a compliment. It's only lately that she's turned touchy, and if you ask me, Mama, I'd say she's quarrelled with the Lieutenant: which will be no bad thing, as maybe now he'll be able to spare a mite more of his time to stopping blackguards like Frost amassing a fortune out of slaving, and less to mooning around after Cressy.'

'Oh, come now, Clay,' interposed the Consul mildly. 'I reckon the Lieutenant does his best, and as for Frost, from all accounts he's turned his attention to other lines of business lately. Selim tells me there's talk in the city that he made a fancy profit out of some cargo he carried on this latest trip, and I gather it can't have included slaves – eh, Hero?'

He looked enquiringly at his niece, who said crisply: 'No. I fancy he was smuggling firearms.'

She was aware of Clayton's swift, startled movement, but if he had meant to say anything he was forestalled by his step-father who said sharply: '*Firearms!* What makes you think that? Did you see any?'

'No. But I told you about the *Virago* stopping one night to take something on board from another ship, and then landing it somewhere else the night before we reached Zanzibar.'

'But you said you hadn't the least idea what it was. What's made you change your mind about it all of a sudden?'

Hero hesitated, regretting that she had mentioned the matter. She had spoken hastily and without thinking, and she had no desire to confess at this late date (or at any other for that matter) that in defiance of a direct order she had called at Captain Frost's house. Faced now with an awkward question, she prevaricated; falling back on a description of the mysterious packages that she had seen landed by moonlight from the *Virago*, and asserting mendaciously that on thinking it over it occurred to her that they might have contained muskets.

'Don't you believe it!' said Clayton shortly. 'Swords and spears, possibly – or even bows and arrows. But not muskets. Why, half these savages wouldn't even know how to load such things, let alone fire them.'

He laughed derisively, but his step-father failed to be amused and remarked tartly that such an observation was foolish in the extreme. 'It don't do to forget,' pointed out Mr Consul Hollis, 'that the white community on this Island is a mighty small one, with little or no means of defending itself. So if firearms are really being smuggled in to the natives, it is a matter that may concern every one of us.'

His wife gave a small gasp of alarm and her plump hands flew to her bosom. 'Surely you cannot mean a *rising*, Mr Hollis? But there could be no grounds for such a thing. Not against *Americans*.'

'You're plumb right, Mama,' agreed Clayton. 'For the reason that we, at least, have no colonial ambitions in this part of the world, and are only here on account of trade and to keep an eye on our whaling interests. We've certainly no intention of interfering with the local Government, and we aren't oppressing anyone or planning to oppress anyone. If they don't want us here they'd only have to say so. They don't have to shoot us!'

The Consul seemed about to retort vigorously, but a glance at his wife made him change his mind. Instead he lit a cigar, taking his time over the operation, and then settling himself back in his chair, said comfortably: 'I guess you're right, Clay. Maybe it's all this intrigue and skulduggery that goes on around here that occasionally gets one to feeling that we're some sort of a lone garrison, holding out in hostile Indian territory.'

'Oh, don't say that,' shuddered Aunt Abby. 'There is no resemblance at all. And even if we *were* in such a position – which of course we are not – I would refuse to believe that any white man, however depraved, would sink so low as to sell firearms to the blacks, knowing that they might be used against men and women of his own colour.'

Hero pulled a scornful grimace and said caustically: 'I wish I could agree with you, Aunt, but I do not think that any such consideration would weigh with Captain Frost. He appears to be entirely devoid of patriotism or morals – or indeed any proper feeling – and I am persuaded he would only see it as a matter of personal gain.'

Clayton's brows rose, and he laughed and said: 'So you've had a change of heart, have you? That's a relief, because at one time it seemed as if you were all set to champion him. But you've certainly hit it straight now. I reckon Roaring Rory would sell firearms to a gang whom he knew were plotting to rob his own mother, provided he could get a good enough price. What I don't believe is that anyone would be in the least likely to pay good money for weapons to use against a harmless handful of white traders, or the undefended consulates of a few friendly nations.'

'Always provided that they believe us to be friendly,' said the Consul slowly.

'What do you mean by that, sir?'

Mr Hollis shifted restlessly in his chair, and once again his wife's plump hands flew to her agitated bosom; for Clay's father, Stanislaus, had spent some years in an isolated trading post in the heart of what had then been Iroquois Territory, and he had often told her tales of risings and massacres, and white men – one of them his own partner – burnt at the stake by whooping, yelling Redskins.

Abigail had never forgotten those stories, and ever since then all coloured races were, in her eyes, 'savages' and potential murderers, who were perfectly capable of going on the warpath against any white men foolhardy enough to enter their territory. She had protested strongly at Nathaniel's accepting the post of Consul in Zanzibar, and even though she had eventually been persuaded that her fears were groundless (and had, in fact, grown quite attached to the native servants), there were still moments when it disturbed her to realize how overwhelmingly the white community were outnumbered by any one of a dozen Eastern races who together formed the colourful, polyglot population of Sultan Majid's tropical paradise.

Nathaniel Hollis, observing the rapid rise and fall of his wife's ample bosom, replied to his step-son's query with a deprecating wave of the hand and a vague: 'Nothing, nothing. Seems to me the mosquitoes are mighty bad tonight; what d'you say we move indoors?'

Having thus put an end to the conversation, the Consul adroitly avoided any further reference to the subject of firearms or risings by persuading his niece to play the piano. But he was far from putting it from his mind, and on the following morning he paid an unofficial call upon Colonel George Edwards, the British Consul.

Colonel Edwards had been engaged in reading a long and involved complaint from the Colonial Office, but he laid it aside and rose courteously to his feet when his visitor was announced. The British Consul was a thin, spare, soldierly bachelor who spoke five Eastern languages and seven dialects with great fluency, and having dealt with Arabs, Indians and Africans for more years than he could count, he was inclined to regard such men as Mr Consul Hollis as dangerous amateurs in a specialized field.

Mr Hollis, for his part, considered the Colonel a fairly typical example of British complacency and narrow-minded colonialism in action, but nevertheless respected his knowledge of local problems, politics and people, and in the present instance felt in need of his advice. He therefore accepted a chair and a cigar, and produced Hero's theory of smuggled firearms in the guise of a bazaar rumour that had reached his ears and which he thought it his duty to pass on to his British colleague – there being, as far as he knew, no embargo on the import of such things into the Sultan's territories, and therefore no reason for smuggling objects that could have been brought in openly.

'That would depend on whom they were consigned to,' said Colonel

Edwards thoughtfully. 'If they were intended for anyone other than His Highness, I can well understand why they would have been brought in secretly. On the other hand, the rumour may have no foundation, for the *Virago* was stopped and searched before she had discharged her cargo, and Lieutenant Larrimore reported to me that he was unable to find anything questionable aboard. May I ask who your informant was?'

'Oh – er – just servants' tales,' said Mr Hollis vaguely. 'I didn't press for details.'

'Why not? It seems, if you will forgive me, a not unimportant point?'

'Maybe it does. On the other hand I didn't feel like making a big thing of it. It might have started more hares and alarmed my womenfolk, and I thought it better to treat the rumour lightly.'

'Yes, of course,' approved the Colonel. 'Always better not to upset the ladies. I'll make a few enquiries in the town, and if there is any truth in it I shall soon know. These things have a habit of leaking out. No use tackling Frost of course; he'd only deny it flatly. I cannot understand how any Englishman ... Well, that's neither here nor there. I suppose every nation has its share of blackguards.'

Mr Hollis said casually: 'You don't reckon there's any danger of arms being shipped into this island to be used against us foreigners?'

'None whatever,' – the Colonel appeared scandalized at the very thought – 'Why should there be? The people have no quarrel with us.'

'Speaking as an American, they've certainly none with me! But you'll pardon me if I say that the same can't be said of any of the rest of you.'

The Colonel's thin lips tightened and he said stiffly: 'I am afraid I do not understand you, Hollis.'

'Oh, come now! These folk can't all be fools and maybe they're beginning to learn from example. You Britishers have eased into half the countries of the East as peaceful traders and then sent along a Consul to keep an eye on your interests, and before they know where they are, you end up owning the whole damn' place. Look what's happening to Africa right now. It's being used as a Tom-Tiddlers-Ground with just about every nation in Europe grabbing themselves a slice – and then you tell me that there's no danger of the Sultan's subjects turning on the white community! How do you know they're not planning to wipe us all out before they find themselves going the way of India and Burma and South Africa, and a dozen other places I could name? Tell me that?'

The Colonel's leathery features set in rigid lines and his pale English eyes became frostily remote. 'My dear sir, I know these people——'

'I take leave to doubt that,' said Mr Hollis, cutting across the sentence: 'You may think you know 'em, but it wasn't so long ago that your officers and administrators in India were saying precisely the same thing about the Bengal Army. And what happened there? A bloody insurrection that went near to losing you the country.'

'The situation in India,' said Colonel Edwards frigidly, 'is in no way comparable with that which prevails here. We have no power in Zanzibar; nor any wish to assume it.'

'Fudge!' retorted Mr Hollis brusquely. 'The last Sultan ruled an Empire of which Zanzibar and Pemba and the territories on the coast were merely a part, but now one son rules Muscat and Oman and another governs Loher, while a third holds the East Africa possessions. And who had the last word on *that* dandy little arrangement? The Government of India! the *British* Government.'

'My dear sir, the matter was submitted – *voluntarily* submitted – by the rival Seyyids to arbitration by the Government of India, whose verdict merely upheld the late Sultan's will and was undoubtedly a wise one. It was quite time the inheritance was divided up into more manageable proportions, since half the troubles of the last reign were a direct result of the Sultan's long and frequent absences in Zanzibar, which led to a weakening of his authority in Muscat and Oman.'

Mr Hollis shrugged, and said: 'Well, I won't argue with you on that account. And I guess Majid's claim was sound enough even without the Indian Government's verdict. But there are other angles: you British have already managed to reduce the Sultanate's most profitable source of income by restricting the slave trade. You've also intervened to prevent a war between Majid and his eldest brother, and you are behaving in a high-handed and dictatorial manner in Mombasa and the coastal strip. And since I reckon even the Arabs and the Africans are not so unlettered that they can't read the writing on the wall, I don't feel any too happy when I come across a rumour that firearms are being smuggled into this Island. If it's true, then I'd like to know just what goes on and who wants 'em that bad – and why.'

A tinge of red darkened the mahogany suntan on the Colonel's cheekbones, and once again his lips thinned to a narrow line. It was obvious that he was making a strong effort to curb his temper, and it was some appreciable seconds before he could trust himself to speak:

'We have as yet no evidence,' said Colonel Edwards in a strictly controlled voice, 'that any such arms have been landed. But I will certainly make enquiries. However, as you know only too well, the island suffers sorely from the raids of these northern Arab pirates who descend on it every year when the monsoon breaks, and terrorize the population. If there should prove to be any truth in this gun-running rumour, I think you will find that the weapons were consigned to His Highness, who has probably got tired of paying the raiders to go away and prefers to try driving them off with bullets – which he has every right to do.'

'Exactly! You are repeating my own argument, Colonel. He has every right to import arms. But if this rumour is true, they were not imported. They were smuggled. *Ergo* – they were not intended for His Highness, or for any purpose that would bear investigation. And if it wasn't for one circumstance, I'd have been inclined, myself, to say that the buyer was someone who meant to stage an armed revolt and take over the throne himself.'

'You mean Seyyid Bargash? Yes: I am not unaware that he still cherishes pretensions in that direction. Or that he is being encouraged in them by a colleague of ours. I have sometimes wished——' the Colonel checked himself and gave a small dry cough, and after a short pause said: 'We try not to interfere too much with the internal affairs of the Island. And as to Seyyid Bargash, I doubt if Frost would do anything to assist him.'

'Just so, Colonel. Frost is a friend of the Sultan's, and therefore no friend to the Heir-Apparent. Which is the circumstance I referred to, that puts that theory out of court. From all I hear of Frost, he'd sell his own mother if anyone offered him a good enough price, but since it's only the Sultan's favour that has enabled him to stay out of jail, we can be sure that he won't kill the goose who is laying him golden eggs; or sell arms to any of the Bargash faction, who hate his guts! Unless, of course, he's been tricked into selling them to some middle-man, and doesn't know or care who they are for?'

The Colonel shook his head and frowned thoughtfully at the far wall of his office. 'No; whatever else he may be he's no fool, and he knows only too well on which side his bread is buttered – and who butters it. He wouldn't sell that sort of thing to anyone in Zanzibar, or in any of the Sultan's coastal territories either, without being quite certain who was going to use them and why. So you can rest assured that if arms have been secretly brought into the island, they will not be used against the European community. Frost is, after all's said and done, a white man himself; and even if he were so far gone in depravity as to connive at the murder of his own kind, he would not forget that any rising against the Europeans would involve violence and massacre, or that rioting mobs are unlikely to distinguish between one white man and another. A mob is not given to discrimination – particularly an Eastern mob.'

'I am glad you realize that,' observed Mr Hollis dryly. 'It is precisely that angle that has had me a little worried. I don't reckon that anyone in this part of the world has any quarrel with America, but if these Injuns once get started on yelling for the blood of the Palefaces, they're not going to be worried by a little thing like an accent. No, sir! When it's a case of anti-foreign feeling it'll be the colour of my skin that'll count – not my country or my opinions. Or my politics either. And I can tell you right now that I've no desire to get a bullet through my belly on account of the colonial ambitions of the British Government.'

'No danger of that,' the Colonel assured him, smiling reluctantly: 'We shall probably find that the whole thing is a hum. It's true that young Larrimore was only after evidence of slaving when he stopped the *Virago*, but he tells me that he did not neglect to examine the cargo, and that it contained nothing that was not entered on the manifest. He would have had a good many questions to ask had he come across anything in the nature of arms and ammunition, so I think we can be reasonably certain that this gun-running tale is no more than another bazaar rumour, and that your informant was mistaken.'

Mr Hollis would have given a great deal at this point to relate Hero's story of a mysterious rendezvous with a ship in mid-ocean and the later unloading of a number of oblong packages by night and on an unknown shore. But he knew he could not do so, since to tell that tale to Colonel Edwards would mean disclosing that his niece had actually spent ten days on the *Virago*. And being only too well aware of what the European community would make of such an entertaining story, he was damned if he was going to make the British Consul a present of it.

Maybe the Colonel was right and Hero was mistaken in imagining that the *Virago* had landed firearms. After all it was only conjecture. She had no proof, and now that he came to think of it, she did not even know if the moonlit beach she had seen through a hole in the matting was part of the coast of Zanzibar. It could just as well have been the neighbouring island of Pemba – or even somewhere on the mainland; perhaps Dar-es-Salaam, the *'Haven of Peace'* where the Sultan was building himself a new palace to which he could retire occasionally from the cares of state? And in any case, who could claim to understand the thought processes of an Arab? – or indeed of any member of the Eastern races? Certainly not he, Nathaniel K. Hollis, American citizen. He was free to confess that they baffled him. And equally willing to concede that the Sultan, for the sheer love of secrecy and intrigue, might have preferred to acquire by stealth a consignment of muskets that he was perfectly entitled to import openly. There was no understanding these people, and Her Britannic Majesty's Consul, George Edwards, who was foolish enough to believe that he at least did so, was probably as ignorant of their motives as any other deluded Westerner!

Mr Hollis collected his hat and rose. 'Well, Colonel, I'll be getting along. You have relieved my mind, for I admit I was a little anxious.

Gun-running is never a pretty business and it generally spells trouble. Big trouble. People don't buy guns for ornaments – they want 'em for use. But I guess you're right and my informant was mistaken. All the same . . .'

He shook his head, and the Colonel said hastily: 'Yes, yes; I agree that one must not be too sanguine, and I am indeed grateful to you for bringing me this – er – story. If I hear anything further I will certainly let you know. May I hope that your niece will soon be fully recovered from her ordeal? Dr Kealey tells me that she is still keeping to her room. Such a harrowing experience must have put a great strain upon her nerves and constitution.'

'Ah – um – yes,' agreed Mr Hollis. 'She does not like to talk about it. The shock, you know.'

'Of course, of course. I quite understand. We must all do our best to cheer her spirits once she feels strong enough to venture out of doors; and to see that she forgets it.'

Colonel Edwards accompanied his visitor to the door and watched him walk away through the white sunlight and the salt sea wind, and when he was lost to view, returned thoughtfully to his office to sit for a long while, rubbing his nose with a lean forefinger and staring out of the window at the rustling fronds of a coconut palm, dark against the hot blue sky.

Arms and ammunition . . . Yes, it was quite possible. In fact only too probable. They would, of course, have been landed somewhere else, and earlier. On Pemba perhaps, from where it would be an easy matter to ferry them across in *kyacks*. That would account for there being no sign of them when young Larrimore searched the schooner.

Had that renegade, Frost, turned his coat after all, and brought them in for the Heir-Apparent? Or was the Sultan arming himself in secret? The last seemed a more likely solution: and more in keeping with what the Colonel knew of Emory Frost. For if the Bargash faction became aware that the Sultan was strengthening his hand it might give them pause, but as long as they did not know it and imagined him to be unaware of their plotting and unprepared to deal with them, they might be rash enough to attempt another *coup d'état* which, this time, could be put down with savage severity. It was exactly the sort of trap that a man like Rory Frost would enjoy setting. And the Heir-Apparent – rash, fiery, and impatient for the throne – was precisely the sort of man who would fall into it.

There was, of course, always another and more unpleasant possibility. The one that had been causing Mr Hollis some anxiety.

Colonel Edwards had served in India, and he was well aware that the

American Consul's assertion regarding the complacency that had reigned among the British officers and officials stationed in that country in the years preceding the great mutiny of '57, was only too true. Those few who had uttered warnings and prophesied disaster had been denounced as scaremongers or poltroons, while the majority had resolutely shut their eyes, refusing to believe any ill of the men under their command; and died for that belief. But then as he had told Mr Hollis, the case here was entirely different. And even if it had not been, the citizens of Zanzibar – for the present at least – were far too busy intriguing against each other to trouble themselves over plotting the downfall of a relatively harmless handful of Europeans. As for Captain Frost, though unscrupulous in the matter of profits he was certainly no fool where his own safety and comfort was concerned!

The British Consul, satisfied as to the correctness of his reasoning, removed his gaze from the palm fronds outside his windows and sat back in his chair. He would send Feruz into the town for news and dispatch a note to Ahmed-bin-Suraj, requesting him to call at the Consulate at his earliest convenience. Feruz had a love of gossip and an infallible nose for news, and as for Ahmed, few things occurred on the Island without his getting wind of them. He was not only a useful ally but a reliable one, and if there was any truth in this tale of smuggled muskets he, if anyone, would probably know of it.

Colonel Edwards reached for the hand-bell that stood beside the file tray on his desk and rang it briskly.

Mr Nathaniel Hollis, keeping to the shady side of the narrow street and holding his hat against the strong tug of the Trade Wind, was feeling considerably less self-satisfied than his British colleague. His earlier apprehension on the score of a possible 'anti-white' rising had, for the moment, left him, giving place to quite another matter that was causing him no small annoyance. The displeasing discovery that Rory Frost, true to Lieutenant Larrimore's prediction, had put one over on them by that supposedly chivalrous suggestion that the *Daffodil* and not the *Virago* should figure as instrumental in rescuing Hero Athena from a watery grave.

Mr Hollis had himself supported that story and seen it accepted without question by his fellow Consuls and the European community: which until a few minutes ago he had considered to be a matter for congratulation. But it had just dawned on him that if he were now to repudiate it, the unpalatable truth would occasion far more unpleasant speculation than it would have done had it been known from the outset.

It was, in fact, going to be impossible for him to do any such thing, and there was no blinking the fact that Captain Frost had scored a point.

Neither Hero nor her uncle could now accuse him of taking on and secretly disembarking cargo that did not appear on the manifest; and without a direct accusation from one or other of them, that complacent ram-rod, the British Consul, would do nothing.

Mr Hollis arrived at his own front door in a bad temper, and removing his wide pith hat in the dim coolness of the hall, tossed it to a negro servant and sent for his niece. But Hero had gone out. Mrs Credwell and Madame Tissot, his wife informed him, had called a short while ago and had taken both Cressy and dear Hero for a drive.

'At this time of day?' demanded Mr Hollis, considerably put out. 'They must be mad! Do they want to get heatstroke?'

'Oh, but they won't be going far,' said Aunt Abby comfortably. 'There are so few roads where a carriage may go. In fact hardly any, and I wonder why anyone should trouble to keep one. But Olivia only intends to take Hero to pay a call on some of the Sultan's sisters.'

'What does she want to do that for?'

'Well, dear, it's only polite. Being your niece, dear Hero will be expected to call on some of the royal ladies.'

'The ones in Beit-el-Tani Palace, you mean: I might have known it!' said the Consul, exasperated. 'That woman Cholé again.'

'The *Princess* Cholé,' corrected Aunt Abby gently.

'"Princess" my left foot!' snorted her husband. 'Her mother was no more than one of the old Sultan's concubines.'

Aunt Abby closed her eyes and shuddered. '*Sarari*, Nathaniel. Not "concubines". *Sarari* – or *Suri* in the singular, I believe. And their children all rank as Princes and Princesses, dear. Seyyids and Seyyidas, I mean.'

The Consul flapped an impatient hand and said: 'Princesses or not, Cressy's been seeing far too much of those women, and it's got to stop.'

'Nathaniel!' Aunt Abby's voice quivered with indignation. 'I just do *not* understand you. Why, you know quite well that it was you yourself who suggested it when we first came here. I remember you telling us how deplorable it was that people who considered themselves entitled to rule over coloured races evidently did not think that they need meet them socially, and that it was not only shockingly ill-mannered but most short-sighted, and——'

'There's no need to keep telling me what I said!' snapped Mr Hollis irritably. 'I remember it quite well, and in general I am still of the same opinion. But circumstances alter cases. For one thing, I didn't know then that Thérèse Tissot and that Englishwoman had managed to strike up a friendship with a clutch of the Sultan's sisters and cousins – and for another, I didn't figure on Cressy living in their pockets!'

'I am sure Cressy wouldn't *dream* of living in anyone's pocket,' stated Aunt Abby tremulously. 'It is merely that she is young, so it is only natural that she should like to associate with young people. Thérèse——'

'Is thirty if she's a day, and a born mischief-maker,' said the Consul, interrupting her. 'Look at the way she used to roll her eyes at Clay? Never let the boy alone at one time. Forever riding with him or calling, or taking him sailing – it's a wonder old Tissot stood for it. I can tell you, I didn't like it by half, and I was mighty thankful when Clay sheered off. As for Olivia Credwell, she's nothing but an empty-headed ninny whose husband must have been glad to die and get shut of her gush and chatter. A fine pair of friends for your daughter! Why, it's got so that Cressy spends more than half her time in their company, while the three of them together spend a sight too much around at Beit-el-Tani. I don't like it, I tell you. Those Palace women are up to something, and I don't like it.'

'Up to something? Mr Hollis, what can you mean?'

Mr Hollis avoided his wife's startled gaze, and scowling instead at a flamboyant arrangement of orange lilies in a large blue pottery jar, said shortly: 'I don't know. I wish I did!'

He turned away from her and began to pace about the room, his hands clasped behind his back and the jerkiness of his stride betraying his inner perturbation, and when at last he came to a stop it was not in front of his wife, but before a framed engraving of Stuart's portrait of George Washington that hung on the far wall of the room. Mr Hollis stared at it for a moment or two without speaking, and then said heavily and with apparent irrelevance:

'It is not our practice to meddle in the conduct or politics of other countries, or to become involved in their domestic disputes. We should strive to remain neutral; if not in thought then at least in deed. And to avoid any appearance of taking sides, because once we start doing that we shall find ourselves committed all over the globe. Committed, as the British are, to interference and responsibility, oppression and suppression – and war. The founders of our country and a great many of its present citizens were and are men who fled from interference and interminable wars. They wanted peace and freedom, and by God, they got it. But the surest way to lose it is by permitting ourselves to get mixed up in the unsavoury squabbles of foreign nations. It's none of my business if Henri Tissot and that hee-hawing half-wit, Hubert Platt, permit their women-folk to engage in intrigue against the Sultan. But I won't have my daughter getting mixed up in something that's likely to raise a bad smell. Or my niece either.'

'But Nat——!' The words were a protesting squeak, and the Consul swung round to glare at his wife and say loudly:

'Or you either, Mrs Hollis! I won't have it. Why, the way your daughter has been talking of late anyone would think she was canvassing votes for a Presidential election, with Bargash as her own private candidate. She's taking sides, and I've no doubt she thinks it's all mighty exciting – like acting a part in a play about a Wicked Sultan and a Noble Heir. But what she's really doing is getting herself mixed up in the private quarrels of coloured people: primitive, lawless people who don't understand our ways of thinking or living, and have never balked at murdering their own kin to get what they want. Well, I guess she'll have to find something else to keep her amused, because I'm not standing for any members of my family sticking their noses into affairs that are nothing to do with them, or helping stir up trouble against the ruler of a territory to which I have been sent as the accredited representative of my country. It's downright dishonourable foolishness, and by goles, it's going to stop!'

13

The Seyyida Salmé, daughter of the late great Sultan, Seyyid Saïd, the "Lion of Oman", sat cross-legged on a silken carpet in an upper room of Beit-el-Tani, one of the royal houses in Zanzibar city, and read aloud from the *Chronicles of the Imams and Seyyids of Muscat and Oman* . . .

'Then went Seyyid Sultan-bin-el-Imam-Ahmed-bin-Saïd to Newaz, and ordered certain men to go to el-Matrah, there to lie in wait for Khasif and to send him bound to Muscat where he should be imprisoned in the Western Fort and kept without food and water until he died, and afterwards to take his body in a boat and throw it into the sea a long distance from the land. And this they did, to the great delight of the Sultan, who proceeded next to es-Suwaik, which was then in the hands of his brother Saïd-bin-el-Imam, and captured it . . .'

Salmé's soft voice slowed and stopped, and she let the heavy book slide off her knees on to the carpet where the breeze that crept through the slats of the shutter ruffled its pages with a sharply urgent sound.

Save for the flap and flutter of the parchment the green-shadowed, mirror-hung room was silent, and in that silence Salmé could hear other sounds: the clatter of pots and pans and a shrill clamour of voices from the servants' quarters on the ground floor, the wash of the sea, the musical cry of a coconut-seller and the beehive hum of the city. All comfortable, familiar noises that made a background to each day, and that had once spelled peace and security. Once, but no longer.

It was, she supposed, inevitable that there should be quarrels and feuds and noisy differences of opinion in such a family as her father's, for although the old Sultan had for many years only one legal wife, his harem overflowed with *sarari* – concubines of every shade and colour from blue-eyed, pearl-fair Circassians to ebony-skinned Abyssinians – whose children ranked as royal, with the right to call themselves Seyyid or Seyyida. But the enormous swarm of half-brothers and sisters, who together with their mothers, grandmothers, aunts and uncles, cousins, nephews, nieces and legions of attentive slaves, occupied the Zanzibar palaces and overflowed into a dozen royal residences, had on the whole lived happily together under the kindly and benevolent eye of the Lion of Oman, and it was only since his death that things had changed.

It was, thought Salmé sadly, as though all peace and contentment had died and been buried with him. And sometimes she would awake in the night and weep quietly for all that had been lost – for the once great

Empire that her father had ruled and which was now divided between three of his sons; for the gay, careless days of her childhood when quarrels had been transient things, as short and fierce as a fire made of dry grasses, and as quickly over; not slow-burning and deadly like the dissensions that were now tearing apart what had once seemed a happy and united family.

Her abstracted gaze rested on her own small person reflected in one of the great gilt-framed and monsoon-tarnished mirrors that were to be found in all her father's palaces. And seeing the light glint on the jewelled medallion she wore on her forehead, she recalled a long-ago morning; a blue and gold morning at the Motoni Palace, when she had escaped from her nurse and run to see her father without waiting to put on the jewel-studded ornament that should have held her twenty plaits together, or the jingling gold coins that should by right have been attached to the end of each one of them. Her father had scolded her for appearing before him improperly dressed and had sent her back in disgrace to her mother . . . It was the only time he had ever been angry with her. The only instance of anger that she could remember in all those sunny, happy, wind-swept years.

Beit-el-Motoni had been her father's favourite palace, for it lay far out of reach of the noise and stench and bustle of the city, and was encircled by palms, green groves of trees and gardens full of flowers. A tall rambling house, several storeys high, whose windows faced the sea and caught the strong cool breath of the Trade Winds. In its colourful, clock-filled rooms the throngs of *sarari* had lived in friendliness and amity, surrounded by their children, their servants, slaves and eunuchs, and ruled over by the Sultan's only legal wife; childless, ugly, imperious Azze-binti-Seif, the Seyyida.

While their elders sewed and gossiped, visited each other or spent long hours in the bath-houses, the children learned to read and write, to ride their father's fiery Arab horses and sail the light *kyacks* off the coral beaches. And there were always the gardens to play in and innumerable pets to feed and caress – peacocks, kittens, monkeys, cockatoos and a tame antelope.

Life in the Women's Quarter at Motoni had been gay and carefree and luxurious, and there had never been any need to plan for the morrow. The long sunny days, regulated by the five sessions of prayer as decreed by the Holy Book, had followed a settled routine that created of itself a pleasant feeling of safety and permanence, and it had never occurred to Salmé that it could ever end. Yet it had ended. Grave news had reached Zanzibar of trouble in far-off Oman, and Sultan Saïd, together with several of his sons and a great retinue of courtiers, servants and slaves, had embarked for Muscat – Oman's capital city and most valuable possession.

That had been the beginning of the end, and Salmé knew that she would never again hear guns without remembering the sound of cannon firing in farewell as the stately ships sailed slowly past Motoni. The women and children had crowded to the shore to wave and weep and pray for the Sultan's safe return, and after he had gone the great palace had seemed empty and forlorn, as though the heart had gone out of it.

Her brother Bargash had sailed with his father, but the Princes Khalid and Majid were among those sons who had remained behind. Khalid, the eldest of the sons born in Zanzibar, was to act as Regent in his father's absence, with Majid next in succession. And since by now the Seyyida Azze was dead, the Sultan had given authority over his women and the palaces to Cholé, his favourite and most beautiful daughter.

But the days that followed his departure had not been happy ones, for lovely Cholé, with the best will in the world, had been unable to avoid arousing jealousy and resentment among the less favoured women, and quarrels and disagreements had become regrettably frequent. Khalid, for his part, had been over-strict, and once there had almost been a major tragedy when fire broke out in one of the palaces, and the screaming women, attempting to escape, found that the Regent had caused all the gates to be chained and given orders to the soldiers on guard that no one might leave, for fear that the common people might see the faces of the Sultan's women.

There were few who for one reason or another did not pray for Seyyid Saïd's safe and speedy return. But the weeks lengthened into months and the months into years and the news that came from Oman was never good news, and there was no word of Saïd's return. Khalid fell ill and died, and now it was Majid – kind-hearted, easy-going, dissolute and unheroic Majid – who was Regent in his place and heir to the Sultanate.

Saïd had never intended to stay away for so long, for he loved Zanzibar and was at peace there. But the vexed problems of his native land, that had dragged him from his green and gracious Island, held him fast among the barren sands and harsh rocks of Arabia. His old enemies, the Persians, had defeated his eldest son Thuwani's army on land and scattered the fleet that he himself had brought to blockade them by sea; and the British having refused his plea for help there had been nothing for it but to accept the harsh terms the victors imposed upon him, and broken and humiliated to turn at last towards home.

Perhaps he knew that he might never reach his beloved island, or see Motoni again, with the blue seas breaking white on the coral shore and the palm trees bowing to the Trade Wind. Or perhaps it was because he felt old and tired and disillusioned – and defeated. But to the surprise and dismay of his followers he had taken with him on board sufficient planks of wood to make a coffin, and given strict orders that should anyone die on the voyage the body would not, according to custom, be consigned to the sea, but would be embalmed and taken to Zanzibar, and laid to rest there. The great dhows had sailed out from Muscat and turned their carved and painted prows towards the south, and five weeks later the crew of a fishing boat, casting their nets off the shores of the Seychelles, sighted the royal ships and raced before the wind to Zanzibar to bring the glad news that the Lion of Oman was returning home.

There were times when Salmé could almost feel that wind on her cheek and smell the scent of those flowers – the garlands of welcome that they had woven when the news came that her father's ships had been sighted. The palaces had been swept and garnished and a feast had been prepared, and the rich smells of cooking had mingled with the swooning scent of flowers and the heavy perfumes of musk and sandalwood and attar-of-roses that drenched the silken garments of the women. How they had laughed and sung as they put on their finest clothes and their loveliest jewels, and hurried at last into the gardens to stand along the shore, straining their eyes to seaward, and waiting – waiting——

Majid had put out with members of his retinue in two small cutters to meet his father, saying that they would be back before sundown and there would be music and rejoicing and a great feast. But the eager day had drawn towards evening and still the watchers had seen no sails, and as darkness fell lanterns glowed along the seashore and lights glittered on every roof and balcony of the town where the population crowded to greet its returning lord; though it was cold now and the wind was shrill. No one in Zanzibar had slept that night, and when the dawn broke they were still waiting and watching, silent and chilled; straining their eyes to seaward as the sky paled and the sun, lifting at last above the tossing horizon, glinted gold upon the sails of ships . . .

Recalling that day, Salmé could hear again in imagination the shout of joy that had arisen from a thousand throats, only to change, terrifyingly, to a long, desolate wail of woe as the fleet drew nearer and it was seen that from every prow there hung a mourning flag.

It had not been granted to Saïd to see his green, spice-scented Island again, for in the same hour that the fishermen had sighted his ships off the Seychelles, Seyyid Saïd-bin-Sultan-bin-el-Imam-Ahmed-bin-Saïd, Imam of Oman and Sultan of Zanzibar, had died. His body had been washed and shrouded, and after prayers had been said over it, his son Bargash enclosed it in a coffin made from the planks that had been brought from Muscat, and made haste to leave the ship before Majid could reach it: taking the coffin with him and landing secretly on the Island to bury it by night near the grave of his brother Khalid, the dead Regent.

Bargash, thought Salmé, had always meant to be Sultan of Zanzibar, and when he heard of Khalid's death it must have seemed to him like the finger of Fate, for he had never had anything but contempt for weak, kindly Majid, and could not have looked upon him as a serious obstacle in the way of his ambition. But Majid had the advantage of seniority, and the chiefs and elders, and the British, supported his claim. So now he ruled in his father's place and Bargash must be content with being Heir-Apparent. But when had Bargash ever been content with second-best?

Salmé sighed and dropped her small chin on her palm. Her gaze strayed to her beloved half-sister, and rested there; anxious and adoring. Cholé was so beautiful, and she could not remember a time when she had not loved and admired and looked up to her. In the black days of mourning for their father it had been Cholé who had comforted her, and it was Cholé again to whom she had clung when her mother died of the cholera and she had felt orphaned and alone among the sympathetic *sarari* and their noisy, swarming children.

Cholé had taken her into her own little palace, Beit-el-Tani, and had mothered her and petted her, turning her childish admiration for an older sister into adoration for a goddess who could do no wrong. But of late Salmé had been troubled by twinges of anxiety and doubt, for though her love had not diminished, she could not help wondering if Cholé were not letting her emotions overrule her sense of justice, and where all this plotting and scheming would lead them.

It had begun with a quarrel: a trivial difference of opinion between the new Sultan and his beautiful, self-willed half-sister over the ownership of a suite of rooms at Beit-el-Motoni that Cholé desired, but that Majid had already allotted to Khalid's widow, and an emerald necklace that he had given to Méjé and which Cholé said had been promised to her by her father and should have been left to her in his will. Méjé had refused to give them up, and when Majid had offered Cholé a fabulous rope of pearls in their place, she had thrown them at him and swept out of Motoni, vowing never to return.

In their father's day such a quarrel would have blown over in a matter of hours. But in the changed atmosphere that Saïd's death had created it had not blown over. Instead it had stayed and taken firm root, until at length what had started as resentment had turned, on Cholé's part, to a bitter hatred that overcame all restraint and common sense. Caught in the grip of that hatred she had looked about her for a weapon to use against her once-loved brother; and found it in the person of his Heir-Apparent – dashing, handsome, swaggering Bargash, who had always despised his older brother and already made two unsuccessful attempts to snatch his throne.

Salmé was fond of Majid: as Cholé too had been until Bargash and a foolish squabble had come between them. But now that Cholé hated him, her friends and partisans must hate him too, and she had forced Salmé to choose – herself or Majid: there could be no half measures. Salmé had wavered and wept and attempted to avoid a decision, but Cholé had been implacable and in the end she had won, and Saïd's once happy and united family split into opposing camps; intriguing, scheming, spying and being spied on.

Their enmity had by now reached such ridiculous proportions that if a member of one faction wore a new jewel, a member of the other must have a similar or a better one, and if a rumour arose that some supporter of Majid had decided to buy a horse or a house or a plot of land, then a supporter of Bargash would forestall or outbid them for spite. Even the nights were no longer peaceful, for it was by night that they held their secret meetings, and by night that spies and mischief-makers carried tales between them; scratching at doors and casements to whisper scraps of conversation overheard or that moment invented, and to hold out greedy hands for a reward of gold coins, thrust uncounted into the waiting palms.

Money was slipping away like water into parched ground, and wisdom with it, for the Arabic love of intrigue had them fast in its grip and it was as though they were the victims of some illness; a fatal málady that inflamed their brains and ate away their reason, and which they could neither cure nor control.

Cholé's little palace, Beit-el-Tani, was separated by no more than the width of a narrow alleyway from the house in which Bargash lived with his sister Méjé and a small brother, Abd-il-Aziz. And almost as short a distance away stood another owned by Salmé's two nieces, Schembua and Farschu, who had followed her into Bargash's camp. But although the proximity of the three houses had assisted the work of intrigue, it had led to other troubles, for Méjé had become jealous of her brother's attentions to Cholé, and conceiving herself slighted by his neglect, she complained of Cholé to anyone who would listen, and took to warning her brother and his fellow-conspirators that they were rushing on disaster and that no good would come of this dangerous plotting. The result had been more quarrels and still more bitterness. Yet in spite of her jealousy and doubts, Méjé had been too fond of her brother to leave him, and so she had stayed with him; wringing her hands and prophesying disaster, but still loyal and devoted. Unable to change her allegiance even when Bargash and Cholé horrified her by courting the aid of white foreigners.

The small white community in Zanzibar had, theoretically, no power to interfere in any family dispute concerning the succession. But they were not without influence, and Cholé and Bargash, looking about them for any means that might further their cause, decided that they must enlist sympathizers from among them. Hitherto Bargash had always affected to despise the foreigners, while Cholé had refused to meet their women: but now the wife of Monsieur Tissot, the sister of Mr Hubert Platt, and the daughter of Mr Nathaniel Hollis were encouraged to call at Beit-el-Tani.

Cholé hated their visits and endured them only for the sake of the use that might be made of them. She considered the 'white women' – whose skins were barely whiter than her own – to be ignorant and uneducated. For although the two older women spoke passable Kiswahili and more than a little Arabic, their limited knowledge of these languages frequently led them to make gross errors of taste which had to be excused on the score of ignorance, but which were none the less unpalatable for that. As for the American girl, Miss Cressida Hollis, her Arabic was still too limited to enable her to sustain a conversation, and her stumbling efforts exasperated Cholé. But though the visits of these foreigners continued to be an ordeal to her, her young half-sister found them fascinating as well as alarming.

Salmé would watch and listen and smile shyly, envying these women their freedom, and Cholé did not know – no one knew or even suspected – that they were not the only foreigners whom she watched and listened to and smiled at: or who watched and listened and smiled at her! For close to Beit-el-Tani and separated from it only by a lane as narrow as that which divided it from Bargash's home, was a house owned by Europeans, and from her lattice Salmé had often watched the gay dinner-parties given by Herr Ruete, a handsome young German who worked for a firm of Hamburg merchants, and whose unshielded windows faced her own not-always-discreetly screened ones with nothing between them but the meagre width of a cramped Zanzibar street.

She was aware that he could have caught an occasional glimpse of her, for once the lamps were lit in Beit-el-Tani, the delicate carving of the wooden shutters made it easy enough for a watcher to see into the rooms they were designed to conceal – a fact that the women were apt to forget because they themselves could not see out into the darkness, and on hot nights the curtains were often left undrawn. But it was only when he took to coming to his window to bow and smile when she peeped at him through her lattice during the daylight hours, that Salmé realized that young Wilhelm Ruete must indeed have seen her, and been watching her with as much interest as she had watched him.

Once he had even leaned out from his sill and tossed a rose across the narrow canyon that divided them. It was so short a distance that he had been able to throw it accurately through the fretted wooden screen so that it fell at her feet. And when she had summoned enough courage to pick it up she found that there was a scrap of paper tied about its stem, on which he had written in Arabic a verse from a song that she herself had often sung to the strains of a mandolin, and which he must have listened to her singing . . .

> *Visit those you love, though your abode be distant*
> *And clouds and darkness have arisen between you.*
> *For no obstacle should restrain a friend*
> *From visiting often the friend he loves.*

Salmé had put the rose in water, and when it wilted at last she had collected the fallen petals, and carefully drying them, wrapped them in a little square of silk and hidden them in the bottom of her jewel box. They had become a talisman against fear and anger, and sometimes when the fever of hate and intrigue that infected the very air of Cholé's little palace became more than she could bear, she would take them from their hiding place, and holding them pressed to her cheek, think of such things as love and peace and happiness; and of a young man's openly admiring eyes and smiling face. A kind face. Her father had been kind. And Cholé too, and Majid—— But she must not let herself remember Majid's good qualities, because that would be disloyal to Cholé, who refused to concede any virtues to her once-loved brother.

Love and kindness . . . Once there had been so much of both, but where had it all gone? Of all the sisters and brothers and cousins she had laughed and played with, only a handful now remained her friends – those few who had elected to side with Bargash. Would she ever be happy again, wondered Salmé? Would any of them, as long as Majid sat on the throne that Bargash coveted, and Cholé nursed her grievance against one brother and espoused the cause of the other?

Bargash would never give up; never rest until he had obtained what he desired – he had always been like that, and Salmé knew that he could not change: any more than Majid could change, or beautiful, embittered, unforgiving Cholé. Yet she had to admit that until a short while ago she herself had found the emotional, semi-farcical atmosphere of plot and counter-plot exciting and stimulating, for it had helped her to forget the sadness of her father's tragic home-coming and the death of her beloved mother. Bargash and Cholé together had snatched her up out of her grey, twilight brooding into a brightly-coloured world of conspiracy and high romance that seemed more than half play-acting, and she had found the whispering and scheming and the tense, uplifting sense of being involved in great affairs wildly exhilarating and as heady as the fumes of *bang*. She had thought it all a great adventure until . . . until the intrusion of the foreign women.

Salmé lifted her chin from her palm and spoke to her sister; her soft voice unexpectedly loud in the quiet room:

'Why do they come here, Cholé? Why do you encourage them to come, when you don't even like them?'

Cholé turned her lovely head, and it seemed that she too had been thinking of the foreign women, for she laid down the embroidery with which her hands had been busied and replied instantly: 'Because we need help and they can give it.'

'How? How can they *possibly* help us?'

'In more ways than you would think. For one thing, they talk; and their talk often tells us a great deal about how their menfolk think, which is very useful to us. They also hear things that we don't, and carry news to our friends by ways that would be much too dangerous for us to use. And as they support our brother Bargash, they . . .' She hesitated, and then shook her head and picked up her embroidery again.

Salmé said urgently: 'They *what*? What else can they do for us?'

'Nothing else,' said Cholé shortly, and turned to address one of her waiting women, when a mischievous childish voice spoke from the far end of the room where little Abd-il-Aziz lay on his stomach among a pile of cushions, eating sugared almonds and playing with a marmoset: 'Of course there is something else: I'll tell you, if Cholé won't.'

'Aziz!' Cholé had forgotten that this small brother was present, and her voice was half imperative and half imploring, while her eyes flashed a warning that even a child could read. The boy glanced at the five other women in the room, and shrugged and turned back to his pet: 'Oh, all right. But I don't know what you're making such a fuss about, because everyone in my brother's house knows. They've been going on and on about it. Even Efembi says that the only thing *he* doesn't know yet is the price; though Karim thinks——'

'Aziz!'

'Don't *fuss*, Cholé! I wasn't going to say anything. Who was the new white woman who came with your foreign friends this morning? We saw her from my window when their carriage came to your door. She's so tall that Karim thought you were entertaining a man in disguise, but I told him you wouldn't dare: not in the middle of the morning with all the slaves looking on. But she walked just like one. Like this . . .'

The boy sprang up and strode across the room with his chin up and his shoulders back, until his foot caught in the fringe of a carpet and he tripped and fell, and rolled over, laughing. '*Just* like that! except that she didn't fall. I wish she had. I'd have laughed and laughed!'

'Then she would have thought you shockingly bad-mannered,' scolded Salmé, 'and cruel, too. People shouldn't laugh when others get hurt.'

'Why not, if it's funny? That fat slave of Mégé's fell down the stairs with a big jar of boiling water last week, and you should have heard the noise she made! The water splashed all over her, and she rolled about and squalled like a scalded cat, and everyone laughed like anything. You'd have laughed too, if you'd been there.'

'No, I shouldn't,' protested Salmé, shuddering. 'I don't like to see people hurt. It is only you others who——' She stopped and bit her lip, aghast at the words she had been about to say: '– *who are Arabs of Oman, and descended from the Imams and Seyyids of Muscat and Oman who loved violence and cruelty and cunning.*' Yet she too was of the same blood. Though in her the gentleness of her sweet-tempered Circassian mother would seem to have outweighed the fiery strain of her father's line, since she could never find pleasure in another's pain.

Looking from her small brother to her beautiful, implacable half-sister, Salmé was conscious of a cold shiver of apprehension. Was it Majid's murder that was being planned? No, it could not be that! Cholé had promised . . . Bargash had sworn . . .

Yet there had been that frightening incident when a boat in which their brother Majid sat to take the evening air had passed within range of the seaward-facing windows of Bargash's house, and had been fired upon – by Bargash himself! A fusillade of shots had spattered into the quiet water of the harbour, and the Heir-Apparent, taxed with an attempt to assassinate the Sultan, had sworn that he had no knowledge of who was in the boat, because it was dusk, and that he had fired as a joke with the sole intention of startling the unknown occupants. Since no one had been hurt his story had been accepted – by all save Majid, who had resolutely refused to receive him until forced to do so under strong pressure from the French Consul, backed by the Commandant of the French forces on the East Coast of Africa, who had been visiting the island in a warship of thirty guns.

Until this moment it had not occurred to Salmé to doubt Bargash's word, or to regard the incident as anything more than the foolish prank he had asserted it to be, because she had been convinced that her dashing brother would never have missed such an easy mark with half-a-dozen successive shots had he really intended any harm. It was this, rather than his denials, that had reassured her. But now, thinking back, she found herself uncertain; and because she was uncertain she became afraid. Her fear forced her abruptly to her feet and took her across the room to kneel on the wide stone ledge of the window embrasure and peer downward through the carved lattice-work of the wooden shutter.

Beit-el-Tani, like Bargash's house, faced the sea, and looking out at the blue harbour water that broke on the beach a stone's-throw away, Salmé saw a small boat passing. It was almost as though she had conjured it up from her anxious thoughts, for it was just such a boat as Majid had used. A Hindu trader lolled in the stern while his slaves bent to the oars, and she could see their faces quite clearly.

The sight brought her a large measure of reassurance, because it seemed to her that anyone should have been able to hit them with a well-aimed pebble, let alone a shot from a pistol, so that Bargash must have spoken the truth after all – or half the truth, at all events, for she had little doubt that he had known perfectly well who was in the boat and had meant to give Majid a fright! But there was no real harm in that; not if it had only been a joke. But had it been? The sun had not been shining then, as it was now, and without the daylight . . .

Once again doubt crept coldly in, whispering that it had been late in the evening and almost dark, and that it would have been easy enough to misjudge the distance of a moving target in the dusk. Could Bargash – had Bargash——?

Salmé drew back sharply from the window and shivered so violently that her teeth chattered, and Cholé, who had been watching her, enquired if she were feeling ill: 'You haven't been looking at all well this morning. You aren't sickening for a fever, are you?'

Salmé forced a smile and protested that she was perfectly well, but Cholé seemed unconvinced, and dismissing her women she sent the reluctant Abd-il-Aziz back to his brother's house, and as soon as they had gone, turned again to her half-sister and said: 'What are you afraid of, Salmé? Tell me.'

'I'm not. I mean . . .' Salmé twisted her small hands together so that the heavy bracelets struck against each other like bells, and said unhappily: 'It's – it's only that I sometimes wonder where all this plotting and deceit is leading us.'

Cholé laughed and said lightly: 'Why, to victory, of course; where else? – for Bargash and all of us. It won't be long now, and when we have won and he is safely seated in our father's place we shall have time to be happy again, and you and I will be rewarded with praise and power. Bargash will give us anything we wish for – jewels, dresses, horses, slaves, palaces – we shall only have to ask. You'll see!'

'And Majid?' asked Salmé in a half-whisper: 'What will become of Majid?'

Cholé rose with a swift, angry clash of silver anklets, and said harshly:

'What does it matter? Why should we care what becomes of him? The only thing that matters is to depose him. And soon!'

'Cholé, you would not – you would not——?' She could not finish the sentence. She could not put it into words and say baldly: 'You would not have him murdered?' But Cholé was looking at her with eyes that were scornful and understanding – and oddly calculating. Cholé could not afford to lose adherents to the cause that she had made her own, and neither could she run the risk of allowing her young half-sister's sympathies to be aroused on behalf of Majid: Salmé knew too much and was far too tender-hearted. It would be a calamity if she were to change her allegiance and run tattling to Majid. Realizing this, Cholé made a sudden rush, and catching the younger girl into a laughing embrace, hugged her, and then holding her away at arm's length said gaily: 'Do you *really* think I am such a monster that I would actually plot to murder one of my own brothers? Do you?'

Salmé blushed and laughed and shook her head, reassured and caught once more in the web of her love and admiration for this beautiful, fascinating older sister who had always been so kind to her.

'No, of course I don't,' she protested. 'How could I? It was only ... Oh, it was the heat, I suppose; and all the worry ... and then having to try and make out what those foreign women were saying. They are very friendly and kind, and they try so hard; but I don't find it easy to understand them.'

'That needn't worry you!' said Cholé tartly, releasing her, 'for they seldom say anything worth listening to.'

'Why do you dislike them so, Cholé?'

'I should have thought it was obvious. But if you really don't know, I'll tell you: because they are foreigners and unbelievers. Because they lack education, refinement and modesty, and because they are ignorant, loud-voiced and shameless. Because they have no manners, and they move and dress without grace and flaunt themselves unveiled in the streets like harlots. And because they smell unpleasant. There! Does that satisfy you?'

'I think you're too hard on them. They can't help these things, because they don't know any better. Shouldn't we try to enlighten them? We could teach them so much and I'm sure they would be grateful for it.'

'No doubt,' said Cholé with a return to hauteur. 'But I have no desire for their gratitude and nor do I wish to teach them anything. If they want to receive instruction in the True Faith, I've no doubt that the maulvies, if properly approached, would be willing to enlighten their ignorance. But it's no business of mine to teach these vulgar barbarians how to conduct themselves. I receive them only because Bargash feels that they may be of use to us, and as soon as their usefulness is ended I shall do so no longer. That day cannot come too soon for me!'

She gathered up her embroidery and went away, leaving Salmé to pick up and replace the *Chronicles of the Imams and Seyyids of Muscat and Oman* in the great carved and gilded chest from which she had taken it an hour ago, after the foreign visitors had left.

14

'Well, what do you think of them?' demanded Cressy eagerly. 'Isn't Princess Cholé the loveliest thing you've ever seen? so gracious and elegant, and so – so *regal*.'

'She's very pretty,' conceded Hero, who had been mentally comparing the Princess with the girl she had seen at The Dolphins' House; Zorah, whose delicate features and enormous dark eyes seemed to her far more appealing than the Seyyida Cholé's flawless beauty and cold, expressionless gaze. The former might be a harlot and the other a daughter of a Royal House, but if asked to choose between them, most people, decided Hero, would give the palm to Zorah. She said reflectively: 'It seems odd that the Princess Cholé's eyes should be almost grey rather than black or brown.'

'*Mais non*, it is not odd at all,' declared the little Frenchwoman who sat opposite her in the leather-scented shade of the closed carriage: 'I am told that many of the old Sultan's children have eyes of an even lighter colour. It is from their mothers, *vous comprenez*?'

Thérèse Tissot was small and dark, prettily plump and amazingly *chic*. Her clothes and her *coiffeur* were the envy of every other white woman in Zanzibar and it was difficult to make any accurate guess at her age, since she obviously tampered with nature. A combination of rouge, rice-powder and discreetly applied mascara lent her an appearance of youth that was possibly misleading, but though her black eyes were noticeably shrewd and observant, the charm of her smile, her coaxing voice, animated gestures and attractively accented English, could not be denied.

'The *sarari* – the Sultan's women,' explained Madame Tissot to Hero, 'have a name for the children of Circassian mothers. They call them "cats", because of their fair skin and eyes; and the other children are jealous of them.'

'But I understood that Salmé's mother was a Circassian too? She's not nearly as fair as her sister, but I suppose she takes after her father. I felt quite sorry for the poor little thing; she has such a sad mouth and seems so shy, and sometimes she looked positively frightened.'

'Frightened?' Mrs Credwell, the fourth occupant of the carriage, looked startled and said nervously: 'Of what? Oh; I do trust that the Sultan has not found out about anything.'

'Olivia – please!' Cressy frowned a warning and gestured silently in the direction of the dark-faced driver who sat on the box, and Olivia

Credwell said guiltily: 'Oh, dear, I quite forgot. It is so difficult to remember that one must guard one's tongue at all times, and that almost anyone may be an informer or a spy.'

Mrs Credwell was a fair-haired and emotional lady who had been married at seventeen to an elderly bridegroom who had tactlessly succumbed to an attack of typhoid fever during the honeymoon, leaving his widow in poor circumstances. No other offers had come her way, and after fourteen years of unrelieved monotony she had gratefully accepted her sister-in-law's invitation to spend a season or two in the tropics.

Olivia had thought it so *very* kind of dear Jane, and was unaware that Hubert's wife, visualizing the possibility of an elderly and indigent widow battening upon them in later life, had only asked her in the hope that she might attract an offer from one of the European merchants or a visiting ship's captain in Zanzibar – for though already in her thirties and with few pretensions to beauty, she was not ill-looking and would show up well enough in a place where white women were few and far between. That had been three years ago. But no second husband had appeared, and Olivia was still here: occupying herself with the enthusiastic study of Arabic and Kiswahili and a passionate interest in the affairs of the Royal Family of Zanzibar.

Her sister-in-law, who considered her to be a foolish, gushing and sentimental woman, had little time for her, and since her busy brother had even less, she had been left to go her own way and find her own amusements. And though Hubert Platt had aroused himself to mild remonstrance when he discovered that she was making friends among a faction known to be hostile to the Sultan, he had not been sufficiently interested to carry the matter further. Not that his sister would have paid much attention to him if he had.

Olivia had always yearned for romance and adventure, and had found no trace of either in her dull and dutiful youth, or her brief marriage and the drab years of widowhood that had followed it. But now at last she had found an outlet for her frustrated emotions in the tangled and enthralling affairs of half-a-dozen Arab princes and princesses plotting for a throne, and for the first time in her repressed life she not only felt alive, but vitally involved in a whirl of important events. It was an exhilarating sensation and it had gone to her head like a strong drink – and produced much the same effect.

'Oh, what a relief it will be,' breathed Olivia, 'when the people of this lovely island throw off their chains and are free to speak their minds without fear or favour!'

'*Olivia!*' This time it was Madame Tissot who spoke, and Mrs Credwell blushed and abandoned the topic, and turning hurriedly to Hero began to point out objects of interest by the way.

There were few roads in Zanzibar capable of taking a carriage, and few people, in consequence, kept such things. But Olivia's sister-in-law, Jane Platt (who disliked Madame Tissot and was not to be outdone by her), had prevailed upon her husband to import an even larger and handsomer carriage than the one owned by Thérèse, and it was this unwieldy vehicle that now conveyed the four women along a dusty, uneven road shaded by flamboyants and India Cork trees, and turned in at the gates of a large pink-washed bungalow on the outskirts of the town. A sun-blistered notice-board proclaimed it the residence of Mr H. J. Platt of the British East African Coastal Trading Company, but the master of the house was away from home, being absent on a business trip to the neighbouring island of Pemba.

'Jane and the twins have gone with him, and they do not expect to be back for at least a week,' explained Olivia in a conspiratorial whisper. 'And as they have taken the only two house-servants who speak any English, we can meet here as often as we like and feel *quite* safe, for the others speak none at all.'

'Which is not to say that they do not understand it!' commented Madame Tissot warningly.

Mrs Platt's drawing-room was pleasantly cool after the sun-baked stuffiness of the closed carriage, and window blinds of split cane lent it a shadowed peace that was a welcome relief from the rutted, wind-blown roads. A white-robed houseboy served chilled coffee in long glasses, and as soon as the door had closed behind him Olivia said eagerly: 'Now at last we can *really* talk!'

'Are you quite sure no one can overhear?' demanded Cressy, looking anxiously in the direction of the french windows. 'You know that we cannot be too careful.'

Mrs Credwell nodded vigorous agreement, and rising from her chair, tiptoed to the hall door and jerked it open with the dramatic suddenness of one who fully expects to find an eavesdropper crouched on the far side of it, ear to keyhole. But the hall was empty, and nothing stirred on the long verandah outside the french windows except the sea-wind blowing through the arches and a lizard sunning himself on the hot stone.

'Not a soul about,' announced Mrs Credwell superfluously, returning to her chair: 'And now Thérèse, we are all agog. *What* news?'

Thérèse Tissot turned her head to look thoughtfully at Hero, and then glanced again at her hostess, her brows raised in a silent question, and Cressy, interpreting the look correctly, said quickly: 'It's quite all right, Thérèse. You need have no anxiety on Hero's behalf, because I have already told her something of the situation and I know she agrees with us.'

'So Jules Dubail informed me,' said Thérèse with a half smile. 'He was a fellow-voyager of Mademoiselle's, and it seems he discusses much with her and finds her *très sympathique*. All the same I cannot feel that she will wish to fatigue herself with our little affairs, so I would suggest that for this morning we talk of other matters, *n'est-ce pas?*'

'You are afraid she will blab!' accused Cressy indignantly. 'Well, she won't. Will you, Hero?'

'No,' said Hero calmly. 'But I must tell you that if you are engaged in what I think, then Madame Tissot is right to be cautious. You would make a very poor conspirator, Cressy, for you are far too trusting.'

'But Hero, you do agree with us?'

'That the present Sultan should be deposed? Certainly. And from what I have seen of the appalling state of slavery and sanitation that prevails in this city, not to mention the shocking tolerance displayed towards evil-doers, the sooner it is done the better. Always provided that the Heir-Apparent is all that you imagine him to be, because I asked Uncle Nat about him, and he did not seem to be as certain on that point as you are, Cressy.'

'Your uncle, Mademoiselle,' intervened Thérèse gently, 'must of necessity take a view that is more ... how can I say it? ... conservative? He has also a respect for the opinions of Colonel Edwards, who is the British Consul, and doubtless feels that he should support his *confrère's* views on this subject. The Colonel's Government support this man Majid because they say his father named him to succeed here. But who can doubt that had his father been spared, this altogether abominable young man would have been replaced as heir by his half-brother Seyyid Bargash? There is no need for us to say like parrots: "But the law is on Majid's side." What we have to ask ourselves is: "What of Justice? – is Justice also on his side? Or is it not rather upon the side of his suffering people?"'

Cressy and Mrs Credwell, carried away by their friend's eloquence, nodded an enthusiastic agreement, but the question had been addressed to Hero, who said slowly: 'I would still like to be certain that this man Bargash could be counted upon to put a stop to the slave trading that is being carried on here in Zanzibar. That seems to me to be the most important consideration. Can you be sure that he will not allow it to continue?'

Madame Tissot shook her head and said soberly: 'It would be easy for me to lie to you Mademoiselle, and say "Yes, I am sure". But alas, I cannot say that. No one can say it: for this is not a thing that can be changed overnight, and much will depend on the will of his people – very many of whom regard it as a way of life. But of one thing I *can* assure you. If Bargash becomes Sultan he will instantly repudiate the iniquitous treaty with the British that permits the trade to be carried on from this island and its dependencies – and with it, too, the one that binds Zanzibar to pay a yearly tribute to the oldest brother, Thuwani! He will do this because he holds the British responsible for his father's death, declaring that it was their refusal to help Saïd against the Persians that finally broke the old man's heart. And because he believes that they betrayed his father we can be very certain that he will enter into no more treaties with them, and that, I can promise you, will change the whole face of the slave trade in these waters!'

'Yes,' agreed Hero thoughtfully, 'it will indeed ... And I own it is a point in his favour, for I have always considered that treaty to be a crying scandal that reflects no credit on the British. All the same, I have to confess that it would be reassuring to know a little more about his character and capabilities before committing myself to helping him to a throne. I have already been told that as Sultan he could not possibly be worse than his brother – my uncle told me this himself. But is that enough?'

'But I've already *told* you——' began Cressy indignantly.

Madame Tissot quelled her with a look, and turning back to Hero said with an approving smile: 'You are right to be careful, Mademoiselle, and I honour you for it. But it may have to be enough. That is, if you are not prepared to accept our word for it that Seyyid Bargash is an infinitely more intelligent and enlightened man than his dissolute brother, and one who is capable of bringing the benefits of Western civilization to his people instead of leaving them to wallow in a state of medieval squalor. If you doubt me you have only to ask anyone in Zanzibar, and excepting only from Monsieur Edwards – or Majid himself! – you will receive the same answer. But since that would not only take up too much time when time is of great shortness, but could lead to much undesirable talk, I feel it would be better to adjourn this little meeting at once and forget that it ever took place. Better for your peace of mind; and more comfortable for you, no?'

Comfortable! ... The word stung Hero as perhaps no other one could have done.

She had not come to Zanzibar to be 'comfortable'. And the little Frenchwoman was quite right, of course. To be asking searching questions of all and sundry as to whether the Heir-Apparent would make a better Sultan than his brother could only serve to alert Majid and his supporters – among them that slave trader, Frost! – to the possibility of a *coup* in favour of Bargash, which (once warned) they would certainly nip in the bud, and in a manner that was likely to be exceedingly unpleasant for all concerned. No, she could not risk that. And in any case, had she not already been told, and by no less a person than the French Consul's son, that the entire foreign community, with the exception of the British Consul, were in favour of Bargash as ruler? Why, even the *Virago*'s perfidious Captain had admitted that the younger brother was the better man! And Uncle Nat's verdict, though hardly laudatory, had confirmed both opinions . . .

According to Uncle Nat, Majid had 'nothing to recommend him except that he happened to be the son of his father', while Bargash at least possessed sufficient strength of character to inspire respect among the islanders and 'make them toe the line whether they like it or not'. So why should she doubt Madame Tissot, Cressy and Mrs Credwell, who all supported this view, and had all lived in Zanzibar quite long enough to know what they were talking about? – even Cressy, who had been there for a year. Not that she would have been prepared to take her cousin's unsupported opinions on such a matter on trust – or Mrs Credwell's either! But Madame Tissot was a bird of a very different feather, for she was clearly both shrewd and capable, and not in the least likely to be taken in by any sentimental nonsense. If she supported Bargash it would be for strictly practical reasons, and not for any of the romantic ones that motivated Cressy and Olivia Credwell. Of that Hero felt quite certain.

She was aware that the others were waiting for her reply, but though she knew by now what that reply would be, she remained silent for a further moment or two: thinking again, as she had thought on her first day in Zanzibar when she had listened to Cressy's breathless talk of a weak and vicious Sultan and a bold Heir-Apparent, impatient for a throne, 'This, surely, is *the work that is waiting for me to do.*' It could even be that this Frenchwoman, and not Clay, was the one who was destined to help her do it, and that this was the very moment that old Biddy Jason had foretold – the *'time to choose'*. Well, she was ready for it, and she had chosen. She would *'do what she had to do.'*

She said aloud and briskly: 'You must forgive me if I seemed to doubt you. I did not mean to be rude; only to be sure. I feel certain that you are right, and I hope very much that you will not adjourn the meeting, but tell us instead what we can do to help.'

'Bravo!' applauded Olivia. 'That's the spirit, dear Miss Hollis. Action! The time for talk is past and we must turn to deeds.'

'Yes, but *what* deeds?' asked Cressy.

'That Thérèse will tell us. She has news for us; isn't that so, Thérèse?'

'Indeed yes. But first you must swear to me, on your oaths most sacred, that what I shall tell you, you will disclose to no one. To no one at all. Is it agreed?'

Receiving their solemn assurances, she lowered her voice and spoke rapidly and with a wealth of gesture:

Support for the Heir-Apparent, said Madame Tissot, was increasing rapidly among the population, and not only had the powerful chiefs of the el Harth tribe decided to throw in their lot with him, but a very large sum of money had been dispatched to him by his eldest brother, Thuwani of Muscat and Oman, for the purpose of financing his followers. Gold in the form of coins, unminted ingots and plate that could be sold or melted down . . .

Gold! thought Hero. How could she have known – that ragged old crone who made a dubious living telling fortunes to cooks and kitchen-maids in Boston? And yet it was all coming true. First the voyage and then the work. And now the gold . . . the 'gold past counting' that she was to lay her hand on but get no good from. Which was only fair and right. It was the people of Zanzibar who would reap the benefit of it, and she would not have had it otherwise . . .

Thérèse was saying: 'Those who support him must be paid, you understand, since many of them, because of their loyalty, have fallen from favour and lost their employment. There are also many more who wish very greatly to follow him, but cannot do so because they fear to starve. So he has great need of money.'

The gold, explained Thérèse, had arrived safely and was at the moment reposing in the cellar of a house in the city, from whence it must be removed as soon as possible to some safer hiding place until the means could be devised to smuggle it into the Heir-Apparent's house:

'It cannot stay where it is now, for every moment it remains there it is in great danger of being discovered, and the owner of the house in which it lies has become very nervous. He is an Indian merchant, you see. A Banyan; and all these Banyans are afraid of Colonel Edwards, because being British subjects they may not keep slaves, and as their Consul he can demand to search their houses. Balu Ram is a friend of someone who has helped us greatly but whose name must not be known, and this is why he agreed to hide the treasure. But now he hears that the Colonel suspects him of concealing slaves, and so he begs that it should be instantly re-moved – tonight if possible. But where to take it? That is the difficulty, because it cannot be taken to the house of any who are known to support Bargash, in case they may be watched by the Sultan's spies.'

'Could it not come here?' enquired Hero.

There was a brief moment of startled silence, and then Olivia Credwell

171

clapped her hands and said: 'But of course! Oh, you clever, clever girl! What could be better?'

'But Olivia *chérie* – reflect . . . consider . . .!'

Mrs Credwell's flounces whirled: 'I don't have to consider. Why, with Hubert and Jane in Pemba it will be the easiest thing in the world! They don't get back until next week, which will give us plenty of time to decide how to transfer the money to the Prince's house.'

'But these are not small objects, *chérie*. They are chests, large and of a great heaviness. Where would you conceal them?'

'In my boxroom, of course. Jane gave me one where I could store my trunks. It is next to my bedroom and I have always kept it locked because one never *knows*, does one . . . with native servants? No one but myself ever goes in there, and it would be *ideal*, since it is quite shielded from the servants' quarters. Besides, the side gate into the garden is right opposite and no distance away, so nothing could be better.'

'*Bon!* Then Balu Ram shall have the chests brought here this very night. You permit, Olivia?'

'Of course, Thérèse dear. It will be a privilege. *Gold!* . . . Oh dear, I do trust it will be safe? Supposing anyone . . .'

Cressy said uneasily: 'It will not be used to buy anything – anything *dangerous*, will it? I mean – guns, or bullets or anything dreadful like that?'

'Dear Cressy,' said Thérèse affectionately, 'you are so tender-hearted. But you need have no fear. No fear at all.'

'Cressy is quite right,' interrupted Hero firmly. 'We must first be certain of that. I for one could not countenance anything in the nature of violence, and I am sure we are all in agreement over that.'

'Indeed, yes. You may rest assured there will be no violence. The Seyyid Bargash has too great an attachment to his people to permit such a thing, while as for the Sultan – *bah*! The Sultan is of a timidity quite remarkable. No, no, dear Mademoiselle, what is planned is a revolution without blood. A *coup d'état*. That is why so much money is needed, because it is as I have told you: there are here, as everywhere, many people who do not range themselves either on one side or the other, but who may be bought.'

'You mean bribed,' said Hero with a distinct trace of disapproval.

Madame Tissot shrugged her plump shoulders. 'It is the same thing, *n'est-ce pas*? They are poor people and they must eat. Their families must live, and therefore they fear to speak against the tyranny of the Sultan. But if there is the promise of money they will side openly with Seyyid Bargash, whom already they love. And once they have added themselves to those other loyal ones a *coup d'état* arranges itself with no trouble and no blows, for what can the Sultan do if the whole city and every man of all the villages is in support of his brother Bargash? He can only retire peacefully to this new palace of Dar-es-Salaam that he builds for himself on the mainland, while his brother ascends the throne to the acclamation of all, and begins the long and hard task of abolishing the injustices and poverty and serfdom that have afflicted his people for so long.'

Olivia Credwell looked as though she was about to applaud again, but Hero's expression was still doubtful, and Madame Tissot laughed and shook a be-ringed finger at her:

'Is it that you do not think it can be accomplished? Or is it that knowing nothing as yet of the East you think it is not right to buy supporters with money? Well, that is your affair. But for myself, I think it better to buy men than to kill them. We know that the Sultan's party have obtained many muskets, and if the Seyyid Bargash's party were to do likewise there would be only one end to this affair; fighting and bloodshed and many deaths. That, you will agree, we cannot permit, and it is to save the good citizens from such a fate that this treasure has been sent from Muscat. To purchase the support of those who – how do you say it? – "seat themselves upon the fence". You understand?'

'Yes, of course,' agreed Hero; realizing with relief that even such a venal scoundrel as Emory Frost would not contemplate selling arms to the enemies of his most influential protector. But it was disquieting to learn that the Sultan's faction were arming themselves, and the sooner the money from Muscat was in safe hands the better. There was obviously not a moment to lose.

'Then if we are all of one mind,' said Thérèse Tissot, 'it only remains to devise some way by which we may convey them safely into the hands of Seyyid Bargash: which will not be easy, since the Sultan's spies watch the houses of all who support Bargash. They have even stopped and searched vegetable sellers and water carriers and slaves carrying washing, and it is certain that they will never permit chests full of treasure to pass in without question.'

'No, I guess not,' said Hero, pondering the matter. 'But we four should be able to take it into Beit-el-Tani – though not in chests of course. I don't suppose a gold bar can be very large, and we could wear our capes. No one would dare search us; or question our paying calls on the Princesses either. We could carry any number of coins in our reticules, and it should be possible to conceal the larger pieces of plate under our hoops.'

It seemed a workable solution, but Madame Tissot regretfully vetoed it. The chests, she explained, were secured against theft by locks upon which the Seyyid Thuwani had placed his personal seal, and if they had any hand in breaking those seals, and the treasure should later prove to be less than was anticipated, it would immediately be said that the white women had helped themselves to part of it and that it was now plain why they had troubled to interest themselves in the matter. This was a risk they could not take, since like Caesar's wife they must be above suspicion.

Hero cordially agreed, and substituted the suggestion that both Madame Tissot's and Mrs Platt's carriages should be pressed into service to transport the chests one by one, or if possible two at a time, to Beit-el-Tani, from where the Seyyida Cholé could be trusted to see that they came to her brother's hands. Olivia and Thérèse would have to go with them to lend colour to the fiction of a social call, and some arrangement would have to be made whereby they could drive into the courtyard at the back of the palace instead of going round to the front door. There *was* such a courtyard, added Hero, because she had seen it from one of the windows as they were being taken up to see the Seyyidas that morning, and though it was probably a private entrance and not normally used by visitors, the gate leading into it seemed amply wide enough to admit a carriage, and perhaps some story could be concocted to explain their making use of it:

'You could say, for instance, that you did not like being gaped at by crowds; which is a thing that all the local people are sure to understand. Do you think that could be arranged?'

Thérèse Tissot nodded her head and said generously: 'I make you my compliments, Mademoiselle. Certainly it shall be arranged. I myself will see the Seyyida Cholé and she shall give the order. And tonight when it is dark and all are asleep, the gold shall be brought here, yes?'

'Oh, yes indeed!' agreed Olivia, enthralled. 'And now all that we need is a good excuse for paying several visits to Beit-el-Tani during the next few days, before Hubert and Jane return.'

'Lessons!' said Thérèse with a little crow of laughter. 'We learn Court Persian. The Seyyidas have graciously offered to teach us, and so each morning we go to school.'

'That will do excellently,' approved Hero. 'Besides, it will give you the opportunity to confine your calls to the hottest part of the day, and there is something so very *unsuspicious* about the mid-morning. Quite different from the late evening or the night. I suppose the Beit-el-Tani servants are to be trusted?'

'If they could not be, the Seyyidas and their brother, and all who plot for them, would long ago have been betrayed. Of that you may be sure.'

'And your own?'

'They have been bribed,' said Thérèse with a twinkle. 'As we shall bribe Olivia's. It is the best way with these people. If one pays them well they will keep a shut mouth.'

'Then that's all right. Now, are there any other points that we have not yet covered?'

The meeting resolved itself into an animated discussion of minor problems, and any passers-by hearing the babble of feminine voices that proceeded from the drawing-room of the Platts' house might have been forgiven for supposing that nothing more innocuous than a ladies' tea-party was in progress. But the results of that morning's work were to prove far-reaching and anything but innocuous.

The first ripple was felt by Hero and Cressida, who on returning to the Consulate met with a reception that bid fair to rival, in the matter of temperature, the heat of the sun-baked streets outside. The Consul had been waiting for them for at least two hours, during which time his temper had risen to boiling point, and it now erupted in an impressive manner to castigate not only his daughter's too frequent visits to Beit-el-Tani and her friendship with Olivia Credwell and Thérèse Tissot, but the English as a whole, the entire French nation, and every member of the Arab and African races.

Cressy had speedily been reduced to tears, but Hero had remained admirably calm, and waiting until her irate uncle had run out of breath, said placatingly:

'Dear Uncle, I do beg you to forgive me if I am being dense, but won't you *please* tell me what all this is about? I am quite bewildered. And pray stop teasing poor Cressy. All we have done is to pay a short call on some charming Arab ladies, and a longer one on Mrs Credwell, who was kind enough to offer us refreshments. Speaking for myself, I found it all most interesting and have seldom spent a more enjoyable morning, and if we have kept you and Aunt Abby waiting for luncheon, I am truly sorry. But it's been so long since I have been able to enjoy a little feminine gossip that I guess I lost all count of time. You know what we girls are like, Uncle Nat. Once we get to talking . . .'

She paused artistically, thereby avoiding, in time-honoured feminine fashion, the lie direct, and Mr Hollis not only capitulated but offered a handsome apology to his weeping daughter.

'And you *will* let us continue to visit these charming little Princesses, won't you?' coaxed Hero, ruthlessly following up her advantage: 'You have no idea how interesting it is to make the acquaintance of women whose lives are so very different from our own, and I am sure it can do nothing but good for them to see that *all* women are not mere chattels. As for Madame Tissot and Mrs Credwell, I just know they'll be deeply hurt if

Cressy and I decline all further invitations from them, but if you really wish it, of course we shall do so. Won't we, Cressy?'

'No, no,' protested the Consul, hastily retreating from the whole position. 'It's just that I had thought maybe . . . Well, I guess I may have got it all wrong. Now, now Cressy, stop sniffling. I've said I'm sorry I bawled you out. I didn't understand the situation, that's all. I thought – well, never mind. We'll say no more about it.'

The incident, as far as Uncle Nat was concerned, was closed. And he was mercifully unaware that at his niece's suggestion Mrs Credwell, taking unfair advantage of her brother's absence, received that night under cover of darkness and conditions of enthralling secrecy, ten locked boxes, borne to the house on *homali* carts and stowed away in the room provided for her travelling trunks. Or that earlier that day Thérèse Tissot had paid another call at Beit-el-Tani.

The Seyyida Cholé had been unusually gracious and had warmly commended Hero's scheme. Nothing, said Cholé, could be simpler, for Miss Hollis had been correct in asserting that the public arrival of unveiled women to pay calls at Beit-el-Tani might be considered shocking. It had shocked many, and in future a more decorous arrangement should prevail. She would expect Madame Tissot and Mrs Credwell for a lesson in Court Persian each morning, and it was exceedingly fortunate that there should be a route to the back door of the palace that was capable of taking a carriage. Doubtless the All Wise had arranged that it should be so, since the vast majority of the city streets were far too narrow and tortuous to permit the passage of such clumsy vehicles.

Madame Tissot had been dismissed with suitable compliments, and when she had gone Cholé laid aside the embroidered half-mask that she had worn during the interview, and calling for water, washed her hands. After which she ordered all the windows to be opened to their widest extent, and sent down a message to the aged retainer whose duty it was to provide a guard on her gate.

It was a message that presently filtered through the bazaars and streets and alleyways of the city, and would have infuriated the Western Consulates and every member of the European community had it come to their ears. For it said, in effect, that since courtesy and good manners prevented the ladies of Beit-el-Tani from resisting the intrusions of certain foreign women who shamelessly persisted in calling almost daily at the palace, the foreigners would in future be received only at the slaves' entrance. Moreover, they would enter under cover of the servants' porch, which was to be strictly screened in protest against the immodesty of their behaviour and attire, and they had been requested to make their visits in a covered conveyance. Should they at any time attempt to enter by the front gateway, or in an open carriage, they were to be refused admittance and turned away.

Fortunately – or perhaps unfortunately? – Uncle Nat remained in ignorance of all this. And nothing more would have been said on the subject of the Seyyidas had not Clayton, returning from a day's shooting with his friend Mr Lynch, surprised them all by being even more annoyed than his step-father when he learned how Cressy and Hero had spent the morning; and saying as much in terms that rivalled the Consul's earlier words on the same subject. He had ended by strongly advising Hero to have nothing further to do with Madame Tissot or Beit-el-Tani, and when she had demanded to know why in a voice that was itself a danger signal, he had disarmed her by saying that it must always be the concern of any man in love to protect the object of his affections from anything that might cause her the smallest degree of unhappiness.

It had not really answered her question; but Hero had not noticed that. And since she was not at all anxious to discuss the subject, she had accepted it with a charming smile and changed the conversation: which had not satisfied Clayton, who for reasons of his own would have preferred to keep Hero and Madame Tissot apart.

He regretted not warning her against Thérèse before, but it was too late for that now. And though he had every intention of marrying Hero, they were not yet betrothed, and he knew that any attempt to press his authority at this stage would only lead to further quarrels and a worsening of their relationship. There was nothing to do but hope for the best, and that evening he had taken her for a stroll in the garden, and avoiding any controversial subjects, had advanced himself in her good graces by being pleasant and attentive and refraining from any attempt at love-making – though had she been almost any other woman he would not have hesitated, for in the soft purple twilight, with the breeze ruffling her short chestnut curls into an aureole about her head, she was looking more sweetly feminine than he had thought possible. But Clayton was no fool where women were concerned, and he was well aware that her mind was on other matters and that the moment was not propitious for a display of lover-like ardour.

He did not let this worry him unduly, for there was, after all plenty of time. And with a girl of Hero's temperament he knew that he would get there a deal faster by moving slowly. Once they were safely married, things would be very different.

15

Mr and Mrs Hubert Platt and their four-year-old twins had duly returned from Pemba, and Olivia, secure in the knowledge that her boxroom now contained nothing more than her own empty trunks and the normal complement of dust and spiders, had been able to assure them that she had not been dull during their absence.

The *Virago* had left harbour on the day following Hero's visit to The Dolphins' House and was still absent on her own ambiguous affairs, and the *Daffodil*, having been away on patrol duty off Kiloa, had put in again to rest and refuel. Letters had arrived from home, and a superb Arab gelding had arrived unexpectedly at the American Consulate – a gift from the ladies of Beit-el-Tani to the Consul's niece, who had been heard to express a desire to ride in the open country beyond the city.

'Oh, isn't he beautiful! Isn't he *splendid*!' gasped Hero, enraptured. 'But I can't possibly accept him.'

'I'm afraid you can't possibly refuse him,' returned the Consul glumly. 'It would be considered an insult. I guess I should have warned you that you can't go saying things like that to Arab potentates without their jumping in and making you a present of whatever it is they think you want. What's more, you ought by rights to give 'em something as good in return.'

It was difficult to think of a reply to this, for though Hero certainly recalled mentioning to Salmé that she enjoyed riding and hoped to acquire a horse of her own while in Zanzibar, she was well aware that this princely gift was in the nature of payment for services rendered. However, it was clearly impossible to explain that to Uncle Nat, so she assured him that she would think of some suitable gift to send in return, and dispatched a gracefully worded letter of thanks to the Seyyidas.

The horse, renamed Sherif (Prince) in oblique compliment to the Heir-Apparent, who had been indirectly responsible for its appearance, provided Hero with a far better mount than anything obtainable in her uncle's stables, since the Consul was an indifferent horseman, while Cressy's idea of equestrian exercise was a demure trot around the *maidan* or along some safe, sandy road. Aunt Abby did not ride at all, so it was Clayton who invariably accompanied Hero when she rode out past the acres of clove trees and through the long aisles of coconut plantations beyond the city.

She preferred to go in the early morning rather than in the cool of the evening, and they would often be joined by other riders: among them

Colonel Edwards, Jules Dubail and Lieutenant Larrimore, Joseph Lynch (who was a particular friend of Clay's and worked for a firm of spice exporters), Thérèse Tissot and the young German Wilhelm Ruete, half-a-dozen superbly mounted Arab Sheiks and landowners, and, on one occasion, the Heir-Apparent himself; Seyyid Bargash-bin-Saïd.

The Seyyid Bargash was, as Cressy had said, a handsome man; though his complexion was darker than that of many of the Arabs whom Hero had met, and in no way comparable to the ivory paleness of his lovely half-sister, Cholé. But he had a princely bearing and a manner that nicely blended dignity with graciousness, and in his rich robes and mounted upon a wicked looking black stallion he presented an impressive picture of Eastern pride and splendour.

He had asked to be introduced to Hero, and Clayton having performed this office, had addressed her in Arabic; complimenting her upon her supposed command of that language and her proficiency as a horse-woman:

'Some of my sisters,' added the Prince blandly, in English, 'have spoken to me of you. Since when I had hoped to have the honour of making your acquaintance, and to thank you for your gracious interest in their humble affairs. May I hope that you will visit us one day at *Marseilles*?'

'Marseilles? You are going to France?'

'Ah no, no, no!' protested Bargash, laughing. 'You mistake me. It is a country estate not far from here that my father named after some French city; perhaps in compliment to a Frenchman? But it belongs now to two of my sister Salmé's nieces. There is a park there where one may ride, and in the stables many horses. It would interest you, I think. I shall ask them to arrange a party and hope that you and your respected uncle and his family will honour it with your presence.'

He bowed and rode away without waiting for an answer, and Lieutenant Larrimore, who had been near enough to hear this exchange, said quietly: 'I wouldn't, you know. Not if I were you, Miss Hollis.'

Hero turned sharply and looked at him as though she had not understood what he had said, and the Lieutenant, qualifying it, said: 'Seyyid Bargash is a man you want to steer well clear of. I wouldn't trust him any further than I could see him – and even then I wouldn't be sure!'

'Indeed?' remarked Hero non-committally, and jerking her horse's head, rode off to rejoin Clayton: annoyed at being given unsolicited advice by a gentleman with whom she had only a slight acquaintance and did not count among her friends.

She was to receive more of it only two days later, and from an even less welcome source; and this time Clayton had not been with her to offer sympathy. He had remained behind to check some figures needed by his step-father, whom he was accompanying to an official audience with the Sultan later that morning, and Hero had ridden out at dawn with only a groom in attendance. She had confidently expected to come upon Mr Lynch or some other member of the European community before she had gone very far, and had indeed done so: though the gentleman she encountered a mile or so outside the city, riding towards her on a narrow track between thickets of wild coffee, was not one whom she at all desired to meet.

He was wearing Arab dress which was perhaps why she did not recognize him in time to avoid a meeting, and he pulled his horse sideways across the path, forcing her to stop, and said in tones of genuine astonishment: 'Good God – the mermaid!'

The overgrown bushes and the fact that the groom was riding close behind her prevented her from turning back, and forced by these circumstances, Hero said 'Good morning' in a frigid voice, accompanying the words with a slight inclination of the head that was less a greeting than a nod of dismissal.

Captain Frost failed to take the hint and continued to block her path, subjecting her the while to an amused and openly appreciative scrutiny that brought the blood to her cheeks and made her back stiffen with indignation.

'I didn't recognize you, now that your face has returned to normal,' observed the Captain with unpardonable candour. 'It's a great improvement. I'd no idea you were hiding so much admirable material behind a black eye and that impressive assortment of cuts and bruises. Perhaps it was just as well, for if I'd realized what a few weeks of care and cold compresses were going to reveal I might have been tempted to kidnap you after all. You're not a bad looking girl, Miss Hollis, and I begin to regret my lost opportunities.'

He bowed to her from the saddle, and Hero, still angrily conscious of her heightened colour, said with less dignity that she could have wished: 'I do not consider that a compliment, and if you would please move to one side I should like to continue my ride.'

'But it is a compliment,' insisted Captain Frost. 'I never trouble to——'

'Kidnap plain women!' flashed Hero, betrayed into retaliation: 'So you told me once before.'

Captain Frost flung back his head and roared with laughter.

'Did I? I'd forgotten. And you remembered that! Did it rankle so badly? I apologize. But I wasn't to know what I'd got my hands on, was I? You looked like a bedraggled street-urchin, and I thought at first you were about fifteen and barely out of pigtails and pinafores. It was really only when you called at my house that I realized you were a good deal older than I'd imagined. Old enough, in fact to know better. And what I was about to say, when you so brusquely interrupted me, was that I never trouble to tell polite lies. It's a waste of time. But there is something I have been wanting to say to you, so perhaps you will ride a short way with me.'

'No, I will not,' said Hero flatly; and was instantly ashamed of herself for resorting to a childish piece of rudeness. It was one of Captain Frost's more maddening attributes that he should be capable of goading her into losing her dignity and descending to bandying words with him, and she bit her lip and said in a more restrained voice: 'I'm sorry, but I do not happen to be going your way and I cannot see that we have anything further to say to each other. Good day, Captain Frost.'

'Yes it is, isn't it?' agreed Captain Frost affably, making no effort to allow her to pass. 'I regret having to spoil it for you, but although you may have nothing further to say to me I have a great deal to say to you. Would you prefer to dismount and listen to it, or shall we ride on?'

His tone was still affable, but there was a disquieting look in his eyes that did not match it, and Hero became suddenly aware, with an odd sense of shock, that he was angry: deeply and coldly angry. The knowledge brought with it a ridiculous feeling of panic, and she threw a quick, hunted glance over her shoulder, and was preparing to pull her horse's head round when the Captain leaned forward, and catching her reins said more or less the same words that Dan Larrimore had used only two days ago, but in a tone that neither Dan nor anyone else had ever used to her before:

'I wouldn't do that if I were you.'

Hero stared at him, wide-eyed: her cheeks no longer flushed but white with anger and alarm, and her breath coming short as though she had been running. Her fingers tightened convulsively on the ivory handle of her riding whip, but if she had contemplated using it in an unorthodox manner she thought better of it, for there was something in Rory Frost's grimly amused and unpleasantly comprehending gaze that dared her to do it, and convinced her that if she did he was perfectly capable of retaliating in kind. Her grip relaxed and her eyes wavered, and Captain Frost said dryly, and as though she had spoken aloud: 'Very sensible of you.'

He turned his horse, and a moment later they were riding side by side down the narrow track; the leaves brushing against them and the impassive groom following at a discreet distance behind.

It took Hero a full two minutes to master her breathing and gain some measure of control over herself, and when at last she felt capable of speech, she said: 'Well, Captain Frost? What is it you have to say to me? If you have changed your mind on the question of a reward for rescuing me, I will naturally see that it is paid. Provided, of course, that it is not an unreasonable sum. But you would have done better to have approached my uncle.'

'Possibly. I have no doubt he would be exceedingly interested in what I have to say; though it has nothing to do with money, and I should not have been put to the necessity of saying it had I not been absent from the Island during the last ten days and therefore unable to prevent you from a piece of criminal folly. I wonder, Miss Hollis, if you have any idea what you have been doing?'

'I don't understand you,' said Hero blankly.

'You should. I do not for one moment suppose that your uncle, who is a well-meaning little man, has the least idea how and why you came by that horse you are riding. But you must not think that others – myself for one – are equally credulous.'

Hero gasped, choked, and was overtaken by a violent fit of coughing. Recovering herself, she said breathlessly: 'I don't – I don't at all know what you are talking about.'

'Nonsense!' said Captain Frost impatiently. 'You can't play off those airs on me. You know perfectly well what I am talking about, and what I'd like to know is what possessed you to do it? No – don't say "Do what?" or I shall begin to think very poorly of your intelligence.'

'I wasn't going to,' began Hero. 'I——'

'Oh yes, you were. I could see it trembling on your tongue. But if you think you can fob me off with a display of bewildered innocence you are very much mistaken, because I happen to know only too well what you and your friends have been up to.'

'You can't know,' said Hero, startled. 'You're only guessing – you've … What have I been doing then?'

'Playing with gunpowder. And what is worse, with people's lives.'

'*You* can say that?' breathed Hero. 'You, who make money out of buying and selling wretched, helpless people who——' She found herself unable to continue.

Captain Frost laughed shortly and said: 'The Devil rebuking sin, you think? But you must own that I make a living out of it, whereas you have merely acquired a horse. Or did they perhaps pay you a "not unreasonable sum" in addition?'

Hero jerked her mount to a standstill, and taking refuge in sarcasm said scornfully: 'But surely you must know – since you know so much else about me?'

'You did it all for love, did you? Love of what, Miss Hollis? Mischief? Excitement? Meddling? Who were you busy impersonating? Joan of Arc, or Flora MacDonald?'

I won't answer him, thought Hero. *I won't*. But it seemed she could not help herself:

'You don't understand; it wasn't like that at all. You don't know anything about it. Anything at all.'

'Only that largely owing to you – it *was* your idea wasn't it? – a quantity of exceedingly dangerous material has been put into the hands of an ambitious man whose envy and overwhelming conceit make him capable of murdering any number of people in order to get what he wants. You probably thought yourself very clever and got a great deal of pleasurable excitement out of doing it; and I am willing to believe that you had no idea of the issues involved, or what a complicated death-trap of lies and double dealing you had allowed yourself to become entangled in. But I would advise you not to meddle any further with such dirty business. Leave it to those who know what they are doing.'

'Yourself, for instance!' blazed Hero.

'Certainly,' agreed Captain Frost. 'I assure you I am better at this sort of thing than you are, and a deal less likely to make dangerous mistakes.'

'What you really mean,' said Hero furiously, 'is that you have been bribed by the opposite faction, and though you are entirely willing to smuggle in articles that will assist one side, you cannot endure anyone doing the same thing for the other – for fear they might be making more money out of it than you are.'

'But I thought you implied that you had not made any money?' observed Captain Frost gently.

'You know perfectly well what I mean!'

'I do. And I trust you will know equally well what *I* mean when I tell you that this meddling in matters that are no concern of yours must stop.'

'And who is going to stop me, Captain Frost?' enquired Hero in an ominously level tone.

'Your uncle, for choice. I presume he has some authority over you. But should he not feel capable of stopping you I have no doubt Colonel Edwards would be prepared to deputize for him, since this is likely to be one occasion on which they will find themselves in complete agreement.'

Hero forced a light artificial laugh, and said scathingly: 'And do you really suppose that either of them would believe you? – even if they consented to receive you, which I doubt? You must consider me foolish indeed if you suppose that you can frighten me by threatening to take such absurd tales to my uncle or Colonel Edwards, both of whom know far too much about you.'

'And far too little about you, it would seem. You may be right: though I must hope you are not, because otherwise I can see that I will have to

183

deal with you myself. And that, my girl, is likely to lead to a lot of un-pleasantness.'

He studied Hero's compressed lips and flashing eyes with a certain grim amusement, and added pensively: 'You know, you may be a good-looking young woman, Miss Hollis, but you appear to me to be spoilt and a termagant; a combination I find excessively tedious. In fact I doubt if it would appeal to anyone – even Mr Mayo – and I would most earnestly suggest that you strive to conquer these defects before it is too late.'

'Indeed?' said Hero in a voice that sounded as though it had been dipped in acid: 'I'm sorry, sir, that I cannot offer you similar advice, but I fear that in your case it is already far too late. And now, if you have quite finished and are sure that you have no further suggestions to make as to how I may improve my conduct and character, I should like to continue my ride – *alone*! Goodbye, Captain Frost.'

She pulled on the off-side rein, and though she had never used a whip on Sherif before, she used it now, and the horse reared up and round, and raced back along the way they had come, almost oversetting the startled groom, and raising a white cloud of dust for the wind to blow away between the tangled thickets.

A comforting smell of hot coffee and new-baked bread permeated the Consulate, and Cressy, Aunt Abby and Clayton were already seated at the breakfast table. But although Hero's appetite was normally excellent – and never more so than after an early ride – this morning she found herself quite unable to eat.

She had ridden Sherif into a lather and she was hot, dusty and tired, but it was anger and not physical exhaustion that constricted her throat and made it difficult for her to swallow more than a mouthful or two of coffee.

A slave trader! A gun-runner and a self-confessed thief, taking that high-handed tone with her and presuming to lecture her as though she had been a naughty Sunday-school child caught stealing from the collection plate. How had he found out? Who had told him? Would he *really* betray her to Uncle Nat or carry tales to the British Consul? Surely he would not dare to do such a thing. They knew what he was and they would never listen to him. Or would they? If they did, if Uncle Nat were to question her, what was she going to say? Could she refuse to reply to the charge? Maybe that would be the best way out, since she could not possibly betray Thérèse and Cressy and Olivia – let alone the Seyyidas and their brother Bargash, who might all face imprisonment, or worse, if the Sultan came to hear of this.

Yes, that was what she would have to do. If that despicable Englishman came tattling to Uncle Nat she would keep silent, and allow it to be supposed that she considered it beneath her dignity to defend herself against a charge brought against her by such a corrupt and infamous person. (From which it will be seen that Miss Hollis, like many of her sex, held the view that in certain circumstances prevarication and *suggestio falsi* were admissible, but a direct lie was not.)

'What is worrying you, Hero?'

Clayton's voice interrupted her troubled thoughts and Hero started, and looking up found him regarding her with a frowning intentness that told her how plainly she had permitted her own discomposure to show in her face. She attempted a smile and said: 'Nothing, Clay,' but neither the smile nor the lightness of tone she had aimed at were a success, and the frown lines deepened on Clayton's forehead as he watched her:

'Are you sure? You are looking very tired. I wish you wouldn't go riding without me. I am not at all certain that it is safe, or that you will not go too far and overtire yourself in the sun.'

'Personally,' said Cressy, buttering a hot biscuit, 'it's not the sun I mind so much as the wind. I know it helps to keep the house cool, but I'm always thankful when it stops. It's the *noise* . . . all those palm trees rustling and the sound that it makes through the window-shutters and under the doors. And then the surf all day and every day, *crash, crash, crash*, and never any quiet, until I sometimes feel I'd like to scream. You know, Hero, you *do* look very pale. Is the wind getting on your nerves too? Or is it the heat?'

'Neither. But I am a little tired,' confessed Hero. 'I took a wrong turning on the way back, and my groom never said a word because he thought I wished to go that way.'

Clayton said nothing more, but he continued to watch her, and Hero was seized with a sudden and urgent desire to confide in him. It would be so comfortable to have someone to whom she could pour out the whole story and who would take her part and advise her, and tell her that she had been right.

But then would Clayton tell her that she had been right? It seemed far more likely that he would say '*I told you so,*' which would be insupportable. He had advised her against seeing too much of Thérèse Tissot and Bargash's loyal sisters, and he would think how right he had been to do so, and might even consider himself bound to disclose the whole affair to Uncle Nat. Men were never to be trusted in such matters, for they had some very tiresome ideas on the subject of Duty, and she could not risk it. But when it was all over – when Bargash had become Sultan and the Island was more prosperous and better governed, and freed from the disgrace of a shameful Treaty and the pernicious influence of a shameless slave trader – she would tell him everything, and he would be proud of the part she had played in bringing it about. Until then he must be kept in ignorance ... unless Captain Frost betrayed her. If that should happen——

Hero found herself back once more at the same starting point and facing the same arguments, and she pushed her coffee cup away from her with a sudden, violent gesture and rising abruptly, excused herself and left the room. But Clayton had moved with equal swiftness and she had barely reached the foot of the staircase when he came into the hall, and closing the door of the breakfast room behind him said: 'Hero, wait——'

Hero paused reluctantly on the bottom step, one hand on the newel post, and he crossed the hall in three strides and laying his hand over hers, said in a low voice: 'Something has disturbed you, hasn't it? Oh, you need not deny it. It was obvious from the moment you came in. Can't you tell me about it?'

'No, Clay. Not now, please.'

'Why not? You must know that I would wish to protect you from any anxieties. Or if that is not possible, at least to share them with you. It was something that occurred in the course of your ride, wasn't it? It must be, for you were in excellent spirits last night. Who did you meet, Hero? Who has been upsetting you? Was it Thérèse Tissot?'

'*Thérèse?*'

The surprise in her voice was as patent as the relief, and Clayton flushed, and withdrawing his hand said quickly: 'I only thought she might have said something to upset you. She has a reputation for making mischief for the mere love of it, and she enjoys setting people at odds. I know she finds Zanzibar intolerably dull, but it is unfortunate that her search for excitement should drive her to inventing and disseminating items of gossip that she knows will cause trouble.'

Hero said a trifle stiffly: 'That is a grave charge to bring, Clay. You cannot know that, and surely it is unjust to condemn anyone on mere hearsay?'

The flush deepened over Clayton's cheekbones, and he looked away, and said in a repressed voice: 'I would not wish to be uncharitable towards any woman, if only for your sake; and I admit that at one time I thought her much maligned and greatly to be pitied, for Henri Tissot is an elderly bore and she has no children to occupy and console her. I thought that it was our duty to try and make life more tolerable for her instead of criticizing her, but I soon came to see that I was wrong, and that all I had been told of her was true. That is why I did not want you to become too intimate with her.'

Hero removed her foot from the bottom step of the staircase and came to stand beside him. 'How did you come to see it, Clay? Did she tell you herself, or did you discover it from the same people who had maligned her to you before?'

Clay turned his head, and his grey eyes were pained and candid. He said: 'If you must know, she told me something that I knew to be entirely untrue and the purpose of which could only have been to ruin a man's career and a woman's happiness. That is all I can tell you. But perhaps you now understand why I wondered if you had met Madame Tissot when you returned looking so distraught. I thought that perhaps she had been talking scandal about – about Cressy.'

'Goodness no. Why, Thérèse is devoted to Cressy. And anyway it wasn't Thérèse whom I met.'

'Then you did meet someone. Someone who frightened you and upset you.'

'Yes – no! Clay, I would rather not discuss it if you do not mind. Not just yet.'

'Is it something to do with me? Is that why it cannot be told?'

'Now you are being absurd,' said Hero lightly. 'How could it be anything of the sort? It is just *because* it is nothing to do with you that I do not wish to burden you with it.'

'And if I tell you that it would not be a burden, but a privilege?'

'No, Clay. It is something I do not want to talk about at present, but when I do I promise that I will talk of it to you first. There, are you satisfied?'

'It seems I shall have to be,' said Clay wryly.

He took her hand and kissed it, and stood watching her as she went quickly up the stairs, the skirt of her habit trailing behind her and her footsteps making a sharp, hollow sound on the polished treads.

She vanished from his sight round the turn of the landing and he heard the door of her bedroom close behind her, but he did not move and he was still standing there staring thoughtfully into space when his mother and Cressy came out of the breakfast-room.

'What is the matter, Clay?' demanded Aunt Abby sharply, disturbed by the look on her son's face: 'Is anything wrong? Has Hero——?'

Clay's face lost its rigid look and he shrugged and said: 'I don't know, Mama. She will not tell me. Something or someone has upset her. And it is not the sun – or the wind either!'

'Perhaps when you become engaged to her . . .?' suggested his mother tentatively.

'That might come about a lot sooner if Cressy would not encourage her to go around with such persons as Thérèse Tissot,' said Clay with a trace of asperity.

'Oh, pooh!' retorted his sister. 'You're a fine one to talk when this time last year you used to take Thérèse riding almost every day.'

Clayton's mouth twitched in a way that his sister recognized as a danger signal, and he said coldly: 'It is precisely because I know Thérèse better than you do that I do not wish this friendship encouraged. But I fully realize that I have only to express my disapproval of someone for you to take the opposite view – as witness your flirtation with that British bumpkin off the gunboat, whose pretensions you have done your best to encourage.'

'I have not!' colour flamed in Cressy's pretty face: 'I won't have you saying so! And he has only called once since his ship returned a week ago, and then I had a headache and could not receive him.'

'That is true, you know, Clay,' intervened their mother anxiously. 'And when the Lieutenant asked if he might call again and take Cressy riding one morning, she sent down a message to say that she really could not tell when she would feel like riding again. He said that he quite understood, and she has seen nothing of him since because he has not called again; has he, Cressy dear?'

The angry colour faded from Cressy's face, leaving it looking white and woebegone, and she said in a small desolate voice: 'No. No he has not. I thought – I thought . . .'

Her voice wavered and broke, and turning quickly away she ran up the stairs to her cousin's room.

Hero's discarded habit lay on the ottoman and Hero herself, clad in a loose muslin *peignoir*, was standing by the window that looked down at the flower-filled spaces of the garden. She turned and said abruptly, without giving Cressy time to speak: 'Come in Cressy, and shut the door. What is your mother doing this morning? Do you know if she will be staying in?'

Cressy closed the door, and impressed by the urgency in Hero's voice, turned the key as an added precaution against interruption and said: 'I believe Mama intends to take morning coffee with Mrs Kealey. Why, Hero?'

'Because I must see Olivia at once. It should be Thérèse, for she has far more sense. But since both your father and Clay seem so set against her, it will have to be Olivia. And I particularly do not wish Clay to know. If he hears that I have asked to see her this morning he will only start being suspicious, and if Aunt Abby knows she will be sure to tell him.'

Cressy drew a deep breath and put her hands to her throat. 'Then he was right. He said something had happened. Hero, what is it?'

'Something most unpleasant,' said Hero with a shiver. 'But I cannot waste time telling you about it now. We must send a message to Olivia . . .

Ring that hand-bell for Fattûma, please Cressy. When does your mother mean to leave?'

'Not until half-past ten, I believe,' said Cressy, complying with the request.

'Excellent. That should give us plenty of time. And as your father and Clay have some business with the Sultan this morning, it should be quite easy for Olivia to slip over here for half an hour without them knowing. If they should find out they will only think that she called in to borrow a book, or ask for a receipt for that mango preserve or some such thing. Now where did I put my pen?'

Olivia Credwell had arrived at the Consulate an hour and a half later, but not alone: 'I was sure you would not mind,' she explained in a breathless aside to Hero, 'but Thérèse had called to enquire about some seedlings that Jane had promised her – runner beans, Thérèse's husband is very partial to them – and Jane was out, for she has taken the twins to play with the Lessing children, so I brought Thérèse with me. Is that all right?'

'It's providential,' said Hero. 'Provided that no one comes to hear of it. In fact I would prefer it not to be known that either of you came here today. Cressy, where can we be sure of being private?'

They had retired to the little boudoir that adjoined Cressy's bedroom, and having first made certain that there were no servants loitering within earshot, Hero closed the door and said briefly: 'I have to tell you that our secret is known.'

Olivia gave an audible gasp and Cressy turned pale, but Thérèse merely said composedly: 'What secret? That we wish Seyyid Bargash well? Or that we have assisted to deliver the treasure chests from Muscat into his hands?'

'Both. There must be a traitor in Beit-el-Tani. That is why I sent for Olivia. Someone must go there at once and warn the Seyyida Cholé that one of her household is a spy.'

It had seemed vitally important to Hero that her fellow conspirators should learn at once that their activities had been discovered. But Thérèse evidently saw nothing to be alarmed at, remarking that the only thing that would surprise her would be the discovery that there was only one spy at Beit-el-Tani and not twenty, since it was well known that Arabs revelled in intrigue: it was meat and drink to them, and in the present circumstances they would all be spying one upon the other – being paid by both sides and betraying both sides.

'Do you mean you *expected* this?' demanded Hero incredulously. 'You *knew* we would be found out?'

'It was always possible. With such people, what is not? But now that the affair is safely concluded we have nothing to worry about: least of all the gossip of informers who can prove nothing against us. From whom did you learn that all was known? It cannot have been from Monsieur your uncle!'

'From Papa?' squeaked Cressy. 'Oh, Hero!'

'No, of course it wasn't' said Hero hurriedly. 'It was someone I met when I was out riding this morning. I would prefer not to give his name, but he said that he knew all about it – and he did. Everything. At least . . .'

She hesitated, and Thérèse said: 'Do not tell me that you admitted it?'

'Not in so many words. I tried pretending that I didn't know what he was talking about, but it wasn't the least use, for he told me he knew everything and said he supposed I thought myself very clever and – oh, it doesn't matter what he said or what I said or didn't say. The point is that he knew. And he couldn't have known unless someone in Beit-el-Tani has been talking, so I thought you should be warned and that someone should warn those women. But it seems that I need not have worried.'

'Not *worried*?' exclaimed Olivia horrified. 'How could you possibly do anything else?'

'I agree,' said Thérèse. 'How indeed?'

'But you have just said——' began Hero indignantly.

Thérèse held up an imperative hand. 'That was because I supposed that this informer was your waiting woman or perhaps a groom from the stables. But from what you tell us, that is not so; which makes it a matter more serious. It becomes necessary, I think, that you should tell us who is this man?'

'*Not*——' said Olivia in a fading voice, 'oh, not my brother? If Hubert has discovered to what use I put the boxroom during his absence, I should sink with shame! Hero, say it is not Hubert!'

'*Dan!*' gasped Cressy, turning even paler.

'No, it was not,' snapped Hero, goaded. 'It wasn't either of them, and I can't see that it matters so much who it was. The only important thing is that somebody knows.'

'There, *ma chère*, you are wrong,' said Thérèse with decision. 'The important thing is *who* knows. Until we know this we cannot take precautions.'

'What precautions?'

'There are many. *Par exemple*, one can say a little word here or there to inspire a doubt as to this person's veracity or his motives. Or——'

Hero heard her with a sinking heart and a sudden regret that she had not held her tongue about the events of that morning's ride. She was remembering, too late, what Clay had said about Thérèse Tissot's fondness for gossip and trouble-making, and realizing that she did not relish the prospect of either Thérèse or Olivia discovering just how well she was acquainted with the Captain of the *Virago* – or the true story of her arrival in Zanzibar. She took a deep breath, and choosing her words carefully, said:

'If you must know, my informant was a person by the name of Frost.'

'*Rory Frost!* You joke with us, I think.'

'I cannot imagine why you should think so,' retorted Hero a trifle sharply, 'for I assure you I do not regard it as a joking matter.'

'But it is. It is ridiculous! You say it is Captain Rory who discloses to you that all is known? But for what reason? Why should he do this?'

'He threatened me!' said Hero, remembered outrage throbbing in her voice. 'He was impertinent and offensive, and he accused me of meddling in affairs that I did not understand and said that I should leave them to those who did. By which he seems to have meant himself.'

'But of course! Oh that Rory——! You must forgive that I laugh.' Thérèse dabbed at her eyes with a scented scrap of lace and cambric, and after a moment or two controlled her mirth sufficiently to say: 'Did you not know that he is on the side of Sultan Majid? He is Majid's man, and he would dislike very much to learn that while his back is turned we have stolen a march upon him and advanced the cause of Bargash. We need not trouble ourselves over *Monsieur le Capitaine* Rory, and as for who has informed him of this, it is well known that he has many curious friends who repeat to him the talk of the bazaars and the scandals of the palaces – and even what is whispered in the women's quarters. It cannot be helped, and we need not regard it.'

'Oh, thank heavens!' said Olivia. 'Oh, the relief!'

Hero could have endorsed that sentiment with equal fervour, but for a different reason. No one, in the excitement of the moment, had thought to ask about her meeting with Rory Frost. And that, coupled with Thérèse's airy dismissal of him as a possible danger, was for the moment relief enough. It was only after the two women had left that it occurred to her to wonder why Thérèse had been so immoderately amused. She herself could see nothing to laugh at. Nothing at all! And yet Thérèse had laughed . . .

The trivial question nagged at her with irritating persistence for the rest of that hot morning, until Clay and Uncle Nat returned from the Palace and she forgot it.

The night wind, blowing strongly off the land, carried the daytime stench of refuse and sewage out to sea, and only a faint fragrance of cloves and orange blossom reached the roof of the City Palace where Majid-bin-Saïd, Sultan of Zanzibar, took his ease with a friend; comfortably bestowed on a pile of Persian carpets and silk-covered cushions, and eating sweet-meats from a silver dish. Above them the wide sweep of the sky glittered with stars as bright and as numerous as the houris of Paradise, while from below, muted by distance, came the sound of palm fronds rustling in the wind, the crash and croon of the surf and all the many night noises of an Eastern city.

Majid-bin-Saïd removed his turban for greater comfort, and propping himself up on one elbow watched a falling star draw a finger of fire across the blue, and when it had vanished said with a sigh:

'You tell me nothing new. Do you think I do not know? – I who felt the wind of the shot sing through my very hair not once, but again and yet again as my dear brother Bargash fired on me with his own hand from his own window? Of course I know! It is nothing new in my family. It runs in the blood.'

'Maybe. But it is your Highness's blood that will soon be running if you do not put a stop to this plotting and play-acting before it turns into something a deal more dangerous.'

Majid shrugged his shoulders and selecting another sugared date from the contents of the silver dish, said: 'To hear you talk one would suppose that attempted assassination is not dangerous.'

Rory gave a curt laugh. 'Considering he missed you at a range of about thirty yards, I cannot regard that particular attempt as serious. For one thing, the whole business was too slapdash and on the spur of the moment. I imagine he was in the throes of a particularly virulent attack of jealousy and spleen when you happened to come sailing past his window, and it probably looked to him like the chance of a lifetime . . . he's got a pistol or two handy, so he grabs one and starts blazing away, but being in a towering rage, misses with every shot. If he'd planned it beforehand he'd have hired an expert marksman instead of trying to murder you himself – in which case you and I would not be discussing the incident now, because you would have joined your illustrious ancestors and I should be just as far away from your successor's dominions as I could get. But, Allah be praised, he is a damned bad shot!'

'It was getting dark, you must remember,' murmured the Sultan apologetically, excusing his brother's indifferent marksmanship.

'Next time it may not be.'

'Are you so sure that that there will be a next time?'

'As sure as you are.'

The Sultan ate a piece of almond *halwa*, taking his time over it, and having wiped his fingers on a gold-fringed napkin, said hopefully: 'Perhaps he will miss again; for as you say, he is a poor shot. Even as a boy he was a poor shot. How angry he would get when he missed! It annoyed him very much, because he could never bear not to be first in everything. Now I myself have never minded about that. Or not so much.'

Rory said severely: 'Majid, you are digressing. What your half-brother did or did not do in the past is immaterial. It is what he is doing at present that is becoming a deal too dangerous.'

'No more dangerous than before.'

'That is where you are wrong, my friend. I regret to tell you that your brother has acquired the means to launch a full-scale rebellion against you. And though I do not think it is likely to prove over-much use to him, the fact that he has his hands on such stuff may well go to his head and give him the idea that he is now strong enough to let the shooting begin. So it is high time you bestirred yourself and did something about it. Is it not written, *"If there be two Caliphs, kill one"*?'

'You suggest then that I kill him? But, my friend, there is nothing I would like better. Only how can I do so while he enjoys the protection of these foreigners? After he tries to kill me I refuse to see or speak to him, and what happens? A large foreign ship – a ship of thirty guns – sails into my harbour, and a foreign Consul and a foreign naval Commandant call upon me and force me to receive him. You see how it is? My hands are tied by the inability of these tiresome Europeans to mind their own business or to understand that the best and quickest way of settling such matters is with a knife: or if one must, with poison, though that is a woman's weapon.'

'A bullet would be better,' said Rory grimly. 'And no more than he's asked for. However, I see your point. It would raise the devil of a fuss if he were to be murdered at this juncture, and even that old ram-rod Edwards might find it difficult to make out a case for you.'

'You think so?' enquired the Sultan in surprise. 'But why should the good Colonel find difficulty over such a thing? He is no friend of Bargash's.'

'No. But he's a stickler for order and the Letter of the Law. That is why he stands by you and will recognize no other claimant – because your father, on whom be the Peace, nominated you as his heir. But he wouldn't stand for you murdering yours.'

'Perhaps not. He is a thorn in my flesh, the Colonel. He behaves towards me as though he were a teacher or a nurse and I a foolish child who must be lectured and scolded for its own good. He has no sympathy for my position in regard to slaves, and every day he comes with complaints against this man or that who, so he says, has been buying or selling or keeping slaves. Is it my fault that my father's treaty with the English left a gap wide enough for any trader to sail his dhow through? Or that it allowed the free moving of slaves within my dominions, and did not prohibit either their entrance or their embarkation from this Island? Naturally such a situation puts temptation in the way of men who wish to trade in slaves, for though the risks (as you well know) are many, the rewards are great. And my friends and my family tell me that they would be greater still if only the British Consul could be brought to a more peaceful and accommodating frame of mind. He should calm himself by acquiring a wife and breeding many sons.'

'An occupation,' observed Rory dryly, 'that has resulted in anything but calm in your Highness's family.'

The Sultan acknowledged the hit with an appreciative chuckle. 'Ah yes! But that, my dear friend, is part of our Arab character.'

He shook his head in gentle regret and popped another sweetmeat into his mouth: 'We require a son, and if only daughters are born we make prayers and go on pilgrimages, and give money to the maulvies and the soothsayers And if Allah is good a son is born and all is rejoicing. But one son is not sufficient, since he may die young. So another is sired, and another. And always there is great rejoicing, for the mother of a son is a proud woman and the father of many sons has much honour. Yes, all is felicity until the boys become men and the eldest covets his father's place and cannot wait for him to die: and when he gets it his brothers, and the mothers of those brothers plot and scheme to take it from him in their turn. It has happened in this manner for a thousand years – you have only to read the history of the Seyyids of Muscat and Oman to see that this is true. And so it will continue – for just as long as there is any place in all the world that is free of white men behaving in the manner of this Colonel Edwards!'

Rory gave a crack of laughter and said: 'Then your countrymen had better make the most of it, for that isn't going to be long. I fear this is merely a beginning, and that you are in for an era of Western interference and busy-bodying that is going to make anything you've seen yet look like a visit from a favourite uncle.'

'It discourages me that you should think so,' sighed the Sultan. 'Why is it that the white races find it necessary to act towards us in this manner? To covet more land, and to make war and win victories to that end, is a thing I can well understand. But that other, no. For myself, I do not expect them to accept my ideas as to what is right or just or expedient, and neither do I wish to force my own way of life upon them or think that they should admire it – or me. I see clearly that many of our ways would not suit them, for their blood is thin and cold and their thoughts are different. Does one expect a crow to sing sweetly in the moonlight, or a nightingale to eat carrion, just because both are birds and can fly and hatch their young from eggs? Yet saving only yourself, I have never yet met a white man who did not consider that I and my people would derive great benefit by changing our ways and imitating theirs, or who did not try and impress upon me the immense superiority of all white laws and customs. It is very strange.'

'It's not strange at all,' retorted Rory. 'Don't tell me that good Moslems have never attempted to convert Infidels and Unbelievers to the True Faith – and by force as often as not – any time these last six hundred years? It's the same thing.'

'But my friend,' said the Sultan reprovingly, 'that is a matter of *religion.*'

'Ah, but then all white races – Europeans, Russians, Americans, the lot – make a religion of their own particular way of living and thinking, and are as bigoted and pig-headed about it as the most fanatical maulvie who ever preached the Faith. In that sense they are all missionaries, for it is their unalterable opinion that they have discovered the best and only possible road to Progress and the Millennium, and that it is their plain duty to herd all men along it – and to force those who will not tread it willingly with a pistol and a club if necessary, since after all, "it is for their own good".'

'But it would do me no good if I accept these foreign ideas,' protested the Sultan plaintively. 'I lose money and power and peace of mind by it. And their ideas are as different as their gods. Monsieur Dubail says one thing and Colonel Edwards another. Mr Hollis does not agree with either and Herr Ruete will not speak with Joseph Lynch, or Mr Platt with Karl Lessing. It is the same with their priests and their parsons and their missionaries, for some worship Bibi Miriam with chanting and the burning of candles and incense, preaching that all who will not do likewise are eternally damned, while others will permit none of these things and assert that all who do will burn. And between the two are many who balance like jugglers on a tightrope. Yet all, while execrating the others, call themselves Christians – and all, my friend, profess themselves shocked at our ways. Why, I ask you, should we of the East forsake the laws and customs of our forefathers at the bidding of ignorant and contentious foreigners whose own governments and priests cannot agree among themselves? Tell me that?'

'Because,' said Rory unkindly, 'you are not going to be given the option. Not in the long run. You can't argue with a gunboat if all you have is a canoe and a throwing spear – no aspersions on your fleet, you understand, I was speaking metaphorically. There is a certain tiresome and time-honoured argument that has been in use since the dawn of history and can be best summed up by that elegant sentence: "If you don't, I'll kick your teeth in." That, my friend, is what you are up against!'

The Sultan wagged his head and said sadly: 'There are times when I fear you may be right.'

'I wish I only feared it instead of being sure of it,' said Rory with regret. 'This is only the morning of the White Man's Day, Majid. The sun hasn't reached its zenith yet, and it won't sink until every Western nation in turn has done its best to foist its own particular Message onto the older civilizations of the East. And by that time, the lesson will have been learned too well and there will be nowhere left in all the world where a man can escape from Progress and do what he damn' well pleases – or find room to breathe in!'

The thought of it seemed to suffocate him and he came suddenly to his feet, and swinging round to face the low parapet, looked out at the vast sweep of the ocean and the immensity of the far horizon, and threw his arms wide as though to fill his lungs with the free wind that blew off Africa.

He stood there for a full minute, his long body dark against the night sky and his blond head silver in the starlight: then his arms dropped, and he turned back and said with low-voiced violence: 'Pray God I do not live to see it!'

'Or I,' said the Sultan devoutly.

He peered up at the tall figure of his friend, and reaching out a hand that was as soft and plump as a woman's, tugged imperatively at the hem of the gold-embroidered *jubbah*. 'Do not tower over me like a hawk. It is an unrestful attitude and it makes me feel tired. I have had a trying day, and now all I wish to do is to sit quietly and enjoy the night air and some pleasant conversation. Sit down.'

Rory laughed and complied: 'But you needn't think you are going to get round me by telling me what a tiring day you have had. I haven't had a very restful one myself, and I did not come here tonight to make idle conversation.'

'I know, I know. You came here to tell me that my brother Bargash is plotting against me, which I already know. Well, you have warned me and I thank you. Now let us talk of something else. I hear that the English Lieutenant catches Pedro Fernandez with a full load of slaves, and that he takes off all who still live and all the sails as well, so that the ship runs aground three days later in a storm, and Fernandez, who cannot swim, is drowned. Which is an excellent thing, since such men are no better than animals. Why trouble to ship three hundred negroes where only a third of that number can hope to survive, and land those who live in such poor condition that they fetch the lowest prices? It is madness! And poor business, too.'

'It is crass stupidity; which is even worse. But we are not discussing the late Fernandez and his ilk. We are, or were, discussing Bargash. Why are you so anxious to avoid the subject?'

'Because if we continue to talk of him you will only end by making me do something about him. And that I do not wish to do. I am not like you. Or like him. In you it is your white blood that makes you wish to stand on your feet and stride to and fro while I wish to sit. And though my brother and I are equally Arab on our father's side, his mother was an Abyssinian, and it is her dark blood that drives him like a whip. But mine was a Circassian woman, and as placid as a beautiful cow who sits among flowers and chews the cud; which is perhaps why I too prefer to sit – and not be worried to do things.'

'That is just your bad luck,' said Rory inflexibly. 'Because I am sailing again on the dawn tide tomorrow, and as I may be away for a couple of weeks you are going to be worried to do things here and now.'

'I knew it!' sighed the Sultan with a rueful shake of the head. 'Let us leave it until you come back. Then, I promise you——'

'It may be too late by then,' interrupted Rory brusquely. 'No, Majid, it must be now. Now, at once!'

'Very well then, I shall do something. But not tonight. It is impossible to do anything tonight. It is too late – you must see that. Perhaps tomorrow I will think about it. Yes, certainly I will think about it tomorrow.'

'And decide to do nothing until next week, when you will decide to put off deciding until next month – or next year. But it is time that you realized that your brother is not being idle. He's been collecting adherents and bribing your own ministers and officials, and plotting a rising that will clear you off the throne and land you in Paradise a good deal sooner than you bargained for. He's seduced the chiefs of the el Harth tribe and young Aziz and three of your sisters into supporting him, and they've got the whole thing planned. Bargash's house is to be their headquarters, and while your brother has been stocking up firearms, your sisters have been baking scores of flour-cakes that have been handed over by night and stored against a siege. I know you've been watching him in a half-hearted manner and having his servants stopped and searched and some sort of check kept on his visitors, but you've never kept any watch on your sisters or their nieces, and they've been allowed to go where they please and do what they like. And what they like is plotting to depose you!'

The Sultan stirred unhappily among his silken cushions, picking at the gold tassels and frowning, and presently he said: 'So I have heard. My wife and my other sisters and many of my aunts and cousins at Motoni tell me that Cholé has joined Bargash in plotting against me ... Salmé and Méjé too. They keep urging me to punish them, and say that they should be fined, imprisoned, banished, flogged – even strangled! It is strange how vindictive women can be towards each other. Especially towards those with whom they have quarrelled! But I cannot believe ...'

'That what they say is true? I assure you it is.'

'True, yes. But I cannot believe that they mean me any real harm. They are young; and since my father's death, life has not been the same for them. They have sorrowed and been dull, and longed for the old days when we all lived out at Motoni and rode races and sailed our boats and were happy in my father's shadow. And because those times are gone and even God cannot give them back, they are restless and unhappy, and so they pick quarrels with the other women, and with me, and cast about for something with which to fill the long days. Bargash has given them this, and he is a snake that should be scotched (yes, that I know as well as you! – better perhaps, for I have not heard that he has tried to kill you yet!), but with my sisters it is different. How can I be hot against them and visit punishments upon them? Or be angry with little Aziz, who is no more than a child and thinks his brother Bargash a hero? It is better to do nothing and hope that in time they will see how foolish they are being, and it will all die away.'

Rory said brutally: 'The only thing that seems likely to die, and that in a painful manner and in the immediate future, is yourself. And if you are not interested in saving your own skin, I must tell you that I am more than interested in saving mine. Bargash is no friend to me, and if you are going to permit him to raise a revolt against you and become Sultan in your place, then the sooner I cut my losses and quit these waters the better. Just how long do you suppose I'd last here once you were dead?'

The Sultan turned on his elbow and regarded his friend with a sly smile: 'Long enough, perhaps, for you and your crew to fire the town and loot half Zanzibar, and get away before order had been restored?'

'It's a thought,' agreed Rory with a grin.

The Sultan lay back on his cushions and laughed aloud, and wiping away the tears of mirth, said: 'Ah, my friend, what a pity that you were not born an Arab! Had you been, I swear I would have made you Sultan in my place and left you to deal with those twin snakes, my brothers Thuwani and Bargash, knowing that you would do so with complete success.'

'The East India Company,' observed Rory, 'would seem to have dealt with your brother Thuwani with a moderate degree of success, and without any help from me. But no one but yourself is going to be able to stop Bargash, and you'll have to do it at once for there's no time to waste. Even tomorrow may be too late.'

'What do you suggest I do?'

'Send a guard to arrest him.'

'Now? At this hour? My dear friend, be reasonable! It is too late—— It is——'

'If you arrest him by day there'll be a riot. He'll see to that! But in an hour or so the city will be quiet and the beggars and bazaar loafers and all the riff-raff from the African Town will be deep asleep, so that there'll be precious few people about to watch the fun and start any trouble. Besides, I happen to know that he'll have several of the chiefs visiting his house tonight to settle up a few last details and probably collect their share of bribes, and it won't do them any harm to have to explain what they're doing there. Put him in irons and send him off to the Fort in Mombasa under a strong guard, and when the city wakes up tomorrow morning it will be too late for anyone to do much about it. There may be a few isolated demonstrations and an official protest or two, but they'll be easy enough to deal with, for the chiefs of the el Harth, who are his main supporters, are only in it for what they can get, and once they see you mean business and intend to put a stop to their nonsense, they and the other malcontents will come to heel soon enough. Will you do it?'

'I might imprison him in his own house. Yes, that is what I could do. I could send armed guards to surround it and allow no one and nothing to go in or out, not even food, until such time as he has come to his senses. That would serve, too, as a good lesson to my sisters, who would see it and be warned. We Arabs have a saying, "*All the sea is not deep enough to wash away blood relationship*" and they are women – or girls, if you will – of my blood. Of my father's blood. I would not be harsh with them.'

Rory remarked caustically that it was a pity that his brother had not heard of that proverb; or if he had, he evidently considered that murder could do what the sea could not: 'As for your bloodthirsty little blood-relations, blockading their brother is not going to worry them over-much. Particularly as they must know he is well provided with food.'

'With food, perhaps. But water will not be so easy. There is no well in that house, and water evaporates very quickly in this weather. I do not think it would take very long to bring him and the guests in his household to a more reasonable frame of mind. And there is another thing. This store of arms that you tell me he has been collecting; they will be in his house and he would not be able to get them out and distribute them among his followers. Nor would he be so foolish as to fire on my guards once he saw that his house was surrounded, so when he makes his submission we shall have the arms.'

'That's all you know! Don't do it, Majid. Send your men in to take him by surprise and ship him out of the island. Have him locked up in Fort Jesus, or somewhere else on the mainland. Can't you see that as long as he is here on this island you'll have no peace? Have you ever seen a rifle?'

'No, but I have heard of them,' said Majid, relieved at this abrupt and unexpected change of topic: 'They are some new kind of muskets that can kill at five hundred paces, are they not? You shall get me some. They will be most useful when we shoot deer.'

'To fire them,' continued Rory inexorably, using an index finger to emphasize each point in the manner of a schoolmaster lecturing a class, 'one fits a small brass cap over a nozzle, and when the trigger is pulled a hammer descends upon that brass cap, striking it and exploding the fulminate of mercury with which it is filled. The spark from that explosion travels down the nozzle and ignites in turn the charge of powder that expels the shot. It's quite simple – always provided one has the small brass cap! Bargash is like that cap: or, if you prefer it, like the fulminate of mercury. Without him the shot cannot be fired and the weapon is useless. Get rid of him, Majid. If you value your life, send him out of Zanzibar at once. Tonight!'

The Sultan sat silent for a time, and presently he rose and began to pace agitatedly to and fro across the flat white rooftop that still held the heat of the tropic sun.

Below him the heaving harbour water reflected the riding lights of ships and the warm gleam and glitter of the Palace windows, while to the left the city was a spangle of lights and still noisy with voices, music and laughter that would soon give place to silence and sleep. But here, high above the sea and the city, the night already seemed quiet and very still, and the tranquil sky and bright, incurious stars no more than a roof that a tall man might reach up and touch with his hand.

Majid paused in his pacing to look up at it, and wished fervently that people would leave him alone. It was not, he thought resentfully, as though he had ever expected or wanted to become Sultan of Zanzibar, and if it had not been for the death of Khalid there would have been no question of it and he would have been left to live his life in peace. But now that he was Sultan an obstinate streak in him, together with a love of money and ease and the good things of life, made him resolve to retain that position.

Not that there had been much ease so far, and precious little money; for between the exorbitant tribute that, by treaty, must be paid to the senior Seyyid, Thuwani of Muscat and Oman, and the necessity of paying heavy bribes to the raiding pirates from the Persian Gulf who periodically descended upon Zanzibar, and had to be paid to leave again, the Exchequer was in a parlous state and he often wondered where he was to turn next for the mere expenses of everyday life. And now Bargash must plot a new rebellion, and lure from their allegiance no less than three of those little sisters with whom he had played so happily in the days when they had all been children together . . .

He found himself thinking of those days with a passion of longing that equalled Salmé's. The games among the flowering shrubs and fruit trees of his father's favourite palace of Beit-el-Motoni: the laughing, shrieking children who had chased the tame antelope and teased the peacocks, and pelted each other with petals. The riding lessons which, when the boys had learned to master their horses, had aways ended with races – the winner receiving a handful of sweetmeats and uproarious applause . . . Was that where the rivalry had begun, and the bitterness crept slyly in like an insect eating away the heart of a rose, unseen and unsuspected until the day when the flower, full blown, unfolds to disclose the ugly ruin within?

It had taken that vicious fusillade of shots to teach him that Bargash meant to be rid of him and would be content with nothing less than his death, and now he could no longer shut his eyes to it and he would have to do something. To do what he had always hated and would always hate doing: make up his mind, and act.

The lights of the city went out one by one until there were only a few scattered spangles of gold to break the starlit darkness, and except for the surf and the dry, interminable rustle of the palms the night was quiet at last. Along the far horizon a wash of pale light heralded the rising of the moon, and presently, as it lifted out of the sea, the silence was broken by the mournful howling of pariah dogs serenading it from the dark lanes of the city and the slums of the African Town across the creek.

Majid turned from the parapet, his shadow lying black before him on the white level of the roof, and Rory said softly: 'Well?'

'I see that you are right,' said Majid heavily. 'I will send for Nasur Ali and the Commander of my guard.'

'Good,' said Rory, and came to his feet in a single swift movement that suggested the release of a coiled spring. 'And your sisters? Whatever you say, you'll have to do something about them too.'

'No. I will not war with women.'

'Now listen, Majid——'

'No, no, *no*! I will not listen. Bargash, yes – for if he could kill me he would, and it is for that end that he buys muskets and arms his followers. But I too have such things and if necessary I will meet him with them, so for the present I will see that he is arrested, because while he is free I shall clearly have no peace. But I will not punish my sisters, who had it not been for his lies and his wiles would never have turned against me.'

Rory said deliberately: 'And if I tell you that it is those same dear sisters who have already armed Bargash's followers with the weapons you hope to find in his house? What then?'

'I do not believe it.'

'You should. Half the loafers in the bazaar could have told you as much; and if your Chief of Police is not well aware of it, I'm a Dutchman. The only reason they don't tell you these things is that they know you'd prefer not to hear them – and would probably refuse to believe them if you did! Well you can believe it this time, because I'm telling you and it wouldn't pay me to lie.'

Majid wrung his hands in a gesture that was oddly feminine, and his weak, pleasant face was contorted with pain and bewilderment. 'You must be mistaken. You cannot be right, for there is no way in which they could have done such a thing. How could they distribute arms from Beit-el-Tani when they receive no men there other than their brothers? It is not possible. Some evilly-disposed person has been deceiving you.'

Rory said quietly: 'It is you who are deceiving yourself, Majid. The arms were not distributed from Beit-el-Tani. Your sisters and an assortment of their female relatives, accompanied by a large retinue of waiting-women and slaves, have recently made several visits to a certain mosque in the city.'

'This I know. They go to pray for a loved cousin who suffers from a painful sickness that neither the *hakims* nor the English doctor seem able to cure.'

'Do they, indeed! A very convenient sickness. Almost as convenient as the convention that well-born women should only venture abroad after dark and muffled from head to foot in cloaks and head-veils. It was probably an equally simple matter to have the mosque closed to the public for half an hour or so.'

'I do not understand you.'

'It's quite simple. Your relatives have not only been petitioning Allah on behalf of the sick cousin, but they have also been leaving offerings.'

'That too is usual,' said the Sultan stiffly.

'Offerings in the form of firearms? For that is what they have taken to the mosque – for the maulvie to collect and subsequently distribute to the adherents of your brother the Heir-Apparent. It must have been dead easy – what a paradise this is for plotters! Twenty or thirty women bundled up in cloaks and escorted by twice as many slaves, and every last one of them toting a firearm under that mound of material. If you search the mosque now, or your brother's house or Beit-el-Tani, you won't find the smell of a firearm or anyone who will admit to ever having seen such a thing. But that was the way it was done.'

'You have no evidence!'

'None,' agreed Rory equably.

The Sultan made a small baffled gesture and turned away again to stare out at the sea and the sleeping city, and Rory held his peace: aware of the uselessness of further argument and afraid of over-playing his hand and arousing that stubborn streak that was so unexpectedly a part of Majid's amiable, vacillating and entirely unstable character. The silver sweetmeat dish had been overset, spilling its contents across the dark richness of a Persian carpet, and he knelt down and began to pick them up, stacking them into a neat, sticky pyramid, and wondering what he was doing here.

It was a familiar thought and one that was apt to occur to him at odd moments, and always unexpectedly. *What am I doing here? . . .* What is there in me, or tied to me, that should have brought me here to sit in the moonlight on a rooftop in Zanzibar? How much of it is due to my own actions and how much to blind chance? Or is it true, as the Followers of the Prophet believe, that 'what is written, is written' and therefore cannot be avoided?

That last, in Rory's opinion, was neither a comforting nor an acceptable theory, since he would far rather shoulder responsibility for his own actions than ascribe them to the workings of an inscrutable providence that decreed them in advance – and by doing so denied him free will or the blame or credit for behaving ill or well. Those curiously disquieting and damnably recurrent questions 'What am I doing here, and how and why did I get there?' were preferable to accepting his deeds as unavoidable steps in some pre-arranged plan. And yet his long association with Arabs and the East had left its mark on him, for there were times when he found himself tempted to drift with the tide and let events take whatever course they wished, in the comforting assurance that there was nothing that he or anyone else could do that would alter the destined end.

'What is written is written' ...

Perhaps it had been written that he should be absent from Zanzibar during the ten days that might yet prove to be crucial to Majid – and to himself. He should have been more careful. But then one could not legislate for everything, and he had had no way of knowing that the 'best laid plans of mice and men' were about to go a'gley again ... though not, he trusted, in too irrevocable a fashion!

It was a nuisance, of course. A damned nuisance. But not necessarily a disaster. Not unless Majid refused to take drastic action against his brother while he had the chance. It was a thousand pities that he himself could not stay and see this thing through, but he had business elsewhere that could not wait, and the *Virago* must sail at dawn even though this seemed no time to leave the Island. If only Majid——

Rory flicked the pyramid of sweets in a sudden spasm of impatience that sent them flying, and stood up. He did not speak, but his shadow moved on the stonework and Majid saw it, and turned.

The moonlight was bright on his face, and recognizing the expression on it Rory experienced a sharp renewal of impatience and a suffocating and entirely unfamiliar feeling of helplessness. He would have been the first to admit that his desire to prevent Majid from plunging to disaster sprang primarily from self-interest, for it was largely owing to the Sultan's friendship and protection that he had been able to evade the law and behave more or less as he pleased in these latitudes. But apart from that (and the fact he would get no such favours from Bargash), he had acquired a liking for this irresolute, easy-going man who had obtained a throne by default and now looked like losing it by treachery.

Rory might be scornful of Majid's un-Arab-like refusal to deal with his once loved and now actively disloyal sisters as they deserved, but he could recognize and even envy the strength of the family tie that was responsible for it, though family affection in any form was something he himself had never known. There was another factor, too, that bound him to Majid: his respect for the dead Seyyid Saïd, who had nominated this son to succeed him.

Once, during his early years in the Island, Rory had unwittingly done Majid's father a service when a philandering friend of the Sultan's, visiting Zanzibar, incurred the wrath of a local chieftain who clamoured for his head (the offence having involved the virtue, or loss of it? of a flighty daughter, both parties were understandably reticent as to details). The Sultan had been unable to produce the offender because Rory – who had been handsomely paid for it – had already smuggled the man on board the *Virago* and returned him safely to his native land, without anyone being the wiser. The incident had been a trivial one, but the

Sultan, learning later how the escape had been effected and grateful for having been spared the embarrassment of handing a personal friend to the headsman, had been gracious to Emory Frost and presented him, in token of gratitude, with the lease of a house, to be held by him and his heirs for the term of one hundred and fifty years.

No one who had ever met the Lion of Oman had failed to be impressed by him, and Emory Frost had proved no exception. For Saïd's sake, if for nothing else, he would do what he could to save Saïd's son from the death that must inevitably follow on the heels of a successful rebellion. But looking at that son's face in the moonlight, he knew that it was going to be difficult to help a man who would not help himself.

Majid said: 'With regard to Bargash, I will do as you suggest. He becomes too brazen and must be shown his place. As to my sisters, it will be punishment enough for them to see that my displeasure has fallen upon the brother they have supported, and whom their plotting has helped to bring to this pass. Summon my servants and I will do what I must do. You are right – deeds of this sort should be done by night. The day is too glad a time. Good night, my friend. May you sleep better than I shall!'

It was a dismissal, and Rory bowed; touching his forehead and breast, Arab fashion, in a gesture of submission that held no mockery. Turning he went away softly down the steep flight of stone stairs that led down from the roof, to send the drowsy attendants up to their Sultan and let himself out into the street.

A shadow detached itself from among the shadows beyond the Palace gates and fell into step beside him, and another and taller one followed a few paces behind.

'Well?' said Batty Potter.

Rory shrugged his shoulders by way of answer and did not speak.

'Like that, is it?' said Batty sympathetically. 'Ah well, if 'e won't act rough it's 'is own funeral.'

'And ours,' said Rory briefly.

'More'n likely. What's 'is fat-'eaded 'Ighness going to do? Nothing, as per usual?'

'He's sending a guard to arrest his brother tonight.'

'You don't say!' Batty's tone was startled. 'That's better 'earing.'

Rory shrugged again and said morosely: 'I might agree with you if I could be sure he wouldn't think better of it in a week or so and let him go free again. If he'd any sense he'd—— Ah, what's the use!' He glanced over his shoulder and added irritably: 'What are you two doing around here, anyway?'

Batty's cough held a shade of embarrassment. 'Oh – er – me and Ralub we just thought we'd better 'ang around and see that you got 'ome safe. Too many of Mister-perishin'-Bargash's pals in town for comfort. You didn't ought to go roamin' around on your own so much. It ain't 'ealthy, what with all these narsty tempers risin', and speakin' for meself I'm 'appy to think that we'll all be sailing out of 'ere tomorrow.'

'It's more than I am. I'm not at all sure that it's safe to leave just now.'

'Lot safer than gettin' a knife between your ribs,' commented Batty sagely.

'Don't be such an old Job's comforter, Uncle. Seriously, though, it might be a good idea to postpone sailing for a day or two.'

'What? And leave young Danny-me-lad 'anging round 'ere to put a spoke in Suliman's wheel? You must be losin' your mind, Captain Rory! Didn't you promise Suliman faithful that you'd draw the *Daffodil* off so that 'e could get 'is little bit of business safe over? 'E'll be caught for sure if you don't, and you know 'e can't wait. If you let's 'im down, no one round these parts is ever going to trust you again. And if 'e's caught we're finished – the 'ole lot of us. 'Sides, we 'ave to meet Sheik Hamed and 'is friends next week, and if we don't show up 'e'll be that insulted that your name'll be mud with 'im from now till kingdom-come.'

'I know, I know!' said Rory angrily. 'But——'

'And what about them 'orses?' persisted Batty. ''Ave you forgot we was shippin' 'arf-a-dozen of 'em back for Sheik Hussein, and for a nice price too?'

'No, I have not. But you know ruddy well that the horses are only a cover, in case . . .'

'A solid gold one, at that price,' snarled Batty. 'And if we don't fetch 'em on time we'll only 'ave that slippery scoundrel Yacoub sellin' them to someone else, for it's my belief they're all stole an' that's why 'e's so blamed anxious to get 'em off 'is 'ands quick.'

'I wouldn't be surprised,' agreed Rory. 'Oh well – to hell with it! I suppose we'll have to go. Besides, it's time we got Danny out of here for his own good. He's beginning to look all peaked and wan and I don't think his love affair can be prospering. A nice healthy week or so at sea may help him forget the wench and put the roses back into his cheeks.'

Batty threw him a frowning side-long glance and said dourly: 'If I were you, Captain Rory, I wouldn't be too light-'earted about that there young squirt. 'E's a sight smarter than 'e looks, and if you gets to thinking otherwise you'll find you're mistook – and you won't like it. You're gettin' too careless, that's what. All this gallivanting about alone at night, too! *Tch!*'

Rory's bad temper left him, and he laughed and said: 'You ought to be ashamed of yourself, Uncle; playing nursemaid at your age.'

'There's times,' retorted Batty austerely, 'when I'm danged if I don't think you need one! You ought to 'ave told us where you was going tonight. 'Owever, if you've talked that soft-'earted ijjut into locking up 'is barsted of a brother, I'll forgive you this once. Not that I'll believe it till I sees it.'

He ruminated gloomily, and presently voiced a pessimistic opinion that was to prove all too prophetic:

'Bound to make a muck of it some'ow,' said Batty. 'Go off at 'arf cock, like as not, and do the job by 'arves. 'E didn't ought to be Sultan and that's the truth. No more gumption than a chicken, poor lad. *Tch! Tch!*'

The night wind blew the words away, while back in the Sultan's palace the Sultan prepared to prove the truth of them by following Batty's prediction and 'doing the job by halves'.

17

The dawn was yellow over Zanzibar and the crows were already cawing above the rooftops when a frightened waiting-woman burst in upon the ladies of Beit-el-Tani, bringing the news that the Sultan had placed the Seyyid Bargash under house arrest, and that 'All was betrayed!' A dramatic announcement that had the effect of reducing Salmé to tears and sending her niece Farschu, who had been spending the night there, into strong hysterics.

The majority of the household instantly followed this example and began to rend the air with lamentations and shrill keening, until brought abruptly to order by Cholé, who drove them out of the sleeping apartments and bade them hold their tongues if they did not wish to be soundly flogged:

'Where are your wits?' demanded Cholé angrily. 'Is this a time for screams and wailing? Must we shout from the house-tops so that every one of Majid's lackeys may know what this means to us? Be quiet, Farschu! They can have nothing against us as yet, but if they hear you screeching and those silly women howling like apes they will need no further proof to carry to Majid!'

Farschu however continued to shriek and drum her heels on the carpet, and it was Salmé who said through her tears: 'But if Bargash has been betrayed, then we must have been betrayed with him. How can you say that they have nothing against us?'

'Because if they had they would have arrested us also. But there is no guard on our gates and we are free to come and go. You can see for yourself. Farschu, if you don't stop that noise I shall slap you. Salmé, give me that water jar!'

Cholé snatched the heavy blue and white pottery jar, and with an effortless movement of her slender arms splashed the entire contents over the screaming girl and handed it back to her sister. The ear-splitting shrieks stopped abruptly, and Farschu spluttered and gasped and lay still among the strewn cushions, breathing hard and exhaustedly, while Cholé clapped her hands to recall the slaves.

'We must behave as though nothing of great importance had occurred,' decreed Cholé. 'We are distressed at the news; that is only natural. But we know nothing of any plots, and if they wish they may search the house, where they will find nothing. Get up, Farschu; and do not let us have any more tears: they will not help Bargash, but thinking and planning may, so we will think and plan – and be calm.'

Her own calmness and good sense had overawed them, and there had been no more outbreaks of noisy despair. Outwardly at least the routine of the morning had continued as though this day was no different to any other. Baths had been filled with fresh spring water, and garments that had been strewn with jasmine and orange blossom during the night were fumigated with amber and musk and laid ready for their owners to put on.

Salmé had never thought the long ritual of the toilet to be irksome or boring, but today for the first time it seemed endless, and she found that she had to force herself to sit still and submit to the ministrations of her serving-women as they dressed and scented her, combed, oiled and braided her hair, and proffered a selection of jewels for her to choose which she would wear that day. Her mind was a turmoil of panic and apprehension, and it would have been a relief to be able to throw herself face downwards on the floor as Farschu had done, and give way to hysterics. But Cholé would only deal with her as she had dealt with Farschu, and of course Cholé was right. Cholé was always right. They must show a calm face to their enemies, and plan what they could do to save Bargash from the wrath of his brother.

Her toilet finished at last, she dismissed her women and ran to the windows overlooking the narrow lane that divided Beit-el-Tani from the house where Bargash lived with his sister Méjé and his little brother, Abd-il-Aziz. The lane itself was empty, but at either end it was blocked by a crowd of armed men whose muskets showed like an impassable hedge of thorns, and Salmé, leaning out a little way in order to get a clearer view, was suddenly aware that in the adjoining room her half-sister too was standing at her window; her veil drawn across her face so that only her eyes showed wide and black-lashed and intent.

Cholé was not looking down at the empty lane or the armed men, but staring straight ahead of her at the cane-screened windows of her brother's house. There was courage and alertness and a certain steely quality in the tilt of her head and every line of her slender body, and following the direction of that intent gaze, Salmé saw a flicker of movement from behind the split-cane screen. In the next instant a corner of it lifted cautiously and she found herself looking across the narrow gulf of the lane at her brother's face.

It was immediately evident that Bargash had already been discussing something with Cholé, for he shook his head as though in reply to some question she had asked, and Salmé saw her sister smile. The jutting window-sills and half-closed shutters concealed them from anyone standing below, and they spoke softly but clearly, using the Court Persian that would have been unintelligible to the chattering soldiers had any been able to hear it at that range:

'— no, of course I'm not going. He must be mad if he imagined for one moment that I would. When his messengers arrived with an order that I was to sail for Oman at once, before first light, I pretended to agree: I said I'd be willing to leave immediately, only the trouble was that I just couldn't afford to live there because I hadn't enough money. And do you know what that fool did? He sent me ten thousand crowns to help "ease my exile"!' Salmé heard her brother brother splutter with laughter and Cholé say, 'Did you take it?'

'What do you think? *I'm* not a fool! It was a bribe, of course – to persuade me to go quietly. I gave it to Nasur to lock away, and then I told them that I'd changed my mind and decided not to go after all, and we rushed at them and pushed them all out and barricaded ourselves inside, and wouldn't let anyone in again. That's why Majid has posted guards all round the house. He thinks he can starve us out. Well, let him try! I'm not afraid of that boneless puppy! And nor is anyone else – except Méjé, who thinks we should run to beg his pardon and ask him to forgive us.'

'I'm not surprised,' said Cholé acidly. 'She's never stopped warning and whining, and now she's got a chance to say "I told you so!" and urge us all to throw ourselves on Majid's mercy. Are you going to take her advice?'

'*Never!*' The reply came with a sudden, low-voiced violence that made the listening Salmé flinch. 'If Méjé wants to go crawling to Majid she can. I shall do nothing to stop her. But if she goes it will be to plead for herself, not me!'

Poor Méjé, thought Salmé, trembling with a similar and sympathetic fear; how often had she begged them to be careful and warned them how this feud might end? For Méjé too loved Bargash above all her brothers, and it was her fear for him that had driven her to oppose this venture. *We shall have to give in,* thought Salmé, crouched shivering in the embrasure of the window. *There is nothing else we can do, and Majid is generous . . . it was generous of him to offer Bargash the chance to escape, and send him money to help him live in Oman. Perhaps he will be generous again, and forgive us . . .*

Bargash's voice, loud with anger, broke in upon her troubled thoughts as though in answer. 'The rest of you can do as you like. But I myself will never surrender. Our plans are too far advanced and we are too strong. Nothing and no one will make me abandon them now: I mean to go through with it – and I shall win. You will see me Sultan of Zanzibar yet!'

A rush of admiration for this splendid, indomitable brother warmed Salmé, and some of her fear fell away from her. No wonder so many people were ready to follow him and to defy Majid for his sake. He was born to lead and to rule, and perhaps this was only a temporary set-back after all and he would rise above it. She ceased to crouch against the side of the window and straightened up, holding herself as proudly erect as Cholé, and Bargash turned his head, and seeing her, called a greeting:

'Are you for me, little sister? Or do you, like Méjé, think that we should surrender all our hopes and sue for mercy?'

There was a ring of recklessness and excitement in his voice, and as he spoke the sun topped the horizon and shone full on his face, and Salmé saw that his cheeks were flushed and his eyes as glittering and bright as though he had a fever. The contagion of that fever leapt across the narrow gulf that gaped between them and fired her to a like excitement, and she forgot her fears and her sympathy for Méjé, and all at once her cheeks were as hot and her eyes as bright as her brother's, and she laughed and waved her hands and cried: 'Never! *Never!* We will fight them all!'

Bargash laughed back at her, and if there was a quality in his mirth that an older and more experienced person would have recognized as hysteria, Salmé certainly did not notice it. She heard Cholé from the adjacent window call out something that she did not quite catch, and saw Bargash smile and nod. And then the split-cane curtain fell back into place and he was gone.

The news had taken a little longer to travel the scant quarter of a mile that separated the American Consulate from Beit-el-Tani and the Heir-Apparent's house, and it was past eight o'clock when the Consul said casually at the breakfast table, in the manner of one who merely notes the rumour of yet another change of Government in some Balkan State:

'Seems the Sultan's gotten tired of his brother's shenanigans at last. And not before it was time. I'm told he sent a guard last night to surround Bargash's house.'

Cressy, who had been helping herself to buttered eggs, dropped the spoon with a clatter that splashed yellow debris across the tablecloth and down the front of her pink muslin dress, and Hero said sharply: '*Arrested?* Do you mean that he has been thrown into prison?'

'Not quite that,' said her uncle, placidly eating a papaya. 'Though I'm not saying it wouldn't have been a better idea if they'd clapped him into the Fort and been done with it. A few months in a cell might cool him off some and give the rest of us a mite more peace and quiet around here. I'm free to confess that I don't like the look of all those el Harth tribesmen who've been swarming over from the mainland to support him. They're nothing but a wild, trigger-happy bunch who'd think nothing of shooting their old grandmothers if they reckoned there was any money in it. It's a pity something wasn't done about stopping them coming ashore in the first place. The sugar, please Cressy——'

Hero said urgently: 'But what about the Prince, Uncle Nat? What did you mean by "Not quite"? Is he in prison or isn't he?'

'Hard to say. Depends on how long they intend to keep him there; if they can do it at all! He's under house arrest.'

'Oh, thank goodness!' said Cressy in explosive relief. 'What a fright you gave me, Pa. I thought you meant he was in a *dungeon* or something.'

Hero directed a warning look at her young cousin and Clay said: 'Blazes, Cressy, what's there to get so excited about? What's it got to do with you, anyway?'

Cressy caught Hero's eye, blushed hotly and replied in some confusion that she wasn't excited, and that if Clay had the least sensibility he would realize that anyone would be sorry to hear that anyone else had been put into a dungeon, even if anyone——

Hero hurriedly cut through this tangle of explanation by addressing herself in a firm voice to her uncle and enquiring if he meant that Prince Bargash was in fact a prisoner in his own house?

'That's about the size of it,' agreed Uncle Nat. 'There are armed guards all round it and the orders are that no one is to be allowed in or out until further notice. It's created quite a stir in the town. Though I'll bet it's nothing to the stir it created inside that house when brother Bargash woke up in the small hours and found that he'd been out-manoeuvred for once! I reckon he must have been hopping mad. That was a good papaya, Mrs Hollis. One of ours?'

'No dear, from the fruit market I think. Cressy honey, do eat your breakfast before it gets cold.'

Cressy ignored the request and said anxiously. 'But Pa, *why*? I mean, why has the Sultan acted like this? Didn't he give any reason?'

'Half-a-dozen, I expect – you'll allow he's had plenty to choose from. But it's no use asking me. All I know is what Abdul told me when I came downstairs this morning, and as every servant in the house seems to have the same story I guess it's true. More coffee, please, dear.'

The subject appeared to be closed, and when Cressy attempted to re-open it she was frowned down by Hero, who began to talk animatedly of a projected barbecue, and kept the conversation there until breakfast was safely over and Uncle Nat and Clay had retired to the office. But no sooner had Aunt Abby departed to discuss menus with the cook than her daughter burst into agitated speech:

'How *could* you sit there talking calmly of barbecues, Hero? Can't you see how terrible this is? It means . . . why it may mean that the Sultan has

found out about everything! Cholé and Salmé and the gold bars and——
Oh, what are we going to do?'

'Keep our heads,' said Hero crisply. 'Really, Cressy, I could shake
you! You are as bad as Olivia; wringing your hands and betraying the
greatest alarm over any little set-back. Even if you cannot feel calm you
should at least try to preserve an appearance of composure unless you
wish to ruin everything.'

'You know I do not wish to do any such thing,' quavered poor Cressy.
'But I am not calm and collected like you, and I cannot sit around planning parties when – when everything we had hoped for is endangered,
and the poor Prince is under arrest and someone may have betrayed us
all . . . you and I and Olivia and Thérèse too, and the treasure chests may
have been found and——'

A sudden thought struck her and her hands flew to her mouth: 'Hero!
Do you suppose *that* was who it was? Do you suppose he told the Sultan?'

'Who are you talking about?' demanded Hero, perplexed.

'Captain Frost. You said that he knew——'

Rory Frost! . . . yes, Captain Frost knew, and he had said – what was
it he had said? . . . *'otherwise I can see that I may have to deal with you
myself, and that, Miss Hollis, is likely to lead to a lot of unpleasantness.'* Was
this what he had meant? Was this his way of dealing with her and this
the 'unpleasantness' he had threatened? All at once she was certain of
it. She had got in his way by assisting to put the gold from Muscat into
the hands of those it was intended for, and now he was getting his own
back.

'Yes,' said Hero slowly. 'That must be who it was. That – that despicable slaver. Well I'm certainly not going to be defeated by him, so he
need not imagine he has won. He hasn't and he won't; I promise you
that. You just leave it all to me – and to Thérèse.'

'And to Cholé,' said Cressy on a small sigh; adding with unexpected
acumen: 'Cholé is like you and Thérèse: strong, and not afraid of things.
I wish I was like that, but I'm not. Do you think we should call at
Beit-el-Tani this morning, just – just to see what has happened?'

'No, I don't,' said Hero, considering the matter. 'It would look too
pointed and we don't know yet if Cholé and the other girls are under
arrest too. It wouldn't do at all to arrive there and be turned back by a lot
of soldiers. We must wait and see what Thérèse has to say. I feel sure she
will hear all the news and lose no time over getting in touch with us, or seeing that Olivia does.'

Hero had not misjudged Madame Tissot. The morning was barely
half spent when a cautiously worded missive from Olivia Credwell was

delivered at the Consulate, begging the two Miss Hollises to take pity on her boredom and drink tea with her on the following day. She regretted that it could not be this afternoon, but circumstances made it inadvisable that they should meet any earlier, and she was sure they would understand and be discreet. Jane and Hubert, added Olivia, in a postscript black with underlining, would not be in, since they were engaged to go sailing with the Kealeys: 'So we shall be a party of *four*, and *quite private*!'

They had, in point of fact, been a party of eight. And they had not taken tea at the Platts' bungalow, but had been offered sherbet, Turkish coffee and little cakes in a house a mile outside the city and hidden behind a high wall and a garden full of fruit trees, to which they had been driven over execrable roads in Thérèse Tissot's carriage.

The house was owned by one of the late Sultan Saïd's numerous relatives by marriage; an obese old lady who found it impossible to move without the assistance of two strapping negro slave-girls to haul her to her feet or lower her on to a cushioned divan. But the three shrouded figures who rose to greet the foreign ladies turned out to be the Seyyida Salmé, her niece Farschu, and an unidentified and elderly cousin who appeared to be acting as chaperone and lady's maid.

'Cholé could not come, so she sent me instead,' explained Salmé when the greetings, questions and expressions of sympathy were over, the refreshments brought and the slaves dismissed. 'She said that you would wish to have news of us.'

Salmé did not consider it necessary to explain that what Cholé had actually said was: 'You had better tell those silly women that we at Beit-el-Tani are safe, and that they must say nothing of the chests, but keep silent and not lose their heads and talk to their menfolk. Two of them have heads as empty as dry gourds, but the American woman who looks like a boy has intelligence of a sort, and the French woman is as cunning as a mongoose. Tell them everything and see if we can make use of them.'

'We others,' continued Salmé, 'have not been molested, and no one has attempted to prevent anyone from leaving or entering our houses. Though of course we could not be seen going out at this time of day, so Cholé made us borrow some of the servants' clothes as a disguise, and go out unattended by the slaves' door so that we should not be recognized or followed. It is only Bargash's house that is besieged, and the soldiers will allow no one to go in or out of it.'

'But you have spoken to him, no?' said Thérèse, not as if she were putting a question but as though anything else was unthinkable.

'Yes,' said Salmé eagerly. 'Through the windows. They cannot prevent us from doing that, and I do not think they know. It is quite safe, and our brother has been able to send messages by us to the chiefs who are supporting him. He is determined not to make submission to Majid, for he says that there is such a large stock of food in the house that he can hold out for weeks, and that Majid will soon get tired of keeping a great many soldiers occupied all day and all night standing about doing nothing. Of course it is a pity that Méjé and her women are there, for several of the chiefs were trapped in the house when it was surrounded and they cannot move about freely because of her, but must keep to one room on the ground floor, which cannot be comfortable for them. But fortunately the most influential one did not go to the house that night, and we are keeping him in touch with Bargash and giving him money and jewels so that he can buy more support for us.'

Thérèse said curtly: 'That will be of little use if the house that was the headquarters of the movement is surrounded by the Sultan's guards. They will have to find another meeting place; a safer one.'

'We too have thought of that,' replied Salmé with a faint touch of hauteur that recalled her half-sister. 'The estate that is called *Marseilles*, which belongs to Farschu here, and her sisters, is now to be our new headquarters. Bargash has directed that all our followers shall collect there, and that it shall be well stocked with food and fuel and water and anything else we may need. The house is already like a fortress and he thinks it could easily hold several hundred men. And be held, if need be, against a thousand.'

Thérèse made no immediate comment and for a minute or two the others were silent, watching her. Then she gave a small brisk nod and said: '*Bon!* It will do very well. In fact much, much better, and had we arranged this arrest ourselves we could not have improved upon it, since the old plan was always dangerous. Your brother's house was too public a meeting place – I have said so a thousand times. *Marseilles* is far better. And now that the Sultan has placed guards around your brother's house, he and his army and his police will think themselves safe and occupy themselves only with watching it, like a cat who sits before the wrong mousehole. But while they do so you will have to work fast. Your brother Bargash is right to remain where he is and not to come out and surrender himself, for it will give you time to complete all the arrangements. Tell him that the longer he stays there and keeps the Sultan and his ministers occupied with watching him, the more those who are not watched can accomplish. And when all is prepared we shall think of some way to obtain his release. He has food in plenty, you say?'

'Enough for many days,' confirmed Salmé. 'But there is little water, and it will not last.'

'No *water*?' gasped Olivia. 'You mean they have no well? But that is terrible! What can they have been *thinking* of to overlook such a precaution? And in this weather too.'

'They did not overlook it,' retorted Salmé, irritated. 'But they had not expected Majid to strike in this manner, and because of the heat they are already finding that such water as they kept is fit only for cooking and washing, and not for drinking. We do not know what to do about that, and if we cannot find a way to send water to them they will be forced to surrender – and very soon.'

'Oh *no*!' cried Olivia and Cressy in distracted chorus.

'Of course we shall find a way,' said Hero bracingly. 'If you can speak to your brother it must mean that the windows of your houses are near enough for you to be able to pass something across on a rope or a stick. Could you not tie bottles of water on to poles and pass them across?'

Salmé shook her head. 'There are a great many people in my brother's house. Not only he and his friends and advisers, but the chiefs who had been to see them that night, and their attendants too, and little Abd-el-Aziz and his tutor and Méjé and her women, and many, many servants and slaves. How could we send enough water for all these people in bottles tied to sticks? It could only be done after dark, or we should be seen; and it would soon be stopped. We could not give even half of them enough water in the time.'

'But it would be better than *nothing*,' urged Olivia hopefully. 'You could use buckets, and—— No, I suppose that would be too difficult. They'd be too heavy to tie to sticks, and they'd tip over and splash and the soldiers would hear. And worse on ropes, because——'

Hero said: 'Be quiet, Olivia: I want to think.'

The women watched her in silence, as they had watched Thérèse, and presently she said decisively: 'Yes, I guess that will do. It won't be too difficult and it should work. Let me explain . . .'

She did so in some detail, and Salmé and her niece and the elderly cousin listened, nodded and agreed while their hostess wheezed and clucked and chuckled among her cushions like a stout brown hen.

They had left shortly afterwards; the four foreign women in Madame Tissot's carriage, and Salmé and her companions on foot. And on the following night, in the dark hour before moonrise, a silk thread tied to a small lead weight had been tossed across the street from Cholé's window to one a storey below in the opposite house, where it had been caught and wound in by Bargash.

The thread had been fastened to a string which had in turn been attached to a wide, flexible tube of waxed canvas – the manufacturing of which had occupied the greater part of the day and caused some sorely pricked fingers. The whole operation had been performed in commendable silence, and the chattering soldiers whose backs were clearly visible in the lamplight at the far end of the lane, never turned their heads. Not even when the canvas bulged and sagged under the weight of water poured down it by more than two dozen excited women who formed a chain and passed heavy earthenware jars from hand to hand, emptying and refilling them for the space of an hour.

By the time the moon rose and peered into the black gully between the houses, the canvas tube was safely back in Beit-el-Tani, and the Heir-Apparent's household provided with sufficient fresh water to last them through another day. And should any inquisitive person have thought to walk down the barricaded lane, they would have found nothing more suspicious than a few damp patches caused by falling drops, which heat and the night wind obliterated long before morning.

With the urgent matter of supplying the besieged household with water solved, it was possible to press on with the plans for the raising and the collecting of supplies at *Marseilles*, and the women of Beit-el-Tani worked as they had never worked before; kneading and baking until they were exhausted, making hard flour-cakes that were packed into wicker baskets and conveyed by night to *Marseilles* to be stored there to feed the soldiers, freed slaves and volunteers who were being rallied to the Heir-Apparent's cause. Cholé drove them on to greater and greater efforts, and Salmé, who could write, was pressed into service as a secretary and spent her days in corresponding with the chiefs; passing on Bargash's commands, ordering the collection and dispersal of arms and ammunition, and urging the importance of secrecy and speed.

Thérèse Tissot's predictions had proved remarkably accurate. Majid and his ministers and officials had all been far too taken up with surrounding the Heir-Apparent's house (and congratulating themselves on having thus checkmated the malcontents and brought the entire conspiracy to ruin) to trouble themselves over-much with what might be going on in other parts of the Island. They kept a desultory eye on Beit-el-Tani, but paid no attention to the comings and goings of the numerous servants who were employed there, and though surprised that Bargash and his household should be able to hold out for so long without water, confidently expected his surrender at any moment – it being obvious that any store of water laid in before the siege must by now be running very low.

Everything, in fact, appeared to be going according to plan, and Majid was inclined to be grateful for Rory Frost's absence. Rory, he felt, would have nagged at him to take further and more stringent action. But the present situation, though it might with more justice be likened to a stale-mate rather than checkmate, was perfectly satisfactory in that it would not only teach his brother, but his disloyal sisters and their friends as well, the uselessness of rebellion against the properly constituted authority of their Sultan. In addition to which, when thirst at last forced Bargash to sue for mercy, he would emerge a sadder and wiser man and no longer an object of admiration to his followers, since the whole city would be a witness to his humble surrender and the humiliating collapse of his hopes. There would be no glamour attached to it, as there might well have been had he been sent into exile or imprisoned somewhere on the mainland. Moreover, he, Majid, would demand that ten thousand crowns back!

The Sultan congratulated himself on his astute handling of a difficult situation, and turned his attention to an equally long-standing and now urgently pressing problem: the chronic shortage of funds in the Treasury; now further depleted by that bribe to Bargash.

Occupying a throne, mused Majid-bin-Saïd, was not half as pleasant as envious people imagined it to be. And for perhaps the hundredth time since he had ascended this one, he wondered if he would not have been a great deal happier and a lot more comfortable as a private individual.

He would have had no doubts at all about that had he been aware that even as he sat musing on the injustice of life and the emptiness of his Treasury, his brother's supporters had sent word from *Marseilles* that all was at last in readiness for a rising that would, if successful, deprive him of that throne and relegate him to the cold privacy of a grave.

The letter had been brought to the upper room at Beit-el-Tani, cunningly concealed in an orange, and Salmé had read it and turned pale with excitement: 'It is done, Cholé! They are ready! They say they will march on the city as soon as we send word, and while one half of the force surrounds the Palace and takes Majid captive, the other will release Bargash and proclaim him Sultan. Let us send them word to march at once!'

'*No!*' said Cholé violently. '*No!*'

The blood had left her face and she looked pale and drawn, but her emotion, unlike Salmé's, was apprehension and not excitement.

'But Cholé——?' Salme dropped the crumpled sheet of paper and stared aghast. 'Why? What is the matter? We have prayed for this moment.'

'I know. I know! But Bargash must be at their head. We cannot let this begin without him – we must not!'

Cholé struck her slender palms together in a sudden passion of anxiety, and said wildly and as though the words had been wrenched from her: 'I do not trust them! If he were not there to lead them, they might well put one of the chiefs in his place. Who can tell what ambition and opportunity may suggest to a man? And if they march on the city while our brother is still held captive, Majid may give the order for his death in the hope that hearing they have lost their leader they may also lose heart and turn back. We cannot risk it. We must free Bargash first. They will have to wait. Send them word that they must wait!'

There was no excitement in Salmé's face now. Only horror as she too perceived the pitfall at their feet. Who indeed could tell what ambition might not do to men? Look what it had done to Bargash! And who would blame Majid if, with his brother's rebel army advancing against him, he slew that brother while he still had the power to do so?

'Tell them to wait!' repeated Cholé, her voice rising in the scented silence of the upper room.

'Yes, yes; I will tell them,' whispered Salmé, searching with trembling fingers for paper and inkhorn.

She wrote quickly, the scratching of the quill keeping pace with her frightened breathing and the hammering of her heart, and when she had finished she folded the paper small, and wrapping it in a fragment of oiled silk, thrust it into the orange that had contained the original message, and clapped her hands to summon her serving-woman.

'See that it is delivered safely, and with all speed,' ordered Salmé, and slipped a gold piece into the woman's palm.

The soft slap of bare feet on the stone stairway faded and was lost, and Cholé said tensely: 'We must think. We must think! There must be some way out.'

'For Bargash? What way? How can he leave while a hundred or more of Majid's soldiers surround his house?'

'The windows,' said Cholé. 'If we could only get him over here we could—— No, we cannot do it that way. It is too far for a ladder or a plank to stretch between them without danger of it breaking under his weight——'

'A rope?' suggested Salmé. 'If he let himself down with a rope into the alleyway, and we pulled him up with another——?'

'It would be too dangerous, because if the soldiers saw him they would fire. And even if they did not kill him, they would never leave the windows unguarded again, and we should lose our only way of communicating with him. That will not do. It will have to be something else. Something safer . . .'

'No way will be safe,' wailed Salmé despairingly.

'Of course not! But anything will be better than letting the rebellion break out without Bargash to lead it. We shall *have* to think of something. Could we not disguise him?'

'As what? They wouldn't allow anyone out – not even a child!'

'No, but they might allow us in. Yes! – that's how we could do it!'

'Cholé, are you mad?'

Cholé gave a shaken laugh. 'Not mad, only desperate. Listen, Salmé – we have never yet attempted to visit our besieged brother or even ask if we might see our sister Méjé, whose position as a woman in a house now full of strange men must be very difficult.'

'How could we, when we would only have been turned back by the soldiers? *We*, the Seyyidas of the Royal House. The humiliation of it would have blackened our faces before every chattering idler in Zanzibar, and we should never have been able to lift up our heads again. You know we could not attempt such a thing!'

'We could and we must. We must go by night – you and I and Schembua and Farschu too, each of us with a picked band of waiting-women. We can say that we only wish to speak with our poor sister Méjé, and beg the guards to let us through. If we take them by surprise they may give us leave.'

'We couldn't – we can't – they would never permit it! Oh, Cholé, *no*!'

Cholé lifted her small head haughtily and her voice was hot with pride. 'We are, as you so truly said, Seyyidas of the Royal House. And if we, the daughters of Seyyid Saïd, ask it ourselves of the Commander of the guard, how can he refuse?'

Salmé gave a gasp of pure horror. 'You mean to speak to a strange man, unveiled? A common soldier? No, Cholé! It is unthinkable!'

'Nevertheless,' said Cholé harshly, 'we must think of it. And not only think of it, but do it. Send for Farschu and Schembua. There is no time to waste. How many tall women have we among our servants and slaves? We must take two or three with us who are as tall as Bargash; more if possible.'

'There are several among the negro slaves,' said Salmé doubtfully, 'but I do not think any of the other women are particularly tall. It is only white women and negroes who grow as tall as men.'

'*White women*——! That girl who walks like a boy and who showed us how to take the water into Bargash's house. She shall help us again. We must send for her at once! If we ask it as a great favour, saying that we are all very much afraid, but that knowing her to be both clever and courageous – and also a friend to us – her presence will give us the courage we need to carry out this dangerous undertaking, she will surely come. One has only to look at her to see that!'

'But why ask her at all? We don't need her. We have plenty of slaves just as tall as she is – taller.'

'Of course we have!' said Cholé impatiently. 'I wish you would use your head, Salmé! Can't you see that if she is with us, and things go wrong, we need only say to Majid that it was not our plan but hers? That she persuaded us into doing it, and we were afraid to disobey her because her nation is a powerful one and we supposed her to be acting under the orders of her uncle, the Consul? Then Majid will not dare do anything either to her or to us, for fear it is true and that her country may send ships with guns to support Bargash!'

'She will not come,' said Salmé unhappily. 'She would not dare. The water was different, since that was to save men and women from thirst. And of the other matter she had no understanding. But for her uncle's sake she cannot meddle in such an affair as this.'

Cholé said angrily: 'Am I a fool? Do you think that we need to tell her that we plan to free our brother so that he may set himself at the head of an army? There are times when you talk like a child, Salmé! I shall tell her that Majid's advisers are demanding his death, and that we fear for his safety and would spirit him out of the country in order to save him from assassination. These foreigners will believe anything, and she will feel that she has done a noble thing in saving his life. Write at once.'

'She cannot read Arabic well,' faltered Salmé.

'Then send word by Mumtaz to that foolish Englishwoman, the widow, and tell her we must see her. It is all a game to those women; they delight to think that they are at the centre of great affairs, and so they will come. Quickly, Salmé!'

Cholé had not been mistaken. Hero had instantly agreed to go, explaining to the apprehensive Cressy, who urged her to refuse, that with a man's life at stake it was impossible to return any other answer. How would she feel if she were to refuse her help, and then learn later that he had been cold-bloodedly murdered – and all for the want of a little enterprise? It was an excellent plan and she was surprised that those girls had had the sense to think of it: and deeply touched that they should ask for her assistance in carrying it out, not merely on account of her height, but because they felt that her presence among them would give them courage. How could anyone refuse a plea like that?

'You are so brave,' breathed Olivia. '"Hero" indeed – in nature as well as name.'

'Stuff!' said Hero, irritated.

18

Aunt Abby had provided unwitting assistance to the plotters by complaining of a headache and retiring early to bed that night, for in order to avoid disturbing her later, Uncle Nat had abandoned a projected rubber of whist and gone up with her, and the younger members of the party had soon followed their example.

'Now remember, Cressy,' warned Hero; 'you are not to get into a fever if I am a little late getting back, for I shall have Fattûma with me and you may be sure that we shall be back around midnight. And do stop looking so scared. If I'm not, there is no reason why you should be.'

'If you must know,' said Cressy flatly, 'I feel *sick* with fright, and I think you must be mad. But I can see there is no use arguing with you any more.'

'None,' agreed Hero gaily, divesting herself of her hoops and exchanging her black silk dinner dress for something more suited to the night's activities. She kissed her cousin affectionately and, after a few last instructions, let herself quietly out of the room.

The house was in darkness, but by keeping a hand upon the banisters she found it easy enough to reach the hall. Her feet made no noise on the stone stairs or the polished *chunam* of the hall, and the rustle of her dress was too soft a sound to be heard above the night noises of the city. But the door bolts rasped and a hinge creaked a complaint as she let herself out onto the terrace, and she stood quite still for a minute or two, listening, and hearing no movements, drew a breath of relief and closed the door gently behind her.

There was no moon as yet, but the starlight was bright enough to show her the way across the terrace and down the short flight of steps into the garden, where the paths gleamed faintly white between the massed borders of flowers and shrubs. She had forgotten that they were strewn with crushed shells, and the frail stuff crunched under her thin shoes with a sound that seemed magnified out of all proportion by the silence. But the house remained dark, and only a night-jar called harshly from the shadows as she reached the shelter of the orange trees, where a hand came out of the leafy blackness and touched her.

Fattûma had brought the same shoes and sombre outer clothing that Hero had worn once before when she had visited The Dolphins' House, and five minutes later, muffled from head to foot, the two women were letting themselves out through the garden door that the night-watchman had been bribed to leave unlocked.

'I have told him that I go to meet a friend,' giggled Fattûma. 'A man friend. He thinks it is a matter of the heart and that he is helping two lovers, the old fool! But we must be back before it is light, or we shall find it locked against us.'

They did not see many people in the streets, for they avoided the more frequented thoroughfares and kept as far as possible to the lanes and alleyways where there were few lights and no crowds to jostle them. But once Hero suffered a flash of panic when they paused at a street corner, and she looked back and saw a man who was obviously a member of the Western community cross the road behind her. He was wearing what appeared to be a dark cloak over a suit of white tropical duck, and for a moment she was sure that it was Clayton and that he was following her. But the next minute he had turned into a narrow cul-de-sac and disappeared from view, and she realized that in spite of her boasted calm she was allowing her nerves to get the better of her.

If Clay had seen her leave the Consulate he would certainly have caught up with her and stopped her instead of following her. And if she were going to allow her imagination to turn some harmless European clerk into Authority dogging her footsteps, then her conscience could not be as clear as she supposed! which was absurd, because of course it was clear: she was on an errand of mercy – helping to save a man from assassination and his brother from the sin of fratricide. Hero clutched her dark draperies about her, and hurrying forward again was careful not to look back at the next turning.

She was unfamiliar with the route they had taken, but she knew when they neared the harbour, for she could hear the sound of the surf and the voices of the soldiers who were on guard before the Heir-Apparent's house. Beit-el-Tani was dark and quiet, but there were two women waiting for her at the kitchen entrance, and Fattûma touched her on the arm, and whispering that she would stay there until the Bibi returned, squatted down inside the doorway as the women led Hero swiftly up winding stairways and along stone passages to the room where the Seyyidas awaited her.

'You are late!' snapped Cholé; words and voice betraying the extent of her nervous agitation.

There seemed to be a great many women in the room, all of whom appeared to be excited and overstrung, and Hero noticed that at least half-a-dozen of them were negro or Abyssinian slaves: tall women wearing long cloaks and head coverings of coarse blue cotton, whose eyeballs showed white with alarm in their anxious ebony faces. The Arab

223

women were draped from head to foot in dark *scheles* similar to Hero's own, and under their fringed head-dresses their faces looked as white as hers. But their doe eyes flickered and started in the manner of frightened animals and Salmé was the only one to smile at her; though it was a poor enough effort and Hero saw that her hands were shaking and that she could not keep still, but like the rest of the women must walk nervously to and fro, jerking at the fastenings of her cloak and fidgeting with her ornaments.

Poor girl, thought Hero. No wonder the Seyyidas had so urgently desired her company on this venture! They certainly needed one cool Western head to provide moral support and a steadying influence, and she regretted that her lack of fluency in Arabic prevented her from taking immediate command of the whole affair. But since this was not possible, she contented herself with smiling reassuringly and exchanging calm greetings with any of the women she recognized, until told curtly by Cholé to veil her face and cover herself with her cloak.

'It is time we left,' said Cholé, and swept the whole party out; the women silent now except for the staccato slap of heelless slippers and the sound of quickened breathing. Salmé's nieces, who had brought their own retinue of slaves, were already waiting for them in the street outside, and the two processions of heavily veiled and shrouded figures merged together and made their way to the main entrance of the Heir-Apparent's house.

The wind that fluttered the women's dark draperies swayed the flames of the oil lamps burning outside the house, and sent the shadows of armed men leaping like acrobats across the high white walls as the advance guard from Beit-el-Tani reached the door, and were halted by the crossed muskets of loud-voiced soldiers. A moment later the night was full of turmoil, wrangling and noise, and Hero could see the silhouettes of heads crowding the lamplit squares of Bargash's windows, as men in the besieged household leaned out to see the cause of the confusion.

One of Salmé's women thrust her way back through the press, whimpering and indignant, and clawed at her mistress's arm: 'Highness, Highness! they say we may not pass; that there is an order that no one may pass. I have told them that it is some noble ladies who wish to see the Seyyida Méjé, but they do not believe it. They say that if we will not disperse they will unveil us here in the street and deal with us as they would with harlots. We must go back, Highness – it is useless to persist. They are rough men and lewd – we must go back!'

Salmé thrust the woman behind her, and turning to her sister said in a voice that despite all her efforts she could not keep from trembling:

'You were right, Cholé. We must go ourselves to their commanding officer and tell him who we are. It is the only way.'

Several of the more elderly waiting women, horrified by this announcement, fell on their knees and endeavoured to hold them back, but Hero struck away the clutching hands and thrust herself between them, and finding themselves free the sisters ran forward to confront the Commander of the guard.

It was probably Cholé's beauty more than Salmé's dramatic and emotional pleading that reduced the guard to dazzled, stammering subservience, for although no man there could have recognized any of the rigorously secluded Palace ladies, it was instantly plain that these two women were what they claimed to be; daughters of the Royal House.

There was a collective gasp of awe and admiration as the sisters threw back their dark wrappings, and a sudden stillness fell on the crowd as they looked on something that men of their stamp would never see again. Even Hero was conscious of a small shock of admiration and a sudden uncomfortable feeling that she herself was fashioned out of coarser clay. The Sultan's sisters were dressed as she had always imagined that the fabulous Queens and Princesses of the Arabian Nights would be dressed, and the lamplight shone on shimmering silks and gold embroidery and threw back the flash and glitter of jewels. But although Salmé's dark eyes and sad mouth had their own appeal, it was Cholé who took one's breath away; Cholé looking as pale and as impossibly lovely as one of those fragile, heavy-scented moon-flowers that bloom only by night and die before the dawn.

The Commander of the guard, bemused alike by that beauty and his reverence for the Royal Family, found his tongue with difficulty and began to stammer apologies for having attempted to obstruct the path of such noble ladies, while the guards themselves drew back, hands to foreheads and bowing almost to the ground. Cholé inclined her lovely head in regal acknowledgement, and the long procession of women – Seyyidas, serving-women, slaves and Hero Hollis – swept past and were admitted into the Heir-Apparent's house.

They found Bargash in Méjé's room, and bedlam reigning. Méjé and several of her women were in tears, Bargash himself ablaze with excitement and nervous tension, and twelve-year-old Aziz riotous with triumph:

'We saw you!' shouted the boy, jumping up and down with all the inexhaustible enthusiasm of the young: 'We were watching you from the windows and Méjé said they would never let you through, and even my brother was afraid. He was pulling his beard and sweating and cursing—— Yes, you were, I heard you! And old Ayesha there was praying. But I wasn't afraid. I knew you'd do it. I knew they wouldn't dare stop you!

Oh, Salmé, isn't it exciting? Have you got a plan? Why are you here? What are you going to do?'

'Hush!' begged Cholé with a frantic glance at the open windows. 'Close the shutters, or they will hear us. We are going to take you away; now, at once. We have brought women's clothes with us for a disguise, and since those fools below never thought to count us they will not know how many go out with us. Salmé has sent word to the chiefs to bring horses to a meeting place outside the city so that you may escape to join your supporters. But they will only wait there until moonrise, and if we are not there by that time they will know our plan has failed and will disperse for their own safety. So we must go quickly – quickly!'

The words had been too swiftly spoken for Hero to follow, but the gist of them – the need for speed – was completely clear, and she could hardly believe it when Bargash haughtily and flatly refused to wear womens' clothes, declaring that he would die rather than allow it to be said that he, Seyyid Bargash-bin-Saïd, had skulked within the dress of a serving-maid and played the woman. Danger he would face, and death if necessary; but humiliation and disgrace, never! If he was to be shot down by his brother's hirelings it would be as himself – the Heir! 'Do you think I could endure hearing the laughter of those low-bred mercenaries if they should discover me among your slaves, trembling behind a woman's veil? No, Cholé! I will not do it!'

'Men!' thought Hero: and for the first time began to take a less romantic view of the Heir-Apparent. Couldn't he see that every minute wasted in this ridiculous manner was increasing their danger and lessening their chances of success? Was he really going to throw away any hope of escape, and waste all the efforts that these courageous women had made to save him, for the sake of a stupid male quibble? He might assert that to be found in women's dress reflected on his courage and honour, but in Hero's opinion it was the women who were showing themselves the braver sex. And the more sensible one, too!

The minutes ticked away and time slipped through their fingers and was lost, but still the foolish argument went on and on; until at last Hero, angry, exasperated and suddenly beginning to wish that she had never come, said loudly: 'We had better leave him then, and go.'

In the babble of voices her words went unheeded by the chief contestants, but Salmé at least had heard them. And so too had several of the serving-women, who already frightened by the delay, recognized the voice of prudence and began to edge towards the door in the manner of panic-stricken sheep.

It was enough for Bargash. He had the sense to see that in another moment their nerve would break and they would be stampeding from the room and out of the house, taking his only chance of escape with them, and he capitulated. 'But I will not go unarmed. If they try to stop me I shall fight. I will not be taken alive!'

Willing hands rushed to arm him, and pistols and daggers were thrust into his waistband and hung about his neck, and at last a *schele* belonging to the tallest of the women was wrapped about him, leaving only his eyes free.

'You must walk behind us,' said Cholé, 'among those of our women who are nearest to you in size, so that your height will not betray you. And we must talk, all of us, and walk slowly. Remember, we have only been on a visit here and we are anxious on Méjé's account. That is all. There must be no hurrying and no signs of fear.' She motioned to Hero and the three tallest slaves to stand with Bargash, directed little Aziz, also disguised in a *schele*, to walk between two of her waiting-maids, and turning her back on the sobbing Méjé said curtly: 'Let us go.'

They walked out the way they had come; forcing themselves to move unhurriedly and control the trembling of their voices; talking lightly though with little idea as to what they were saying, and wondering, each one of them, if when they reached the guards they would be stopped and the whole desperate enterprise end in shots and terror and spilt blood.

Bargash's own servants unbarred the great carved door, opening it only wide enough to allow the women to pass through. And then they were out in the night air once more, with the sea wind blowing in their faces and the lamplight and the shadows swaying back and forth across their shrouded figures.

It seemed to Hero that the guards had been reinforced and that there were now many more of them massed outside the house than there had been half an hour ago. But she held herself straight, walking erect and tall so that the Heir-Apparent's hunched shoulders and lowered head might appear shorter by contrast. Out of the corner of her eye she saw one of the Sultan's Baluchi soldiers lean forward suddenly and stare, and felt fear trickle like ice-water down her spine. Had he noticed anything strange about the muffled figure that kept pace with her, or was it a glimpse of her own grey eyes that had attracted his attention? She should have remembered to keep them lowered, and she did so now; hoping that if he had seen them he would take her for a Circassian.

'Slowly,' muttered Salmé – for once past the guards the impulse to break into a run had been strong enough to make every one of them quicken their steps, though they were still in full view and by no means out of danger. Hero could hear Bargash breathing as though he had already run a mile, and was annoyed to find that her own breathing was far from steady and her heart beating much too fast. And then at last they had reached the corner, turned it, and were out of sight . . .

'Not yet – not yet!' whispered Cholé urgently. 'We must not run until we are free of the town. There are still too many people abroad, and we must look as though we were only going or returning from a visit to friends. Go on talking as though there was nothing wrong.'

It had never occurred to Hero that they would not return immediately to Beit-el-Tani. She had visualized Bargash being given a more adequate disguise there, and provided with a trustworthy escort to accompany him to some waiting ship that would take him to safety. But they had already passed Beit-el-Tani and were walking through the streets; faster now but still without any appearance of haste; and somehow it did not seem possible to turn back and abandon them at this point. Whether she wanted to or not she would have to stay with them, and she could only hope that Fattûma would have the sense to wait for her, since it began to look as though the whole affair were going to take a good deal longer than she had anticipated.

Swept onward by the hurrying crowd of women she soon lost her bearings and all count of how many turnings they had taken. The houses began to thin out and there were more trees, and then at last the open country stretched before them, grey in the bright starlight, and throwing aside all restraint they began to run towards a distant mass of trees that loomed up darkly against the night sky. As they neared it they slowed to a walk and stopped, sobbing for breath, to veil their faces from the sight of strange men as half-a-dozen shadowy figures moved out from among the trees to meet them. One of these coughed in an artificial manner that suggested a signal, and a man's voice called softly: 'Is it you, Highness?'

'It is I,' replied Bargash breathlessly.

'Allah be praised!'

The fervent exclamation made Hero jump, for it was not a single voice that spoke, but a chorus. Somehow she had not expected that there would be so many men. She had imagined there would be two or three, and the fact that there were more than two dozen gave her a sudden feeling of disquiet. Could *all* these men be escaping on the same ship that night? She did not have time to ponder the question, however, for there were horses waiting in the shadows and this time there were no arguments and no delays. The Heir-Apparent flung off his *schele*, and with barely a word of farewell, took his young brother by the hand and vanished into the darkness. And a moment or two later the jingle of harness and the thud of hooves on dry ground told her that the whole cavalcade had mounted and were riding swiftly away into the night.

The women stood huddled together; waiting, speechless and exhausted, until the last sounds faded into silence; and when they could hear nothing more they turned tiredly to face the return journey across the fields and the open country to the dark, deserted streets of the sleeping city.

The moon was up by the time they reached Beit-el-Tani, and Hero was limping badly as the result of losing one of her shoes while running through stubble. But Fattûma was waiting for her in the hall and they had reached home safely, to find Cressy still awake and in a state of agitation that reminded Hero all too vividly of the scene she had recently witnessed in Méjé's room.

'I thought you were *never* coming!' shuddered Cressy. 'I've been down at least ten times to see that no one had shut the door, and I thought you must all have been caught or shot or—— What have you been doing to be so late? Has the Prince escaped? Is he safe? Is everything all right? What *happened*?'

'Everything!' said Hero briefly, collapsing onto her bed. 'Yes, he's safe, and everything's all right. It went off beautifully in spite of the silly way he behaved; you wouldn't believe how tiresome he was! It should be days and days before anyone finds out he isn't in the house, and by the time they do he'll be half-way to Arabia or Persia, or wherever he's going.'

'Oh,' said Cressy, suddenly deflated. 'Then – then it's all over.'

'Yes. They had horses, so they're probably safely on board some ship by now.'

'I didn't mean that. I meant ... everything else. The Prince will never be Sultan now, and everything will be as bad as before and never get any better.'

Hero stood up, wincing, and began to remove her dress. She said thoughtfully: 'I'm not so sure about that. You know, Cressy, we may have been wrong about the Prince. After all, a great deal of what we know about him is only what his sisters have told us. And one can see why they all dote on him, for he is exactly the type of dashing, dare-devil younger brother that sisters would spoil and adore – particularly Eastern sisters! But though I admit that I thought it an excellent idea to have him as Sultan instead of Majid – and I still think he would make a better one – anyone who could behave so ... so downright *ridiculously* as that man did tonight cannot be held to have a great deal of common sense. He carried on like a schoolgirl in a tantrum, and I am not at all sure that he is the right person to institute reforms. So I guess it's just as well that he's gone and I only hope he reaches the ship in safety. Goodness, am I tired! I feel as though I could sleep for a week. Good night, honey.'

She crawled thankfully between the sheets, conscious of having done her duty and happily unaware that the Heir-Apparent and his entourage had safely reached not a ship, but *Marseilles*, and that his escape had not, as she so confidently supposed, gone undetected. For a Baluchi soldier who had stood at the gate and watched the women pass out had recognized, in one brief moment between the slipping of a fold of cloth and its hurried replacement, the face of Seyyid Bargash-bin-Saïd, half-brother and Heir-Apparent to His Highness the Sultan.

The Baluchi had not raised an immediate alarm, since he, like Hero Hollis, had believed himself to be witnessing the escape of a man whose sole intention was to fly the country. And having served for several years under the Seyyid's father, his loyalty and respect for the dead Lion of Oman had been strong enough to persuade him to hold his tongue and give his late Sultan's son a chance to reach safety. But morning had brought the country-folk flocking into the city with their loads of grain and fruit and vegetables for the market, and they had brought with them tales of unprecedented numbers of Arabs seen hurrying towards *Marseilles* – armed and eager men on foot and on horseback, accompanied by slaves carrying swords, muskets and provisions enough for an army . . .

The Baluchi soldier, listening to those tales, realized that the Seyyid Bargash had not flown the country, but escaped to lead an armed rebellion, and he had hurried to the Palace to confess what he had seen.

Two hours later a frightened eunuch scratched at Cholé's door with the news that every detail of her brother's escape and his sisters' part in it was known to the Sultan, and that his ministers were already meeting to decide what action must be taken: 'They have sent for the British Consul,' stammered the eunuch, 'and it is said that he is urging His Highness to take strong measures, and will lend guns and English sailors from a ship that is expected to arrive within a few days.'

The guards had been withdrawn from Bargash's house, and in the Palace the Sultan, pallid with alarm and indignation, poured his troubles into the unsympathetic ear of Colonel George Edwards, and received in return the same comments and advice that his ministers and councillors had already given him.

'I have repeatedly warned your Highness,' said Colonel Edwards stiffly, 'that your leniency in the matter of your brother has been sadly misplaced. But as you have so far chosen to ignore my warnings, you cannot now expect me to express astonishment at what has occurred. It was only to be expected, and I am not in the least surprised.'

'You knew of this plot, then?' demanded Majid indignantly.

'As much as your Highness knew. There has never been over-much secrecy about your brother's proceedings; or, for that matter, his intentions. I am well aware that your ministers have been pressing you to take action against him for months past, and I can only join them in urging you to lose no further time about it, since every hour that you waste is to his advantage. He is obviously counting upon outside support, either from Muscat and Oman or – or from some European nation. And though at the moment you can muster considerably more men and armaments than he can boast of, if you allow him to entrench himself in a strong position and remain there unmolested, collecting more supporters daily with promises of pay and the prospect of plunder, and waiting until even stronger reinforcements arrive from outside the Island, your throne is lost. Your Highness must act at once.'

It was always easier to advise Majid to take action than to get him to the point of acting. But the news that his brother had forced the slaves on the plantations bordering on *Marseilles* to join him, and had set them to cutting down the coconut groves to build a stockade about the house and destroying the clove plantations so that they might not be used to cover a hostile advance, finally drove him to collect a force of five thousand men and reluctantly accompany it to Beit-el-Ras, a royal estate on the coast some eight miles from the city.

Bargash's undisciplined supporters, undeterred by this move, embarked on an orgy of looting and destruction, and Colonel Edwards sent off a dhow with an urgent message requesting the immediate presence of any Royal Navy vessel that might chance to be in the vicinity. And as panic spread through the undefended city, Hero Hollis realized with horror that this ugly and terrifying situation was something that she herself had helped to bring about.

19

Lieutenant Daniel Larrimore, having tailed the *Virago* as far as Ras Asuad and then lost her, turned back to patrol the narrow waters that separated the islands of Pemba and Zanzibar from the Sultan's mainland territories. The *Virago*, he argued, was bound to return that way, and if Captain Frost supposed the *Daffodil* to be lurking for him somewhere north of Mogadishu, so much the better.

It had been close on sunrise when the dhow sighted them, and full daylight by the time she ranged alongside and sent over a messenger carrying a single sheet of paper, stamped with the Consular seal and bearing Colonel Edwards's urgent request for immediate assistance. The messenger reported that another naval vessel, H.M.S. *Assaye,* had already been contacted and should by now have reached the Island, but added that the situation being serious, he thought that any reinforcements would be welcomed: a view with which the Lieutenant found himself in so much agreement that he instantly abandoned any further ideas of waylaying the *Virago*, and gave orders for the *Daffodil* to make all speed for Zanzibar.

Dan was well aware what the motley crew of freed slaves, petty criminals and el Harth tribesmen who composed the bulk of the Heir-Apparent's forces would be capable of once they got out of hand, and his heart contracted with fear at the thought of Cressy in a town that might even now be given over to riot and rape at the hands of a murderous, greed-crazed mob of looters, who would think nothing of burning it to the ground. It was a situation that he could hardly bear to contemplate, and he cracked on more sail and yelled down the hatchway for more steam – and cursed Rory Frost with more than ordinary virulence, because it was entirely on his account that the *Daffodil* had been three hundred miles from Zanzibar on the night of the Heir-Apparent's escape.

The sloop made harbour shortly before midnight, and Dan, who had been visualizing the city in flames, was unspeakably relieved to find it looking much as usual, with the waterfront silent and the few men there asleep. But despite the lateness of the hour he had gone immediately to the British Consulate to report his arrival, and had found Colonel Edwards awake and engaged in writing an acidulated dispatch to the Foreign Office.

'Glad to see you, Dan,' said the Colonel, and looked it. 'Did you fetch in by chance, or did you get my message? I sent Jahia off to see if he could make contact with any Navy ship in these waters.'

'He sighted us early this morning, sir, and we got here as soon as we could. I thought I might have some difficulty in getting to your house, so I brought a couple of bluejackets with me. Is the situation really bad, sir? The town seems quiet enough.'

'The town,' said Colonel Edwards austerely, 'is in a state of anarchy and the situation is thoroughly unpleasant to say the least of it. And as if that were not enough, Monsieur René Dubail called on me today to inform me that he had heard from a reliable source that I had been urging the Sultan to launch an attack on his brother's forces and proposed to offer him aid in the form of guns and men from the *Assaye*. He wished to know if this was true, and upon my replying that for once his information was entirely accurate, he had the effrontery to object to what he was pleased to call my "unwarrantable interference in a domestic matter that was the sole concern of the Sultan's Government and subjects, and nothing whatever to do with the British Crown".'

'Good God!' said Lieutenant Larrimore, scandalized. 'What can he be thinking of?'

'You may well ask. He further informed me that if I persisted in my efforts to promote civil war on behalf of a man who had no legal right to the throne – by which he meant the Sultan – it would leave him no alternative but to place the Heir-Apparent under the protection of his own Government.'

'He must be mad,' announced the Lieutenant, taking the most charitable view: 'The heat, I expect.'

'Nothing of the sort. This isn't the first time I've come up against him. Though it is the first occasion on which I have permitted myself the luxury of losing my temper. I asked him how he could even contemplate offering his country's protection to the rebel subject of a ruling monarch, and pointed out that the Sultan had himself asked for my advice and assistance, and that he had every right to do so if he wished, since he was as much an independent sovereign as Louis Napoleon. Monsieur Dubail said the comparison was an insult, so I told him that he might call it what he liked, but it was still the truth. He did not like it at all, and the whole thing was most unfortunate: deplorable! "*Legal right*" indeed! It is just as well that this is not a matter that our respective countries would ever consider going to war over.'

The Lieutenant, whose mind had been occupied with other things of late, frowned and said: 'But surely, sir, there was never any question of Bargash being the rightful heir?'

'Oh, he was referring to the elder brother, Thuwani, whom Bargash once pretended to be acting for. No question of that now, however. Bargash is playing this hand for himself and no one else. But I must not keep you. You will be wanting to get back to your ship to get some sleep. About tomorrow . . .'

Dan received his instructions and left; heroically resisting an impulse to make a detour that would take him past the American Consulate, and wondering when, if ever, he was going to be forgiven for having criticized Cressy's too frequent visits to Beit-el-Tani. It had been a mistake to do so, and he had paid for it. Yet how could he possibly have held his tongue? Cressy was so innocent and trusting – so sure that she was helping to further the cause of friendship and understanding between East and West. He could not have stood aside and kept silent while she became involved in the ugly web of plotting and conspiracy that was being woven by Bargash and his friends. But his well-meant warning had merely resulted in a quarrel that was making it very difficult for him to present himself at her house again. Dan's heart and his spirits sank at the thought, and he could almost wish that he had returned to find Zanzibar in flames so that he could have had the privilege of rescuing her from a burning building, or saving her single-handed from a rioting mob.

He managed to snatch a bare hour of sleep that night, and at first light joined the small flotilla in which Colonel Edwards, together with the Commander of the *Assaye* and as many officers as could be spared from duty, proceeded up the coast to the Sultan's camp at Beit-el-Ras to call upon His Highness.

The interview proved tolerably satisfactory, in that it had resulted in the Sultan striking camp and moving off with his entire force to attack the rebels. Dan and several of the younger officers had been requested to accompany him, and the cumbersome amateur army marched away from the coast through groves of palm trees, fragrant plantations of cloves and oranges, tangled thickets of jungle greenery and rough stretches of open country, towards the centre of the island and rebel-held *Marseilles*.

By mid-afternoon they had covered roughly ten miles, and after a halt and a brief conference it was suggested that the British contingent should ride ahead to reconnoitre, and led by a reluctant guide they left the track and rode off at a tangent towards a grove of trees that lay just beyond the boundary of the *Marseilles* estate. There had been a farmhouse near the grove, but it had been recently burned and now lay blackened and deserted; the ashes still hot to the touch and a thread of smoke drifting up from a charred beam that had once been part of the roof.

It was a sobering sight, for it made the rebel force a reality and not merely something that had been spoken of in words but whose existence had yet to be proved. There was nothing unreal about the burned and looted building whose shell made an ugly blot against the lush green of the trees. And neither was there anything illusory about the vicious whine and crack of a dozen musket balls that greeted the advance party as they emerged on the far side of the grove. They were well out of range, but the horses did not take kindly to the sound of the shots, and Dan lost patience with his plunging animal, and dismounting, handed the reins to his coxswain, Mr Wilson, who had accompanied him, and went forward on foot to study the rebel position. It looked to him a good deal stronger than they had been led to suppose, and staring at it through eyes narrowed against the dazzle of the hot sunlight, he realized that subduing it was likely to prove a more serious matter than anyone had suspected.

The stretch of ground that lay immediately ahead provided little in the way of cover, for the palm and clove trees that a short time ago had made it a green and pleasant place had been ruthlessly destroyed to allow an uninterrupted field of fire, while the house itself might almost have been a fort, so well was it constructed for defence. Large, two-storeyed and solidly built, it was flanked on either side by several detached buildings and outhouses, and surrounded by a high wall that Bargash's men had evidently loopholed and protected with parapets of sandbags.

There was also a formidable outer stockade of recently felled palm trunks, and Dan regretted that he had not thought to bring a telescope with him, since at this moment it would have proved a far more useful piece of equipment than the ceremonial sword that had been an active irritation ever since he had buckled it on at dawn. But even without one he could make a reasonably accurate guess at the amount of opposition the Sultan's force were likely to encounter in any attack on the position; if – which he began to doubt – they could be persuaded to attack it at all!

The sunlight glinted on the brass barrels of at least three guns that had been mounted near the outer gates, and the enclosure was alive with armed men. He could see muskets and dark faces at every window, and the men peering down from between the sandbags that reinforced the low parapet on the roof continued to fire at him. An occasional spent ball dropped into the grass or struck the rocks at his feet, but as he was still out of musket range he remained where he was, for there was one important point that needed to be made clear; did they or did they not possess rifles? He thought it unlikely, since the Lee-Enfield rifle was still something of a novelty in the East, and though they were now in general use in the British Army in place of the antiquated 'Brown Bess' (and had been issued with disturbing results to the East India Company's Bengal Army), they were not as yet being manufactured for sale abroad. But it was always possible that some might have found their way here and fallen into the hands of the rebels, for they commanded high prices and there was a brisk trade in stolen army rifles smuggled out of India to Afghanistan, Persia and the Gulf.

The Lee-Enfield's range was far greater than that of the old-fashioned musket, and Dan was well aware that in offering himself as a target he would be taking a considerable risk. But it was one that would have to be taken, because if the defenders of *Marseilles* possessed rifles it was going to make a deal of difference to the Sultan's gun crews. And since he was convinced that no one armed with a Lee-Enfield would be able to resist using it on a tempting target, and it was not in his nature to order another man to run a risk that he, personally, would choose to avoid, that target would have to be himself.

A few nerve-racking minutes later, having induced the insurgents to waste a quantity of ammunition on him and proved to his own satisfaction that their armament did not include rifles, he turned and walked thankfully back to where the remainder of the party waited at the edge of the grove:

'We'll have to get a couple of guns and some rockets up here,' said Dan. 'No good storming that place until we've blown a hole in it. Let's get back.'

It had taken the best part of an hour to manhandle the guns into position, and by the time they had done so they were drenched with sweat and grey with the gritty dust of the open country, and Dan, who in company with the rest of the naval contingent had discarded his coat, hat and sword belt, and was working in his shirt sleeves with a borrowed scarf wound turban-wise round his head against the relentless glare, was feeling far from confident as to the outcome of the engagement. The Sultan's troops were for the most part untrained and undisciplined men with few ideas on the subject of organized fighting and none at all on tactics, and already a body of them, rushing forward to the attack on their own initiative and without waiting for the guns to make a breach for them, had met with a withering fire that had left the ground in front of the palm stockade strewn with dead and wounded.

This disaster had effectually discouraged any further advance, and now that the guns were at last in position Dan discovered that it was he and his fellow officers who would have to man and fire them, for with the exception of a handful of Turkish gunners the Sultan's troops (who had received a salutary lesson and were not anxious to have it repeated) remainly firmly in the rear and refused to move.

The hour that followed was a torment of dust and din, and though at sunset the wind died and the air became cooler, the evening reeked with the stink of black powder and the smell of blood, and the guns had become almost too hot to handle. The crews had worked under continuous fire from the roof, the loopholed walls of the main buildings and the well-served brass guns by the gateway, and Dan's left arm had been put out of action by a splinter of rock sliced off by a shell that had landed less than five feet away and killed a Turkish gunner.

Three of the naval officers and two more Turks had been wounded by the scrap-iron which the rebels were firing in place of round shot. But their casualties were negligible when compared with those they had inflicted on the garrison of the besieged house, and though the pursuit and arrest of slave ships had accustomed Dan Larrimore to unpleasant sights, he was young enough to wince and sicken at the sight of the bloody devastation wrought by round shot and rockets landing among a dense mob of shouting men.

There must, he thought, have been anything up to five or even six hundred men inside the walls of *Marseilles*. Arabs of the el Harth tribe, raiders and Bedouins from the Gulf, and terrified African slaves who screeched and ran to and fro like panic-stricken animals, striving to take shelter behind walls and outhouses. But they would soon have nowhere to hide, for now at last the way was open: the outer gate a mass of rubble and pieces of what had once been men, and the inner doors smashed to splinters.

Now, for once, it was Majid who called for action – and could not persuade his troops to move, though he placed himself courageously at their head and urged them to follow him. Waverer and man of peace as he was, the Sultan yet had sense enough to see that an attack at this moment would be met by little resistance from his brother's demoralized forces. But the disastrous sortie of the earlier afternoon, the deafening crash of gunfire and the crackle of musketry that had rolled over them ever since, and above all the sight of their own dead and wounded, had sapped his troops' courage, and neither threats nor pleading could persuade them to advance.

'For Christ's sake——!' muttered Dan between clenched teeth, 'can't they see that all they've got to do is to walk in? The place is a shambles! At least half of those poor devils in there must be dead or dying, and they can probably take it without firing another shot. Or do the chicken-livered bastards expect us to take the bloody position for them? Why the hell we should be expected to do their dirty work for them I don't know, but if they won't, I suppose we shall have to try.'

He looked round at the handful of smoke-blackened, powder-grimed, exhausted ragamuffins who had set out only that morning suitably attired to attend an audience with a reigning monarch, and knew that they could not advance unsupported. There were too few of them; and those few too young and tired and dishevelled to impress even the battered garrison of *Marseilles*, who seeing such a ragged remnant advancing against them would draw encouragement from the sight, and shoot them down at point-blank range. And yet . . .

It was getting dark and the battered house seemed to move with a curious up and down motion as though the ground was not quite solid. But now that the wind had died it should be still. He could not understand why it did not stay still. His left arm was caked and sticky with half-dried blood, and the tourniquet that Massey had applied above the ugly ragged gash was biting into his flesh and causing him a great deal of pain. He tried to move the fingers of his left hand and discovered that he could not do so, and once again the distant house swayed dizzily before his eyes and he found himself thinking that if there were any men left alive in it they must surely fall off the roof and out of the windows. Perhaps they were all dead, and if so there was really no reason why he and his fellow officers should not occupy the place themselves. *Finish the job*, thought Dan hazily. *That's right – finish it . . .*

He said: 'Wait here while I take a look. May as well finish . . . finish the . . .' The Assistant-Surgeon caught him as he fell.

'No you don't,' said the Assistant-Surgeon grimly. 'Or the rest of us either. We've done the spade work for them and they can damn' well do the rest themselves. Home, I think. And not on those blasted horses either! The least our cautious allies can do is lend us a reliable guide and some decent animals, and the sooner we all get back on board the better.'

They had got back – the majority on horses from the Sultan's own string and the four injured officers in a creaking bullock cart, while behind them the Sultan's forces prepared to camp for the night, leaving the dead lying sprawled before the broken walls of *Marseilles* and the wounded to crawl painfully away under cover of darkness.

It had been a slow and uncomfortable journey, and Dan, who had lost a good deal of blood and was unconscious for most of it, was surprised to find how relieved he was to see so commonplace a sight as the riding light of his own ship reflected in the grey harbour water. He had submitted impatiently to having his wound washed and dressed, and as soon as that unpleasant operation was over, stumbled to his bunk with the observation that at least the next few days were likely to prove peaceful.

But he was wrong, for the next few days were anything but peaceful.

The morning dawned hot and windless, and in the city the shops were still closed. Nervous citizens kept their doors barred and their shutters bolted, while panic-stricken ones besieged the harbour offering large sums in return for a passage to the mainland. And in his camp near *Marseilles*

His Highness the Sultan, having again failed to persuade his troops to advance, sent an urgent message to the British Consul asking for the assistance of Her Majesty's forces.

'Wants us to pull all his chestnuts out of the fire for him,' grumbled Colonel Edwards. 'Well, I suppose we shall have to do so, because if we don't there's no knowing what sort of mess he'll end up in.'

'Pretty good mess already,' commented the Commander of the *Assaye*. 'Four of our own men wounded and sixty of his killed or injured – and God alone knows how many losses on the other side. Not bad for a minor skirmish! What assistance do you propose to send him, sir?'

'That's up to you, Commander. As many of your men as you consider necessary to capture the position.'

'From all I hear, a petty officer and a dozen bluejackets could have done it yesterday evening,' said the Commander disgustedly. 'But the rebels will have had well over twenty-four hours in which to pull themselves together and reorganize their defences before we can get out there again. Oh well, I'll see what we can raise, and with your permission we'll send 'em off at first light tomorrow.'

The following dawn had seen another naval contingent setting off for the Sultan's camp: this time consisting of twelve officers and one hundred petty officers and seamen, armed with rockets and a twelve-pound howitzer and commanded by a senior officer from the *Assaye*. They found Sultan Majid angry and ashamed and his followers sullen and uneasy, but although the atmosphere had been considerably lightened by the sight of the British contingent, only the Sultan and three of his ministers expressed the intention of accompanying them to the attack. The troops had declined to move, and standing prudently back they watched their ruler and his white reinforcements move off in the direction of *Marseilles*, and listened anxiously for the sound of firing.

There was no firing. The advancing force halted at the edge of the grove while their commanding officer scanned the ruined buildings through a telescope, but save for a number of lethargic vultures nothing moved, and he could see no sign of any defenders. Suspecting an ambush, he held half his men in reserve and sent the rest forward under cover of the howitzer. But *Marseilles* was deserted. Not even the dead remained, for kites and crows, vultures and pariah dogs had already feasted a full day off the bodies of those who had been left unburied, while rats, foxes and a leopard had been there by night to finish the work that those earlier scavengers had left undone. A sickening stench of corruption pervaded the hot stillness and the drone of a million flies was loud in the silence.

Majid looked about him and spoke in a whisper, as though he feared to break that stillness. Or perhaps he was only speaking to himself – or to those children whom he had played with as a child; the brother and the sisters who had tried to depose him:

'This used to be such a beautiful house,' whispered Majid. '. . . so happy. So – so gay.'

He turned to the silent ranks of watching seamen and his voice shot up, high and imperious: 'Blow it up! Smash it into dust with your cannon! I do not wish so much as a stone to remain. Let it be destroyed: and then perhaps one day the trees and grass will grow again, and hide it.'

He walked away with his ministers; a small, undistinguished figure in the harsh sunlight, and did not wait to see the blood-stained shell of *Marseilles* dissolve into fragments in a series of crashing detonations and a darkness that momentarily shadowed the bright day.

In the city Colonel Edwards and Commander Adams of the *Assaye*, who had accompanied the naval contingent as far as Beit-el-Ras before hurrying back to see what measures they could take for the safety of the citizens, had been met by the news that the rebels had evacuated *Marseilles* under cover of darkness and were now ready to make their submission to the Sultan. Also that the Heir-Apparent, finding himself deserted by the majority of his followers, had returned in secret to his house in the city and was in hiding there.

'You don't think that's only a rumour?' suggested Commander Adams.

Colonel Edwards shook his head. 'No, Feruz is the best spy I've got, and if he says Bargash is back, you may be sure it's true. Well, there's only one thing to do, and the sooner it's done the better.'

'What's that, sir?'

'Put a strong guard of the Sultan's Baluchis on that house, and get off an urgent message to His Highness asking him to send someone with authority to enter it and take the Heir-Apparent into custody. If you can spare another petty officer and about half-a-dozen of your men, I'd like to put them on night guard so that we don't have any repetition of that ridiculous nonsense of allowing a covey of women to get into the place under the pretence of paying a social call. I don't imagine that *your* men would let anyone in.'

'Or out,' said the Commander grimly. 'I'll get back and see to it at once.'

'Thank you. That will be a weight off my mind. We don't want to let him slip through our fingers again. I'll get that letter off immediately and go along to the Palace and wait there for whoever His Highness sends to effect the arrest. It won't be easy, and I do trust he will have the sense to send someone of sufficient standing to command respect, and not some royal stripling who will be refused admittance.'

Majid did not send a royal stripling, but a near relative. Seyyid Sûd-bin-

Hilal, a kindly, middle-aged and much respected man, who arrived towards midnight with an escort of two hundred men and orders from the Sultan to capture his rebellious Heir-Apparent at all costs, but to make the submission as easy as possible for him.

Seyyid Sûd had greeted Colonel Edwards with grave courtesy and startled him by the gentle announcement that he proposed to go immediately to Bargash's house, but alone.

'We must not forget, my dear Colonel, that he is still the heir, and a son of our late great Imam – to whom may God grant the highest reward and admit to heaven without bringing him to account. It is the wish of His Highness that his brother should be given the opportunity of surrendering with honour, and this is why I must go alone and unarmed. We know that Seyyid Bargash and his followers have many guns with them, and if I go to take him with troops he may open fire upon them, which must be avoided at all costs. There has been too much bloodshed already. But I am older than Seyyid Bargash, many years older, and if I go to his house alone and he sees that I have no weapons and no armed guards, he may admit me and listen to what I have to say, and accepting His Highness's terms, surrender himself to me. That is what we must hope for.'

'He won't do it,' said Colonel Edwards with curt conviction.

'You think not? I trust you may be wrong. But I hope you will agree that he must be given the opportunity to do so. It is always better to risk something – in this case no more than an affront to my own pride – in the hope that if an enemy is offered a way of honourable retreat he may accept it in preference to continued violence and the taking of more lives.'

'And if he refuses?'

'Then we shall have no choice but to take him by force. That task I shall place in your hands, but tonight we shall try my way.'

He turned to exchange the coat he had travelled in for a more formal one that was richly embroidered in gold thread, and Colonel Edwards said abruptly: 'What terms does His Highness offer to Seyyid Bargash?'

Sûd-bin-Hilal settled the robe on his shoulders, and smoothing his greying beard said gently: 'His Highness the Sultan, whom may God preserve, has told me to tell his brother that in spite of all he has done, he will be pardoned if he will foreswear all rebellious plans for the future.'

'*Hmm*,' grunted the Colonel. 'Then all I can hope is that the offer is refused, for a more preposterous one would be hard to conceive. If he accepts those terms he isn't likely to keep them for more than a week – possibly not more than an hour. You'd think His Highness would realize as much by now.'

Sûd shrugged and smiled a small, tired smile. 'His Highness the Sultan,' he murmured, 'is a man of peace.'

'His Highness the Sultan,' snapped Colonel Edwards, exasperated, 'is precisely the kind of man whose desire for peace is an incitement to violence. Any man who owns what others avidly covet should take reasonable precautions to safeguard it, or else give it away. If he will do neither, he cannot complain when he discovers that Allah made thieves as well as honest men!'

Seyyid Sûd-bin-Hilal spread out his hands in a gesture that both deprecated and accepted, and went out into the quiet night to make his appeal to a rash, egotistical and desperate man. It had proved fruitless. The *débâcle* at *Marseilles* had taught the Heir-Apparent nothing, and he was still convinced that he could rouse the Island against his brother and seize the throne: *Marseilles* had been a miscalculation, no more.

He had been excited, boastful and insulting, and Sûd was forced to the regretful and humiliating conclusion that his mission had, after all, been a grave mistake, and that he had misjudged both the situation and the Heir-Apparent. For the fact that he had come alone and unarmed, bearing terms that were (as the British Consul had not hesitated to point out) generous to the point of folly, had merely served to convince Bargash that his brother was not only afraid of him, but too uncertain of his own position to attempt strong measures, and that continued defiance would yet win the game.

Tolerance and mercy were things that Bargash had never understood and would always confuse with weakness. And now he was more certain than ever that he had been right, since was not Majid suing for mercy? – begging him to apologize and promise to be good, as though he were some naughty child who could be coaxed with sweets? His brother's position must be a parlous one indeed if he could afford to take no sterner action than this!

Bargash was not in the least repentant; and now he was no longer afraid. He laughed in Sûd's face, telling him that he must be as great a fool as Majid if he thought to trick him as easily as that; and the Sultan's envoy returned sorrowfully to the Palace in the yellow dawn, to report the failure of his mission.

'Told you so,' said Colonel Edwards, who having passed an uncomfortable night dozing fitfully in an ante-room of the Palace was not in the best of tempers. 'And I won't say I'm sorry. The only thing that young man understands or will ever understand is force, and it's also the only thing he respects. If His Highness had taken a strong line at the start none of this would ever have happened and a good many lives would have been saved. Never pays to go prattling of mercy or turning the other cheek to the Bargashes of this world. They haven't the faintest idea what you're talking about, and they'll write it down as weakness every time. What do you propose to do now? I can't handle this without a direct order from the Sultan, you know.'

'I have His Highness's authority to give you that order,' said Sûd. 'If I should not succeed, I was to place the matter in your hands. I have not succeeded, and now it is for you to do as you think fit.'

Colonel Edwards restrained himself from saying: 'And about time too!' and having bowed instead, left the Palace and hurried back to his Consulate to snatch a few hours sleep, eat a late lunch and make arrangements for taking the Heir-Apparent's house by storm.

The naval contingent had not yet returned from Beit-el-Ras, but the *Daffodil* and Lieutenant Larrimore were still in harbour, and Colonel Edwards hoped that young Larrimore was by now feeling more the thing and sufficiently stout to take charge of a landing party. He was in the process of addressing a note to the Lieutenant when Mr Nathaniel Hollis called in to enquire as to the fate of the insurgent forces.

'There have been at least half-a-hundred rumours flying round town,' explained Mr Hollis. 'All of 'em different and each one worse than the last. So I figured I'd better check up on 'em. I understand your Navy boys have been sorting things out a piece?'

He listened attentively while Colonel Edwards gave him a brief résumé of the situation, and having expressed approval of the proposed measures, took his departure with the comfortable feeling that for the first time in several days he would be able to cheer his anxious family with some good news. But though it had certainly cheered his wife, its effect upon his daughter had been entirely unexpected, for Cressy had instantly burst into tears and fled from the room.

'What in thunder's gotten into the girl?' demanded her father, considerably startled. 'She feeling ill, or something?'

'I guess it's only nerves,' apologized Aunt Abby. 'It's been very upsetting for all of us; what with all that shooting, and not being able to leave the house, and no butter or milk and the servants getting downright hysterical.'

'If you ask me, she wanted that fellow Bargash to win,' observed Clayton. 'That's what's upsetting her.'

Hero alone had made no comment. She had been markedly silent and distrait ever since the morning that her uncle had told his assembled family of the Heir-Apparent's dramatic escape to *Marseilles*, for it had shocked her profoundly to find that she had been duped and deliberately lied to, and that there had never been any question of Bargash escaping from certain death or leaving the Island. It was also far from pleasant to realize that she had been made a fool of. But worst of all was the realization that the 'bloodless revolution' that Thérèse had once spoken of –

the swift *coup d'état* that was to result in a transfer of power in a matter of hours and without a shot being fired – had already led to looting and riot, a complete paralysis of the normal life of the city, and the brutal murder of a respected Hindu merchant.

There had been no reliable news for the past few days, but Hero knew something of the provisioning of *Marseilles* and of its strength and impregnability, and when the Consulate servants had retailed rumours of widespread support for Bargash and panic among the Sultan's supporters, it had seemed to her that Majid could not possibly win, and she had expected hourly to hear that he had abdicated.

The news that his reluctant army, having been reinforced by a small detachment of English naval officers, had forced a battle, inflicted severe casualties on the garrison, breached the walls of *Marseilles* and driven the Heir-Apparent and his supporters to flight, was entirely unexpected, and the recital of it appalled her no less than Cressy. She could not understand how Uncle Nat could sit there and tell it as though it were nothing more than an unfortunate incident; let alone express satisfaction at the measures that Colonel Edwards was planning to take in order to effect the arrest of the fugitive.

Hero might react less emotionally to the news than Cressy, and it was true that she had been feeling a good deal less kindly towards the Prince of late. But she sympathized deeply with her cousin's distress, and as soon as she could do so, she excused herself and ran upstairs to comfort her. But Cressy's door had been locked and she had returned no answer when begged to open it.

Hero gave up the attempt and went downstairs again: unaware that the room was empty and her cousin already half-way to the harbour.

20

The sky was pink and green and gold with the sunset, and the streets were very hot, for there had been no wind for the last two days.

Normally, the approach of evening brought people out of their houses to stroll and talk in the cooler air. But today there were few women and children to be seen and no loiterers, and the men all seemed in a hurry: too much of a hurry to spare more than a curious glance at the white woman whose grey, hooded cloak covered her muslin dress and partially concealed her face.

Cressy had never before been out alone and on foot, and at any other time the very thought of walking unaccompanied through those filthy, crowded streets, being jostled and stared at by dark-faced men of a dozen Eastern races, would have horrified her. But she was not thinking of it now. She was thinking only of how she could reach the *Daffodil* and speak to Dan Larrimore. Which had, after all, proved easy enough, for the *Daffodil*'s jolly-boat was waiting at the water-steps, and a startled coxswain, who knew Miss Cressida Hollis by sight, was persuaded without much difficulty to convey her out to the ship.

It was Dan who had been difficult. He had said 'Yes, who is it?' when the coxswain tapped on the cabin door, but the tone of his voice had been so forbidding that Cressy had brushed past her hesitant guide for fear that he might actually refuse to admit her.

Dan had been quite as startled as the coxswain, and had taken no pains to conceal it; which Cressy put down to the fact that she had caught him at a disadvantage, for he was in his shirt-sleeves and wearing what she took to be a bathrobe flung hurriedly about his shoulders. But she was too distraught to pay the least heed to such details, and in any case her own unchaperoned appearance at this hour was sufficiently irregular to make Lieutenant Larrimore's unconventional attire a matter of no account.

The coxswain, taking note of his commanding officer's stupefied expression, retreated hastily and closed the cabin door behind him, and Cressy said: 'I know that I should not have come, but I was so upset when I heard what had happened that I just *had* to see you.'

Dan continued to stare at her in frowning silence, and something in his face made her say sharply: 'Are you all right?'

She saw his expression change with startling suddenness, as though she had said something unbelievably wonderful; something too good to be true.

He said unsteadily: 'It isn't anything. I'm all right. It's nothing to worry about.'

'How *can* you say such a thing?' demanded Cressy distractedly. 'It may not be anything to you, but it is to me!'

'Is it?' asked Dan gently. 'Then it was worth it. I didn't know you'd feel like that. I didn't know you cared at all.'

'You did know! You've always known. That was what we quarrelled about. You knew very well how I felt about it all. And I haven't changed. That's why I came here to tell you that you can't do this. That you mustn't!'

The glow faded from Dan's eyes and was replaced by a curious still-ness, and he said carefully: 'I seem to have made a mistake. What are you here for, Cressy?'

'I've just told you. To ask you not to do it. To *beg* you not to. You could refuse if you wanted to. Colonel Edwards isn't anything to do with you really. I mean, he's not in the Navy, or – or anything like that, and you could always leave harbour and say you were needed some place else, couldn't you? You're supposed to be hunting slavers, so you could say that you had heard one was on its way to—— Oh, to Madagascar or the Gulf, anywhere – and that it was your duty to intercept it. And it *is* your duty; it is! This isn't. Zanzibar doesn't belong to you or your country. It's nothing to do with you and you've no right to interfere!'

She saw that Dan was looking oddly drawn and somehow a great deal older than she had imagined him to be, and found herself thinking that this was how he would look in ten years' time – or twenty.

He said: 'Will you excuse me if I sit down?' and did so without waiting for her permission, jerking the bathrobe further across him with his right hand. 'I think you'll have to make yourself a little clearer. What is it that you want me to do – or not to do?'

There was a remoteness in the tone of his voice that disconcerted Cressy, and she looked at him doubtfully. She had never heard anyone speak in quite that voice before, and she realized with a little shock of surprise that he was no longer a friend, or even an acquaintance. He had suddenly become a stranger about whom she knew nothing, and the eyes that were raised to her face were empty of all expression. Yet if he were once not the person she had thought him to be, not a man whom she had once con-fidently imagined to be in love with her, how could she ask favours of him? And if she did ask, was there any reason why he should be disposed to grant them?

Cressy discovered that the air in the cramped little cabin was intolerably close, and pushing the hood back from her head with a nervous gesture she tugged at the ribbons that fastened it under her chin, as though they impeded her breathing. The sun slid below the horizon taking the gold from the day, and all at once the cabin was full of blue twilight and the sound of the tide chuckling softly against the anchor chain.

Dan said: 'Well?'

'Papa said . . . Pa told me——' began Cressy uncertainly: and paused again, biting her lip and pleating the ribbons with careful fingers.

'Yes?' The query was not in the least helpful and was not intended to be.

Cressy flushed and said: 'Colonel Edwards told him that – that the Sultan's men had refused to attack the Prince's troops.'

'The rebels, you mean,' corrected Dan dryly.

Cressy flashed him an angry glance and said defiantly: 'No, I don't! I mean Prince Bargash's supporters. And he said that when they wouldn't do anything, you and a party of your people fired on them and drove them out of *Marseilles*, and killed a great many of them. Did you do that?'

'We did. Is that what you wanted to ask me?'

'No. I – he . . . Colonel Edwards told Papa that the Prince had come back to his own house and that you were going to arrest him tomorrow. He said you were going to anchor right opposite his house and open fire on it. Like you did on *Marseilles*.'

She paused again, as though she hoped that he would deny it. But Dan made no comment: partly because the British Consul's instructions had not yet reached him and this was the first he had heard of it, but largely because there was nothing to be said.

Cressy held out her hands in a sudden childish gesture of pleading that touched his heart, and at the same time pitchforked him into anger because she had no right to come here and ask impossible things of him: things that he could not grant and that she would hate him for not granting. He would so gladly have given her almost anything else she might ask of him – including his life if she had cared to demand it! But not this . . .

Cressy said: 'Dan, please – *please*! You can't do it. You can't kill a whole lot of people who have no quarrel with you and are no concern of yours, just because you think one man should be their ruler and they prefer another. Let them settle it among themselves. It's their country, not yours. You don't have to interfere.'

Dan said curtly: 'I have to obey orders.'

'But you've no *right* to interfere!'

'I'm not interfering. I'm obeying orders.'

'But if the orders are wrong? – if they are unfair?'

Unfair! thought Dan with another spasm of anger and despair. How could she talk about being unfair when she could come to him now, looking pale and desperate – and utterly, heart-breakingly young and sweet and lovely? When she knew, she *must* know, how much he loved her and how hard it was to resist her ... Unfair! What did women know of fairness or unfairness if they were prepared to use a man's love as a lever to get what they desired?

He said harshly: 'Who is to be the judge of that? You? You don't know what you are talking about, Cressy. You are being sentimental about something you do not understand, and thinking with your heart and not your head. I'm not going to argue the rights and wrongs of the case with you: I tried to do that once before, you remember, and it only ended by my offending you.'

'Because you were being prejudiced,' said Cressy hotly. 'You didn't want me to be friends with the Prince's sisters because you and your Colonel Edwards don't happen to like him, and you were afraid that I might hear something to his advantage – see *his* side of things for a change.'

'No,' said Dan evenly and without emotion. 'I was afraid that you might get involved in a dangerous and unsavoury affair; and I can only hope you have not done so.'

'Well I have! – if you mean that I sympathize with the Prince and think that he is a far better man than that horrible brother of his, who everyone knows is weak and mean and selfish and is doing nothing for his people, and won't spend any money except on himself, and——'

She paused for breath and Dan said tiredly: 'I suppose you got that from his sisters, too? It's no good, Cressy. You had better go home. I can't help you. And even if I could, it would still be no good, because if I took the *Daffodil* out tonight someone else would carry out the orders in my place.'

'No, they wouldn't. That's why I came here. That's why I *had* to see you. Pa says that Colonel Edwards told him that the other ship and the Sultan's own warships draw too much water, and that's why he had asked Colonel Edwards to use yours instead, because the *Daffodil* can go right in close to shore and his can't. So you see if you weren't here it would be all right. Dan, couldn't you? Wouldn't you for ... for ...' The blood came up in a hot rush to her pretty, pleading face, and she finished in a barely audible whisper: 'For *me*?'

She saw Dan flinch as though she had struck him, but he did not speak. He only looked at her, and the silence stretched out like a violin string that is slowly drawn taut, until she could hear the ticking of the flat gold pocket watch that lay on the desk between them, and once again the whisper of the tide.

He was not going to answer her, but his silence was the refusal that he would not put into words, and now it was no longer only her cheeks that were hot, for her whole body seemed one burning blush of shame. She had made a personal thing of her plea, and he had refused her. He was not in love with her after all. He probably never had been and she had only imagined it. And imagined, too, that because of it she could, if she tried, twist him round her finger and make him do anything she asked, because it was she, Cressida Hollis, who asked it.

Cressy pressed her hands together, trembling with humiliation and hurt, and forcing back the angry tears that glittered in her eyes and must on no account be allowed to fall, said in taut, brittle voice: 'I suppose I should have known better than to ask a favour of you. The British enjoy bullying, don't they? And interfering. And running other people's countries and sending gunboats to deal with anyone who disagrees with them. You didn't stop and think before you opened fire a few days ago on several hundred defenceless people who had done you no harm, did you? You just obeyed orders and killed them. And you'll do just the same tomorrow, even though there are women in the house. Méjé is there, and her servants. And a little boy of twelve. But that won't stop you, will it? You'll kill them without a qualm, and the Prince too and all the people who have stayed by him and been loyal to him, just because you are ordered to. You're no better than a public hangman and I hope I never have to see you again!'

She dragged the hood over her curls, and Dan said in a colourless voice: 'I'll get someone to see you home.'

'I don't need anyone to see me home, thank you.'

Dan gave a short laugh that held no amusement, and said: 'You'll need a boat; unless you intend to swim.'

He got to his feet with a palpable effort, and as he did so the bath-robe slipped a little and she saw for the first time that his left arm was in a sling. For a moment her heart seemed to check and stop, and she said breathlessly: 'You're hurt! How did you—— were you ... were you wounded in the fighting?'

'I was,' said Dan. 'By those poor "defenceless creatures" you are so concerned about. And since it seems that their enemies are yours, it will console you to know that I was not the only one, for they somehow managed to kill or wound over sixty of their attackers.' He walked past her to jerk open the cabin door and send for Mr Wilson, whom he instructed to see Miss Hollis safely back to her father's house.

The boat that took her away passed the British Consul's skiff coming out, and the seaman who brought Colonel Edwards' letter to Lieutenant Larrimore's cabin found it in darkness in the deepening twilight, and his commanding officer sitting with his head on the desk and his face hidden in the crook of his right arm.

*   *   *

As the clear, pale light of morning brightened over the green Island and the placid sea, the muezzin's voice arose from the minaret of the mosque calling the Faithful to prayer, and throughout the city good Moslems left their beds and stood facing Mecca to murmur obediently: '*Here am I at thy call, O God*——'

Cholé had risen with them. But when her prayers were said she had not returned to her bed to sleep again, for she knew that today sleep would elude her as it had eluded her for the greater part of the two last nights. She had witnessed from her window the humiliating reception and ignominious retreat of Majid's ambassador, and had placed the same construction upon that ill-fated essay in diplomacy as her brother Bargash had done. And when on the following night Méjé, leaning from her lattice in the dark, had whispered the details of Sûd's visit, she had been as sure as Bargash himself that he had been right to reject such a pusillanimous offer, since it was clearly not the action of a man who held the winning hand, but of one who was afraid and who hoped to gain by fair words what he could not gain through strength.

Fortified by this conviction, Cholé's spirits had soared once more and she had lain awake in the darkness, feverishly thinking and planning for Bargash, and refusing to entertain the prospect of failure. It was still unthinkable to her that the brother whom she had quarrelled with and now hated should triumph over the brother she loved, and even now, after the crushing defeat at *Marseilles*, she would not admit that such a thing was possible. There was still hope – Sûd's abortive mission had proved that! There would be some way out. There *must* be some way out! Some twist of fate that would turn defeat into victory.

Cholé had tossed and turned and agonized, and fallen at last into an exhausted sleep from which dawn and her women had awakened her barely two hours later. But her prayers being said, she had gone to the windows that gave onto the harbour, to lean on the sill and breathe the fresh air of morning and hope that the day would bring a solution to the tangled problems that had haunted her all night.

The sea was a milky opal in the dawn, and the harbour full of ships that rocked gently to the barely breathing swell, appearing no more substantial than silhouettes cut from dark paper and pasted on looking-glass. Dhows, mtepes, batelas, feluccas, wind-jammers and brigs; each one drowsing above its own mirrored reflection. Behind them, threading its way through the three tiny islands that guarded the entrance to the harbour, a solitary schooner under jib and staysail drifted in on the tide, and Cholé watched it idly for a moment or two, and then recognizing it, frowned. The *Virago*'s owner was a friend of Majid's and therefore by inference an enemy, and she could have wished that he had not chosen this moment to return, for they had enough enemies to contend with already and the arrival of another was an unpropitious omen. She gave a small superstitious shiver at the thought, and looking quickly away, saw the *Daffodil* ...

It was surprising that she had not noticed it at once, for it lay close in shore and immediately opposite her brother's house: its guns trained on the barred door and shuttered windows, and a boat-load of armed seamen already rowing away from it. She watched uncomprehendingly while the men disembarked, and saw a naval officer detach himself from among them and walk alone to the gate – the Sultan's Baluchi guard parting to let him through – and heard him call out to the Seyyid Bargash to surrender. And it was only then that she realized what had happened. Majid had appealed to the British to arrest his brother, and all was indeed lost.

Salmé, entering, found her sister pacing frantically to and fro, wringing her hands and crying; her lovely face so ravaged with grief as to be barely recognizable and her voice harsh with tears: 'It is over,' sobbed Cholé. 'It is over! We have lost! It is over——! What are we going to do? What will become of us all?'

She began to rock herself backwards and forwards, and Salmé looked from the window and saw the end of everything they had planned. The end of hope and the end of all their dreams ... 'Méjé was right,' whispered Salmé. 'She is the only one who has been right. She said Majid's terms were generous and that Bargash would have been wise to accept them. We have all been mad and foolish, and now——'

Her voice was drowned in a crash of shots, and the morning that a moment before has seemed so quiet was suddenly a bedlam of noise, for the bluejackets were firing at the shuttered windows, and the crack and whine and smack of bullets were barely louder than the shouts of men and the terrified screams of women.

Cholé broke into hysterical weeping, and as the din of the firing increased she put her hands over her ears and ran from the room. But the whole house was awake and alive with sounds that could not be shut out, and everywhere she looked there were shrieking women who cowered in corners or tried to hide themselves behind curtains and hangings. In their screams and the remorseless crack of the rifles she heard at last the knell of all her fevered dreams and glittering ambition, and knew that there was no longer any hope for Bargash except in submission. The English had not yet used the guns that were trained on the house, but they would do so if he persisted in his refusal to surrender. They would use them as they had done at *Marseilles*; to batter down the solid stone walls and smash the men who hid behind them into into ugly, bloodstained fragments. It must not happen here! She must do something to stop it. She must persuade Bargash that his only chance was to surrender . . .

She fled to a side window, and leaning from it, screamed across the narrow gap until at last she was answered and her brother's contorted face glared back at her, mouthing wild words:

No! he would not give himself up. Death was preferable and he would sacrifice his whole household rather than surrender! Méjé, Aziz, servants, slaves and supporters – they should die with him! It was the least they could do after the way he had been betrayed . . . *Yes*, betrayed! None of this was his fault. Not one jot of it! He had been tricked by that scheming white man who had sold him worthless weapons. By the imbecility of the el Harth who had lacked the wit to know how to use such new-fangled firearms and supposed that he would be able to explain all when he came, or bring different ammunition; and had then blamed him for their own stupidity – the sons of apes and noseless mothers! But let everyone beware, for he was not yet defeated! He still had many sympathizers in the city and more in the villages, and they would certainly have heard the firing and already be hastening to his side to slay the foreign sailors and overthrow Majid. Cholé would see——!

Listening to her brother's extravagant ravings through the din of firing and the sound of bullets ploughing into furniture and splintering vases and mirrors, Cholé was seized with the terrifying conviction that Bargash had lost his grip on reality and was no longer sane, and she began to cry again and to beg and implore in a voice that was alternately choked with tears and shrill with panic.

Perhaps it was her frantic pleading that at last persuaded him. Or possibly it was the ominous smell of smoke and a belated realization that the beleaguered house could all too easily catch fire and burn down about them. Whatever the reason, she saw his face change. The frenzy drained slowly out of it, leaving it as slack and emotionless as a dead man's, and she knew that she had won:

'Tell them to stop firing,' said Bargash dully. 'I will surrender . . . but not to Majid. I will never surrender to Majid. It must be to the British Consul, or to no one.'

Cholé did not wait for further words. She turned from the window and ran out of the room and along the passages, tripping over boxes and scattered bundles of clothing, thrusting aside kneeling women and only pausing at the bottom of the last flight of stairs to snatch a cloak and a veil from a praying slave. A moment later she had crossed the courtyard and brushed past the cowering gate-keeper, and was running through the streets towards the British Consulate.

She knew that what she was doing was contrary to every tenet of Arab etiquette and violated every rule of feminine modesty. But to Cholé as well as to Bargash, the humiliation of begging assistance and mediation from a foreigner was preferable to humbling themselves before Majid. Behind her she could hear voices shouting above the crash and crackle of musketry: '*Aman! Aman!*' (peace) and she knew that they came from Bargash's house. His people must be calling to the sailors to stop firing, and she paused for a moment in the deserted street to listen, gasping and breathless, and heard the sounds thin and stop. And all at once the morning was strangely silent.

It is all over, thought Cholé. *We have lost* . . . She began to run again, but more slowly now, because she was blinded by tears; and by the time she was ushered into the British Consul's presence she was crying so uncontrollably that it took that embarrassed bachelor a full five minutes to discover what it was that she was trying to tell him.

Colonel George Edwards, small and spare in the hard sunlight, stepped briskly up to the carved and bullet-scarred door of the Heir-Apparent's house and tapped peremptorily upon it with his walking stick; and when at last it creaked open, Bargash came out weeping, and handed his sword to the Consul.

Dan and a party of the *Daffodil*'s men escorted the defeated rebel to the Palace, and having given him into the custody of the Sultan's guards, returned to their ship. And it was only as the *Daffodil* moved back to her moorings that Dan saw the *Virago*, and realized that Captain Frost had returned. But by then he was too tired to care.

He glanced at the schooner where she rode at anchor between a two-masted Arab dhow and a gaily painted *baghlah* from Cutch, and wondered fleetingly what shady business her owner had been engaged in on the coast north of Mombasa. He took it for granted that it had involved some questionable chicanery, and also that any cargo Rory Frost had landed or was about to land would be found, on inspection, to be blameless. All the same he would, on a normal occasion, have inspected it. But now he found that he could raise no interest in the *Virago* or the transactions, illegal or otherwise, of her Captain. Or, for that matter, in anything else. He was feeling ill and bad-tempered and inclined to think that life was a dreary and savourless business; and his arm was giving him a good deal of pain, for he had refused to keep it in a sling and gone ashore that morning with it thrust uncomfortably into a sleeve that had not been designed to accommodate bandages.

'I see Rory's back,' observed the Assistant-Surgeon meditatively: 'A pity we lost him. Young Ruete says that he's brought back half-a-dozen horses from somewhere over on the mainland, and that they were landed an hour or so ago, just before we got back from the Palace. Sounds innocent enough. But then Rory's transactions always do. It's the smell of them that's wrong. What do you suppose he's been up to?'

'I've no idea,' said Dan indifferently; and went down to his cabin to try to snatch a little rest before going ashore once more to accompany Colonel Edwards and Commander Adams of the *Assaye* to the Palace.

Majid returned to his city that same afternoon in impressive state; attended by his ministers and escorted by his troops and the British naval contingent who had left to fight a battle and stayed to blow up *Marseilles*. The grateful citizens, thankful to see the end of hostilities, received them as though they had been a conquering army returning loaded with laurels, and they marched through cheering crowds and a rain of flowers and rice that showered down upon them from every balcony, window and rooftop. The foreign community too had turned out in force to watch the festivity and raise their hats as the Sultan rode by. Among them Monsieur René Dubail with his family and the members of his consulate; for whatever his private feelings on the matter, Monsieur Dubail, as the diplomatic representative of his country, had no intention of appearing to snub the winner of the recent contest, even though his Government had favoured the cause of the loser, and for reasons of their own would have greatly preferred see Bargash in the role of victor. Well, that could still happen one day, thought the Consul philosophically. Time was on his side and he might yet inherit his brother's throne in the normal manner. In the meantime, however, policy dictated that Majid's triumph should be accepted with a good grace, and Monsieur Dubail therefore lifted his hat, smiled indulgently and bowed as the Sultan passed.

Back once more in his Palace Majid had called a Durbar of princes, chiefs and nobles to decide what had best be done with his rebellious brother. He had refused to consider such penalties as death or imprisonment, and at its conclusion summoned the British Consul to hear the Durbar's decision. 'We are all agreed,' he informed Colonel Edwards – not entirely truthfully. 'And it is our desire that my brother, Seyyid Bargash, be given into your charge, and that you should do with him what you think fit.'

If the Colonel was unprepared for this bland transference of responsibility he did not show it, but bowed and suggested that, in his opinion, the best method of dealing with the Heir-Apparent and restoring peace to His Highness's dominions would be to desire the Seyyid Bargash to sign a formal undertaking never to plot or wage war against the Sultan again, to quit the Sultan's territories and to proceed to any port that the British Consul might select.

The document had been signed in the presence of the packed Durbar, and having taken a solemn oath on the Koran to abide by it, Bargash listened in silence while Majid ordered him to embark for India on the *Assaye*. After which he walked out with an escort of the Sultan's troops to say farewell to his sisters.

Cholé had wept so many tears during the last frantic hours that she had none left to weep. But her dry-eyed despair had been more heart-rending than Méjé's noisy lamentation or Salmé's broken sobs, and Bargash had torn himself away at last, racked with grief and emotion and raging against Fate and all those who had failed him. Little Abd-il-Aziz had not been one of these, for the boy had pleaded to be allowed to go with his older brother into exile, and Majid had given his consent.

They had embarked together, and from the windows of Beit-el-Tani their sisters had seen them go, and watched the *Assaye* weigh anchor and move slowly out of harbour on the evening tide, her sails rose-pink in the sunset and her wake a silver ribbon across the darkening sea.

'He is gone,' whispered Cholé. 'It is all over. Everything is finished . . . it is the end.'

But though the great enterprise was over and Bargash had gone, the aftermath had still to be faced. And even Cholé could not have known how bitter it would prove to find themselves alone and ostracized.

Their riches had been dissipated, and many of their slaves whom they had armed and sent to support Bargash had been killed or wounded at *Marseilles*. Their friends fell away from them and their foes watched them jealously for fear that they might instigate new plots; even the merchants of the city would call no longer at Beit-el-Tani except under cover of darkness. Worst of all, their support of Bargash had lost them the loyalty and affection of all those half-brothers and sisters, relatives and connections, who had made up the gay and heterogeneous family of Sultan Saïd, and they were never again to be part of it. Only one person had stood by them, and that, by the irony of fate, the one who had most cause to hate them.

Majid could not be persuaded to punish his sisters, though his ministers and his family complained that he was weak and ineffectual, and the townspeople who only a few days before had pelted him with flowers and greeted him as a victorious General laughed at him in the bazaars, and despised him for his clemency.

'It is all over,' Cholé had said. 'Everything is finished . . . It is the end.' And for her this was true. But for Salmé it was a beginning: because now once again she had leisure to steal up to the rooftop after sundown. Not to mourn for Bargash and the ruin of their hopes, as Cholé was doing, but to watch a young man from Hamburg entertain his friends in a lamp-lit room on the far side of the street.

In the anxious days of the conspiracy she had been too busy to go, for there had been so many letters to write and so many plans to be made. But Beit-el-Tani, once a burning centre of excitement, activity and intrigue, was quiet now, for no one visited Salmé and her sister any more, and their days were long and empty and idle.

There was time now to think and to regret. And Cholé wept her beauty away while Méjé moaned and lamented, explaining over and over again to anyone who would listen that she had always known that this would happen – she had told them so, and she had been right! But for Salmé there was time to think of young Wilhelm Ruete, and to peep at him through the chinks of the shutter that guarded the passage window. Time now – too much time – to watch him and his friends from the darkness of a flat-topped roof. A roof so near her own that by leaning over the parapet and stretching out her hand she could almost have touched the hand of – of someone who had done the same from the opposite side of the street . . .

> Visit those you love, though your abode be distant,
> And clouds and darkness have arisen between you . . .

No man of her own race would say such words to her now, for what Arab of rank would wish to marry a woman who had been concerned in the rebellion, and was no longer rich or received by her own relations? The clouds and the darkness had indeed arisen, and Salmé, who was young and sad and very lonely, watched Wilhelm Ruete and dreamed impossible dreams.

'One can't help feeling sorry for the poor little thing,' said Olivia Credwell, drinking morning coffee at the Hollises. 'None of the Sultan's family will speak to any of them now, and Cholé seems to have been *most* unkind to her, and accused her of disloyalty or something. You can see that she's terribly distressed about it all. I'm teaching her to speak English, and she says she would like to learn German too, so I've asked Frau Lessing to tea on Thursday to meet her, and I do hope you will both come too. She would be *so* happy to see you.'

Hero had returned a non-committal answer, while Cressy continued to stare out at the garden as though she did not know that she had been addressed, and said nothing at all. But their lack of enthusiasm passed unnoticed by Olivia, who said a trifle anxiously:

'I did ask Thérèse, but she won't come, because she says that now that the whole thing has failed – the rebellion I mean – we would do much better to keep away from Beit-el-Tani and not be too friendly with anyone who had anything to do with it. But then as we *ourselves* had something to do with it, I don't see how . . . I told her I thought she was being a little hard, but she assured me that on the contrary she was only being wise. Oh, well——!'

Olivia paused to heave a deep sigh, and then added with regretful honesty: 'I fear that I myself have *never* been very wise. I think being kind is better, and I really do feel that we should all try and be as kind as possible to poor little Salmé. And to the others, of course.'

'The others don't want us to be kind to them,' said Hero. 'They've made that perfectly clear!'

'Yes, indeed,' agreed Olivia with another sigh. 'You would think, after all we have done for them . . . Do you know that Cholé *positively* refused to see me when I called to commiserate? Naturally, I assumed at the time that she was feeling too upset to see anyone. But now I believe it was quite deliberate, because I have been several times since then and she has always sent someone to say that she cannot see me – and almost rudely, too! I cannot think why she should behave in such an odd manner after all that one has tried to do. Though of course I do feel terribly sorry for her.'

Mrs Credwell extracted an acceptance to her tea-party and went away, and Hero said: 'The trouble with Olivia is that she really cannot see why Cholé does not wish to see her.'

'Can you?' asked Cressy listlessly.

'I think so. I guess it's because Olivia is English and Cholé can't forget that.'

Cressy continued to gaze unseeingly out of the window at the sunlit garden where the butterflies lilted idly about the jasmine bushes and the over-blown roses, and after a minute she said almost inaudibly: 'Olivia tried to help them.'

'I know. But it would be asking too much of Cholé to expect her to forget that it was the English Consul and English seamen who defeated her brother and helped kill a whole heap of his men. And the English, too, who have shipped him off to one of their own Colonies, where I've no doubt they'll keep him to fit in with future plans of their own. They hadn't the least right to interfere, and when I think of them opening fire on that house——'

'*Don't!*' said Cressy in a suffocated voice.

'I'm sorry,' apologized Hero contritely. 'I know you feel as badly about it as I do – you couldn't possibly feel worse, because you haven't anything to blame yourself for, and I have! But at least you did your best to prevent the Prince's house being fired on, and you will always be able to console yourself with that.'

'Yes . . . Yes, I can always console myself with that, can't I?'

There was an odd note of hysteria in Cressy's voice, and Hero said in some astonishment: 'You aren't still thinking about that Lieutenant, are you Cressy?'

Cressy did not reply, and presently Hero said earnestly: 'I assure you honey, he is not worth worrying your head about. Any man who could permit himself to be used in such a manner is no better than a hired bravo, and the sooner you forget him the better. I am not saying that it was not exceedingly courageous of you to try to persuade him not to act the part of a mercenary, but you might have known that it would prove useless. I do not think he is at all the sort of person whose better nature one could appeal to. Too hide-bound and unimaginative. And solid.'

'I should not have gone,' said Cressy in a whisper.

'There I *cannot* agree with you!' said Hero vigorously. 'We should always do what we conceive to be our duty, no matter how painful the consequences. You were quite right to make the attempt.'

Cressy gave a small, hysterical laugh and turned from the window, and Hero was shocked to see how white and stricken she looked. She said on a high note:

'That is what Dan said. Don't you see, that was exactly what he said. And that is why he did it! We talk a lot about people having "a sense of duty", but it seems that when an Englishman is said to have one, he really *has*. It's very funny, isn't it?'

She began to laugh and found that she could not stop.

21

The picnic had been Aunt Abby's idea. They had all, she said, been cooped up indoors too long and Cressy was beginning to look downright peaked. But now that the Bargash rebellion had ended and the city returned to normal, there was no longer any reason why the girls should not get into the open country and breathe a little fresh air. Dr Kealey, whom she had consulted over the matter of her daughter's pale cheeks and loss of spirits, prescribed an iron tonic and sea bathing, and suggested that more exercise and less sitting about in shuttered rooms might be beneficial to all the ladies. A piece of advice which her husband heartily endorsed:

'There's been a damn' sight too much moping around, if you ask me,' said Uncle Nat, who had not in fact been asked, 'and it's getting my goat. Why the heck any daughter of mine has to go around looking like a drowned kitten just because a good-for-nothing Arab rebel has gotten his just deserts, I'll be darned if I know! She'd no business taking sides in the first place, and even less business carrying on mooning and sulking because the candidate she fancied has taken a licking.'

'I don't *think* it's that,' said Aunt Abby, pondering the matter. 'Though of course, being so friendly with those sisters of his, she was disappointed for their sakes. But you have to admit that the whole affair was most unpleasant . . . and not being able to put a foot out of doors, either.'

'All the more reason for putting one out now. Besides, the rains will be starting up soon, so you'd better all get out while you've got the chance, because once they get going you'll have to stay indoors whether you want to or not. It's a pity your daughter can't learn to keep herself occupied in the way my niece can.'

Aunt Abby, recognizing the implied rebuke of that 'your' sighed and said submissively: 'Yes, indeed. Dear Hero is really a most industrious girl. She tells me that it is quite clear that until she masters the language she can do little practical good in Zanzibar, and she has certainly been applying herself most seriously to her studies. She was asking Dr Kealey a great many questions when he called this morning, and I am afraid she means to do something about the local sanitation: I know she used to help in that hospital, but I still do not think it is a very suitable subject for a young girl, though when I tried to change the conversation she told me that I had no social conscience. I do hope that is not true, but I own I cannot get so – so angry about things. Not that Hero gets angry. She is much more like your brother in that. She just decides what is right and is quite calm about it. And firm,' added Aunt Abby with another faint sigh.

'Gets that from her Aunt Lucy,' commented Uncle Nat with a grin: 'Lucy was always right, even in the schoolroom; no arguing with her. No arguing with Hero, either!'

'I confess I do not try,' admitted Aunt Abby simply.

'Clay does,' said her husband with a short laugh.

Aunt Abby looked worried. She had thought for so long that Hero would be just the wife for Clay, but now, suddenly, she was not so sure. There was still the money of course: Harriet's fortune and now Barclay's handsome competence. She had always hoped that Clay would marry a well-endowed wife, because whatever people might say to the contrary, money made a great difference to life, and Clay was ambitious and handicapped by the lack of adequate private means. But Abby was not mer·cenary, and though at the time she had been bitterly offended by her brother-in-law's insistence that Hero and Clayton were totally unsuited to each other, of late she had begun to wonder if perhaps Barclay had known his daughter a great deal better than she knew her son, and that what he had really meant was that Hero would not suit Clayton.

Abigail Hollis, after the manner of mothers, looked at her son through spectacles so strongly tinted with rose that it is doubtful if she ever saw his true colouring at all. But at least she knew something of his character and tastes, and this knowledge had led her to suppose that what dear Clayton needed was a wife who would settle him down and act as a safe anchor to hold him back from sailing off into dangerous and uncharted seas. She had thought once that Hero would be just the right girl to do this. A steady, sensible young woman who would be able to counteract a certain instability that her son had inherited from his dashing father. But the more she saw of her niece the less certain she became that a marriage between them would prove a success.

Money and high ideals were all very well, thought Aunt Abby uneasily, but would not a little more docility – a little more tolerance, leavened perhaps with a dash of frivolity – be even more desirable? Aunt Abby suspected that Hero might not be tolerant, and the prospect distressed her. Though it did not appear to worry Clay, and after all, he was the one it would most affect. Unless he had thought better of the whole idea? Now that she came to think of it, he was very often out these days and on the whole saw less of Hero than might have been expected. But then perhaps he was merely being wise, for propinquity was something that one could have too much of, and posssibly it might be better if he did not come on the proposed picnic. She would make it an exclusively feminine party (so that they could follow Dr Kealey's advice and find some secluded beach from which they could bathe), and announce it for next Tuesday, as Clay had already arranged to go shooting with Joe Lynch on that day.

Mr Hollis, who disliked eating his meals out of doors, had warmly approved this amendment, and his wife issued invitations to Mrs Kealey, Frau Lessing, Olivia Credwell and Jane Platt, and forgot her anxieties in plans for the preparation of cold pies, desserts and fruit drinks. The German Consul had lent them his own felucca, the *Grethe*, whose crew were trustworthy members of the Consulate guard, and on the following Tuesday Aunt Abby embarked her party and her picnic baskets and set off to sail gently up the coast and spend a refreshing day in the open air.

The weather had been perfect for such an expedition. The wind that day was no more than a gentle breeze, sufficient to temper the heat to tolerable proportions, but not, the hostess noted thankfully, capable of producing waves that were large enough to cause any discomfort to the *Grethe*'s passengers. But though Aunt Abby's first care had been for the comfort of her guests, she had not been too occupied to notice her daughter's behaviour as the *Grethe* moved down the harbour; or too simple to divine its cause.

The felucca had passed within less than a dozen yards of the *Daffodil*, and as they approached it Cressy had quickly changed her seat for one on the far side of the boat, and then looked back again as though she could not help herself: her face betraying her as clearly as though she had shouted her thoughts aloud.

Oh dear! So that's *it! I was afraid so*, thought Abigail. How agonizing the heart-aches of youth could be, and how comfortable it was to be done with all that. Though it did seem a little unfair that one should have to suffer the same pangs at second-hand on behalf of one's children. First Clay and now Cressy——! And neither of them, in their mother's opinion, likely to be much happier in the near future.

For her own part, Abigail had taken a liking to Daniel Larrimore, whose manner towards her had always been admirable and whose patent devotion to her daughter she found touching. She had warmed towards him, and might easily have grown fond of him had not Clayton and Nathaniel's dismay at the very idea of losing Cressida to a 'foreigner' made her feel that she should not give him any encouragement. But although there had been a time when the *Daffodil*'s arrival in harbour had been a signal that Lieutenant Larrimore could be expected to call at the American Consulate within the hour, he had not been there for some weeks now, and she had allowed herself to hope that the whole thing had died a natural death. Which, taking the viewpoint of her husband and son into account, was a distinct relief, since she herself had always suspected that her daughter was not nearly as indifferent to the Lieutenant's attentions as she would have her family suppose.

Scanning Cressy's strained face she was sure now that her suspicion had been correct, and she wondered what could have gone wrong. They had obviously quarrelled about something, but as she did not believe in forcing confidences and Cressy had not as yet chosen to confide in her, there was nothing much that she could do except hope that it would pass as these things did – though she knew that when one was young it was difficult to believe that. Cressy and Clayton . . . Aunt Abby sighed, and glancing towards the girl whom her son hoped to marry, was as startled by Hero's expression as she had been disturbed by Cressy's.

Hero too was staring at a ship; and although her aunt had no reason to recognize the *Virago*, she was immediately aware that this must be the one on which Hero had spent an uncomfortable ten days after her rescue at sea. Nothing else could account for the forbidding expression on her niece's face, and though Aibgail fully shared Hero's opinion of the *Virago*'s owner, she could not think it right that any young woman should look so – so coldly implacable. Especially one who might decide to marry her son! It augured a temper and disposition that was ill suited to dealing happily with such a person as Clay, and Aunt Abby trembled for both of them and was conscious of a sinking feeling of guilt, in that it was she herself who had pressed her niece to come to Zanzibar.

Oh my! thought Aunt Abby helplessly. *Oh my——!* Her pleasure in the glittering day had been quite spoiled, and she found herself wholly unable to enjoy the charming views that slid past them as the felucca won free of the harbour and turned northward up the coast.

So he's back, is he! thought Hero, staring at the *Virago*. She might have known it! Captain Frost had presumably made a nice profit out of providing the Sultan with arms to put down the recent rising, but she noticed that he had taken good care to be absent when it occurred. And now here he was back again: basking once more in the protection of his friend Majid, and able, in consequence, to continue his slave-trading activities with the minimum of risk and the maximum of profit. She wondered, as Dan had done, what questionable cargo his ship had been carrying this time, and presumed that it would be men rather than muskets.

The rising would have provided him with an excellent opportunity to bring in any number of slaves under the very nose of authority, since the British Navy, reflected Hero resentfully, had been far too taken up with shooting down the hapless supporters of Seyyid Bargash to pay the least attention to such minor matters as slave trading!

The fact that the Sultan's victory over his brother meant a corresponding rise in the fortunes of Captain Frost seemed to her one of the worst aspects of the whole affair, and she considered it high time that someone, preferably the British Consul, did something about it. After all, the man was English, and since the British authorities were empowered by their Government to put down slavery and mete out summary justice to any of their subjects caught shipping, selling, buying or owning slaves, she could not understand what they were about to allow such a person to remain at large. It not only made a mockery of justice, but was an open admission of incompetence or blatant national partiality.

The opinion once advanced by Thaddaeus Fullbright that they were waiting for proof could be dismissed as ridiculous, – together with his assertion that Dan Larrimore would get it one day because he was the 'persevering kind'. Well, if the Lieutenant had failed to get it by now, he was not really trying and it was quite time someone else took a hand. She had a very good mind to see if she could not do better herself.

Hero removed her hat to let the breeze blow through her curls, and leaned back in the shade of the sail to ponder the problem.

If the *Virago*'s Captain were running cargoes of slaves he was obviously hiding them in a place where no one had yet thought to look, and that place was almost certainly somewhere on the Island. Probably the house of some Arab acquaintance, for Colonel Edwards's authority over all British subjects would make it too dangerous to permit of slaves being hidden in any house that might be searched. It was therefore merely a question of discovering 'Who' and 'Where' – which should not be so difficult, since the Island was far from large.

I'll speak to Fattûma about it, decided Hero. Fattûma heard all the gossip of the bazaars and might be able to pick up some information. And there was also Thérèse, who had spoken of spies being employed by Cholé and her sisters to keep them informed of their enemies' plans, and implied that it was common practice in Zanzibar. If that were true and information could be bought, then she would discuss the matter with Thérèse and set about buying it herself. And once the evidence was obtained it could be handed to Colonel Edwards, who should be able to arrange to catch Rory Frost red-handed and thereafter have no difficulty in effecting his arrest and deportation.

Hero was not so foolish as to imagine that putting one slaver out of business was going to make an appreciable difference to the trade, or reduce by more than a fraction the number of wretched captives who yearly passed in and out of Zanzibar on their way to the auction block and a life of servitude. She was fully aware of the size of the problem and the appalling difficulties of cleaning such an Augean stable; but at least she would have struck a blow against white participation in the revolting traffic, and to remove even one cause of offence was something, even though nine hundred and ninety-nine remained to deface the name of humanity.

Coloured slave traders, thought Hero from the lofty standpoint of the West, could hardly be expected to realize the full enormity of their actions, and therefore some slight excuse could be made for them on the score of ignorance. But Western slavers ... *White men——!*

'That's Motoni over there,' said Olivia, pointing with one hand and holding on to a flapping, rose-trimmed hat with the other: 'Beit-el-Motoni. Salmé told me that it was her father's favourite palace, and it's where she and Cholé and the rest of them spent most of their childhood. I think it's so sad to picture them all playing together and not knowing that they'd grow up to hate each other, don't you?'

Hero started guiltily, and abandoning her reflections said contritely: 'I'm sorry, Olivia. I was thinking of something else. What were you saying?'

'Nothing very interesting,' admitted Olivia candidly. 'I was only pointing out the sights. That pavilion over there, and the long untidy-looking houses among the trees; that's one of the old Sultan's palaces. And there's another one a bit farther on – look, you can see it ahead, just beyond those far trees. That's Beit-el-Ras. Hubert, my brother, says that Sultan Saïd was still building it when he died and that now it will never be finished. It does seem a pity doesn't it?'

'I suppose so,' said Hero without much interest. 'Isn't that where Majid's army camped the other day?'

'Yes. And they must have made a dreadul mess of it – five thousand men, and all those horses and carts and cooking fires and so on. But then I expect it was a mess already, because Hubert says they're always digging up bits of Beit-el-Ras in the hope of finding the treasure, though so far no one has come across even a trace of it.'

'Treasure? What treasure?' enquired Hero, reacting predictably to a word that for centuries has held a potent magic for all mankind.

'Hasn't anyone told you about that yet? Why, I thought everyone knew it. Hubert says it is just a "yarn"; but all the Arabs believe it. The old Sultan, Seyyid Saïd, collected an enormous amount of treasure, and no one knows what he did with it except that he hid it somewhere, but a lot of people believe that he buried it at Beit-el-Ras and that if he hadn't died at sea he would have told his heir where it was. Majid, I suppose. But as he didn't get back here alive no one knows where it is, though his whole family are quite *convinced* that the British Consul knows. Not Colonel Edwards; another one who had been a great friend of the Sultan's. They say that the Sultan kept on calling for him when he was dying and that made them think—— But of course Hubert says it is all nonsense and there probably wasn't any treasure in the first place. Or if there was, he'd spent it. I'm afraid Hubert is sadly unromantic, and I cannot think why Jane——'

Olivia broke off abruptly, recalling that her sister-in-law was seated within a few feet of her, and turning hurriedly away began to enquire after the health of Frau Lessing's children, while Hero, released from the necessity of making conversation, propped her chin on her hand, and gazing out at the lovely coastline, thought how strange it was that so much beauty and such appalling squalor and cruelty could exist side by side.

A mere mile or so behind them lay the rubbish-strewn waters of the harbour and the reeking alleyways of the city. But here the sea was sapphire, veridian and jade, and the breeze smelled sweetly of cloves. Below the felucca's keel the coral reefs were bars of purple and lilac and lavender, and a strip of white sand three fathoms down was a wide wash of cerulean, freckled with the sequin-shimmer of darting fish. The surf broke cleanly here, uncluttered with ugly flotsam, while the palm-fringed, flower-spangled shores that basked in hot sunlight and cool shadow had the untouched beauty and innocence of Eden.

Lulled by the drowsy swish of the sea and the warm, scented breeze, Hero drifted off into a light sleep . . . and was suddenly back in the cabin of the *Virago*, struggling to remove a heavy matting screen that prevented her from looking out through the open porthole. Beyond that matting, she knew, lay a starlit sea and a white house among dark trees, and someone was rowing bodies ashore and carrying them up to the empty house: the bodies of dead men. It was imperative that she should see who that someone was, and she tore and pushed at the coarse matting until at last a hole began to appear in it and the darkness thinned, and she could hear a voice speaking: Aunt Abby's voice. But what on earth could Aunt Abby be doing on board the *Virago* . . . ?

'I think we might stop soon,' her aunt was saying. 'Somewhere on the far side of those rocks, perhaps?'

Hero awoke with a start to find her fingers clenched on the coarse straw of her hat brim. But her dream was still with her. It had not vanished with her waking, for she was still looking at the same view . . .

It took her a full minute to realize that the house and the trees and the curve of the beach were not a figment of her imagination, but real and three-dimensional; that she was looking at the identical place that she had seen once before (and dreamed that she was seeing again) through a slit cut painfully with a pair of shears in a heavy piece of coconut matting.

There could be no mistaking it. The starlight had concealed details that the midday sun made plain, and the majority of Arab houses were built to much the same plan. But there could not be two identical houses, both high and white with flat, castellated roofs, standing among trees and protected from seaward by a massive wall that appeared to be part of an ancient fort and rose sheer from the rocks on the seashore. A wall with a guardhouse at one end of it.

The beach too was familiar: a crescent of shelving sand, ending on either side in tall, misshapen rocks of wind-torn coral and cliffs topped by casuarina, screw pine and ranks of rustling palms. She could not be wrong ... this was the bay and that was the house. And there was the beach where the muskets had been landed! She had found the secret hiding place where the *Virago*'s contraband was kept concealed until such time as it could be safely distributed to buyers.

Hero drew a long shuddering breath, and for a moment she was almost afraid. This was more than a coincidence: it must be! This was *meant*! She did not pause to consider that in the normal course of events she was almost bound to pass this way one day, and that there was nothing in the least miraculous about it. It seemed to her, on the contrary, that Providence had led her straight to this spot, and for the express purpose of saving countless men, women and children from being sold into slavery by an unprincipled rogue.

All she had to do now was to discover the name of the man who owned that house, and then go to the British Consul with the whole story – or, better still, to Lieutenant Larrimore, who could hardly fail to act upon such information. It might take him a little time to prove any connection between Captain Frost and the owner of the house, but sooner or later the Captain or some member of his crew was bound to visit it. And then the very next cargo of cowed and helpless captives that Emory Frost disembarked or took aboard in that bay would be his last.

She shivered suddenly, and jumping to her feet caught at Mrs Kealey's sleeve, and said:

'Whose is that house over there? Who does it belong to?'

'I've no idea,' said Mrs Kealey, glancing at it without interest.

'One of the local landowners, I expect,' offered Olivia, overhearing the question, 'all the houses in this part of the island are owned by rich Arabs. Do put your hat on, Hero. You'll get shockingly sunburned.'

They were already past the house, and ahead of them, on the far side of the rocks that shielded the bay, lay a long irregular strip of beach shaded by coconut palms and full of unexpected little inlets and deep, rock-fringed pools that the tide had left behind.

'Surely someone must know who it belongs to?' insisted Hero urgently. But no one seemed to know. It was just a house; and apparently an empty one, for the windows were closed and shuttered and there was no sign of life. The crew of the felucca, when interrogated, professed to be equally ignorant, though one of them muttered something that Hero did not catch and another grinned behind his raised hand.

'What was that?' demanded Hero. 'What did you say?'

The man looked blank and shook his head, and Hero appealed again to Olivia: 'Livvy, you ask him. I'm sure he knows.'

Olivia appeared a trifle surprised at her insistence, but complied amiably enough and reported that the man said the house was known as *Kivulimi*.

'Kivulimi's house? Is that the owner's name?'

'No; just *Kivulimi*. It means "The House of Shade". Because of all those trees about it, I suppose. Oh good, we're going to stop here——'

'But who does it *belong* to?' persisted Hero. 'Ask him who it belongs to, Olivia. They pretend not to understand when I speak to them.'

The man shrugged his shoulders and spread out his hands, and Olivia said: 'He doesn't seem to know. Why are you so interested, Hero? It isn't a ruin or a palace or anything like that.'

'I thought I'd seen it before.'

'When? Oh – you mean when you arrived on the *Daffodil*? I expect you did pass it. But then I always think all these houses look exactly alike. What a lovely beach! Now, if we can find a nice place to bathe——'

The felucca edged in as close as it dared and dropped a clumsy iron anchor over the side, and the small boat that had been towed behind it was pressed into service to convey the ladies and their picnic baskets ashore. Aunt Abby selected a sheltered spot where the palms laid a carpet of shade on the sand and an outcrop of coral rock screened the party from the men on the felucca, and despite some anxiety on the score of octopuses, sting-rays or jelly-fish, Cressy, Hero, Olivia and Millicent Kealey bathed in one of the deep pools left by the tide.

The afternoon heat had been tempered by the breeze, but it was still too hot to make anyone feel energetic, and luncheon having been eaten a pleasant torpor descended upon the assembled party. Olivia, who dabbled in art, took out her paints, while Cressy retired to a seat on a fallen palm tree with a book and her own troubled thoughts. The four older ladies settled down to a pleasant nap, and Hero, who had made up her mind a full two hours ago as to what she intended to do, went for a short stroll along the shore.

'You won't go too far, will you honey?' murmured Aunt Abby, already half asleep: 'It might not be safe. Are you quite sure you would not like someone to accompany you?'

'Quite sure,' said Hero with sincerity. 'I don't intend to go far, and if I see anything alarming I shall come back at once.'

'That's right, honey,' approved Aunt Abby drowsily. She shut her eyes, and Hero, retying the wide straw hat firmly over her curls, set off down the beach in the direction of The House of Shade.

It had not taken her long to reach it, for though the felucca had kept on its way for half a mile beyond the bay where the house stood, the boat had landed the picnic party some distance back in order that they might bathe out of sight of the felucca's crew, and the wind-worn rocks that marked the northern end of the bay were barely a quarter of a mile from the spot that Aunt Abby had finally selected.

Hero rounded them cautiously, and scanning the fortress-like outer wall and the blank, shuttered windows of the house, decided that the whole place was empty. Empty and quiet and deserted. Behind her the soft crash and drag of waves falling on a shelving beach provided a pleasant accompaniment to the whisper and rustle of leaves and palm fronds, but both seemed only to accentuate the warm, sleepy, scented silence of the hot afternoon, and nothing moved on the curve of the bay except the surf and the little white sandcrabs.

She had never intended to do more than take a closer look at the house from the shelter of the coral rocks, and while keeping out of sight herself, examine the approaches to see if there was anything that would lend support to her suspicions. If there were newly landed slaves imprisoned behind that wall there would surely be some sign of them. Voices, muffled cries and wailing; the stench of dirty, terrified, sweating black bodies penned up in some locked cellar. But there was no sign or sound to indicate the presence of any occupants in the silent house: no thread of smoke or smell of cooking. Nor, strangely enough, was there anything sinister in that silence. If there had been, Hero might have behaved very differently; but even the blind, shuttered windows merely gave the house a curious impression of peace. A drowsy, withdrawn look; as though it had retreated behind its trees and its guardian wall and settled down to dream and wait, and listen absently to the voice of the Trade Wind crooning through the quiet rooms and under the empty archways.

Kivulimi ... the syllables held a lilting charm that caught Hero's fancy, and she repeated them under her breath. They had, she thought, something of the same singing quality as the surf and the swaying palm fronds, and she was surprised and a little ashamed of herself for entertaining such an absurdly fanciful idea. Yet there was something about the silent house that was intriguing as its name, and which drew her out of the safe shadow of the rocks and across the open sand, to stand at the foot of a path that led up over the rocks to a small, iron-studded door that was set deep in a recess of the outer wall.

It was the fact that the door stood ajar that decided her. Had it been closed she would probably (though by no means certainly) have turned back. But looking at it she could catch a glimpse of sun-dappled shade and the crimson fire of hibiscus beyond it, and suddenly she was no longer Hero Hollis, but Eve or Pandora or Bluebeard's wife. She stood quite still for several minutes, not in doubt, but to listen, and hearing no sound but the surf and the sea wind, ran lightly up the steps.

The heat of sun-baked stone burned through the thin soles of her slippers, and as she pushed open the door the iron hinges creaked plaintively in the silence. But though the sound startled her it did not stop her, and she stepped over the threshold out of the glare of the beach and into cool greenness, and found herself standing in a garden full of narrow winding paths, overgrown flowerbeds and innumerable trees.

It seemed she had been right in thinking that the wall that bounded it was part of an old fortress, for she saw now that it was a great deal older than the house, and was, on this side, overhung with flowering creepers and honeycombed with archways and cells that must once have been guardrooms and granaries and stables for horses. The sight of those dark, stone cells revived all her momentarily forgotten suspicions, and she tiptoed along a path that ran parallel to the wall and peered cautiously into several of them. But it was soon plain that they were unoccupied except for spiders and bats, and that no one could have entered them for some considerable time, for the weeds that grew up to the doorless arches were tall and undisturbed, while the heavy veils of bougainvillæa, jasmine and trumpet-flower that overhung them had not been cut back or broken.

Hero turned away from them, and lured by a gleam of water, followed another path that brought her to the edge of a shallow pool flanked by stone birds and full of fallen petals, where gorgeous scarlet dragon-flies sunned themselves on the lily pads. On the far side of the pool lay a tangled wilderness of flowers: hibiscus, zinnias, roses and coral plant, a blue mist of plumbago and a white fountain of jasmine that filled the shade with heavy sweetness; and glimpsed between tree-trunks and a lace of leaves, a short flight of steps leading up to a long, stone-built terrace that fronted the house.

The wind whispered in the branches of peepul and jacaranda, orange, tamarind and rain tree, but it could not disturb the tranquillity of the warm, flower-filled greenness below, and it seemed to Hero that garden, terrace and house alike might have belonged to that Princess of fairy-tale, Aurora, who pricked her finger on a spindle and fell asleep for a hundred years while the briars grew up about her.

The thought was not a particularly pleasing one, since it recalled the fact that her ebullient cousin, Hartley Crayne, had nicknamed her 'The

Sleeping Beauty': kindly explaining that he 'reckoned she was sound asleep behind her hedge of prickles, and that any Prince who had the idea of waking her up was going to have to take a goddamned hatchet to hack his way through 'em!'

'Might even try it myself,' Hartley had added, 'if I weren't so doggone idle. I'm all for the waking up with a kiss, but chopping down thorn trees ain't in my line.'

Hero had not considered it in the least amusing, and she grimaced at the recollection; and then smiled, thinking how absurd it was to be brooding on Hartley's impertinences in a garden in Zanzibar! It must be all these roses . . .

A spray of them, yellow and sweet-smelling, caught at her skirts as she turned from the pool, and she bent to disentangle them—— And was suddenly still; her hand rigid on the hem of her black poplin dress and the smile frozen on her face: staring incredulously at a pair of booted feet whose owner stood motionless among the tree shadows on the far side of the rose bush.

For a dreadful, dragging moment it seemed as though the sight had deprived her of all power of thought or movement, and she could only crouch there, staring, while her heart raced and her breath caught in her throat. Then she straightened up swiftly, hearing the lace of her petti-coat rip, and met the level gaze of a pair of pale and disconcertingly cold eyes.

22

'Good afternoon, Miss Hollis,' said Rory Frost politely. 'This is an unexpected pleasure.'

'So I *was* right!' Hero's voice was barely more than a gasp and these were not the words she had meant to say: 'This *is* the house – I knew it must be!'

The incoherent sentence appeared to be perfectly clear to Captain Frost, for he said without surprise:

'I imagined you would recognize it if ever you saw it again. It was a clear night. How did you get here?'

'We were picnicking. We came by boat and I saw it as we passed.'

'And dropped in to call? How very friendly of you,' said Captain Frost urbanely.

Hero flushed and realized that once again, and instantly, this obnoxious man had made her lose her temper. Well, this time she would not show it. Outwardly at least she would remain perfectly calm, and in full control of herself and the situation. She saw a corner of Rory's mouth twitch and received a swift and disconcerting impression that he had read her thought unerringly and was amused by it. But putting the suspicion firmly aside she said in an admirably composed voice: 'Nothing of the kind. I was merely interested to know who it belonged to; and as no one seemed to know, I walked along the beach to see if there was anyone here.'

'And walked in when you decided there was not. Don't you think that was a little foolhardy of you, Miss Hollis? It might so easily have been misunderstood.'

'I didn't mean to. But the door was open and——' Hero checked, annoyed to find herself on the defensive.

'And you couldn't resist it. I quite understand. But if you make a habit of walking into any house whose owner is careless enough to leave the door ajar, you could find yourself in a deal of trouble in this part of the world. You might, for instance, find yourself being added to some impressionable gentleman's harem. Or even kidnapped and held for ransom!'

Hero did not miss the gibe implicit in that last remark, but she held to her resolution, and refusing the bait said with unimpaired calm: 'Do you think so? I am disappointed, for I had always heard that Arabs had charming manners.'

'So they have, as a general rule. But they also have strong appetites and hot tempers, and are inclined to resent the presence of anyone whom they might suspect of spying.'

'I was not "spying"!' flared Hero indignantly.

'No? You must forgive me. It was probably the extreme caution with which you peered into those old guardrooms under the wall that gave me the idea. What did you expect to find in them, by the way?'

'Nothing,' said Hero, considerably put out. 'I mean, I was merely interested. The place looked so – so old.'

'It is old. If you mean the outer wall. I believe it was once a fort in the days when Portugal was a great colonial power. But the house itself was only built about twenty or thirty years ago; and by an Arab whose manners were anything but charming.'

'Oh? Who was that?' enquired Hero with deceptive carelessness.

'A gentleman called Ali-bin-Hamed; if it is of any interest to you.'

It was of considerable interest to Hero, but she did not say so. She carefully committed the name to memory and reflected with some satisfaction that she had not only got what she had come for, but received, by inference, additional proof that Captain Frost was on excellent terms with the owner of the house. If Lieutenant Larrimore and Colonel Edwards could not put two and two together when they heard of this, she would be very much surprised. And so, she hoped, would Emory Frost, who obviously knew a great deal about the house and had rashly admitted as much.

She discovered that he was observing her with a speculative look on his narrow, sunburned face, and he said pensively: 'I wonder what you are thinking of now? "Nothing" again, I suppose?'

'Not at all. I was merely wondering what you were doing here.'

'Did you think I was landing some questionable cargo in broad daylight? Surely you know me better than that!'

'I do indeed,' agreed Hero cordially.

Captain Frost laughed.

'That's one thing I like about you, Miss Hollis. You have no ladylike qualms about hitting from the shoulder. Or, for that matter, below the belt. If you must know, I was engaged in nothing more sinister than enjoying a quiet siesta in a spot that I have always found to be pleasantly peaceful and, until this afternoon, private.'

Hero ignored the insulting implication of the last word, and enquired coolly if he made a habit of coming here even when the house was obviously empty and his Arab friend not in residence.

'What Arab friend?'

'Ali-bin-Hamed.'

'You mean the late unlamented Ali-bin-Hamed. I am afraid he went to his reward a good fifteen years ago, as the result of setting a booby-trap for an unsuspecting guest and carelessly walking into it himself. And I imagine his reward is keeping him uncomfortably warm.'

Hero frowned and said impatiently: 'His son then. Or whoever owns this house now.'

'I do,' said Rory Frost.

'*You?*'

'Do you really mean to say you didn't know?' Rory's eyes were amused. 'No, I can see you didn't. And I should be interested to know why the information is such a disappointment to you. It is, isn't it?'

'No. Yes——! I mean . . . When did you——?' she stopped again and bit her lip.

'When did I acquire it? Oh, about five or six years ago.'

Five or six years ago! Then there could be no secret about it and people like Colonel Edwards and Dan Larrimore must not only know of it, but given the slightest excuse, would undoubtedly have had the house searched from top to bottom: which meant that this could not be where he hid the slaves. And yet he had landed muskets here, and by night – she had seen that herself. She had only to tell . . . But that was no good either, for there was no law against it, and this was his own house and his own beach.

It was an effort to conceal her discomfiture, but she did so and said stiffly that it seemed to be a charming property and she was sure he must find its position most useful to him. She was sorry to have disturbed his siesta and would certainly not have trespassed had she known that she would find him here.

'I am well aware of that,' said Captain Frost grimly. 'And I won't ask you what you were doing here, because I think I can make a fairly accurate guess. I imagine you came here to find out who this place belonged to, because you once saw a certain cargo being landed here by night and suspected that other cargoes might be concealed here. That it might, in fact, be a barracoon, and you strongly disapprove of slave traders. That's right, isn't it?'

'I seem to remember you asking me that question before,' said Hero, choosing to misunderstand him. 'And I also remember telling you that I do not "disapprove". I *abominate* slave trading – and all who engage in it.'

'So you gave me to understand. Why?'

'*Why?* You surely cannot mean that! The reason must be obvious to any thinking person, and how you can ask such a pointless and – and *abysmally* stupid question I cannot conceive. Good day, sir.'

She gave him a curt nod and would have turned and left him, but she had forgotten the spray of briar that was still entangled in the lace of her petticoat. And as she paused to free herself, Captain Frost stepped lightly over the intervening roses, and catching her wrist in a grip that felt as unyielding as a steel trap, said equably and in a voice that was strangely at variance with that inflexible grasp: 'If you knew me better you would realize that I never ask pointless questions. I happen to have a particular reason for being interested in your views.'

Hero looked from his hard fingers to his equally hard face, and managed with considerable difficulty to control a terrified impulse to scratch and kick. But since it was obvious that any such action would only end in humiliating defeat, she forced herself to stand still and say calmly: 'You are hurting my wrist.'

A flicker of something very like admiration showed briefly in Captain Frost's face, and he smiled faintly and released her. Hero snatched her hand away and rubbed the angry marks his fingers had made, but she did not again make the mistake of attempting to leave, and Rory looked at her reflectively for a moment or two; thinking illogically and with a curious sense of surprise that he had not remembered that her eyes were grey or that they had small green flecks in them, and that he would not forget it again.

He said meditatively: 'Leaving aside the larger issues, why, specifically, do you abominate slave traders? Because they make money out of it?'

'No.' Hero's voice was ice. 'I told you once before and I am quite certain that you have not forgotten it. But if you really wish to hear me repeat it I shall be happy to oblige you. I abominate them because they are personally responsible for the death and agony and degradation of thousands of people. Of innocent human beings who have done them no harm and with whom they have no quarrel. Because they callously condemn to appalling suffering and misery——'

'Yes, that's what I thought. I just wanted to make sure I hadn't got it wrong. Then perhaps, Miss Hollis, you can tell me how it is that, while holding such views, you have recently been doing your damnedest to make yourself personally responsible for the death or mutilation of several hundred human beings who cannot have done you any harm, and with whom – as far as I know – you can hardly have quarrelled? And furthermore, why you should have thought fit to assist in the extension of a trade you profess to abhor? I will absolve you from the charge of doing either of these things for the sake of personal profit; though that at least would have been a more understandable motive than a mere love of meddling. But I confess I find it interesting.'

Hero said blankly: 'I think you must be mad! I have not the least idea what you are talking about, and I cannot believe that you have either. May I go now? It is getting late.'

Captain Frost ignored the request and said unpleasantly: 'I advised you once before against meddling in matters that you do not understand, but it seems that you are a young woman who will not take advice. So you can oblige me now by explaining how this tender conscience of yours permits you to assist in smuggling a considerable quantity of arms into the hands of an irresponsible mob of conspirators, while at the same time absolving you from any feeling of responsibility for the deaths that were a direct result of that action?'

'I didn't! – I never touched . . . It *wasn't* arms!' Hero's indignation led her into passionate incoherence: 'It was votes! – I mean people. I mean——'

'You mean,' interrupted Captain Frost scathingly, 'that you expect me to believe that you helped to smuggle ballots into Beit-el-Tani – or bodies?'

'I don't expect you to believe anything!' said Hero hotly. 'And I don't care what you believe. Of course if wasn't bodies or—— It was money. To pay for food and to get people to support the Prince – the ones who couldn't afford to do it for nothing – so that there needn't be any fighting. It was *your* people – your bullying Navy and your tiresome Consul who started all the shooting and killing. If it hadn't been for them——'

She stopped abruptly, disconcerted by the expression on Captain Frost's face and conscious of a dreadful sinking of the heart and a frantic desire to put her hands over her ears and refuse to listen to anything else.

Rory said softly: 'You really believe that, don't you? What a gullible little cat's-paw it is! Do you mean to say that it never even occurred to you to open one of the chests that you helped to smuggle into Beit-el-Tani? Not even one?'

'They were locked; and——' Hero caught her breath and her eyes were suddenly wide and appalled. She said in a whisper, and as though she had to convince herself rather than him: 'It was *money*!'

'It was rifles,' said Rory Frost.

'I don't believe you.'

'I think you do,' said Rory grimly.

'No,' said Hero in a choked voice. 'No! Oh no!'

'What story did they tell you to keep you from opening the boxes?'

'They said that the Arabs might think——' she stopped again, remembering that it was Thérèse who had said that: Clayton had warned her against Thérèse . . . and against Cholé too; and the others . . .

Rory said: 'That you might have stolen part of the contents? And you swallowed that, and helped them to put two hundred rifles into the hands of a man who needed only that encouragement to start an armed rising!

And now I suppose you are going to say "Please, I didn't know," and forget the tiresome maxim that says, "*Ignorance of the law excuses nobody*".'

'I wasn't – it *was* money. It must have been!'

'In chests that size? Don't be silly! They were rifles all right. And as if that wasn't enough, you actually took a hand in helping Bargash to escape to his followers and touch off a rebellion in which a hell of a lot of men died. And then you prate to me of the brutal behaviour of that old fool Edwards and a handful of callow young officers, who had the unenviable task of preventing half the island going up in flames and putting a stop to what you and your friends had done their best to start. If you'd known the first thing about the el Harth you'd know that they don't give a curse for any son of Sultan Saïd, and were only out to get rid of his entire family and grab power for themselves, while half the rest of Bargash's followers were merely hoping for loot.'

Hero's face was painfully white and she did not appear to be listening to him. She said in an almost inaudible whisper: 'No. No, of course it isn't true. Thérèse would never . . . She *promised*!'

Rory's laugh was as curt and brutal as an ugly expletive. 'Dear Thérèse! she's an intriguing creature in both senses of the word. She is also – in addition to being hard-headed and unsentimental – an intensely practical and patriotic Frenchwoman, whose husband's firm has a large stake in sugar and would therefore dearly like to remove Majid, because Majid has the support of the British, and the British have set themselves to put an end to slavery. That is why Monsieur Tissot and his friends (and incidently, his Government!) elected to support the eldest son, Thuwani, when he tried to claim the whole of his late father's territories instead of being content with his own lion's share of the inheritance. And why, when Britain's East India Company stepped in and sent Thuwani's warships back to port, they turned their attention to Bargash instead.'

'Because he would have been a better Sultan,' declared Hero defiantly. 'He would have done something for his subjects and started reforms and – and been strong where his brother is weak, and been a progressive ruler instead of a backward and medieval one!'

'Is that what they told you? Poor Miss Hollis! That's what you get for being innocent and credulous.'

'Why shouldn't it be true?' demanded Hero passionately. 'Why should you be so sure you are right just because you took care to make friends with Majid so that you couldn't be run out of the island? The Prince *would* have made a better Sultan!'

'From the Arab point of view, yes,' agreed Rory. 'They've always been in favour of ruthlessness and cunning. But the other attributes with which you have endowed him are purely imaginary, and Thérèse knows that even if you don't. There is one reason, and only one, why her husband's firm would prefer to see either the Seyyid Thuwani or Bargash, whom they regard as Thuwani's deputy, in Majid's place as ruler of Zanzibar and the mainland territories. Because either would permit, for a consideration, the shipping of African slaves to work the sugar plantations on Bourbon and La Réunion. *Now* do you understand?'

'No . . .' Once again Hero's voice was a whisper. 'You can't know that. You are making it up. I've never heard of Réunion, and it's probably only something that you——' her voice failed her.

'There would appear to be a great many things you haven't heard of,' said Rory unkindly. 'But for your information, the islands of Bourbon and La Réunion are French possessions, and His Imperial Majesty Louis Napoleon – or his Government if you prefer – have permitted the importation of negro slaves under the pleasing title of '*Libres engagés*'; which is supposed to mean that they have freely volunteered their services, though the results are precisely the same as before. The negroes are purchased by native agents all along the Mozambique coast, and herded aboard French ships, where they are asked if they are willing to engage themselves for a term of ten years. And since they do not understand a word that is spoken to them and have been ordered by the dealers to nod when spoken to – which normally means 'no' to an African and not 'yes' as it does to us – this is taken for consent. They are thereupon registered and numbered, and forwarded in shiploads to the plantations; where they do not survive for long. Do you know how many slaves are needed to work the plantations of La Réunion alone? A hundred thousand! And as they reckon the average life of a slave there as five years, they need twenty thousand new ones every year. They need them so badly that they send French men-of-war to escort the slave ships safely to port, and intrigue against Sultan Majid because England supported his nomination. And they have created such a demand for slaves that the prices have risen to a point where the tribes have found it more profitable to hunt and kidnap their neighbours than to bother with more normal methods of earning a livelihood. That, my public-spirited young woman, is what you and your friends have been doing your damnedest to assist. It's an entertaining thought, isn't it?'

'I . . .' began Hero, and found that she could not continue.

Captain Frost laughed. 'Yes, ironically enough, *you*, Miss Hollis. Your enthusiastic and uninstructed meddling in the Bargash plot helped to bring a good many men to their deaths, and had it succeeded you would have had a share – admittedly a very small one, but still a share – in the capture and disposal of a vastly increased number of negro slaves for the

277

French Colonies (and I daresay for a great many other places as well) by anyone who cared to join in.'

'Such as yourself!' said Hero in a shaking voice.

'Such as myself,' agreed Captain Frost affably.

Horror and disbelief had assailed Hero in turn and served for a brief space to submerge her anger. But now it returned again as she recalled that the man who stood there lecturing her as though she had been a guilty schoolgirl was, by his own admission, a thief, a slave trader and a libertine, and for all she knew, a pirate as well! Yet he dared to take her to task for becoming innocently involved in something that he himself had knowingly engaged in for years – and for profit.

The colour flooded back to her white face and she said furiously: 'You have had a great deal to say in my dispraise, but at least I intended no harm, while you——! How did you know that there were muskets in those boxes? If there were (which I do not have to believe) it could only be because they were the ones that you yourself had smuggled into Zanzibar and carried up to this very house. *Your* house! And yet you dare suggest that I had a share in the death of men who could only have been armed with muskets that you yourself must have sold to Bargash.'

'Not to Bargash,' corrected Rory equably. 'To an agent who I believe re-sold them to Seyyid Bargash at a nice profit.'

'Then you admit it!'

'Why not? I can't see that because you prefer to shirk your share of the responsibility for their transfer to Beit-el-Tani, I should do the same over my part in the transaction.'

Hero gave a scornful and triumphant laugh and said: 'There——! I thought you were lying and now I know it. Those boxes were *not* the ones I saw you landing here.'

'Of course they weren't. But their contents were. And don't say "I don't believe it" again, because that remark is getting a little monotonous. I assure you I know who bought them and who re-sold them and to whom. And also that it was you who devised a way of getting them to Bargash.'

'And you can admit that, and still have the – the *audacity* to accuse me of responsibility for the deaths of men to whom *you* sold muskets, for money?'

'Ah, but you see,' said Rory, 'they weren't muskets. They were rifles.'

'I don't see what that has to do with it!'

'You wouldn't. But it happens to have a great deal to do with it. I was asked if I would be willing to supply, secretly, a certain number of firearms for a purpose that was not named, but which was nevertheless perfectly clear to me.'

'So you knew – you knew all the time!'

'My good girl, not being a credulous spinster, of course I knew. It needed no great intelligence. But a handsome sum of money was mentioned, and I have made it a rule never to refuse a good offer.'

'Even though you pretend to be a friend of the Sultan's? Even though you say you knew that the muskets would be used against him?'

'Rifles,' corrected Captain Frost blandly.

'Why do you keep saying that? They can still kill people.'

'Not these ones. At least, not until someone can collect a reasonable supply of fulminate of mercury and get down to manufacturing some caps. You see, Miss Hollis, I was not asked to supply the necessary ammunition; only "firearms". Two hundred of them, to be precise. An acquaintance of mine undertook to provide the ammunition, but owing to a – er – misunderstanding, and the fact that a rifle is still something of a novelty in these parts, he supplied ammunition that was suitable for muskets but not for rifles. You see the point?'

Hero stared at him in incredulous disgust; the classic curve of her lips pressed into a tight line and her grey eyes stony. She said: 'Clearly! It was, in fact, a deliberate fraud, designed to cheat your buyer into paying this "handsome sum" you say he was offering, for goods that were entirely worthless.'

'Not entirely – a rifle is still worth its own weight in Cape dollars, and they were in perfectly good condition. It was merely unfortunate, from the viewpoint of the final purchaser, that they could not be used until the proper caps and the correct ammunition were available.'

'But you——'

'I, Miss Hollis, carried out my part of the bargain and delivered two hundred firearms to my client. They were then sold again: and but for your unlooked-for interference the whole transaction would have been as harmless as it was lucrative. A large part of the money sent by Thuwani for the purpose of financing a rebellion – Oh yes, he sent funds! – would have been uselessly frittered away. For when old Abdullah-bin-Salim and the chiefs of the el Harth laid eyes on those rifles, they would have discovered that they couldn't be used with the ammunition they had recently collected and paid for, and they would have held their hands until they could get or manufacture the right variety. Which, believe me, would have taken a considerable time, and provided enough delay to take the heart out of a very large number of Bargash's supporters, who had been getting noticeably restive and were almost ready to throw their hands in or go over to the other side. However, thanks to you and your fellow heroines, the rifles got into the hands of those silly women at Beit-el-Tani, where Bargash was shown them by night. All two hundred of them piled up in a beautiful, martial heap.'

Hero said helplessly: 'I don't see what difference that could make. If he saw them, he'd have known . . .'

'He hadn't seen the ammunition – for the simple reason that it had been delivered separately to one of his civilian supporters at a house outside the city. Anyway, he apparently didn't take the trouble to examine the rifles. One look at them seems to have been enough to send him tipsy with confidence. And since they were removed almost at once to be distributed by ones and twos, not to the chiefs but to the rank and file – who probably imagined that one or other of their leaders would show them how to use these magical new weapons – it isn't difficult to understand why the mere fact that they got their hands on no less than two hundred of the things was just what the rebels needed to galvanize them into hauling up the anchor.'

Hero drew a deep breath, and after a long pause said unsteadily: 'I can understand one thing, at least. That you are entirely unprincipled and prepared to take any risk or perpetrate any fraud in order to enrich yourself. But I cannot see how you have the effrontery to take me to task when your own behaviour is wholly indefensible.'

' "*Video meliora proboque, deteriora sequor*",' quoted Rory with mock regret.

'If I knew what that meant, I might agree with you.'

'I apologize. I imagined that with a name like yours you would have received a classical education. It means "I see the better course and approve it: I follow the worst." But at least I do it with my eyes open! And now, if you will forgive me, I shall have to leave you to find your own way back to your aunt. The door is over there and I should be grateful if you would close it as you go out – just in case any other members of your party should find it an inducement to trespassing. Good day, Miss Hollis.'

He sketched the briefest of bows, and turning on his heel walked away down the flower-bordered path and up the short flight of steps that led to the terrace, leaving Hero standing among the shadows with her skirts still entangled in the trails of yellow briar and feeling like a dismissed kitchen-maid.

The sound of his footsteps echoed under an unseen archway and were gone, and Hero tore at the roses, pricked her fingers and ripped another long tear in the frail muslin of her petticoat, and gathering up her skirts, fled from the garden: slamming the door behind her and stumbling down the rocky path to the beach, her mind a turmoil of anger and shock and her lips moving in foolish, sobbing whispers: '*I don't believe it . . . I won't believe it . . . I don't believe it . . .*'

23

'I don't believe it!' insisted Hero stubbornly. But in the end she had to believe it. Or at least some part of it, for Uncle Nat, appealed to that same evening, had supported a good deal of what Captain Frost had said:

'Why yes,' said Uncle Nat, 'I guess that's so. The French have always wanted a footing on the mainland around these parts, and there's nothing they'd like better than to dethrone the Sultan and put an end to British influence here. After the old man died they hoped to get rid of Majid in favour of Thuwani, and see Zanzibar and her East African territories declared a dependency of Muscat again, so that they'd get the secession of a port from the new and grateful ruler – with the right to ship slaves from it. In fact they've been a blame nuisance, one way and another.'

'But – but the French were the first to try and stop the slave trade!' protested Hero, dismayed. 'You *know* that's so, Uncle Nat. I remember Miss Penbury telling me that they made the very first anti-slave laws in Europe, when the National Convention abolished negro slavery back in the seventeen-hundreds. You can read about it!'

'Well, you know how it is with these things,' said Uncle Nat easily. 'It's all a question of politics. I guess it seemed a great idea to abolish slavery when they were cooking up a revolution: "Liberty, Equality, Fraternity" and all that. But it got put back on the books a few years later by the Consulate; and you can read about that too! *Conformément aux lois et règlements antérieurs.* It's been an "On again, off again" arrangement ever since, because the Republic officially abolished it again, but there's no blinking the fact that this *"engagés"* system of theirs is just another name for the same thing. They need negro slaves for their colonies and they're going to get 'em, come hell or high water! But they'd get 'em a sight easier if they could get a foothold on the coast, which they won't manage to do as long as Majid is on the throne, on account of him leaning towards the English.'

Hero said in a stifled voice: 'Why did you never tell me this before, Uncle Nat?'

'I guess you never asked. And how is it you're so interested all of a sudden, anyway?'

'I'm not . . . I mean, I've always been interested. People have to be, if it's ever to end. This selling human beings like – like cattle and not caring if they live or die. You have to care about cruelty; you *have* to! But

281

I didn't know about the *engagés* and Réunion and – and . . .' Her voice wavered on the verge of tears.

'No need why you should bother your pretty head about such things,' said Uncle Nat infuriatingly. He had always adhered firmly to the view that women should confine their energies to what he vaguely termed 'womanly pursuits', and these apparently did not include anything outside the home. He had strongly disapproved of Hero's mother, Harriet, and now he looked long and thoughtfully at his niece, and clearing his throat with a shade of embarrassment said carefully:

'You know, Hero, this may sound like some kind of a sermon, but it don't do to start blaming any one nation more than another for a thing like the slave trade. Before you get your dander up you've got to remember we've all been in it. And by that I mean Mankind! Even the negroes themselves are in it – up to their necks, and I don't mean their slave-halters either. The African tribes have preyed on each other in order to supply the traders, and made a mighty good thing out of selling their own people into slavery. Arabs, Africans and Indians, the British and the French, Dutchmen, Spaniards and Portuguese, North and South Americans – there isn't one of 'em can show a clean pair of hands, and it's as well to remember that. Why, our own Thomas Jefferson, at the very time when he was speaking and writing against the slaving activities of the English, owned more than eighty slaves himself – and explained that though he hated the whole system he just couldn't afford, for financial reasons, to free his own negroes! We're all tarred with the same brush, and there's a sound old saying about "people who live in glass houses" that we'd do well to remember before any of us start in reaching for stones. And I guess that goes for a heap of other things besides the slave trade! One way or another, all our houses are glass.'

'I – I suppose so,' said Hero desolately. Her own had certainly been; and she spent a sleepless night brooding on Captain Frost's horrifying revelations and Uncle Nat's confirmation of them, and convicting herself at least of manslaughter if not actually murder. She had been unbelievably stupid and stubborn, and Clay had been right . . . Clay had tried to warn her and she had refused to listen to him, because she had imagined herself to be settling the destiny of the Island for its own good, when all the time she was merely being used and made a fool of by Thérèse Tissot, Cholé and Bargash, who had tricked her as easily as though she had been a conceited child. And she could not even acquit herself of behaving like one, because surely even a child should have seen through that story of the treasure chests that must not be opened.

Had Olivia known? Somehow Hero did not believe it. But the reflection that Olivia and Cressy had been equally gullible did nothing towards lessening her own agony of remorse and self-loathing, for she had thought herself so much cleverer and far more capable than either of them, and had considered Olivia Credwell to be an empty-headed, sentimental creature, and Cressy a silly child. Yet her own behaviour had been marked by a sentimental silliness that she could hardly bear to contemplate: *criminal* silliness! for she had done a great deal of harm. What could have possessed her to lend herself to pulling other people's dubious chestnuts out of the fire? She should have known: she should have suspected. *'Ye'll have a hand in helpin' a power o' folk to die ...'* Biddy Jason had known! All those long years ago she had known, and this is what she had meant——

'A power of folk' ... How many men had died inside the walls of *Marseilles* and on the parched ground between the raw stumps of clove trees and coconut palms that had been hacked down to clear a field of fire for Bargash's men? Two hundred? – three? – four? Her own part in the rising had been so trivial that her share of the responsibility must be equally small: a minute proportion of the whole. But then guilt was not a thing that could be measured out on a pair of kitchen scales or split like a hair under a microscope, and perhaps if you allowed yourself to have even a fractional share in something that resulted in the death of others, you were morally responsible for the whole. If that were so, she must shoulder the blame for everything that she had in any way helped to bring about, and the fact that she had not known what she was doing could not be held to excuse her. *Ignorance of the law excuses nobody ...* Captain Frost had said that.

Quite suddenly, lying there in the dark, she realized that at least one of the questions she had asked herself was answered. The reason that she had thrown herself so blindly and hastily into this disastrous affair was less for the sake of sympathy for the suffering citizens of Zanzibar, than for a personal detestation of Captain Emory Frost of the *Virago*. It was as simple – and as humiliating – as that!

Rory Frost embodied everything that she had learned to hold in abhorrence: slavery and the white men who helped to keep the horror alive and make fortunes from the tragedy and suffering of captive negroes: dishonesty, profligacy and miscegenation: the English, who had attempted to force iniquitous laws on free-born Americans, burned the White House and fired on peaceful farmers. And as if that were not enough, he had made fun of her, lectured her and treated her with casual disrespect, had the effrontery to admit his crimes without a trace of shame or apology, and worst of all, to be a man of birth and education.

That last still seemed to Hero less forgivable than a coloured mistress and bastard children, since it stripped him of all excuses and branded him as someone who, as he himself had said, could see the better course yet deliberately follow the worst. Because all this had outraged her, she had allowed herself to embark on a personal vendetta that had blinded her to everything else and completely destroyed her sense of proportion. It was a singularly unpleasant reflection, and for the first time in her life Hero took stock of herself – and did not like what she saw.

One result of her unhappy meditations was that Clayton Mayo appeared in a far better light than at any time since the days when she had first imagined herself in love with him.

Clay had tried to warn her for her own good, but he had never reproached her, and except for the unfortunate scenes that had marked the day of her arrival, remained unfailingly considerate. He had not pressed any claims or thrust himself upon her notice, and in her present state of self-abasement he began to seem the only stable thing in an uncertain world, for he not only loved and admired her, but he would protect her from her own impetuousness, and apply balm to her wounds by making her feel cherished and adored – and safe! Though why she should suddenly desire safety she did not know. She only knew that the need was there and that Clay would satisfy it.

Whether she loved him or not was something she still could not be sure of. But then Aunt Lucy had once told her that it was quite unnecessary to be in love with the man one married, while as for feeling any *passionate* attachment, that was neither necessary nor desirable: respect and affection were more than sufficient, and provided those were there, love would inevitably follow. Since Aunt Lucy's own marriage appeared successful enough, no doubt she was right. *I will speak to Clay tomorrow*, thought Hero.

The decision brought her an enormous sense of relief, and as daylight brightened behind the drawn window blinds and the birds began to stir and twitter in the garden, she was able to fall asleep at last.

But it had not proved as easy to speak to Clay as she had supposed, for she had slept late, and by the time she came downstairs he had already gone out and no one could be sure when he would be back: probably not until late afternoon said his mother a shade tartly, since he was engaged to lunch with Joe Lynch. Aunt Abby did not approve of Mr Lynch. She considered him wild to a fault, and did not believe that he was a good influence on dear Clay, for Joe had the reputation of being a gambler and a 'gay dog', and she deplored her son's partiality for his company and had cherished the hope that Hero's arrival might put an end to that connection.

'I am afraid,' explained Aunt Abby apologetically, 'that Clay has to go out a great deal. Not only on business, but in order to keep in touch with the various European interests here ... so necessary when one is abroad. In fact your uncle considers that social contacts are often as important as business ones – don't you, Nathaniel?'

'One gets a lot of useful information that way,' agreed Uncle Nat mildly. 'More than one gets in the way of official interviews, as like as not. You need to know what goes on in a place like this, Hero, and Clay's been a great help to me in that way. He gets around and gets to know the folk, and they'll often say a heap more to him than they will to me. But I'm free to own it keeps him out of the house a good deal, and I hope you don't think he's been deliberately neglecting you, miss. You ought to know that he'd rather be right here in this room if he had the choice!'

Hero blushed and laughed and Aunt Abby gave her husband a repressive glance and said: 'I am sure Hero realizes that if Clay is not here more often it is because he has his duties to see to, and not because he prefers to be elsewhere.' But in fact Hero was not too sorry to find that Clayton would be away that morning, for there was someone else whom she intended to speak to, and she suspected Clay would disapprove and try to stop her. His absence made her projected visit much easier, and having obtained her aunt's permission and fobbed off Cressy, who wished to go with her, Hero sent for Sherif, and accompanied by her groom, rode over to the Tissots' house.

Thérèse had been seated at the writing-table in her own little sitting-room, busy with her household accounts, but when Hero was announced she flung down her quill, and springing up, greeted her with exclamations of hospitable surprise. 'Hero, *chérie!* This is indeed an unexpected pleasure. How charming of you to call. You will drink chocolate with me, no?'

'No,' replied Hero curtly.

Madame Tissot's eyebrows rose, and then realizing from her visitor's forbidding expression and the curtness of her refusal that this was not to be a social call, she dismissed the servant, and when the door had closed behind him said lightly: 'Well, Hero? What is it that you have to tell me? Is it that something else has gone wrong?'

'You know very well what is wrong!' said Hero stonily.

'Do I? Of that I cannot be sure. But I see very clearly that you are much upset. And angry, too. So why do we not both seat ourselves, and then we can talk together calmly and sensibly? That will also be more comfortable, is it not?'

'Thank you, but I prefer to stand,' said Hero icily.

Madame Tissot cocked her head a little on one side and studied her uninvited guest for a moment or two in silence. Comprehension and a faint suggestion of malicious amusement glimmered in the observant gaze of her shrewd dark eyes, and then she shrugged and said: 'As you wish. But you must forgive me if I do not, for I find that to converse upon one's feet can be very fatiguing.'

She subsided gracefully into the nearest chair, and having arranged the artfully simple folds of her morning gown to their best advantage, linked her small, capable hands in her lap, and leaning back, looked up at her youthful visitor with an expression that, while nicely blending politeness with interest, somehow managed to convey the impression that Hero was some erring schoolgirl summoned to explain herself to the Headmistress. But Miss Hollis had confronted far more formidable opponents than Madame Tissot, and she was not in the least intimidated by the fact that Thérèse was a good deal older than her and considerably more experienced in the ways of the world. Although now that it was too late she regretted refusing that invitation to be seated, for there was no denying that it put one at a disadvantage to be standing upright when confronting an adversary who lolled at ease in a comfortably upholstered armchair. But she had no intention of allowing such a trivial circumstance to prevent her from speaking her mind: any more than the fact that she had thought herself to be a prisoner on the *Virago* had prevented her from speaking it to her supposed kidnapper, Captain Emory Frost! No one would ever be able to say of Hero Athena that she lacked the courage of her convictions.

'I have just found out,' she announced in measured tones, 'that you not only told me a great many lies, but tricked me into helping you do something so terrible that it will be on my conscience for the rest of my life. I hope you do not intend to deny that you knew very well what was in those chests that we smuggled into Beit-el-Tani, and precisely what they were going to be used for?'

'*Deny?*' exclaimed Thérèse in unaffected surprise: 'Why should I, when I think it arranges itself very cleverly? Is that all you wished to tell me?'

'*All*——?' gasped Hero, more shocked by the truth than she had been by the lies: 'You call that "all"? How could you do such a thing?'

'I feel sure you must know that; seeing that you have discovered so much!'

'I do indeed!' retorted Hero, her temper getting the better of her. 'I wouldn't believe it at first. I couldn't! But when my uncle said—— I don't understand how any woman could bring herself to tell such barefaced lies ... To be so – so heartless and unprincipled and downright *wicked* as to——'

'Ah, bah!' interrupted Thérèse, irritated: 'Your trouble, Mademoiselle, is that you do not understand anyone who does not think as you do.

You also possess a credulity quite remarkable – one sees that in the twinkling of an eye. A child could deceive you! Did I not tell you myself, on the day we first met, that it would be very easy to lie to you? *Mon Dieu!* and was it not true!'

Hero's face paled with horror as she remembered that Thérèse had indeed said something of the sort, and that she had taken it as proof of the speaker's honesty! She said in a choked whisper: 'And you don't even mind admitting it.'

'Why should I? I have nothing to be ashamed of. It is you who should be ashamed – of being so gullible!'

'And you for not knowing what shame means!' cried Hero. 'You are completely brazen! You lied to all of us. Every single thing you told us was a lie, and you deliberately helped to plan and launch a rebellion that led to the death of heaven alone knows how many people ... *hundreds!*'

'And you also, is it not so?' retorted Thérèse acidly, '– and with less reason! Me, I had a good reason. But yours, Mademoiselle, would seem to be a love of meddling with matters that do not concern you ... "Putting the finger into the pies of others". It is your hobby, I think.'

'Then you think wrong! To me it is a – a crusade, and I intend to do everything in my power to put an end to slavery. While you mean to see that it continues, and you don't care how much misery and human suffering and evil is involved. You'll lie and scheme and cheat to ensure that it does. And you call that a "good" reason for your indefensible behaviour!'

'Ah, but then I, Mademoiselle, unlike you, am not a sentimentalist. I do not think with the heart as you do. I think with my head – and for my country. To me, this matter is one of politics: of policy. And me, I neither make those policies nor decide the issues. That is done in Paris, and by far wiser heads than mine – by the Government and the servants of the Government. But what they decide, I support: which is something that you, *chère* Hero, should sympathize with, for was it not a citizen of your own great nation who said those famous words "our country, right or wrong!' ... and to great applause, *n'est-ce pas?*'

Hero said scornfully: 'You really mean that, don't you. That to you this whole cruel, murderous business was merely a matter of politics. *Politics!*'

'*Mais certainement.* What else?'

'And all those poor wretches who died at *Marseilles*, and the hundreds of thousands who will die and have already died because of your country's sugar plantations, mean nothing to you? Nothing at all?'

Thérèse shrugged again and said coolly: 'One has to be a realist in such matters, so I do not permit myself to lose sleep over what is a fact of life and a question of business interests. And now, if you are quite sure that there is nothing else that you wish to take me to task for . . .?'

'Nothing,' replied Hero, 'that I know of! Though I feel sure that any person as devoid of principle and common humanity as you have shown yourself to be must have a great many sins on their conscience – if you have one, which I doubt. However, that is hardly my affair.'

'You do not know how greatly it relieves me to hear you say so, *ma chère*. I had feared that there might be more!'

There was an unmistakable note of mockery in Thérèse's purring voice and she passed the tip of her tongue over her lower lip in the manner of a cat who has been lapping stolen cream: 'Then perhaps you will not mind (since I too can be curious) if I put one little question to *you* before you leave? *Bon!* It is this: why is it that you are here in Zanzibar, concerning yourself with your "crusade", when, unless I too have been deceived and lied to, there are in your own country very many planters who depend for their labour on slaves whom they import in vast numbers in slave ships – paying good prices and thus encouraging this trade that you profess to abhor? Me, I am here because my husband's firm sends him to this island. But you, it seems, are not even betrothed to Monsieur Mayo. Yet you are here; espousing the cause of the slaves in Zanzibar rather than those who work for the owners of plantations in your own country. This I find very curious, and I would be happy if you would explain it to me.'

'I——' began Hero, and stopped: realizing in the nick of time that Thérèse was deliberately trying to turn the tables on her by goading her into going onto the defensive: and had very nearly succeeded, for it was a hard struggle to hold back the words that were jostling for place on her tongue. But it was Madame Tissot, and not she, Hero Hollis, who was in the dock and guilty, by her own admission, of lies and trickery and actively assisting the vile traffic of slave trading. It had been a grave mistake to cross swords with such a devious and unprincipled schemer, and she should have known better than to attempt it. But at least she was not going to give Thérèse the satisfaction of hearing her defend herself against those intentionally provocative charges. She bit back the furious words that she had so nearly spoken, and pressed her lips tightly together. And immediately, as though her thoughts had been clearly printed on her face, Madame Tissot broke into malicious and obviously genuine laughter.

Hero stared at her with loathing, and then turning on her heel, swept out of the room without another word; her eyes bright with anger and her mind in a turmoil of wrath, indignation, and – it must be owned – sheer frustration. Because the worst of it was that as Uncle Nat's niece she would have to attend a great many functions at which that despicable woman was almost bound to be present, for owing to the smallness of the

Island's Western community, all social gatherings were apt to consist of combinations of the same handful of people. And since it was clearly impossible to denounce the villainess of the piece without betraying Cressy and Olivia Credwell, not to mention gravely embarrassing her uncle and aunt, she would frequently find herself in Madame Tissot's company, and in circumstances that would make it impossible to cut her.

'But there is no reason why I should ever speak to her again,' decided Hero, 'and if she is invited to our Consulate, I need only say I have a headache.'

Clayton's duties had kept him occupied until well after sunset, and since he returned late for dinner Hero had no opportunities for private speech with him until the meal was over. But gazing at him in the soft glow of the candles she no longer saw him as a man she might one day decide to marry, but as the man she was going to marry: 'For better for worse ... to love, cherish and obey until death do us part ...' It was in some ways a daunting thought, but in another a comforting one because of its comprehensiveness and finality.

To love, cherish and obey. She would certainly resolve to cherish and obey. But to love——? Could she promise to do that if she were still not sure? Whoever had originally written those words had not considered doubts, and they must have been spoken down the centuries by innumerable women who had not been in love when they said them, but who had, if Aunt Lucy were right, learned to do so later. And it would be very easy to love Clay.

The candle-light was making him look a little flushed and more than ordinarily handsome, and tonight he was obviously in good spirits, for he kept up an uninterrupted flow of conversation: teasing Cressy, rallying his mother on the subject of her bathing picnic, informing Hero that Jules Dubail had referred to her admiringly as *La belle Grecque*, and regaling his step-father with some of Joe Lynch's latest after-dinner stories – the latter to the evident agitation of his mother, who suspected that he had been drinking and kept glancing anxiously at the two girls.

Aunt Abby need not have worried, for her daughter and her niece were both far too occupied with their own thoughts to pay much attention to her son's anecdotes. And though Hero was watching him she was not really listening to what he was saying, and except when directly addressed would probably have remained inattentive to the end of the meal, had it not been for the introduction of a name that caught her attention as abruptly and unpleasantly as though she had been sleep-walking and had run into a wall in the dark.

'. . . one of Frost's women,' said Clay.

'How do you know?' enquired his step-father.

'Saw her once before,' said Clay with a reminiscent grin. 'She was looking out of a window of that house of his in the city. The one they call "The Dolphins' House". Loveliest thing imaginable – give you my word! Eyes the size of saucers and skin like . . . Oh, I don't know; gold, ivory, cream? And a yard and a half of the blackest, silkiest hair you ever saw. She jumped back when she saw me staring, but it wasn't the sort of face you'd be likely to forget, and I recognized her as soon as I walked into Gaur Chand's shop. She was in that back room that they keep for their purdah customers, but the door blew open in the draught and there she was, looking at silver bangles or something of the sort. So I walked in and introduced myself, and she pulled her veil over her face and acted as though she'd been somebody's virtuous daughter instead of just another of Frost's fancy strumpets.'

'Clay, dear!' gasped Aunt Abby indignantly: 'I will not have you using expressions like that in front of the girls. Or mentioning that sort of woman either. Mr Hollis——!'

Uncle Nat, thus appealed to, wagged a placating hand at his ruffled wife and said: 'No need to take on like that, Abby. The girls are both quite old enough to know that there are such creatures around. They're out of the schoolroom now.'

'Even if they are, I still do not consider this a suitable subject for mixed company.'

Clayton laughed and said: 'Darling Mama, you seem to forget that this is not Boston. We're in Zanzibar, where such things are taken for granted and every man who can afford it has a harem. Look at the local Royal Family – not one of 'em what *we'd* call legitimate. Why, they say the old Sultan fathered a hundred and twelve children in his day, and left seventy concubines to mourn him when he died.'

'No, Clay!' protested Aunt Abby. 'No, really dear, I will not have it. I know that word is in the Bible and that Arabs may not think anything of having them, but then this man Frost is not an Arab, which puts the whole thing on *quite* a different footing – a most objectionable one – and I would prefer you to talk of something else.'

'Of course it's different. If she'd been a member of some Arab's seraglio I'd have referred to her as a *sarari*. But as the fancy-lady of a white-trash slaver she's no more than a——'

'Clayton!'

Clayton laughed again and said: 'Very well, Mama. I apologize. What shall we talk of instead? The weather, like Colonel Edwards and the Kealeys and the Platts? Or food, like the Lessings? Or women, like Jules and Joe and —— No, that's taboo, isn't it? It'll have to be the weather. Mohammed Ali tells me that the rains will be here before the end of next week. I told him it was too early, but he swears he can feel it in his bones. Let's hope he's right. It'll be a relief to get some of the garbage washed off the streets and to feel cool in the daytime instead of only at night. What d'you say we go for a ride tomorrow, Hero? Will you come?'

Hero recovered herself with a start. She had been thinking with angry resentment of men like Emory Frost and the Arabs of Zanzibar, who treated women as creatures to be bought and used and discarded; sad, hapless, servile creatures who had little or no say in their own destiny and must accept a man's embraces and bear his children whether they cared for him or not. *'One of Frost's women'* – a cold shiver of puritanical disgust made her flesh shrink and crawl, and she was once again sharply aware of the need to escape to safety.

Clay said again: 'Will you, Hero? Please.'

She did not know what he had asked her. Only that it was a question. And she answered it as though it was the one question that every woman wishes to hear. She said: 'Yes, Clay!' And having said it experienced an enormous sense of relief and of laying down a burden.

If Clayton was a little startled by the tone of her response he did not show it, and half-an-hour later, in the cool of the garden where the scent of orange blossom provided a suitably bridal note, he had put into words the question that Hero had already answered, and, though not aware of this, had been accepted for the second time that evening.

It would have been untrue to say that he was surprised, for although he had harboured some doubts when he had first sailed East, he had been confident of the outcome from the moment he had heard of Barclay's death and Hero's acceptance of his mother's invitation to visit Zanzibar. But her capitulation at that moment was a trifle unexpected, since he had, on the whole, seen little of her during the past few weeks. There had been other things on his mind, and as Hero had been preoccupied and obviously in no mood for dalliance, he had thought it better not to press his suit, but to treat her instead with affectionate deference and allow her time to look about her and feel more settled.

The effect that his lover-like behaviour had produced on the day of her arrival had taught him the unwisdom of rushing his fences, and having realized that she was not yet ready to fall into his arms, he had been prepared to wait until the novelty of her situation and surroundings had worn off and she was disposed to pay proper attention to him. This policy had plainly been the right one, and Clayton congratulated himself on his handling of the affair and was not more than mildly impatient when, on attempting to embrace his newly promised wife, he had been held off with a display of maidenly modesty that in the circumstances he considered excessive, if not actually ridiculous.

It was going to be the devil of a nuisance, he reflected, if Hero were going to prove as genuinely frigid as her startled reaction to any physical contact would suggest. But the time to deal with that problem would come later; and in the meantime, if she wished to be treated like a Vestal Virgin until the ring was on her finger, he was prepared to humour her. It would not be for long, and as he had no intention of frightening her into changing her mind, he contented himself with kissing her hand with affectionate fervour and doing no more than brush her cheek with his lips.

The news of the engagement had a mixed reception from his immediate family. His mother was unable to prevent her pleasure being modified by doubts, and though congratulating him, was a little tearful. Nathaniel Hollis frankly considered the match an excellent thing and his step-son a lucky man, and Cressy temporarily abandoned her apathy to embrace Hero passionately and declare in one and the same breath that she was so glad – so *very* glad – and she wished she were dead!

The European community, with one or two exceptions, welcomed the news with enthusiasm, since it presented an admirable excuse for the giving of parties, and Clayton and his betrothed were entertained at a series of dinners, luncheons, tea-parties and receptions, and received the congratulations of a large number of Arab and Asian notables.

Olivia Credwell was sentimentally ecstatic, but Thérèse Tissot's written felicitations contained a distinct note of acidity, and there had been no word from the Seyyida Cholé. Or from Lieutenant Daniel Larrimore either, for the *Daffodil* had left harbour – slipping out quietly on the evening after Aunt Abby's picnic party, and without her commanding officer having paid his customary farewell call at the American Consulate.

The *Virago*, on the other hand, was still at her anchorage in the harbour, and her Captain was frequently to be met with riding through the town with Hajji Ralub or lounging on the sea wall deep in conversation with a motley selection of Arabs, Banyans and Africans, and usually accompanied by Batty Potter and several of the more villainous-looking members of his crew.

Mr Potter had accosted Hero outside a silversmith's shop in the city one evening, where she had gone in company with Olivia, Hubert Platt and Herr Ruete to purchase a trinket designed as a birthday present for Mrs Jane Platt.

Batty had tugged at her sleeve and demanded in a hoarse whisper, redolent with rum, if it were true that she had engaged herself to marry Mr Mayo, and on receiving a hurried affirmative, said sadly: 'There now, I was afraid you 'ad. If you was to ask me, you're makin' a mistake and you'd do better to call it off before it's too late. That's my advice, miss. Call it off. You won't suit. " 'Andsome is as 'andsome does," is what I says. But lor! – women never 'as no more sense than a chicken when it comes to a good-looking young cove.'

'You don't even know him!' retorted Hero in an indignant undertone.

'Not to speak to,' admitted Batty. 'But I knows you, miss. Werry well I knows you, after 'elpin to spill the water out of you and mendin' your duds and 'acking off your 'air, and chewin' the rag with you on the after 'atch. Ah well, once you fancies you're in love it's all up with you, as I knows to me sorrow. But then I never loses me 'ead and marries 'em! or not proper – exceptin' when I was too young to know any better. Well, I 'ope you'll be 'appy, miss.' He shook his head in the manner of one who has grave doubts, and added: 'But don't say as I didn't warn you. Marriage ain't never what you thinks it is. Not by no means!'

Mr Potter sighed regretfully, mopped his forehead and remarked that it was 'cruel 'ot weather', and nodding a brief farewell was lost to sight among the colourful crowd that thronged the street.

Young Herr Ruete, who had seen him go, said: 'Who is that old man who speaks with you? Does he require something?'

'No,' said Hero hastily. 'It was only someone who was passing. He – er – said something about the weather: that it was very hot.'

'Ah – an Englishman!' laughed Herr Ruete. 'The heat is indeed oppressive today, but soon it will rain. *Lieber Gott!* how it will rain. You will presently see.'

There had been no clouds for several days; and no wind. But a haziness had dulled the clear blue of the sky, and the heat, as Wilhelm Ruete said, had become stifling and oppressive. Even at this hour of the evening Hero could feel the sweat trickling down between her shoulder blades, and she was grateful to her aunt for persuading her to discard her mourning in favour of lighter and paler-coloured muslins. Black poplin was certainly unsuitable wear in such a trying climate. And even less suitable, as Aunt Abby had pointed out, for a newly betrothed young lady:

'You would not wish people to suppose that you regret your decision, I hope?' she had coaxed. 'Because that is what they might suppose if you do not put off your mourning. Black is *quite* unsuited to betrothals and bridal plans, and I am persuaded that your dear Papa would have fully agreed with me.'

Hero had capitulated and packed away her mourning; and with it, she hoped, all regrets. The past was over, and she was about to enter a new life in which she would no longer be her own mistress, but Mrs Clayton Mayo, pledged to love, cherish and obey her husband until death did them part. A dress of lilac-coloured muslin, worn with a chip-straw bonnet trimmed with violets and tied under her chin with ribbons of the same shade, had bridged the gap between full mourning and the time when she might venture to wear gayer tints, and Clay had been pleased to commend the result.

She looked so charming, he informed her, that it was a matter of great regret to him that business in another part of the town prevented him from accompanying her on the expedition to the silversmith's shop. But they had in fact caught a glimpse of him on their way back to the Consulate, for they had returned by a different route and had seen him emerge from a narrow lane just ahead of them, walking quickly and looking angry and preoccupied. He had disappeared down a side-street before they could catch up with him, and Mr Platt, peering short-sightedly after the retreating figure in the dust-coloured suit and wide-brimmed hat, said: 'Isn't that Mayo? I hope he is not looking for you, Miss Hollis. I promised him that you would be safe with us, but he may not trust us with such a precious possession!'

He accompanied the remark with a little tittering laugh, and Hero smiled politely and was about to reply when they reached the entrance to the lane and were brought to a halt by a horse and rider who were emerging from it. The lane was a cul-de-sac, and the rider, clad in a light brown habit and wearing a small hat with a heavy veil, was Madame Tissot.

Thérèse checked her horse to exchange a few pleasantries; explaining that she had lost her way in this abominable maze of streets but had been fortunate enough to encounter Miss Hollis's fiancé, who had kindly re-directed her. She accompanied the party as far as the Consulate, threading her horse between the amiable and apparently aimless crowds and keeping up an uninterrupted flow of small-talk, but as Hero, who had not spoken, did not invite her to come in, she had left them there; including them all in a graceful bow and cantering away in the direction of her own house.

Clayton had said nothing of the incident when he returned an hour later, and Hero had refrained from mentioning it, for she knew that he disliked Madame Tissot and she did not for a moment believe that Thérèse, who knew the city almost as well as Fattûma, had lost her way. It was far more likely that she had seen Clay take that turning and had followed him in order to force him into conversation with her, or to issue an invitation to one of her 'receptions' that he might have difficulty in refusing to her face. And since Hero did not think Madame Tissot would take kindly to being rebuffed by someone who had once treated her with thoughtful consideration, she felt truly sorry for Clay and took pains to be particularly pleasant to him that evening.

The heat had not abated with the coming of night and the stars were not as bright or as clear as usual, but appeared dim and small in the moonless dark, and, for once, very far away. Hero had set her bedroom window wide in the hope of catching a breath of breeze, but there had been no wind. Only the cloying scent of frangipani and orange blossom from the Consulate garden, and underlying it a faint and unpleasant stench of sewage, salt water and corruption that was the smell of Zanzibar. Someone was singing in a house on the far side of the garden wall; a woman's voice, high and sweet, accompanied by the thin, twangling music of a *kinanda*. And from somewhere much further away, the monotonous *tunka-tunk* of a drum provided a measured counter-point to the quavering song.

Listening to that throbbing beat, Hero remembered an evening on the *Virago* and Batty Potter telling her some absurd tale of the sacred drums of Zanzibar that sounded a warning of their own accord when disaster threatened the Island. It did not seem quite so absurd now; though no ghostly hands were responsible for the present sound, for it did not come from some hidden cave in the hills near Dunga, but from the purlieus of the city: a rhythmic and familiar accompaniment to the no less familiar sounds of voices and laughter, the braying of a donkey and the squawling of a pair of alley-cats who were conducting a courtship among the pomegranate trees.

Hero blew out the lamp, and pulling back the thin muslin curtains, looked out into the hot darkness and thought how strange the night noises of the city sounded now that the surf and the palm fronds were silent. And how far away Hollis Hill and Boston seemed – as though they were not only part of another continent, but part of another world: a new, clean world, uncluttered by the dirt and disease and the old, dark tyrannies and ugly superstitions that still crept and swarmed and spawned within a stone's-throw of her window.

She shivered at the thought, and for the first time found it frightening rather than challenging. It was not going to be as easy as she had once imagined to clear away the dirt and delusions that men had lived with and tolerated and clung to for long centuries. Or to alter the rules and precepts that had governed the lives of countless generations.

Hero sighed, and was about to turn away from the window when a faint sound from somewhere immediately below her attracted her attention and made her pause to listen. It was only a very small sound, and had it not been for the humiliating memories it evoked it is doubtful if she would have picked it out from among the multitudinous night noises of the city. But the surreptitious rasp of that particular bolt being eased from its socket was familiar to her, for she had drawn it back herself, and with equal caution, on the fatal night when she had crept out of the house to go to Beit-el-Tani.

The Consulate was in darkness, and the last light to be extinguished had been Hero's own. But the side door that led out of the hall on to the terrace was being quietly opened, and as quietly closed again.

Hero caught the muffled squeak of the hinge and the little click as the latch caught, and she leaned out to peer downwards. But nothing moved among the shadows, and when a moment or two later her ear caught the soft crunch of quick, cautious footsteps on the crushed shell of the garden paths, she was startled to realize that someone had walked softly along the terrace and down the steps without her seeing or hearing them.

A dark shape accompanied by a spark of light showed briefly against the paler masses of the flowerbeds, to be lost to sight almost immediately among the orange trees at the far end of the garden. Hero waited for the creak of the garden gate, and when it came was startled to find herself shivering. Which was, she told herself, absurd, because it could only mean that Uncle Nat's personal servant Joshua, who was supposed to sleep at night on a palliasse on the back landing so as to be within call in case of emergency, had waited until his master was asleep and then left the house for some assignation in the city.

Had it been someone entering the house it would have been a different matter, for then she would have had ample cause for alarm. But someone leaving it could only be a member of the household who had crept out and intended to return, and it would be both foolish and unkind to go waking up Clay or Uncle Nat in order to get Joshua or the night-watchman into trouble. All the same the incident disturbed her, and the smell of the city and the scent of cloves and strange flowers that permeated every corner of her darkened room was suddenly a part of it: the odour of mystery and corruption, and the East . . .

Hero shivered again, and drawing the curtains against the night, went back to bed, but could not rest: until all at once it occurred to her that the man she had seen leaving the house so quietly had been smoking a cigar. Then it must have been Uncle Nat or Clay, and there was nothing to worry about. Except why should Clay . . .

Hero yawned and was asleep.

24

' "*At sea north-east winds blow Sabean odours from the spicy shore of Araby the blest,*" ' declaimed Emory Frost, gesturing with his glass. 'And I wonder just what Milton would have made of the paradisiacal odours if he'd ever got a good whiff of Muscat on a hot night? Or of this salubrious spot, either!'

He lifted his head and sniffed the night air. 'The wind has changed. There will be rain tomorrow – the monsoon is here.'

Majid licked his forefinger and held it up, and after half a minute dropped his hand and said: 'You imagine it. There is no wind: not so much as the smallest breath. You are drunk, my friend.'

'Possibly. But not too drunk to feel the air change. It will blow soon enough, and in a day or two your abominable sewer of a city will be fit to live in again.'

Majid shrugged and said carelessly: 'A sensitive nose would seem to go with a white skin. A bad smell in the streets does not worry us over-much. It passes, and does no harm.'

'There you're wrong: it does a deal of harm. It breeds sickness.'

'*Bah!* You are as bad as that English doctor and the good Colonel Edwards – and the new American lady who looks like a youth in women's clothes and worries my poor ministers with complaints about the evil things that people throw into the streets or on to the beaches. Where else should they throw them? They cannot keep such stuff in their houses – imagine the odour! And when the rains come all will be clean again.'

'Until the rains cease and the dry season returns. I know! You're an idle lot of ruffians.'

'Would you have me waste the revenues on pulling down old houses and building sewers? Or paying armies of slaves to carry away the refuse daily?'

'Good God, no! I'm not complaining. Or not much. There may be times when the stench gets a bit much for me, but rather that than a stink of Progress and Carbolic. Besides, I understand you've spent the revenues already. Or am I wrong?'

Majid sighed heavily. 'Alas, no. You are right. But even if I had not, my people would laugh at me for wasting good money on such things as the removal of filth. Nor would they thank me for interfering with their ways. The English doctor tells me that if I would but force my subjects to keep the streets free of waste matter and evil smells there would be less sickness and fewer deaths, and more children would live to grow up and more men and women live to grow old. To heal the sick is good; but to tamper in such a manner with the plans of God is certainly foolish, since is not the All-Powerful also the All-Wise? If there were no more sickness, and no babes are carried off in youth but all live to be strong and old, there will arise great trouble in the world, for any fool can see that in time there will not be sufficient room for all.'

Rory said: 'Allah will doubtless be able to devise other ways of keeping the population within bounds. And if he should not, they can safely be trusted to see to it themselves. It's one of the things they've always been good at.'

Majid acknowledged the jest with a twisted smile. 'That is true. It is because they will not learn to accept the world as God made it, but must for ever be meddling with it; as though Allah and his Prophet did not know what was best for them and for it. And the worst of the meddlers are those from the West. You may not believe me, but do you know what that tall woman who is the niece of the American Consul has been doing?'

'Only too well!' said Rory with a grin. 'She conceived it her duty to assist your brother Bargash, in the expectation that he would prove a more enlightened ruler than yourself and agree to put an end to the buying and selling of slaves.'

'*Bargash?* But he would have—— She cannot have known his mind!'

'She didn't. I think your sisters and Madame Tissot gave her that impression for their own ends.'

'She must be mad, poor woman. I knew that she had interested herself in the affair, but I had imagined it to be out of affection for Cholé, who is very beautiful. But it was not that I meant. No; she has been buying slaves through her uncle's gardener, a rascally negro by the name of Bofabi. The man is himself a freed slave, and therefore she seems to imagine that because of this he will feel more sympathy for his own kind than an Arab, and thinks that once he has bought them they are free. She does not know that he owns a small shamba outside the town, and that with the money she gives him to buy these people, and to feed and keep those he buys, he has bought more land on which he makes these slaves work hard for him, so that soon he will be rich. He tells her that he has paid high prices and has bought more slaves than he has in truth done, and pays money to her woman, Fattûma, to tell her how well and happy are all those he has bought and freed. She must indeed be afflicted by Allah!'

'On the contrary,' said Rory. 'She is afflicted by a desire to assist her fellow-men and help to right the injustices of the world. It is the crusading spirit. Very laudable – and damnably uncomfortable!'

'Not for Bofabi and the serving-woman,' commented Majid. 'They are both most comfortable. Though I do not think the slaves are, for Africans are devil-worshippers and do not know how to treat slaves. Someone should tell her that.'

'She would not believe it. She believes only what she wishes to believe.'

'Then her relatives should get her a sensible husband. A strong man who would beat her when she behaves foolishly. All women need husbands.'

'This one is not a woman. She is an admirable piece of statuary, and what she needs is a Pygmalion.'

'A what? I do not understand.'

'According to the Greeks, a sculptor of that name fell in love with a beautiful ivory statue, and persuaded some Goddess – Aphrodite, I think – to breathe life into her. After which he married her and named her "Galatea". But the lady in question is probably doomed to remain ivory for the rest of her life, since I doubt if Mr Clayton Mayo will be sufficiently interested in turning her into a Galatea. I should say he is a deal more interested in her fortune: though I may be wrong. You know, this brandy of yours is quite tolerable. Over-scented, but I've tasted worse. Here's to your very good health.'

The Sultan and Captain Emory Frost were seated in a private audience chamber of the Palace: a high white room with arched, open doorways hung with silk curtains, and wide windows giving on to a view of the sea. Oil lamps in pierced bronze holders hung motionless from the ceiling, reflecting themselves in the inevitable gilt-framed looking-glasses and attracting a horde of winged and crawling creatures from the darkness outside. Moths, beetles and other night-flying insects whirled and fluttered in a golden haze around each lamp, and a dozen gecko lizards darted and snapped on the ceiling, bloating themselves with the winged feast. But the lizards and the hypnotized insects provided the only movement in the hot night, for beyond the windows the black silhouettes of palm trees stood still and unstirring against the dark sky and the dim, unblinking stars, and inside the silk curtains hung motionless in the archways.

The two men lay relaxed in careless undress, the Sultan on a low divan among an assortment of cushions, and his guest, for greater coolness, on the floor. Rory had been drinking perfumed brandy for the best part of an hour, and though it had made him feel pleasantly carefree it had not yet thickened his speech or blunted his faculties, and studying Majid with half-closed eyes, he harked back to an earlier thought and said lazily: 'Why should the prospect of the rains trouble Your Highness?'

'It is not the rains,' said Majid mournfully.

'What then?'

'The winds that bring them and the thought of what those winds will bring: the dhows of those *shaitans* – those devils from the Gulf.'

'They may not come,' said Rory easily. 'After all, they didn't come last year, did they.'

Majid made a small petulant movement. 'That is why I am afraid. Because they did not, they will surely come this year – and be doubly rapacious.'

'With any luck they won't, for they don't like the British Navy and the *Daffodil* has been hanging about here too much of late.'

The Sultan sighed and relaxed. 'That is true. She has been capturing many slavers of late. Six in the last month.'

'Hell-ships all,' said Rory cheerfully.

'So I understand. The Lieutenant is very lucky. Or else his information is unusually good. He is always there in the right place and at the right time.'

'Not always,' grinned Rory.

The Sultan gave him an odd oblique glance, and frowned. 'You should be more careful, my friend, or one day someone will inform upon you. Then it will be *your* name that some waterfront idler will whisper to the Lieutenant as he passes, and your ship that he will be waiting for at the right time and the right place. It is a dangerous game that you play.'

'I know. That is why I play it carefully.'

'You have need to. The Lieutenant would give a great deal to catch you. I might even be tempted to sell you myself! How much do you think he would pay?'

He chuckled maliciously, and Rory laughed and said: 'Not enough to make it worth your while, I'm afraid.'

'Perhaps that is why I do not do it. But I could wish the *Daffodil* were here now.'

'Personally, the less I see of young Larrimore the better. He's one of the bulldog breed, blast him. Gets his teeth in and won't let go. He's got 'em into me and he's the very devil to shake off. Did Suliman get in safely?'

'So I understand. Officially, of course, I know nothing. But I hear that he landed a hundred and fifty slaves in excellent condition, and that all of them have fetched high prices. I cannot understand why Colonel Edwards should make so great a fuss about a few slaves. We Arabs have always kept slaves; it has been part of our life for a thousand years and more, and our whole concept of society is bound up with it. The Prophet himself did not forbid it – it is only their ill-treatment that is forbidden. Yet every day the Colonel worries me with complaints: I find it very tiring. You do not think that you could let it be known that you will take off some slaves in a few weeks' time for sale in Persia?'

'Good heavens – why?'

'So that the good Colonel will send messages at once to tell these gunboats to return and entrap you. I confess I should feel easier in my mind if I knew that one would be near, so that the raiders would hear of it and keep away.'

'Why not get your own ships to chase them off? They could do it.'

Majid said crossly: 'Now you are mocking me. You know they would not. These devils of pirates are wild and lawless men who have guns and knives and care for no one, and my men have no desire to be killed.'

'Neither have the townspeople any desire to have their women and children stolen and their slaves kidnapped, or their houses robbed and set on fire. But if the raiders come it's either that or fight them. Unless you intend to buy them off again?'

The Sultan flung his hands out in a despairing gesture. 'How can I, when you know that I have not the money? A fortune it cost me last time. A fortune! But the Treasury is empty, I am deep in debt, and I do not know where to turn for so much as a gold piece, so if these *shaitans* come they will sack the town and perhaps burn it, for I can neither fight them nor bribe them. They will stay and do what they will in the city, and only leave when they have taken their fill of goods and women and slaves to carry back to the Gulf. You do not know what they are like! You and your ship have been elsewhere whenever they came before, and your house being strong and well guarded, they leave it alone. But others have not been so fortunate.'

Rory shrugged and refilled his glass from the bottle that stood on the floor beside him. It was true that he had never been present when the Arab pirates from the Persian Gulf made their annual raid on Zanzibar. He had taken good care not to be. The north-east Trade Winds that brought the monsoon sped the pirate dhows down the coast of Africa, and they descended like locusts on the Island to kidnap children and procure slaves: camping outside the city like a hostile army and swaggering through the streets, brawling, murdering and looting. No child, slave or personable woman was safe from them, for what they did not choose to buy they stole, and at the first sight of their sails all who could do so hurried their children and young slaves to safe hiding places in the interior. But despite every precaution, many were kidnapped daily and carried off to the dhows. The poorer quarters of the town suffered most, since undefended houses were frequently broken into and victims forcibly abducted; and it was a brave man indeed who dared leave his house after dark while the raiders remained, for they stepped aside for no one, and even the Sultan's guards took care not to interfere with them.

Majid said angrily: 'It is all very well for you to shrug your shoulders. I tell you, you do not know what they are like! They are like a pack of wild dogs. They go armed about the city so that my guards, being afraid for their lives, will do nothing. And if they were not afraid, and fought them, it would be worse, since if any hindered them they would attack in force and burn the town and perhaps even my own palace. There are hundreds of them. Thousands! Strong, wild, lawless men who——'

Rory raised a protesting hand: 'I know. I heard all about them last time. And the time before – and the time before that.'

'They will be worse this year,' said the Sultan pessimistically, 'because they will know that I cannot give them money. Everyone knows. I cannot even pay for the building of my new palace at Dar-es-Salaam.'

'I thought you used slaves for that? And convicts.'

'I do. But even they must be fed, and I now owe so much to those who have supplied food and stone and marble that they give me no peace. There is also the tax that I am bound by treaty to pay to my brother Thuwani, and if I cannot pay that – and how can I? – he too will make trouble. Money ... money ... *money!*' Majid raised his clenched fists to heaven: 'How I have come to abominate that word! I tell you, my friend, I think of nothing else all day and all night, and therefore I do not sleep and my appetite has gone. How can one be a ruler when there is no money to pay for one's own amusements, let alone all the rest? Where am I to turn? Where? – tell me that!'

Rory sat up suddenly, knocking over the brandy bottle in the process, and said: '*Pemba!* ... I knew I'd forgotten something!'

'How do you mean, Pemba?' enquired the Sultan sulkily. 'If you mean the revenues from the last clove crop, they were disappointing. And I have already spent them!'

'No, it wasn't that. It was something I heard from a man I met in a back street in Mombasa one night, when we stopped to take on fresh water for those horses. I can't think why I didn't remember it before – except that I was fairly drunk at the time and it seemed a lot of nonsense anyway. But there might be something in it.'

'In what? What has this to do with Pemba? I do not understand what you are talking about.'

'Money – I think,' said Rory. He looked at the fallen bottle as though he did not see it, and presently stretched out a hand to lift it and hold it up to the light. But what little remained of its contents had soaked into the carpet, and he pitched it carelessly out of the window and clasped his hands about his knees; his blond brows wrinkled in thought and his gaze fixed on a large beetle that had stunned itself against a lamp and was describing foolish, buzzing circles on the polished *chunam* floor beyond the edge of the rug.

The silence and that small, futile sound began to get on the Sultan's nerves, and after a minute or two he said irritably: 'Stop staring at that insect! What had you forgotten? What is this about money?'

Rory lifted his head and his eyes were no longer blank and unseeing, but alive and very bright, and his voice held an odd note of excitement:

'What would you offer me if I could show you how to get your hands on a fortune? Enough money to pay the tax to Thuwani and bribe off any number of pirates, as well as keeping yourself in funds for the next twenty years or so?'

Majid abandoned his lounging pose and sat up stiffly, staring as though he were not quite sure that he had heard aright. He said: 'You think you can do that?'

'I'm not sure. But it's possible.'

'Half!' said the Sultan promptly. 'If you can do this, you shall have half.'

'Is that a promise?'

'It is an oath. I do not believe that you can do such a thing, but if you can, I swear by the beard of the Prophet and my dead father's head that you shall take half.'

'Fair enough,' said Rory, 'and I may even live to claim it. This man I met in Mombasa . . .' He was silent for a space, as though collecting his thoughts, and then he said slowly:

'It was late at night, and he lurched into me and fell flat on his face under my feet. I thought that he too was drunk, and swore at him. But he'd been stabbed. He was an old man, and there was blood all over his back: it looked like embroidery until I put a hand on him to help him up. I turned him over and made him comfortable. There was nothing else I could do for him; but he held on to my sleeve and kept muttering, so I stayed with him until he went. He'd apparently got into a street fight and someone had stuck a knife into him. Told me he came from Pemba, and that his elder brother was a famous *Mchawi* – a wizard who had been consulted by your father about that drought business with the Mwenyi Mkuu, and was the only one who knew the secret. I asked him what secret – more for something to say than anything else – and he grinned and said the one that everyone wanted to know. The Imam Saïd's secret. Then he babbled a lot of nonsense about it being all very well for his brother to say that gold was no good to anyone and better underground, but there were others who could use it, and he for one did not despise riches. And after a few uncomplimentary remarks about his family he started to cough up blood, and died. I left him there and came back to the ship; and what with waking up the next morning with a head like a cauldron full of red-hot shot, and one of the horses going sick, and then getting back here to find your beloved brother conducting a private war with the British Navy, I haven't thought of it since.'

'And you are thinking of it now because . . . ?' Majid seemed unable to finish the sentence.

'Because it occurs to me that the man may have been referring to your late father's treasure.'

There was a long silence in which the angry buzzing of the beetle and the flutter of moths' wings beating against a lamp was once again startlingly audible, and then the Sultan let out his breath in an explosive sigh. His eyes were as bright as Emory Frost's and his hands shaking. He said in a harsh whisper: 'It cannot be true – it could not be!'

'Why not? No one has ever believed that your father would have hidden that treasure without anyone knowing about it. He must have had some help, even if the reports of its size are less than half true.'

'It is said that they died.' Majid's voice was still no more than a whisper. 'There is a tale that there were only two men, both deaf and dumb and both afflicted by Allah.'

'Mad?' enquired Rory.

'Simpletons only. Strong in body, but with the wits of young children, and therefore well chosen for such a task. It was said that it took them a score of nights to bury the treasure, so great was its size, and that after it was done my father sent them out of the country, to Muscat, but that the ship ran aground in a great storm off the island of Socotra, and was lost with all aboard her.'

'Very convenient,' commented Rory. 'But I still don't believe that your father – may he rest in peace – would have hidden a sizable fortune without taking at least one other person into his confidence in case of accidents.'

Majid shook his head. 'We have always thought that when he buried it he meant to tell his heir upon his death-bed, and could not, because he died at sea and in the arms of my brother Bargash. My father would have known that had he told my brother, or any that were with him, Bargash would have grasped both the treasure and the throne. If any man knew the secret it was the Englishman who was British Consul here at that time, for my father held him in great friendship and called upon his name as he lay dying. But the Englishman lied and denied it, and now he is back in his own country, and the treasure, if it is anywhere, is with him.'

Rory gave a short laugh and came to his feet, kicking aside his empty glass. 'Don't you believe it! I knew the old ram-rod better than you did. A damn' sight too well! Told me I was a disgrace to his nation and tried to get me deported from the Island. Worse than the present incumbent, though you wouldn't think that possible. You may not like to believe it, but you can take it from me he was the kind of upright idiot who'd cut his throat before he'd steal sixpence, even if he were starving. I know the breed – and so did your father!'

'But he might still have known.'

Rory made a sweeping, scornful gesture of negation with one hand. 'If he had, he'd have told you. Because there wouldn't have been any point in your father confiding in him except to ensure that someone knew the secret, and could be trusted to hand it on to his heir supposing he should die in Oman, or before he could get back here. And as you were not told it, your father didn't tell him. That, as Uncle Batty would say, is as plain as the nose on your face. All the same, I bet he told someone, and I'm putting my money on it being that witch-doctor.'

Majid pulled at his lip, his eyes glittering with excitement and his brows wrinkled in doubt, and at last he said pensively: 'It is true that the greatest witch-doctors in the world live in Pemba. It has always been renowned for its wizards and warlocks, and my father had great faith in them and often consulted with them on matters of spells and magic and the secrets of the past and the future. There was one whom he visited often and who once came to Motoni, and if he told anyone, he would have told that man. But why?'

'Don't ask *me*. Perhaps he wanted a spell put on it.'

Majid's head jerked round as though it had been pulled on a string. 'That is it! Yes, that is it . . . a spell to keep it safe from discovery and the hands of thieves. I remember hearing that the man could summon demons and that he was famous for such spells. You are right, my friend. There is someone who knows.'

'Well, there we are,' said Rory. 'All you've got to do is to trace the man, find out if he had a brother who died recently in Mombasa, and then get him to talk.'

'But how – how?' the Sultan struck his hands together and the sweat glistened bright on his excited face. 'To trace him will be easy. But if he will not talk——? He may not, else why has he not spoken before? Knowing that my father's dead and that I am Sultan, he has still kept silent. That can only mean that he does not intend to speak of it to anyone. So what if he holds to that and will not tell?'

Rory laughed unpleasantly and said: 'Threaten him with a dose of his own medicine. You'll find that he'll be only too ready to spit up all his secrets rather than face the sort of treatment that he and his kind have been handing out to their wretched victims for years. Or are you afraid to threaten a witch-doctor?'

'I would be a fool if I were not,' said Majid, shuddering. 'And you too would be wise not to treat such men lightly.'

'I don't,' said Rory briefly. 'But then I don't treat money lightly either, and in this case it looks like being one or the other. Do we risk offending the powers of darkness, or give up the treasure? Or if you prefer to put it another way, which are you most afraid of? Being cursed by a witch-doctor, or overrun by pirates and infuriating your brother of Muscat and Oman by failing to pay your yearly tribute money? Though mind you, if you'd take my advice you'd refuse to pay Thuwani another penny, treaty or no treaty!'

Majid said crossly: 'So you have often said. But then *you* have nothing to fear, since he is not your brother.'

'No, thank God.'

Majid smiled wryly and said: 'You may well do so. It shall be the money then.'

'Good. I shall leave the details to you and only remind you that if you hope to use some of it to buy off the Gulf pirates, you haven't got too much time. Look over there——'

He jerked his chin in the direction of the curtained archways and Majid turned and saw that the thin silk was beginning to move at last; billowing out on a draught of air that stole through the hot rooms and set the lamps swaying.

Rory said: 'It's blowing from the north-east. I told you it would rain tomorrow. If these bastards are coming this year they'll be setting out soon enough, and they won't take so very long to get here with the wind behind them.'

Majid watched the swaying curtains for a moment or two, and then rose from the divan and crossed over to the windows to look out into the night. The stars were still visible, but the palm trees had begun to whisper and rustle and the distant noises of the city came unevenly as the breeze blew and died and blew again, like a man breathing.

He turned back to look at Rory and said abruptly: 'If he should say he will not come here, would you yourself fetch him for me?'

'No,' said Rory promptly. 'I can always find a use for money, but I don't need it as badly as you do, and though there are not many things I stick at, kidnapping a witch-doctor is one of them. I've put you on the trail, so it's only fair that you do the next part. And if you get the information I'll help you collect the booty.'

'How do you know that I will tell you if I get it? I might say that the man did not know – and he may well not! – and then go by stealth and remove all the treasure, leaving you none.'

Rory laughed and said: 'For one thing, you have sworn an oath. And for another, I shall watch you like a hawk to see that you don't get the chance.'

'So?' Majid smiled, and regarded the tall man with shrewd, appraising eyes and a touch of envy: 'My friend, it grieves me to say so, but you are a scoundrel. Yes, a reckless, ruthless scoundrel, and had you been born an Arab you would surely have risen to be a great King or a Commander of Armies, instead of only the Captain of a disreputable ship that will undoubtedly one day be sunk by the guns of your own people. It is agreed then: I will consent to do the – ah – "next part" for you.'

'For us both,' corrected Rory. 'And you are wrong, for I have no desire to be either a King or a Commander of Armies. I am content with what I have.'

'With so little?'

'With freedom; which is no small thing. Here I am free to go where I will and do what I like, and to make and break my own laws. Or anyone else's, if I choose.'

'You are a romantic, my friend.'

'Perhaps – if to be a romantic is to relish experience and danger, and dislike rules and restrictions and the cramping hideousness of life in the so-called "civilized West". You don't know – you couldn't begin to understand – the smug self-righteousness of those who live there. The sweets of Progress that can turn a green country into an ugly commercialized ash-heap. The endless laws churned out by pompous fools in Parliament that aim at making every petty peccadillo into a crime. The interference and the prying! The——'

He stopped and gave a short laugh. 'I'm sorry. I must be drunker than I thought. I'd better get out before I start thumping the table and giving you my views on societies whose sole object is the suppression of something someone else likes to do. You don't have them yet in your part of the world, but you will. You will! Someday someone is going to see that you get the blessings of Progress, Western style, whether you want it or not. And if you don't want it you'll get it crammed down your throat with a rifle butt.'

Majid looked at him with a slow, sly smile, and said softly: 'That is not all the truth. There is something else. A reason. What is it that you do with all the money you make? – that which you do not spend?'

'Count it,' said Rory. 'What else? Are you hoping for a loan? If so I must regretfully tell you that you won't get it. Or not from me, anyway.'

'No, no. I am not such a fool as that. You mean to make your fortune, do you not? And when you have made it, what I wonder will you do with it? What is it that drives you?'

'Pure greed,' said Rory lightly. 'I am a miser at heart. Or do I mean a magpie? That brandy of yours is making me too talkative, so I shall wish you a very good night. *Kua-heri! yá Sidi.*'

He saluted the Sultan and went out into the uneasy night, stumbling a little on the stairs, and did not speak when Batty's faithful shadow moved across the pool of light by the side gate where three members of the Palace guard whiled away the hours playing cards.

The breeze had strengthened, but it was still blowing in uneven gusts, and the sea was beginning to slap against the harbour wall in small, jerking splashes, turning the reflected lights of the ships from placid streaks of gold to glinting fragments that danced and jigged and leapt as the wind ruffled across the water. The air was perceptibly cooler and the streets had emptied, and Rory listened to the sound of his own footsteps and the faint echo that was Batty's cat-like tread, and thought of the things that brandy had made him put into words: that restless craving for excitement and danger. The desire to break a law for no better reason than because it was a law. The urge to flout convention, and to escape – above all, to escape . . .

He had been six when his mother had run away with a dancing master and life had changed for him overnight. She had been pretty and gay and selfish, but she would have spoiled him if she had had her way, and he could not believe that she had abandoned him to the angry, autocratic father whom he had always been afraid of. He had been sure she would return one day, and it had taken him a long time to realize that she had gone for good and would never come back.

The next two years had been grey ones, for his father had dismissed both nurse and governess – his reason being that they had been selected by his wife and must therefore be unreliable – and substituted an elderly tutor who disliked children and showed it in many small, mean ways. Rory had hated Mr Eli Sollet with a small boy's helpless, simmering hate, and had imagined that the world could not hold anyone worse: until his father died of an inflammation of the lung, contracted out duck-shooting on the marshes, and left his son to the care of his only brother, Henry Lionel Frost, with whom he had not been on speaking terms since the day that Henry had chosen to make a few critical remarks on his elder brother's choice of a bride . . .

At the time, Rory's father had been convinced that this disapproval of his Sophia had its roots in spleen, since it had long been an accepted fact that he would die a bachelor, and Henry, who had two sons of his own to think of, had always looked upon himself as his brother's heir. But the scandal of Sophia and her dancing master had proved his criticisms to have been well founded, and the senior Emory, on his death-bed, had made what seemed to him an adequate acknowledgement of this by appointing him sole trustee and guardian of his only child. The years of bondage had begun.

Uncle Henry, his acid-tongued wife, Laura, and their two stout and over-indulged sons had made the eight-year-old Rory look back upon the reign of Eli Sollet as a period of almost halcyon peace. His cousins were both older than himself, and they had bullied him unmercifully but had no hesitation, when he retaliated, in running screaming to their mother, who punished him with outraged severity.

What am I doing here? How did I get here? Why? thought the boy Rory, locked in a dark attic with a slice of bread and a glass of water for long cold hours, sore from a whipping and burning from a deep sense of injustice. It was a thought that was to recur with great frequency during the years that followed, and one to which he never found an answer.

The years had dragged by intolerably slowly: punctuated with monotonous regularity by floggings, angry tirades and endless days spent locked in his room or the attic on a diet of bread and water, with a lesson to learn by rote – a chapter from some improving work or several pages from a volume of collected sermons (Uncle Henry and Aunt Laura were both genuinely convinced that Sophia's son could not have avoided inheriting a large part of his immoral and unmentionable mother's disposition, and that it was their duty to eradicate or at least subdue that evil taint with every means in their power). They had locked him in with the New Testament on one occasion, but had not repeated the experiment, and the thrashing that had followed had been more than usually severe, for he had returned it to them with a page turned down at the twentieth chapter of St Luke and part of the fourteenth verse heavily underscored in indelible pencil: *'This is the heir: come, let us kill him, that the inheritance may be ours.'* Rory was growing up.

The only comfort he had found in those black years had been his discovery that all books were not long-winded sermons or dry-as-dust treatises devoted to improving the sinful, and he had read voraciously; smuggling books out of the library and hiding them under his mattress or on the top of the cupboards, and devouring them in secret. They became his escape from an intolerable world, and with their help he lived a hundred lives: Lancelot and Charlemagne, Marlborough and Rupert of the Rhine, Raleigh, Drake, John of Gaunt and Henry the Navigator. He fought battles with the Roman Legions, scaled the Alps with Hannibal and sailed into the unknown with Columbus, scuttled Spanish galleons with Francis Drake and charged with the Guards at Waterloo. He had

been barely twelve when he had opened a book at random and read four
lines that he had known were written expressly for him:

> By a Knight of Ghosts and Shadows
> I summoned am to tourney
> Ten leagues beyond the wide world's end.
> Methinks it is no journey.

He had read it over and over again, fascinated to find that something
said in verse could make such piercing sense. But though his journeys
had been easy enough to make in the spirit, they had been hard to make
in the flesh. Five times he had run away only to be ignominiously captured
and brought back. And when at last he was sent away to school, the three
years he spent at an establishment noted for its success in crushing the
spirits of recalcitrant and unmanageable boys had seemed a paradise compared to his uncle's house.

It had been a strict and brutal school. Run more on the lines of a re-
formatory than a seat of learning, by mean and unimaginative men under
a headmaster who, though preaching in the school chapel as one in the
full confidence of the Almighty, underpaid his assistants, saved money on
food and amenities, and believed with Uncle Henry that inflexible strict-
ness, harsh corporal punishment and near-starvation was the only way to
deal with difficult boys. But four years under his uncle's roof had inured
Rory to all these things, and he had swallowed such learning as was offered
him with an avidity that would have disgusted his schoolmates had it not
been for the fact that he had also learnt to use his fists with a skill that
had taught them to leave him severely alone, and a ferocity that no subsequent punishments had succeeded in curbing.

He had been fifteen when he decided that he had had enough of school
and Uncle Henry, and on the night following that decision he had climbed
out of his dormitory window, slid down a conveniently placed drainpipe,
scaled two walls and walked out into the world a free man. And that time
he had not been caught or brought back . . .

The north-east Trade Wind that stirred up the evil-smelling dust of
Zanzibar and woke the palms to rustling music, was a very different wind
from the cold north-easter that had once blown icy raindrops into the
face of a boy who plodded along in the darkness, making for the nearest
seaport. But recalling that long-ago night and the dungeon years behind
it, Rory felt again a tremor of the fierce determination that had possessed
him then. A determination to escape and live his own life in his own way,
and never again to allow another man or woman to tell him what he must
do, or punish him for not doing it.

He had lived ever since by his family's motto; taking what he wanted when he wanted it. And he had never let sentiment or remorse or any scruples stand in the way of his desires, or permitted anyone to order or own him. Love, friendship, affection, were all dangerous things if one let them get too great a hold on one, so he had seen to it that they should not do so. For his charming, selfish mother had taught him early a lesson that he had never forgotten – that pain inflicted by someone loved and trusted is deeper and more unendurable than the worse savageries that can be committed by those one hates or cares nothing for. He had no intention of allowing his own emotions to become either a weapon that could be turned against him or a tie that could hold him against his will, and there were even times when he resented Batty, Ralub, Zorah and the child Amrah, because in their several ways they implied a claim on him, and he would not admit any such claim: least of all through his affections. Faithful Batty, loyal Hajji Ralub, adoring Zorah, and Amrah – Amrah who was his own daughter . . .

The child had been a mistake: his mistake, and a bad one. He had never paused to care or consider whether his casual amours were productive of anything more than the gratification of a passing desire, and he had certainly never thought of it when the starving, terrified creature he had bought in an idle moment off an Arab slave trader had grown into a lovely and desirable woman. He had taken her because it pleased him to do so.

Rory had had other mistresses; and possibly other bastards, though if so he was unaware of it. But Zorah had differed from the others in that she belonged to him. She was as much a part of his household as Batty and Ralub, his servants and his crew and Murashi, the white cockatoo. He had bought her, and she had no other home, and though he had tried, once, to trace her people, it had proved an impossible task and he had abandoned it. And then she had grown up and without his quite realizing it taken over the management of The Dolphins' House from the fat, idle negress who had been in nominal charge, and within a year of her becoming his mistress, Amrah had been born.

He could still remember the shock it had given him when she had told him with shining pride that she was carrying his child: his sudden involuntary spasm of revulsion. 'It will be a son,' said Zorah. 'It cannot be otherwise, for I have prayed for a son and made offerings, and surely my prayers will be granted.' But he did not want a son and he did not want to see Zorah bear one. Not his child; someone who would have a claim on him and grow up to carry his blood into a future that he could only view with hostility and distrust. Someone who would be a responsibility and a tie – looking to him for advice, affection and security.

If he could have sent Zorah away then he would have done so, and as

311

he could not, he had absented himself from the Island as often as possible and had not been there when the child was born. Amrah had been three months old when he had first seen her, and though the baby's sex had been a bitter disappointment to Zorah, Rory had been strangely relieved. Any child was bad enough, but a girl was the lesser of two evils, since she would belong more to her mother and so be less of a tie. But the little creature had been startlingly like him, and as she grew older she had become more so, and it had been an effort to prevent her from getting her small fingers on his heart.

'*With a host of furious fancies, whereof I am commander, with a burning spear and a horse of air to the wilderness I wander . . .*' The words that had first made poetry live for him repeated themselves in his brain and were still with him. He was still Tom-a-Bedlam, singing them in the streets of Zanzibar. '*Whereof I am commander*' . . . That was the secret! To exercise complete control over one's heart: to possess oneself, rejecting the tyrannous or clinging claims of others, and to wander in the wild and lawless places of a world in which there would soon be no wildernesses, but only walls and laws and factory chimneys. He could see it coming and feel its encroaching breath as clearly as he had felt that faint, barely perceptible change in the hot, heavy stillness and known that the currents of the air had changed and soon the wind would rise. There would be no escaping it, and nowhere left where a man could breathe – and go to the devil in his own way!

He said abruptly: 'Batty, what would you do if you had a hell of a lot of money?'

Batty did not reply to the question immediately, but after pondering over it for a space, he said thoughtfully: 'Now that I comes to think of it, I don't know as I'd want an 'ole 'eap of money. Enough's enough, I reckons. What 'ud I do with it – my age?'

'You mean you wouldn't fancy yourself as a bloated plutocrat with a carriage-and-pair and a house full of butlers and footmen? There's nothing you'd like that you haven't got?'

'Well now, I won't go so far as to deny that there's times that I'd like to see old London town again, and 'ear Bow Bells ring and walk down Cheapside. But what would a cove like me do with butlers and footmen? An 'aughty lot they are, and I'd rather 'ave that old scoundrel Jumah any day. I clips 'im when I thinks 'e needs it, and 'e answers back as saucy as a sparrow, and no 'ard feelings on either side. I reckon I been livin' this way too long to fancy settlin' down in mansions with footmen, and as long as I 'as enough to keep me from the work'ouse in me old age, I won't say as I wants much more than I 'ave right now.'

'Uncle, you're a man of sense. About the only one I've ever met!'

'What you mean is, I ain't a blinkin' fool,' sniffed Batty: and added ruminatively: 'If I was younger, now, I might get to thinkin' that money would buy me an 'areem full of beauteous wimmin, and enough rum to keep me as drunk as a royal Dook. But I've 'ad me share of females, and though I ain't saying as I don't enjoy a nice tumble with a likely wench now and then, it ain't what it used to be, and that's the truth. Grub and terbaccy is as good, and maybe better. Still, there's somethin' about money – "filthy lucre" it may be, but it gets you; and I dare say if someone was to offer me a ruddy great fortune on a platter I wouldn't 'ave the 'eart to turn it down.'

'That's the trouble,' said Rory, and laughed.

'Why? Anyone been offerin' you a fortune lately?' enquired Batty, interested.

'More or less. And on a platter.'

'Must be a catch in it,' decided Batty, shaking his head pessimistically. 'No one don't go 'andin' out fortunes for nothing. You know what's the trouble with you, don't you Cap'n Rory? You been on the booze again, that's what. You'll wake up with a shockin' 'ead in the mornin': and no fortune neither – though what you'd do with one I don't know.'

'I do!'

'And what's that?'

'What I've always meant to do one day – go back to England and put the law on dear Uncle Henry.'

'There! I knew you was drunk. Why, 'e'd turn the Peelers on you quicker than a flash. Ten years you'd get. Maybe twenty!'

'He hasn't any proof. Besides, he wouldn't dare charge me.'

'That's what you 'ope. But what about me? I ain't 'is loving nephew.'

'Don't be an old fool, Uncle. He doesn't know anything about you.'

'Maybe not. But the Peelers do, and they 'ave 'orrible long memories, God rot 'em! I know – I've 'ad experience: which is more than anyone could say of you, if you're fool enough to go puttin' your 'ead back into the basket. You ain't reelly thinkin' of going after 'im, are you?'

Batty's voice was suddenly anxious, and Rory gave a short and ugly laugh. 'I've thought of nothing much else for years! And I'll do it one day – unless he cheats me by dying before I get the chance. But it's going to take a lot of money to fight Uncle Henry in the courts, and make him account for his stewardship and cough up the family estates on which he and my dear cousins Lionel and Walter have established squatter's rights. Justice comes high in the Home of the Free!'

'You can't do it!' said Batty distressfully. ''E'll 'ave the law on you for snitchin' all them spoons and stuff and swipin' your aunt's jools – sure as check!'

'Let him try! But you don't have to worry Batty. I'm not going to do anything about it at the moment. It's just one of those day-dreams, and it can wait. It's waited long enough, God knows!' He began to whistle very softly through his teeth, and presently he broke off in the middle of a bar to say: 'You know, Batty, it's time we moved off somewhere else. This island is getting a bloody sight too civilized. Foreigners and sour faces wherever you look; British gunboats cluttering up the harbour and a damned officious British Consul poking his nose into peoples' private affairs. Yanks, Frogs and so on jostling for elbow-room on the *maidan*, and soon we'll have a swarm of missionaries preaching Salvation. It's played out, Batty. It's beginning to stink of law and order, and for myself I prefer the smell of sewage.'

'*Hum*,' said Batty doubtfully, rubbing his nose with a gnarled forefinger. 'I'm not sure that you ain't right. Where was you thinkin' of going?'

'Persia – Arabia – Borneo – China. The Mountains of the Moon! What does it matter? Central Asia, perhaps.'

'Couldn't take the *Virago* there,' commented Batty judicially. 'I wouldn't like that; I've got used to the old bitch. Mind the step now – we're 'ome. And if I was you I'd put me 'ead under the pump before I went to bed. Might sober you up a bit. *Fortunes*, indeed!'

True to Batty's prophecy, Captain Emory Frost awoke the following morning with an evil headache and a jaundiced view of life. But his own prediction was also fulfilled, for he found the shutters of his room barred against driving rain, and the north-east Trade Winds roaring across the island.

The rain poured off the roofs and balconies of Zanzibar in a thunder of falling water; washing away the dust of the burning days and leaping in cataracts to the streets below, where the gutters flooded and the dirt and debris of months swirled away on a rushing torrent; racing down the narrow lanes to pour into the sea, and carrying with it a tide of filth and garbage and all the unspeakable flotsam and jetsam of the city.

Within an hour the streets were swept clear, and a day or two later beaches that for weeks past had been no better than vast, malodorous middens were clean sand and rock and shingle once more, and the harbour was no longer awash with foulness, but smelt only of the sea.

25

To discover which of Pemba's notorious *Mchawis* had been consulted by Sultan Saïd in the matter of the great drought had been easy enough, for although at the time many had been consulted, only one, the youngest, was still alive. It had also been a simple matter to verify that this same man had visited the late Sultan during the last years of his reign, and possessed a brother who had recently met a violent end in Mombasa. But it had proved quite a different matter to get him brought over from Pemba to Zanzibar.

Majid's messenger had returned bearing the witch-doctor's barely polite excuses, and when a direct command had also been ignored, there had been nothing for it but to kidnap him. Though that too had presented considerable difficulties, since few men were prepared to risk the terrible fate that might befall those who mishandled a wizard known to have authority over devils, ghosts and demons. It had been done eventually by two malefactors under sentence of death, who had been promised a free pardon, a handful of gold and a passage to Muscat in return for their services. Fearing demons less than death, they had brought the bound and gibbering witch-doctor under cover of night to a disused storehouse in the grounds of the old palace of Beit-el-Ras.

The vaulted stone chamber with its ruined gutters and damp-streaked walls had been built underground for greater coolness, and had once, long ago, been used for the storage of fruit and oil and such foodstuffs as kept better in a low temperature. It stank of mildew and rotting vegetation, the dank smell of stone and the acrid scent of charcoal and hot metal: and later of other and more noisome odours; burning flesh, blood and sweat and human excreta. For the wizard proved obdurate.

Majid, to give him his due, had never seriously imagined that it would come to this. After all, as the son who succeeded Seyyid Saïd as Sultan of Zanzibar, he was entitled to his father's treasure, and there was no reason why the *Mchawi* should object to disclosing its hiding place to the legal heir. He therefore ordered the man's bonds to be removed, apologized and promised suitable compensation for the somewhat arbitrary manner in which the wizard, due to his own intransigence, had been brought over from Pemba, and having fully explained the circumstances that had made this necessary, requested the *Mchawi's* co-operation.

It was not forthcoming. The witch-doctor was not only furious over the way he had been abducted, but insolent, unco-operative and quite impervious to reason. The late Sultan, he declared, had intended the treasure for his own use and requested that a spell be put upon it to ensure that its hiding place was not discovered by anyone else. He had left no instructions as to who, if anyone, should inherit it after his death, and that, as far as the *Mchawi* was concerned, was that. Majid had attempted to reason with him, and when that had proved useless tried bribery, threats and cajolery by turns. But all to no effect. The *Mchawi* remained adamant, and there is little doubt that had he initially denied all knowledge of where the treasure was hidden, Majid would have decided that he was following a false trail and given up. But men had cringed and grovelled and gone in terror of the wizard for too long, and far too many of them had died terrible deaths at his hands or by his orders, for him to believe that anyone, even the Sultan, would dare to do more than threaten him. Secure in that belief he not only haughtily admitted his knowledge but boasted of it; and thereby sealed his fate. For having committed himself so far, fear and avarice had driven Majid to translate threats into action.

It was a long-drawn-out and ugly business, for the wizard, though ancient and white-headed, was also unbelievably stubborn. He shrieked and writhed and screamed to his familiars to aid him, and between bouts of pain called down horrifying curses upon the heads of his tormentors and chanted the song that begins '*Hodi Muamu. Nakuja Kuamsha na ni ujima*', that is used to summon devils. But his devils did not aid him. Majid trembled and muttered charms, and countered with the '*Watenda je hapa*' that drives them away: though recalling some of the more unpleasant activities of the witch-doctors of Pemba, and the many victims who had in their day suffered worse terror and tortures at the hands of the shrieking creature who writhed in the red glow of the brazier, he was not disposed to waste any pity on him.

Considering the wizard's age, the hideous, nerve-racking affair took an unconscionably long time. But the half-breed dwarf and the huge negro, both of whom combined a talent for torture with a physical defect that proved invaluable in their profession – they were stone deaf – eventually succeeded in bringing him to see reason, and what was left of him talked . . .

'So it *was* true!' muttered Majid under his breath, and brushed the sweat from his forehead with a shaking hand. His face was wet and pallid in the dim light and he was shivering as though with ague. The solitary lamp that hung from a staple on the damp wall was less bright than the coals that burned in a brazier on the stained flags beneath it, but although the room was below ground level and the massive door at the top of the steps that led down to it had been closed and bolted, a faint draught had found its way in, and the flame of the oil lamp swayed to it, sending the shadows of three men crawling over the walls, and giving an uneasy suggestion of movement to the huddled body of the fourth. Majid wondered if the man were dead, and thought that it would be as well if he were. And also that Rory was not going to like this! The flame began to gutter and burn low and he turned and went up the stairs, and drawing back the heavy iron bolt, jerked open the door to let a rush of cool, rain-scented air into the fetid atmosphere of the cellar.

It had been black night when he had closed that door, but now morning was already pale behind the blanket of the rain clouds, and the ragged casuarinas and dripping palms showed grey and ghostly against the long stretch of sodden grass that lay between the ruined storehouse and the unseen shore where the sullen tide surged and muttered among a tumble of coral rocks. It would be daylight soon – too soon. Majid returned and gestured a dismissal to the grotesque pair who squatted silently in the shadows, and they rose obediently and preceded him up the steps to the door. But before they reached it the dreadful figure on the floor stirred and lifted its head, and Majid checked, drawing in his breath in a gasp that was almost a scream.

The glow from the brazier glinted on the man's rolling eyeballs so that they too seemed to burn red like live coals in the greying face, and he spoke in a hoarse whisper that anywhere else would have been barely audible, but that in the silent place seemed over-loud:

'Hear me, oh ghosts and devils! Hear while I curse it! As it has brought me to my death, so may it bring evil and woe to all who think to use it for their own ends. Unless it be left to lie in the dark it shall bring no good, and he who would use it shall only use it for evil ends and to create more evil . . . Hear me, O Demons of the Trees! Hear me, all ghosts and spirits! *Wenzi wetu watungoja nawe toka hima . . . hima!*'

The cracked voice rose steadily and uncannily until it stopped on a last high note that rang and echoed under the vaulted roof, and the man fell back, and was dead.

Majid turned and fled up the stairs, and thrusting his henchmen out into the wet dawn, swung the door to behind them. It closed with an eldritch shriek of rusted hinges that seemed an echo of another and uglier sound, and he cursed under his breath and drove home the bolts with hands that trembled uncontrollably, and turning from it hurried away into the dripping greyness with the dwarf and the negro trotting at his heels . . .

He had been right in assuming that his friend would not approve the lengths to which he had gone to extract information from the *Mchawi*, for Rory, summoned to Beit-el-Ras to hear the result of the interview, had been gratified by the news that his guess had proved correct, but brutally outspoken as to the methods employed in persuading the wizard to speak.

'What did you expect me to do? Let him go again?' demanded Majid, aggrieved. 'He would not speak and he was insolent and obstinate. And what I did to him was no more than he in his day has done to others. To many, many others!'

'Maybe. But you didn't have to kill him, did you?'

'I tell you, it is better that he died! Had he lived, how could I have permitted him to go free? He would have returned to Pemba and his fellow warlocks, and . . . No, no! It would have been too dangerous. It is better this way.'

Rory said brusquely: 'Well, it is done now, so there is no point in arguing about it. Where is this treasure?'

They had met, for the sake of greater privacy, in a small open pavilion in the garden where there was no possible cover for eavesdroppers, and Majid had dismissed his attendants. Nevertheless, he glanced cautiously about him before replying, and lowered his voice to a whisper that was barely audible above the murmur of the surf:

'It is in a cave,' said Majid; and stooping, drew with his finger on the dust of the pavilion floor: 'Here there is a well, and here a mango grove: and to the left there is a tall rock with a tree growing from it. He said we could not mistake it.'

'Let's hope he was right,' observed Rory, rubbing the map out with his foot. 'Do we go now, or by night?'

'By night,' muttered Majid. 'It is better that no man should know, because if it is heard that I have found my father's treasure there is no knowing what might happen. My brother Thuwani would increase his demands, and—— No, no. It is better to keep such a matter secret. We can carry it away ourselves – if it is still there and that warlock, knowing its hiding-place, has not spirited it away for his own use.'

'That at least he will not have done,' said Rory with a curt laugh, 'for if he had, he wouldn't have wasted his last breath putting a curse on the stuff!'

Majid shivered again and looked sharply over his shoulder, as though he feared to see the witch-doctor himself, or perhaps his ghost, standing behind him. 'You are right. It will be in the cavern where he said. Bring horses and wait for me in the mango grove by the well. We shall need no more than a rope and a crowbar, and those I will bring.'

Rory bowed and took his departure; walking away across the wet grass between the tall columns of the palm trees to the beach where the *Virago*'s dinghy lay drawn up on the shingle, and Batty Potter waited to take him back to the city.

The remainder of the day had been hot and still and unbearably humid; but Rory had slept through the greater part of it, and being untroubled by nerves had not dreamt but awoken refreshed; to hear the familiar sound of rain drumming steadily on the roof of The Dolphins' House. It had slackened off towards sundown, and the clouds had lifted to show a narrow streak of gold above the slate-grey sea, and later, as he rode through the ankle-deep mud of the road that ran westward towards Beit-el-Ras, they parted to disclose a wide pool of newly washed sky in which a scatter of stars swam serene and brilliant.

He had taken Batty and four spare horses with him, and Majid, who was accompanied by the two deaf mutes, had not kept him waiting. They left their escorts to keep watch in the shadows of the mango trees, and going forward alone were surprised by the ease with which they reached their goal.

The Island was honeycombed with underground caves, and without the *Mchawi*'s detailed directions they might have searched for a lifetime without finding the way into this one. But given those directions it had been a simple matter, and within a remarkably short time the light of their one oil lantern fell on the hidden, hoarded treasure of Sultan Saïd, and threw back a multicoloured sparkle that shamed the stars.

'Your father, may he rest in peace, knew what he was about,' observed Rory, finding his voice after an awe-struck interval. 'Where in the name of seven thousand and seventy angels do you suppose he managed to collect all this from? It looks like the loot from the sack of ten cities.'

He received no answer, for Majid had not even heard the question. He was on his knees lifting the scattered jewels and letting them run through his fingers like rivers of light: watching the flame of the lantern flash and glitter on gem-set sword belts, scimitars with diamond-studded hilts, necklaces, rings and brooches of pigeon's-blood rubies, carved emeralds, sapphires, turquoises, moonstones and amethysts, and rope upon rope of shimmering pearls.

Rory glanced at the jewels and the chased goblets, the glittering weapons and chests of uncut gems, and disregarded them. For beyond them, piled up in a staggering heap that reached from floor to ceiling, lay bar upon bar of raw gold; crudely shaped ingots from the accumulated loot and tribute and treasure of centuries, that had been melted down to make it more portable and added to year by year. Jewels were alluring things, for apart from their value their sparkle and colour and glowing, baleful beauty charmed men's eyes and hypnotized women. But for himself he preferred the gold.

He got it. Or the greater part of it.

Majid had always loved beautiful things, and the shapes and colours and glittering splendour of the lovely treasures that were the work of master craftsmen, of jewellers, goldsmiths, swordsmiths and the like, lured his eye and captured his heart to the exclusion of the clumsy yellow ingots that represented fabulous riches but were without beauty or form. Besides, there were plenty of gold coins; moidores, guineas and ducats. And a profusion of silver dollars, blackened by the years but ringing melodiously when struck against stone. He was satisfied with those and as many ingots as he could carry in a single saddle-bag, and gave Rory the rest – together with a necklace of delicate gold filigree work set with seed-pearls, topaz and tourmalines. A pretty trifle of no great value that Rory had thought would please Zorah.

'That stuff will be heavy. Will you take it now?' asked Majid carelessly, holding up a collar of pearls and diamonds fringed with tallow-drop emeralds, to watch it flash and scintillate in the lantern light. 'Or shall you leave it here until you can take it away by sea?'

'I'll take it now. I've got six horses out there. Four of them pack animals with saddle-bags. The sooner we move this stuff the better. You say those two servants of yours are reliable, but there are few men I would trust once they had laid eyes on this; and if we come here again and again we shall be followed and there will be talk.'

Majid nodded without taking his eyes off the shimmering glory in his hands: 'You are right. But we cannot take all this in one night.'

'We can try,' said Rory laconically.

It had taken him all night, but with Batty to help him he had done it. And because The House of Shade had been little over a mile and a half away, they had taken the gold there; thrusting it into a ground-floor room leading off the central courtyard, where the window shutters were further reinforced by iron grille work and the doors were stout. Daud-bin-Saud, the caretaker, an elderly Arab who had once been the *Virago*'s second mate and now occupied two rooms in the thickness of the old wall beside the main gate, had admitted them, and having been told that his services were not required had gone back to his bed, being too familiar with Captain Frost's ways to be curious.

Majid had brought gunny bags and deep wicker baskets such as are used to carry fruit and vegetables to market, and when he had filled them with treasure with his own hands Rory had carried them out one after another from their hiding place, from where they were removed to a wing of the Palace of Beit-el-Ras.

Once again it was grey daylight before they were done, and they had gone their separate ways in the pouring rain, too exhausted to feel exhilarated. And that day Rory had slept at *Kivulimi* with a pistol in his hand, while Batty snored gently, his back to the door that guarded an Emperor's ransom in gold.

The weather had changed that afternoon, bringing one of those brief, shining intervals that broke the grey monotony of rain clouds and sultry, breathless heat like a green oasis in a weary desert. A fresh wind swept the sky clean, and on every tree, shrub and creeper in the garden of The House of Shade the sunlight blinked and blazed on a million raindrops; sucking up the moisture from the paths and the pools that lay on the stone-flagged terrace, and drying out the sodden window shutters.

Rory could feel the sun hot on his shoulders as he stood in the doorway of the room that Batty's slumbering form had protected for the last eight or nine hours, and stared incredulously at its fabulous contents. The thing that had seemed reasonable enough by darkness and the light of a ship's lantern seemed unbelievable and entirely fantastic by day, and looking at those roughly shaped bars of metal he wondered if he were still asleep and dreaming.

He stooped slowly and picked one up, balancing it in his hand and feeling the weight of it, and then taking the knife out of the sheath at his belt he tried the sharp edge of the blade on the metal, and knew by the ease with which it cut that the gold was pure and had not been adulterated by alloys.

Tossing it down again, he saw it dent where it struck the stone floor; and for a fleeting moment the dead-weight of that fabulous pile seemed to press upon his shoulders and drag him down, and he was aware of a feeling of lost freedom and a sharp nostalgia for the reckless, care-free past. It was gone almost as quickly as it had come, but it left an uncomfortable taint behind it, and he wondered if life would ever be the same again, or hold again the same tingling sense of adventure that had thrilled through him when he had dropped over the wall of Dr Maggruder's 'Academy for Young Gentlemen' on a cold November night almost twenty years ago, and which had never really left him from that hour.

With the help of those ingots he could now have his revenge on the Unjust Steward, Uncle Henry, and pay off the long score of his childhood. He could sell the *Virago* and buy a larger and swifter ship – but to what purpose? There was no longer any necessity to make his fortune, and he had never run cargoes just for the sake of running them. Need had played a large part in it, and profits had been the object; the bigger the better. But now there would be no further reason to buy or sell; to drive hard bargains or to dodge the ships of the Cape Squadron.

He could afford to pension off his crew, square his account with Uncle Henry, and settle down – if he had ever wanted to do such a thing, which he had not! But though he had frequently cursed the *Virago* for an ill-found, wild-steering, bloody-minded bitch, he, like Batty, had grown attached to her, and the thought of selling her to some Arab trader, who would run her on a reef or lose her in a gale the first time she played her tricks on him, was suddenly unthinkable. As unthinkable as giving her to Batty and thereby losing both of them; leaving them behind while he went . . . where?

Memory presented him momentarily with a picture of a house with twisted chimneys and ivied walls, set among tall elm trees and the deep green of English oaks: a house in which he and many generations of his family before him had been born, and which was still his by law despite the fact that Uncle Henry continued to live there and to regard it as his own. He had meant to return and claim it when he had made his fortune, and he had made it last night: or acquired it, anyway. It lay piled before him in careless profusion on the floor of a small shuttered room in a house in Zanzibar. Enough gold to buy him anything he wanted and take him anywhere in the world . . .

A shadow fell across the flagstones and the ingots of raw red gold, and Batty's dry little cough broke the afternoon silence of the sun-baked courtyard. Rory turned:

'Well, Batty – there it is. That's the fortune you were being so sceptical about not so long ago. What are we going to do with it?'

Batty cleared his throat and spat a stream of tobacco juice at a butterfly sunning itself on a spray of the petra that fell in a mauve cascade from a stone urn on the verandah above. 'Ain't none of my business, Captain Rory. It's your own look-out.'

'There's enough for both of us, Uncle. For all of us, if it comes to that.'

'Not for me,' said Batty firmly.

'Don't be a pig-headed old idiot. You helped me get it and you can take as much of it as you like. Go on, help yourself.'

Batty took a quick step backwards as though to duck an attack, and shook his grizzled head with considerable emphasis: 'What, take a slice of that stuff after what you told me last night? After that *Mchawi* puts 'is dying curse on it? Not me! I ain't an overly superstitious cove, but I wouldn't 'ave laid me 'and on that stuff, 'cept that I knows you when you gets the bit between your teeth, and I knew you wasn't reasonable to argument at the time. 'Sides, I didn't know then what I knows now. If you takes my advice you'll 'eave the 'ole bloomin' lot into the sea and forget about it. It'll be safe there.'

Rory stared at him in blank astonishment, and then broke into laughter. 'By God, I really believe you mean that. Come off it, Uncle! You can't believe that sort of mumbo-jumbo. Be your age!'

'Which is more than twice yours, young feller-me-lad! If you 'ad a few more of my years you'd maybe 'ave learned more sense. Mumbo-jumbo it may be, but I been to Pemba an' I seen a mort o' things that there ain't no accounting for and which I 'aven't liked. I don't 'old with parsons and missioners and such, but after two nights on Pemba I comes back 'ere and I says me prayers – *earnest*! You don't 'ave to laugh. I don't scare easy, but some of the things I seen there – and more that I 'eard – I don't want to see nor 'ear again. Not nowise!'

'They were pulling your leg, Batty,' said Rory grinning. 'I had no idea you were so credulous. Did they try to sell you a love potion, or offer to mix up a charm that would rid you of one of your enemies?'

Batty shuddered: a movement that in the bright sunlight was strangely shocking. His nut-cracker face seemed to shrink and grow pinched, and he said: 'If you knew what them devils put in their messes you wouldn't think it so bleedin' funny. They makes them out of corpses, that's what! – corpses which they buries first and then digs up and 'angs on trees until they rots. I *saw* 'em, I tell you! And you could smell 'em at night. I've 'eard tell as they eat them, too . . . *Ugh!* fair makes me skin crawl. And there's worse things that I could tell you——'

'You needn't bother,' said Rory. 'I know. But you have to be a naked savage, or the next thing to it, to believe that they can do even a quarter of the things they'd like you to think they can.'

'A quarter would be enough!' said Batty with conviction. 'More than enough! Foolish I may be, but I ain't a big enough fool as to try spendin' any of that damned gold. I don't want no part of it an I ain't taking no part of it. Not a farthing's worth. And I'm telling you straight, Captain Rory, if you 'as your wits about you – which I doubts – you won't go touchin' it neither.'

'*Bah!*' said Rory.

Batty shrugged and gave up. He had seen that particular look on the Captain's face before, and he knew it too well to waste time in further argument. He expectorated again, but with less violence, and said in a more reasonable voice: 'Were you thinking of moving it somewhere, or are you going to let it lay there?'

Rory turned to contemplate the ingots again, and shook his head. 'No, we can't leave it here. It would be too easy to break down that door with the house empty, and I don't want to stay out here just now.'

He brooded for a moment or two, and then said abruptly: 'Where's that old scoundrel, Daud? He's sound enough, but I'd rather he didn't see this.'

'That's what I thought,' nodded Batty. 'I sends 'im off to get a load of fodder for the 'orses, and one or two other things that'll keep 'im busy till nightfall.'

'Good. Then let's get started.'

'Where to?' asked Batty suspiciously.

'I'm going to shift this stuff down to the seaward wall of the garden, and you're going to help me. You know those old guardrooms? – well one of them has a sort of oubliette under it. I found it by accident one day. Dropped a coin on the floor, and it rolled away and got caught in a crack between two stones in a recess against the back wall – the sort of place that probably had a bench in it once. When I went to pick it up it slid through, and a second later I thought I heard it hit something that sounded as though it was quite a way below. So I dropped another to make sure, and after that I got a crowbar and prised the stone up, and found that someone had had a hiding-place made for his wine or his valuables – or possibly for a temporary bolt-hole in time of trouble. I didn't say anything about it because I thought it might prove useful one of these days, and it seems I was right. We can pitch this stuff down there and no one will ever find it. Come on.'

Batty had improvised a crowbar and they carried the first load down through the tree shadows and the winding, overgrown paths of the garden, and carefully lifted the tangled mass of bougainvillæa that curtained the entrance to a ruined stone cell. The stone had settled back into place and blown dust had lodged in the crack down which the coin had slipped, providing a foothold for a crop of toadstools. It had not been as easy to lift as Rory remembered, but it had moved at last, and disclosed a black space that ran back under the wall and appeared to be partly cut out of the rock on which the fortress had been built.

They had made a good many trips, for the ingots were heavy; and when the last of them had been thrown into the darkness they replaced the stone and filled the crack with earth, and scattered dirt and rotting vegetation over it. Rory looked thoughtfully at the recess and said: 'We could fill that in, you know. That would make it safer. Or better still, fit a stone slab in the bottom of it with mortar, to make it look as though there had always been a step there. Something must have stood there once, and there are plenty of those stone blocks lying around the place still. But that'll do for the moment.'

They let the bougainvillæa drop back and screen the doorless entrance again, and Batty said 'You don't 'ave to worry. The next time it rains the 'ole place'll be a mess of green again, and things grows so fast in this 'eat that in 'arf an hour no one'll ever know you been near it.' He stumped away up the crushed-shell paths, and gaining the house again, washed his hands with elaborate thoroughness as though he feared that some particle of the gold might have adhered to them to bring him ill luck. 'You take my advice and leave it there and forget it,' growled Batty, but without hope.

'You ought to know I never take advice,' retorted Rory with a grin. 'Stop wailing like a banshee, Batty. There's nothing for you to get worried about. Since you won't take any of the stuff, you're quite safe from ghosts and curses, and as I don't believe in either they aren't likely to harm me. Try and look a little cheerful and realize that I've made my fortune.'

'*Hmm*. If 'e lets you get away with it. And I don't mean that witch-doctor, neither. 'Oo's to say the Sultan won't go changing 'is mind and want it all back again? Seems to me 'e 'ands it to you werry careless-like last night.'

'He could well afford to. You ought to see what he kept! He regards that stuff down there as mere chicken-feed.'

'Maybe 'e does. But what 'appens when 'e's spent 'is lot, or lost it? I wouldn't trust 'im a yard; not once 'e's wasted 'is share on riotous livin'.'

Rory laughed, but the laugh ended in a frown, and he said: 'It's a thought, Batty. There's more solid sense in that head of yours than one would suspect. I'll make a point of visiting His Highness before he starts to think over things too deeply, and get him to put it in writing – just in case of trouble. We'll start as soon as Daud gets back.'

The caretaker had returned shortly before sunset and had helped saddle the horses and fetch the pack ponies, and it was as they were riding along the road toward Beit-el-Ras that Rory pulled a handkerchief out of his breeches pocket, and something that he had wrapped in it, and forgotten, flashed in the last ray of the setting sun and fell into the caking mud of the roadway.

He reined in, and Batty, following suit, dismounted and retrieved it. 'Where did you get this?' enquired Batty, swinging the fragile trifle in one horny hand.

Rory leaned down and took it from him without replying. He had forgotten all about the necklace, and now he sat silent, swinging it from one finger and admiring the delicacy of the goldsmith's work and the artistry that had frosted it with seed-pearls and fringed it with leaves and blossoms of topaz and tourmaline. It was a lovely thing and would become Zorah's fragile beauty far better than the magnificent and infinitely more valuable ones in diamonds, emeralds and rubies would have done.

Batty spoke again, and in a sharper voice: 'I said, where did yer get it?'

'This? Oh – same place.'

'Ho! Prigged it when 'e weren't looking, did you?'

'No, I did not, blast you! What the hell do you take me for?'

'It wouldn't be the first thing you'd lifted,' retorted Batty, unimpressed. 'Nor yet the last, if I knows you!' He scrambled back into the saddle and kicked his horse into a gentle trot. 'I thought you told me that 'Is 'Ighness took all the jools and such-like stuff.'

'So he did: but I took a fancy to this, and as it isn't particularly valuable he let me have it.'

'What you want a thing like that for?'

'To give to Zorah.'

'*You never!*' Batty's leathery face paled and he leant from the saddle and made a grab at the necklace.

Rory snatched it away and returning it to his pocket said irritably: 'Don't be a fool Batty, you'll break it.'

'Give it me, Captain,' pleaded Batty, his eyes bright and frightened and his voice hoarse with anxiety: 'Let me 'ave it. I'll – I'll buy it off you, honest I will.'

'For God's sake, Batty, what *is* all this? This isn't part of the gold,' said Rory, impatient and suddenly exasperated. 'And anyway, she didn't have anything to do with taking it; this'll be a gift.'

'It's bad luck,' insisted Batty stubbornly. ''Ow can you give it to 'er when you knows there's bad luck on it? You give it me and I'll buy you something just as pretty. Give you my word I will.'

Rory scowled at him, but abandoning his intention of cursing Batty in a manner that would have put the late warlock's efforts in the shade, laughed instead, and urged his horse to a gallop. The matter was not mentioned again, but Batty's face remained surly and troubled and he relapsed into a silence that was anything but companionable. And as the sunset faded and the swift green twilight closed down upon the Island he glanced over his shoulder more than once, as though he feared that the witch-doctor's demons might be padding after them in the dusk.

Beit-el-Ras was already falling into ruins, for like so much Arab work it had been left unfinished, and Majid seldom went there; preferring his city palace or the home of his childhood, Beit-el-Motoni. Wind, rain and heat, damp and neglect, had been hard at work on its walls and windows and rabbit-warren of rooms, until now even the kindly light of candles and oil lamps could not disguise the fact that its day would soon be over. But in the wing at present occupied by the Sultan something of its old magnificence remained, for here silken hangings disguised damp-stains and flaking plaster, the floors were strewn with carpets from Tabriz and Samarkand, while lamps burning perfumed oil stood on tables of ebony and sandalwood inlaid with ivory, silver, or mother-of-pearl.

Half-a-dozen huge wooden chests, carved, polished, and ornamented with brass-work and heavy bronze locks, stood ranged against one wall, and Majid himself was seated cross-legged upon a pile of Persian rugs, supporting himself on a gold-embroidered bolster and several cushions, and engaged in admiring a selection of richly jewelled daggers. He nodded affably to Rory, and waving him to a similar pile of cushions a few feet away, said: 'You will eat with me, and we will talk later.'

The meal had been long and elaborate, and when it had been cleared away Majid belched comfortably and relaxing against the cushions, began once more to toy with the daggers; turning them this way and that so that the lamplight struck brilliant sparks of red, green and violet light from the diamonds, and woke the pigeon's-blood rubies to baleful life.

'I see that you at least are not afraid,' remarked Rory, watching him.

'Of the *Mchawi*'s curse?' Majid examined the setting of a carved emerald with careful attention, and then said slowly: 'Yes – and no. For you see, he had put a magic on that hiding-place for its safe keeping, yet we two were able to enter and to remove these things without harm, and his spells did not prevent us. So I have thought that because I am my father's heir, and he must surely have meant me to know where his treasure lay hid so that if need arose I might make what use of it I pleased, the magic was powerless against me. And if that is so the curse will be also, since why should my father have wished to withhold his riches from me, who by his wish succeeded him?'

'So you think that absolves you from any evil consequences?'

'I believe that it may. That is why I say "No, I am not afraid". But I also say "Yes, I am", because I have a fear that such a man can wish evil for its own sake, and so perhaps ill fortune may fall upon me.'

'But you consider these jewelled things are worth it?'

Majid made a gesture of negation. 'It is because I know full well that evil awaits me on either path. If I let the treasure lie, I reap evil from my people and the pirates and my brother Thuwani – because I have no money. But with a small part of these things I can buy relief from all three, and much pleasure for myself. Therefore I accept the lesser evil.'

Rory grinned and said: 'That seems simple enough. But what about me? No reason why the *Mchawi*'s familiars shouldn't get to work on me.'

'None,' agreed Majid placidly.

Rory laughed in genuine amusement and said: 'And you don't give a damn either – not as long as you're all right. And why should you? I don't myself. I haven't seriously believed in wizards and warlocks in the past, and I don't intend to start now. Not if it means giving up my share of the loot. I'm sticking to that. But there's something else I want from Your Highness.'

'Another necklace?' enquired Majid doubtfully.

'No. I want a paper from you, signed and sealed, to say that the gold is a payment, or a free gift, to Captain Emory Frost of the *Virago*, in return for services rendered to the State. Will you grant me that?'

'Assuredly. But why? You have the gold.'

'At the moment. But there may come a time when others may contest my right to it.'

'It may be that you are right. I will give you such a paper: my scribes shall prepare it.'

'As a matter of fact, I've prepared one myself,' said Rory blandly. 'I thought it would save time. It's in Arabic, with an English translation just to be on the safe side. All it needs is your signature and seal, and your thumb-print to make it really water-tight.'

He drew a folded sheet of parchment out of his breast pocket and handed it over to the Sultan, who read it with interest and complimented him on his Arabic script. Rory bowed his acknowledgement and the Sultan clapped his hands to summon a slave and, when the materials were brought, signed his name with a reed pen, pressed his thumb-print below it, and watched while the royal seal was applied to the foot of the paper. 'Are you now satisfied, my friend?' he enquired, handing it back.

'Entirely, thank you. I like to make sure of things: whenever it's possible.'

'And now that you are sure, perhaps you will grant me a favour in return; yes?'

Rory looked up quickly, the shadow of a frown between his blond brows: 'What is it? you know I will if I can.'

'Oh, it is nothing difficult,' said Majid airily, 'but I should be pleased if you could take your ship to Dar-es-Salaam where as you know they are building me a new palace, which I can now afford to complete, and see how the work progresses.'

He stopped, as though that was all that he meant to say, and picking up a short, curved dagger with a hilt that was a parrot's head fashioned from emeralds, affected to be interested in the design.

Rory said: 'And——?'

Majid smiled and tossed the dagger away: 'You know me too well, it seems.'

'Well enough to know that you would not bother to send me on such a trivial errand if that was all there was to it,' said Rory dryly. 'What is it you want?'

'Information. I have heard that a certain Hajji, one Issa-bin-Yusuf, who is a much respected man and has a house within a mile of where my palace is being built, is in league with these Gulf pirates, and that it is he who gives them their information as to the number of slaves they may find here, and whether it is worth their while to buy or steal. Also which households possess young slaves and well-looking children, and which are well guarded and dangerous to plunder, and which are not. If this is true, and not a lying rumour spread by his enemies, then he will know of you as one who has also dealt in slaves, and you may approach him in that manner.'

'And if it is true?'

'Find out if the raiders will come this year, and how soon, and what they will take to leave this island in peace and buy or steal their slaves elsewhere. See, I will give you this——'

He thrust a hand under the cushions and produced a small brass-bound box, and opening it, spilt its contents on to the carpet: a dazzle of cut and uncut gems that lay in a pool of light, twinkling and glowing with colour. Diamonds, emeralds, balas and pigeon's-blood rubies, amethysts, sapphires, alexandrites and opals. And among them a dozen pearls of a size, lustre and purity of colour that Rory had never seen equalled.

'It should prove enough, I think, to persuade them to go elsewhere,' said Majid, thoughtfully appraising the value of the lovely fragments of colour. 'But there is no need to show them all, since half may be enough. That I will leave to you.'

Rory sat looking at them in silence, and Majid watched him anxiously and gave a small sigh of relief – or was it regret? – when at last he reached out a hand, and sweeping them together, restored them to their box and closing the lid said: 'I'll see what I can do. But isn't there something that you haven't taken into account?'

'That you might keep them?'

'Well, there is that,' grinned Rory, 'though it wasn't what I was thinking of just then. Doesn't it occur to you that the sight of these stones may serve to whet their appetites, and that they may take them and then come over here to see if they can't get a few more? If they think you have any more.'

Majid pondered, pulling his lip and frowning, and at last he said: 'If you sat in my place, what would you do?'

Rory grinned at him. 'That's a damned silly question, when I've told you often enough what I'd do.'

'Yes, yes,' said Majid impatiently. ' "*Fight them! Do not permit them to land. Send out ships to meet them and to fire upon them if they will not turn back!*" I have heard the like for too long, and again I tell you that it is foolishness. If I could not persuade my soldiers to advance against my brother's supporters at *Marseilles*, though I placed myself at their head and the guns of the English had broken down the gates for them, how do you think I can spur them to fight these pirates of whom they are even more afraid? Besides, too many of my people here sell them slaves for good money.'

Rory shrugged and said: 'In that case, if I may say so, your people here deserve everything they get, and until they are prepared to do something about defending themselves and their property, I'd leave them to take the consequences. After all, you're all right: they don't touch the Palace.'

'No. But when they have gone the people are angry, and it is I whom they blame for permitting such raids. As though I could stop three thousand men and more with my two hands! Allah, what foolishness! And what if these pirates become too vain-glorious and fire the town, as they have threatened to do before now? My Palace might burn too, and trade would be destroyed and the revenues dry up. We should be ruined! So do not let us have any more talk of fighting them.'

'Or of bribing them to stay away, either. Unless you can trust them to abide by their bond once they have those gems in their hands. Can you do that?'

'No,' admitted Majid gloomily. 'They are the sons of jackals and she-devils, and good faith is not in them.'

He reached for the box, and thrusting it back again under the cushions, said: 'You advise me then to submit?'

Rory gave a short laugh: 'That's something I wouldn't advise my worst enemy to do! No, I've got a better idea.'

He glanced over his shoulder and then at the curtained doorways, and Majid, interpreting the look, clapped his hands and gave a brief order to the servant who answered the summons, and when the doors had been closed said: 'Now they will not hear, so you may speak freely. What is this better idea that you have?'

Rory lowered his voice to an undertone and spoke softly and to the point, and when he had finished the Sultan's smile became a chuckle, and finally a full-throated laugh:

'My friend,' said the Sultan. 'My very dear friend, you are a son of Eblis and the father of cunning, and I will do as you say. You shall arrange it for me. And if they come, you will send me warning? I would not wish to be unprepared.'

'I will do that.' Rory came to his feet and stood looking down at the plump, olive-skinned man who sat cross-legged and chuckling on a throne of silken rugs and gold-fringed cushions, and was caught once again by that sudden and unpredictable sense of surprise. What was he, Emory Tyson Frost, son of Emory Frost of Lyndon Gables in the County of Kent, doing here in this outlandish setting? He laughed aloud, but at himself rather than with Majid, and saluting ceremoniously, turned and went away, walking with the slow unhurried stride that is the hallmark of Arabs and sea-faring men.

The curtain lifted and fell again behind him, and presently the Sultan slid a hand under the cushions, and drawing out the box of jewels, opened it and fell to studying them once more with a deep sense of satisfaction and an admiration of their beauty and purity of colour that went far beyond his keen appreciation of their value in terms of money. Yes, his friend was entirely in the right. Why should it be only the Sultan of Zanzibar who was compelled to pay out large sums from his private purse to purchase immunity from the Gulf pirates? It was surely only fair that the townspeople (particularly the Banyan merchants and the rich Arab landlords, who owned many slaves and were the chief sufferers from such raids) should shoulder a share of the burden, since they appeared unwilling to defend their property at the risk of their lives.

Until now, each man had hoped that by hiding his slaves and doing nothing to annoy the enemy he might escape their depredations, and that it would be his neighbour and not himself who would suffer. With the result that no concerted effort to deal with the pirates had ever been made, or (unless Rory Frost's plan succeeded) ever would be made by the Sultan's subjects. The raiders would continue to come year after year, and each time it would be his, Majid's, money that would be expended in buying them off. And when the bargaining was over and they left at last, his frightened, angry and demoralized subjects would emerge from behind the barricaded doors of their houses to count the cost in stolen slaves, kidnapped children and looted goods, and turn on him, their Sultan, with outcries and complaints and demands that strong measures be taken to prevent any further recurrence of these outrages.

But if all went well perhaps next year they would be prepared to take a hand in putting a stop to these annual disasters, instead of confining themselves to complaining about them afterwards. It would be interesting to see.

26

'It is beautiful!' breathed Zorah, touching the filigree necklace with delicate, henna-tipped fingers and staring entranced at her reflection in the looking-glass.

The height of the room, with its Moorish arches and long stretch of cool *chunam* floor, made her appear even smaller and slighter by contrast, and Rory watched her and frowned; thinking that for all the early-flowering maturity of her Eastern blood, her absolute authority over his servants and the fact that she was the mother of a four-year-old daughter, she was still, by Western standards, little more than a child.

He had no idea how old she was, for at the time he had bought her she had been no more than a starving, terrified bundle of skin and bone, with the face of an old woman and a frame that might have belonged to a child of five. The negro slave dealer had told him that she was ten or twelve years old, and if cared for and well fed would 'soon be a woman'; and Zorah herself had first said that she thought she was fourteen, and later that perhaps she was two years younger than that – or it might be two years older? – she did not know. But the slave dealer had been proved right as to the beneficial effects of care and good food, and since women in the East ripen earlier than those who live in colder climates (often being wives and mothers at a time when a Western girl of similar age would be wearing pinafores and studying her lessons in the schoolroom), it had been difficult to know which estimate of her age had been the right one; Zorah's or the slave dealer's. Or Rory's own, which had originally been considerably lower than either.

Glancing at her reflection as she stood admiring the effect of the filigree necklace, he thought with a pang of guilt that perhaps his initial guess had been right, for she looked like a child in fancy dress. A lovely child wearing trousers of emerald-green silk below a tunic of cloth-of-silver the colour of moonlight: slender wrists and ankles encircled with bracelets of gold and spun glass, and about her neck the shimmer of seed-pearls, topaz and tourmaline.

She turned her head and smiled at him, her face alight with pleasure and her fingers caressing the trinket as though it were a sentient thing, and said again: 'It is beautiful!'

'It borrows beauty from the wearer,' said Rory, reaching for that caressing hand and kissing it lightly.

A warm flush of rose coloured Zorah's cheeks, and her smile was no longer one of pleasure but of pure happiness.

'That is not true, my lord, for it would lend beauty to a Queen. But it is sweet to hear you say it, when of late I have thought . . . I have feared . . .' Her soft voice faltered and her lashes dropped like dark curtains.

Rory took her chin in his hand and tilted up her face, but now she would not look at him. He said: 'What is it that you have thought, my bird?'

'That you – that your slave had lost favour in your sight.'

'That is foolishness, little heart. And since when have you been a slave?'

The black lashes lifted swiftly and her eyes were wide and passionate and adoring: 'Always! From that first hour – and until the last. You may give me my freedom ten times over or ten thousand times, but it cannot alter that. I am still your slave, my lord and my life, and if I lose your favour I die!'

Rory's hand dropped and he bent to kiss her cheek, but her arms flew up to clasp him and cling about his neck, and all the scented quivering softness of her slight body pressed against him in wild hunger and desperation. It was not only desire for his love and for its active demonstration that drove her, but the hunger to bear him a son and shame that she had not done so, and since Amrah's birth had failed to conceive another child. She knew that she was not to blame for this, and yet she blamed herself; since surely it must be something lacking in herself – some beauty or grace or physical allure that she had once possessed and had now lost – that was responsible for his changed attitude towards her; for the infrequency of his desire and the casual kindness that had replaced passion?

She was not unaware that there were other women, for he had never attempted to disguise the fact, and in Zorah's world, as in all the East, men were polygamous. She might wish in secret that they were not, but it was against both nature and tradition to expect them to be otherwise, and who was she to murmur if her lord distributed his favours to other women? Even to white women?

It was said that white women were sexually cold and unversed in the ways of love, yet it was of them that she was most afraid, because though the Sidi could speak and live as an Arab, he was of their blood, and it was her terror that he would one day find himself a wife from among them and return to his own land. But if she could only bear him a son, that fate might be averted. All men desired sons: strong, brave, handsome boys to carry on their line and reflect credit upon them. Daughters were pets and playthings, and if they were beautiful their value and their claim on a father's affections might be enhanced thereby. But they could never replace a son, and Amrah was not beautiful as Zorah understood beauty. She was too like her father and she should have been a boy. Ah! – if only the All-Wise had seen fit to make her a boy, what a son she would have been!

Zorah, who adored the child, knew that Rory's affection for his daughter, though real enough, contained something that she could not understand; a baffling quality of restraint and wariness as though, almost, he were afraid of her or of caring too much for her. And because she did not understand it she explained it to herself, with the philosophy born of uncounted generations of women who have believed themselves to be inferior beings, devoid of souls and created only for the service and pleasure of men and the bearing of children, as stemming from the fact that Amrah had disappointed him by being a girl. Had she been a boy he would have loved her and been fiercely proud of her strength and sturdiness and quick intelligence: Zorah was sure of that. And sure, too, that it was only disappointment that brought that curious closed look to his face. A look that she had noticed often enough, and that would come without warning when he had been playing with the child, or merely watching her as she teased the white cockatoo or raced in delighted, laughing pursuit of one of Pusser's kittens. And when it came he would get up abruptly and leave the room, and often he would leave the house and not come back for a day – or a week or a month.

He looked like that whenever Amrah spoke to him in English, and the first time she had done so he had been furiously angry with Bwana Batty, who had taught the child her letters with the help of a coloured picture-book. And with Zorah herself, who had taken her to a woman missionary on sick-leave in Zanzibar, day after day during the months that he had been absent at sea, so that she might learn her father's tongue from that unexpectedly broad-minded and tolerant spinster, Miss Dewlast, who had laboured to save souls for the God of the White Men, and died before she could return to Africa.

It was the first and only time that Rory had ever been angry with her, and Zorah had been crushed by his displeasure, for she had kept the lessons secret until such time as the child could speak the barbarous tongue with reasonable fluency, and had meant to surprise him. She had done so; but not in the way she intended, and had it not been for Batty Potter, Amrah might well have forgotten all she had learnt. But if Zorah was crushed and contrite, Batty was not. That portion of Mr Potter's heart that did not belong to Captain Emory Frost, Hajji Ralub and the *Virago*, had been given unstintedly to Amrah, and he loved the little creature as he had never loved anything else in all his long and disreputable life – certainly not any of his own miscellaneous offspring! His devotion was a fresh and unexpected flower to find blossoming on such dubious soil, but it had taken firm root; and while Zorah wept, Batty had been truculent:

'I never 'eard such muckin' rubbish in all me bleeding puff!' declared Batty, outraged. 'And the sooner you shuts your trap and gives over, the better. You fair makes me ill! Why shouldn't the nipper learn to speak like a Christian? She's your daughter – or so I been told.'

Rory had replied furiously that it was precisely that fact that gave him the right to bring her up as he chose, to which Batty had retorted with a single, exceedingly crude epithet.

'What you means,' added Batty shrewdly, 'is that you'd like to keep 'er all Arab, so that you can keep yourself 'appy by makin' out to yourself that she's all Zorah's and you ain't noways responsible. Well, you ain't going to do it! Not while I 'as me strength. That kid 'as every right to choose where she belongs, and by goles I'll see she 'as it. If you loved 'er proper it would be different; but you don't. And if you're thinking of telling me to 'op it, you can think again, because I ain't a'going to!'

Batty had won, and Amrah spoke English, Arabic and Kiswahili with equal facility, though with a tendency to drop her aitches in the first of these. But Rory still kept out of reach of loving her as Batty and Zorah loved her: shying away from that emotion as violently and instinctively as an unbroken horse shies away from the human who advances with sugar in one hand and a halter in the other. And still Zorah thought: 'If she had been a boy——!' and longed for a son who would bind him . . .

Rory held the slim, passionate body in his arms and stroked the soft hair that felt like silk and smelled of frangipani blossoms, but above her head his eyes were abstracted, for his thoughts had left Zorah and The Dolphins' House and Zanzibar, and forgetting even the gold that lay hidden in the sea wall at *Kivulimi*, had leapt forward to the mainland and Dar-es-Salaam, the 'Haven of Peace', where Hajji Issa-bin-Yusuf, that rich and respected Arab landowner, lived luxuriously in a house among the coconut groves and orange orchards, and might, or might not, be the friend and ally of the pirate raiders from the Gulf.

Clinging to him and comforted by his arms and that slow, caressing hand, Zorah still sensed his preoccupation, and knowing that he was not thinking of her or of love, she pressed closer to him and kept her face hidden against him that he might not see the tears that she had always striven to weep only in secret, and now could no longer control. He had not seen them, or even known that she was crying. And when at last she had steeled herself to draw away and meet his gaze, he had released her without question, and she saw that his look was fixed on the far horizon and the wide expanse of sea that lay beyond the open windows, and that he was barely aware that she was no longer in his arms.

He had spent the night on board the *Virago*, and the following evening had sailed out of the harbour towards the sunset; heading due west for no better reason than that Dar-es-Salaam lay to the southward and Captain Emory Frost had acquired a rooted objection to advertising his destination – even on those rare occasions when he was not engaged in doubtful transactions.

Amrah had begged to be taken with him, and on being refused had stamped her foot at him and scowled in a manner that twenty generations of Frosts would have instantly recognized. It was so exactly a reproduction of Rory's own, when in a black mood, that Batty had wheezed and chuckled and informed her that she was a chip off the old block and no mistake, and that one day he would take her himself even if he had to smuggle her aboard in a sea-chest, but that meanwhile he would bring her back the best present that money could buy.

Zorah had returned Rory's perfunctory parting kiss with passionate fervour, assuring him as always that she would pray hourly for his safety and his swift return. And it was only as he turned to go that he realized that she was still wearing the filigree necklace, and was unaccountably disturbed. He had treated Batty's warnings on the subject with considerable impatience, but now it seemed as though he himself was not entirely immune from superstition, because he came back to her, and gripping her slim shoulders turned her about, and unfastening the catch removed the necklace and flung it across the room.

'It is not worthy of you,' he said shortly in answer to Zorah's cry of protest. 'I will bring you something better. Do not wear it again, my pearl.'

He kissed her again, and this time some instinct of protection made him hold her hard against him, crushing her so that for a moment she could not breathe, and kissing her with a roughness that disguised a sudden tremor of fear. It had left her happier than she had been for many months, and when he had gone she had retrieved the necklace and attempted to fasten it about her throat again, because it was not only his gift to her, and therefore a proof of his love, but too beautiful in itself to be hidden away in some sandalwood box. But it had also proved to be too delicate for such rough treatment. She found that one of the topaz-set blossoms had been snapped off and the catch had been broken so that she could not fasten it again, and tying it instead with a piece of silk she decided to take it the very next day to Gaur Chand the jeweller, to be mended.

Colonel Edwards, walking briskly along the waterfront to take the evening air, observed Captain Frost's schooner threading her way between the anchored dhows in the habour, and pausing to watch her, thought: *'Wonder what that feller's up to now?'* And ten minutes later Majid-bin-Saïd, Sultan of Zanzibar, looking from a window of the city Palace, saw the *Virago* spread her sails before the evening breeze, and knowing something of her owner's mind, smiled to see the ship head westward.

Hero too had taken advantage of the break in the monsoon to walk along the seafront with Clayton, and watching the schooner glide away from its moorings she felt that with its departure the air became cleaner and more breathable; a thought that was evidently shared by Clayton, who said trenchantly: 'That's one less bad smell in this town! If it rained around once a week, and trash like Frost and his crew were run out of the place, it might be a little less of a hell-hole. I can't wait to get you out of it.'

But it did not look like a hell-hole that evening, thought Hero; and although a day or two ago she would have been ready to agree with him, she looked now across the quiet, wind-ruffled water and out towards the rose-pink horizon, and was not so sure that she wanted to get away from it. There would be rain again soon; perhaps tomorrow. But for the moment the sky overhead was clear and the enormous banks of cloud that piled up one above the other to the east of the island were ablaze with the sunset; a glory of gold and apricot that stained the sea and turned the white-walled town and the grey trunks of the coconut palms to a vivid, glowing coral against the quiet aquamarine of the evening.

A single star trembled like a drop of brilliant dew above the purple and blue of the distant tree-tops, and as the colours faded and the twilight swooped down upon Zanzibar, lights flowered in the town and on the dark shapes of the great dhows that lifted and sank to the breathing of the tide, and where a moment ago there had been one star there were now a thousand; each one enormous, steady and impossibly brilliant. A muezzin's voice called from the minaret of a mosque, clear and high and with a haunting cadence that was as strange and exotic to Western ears as the green, coral-built island with its dark groves of spice trees, swaying palms and scented orange orchards was to Western eyes. And as the last echoes died away, the *Virago*'s sails melted into the dusk and were gone, and Hero relaxed her clasp on Clayton's arm, and turning away from the sea an l the darkening harbour, walked back with him through the shadowed streets.

The frangipani tree that fronted the Consulate was silver in the swiftly falling night, and the scent of its fading blossoms filled the warm air with a fragrance that Hero had once considered cloying but which tonight appeared strangely sweet and for some reason curiously disturbing. Pausing to look up at it, it seemed to her that the stars hung so low in the sky that they were caught in its tangled branches, and that she had never realized before what beauty meant.

She stood there staring at it for so long that Clay became impatient, and grasping her by the elbow, urged her into the house. And the next day it rained again: and the next and the next. A warm deluge of falling water that stripped the last white blossoms from the tree and left it standing stark and grey and ugly in half an acre of splashing mud.

The *Virago* had taken a full two weeks to reach Dar-es-Salaam, for once out of sight of the Island Rory had turned her northward into the wind, and only after several days fetched about to run in on Lamu and Malindi, and after that Mombasa; picking up a variety of interesting information on the way, a good deal of which supported the theory that Hajji Issa-bin-Yusuf of Dar-es-Salaam was deeply implicated in the so-called 'trading' ventures of the pirate dhows from the Persian Gulf.

He had also let it be known that he himself was prepared to pay good prices for selected slaves and had gone as far as to inspect some that had been brought up secretly from the south, and were on their way to Arabia provided that the trader, an Arab from Kilwa, could dodge the ships of the Cape Squadron; too many of which had taken to patrolling those waters.

There had been news, too, of Lieutenant Larrimore and the *Daffodil*. Dan had apparently intercepted no less than seven slavers during the past few weeks, and having impounded their cargoes, run the dhows into shallow water off Lamu and released the slaves – most of whom, Rory concluded cynically, would probably have been recaptured by some other trader within the next day or so. But the *Daffodil*'s assistance could not be counted upon in the matter of discouraging the pirates, for she had drawn off to the southward and was not expected back for some considerable time; and Rory reflected with some annoyance that it was ironic that Dan should remove himself on the only occasion when his presence might have proved a help rather than a hindrance to his, Rory's, own particular schemes.

It was in Mombasa, in the house of a Persian courtesan, that he heard a rumour that a fleet of pirate dhows had already left the Gulf and was bound for Zanzibar by way of Bunda Abbas, Kishim and Socotra, and so down the coastal waters past Mogadishu and Mombasa – from where they would skirt Pemba and swoop down upon Zanzibar with the north-east Trades at their back. They could be expected within a matter of weeks, depending upon the weather and the chances of trade encountered on the way. Two weeks perhaps, or four – or five? Allah and the masters of the dhows alone knew. But they would come. That at least was sure, for slaves were scarce that year, owing to a great plague that had smitten the tribes in the interior and was decimating the land. Some said that it had begun on the shores of the Red Sea and had crept slowly southward along the caravan routes of the slave traders, while others held that it had been bred somewhere in the unexplored lands that lay behind the Mountains of the Moon, and spreading outward had killed off whole villages, so that a man might travel for a hundred days and find only bones and the bodies of the dead in deserted huts and in the fields that the jungle was already reclaiming.

Rory heard that many slavers who, with their caravans and followers, had left the coast to conduct their habitual raids on the interior had not returned, and no word had come back to tell of what had befallen them. And that it was whispered that the centre of the vast continent was empty of men, and that the great carnivorous cats and all other eaters of carrion had become so bold and savage from gorging on human flesh that neither fire nor muskets could protect one from their attacks.

'Wherefore it is sure,' said his informant – a garrulous Banyan from Cutch who dealt in ivory, hides and spices – 'that these Gulf raiders will fall upon Zanzibar this season. For where else shall they find sufficient slaves for their needs, if it is true that the gods have thought fit to send a plague to slay all the black men and give the great land over to lions and other wild beasts?'

'I too have heard this,' nodded the Persian courtesan. 'Though it may be no more than a traveller's-tale, since I have met none who have seen it with their own eyes, and it is always the other man who has met a man who has heard it told by a third.'

The Banyan smiled thinly, and drawing out a small copper betel-box, prepared himself a wedge of crushed nut wrapped in a leaf, popped it into his mouth and said: 'And yet what of Jafar el Yemini? and Hamadam? and Kabindo the Nubian, and a score of others? Slave traders and dealers in gold and ivory, who set out many moons ago and have not returned? If it is a traveller's-tale, where then are the travellers? Those who have seen it with their own eyes are themselves dead of the plague; of that we may be sure! Presently it will reach the coasts and come to Mombasa; wherefore I myself intend to return to my own country for a time, taking my family with me, though at this season of the year the voyage is long and unpleasant and I am always sick at sea. But one recovers – which is more than can be said of the black cholera!'

The woman looked uneasy and muttered a charm, and the Banyan smiled again, patronizingly, and turning back to Rory said: 'But Zanzibar, being an island, will be safe from the sickness, and the town is rich and there are many slaves. These pirates will know that though every slave in Africa were dead there would still be sufficient in Zanzibar to fill their dhows and sell for much money in Persia and Arabia. They will come down upon the Island like an army of locusts, and return filled.'

The *Virago* had left for Dar-es-Salaam at dawn the next day, where her Captain, having first wasted a certain amount of time ostensibly inspecting the building of the Sultan's new palace, made a few discreet enquiries among the citizens of the little town, and eventually achieved his object and made the acquaintance of the respected and respectable Hajji Issa-bin-Yusuf.

The Hajji had been both polite and hospitable to the European slave trader whose name and reputation were well known in those parts – as was also his friendship with the new Sultan of Zanzibar – and finding that the Englishman not only spoke both Arabic and Court Persian as though born to them, but could quote from the Persian poets and was as familiar as the Hajji himself with the Koran, he had unbent still further and invited him to stay at his house.

Issa Yusuf's house lay within easy reach of the new palace and was large and cool and greatly to be preferred to the hot cabin of the *Virago*, and Rory had enjoyed himself. He did not intend to broach the matter of his visit until the acquaintance had ripened to a stage where it became possible to do so without offence, but it was, in point of fact, Issa Yusuf himself who had made the first move. The Hajji had taken his guest on a leisurely tour of his estate during a break in the rains, and as they rode slowly between the orderly ranks of coconut palms while the earth steamed in the hot sunlight, he said affably and unexpectedly: 'Now that there is no one near who can overhear us, perhaps you will tell what it is that His Highness the Sultan – whom may God preserve – requires of me? You are, I think, in some sense his emissary.'

Rory's brows shot up and he turned in the saddle to regard his host with as much amusement as surprise: 'Now how did you know? If that is not an indiscreet question?'

The Hajji laughed silently, his stout shoulders quivering to his repressed mirth. He was fat and elderly and his white beard had been dyed with henna to an improbable shade of scarlet, but one could still see that in his youth he must have been a lean, fiery and dangerous man; and though both leanness and fire had vanished the danger was still there, lurking dormant but by no means dead under the layers of fat and the deceptive affability, and only betraying its presence in an occasional flash of the dark, hooded eyes.

'Few questions are not,' said the Hajji. 'Even the one I have asked you may be indiscreet; though if so I must hope that you will make allowances for old age and forgive the discourtesy.'

'There is no discourtesy in truth,' said Rory politely. 'I am indeed in some sort an emissary of His Highness of Zanzibar, but the position is delicate. We – he – had heard that you might have friends among certain northern Arab raiders——'

'Traders,' corrected Issa Yusuf blandly.

Rory bowed: 'Arab traders, who make a practice of descending on His Highness's dominions at a time when the north-east Trade Winds guarantee them a swift passage to Zanzibar, and who create a great deal of trouble for His Highness and his subjects.'

'By offering good money for slaves? But that is only business. And good business, surely, for those who sell?'

Rory laughed and said: 'Hajji, are we to talk as though we were children and strangers? Or shall we speak truth and get to the heart of the matter?'

Issa Yusuf's little eyes narrowed for a brief moment, and then he chuckled fatly and said: 'They told me you were a bold man and an impatient one.'

'And also, I hope, that I can be patient enough when it suits me.'

'That also. Let us get to the heart of the matter.'

'Good. Your friends, then, though they come ostensibly to purchase slaves and have been known to pay reasonable prices, steal far more than they buy, and of these many are children whose parents raise a great outcry against the Sultan. They also rob and slay, and while their dhows fill the harbour there is no peace in the island and all men go in terror of their lives. That you must know to be true.'

The Hajji shrugged and spread out a fat wrinkled hand in a deprecatory gesture. 'I have heard that such things happen. But not that His Highness's house or the houses or property of any of his family have suffered theft or damage. Or, if I may say so, your own.'

'My own,' said Rory grimly, 'is adequately defended, and I would not advise anyone to molest it, since they would do so only at great risk to themselves. As for His Highness, he lives by the revenues received from his people, and if the city and the estates suffer loss, then sooner or later that loss is visited upon him. And though his own property and his person may not have been molested by these – traders – it is His Highness who has hitherto been compelled to pay large sums from his private purse to buy them off and persuade them to leave.'

Issa-bin-Yusuf shrugged again and said: 'If what I hear is true, they have spent those sums on buying more slaves from His Highness's loyal subjects, who have never been averse to selling. So his money has at least remained in the island.'

'But not in the Treasury; which, as you must undoubtedly have heard, has become sorely depleted of late owing to certain family troubles: the matter of the yearly tribute that is paid to His Highness's half-brother,

341

Seyyid Thuwani of Muscat and Oman, and lately the affair of Seyyid Bargash. His Highness's private purse is also sadly lean, and he is finding it difficult to meet the normal obligations of daily life and keep up even an appearance of state. His affairs are, to be frank, in a parlous condition, and I cannot see that there is any chance of his paying your friends——'

'My acquaintances,' protested Issa Yusuf, looking pained.

Rory accepted the correction with a brief inclination of the head: '– your acquaintances to reduce their depredations and refrain from terrifying the townsfolk and wrecking the economy of the Island.'

'And you hoped that I might be able to persuade my – er – acquaintances to stay away this year? I wish I could do so! But I am afraid it is impossible. Quite impossible.'

The Hajji heaved a regretful sigh and managed to look so sincerely distressed that Rory's sense of humour got the better of him and he laughed aloud, and so infectiously that his host was betrayed into another bout of silent, shoulder-jerking mirth that ended in a wheezing and audible chuckle.

'But it is true,' insisted Hajji Issa, recovering himself. 'I regret exceedingly His Highness's financial troubles, and I sympathize with him in his misfortune. But the dhows have already sailed and I could not turn them back if I would. My – acquaintances have their living to make, and they are hard and unsentimental men who would not listen to an old, fat man such as myself, even if I were foolish enough to try and dissuade them. I can, alas, do nothing for you.'

'You will forgive me if I disagree,' said Rory with a grin. 'I have no intention of asking you to use your influence to keep them away from the Island. For one thing I don't believe you could do it even if you wanted to; which I am well aware you do not! But your friends – I beg your pardon – your acquaintances, have so far contented themselves with robbing the poorer section of the community. Such houses as they have broken into have mostly been in the bazaar quarter of the city and ill guarded, and they have left the richer merchants – the Banyans and the big Arab landowners and nobles – severely alone, confining themselves to preying on those who are less able to defend themselves.'

'It may be,' said Issa Yusuf vaguely. 'I have not been there myself and so I do not know about these things; though it seems to me a wise course to refrain from attacking the strong. But you did not come here only to tell me this?'

'No, Hajji. I came here with the intention of making your acquaintance, because I had heard that you were a shrewd and sagacious man, and I thought that together we might work out some more equitable arrangement.'

342

Issa-bin-Yusuf looked an enquiry but did not speak.

'It seems to me,' said Rory pensively, 'that if some of the richer and more influential members of the community were to suffer a heavier loss, it might encourage them to contribute part of their wealth to a fund that could be used by His Highness to buy back, for a fair price, any kidnapped children, and also to persuade your acquaintances to shorten their stay and do their trading elsewhere. And as any money they receive would, as you have so truly said, in all probability be spent on buying more slaves from His Highness's subjects, the people should have nothing – or not much – to complain of.'

He smiled pleasantly at Issa Yusuf, who for all his cunning did not know that smile, and was deceived by it as others had been. 'Naturally,' said Rory gently, 'since some of the richer merchants occupy unpretentious houses and do nothing to advertise their wealth, your acquaintances would wish to know which of the houses in the town would most repay their attentions, and to what villages and hiding places in the interior slaves and valuables have been taken for safe-keeping.'

Issa-bin-Yusuf drew rein at the edge of a fragrant orange grove, and sat silent for a while, stroking his beard and gazing thoughtfully into space while Rory waited, sitting relaxed in the saddle and idly watching the slow progress of a chameleon that was edging itself along a broken branch in pursuit of a large black and gold butterfly sunning itself just out of range of that whip-lash tongue. He knew when Issa Yusuf's sly old eyes slid sideways under the wrinkled, hooded lids that were so like an elderly eagle's, but he gave no indication of it and endured that suspicious scrutiny without altering his own expression. As he had just said, he could be patient when it suited him, and he hoped that the bait would prove sufficiently tempting to lure Issa-bin-Yusuf and his friends into snatching and swallowing it without perceiving the concealed hook.

The chameleon, having gauged its distance, took a firm grip on the branch, and a split second later the butterfly had vanished and the chameleon was wearing a pair of black and gold wings on either side of its closed jaws. Its blank unblinking look had not altered, and neither did Rory's as Issa-bin-Yusuf took the bait . . .

'Would there,' enquired Issa-bin-Yusuf softly, 'be a way to ensure that such houses were not too well guarded on certain nights?'

Rory permitted himself to laugh again. He turned his head and met Issa Yusuf's shrewd, calculating gaze with eyes that were bland and amused. 'I think it could be managed. But there must be no killing and no setting houses on fire, for if the merchants die and the city burns, the Sultan will be ruined and the Island with him. And we have a saying in my country that it is foolish to slaughter a goose that lays golden eggs.'

He offered the maxim deliberately and wondered for a moment if he had gone too far. But Issa Yusuf, having pondered it, began to laugh and broke once more into his wheezing chuckle. 'I think we can deal together,' said Issa Yusuf, and wiped a tear of mirth from the corner of one eye: 'As you say, it is not right that His Highness should carry the full burden of expenses while others who can well afford it escape with full purses. Yes, certainly we should make a more equitable arrangement.'

'And a more profitable one,' murmured Rory.

'Assuredly. Assuredly! For if His Highness's Treasury is as empty as you say, and the rich and powerful, suffering little from the visits of these traders from the Gulf, will not assist him, where is the money to come from to sweeten the traders' departure?'

'Where indeed? I see that we are agreed. And if the merchants and nobles should pay into the Treasury a little more than the masters of the dhows require for that sweetening, and for the ransoming of such children whose parents may raise too great an outcry, then His Highness too will have no cause for dissatisfaction.'

Issa Yusuf's mirth threatened to deprive him of breath, and he rolled in the saddle, coughing and grunting, and when he had recovered himself he said: 'I see that His Highness is also a shrewd man of business. It is a pleasure to deal with him, and I shall do my best to assist him. I am expecting a friend – yes, an old friend from Kuwait – in a few days' time. He makes a point of visiting me when he comes south to trade, and if you would honour my humble house with your illustrious presence until such time as he comes, I know that you will be interested to meet him.'

They had returned to the house in perfect amity, and Captain Frost, reporting the further delay and the reason for it to Mr Potter that evening, observed that he could only hope that the Hajji Issa-bin-Yusuf's old friend from Kuwait would be equally blind to the fact that there was a catch in it.

'What catch?' demanded Batty suspiciously.

'Think it over,' advised his Captain briefly, and went out to give certain instructions to Ralub which resulted in the unobtrusive departure, some three hours later, of a small fishing boat that slipped out of the harbour shortly before moonrise, headed for Zanzibar and carrying the news that the pirate dhows might be expected before the week was out.

Batty was still scratching his head and looking thoughtful when he returned to the cabin, and Rory said unkindly: 'Worked it out yet, Uncle?'

Batty shook his head, and Rory said fervently: 'Thank God for that!'

'And why, I should like to know?' snarled Batty, nettled.

344

'Because if it hasn't occurred to you, the chances are that it won't to them – until it's too late.'

'Well come on, can't you? Stop pattin' yourself on the back and let's 'ear what it is.'

'Ever heard of the goose that laid the golden eggs, Batty?'

'I 'av not. And what's more I don't believe——'

'Neither had my respected host. The allusion went straight over his venerable head, though I was afraid for a moment or two that he was going to get it. But he only saw one side of it: the wrong one, I am thankful to say. The citizens of Zanzibar will go on finding their harbour full of pirate dhows, and the place swarming with raiders, just as long as they sit on their hands and thank Allah that the next man's slaves and children have been stolen, and not theirs. But this time the ones who usually escape with no more than a fright and a bit of inconvenience are going to find themselves robbed and beaten; and when they put pressure on the Sultan to pay over large sums to buy the pirates off, they are going to be told that they themselves will have to supply the money to do it with. Or a share of it, anyway.'

'Which they won't do,' grunted Batty.

'Oh yes, they will: if it's that or losing everything they've got and having the town burned over their heads. They'll do it all right once they get that point straight. But they'll hate doing it. My God, how those fat Banyan merchants and idle Arab nobles will hate it! They're the ones who have managed to escape the worst of it so far, and it will be like drawing eye-teeth to get money out of them. They'll do it this time because they'll have to, but I don't think they'll do it again. Next time they'll probably prefer to fight and put a stop to it once and for all, and Issa-bin-Yusuf, and his old friend from Kuwait and his business acquaintances from the Gulf, will find that they have killed the goose, and with it the golden eggs. Simple, Batty, isn't it?'

Batty ruminated for a while, and then a slow smile split his nut-cracker face and he said: 'Simple it is. And I reckons you're right. If there's one thing them Banyans and rich Arabs 'ate it's forkin' out the rhino, while as for those 'oo send their kids and their best slaves to their country 'ouses soon as ever the dhows 'eave in sight, they never yet been 'it where it 'urts, and they ain't going to like it. Not 'arf, they ain't! There's such a thing as being druv too far.'

'Let's hope so. And now we'd better get down to producing a list and a set of careful directions for the benefit of this visiting gentleman from Kuwait. Call Ralub, and we'll see what we can do.'

Between them they compiled a list that included the names of any rich landowner, merchant or noble who had so far escaped spoliation by the pirates or was known to have made money from them through the sale of slaves; adding such details as the location of houses in the city and the exact whereabouts of country estates and hiding places in the interior of the island. In addition they devised a method of obtaining entrance that stood such an excellent chance of proving effective, that Ralub was driven to observe regretfully that it was a pity not to try it out for their own benefit instead of handing it, with its rich rewards, to a horde of thieves and cut-throats from the Gulf.

'It is that,' agreed Batty with a sigh, 'but no good never come from fouling your own nest, and speaking for meself I don't fancy being run out of one of the few places that's been an 'ome-from-'ome to me.'

'They'll run us out soon enough if they ever get to hear about this!' observed Rory, appending a sketch-map of the estate of an idle, lascivious and pleasure-loving sheikh whose practice it was to withdraw into the country at the first sign of trouble, leaving a few of his older and less useful slaves to stand their chance in his town house, and who had long been suspected of kidnapping likely children from the villages and selling them to the raiders.

'They will not hear of it,' said Ralub. 'And if they did it would make no difference, for those who have suffered in other years would be on our side, and if by this we rid the Island of these locusts we shall all be the gainers. Write down Mahmud Ferjiani. The old toad pays no taxes and pretends to be a poor man, but it is said – and I believe it – that he owns half the houses in the Street of the Harlots in Mombasa, and that it was he who stole Ali Mohammed's two girl-children for one of these houses, knowing that the pirates would be blamed for it when last they came. His doorkeeper is known to me and I think that we can arrange for the latch to be off one night.'

Issa-bin-Yusuf's friend from Kuwait had arrived two days later. A man as lean as Issa Yusuf was fat; gaunt and grey as an elderly wolf, and with all a wolf's ferocity and cunning in his cold eyes. He had been introduced as Sheikh Omar-bin-Omar, and Rory had suffered a slight qualm on seeing him and had momentarily regretted that rash remark about the goose and the golden eggs. It seemed to him that this was a man who might well see further than Issa Yusuf had and follow it to its logical conclusion. But either his host had not thought fit to repeat it, or it had once again been accepted at its face value and the Sheikh's greed had blinded him to other issues. He expressed deep concern over the matter of the Sultan of Zanzibar's depleted Treasury and lamentable lack of private funds (a situation with which any gentleman must sympathize), and announced himself delighted to co-operate in any scheme that might assist His Highness to overcome his difficulties and ensure that his wealthier subjects bore a fair share in any financial arrangement between the Palace and the raiders.

'Traders,' murmured Issa Yusuf automatically, but was disregarded.

'There is one thing more,' said Captain Frost, thoughtfully weighing several folded sheets of paper in the palm of his hand.

'Your share?'

Rory shook his head and laughed. 'For once, I am doing a favour to a friend. But as it will be a profitable one for you, I require something in return for the information I have here in my hand and for any other assistance that I or my crew may give you later.'

'You have only to ask,' said the Sheikh with a lordly wave of a hand that was as thin and curved and predatory as the talons of a bird of prey.

Rory bowed gravely in acknowledgement. 'I require the safety of my own house and of any belonging to my crew, and an assurance that no white foreigner will be in any way molested.'

'It is granted,' said Omar-bin-Omar magnificently, and held out his hand for the papers.

They had sealed the bargain with cups of Turkish coffee, glasses of sherbet and a varied assortment of highly spiced and richly assorted dishes, and Rory had enquired as to how soon the dhows might be expected.

'In two days' time,' said Omar-bin-Omar, sipping coffee. 'Or it may be less. And you return to Zanzibar – when?'

'When it pleases me,' said Rory dryly.

Omar-bin-Omar scowled, and then laughed. 'But this assistance you have promised?'

'You have it in your hand. As for the rest, I am sending two of my most trusted men to make any arrangements that are necessary.'

'Then you will not be returning yourself?'

'I can see no reason for doing so. There are other matters that require my attention.'

No more had been said on that head, and on the following morning Rory had offered suitable thanks to Hajji Issa-bin-Yusuf for his hospitality, and returned to the *Virago*. In view of the particular circumstances it would, he considered, be a deal safer and more sensible to stay well clear of Zanzibar while the pirate dhows filled the harbour. Majid, warned of their arrival, could be trusted to deal with the situation without any further prompting, and he had no fear that Omar-bin-Omar would break his word respecting the safety of his house and possessions and those of his crew; or of the Western community either. There was, in such matters, more honour among thieves than is normally found in honest men, and he would wait for news of the pirate fleets' arrival and then sail south to Durban for a spell, to enquire as to the European market prices of raw gold and the best way of converting unminted metal into foreign currencies.

But in the event he neither sailed for Durban nor kept clear of Zanzibar. For in the same hour as the dhows were sighted, bearing down like witches on the wind, Igzaou the Abyssinian, who had carried Rory's warning of their imminent arrival to Majid, returned from the island with evil news.

He had not dared bring it himself to the Captain, and it was Batty who brought it. Batty with his brown, wrinkled face distorted with fury and his thin body shaking with rage: 'It's you what done it,' cried Batty hoarsely. 'I told you not to give 'er that necklace, didn't I? But would you listen t'me? Not you! you crooked, cock-sure chouser, you!'

Rory turned to stare at his distraught henchman in some surprise, and said shortly: 'Go to bed, Uncle; you're drunk.'

'Drunk am I?' So'll you be when you 'ears what I 'ave to tell you. She's dead, d'you 'ear? . . . *dead!*'

Rory rose abruptly and stood very still for a long, dragging minute. Then he took a swift stride forward and gripping Batty's bony shoulders shook him with a violence that made the little man's teeth rattle. 'Who's dead? What are you talking about?'

'Zorah. That's 'oo!' There were tears in Batty's eyes.

'I don't believe it.'

'It's true, I tell you. Do you think I'd lie about a thing like that? The barstards – the bleedin' barstards . . .!' Batty's voice broke.

'Who told you? How did it happen?'

'Igzaou. 'E just come back. 'E wouldn't tell you 'imself. Ralub and me we don't believe it neither when 'e tells us, but it's true all right, and it were that there necklace. I told you – I *told* you . . .'

Rory shook him again savagely. 'What happened?'

Batty gasped and made an effort to control himself. 'It were like I said. Seems you broke that necklace before you leaves; did you?'

'What's that got to do with – I may have done. Go on.'

'Zorah she took it to Gaur Chand's shop to be mended, and on 'er way back she were kidnapped.'

Rory's face was suddenly as grey and bloodless as Batty's; and as old. He said again, and quite steadily: 'Go on.'

'She were missing for two days, and when she come back she acted wild-like and wouldn't eat nor drink, but cries and carries on, and 'er woman, Dahili, says a man 'ad 'ad 'er. 'E kept 'er for two days in an 'ouse in the city, and then 'e give 'er an 'andful of money and turns 'er loose.'

Rory said harshly: 'For God's sake get on with it!'

'Dahili says she gets it into 'er 'ead that she's been got with child, and she does something to 'erself to get rid of it, and it's that what kills 'er. She dies the night before Igzaou gets in. And now 'oo's to look after me baby? 'Oo's there to care for Amrah? Not you! You don't care for 'er – you never 'ave! She only 'ad 'er Ma . . . and me.'

Rory said in a whisper: 'Who did it? Do they know who did it?'

'She wouldn't say – except that it were a foreigner. Dahili says it were a white man.'

'*What!*' Rory's fingers bit into Batty's flesh and made him wince with pain, but he made no attempt to pull free. He said: 'That's what she told Igzaou. She were with Zorah when she were took. They was coming out of the shop when three blokes sets on 'em, and one fetches Dahili a clip which knocks the wind out of 'er so's she can't do nothing, while the others shoves a cloth over Zorah's 'ead and slings 'er up and runs off with 'er. And Dahili she says she'll swear as those two were whites, though they was dressed as Arabs. But on account of 'er dropping the lantern and its being dark she didn't see no faces, so she don't know no names, but that there weren't no foreign ships in 'arbour . . .'

'We can find out,' said Rory softly.

He stood for a long time gripping Batty's shoulder and staring above his head at the open door and the companionway beyond; seeing Zorah's small face and her dark adoring eyes, and all the slender loveliness that had meant so little to him. A white man . . . two white men . . . perhaps three. Men to whom all coloured women were 'nigger girls'. And if there had been no foreign ship in the harbour they were not some casual seamen, but men from the trading firms or the consulates. White men resident in Zanzibar, to whom Zorah would have seemed fair game: a harlot. A coloured harlot. White men . . .

Rory's eyes narrowed and his lips drew back from his teeth in a smile that sent a sudden shiver through Batty's meagre frame. The slight movement brought him back from whatever place he had been wandering in, and he released Batty with an abruptness that sent the older man staggering back against the wall, and ran from the cabin. Batty heard his feet on the deck outside and his voice shouting an unintelligible order, and following more slowly was in time to see him leap down into a hastily lowered boat to be rowed away to the water steps.

'Where is he going?' asked Ralub, listening to the quick splash of the oars.

'Gawd knows,' said Batty tiredly. 'Maybe 'e just wants to be alone.'

But it was the Sheikh Omar-bin-Omar, and not solitude that Captain Frost had gone in search of, and coming up with him as he was about to take his departure from Issa Yusuf's house, he broke unceremoniously across the polite and protracted farewells.

Omar-bin-Omar was accustomed to the hot, swift-flaring rages of his own people and could recognize them. But he had never before seen a man in the grip of a cold, killing rage, and he was puzzled by an emotion that he could not understand yet knew instinctively to be considerably more dangerous than any display of uncontrolled fury would have been.

'I have come,' said Captain Frost tersely and without preamble, 'to ask a favour of you.'

Omar-bin-Omar's interested gaze became suddenly blank, and he murmured a vague formula to the effect that his house and all that was his was at Captain Frost's disposal.

'I have no need of your house or anything that is yours,' said Captain Frost in a hard and entirely expressionless voice: 'I asked a favour of you once before – that you would see that no white foreigner in Zanzibar was molested. I should like you to forget that request.'

'You mean——?' began Omar-bin-Omar, taken aback for perhaps the first time in forty years.

'I mean,' said Captain Frost deliberately, 'that you will be doing me a personal favour if you would request your friends from the Gulf to put the fear of God and the devil into every white man in Zanzibar!'

Omar-bin-Omar recovered himself and his teeth showed briefly in a wolfish grin; for behind the clipped, colourless voice and stony gaze he had seen something that he understood and could sympathize with – a savage desire for revenge.

'It is granted,' said Omar-bin-Omar graciously.

27

The north-east Trade Winds that brought the monsoon rains, and drove the great dhows down the long coast of Africa as it had driven them for two thousand years, unchanged and unchanging, brought also a steaming, enervating heat, until it sometimes seemed to Hero that everything she touched was damp, and that it was months instead of weeks since she had last worn a garment that could be called dry.

The sheets on her bed, her thin cotton undergarments and the flimsy muslin folds of her dresses felt limp and clammy, and a pair of shoes removed at night grew a white film of mould before the following morning. Mildew attacked her gloves and shoes, the backs of books and anything made of leather, while metal rusted and polished wood grew dim, and toadstools sprouted in impossible and improbable places. But it was not only inanimate objects that deteriorated in the heat and humidity, for Hero was shocked to discover that it had an equally detrimental effect upon the character and habits of the white community, and that she herself was by no means immune to its insidious encroachments.

It had been easy enough to feel brisk and energetic, and critical of the idleness and apathy of others, while the sun shone from a cloudless sky and the nights were clear and cool. But the hot damp days and breathless nights had left their mark on her, and now the laziness of the native population, together with its ability to think up excuses for delaying any task until tomorrow – or the next day or the next week – no longer appeared so reprehensible, because she found that she herself was becoming idle. Idle and more tolerant.

Even the custom of an afternoon siesta, which she had once considered a disgraceful waste of time, had become so much a habit that she sometimes wondered if she would ever be able to break herself of it: though on reflection it still seemed absurd to her that she should be able to sleep away three hours of daylight in addition to retiring early each night and, on the whole, sleeping soundly enough until six or seven o'clock on the following morning.

There were still just as many things that needed to be done: abuses and misuses of justice which no one cared to put right; abominations that should be stamped out, and matters of sanitation that the rains had not solved and barely alleviated. Slavery still flourished, and though Colonel Edwards protested repeatedly to the Sultan, men, women and children continued to be openly shipped to the island and sold in the

Zanzibar Slave Market. 'It's been going on for two thousand years or so,' said Nathaniel Hollis, 'and if it takes another twenty years, or fifty – or even a hundred – to stamp it out, it won't be surprising. Custom is a mighty deep-rooted thing.'

'I suppose so,' said Hero desolately: and gave Fattûma more money to give to Bofabi the gardener for the purchase and freeing of slaves. 'Tell him only the ones whom no one else will buy, Fattûma. To save them from being sent away in the dhows.'

'They will bless your name for your great goodness,' Fattûma assured her, pocketing the money and deciding that she could on this occasion safely retain half, since the sum was an even larger one than usual. What a fool the Bibi was! And what a pity that she would soon be marrying the Bwana Mayo and leaving Zanzibar . . .

The wedding was still a long way ahead; the date having been fixed for the end of May when the *Masika*, the 'Long Rains', would be over and five months of cool sunny days and pleasant nights set in. Clayton would have preferred an earlier date, but Hero had been obdurate, for the heat and humidity that the north-east Trades had brought with them made her shrink from embarking on such a delicate and personal relationship as marriage at a time when the climate was trying enough to make normal living no easy matter.

Her aunt had unexpectedly supported this decision, though for a different reason. Nathaniel Hollis's tour of office, already extended by a year, would be over by midsummer, and then they could all return to the States together and be home by September – long before there was any possibility of the voyage being complicated by the imminent arrival of a baby. 'For one has to think of such things,' confided Aunt Abby to Millicent Kealey, the doctor's wife, 'and if Clay had won his point and they had decided on getting married at the New Year, there is no telling but that dear Hero might have made me a grandmother during the voyage. Whereas if they wait to be married until the end of May or the first week in June, there can be no danger of her being in anything more than a delicate situation.'

It was a point that had not even occurred to Hero. She had been conscious only of a desire to postpone the wedding day until it was possible to think more clearly, and to rid herself of this unnatural mental and physical inertia which she felt sure was the result of the damp heat and the long hours of idleness. At the moment she did not feel capable of deciding anything. Which was in itself surprising enough, since she had always prided herself on knowing her own mind.

She began to wonder if perhaps the climate of a country was something that should be taken into account when one judged its inhabitants, since it could not fail to have an effect upon them. As it was having, after so short a time, upon herself! And on Cressy too, who was visibly wilting: though Hero was not entirely sure that it was only the humidity that was responsible for her cousin's pale cheeks and listless manner. But then most of the other European women looked equally wan, and even her own flawless complexion was beginning to suffer from the heat and the pouring rain and the enforced inactivity.

They seldom saw Thérèse these days, but Olivia continued to be a constant visitor, and it was she who brought them the news that the lonely little Princess Salmé had taken to meeting young Wilhelm Ruete after dark, and that they had fallen in love.

'Isn't it *romantic*?' breathed Olivia rapturously. 'We've all been so sorry for her, poor little thing, because of course none of the Royal Family will speak to her now, and even Cholé has quarrelled with her because she said that she thought after all that they had been wrong over Bargash and ... But she has been going up to the roof of Beit-el-Tani every evening, and Mr Ruete has been going up to his, and they've been able to talk to each other because the roofs are so close. He's been teaching her German, and now they are in love and he wants to marry her. Don't you think it's *wonderful*?'

'Oh, *yes*,' said Cressy, unaccountably shedding tears.

'Oh no!' said Hero, distressed, 'for how can he possibly marry her? It would never be allowed. He must know that.'

'Well he does, of course, and so does she, and it's making her dreadfully unhappy. They've managed to meet sometimes ... in our house you know. But Hubert says it's exceedingly dangerous and he doesn't at all like them taking such a risk, because if it ever came out that they were seeing each other they'd probably both be ... Well, I don't suppose they'd be *killed*, but ...'

'That's just what I mean,' said Hero. 'You ought not to encourage it, Olivia.'

'Oh, but I'm *sure* something can be done. Love will find a way,' declared Olivia, with a sentimental confidence that had not been misplaced, for a way was found a week later.

A British ship had put into harbour, and Salmé took advantage of a holy day to go down to the sea with her maids to make the ritual ablutions proper to the occasion. She was seized and carried on board by British seamen, together with a hysterical maid (*'Lord how she screeched!'* recalled an enthralled sailor, writing home), and a few minutes later the ship had sailed for Aden where Salmé was to meet and marry her lover, and to be baptized a Christian.

The city had not taken it quietly.

Anti-European feeling rose so high that it became dangerous for a white face to be seen on the streets, and a furious mob of Arabs milled about the German Consulate, shouting insults and demanding vengeance, while the alarmed Europeans kept prudently to their houses, locking their doors and keeping their shutters closed. But though the majority of the Sultan's subjects considered that the behaviour of the Seyyida Salmé had brought a greater shame upon the Royal House than her support of Bargash, Majid himself had not been able to find it in his heart to condemn her.

'There must be a great deal of good in him after all,' reported Olivia: 'Which is a thing I never suspected. I know that his advisers wanted him to punish her over the Bargash affair, and he wouldn't, but Hubert says that this is really *far* worse from the Arabs' point of view, and that they are all terribly shocked. But it seems Majid has actually helped Wilhelm to leave the island safely and sent him off to Aden to join her. And he is going to send her dowry and a lot of jewels and things to Germany – which of course he needn't do – and Hubert says the whole family are *furious*!'

'Perhaps we were all wrong about him, after all,' whispered Cressy, dabbing her eyes. 'We must have been, if he can be so noble and forgiving.'

'Yes, indeed,' agreed Olivia warmly. 'And I am *so* happy for poor little Salmé! It must seem like a fairy-tale to her . . . they are so much in love. And only think how wonderful it will be for her. Living in a comfortable modern European house in a rich and civilized country, after *this*——!'

She waved a disparaging hand in the general direction of the city, and Cressy and Aunt Abby nodded their agreement. But it occurred to Hero that they might all be wrong, and she wondered if Germany would really seem so wonderful to the little Arabian Princess whose father had been Seyyid Saïd-bin-Sultan, the Lion of Oman?

Would the cold climate of the West, the grey, brick-and-stucco houses, the gas-lamps, greasy streets and drab Western clothing hold much allure for a girl who had been born and brought up in an Eastern palace, where the windows looked out across green and scented gardens to a wide sea full of coral islands and the white wings of ships? Somehow Hero did not think so, and for the first time it occurred to her that there were aspects of Western cities and Western civilization that might appear as ugly, crude and appalling to Eastern eyes as Zanzibar and some of its customs had appeared to her. She herself had been profoundly shocked by so many things in the Island. But what would Salmé think of the rows of mean streets that were an accepted part of every European or American city? – the sordid slums and overcrowded tenements, the cheap saloon bars, the brothels and the street beggars? Were the well-fed black slaves of the Zanzibar Arabs so much worse off than the wizened children of 'free' whites, who worked in factories and mines? And would Salmé think that a grimy, fog-filled and smoke-blackened market in some industrial town was so much to be preferred above the hot, teeming, colourful bazaars of her native Island?

It had never before seemed possible to Hero that there could be any comparison between life in the East and the West that was not greatly to the West's advantage. But now she found herself thinking about it from the standpoint of a girl who had been born in Zanzibar and known no other country, and who would soon be exchanging her bright silks and exotic jewellery for sober dresses of heavy, dark-coloured woollen cloth, and landing at the teeming, industrial port of Hamburg, where the docks would be full of merchant ships and the sky heavy with smoke from factory chimneys, and where there would be poverty, drunkenness and crime as well as gas-lamps and opera-houses and the opulent mansions of the rich.

'Poor Salmé!' said Hero softly. 'I hope she will not be too homesick, and that her husband will be good to her and make up to her for all that she has given up for him.'

'*Given up?*' exclaimed Olivia in surprise. 'I can't see that she has given up anything. I think she's done very well for herself running off with that nice young German, and I expect they'll make a great fuss of her in Germany because she's a Princess, and she'll be wildly happy and only too glad to escape from this horrid, hot, tuppenny-ha'penny little island. I'm beginning to look forward to leaving it myself, though once I used to think that it was quite charming and romantic . . . except for the dirt of course. And the smell. But one cannot *trust* these people. All these riots and disturbances and everything. I confess I shall be thankful to leave.'

Aunt Abby said soothingly: 'But it is all over now, and everything has calmed down.'

'Until the pirates come,' said Olivia with a grimace.

'Oh, dear heavens!' gasped Aunt Abby, her face paling and her plump shoulders quivering in alarm: 'If I hadn't clean forgotten about those varmints! Yes, I guess they'll be here soon. But then maybe they won't come this year. And in any case, they never harm *us*, do they? Though of course they behave *abominably* to the poor townspeople. But the first year we were here the Sultan gave them a substantial sum of money to go away again, and though I know a heap of people seemed to think that he should not have done so, I myself think it was mighty sensible of him.'

'Perhaps he'll do it again,' said Olivia hopefully. 'I used to think that

it was very craven of him, but now . . . Well after all that fuss over Salmé –
and before that, Bargash – and not being able to go out for two whole
days because of anti-European feeling, one really begins to feel that if
peace can be bought for money then it is what Hubert calls a "*good buy*".
Or is that very poor-spirited of me?'

'Not at all, dear,' said Aunt Abby warmly. 'I am sure that any sensible
woman would agree with you, and we must hope that His Highness will
pay these nasty creatures to go away again. That is, if they come.'

But there was no '*if*' about it, thought Hero with a faint shiver of disquiet. The news that they were on their way must already have reached
the Island, because only that morning she and Clayton, snatching the
opportunity offered by a break in the rains to take an early ride, had passed
anxious groups of people leaving the city: the children and the more
valuable slaves, and in some cases the wives and concubines, of well-to-do
merchants and rich Arabs of Zanzibar, on their way to safe hiding places
in the interior where they would remain until the raiders left.

She had watched the panic-stricken exodus with a certain amount of
scorn, for in spite of all that she had heard of the pirates and their ways,
it still seemed to her quite preposterous that the Sultan and his subjects
should tamely submit to this annual infliction as though it was some inevitable visitation of nature, like the heat or the monsoon rains, that no
one could do anything to prevent. This was, after all, the nineteenth century, and it was high time that such medieval institutions as piracy were
put a stop to! All that was needed was a little firmness and resolution.
But there had been no indication of either quality in the anxious, hurrying
groups of people who were seeking safety in the interior of the island,
and it was only too obvious that they had no intention of making a stand
against the raiders.

Her aunt was saying: '. . . as for any further ill-feeling towards the consulates, Colonel Edwards assured me only yesterday that there was no
longer any danger of anti-white demonstrations, and that we could all go
about quite freely again. Why, Clay took dear Hero out riding only this
morning, which he would *never* have done had there been the least likeli-
hood of trouble. Mr Hollis always says that these people are really just
like children; they get excited and worked up, and then it all blows over
and they forget about it and are once more as good-tempered and cheerful
as though nothing had happened. And he is right, of course. One sees it
so clearly.'

Aunt Abby appeared to derive considerable comfort from this sage
observation, but Hero could recall nothing in the least child-like in the
harsh, hawk-faces of the Arab seamen whom she had seen in the streets
that morning. Or, for that matter, in the frightened and apprehensive

ones of the Banyans, Somalis, negroes and Arabs whom she and Clay had passed on the unmade roads beyond the city. But there was no point in upsetting her aunt by saying so; and in any case, the pirates had never yet molested any member of the small white community on Zanzibar, so they themselves had nothing to fear.

A month or two ago such a reflection would not have occurred to Hero; or if it had, would have been indignantly dismissed as being both selfish and callous. But the same apathy that she blamed on the climate would seem to have been slyly at work undermining her capacity for indignation, because she discovered with an odd sense of surprise that she could not feel over-much anxiety on behalf of the Sultan's subjects, who greatly outnumbered the pirates and ought to have enough gumption not to put up with such nonsense. She had been far more anxious over the fate of the unmentionable Captain Frost's small daughter, Amrah; though why she should have troubled herself over the little creature she would have been at a loss to explain.

Fattûma had brought her some garbled story about the child's mother dying suddenly and under suspicious circumstances, and Hero knew that the *Virago* was not in port. It was no concern of hers, and every instinct revolted against having anything further to do with that house or with anyone in it. But somehow she could not get the thought of the lonely child out of her head. With its mother dead and its father absent, and no one but the servants to look after it, its situation seemed to her a tragic one, and though she knew that Clay would never have permitted such a thing had he known, she had paid another visit to The Dolphins' House.

Her conscience had troubled her a little, for she did not like having secrets from Clay. But she had at least satisfied herself that the child was being well cared for; and she had not repeated the visit, for though Amrah had greeted her appearance with delight, the servants had been markedly uncommunicative and had professed not to understand her when she had asked questions about the death of the child's mother. Hero hoped that this did not mean that the woman had died of some infectious disease, because if so Amrah ought to be removed at once, and she herself might well endanger everyone in her aunt's house by carrying the contagion back with her; but Fattûma had assured her that it had been an accident. All the same, thought Hero, someone really should take charge of that child, and it was too bad that . . .

'Hero, you are not listening!' said Olivia with mock severity. 'It is your wedding gown we are discussing!'

'I'm sorry,' said Hero hastily, waking with a start to the fact that the pirates had been abandoned in favour of the more interesting topic of fashion.

During the next twenty minutes she did her best to take a proper interest in the question of pearl clusters and pagoda sleeves, but only to discover, with an uneasy sense of guilt, that such things as the cut and style of her wedding-dress, and what colours would best suit Cressy as her bridesmaid and Olivia as Matron-of-Honour, seemed of much greater interest to others than they were to herself, though she knew that by rights she should be enthralled by them. The fact that she could not feel anything more than a vague indifference, and that it did not seem to matter in the least to her whether she wore silk or muslin for the occasion, or decided in favour of a veil or a bonnet, did not mean, she hastened to assure herself, that she did not wish to marry Clay, because of course she did! But there was plenty of time – days, weeks, months of time – before the 'Long Rains' and the end of the hot weather would bring her to her wedding day, and she did not have to think too much about it yet. For the moment it was enough to sit back and relax, and to enjoy Clay's devotion, and endure the heat.

It was sometimes difficult to do the latter; but as for Clay she could not, she decided, have made a better choice of a husband, for although he was unfailingly attentive and charming, she was relieved to find that he did not consider that their betrothal entitled him to indulge in embarrassing displays of affection, for she knew that she could not have borne to be kissed and embraced as a matter of right – if at all. She had always had an instinctive shrinking from such demonstrations, and it was both comforting and reassuring to find that her future husband shared her tastes and was not one of those romantic gentlemen (so frequently met with between the covers of novels), who were for ever clasping their sweethearts to their manly chests and smothering them with passionate kisses.

Clay's occasional kisses savoured more of affection and respect than of passion, and he confined himself, correctly, to bestowing them on her hand or her cheek rather than her lips. Which augured well for their future happiness, and Hero was thankful that both she and Clayton were rational, level-headed and thoughtful people who put first things first. Not like poor silly little Cressy, who provided a sad illustration of the unwisdom of permitting emotion to take precedence over good sense!

Cressy had obviously been foolish enough to fall in love with Daniel Larrimore, without pausing to consider that once the first flush of romance had faded, she would be certain to discover that an English naval officer not only had little in common with her, but was unlikely to be able to offer her anything but an unsettled and uncomfortable life, full of separations and temporary lodgings in outlandish ports. Hero was sincerely sorry for her young cousin, but looking at her now as she sat listening to Olivia's chatter, she could not help thinking it an excellent thing that the romance had not prospered. And that it would be an even better thing if the *Daffodil* were not to return to Zanzibar until after the Hollises had left!

She was not to know that less than twenty-four hours later she would have given much to see the *Daffodil* riding at anchor in the harbour, and Dan Larrimore and his bluejackets marching through the town. For dawn had brought the dhows. The dark, high-prowed ships that were little different from those that sailed along the coasts of Africa seven centuries before the birth of Christ, to trade in slaves and ivory and gold from fabled Ophir.

They swooped down upon the Island, their sails curved like the crescent moon that is the emblem of Islam, and their savage crews beating drums and flying the green flag of a Faith that was younger than their ships: sweeping in on the wind like a great flock of carrion birds; fierce, predatory and ruthless, hungry for flesh. Filling the harbour with a tossing forest of masts, and the streets with swaggering, hawk-nosed men who brandished swords and carried sharp-edged daggers in the folds of their waistcloths.

'They won't do us any harm,' said Nathaniel Hollis, repeating his wife's words of the previous day. 'They know better than to molest any white folk.'

But this time it seemed that he was wrong, and that they did not know better.

'I don't understand it,' fumed Colonel Edwards, calling on his colleague two days later. 'This is unprecedented. *Outrageous!* Two of my servants have been injured and several Europeans attacked in broad daylight on the streets. I don't know what has got into these ruffians, and I think it would be advisable for us all to keep within doors until the situation is brought under control. I have protested most strongly to His Highness and demanded a guard of Baluchis to protect my Consulate. I suggest that you do the same.'

'Not me,' declared Mr Hollis firmly. 'I don't believe in asking for trouble, and if you'll forgive me for saying so, it's my belief that a guard at the door would be taken as an admission that I was afraid of being attacked – which I am not. They've got no quarrel with us, and I don't intend to sell them the idea that they have!'

Colonel Edwards's leathery face reddened indignantly at what he took to be a politely phrased reflection upon his own courage, but he controlled himself with an effort, and remarking frostily that for his part he had always considered that there was much to be said for the old adage that Discretion was the better part of Valour, took his leave and returned to his own Consulate in a state of considerable perturbation.

The Colonel had always looked upon the yearly arrival of these piratical hordes of northern Arabs as a recurring disease that was quite as unpleasant, and not infrequently as fatal to the Sultan's subjects, as the plague; and though it never failed to horrify and infuriate him, he had come to accept it as a necessary evil that only time and the onward march of civilization could cure. But he was sorry now that he had not requested that the *Daffodil* or some other naval vessel remain in the vicinity, because this year there was an ominous difference in the attitude of the cut-throat crews who poured out of the dark, rakish hulks of the dhows and invaded every street and alleyway of the city.

They had always been numerous and insolent, but now both their numbers and their effrontery had increased beyond all bounds, and in contrast to other years their attitude towards the European community appeared to be one of open hostility. Colonel Edwards did not like it at all: or understand it, for it seemed to him that there was something behind it: a reason and a plan, and not mere arrogance and braggadocio or mischief for the love of mischief.

It was towards dusk of that same day that he saw a familiar shape against the green of the evening sky and knew that the *Virago* was back. And wondered why? Emory Frost had always been careful to avoid the Island during the period of the annual slave raids, and it was rumoured that he paid 'protection money' to the pirate traders for the safety of his house and his servants. It was curious, thought Colonel Edwards, that he should have elected to return this year; but perhaps he too was aware of a different feeling among the invading horde, and feared that even locked doors and barred windows might not be sufficient to protect his property on this occasion. Or possibly the death of that slave-girl (what was her name? – Zara? Zorah?) had brought him back, for it seemed that there was a child, and it was reasonable to suppose that even such a pernicious renegade as Rory Frost of the *Virago* possessed some parental feelings for his offspring.

Colonel Edwards had heard of the woman's death through his spy, Feruz Ali, whose business it was to know all the gossip of the city. Feruz had added an absurd story to the effect that she had been abducted by some European and subsequently killed herself, but that was obviously just another bazaar rumour arising out of the anti-European feeling that had gripped the town following the Seyyida Salmé's elopement with young Ruete – an episode, now that he came to think of it, that might also account for the present hostility of the pirates.

The Colonel paid another visit to the Palace on the following morning, and did not enjoy the experience. It had actually looked at one time as though his escort of a dozen armed Baluchis was not going to prove sufficient to protect his person from man-handling by the mob, who yelled insults at him as he passed and brandished swords and old-fashioned matchlocks in a threatening manner. The Sultan too had been in a difficult mood, though for once he seemed impervious to the dangers of the situation and betrayed none of the trembling agitation of former years. Or indeed, any readiness to bribe the raiders to cease their depredations and withdraw.

'It is Fate,' said the Sultan airily. 'I can do nothing. But since it is written in the Sura of the Djinn: *No man shall live to laugh at his own evil,* these sons of dogs will surely reap the reward of their wickedness and pass not to Paradise but to Jehanum. We must content ourselves with that.'

This cheerful indifference and total lack of alarm puzzled the Colonel even more than the behaviour of the raiders, and he returned to his Consulate with the feeling that he had missed a clue somewhere. An obvious clue that should not have escaped his notice had he been more alert and more closely in touch with the feeling in the city. Perhaps he was getting too old for the work; too tired and run down, and too disheartened. It was high time he retired and let a younger and more optimistic man take his place.

Walking back through the mob of snarling, hostile strangers who filled the narrow streets, he caught sight of the *Virago*'s English Captain in close converse with a gaunt, grey-faced Arab who wore a black *jubbah* liberally and splendidly embroidered with gold, and who was, so one of his Baluchi guard informed him, Sheikh Omar-bin-Omar, an associate, in some sort, of the northern pirates.

It was noticeable that the Captain, despite his blond hair and the fact that he was wearing European dress, was not included in the crowd's anti-European hostility, but appeared to be treated as one of them, and Colonel Edwards thought disgustedly that it was all of a piece: there was, after all, little to choose between an Arab pirate and a renegade English slaver, and of the two he preferred the pirate. But later that afternoon he had sent for Emory Frost, because two European employees of trading firms and a young secretary from the French Consulate had been severely injured by the raiders, the houses of three rich and influential Zanzibar merchants (two of them Banyans holding British-Indian nationality) had been broken into and looted of hidden valuables, and Feruz had relayed a curious and disturbing rumour that he had picked up in the bazaars ...

It went against the grain to hold any communication whatever with Captain Frost, and Colonel Edwards was inclined to doubt whether Frost would, in fact, agree to talk to him. He suspected that his summons would be refused if not ignored, and was prepared if necessary to send a squad of Baluchis to bring the man to his office by force. Or if that proved impracticable, to go as far as calling at The Dolphins' House himself. But in the event neither action proved necessary, for within an hour of his letter being despatched, Captain Emory Frost, accompanied by a wizened little Englishman and a tall, hatchet-faced Arab, presented himself at the British Consulate.

On first sight Colonel Edwards had suspected the Captain of being more than a little drunk, for he smelled strongly of spirits and walked with the deliberation of a man who is giving his attention to keeping on a straight line. But he appeared to be in full possession of his faculties, and observed insolently that it was a signal honour to receive a pressing invitation to call upon so distinguished an official as the British Consul.

'It was not intended as such,' said the Colonel dryly.

'No? I am disappointed. Though I rather thought it could not be a mere social gesture. What is it you want, then?'

'I have heard,' said the Colonel carefully, 'that you have a friend – or should I say an ally – among the captains of the dhows who have anchored in the harbour. Sheikh Omar-bin-Omar.'

'I am acquainted with him, yes.'

'So I realized when I saw you talking to him in the town this morning. If I had not seen that I might not have placed any credence in a report that was brought to me this afternoon. A report that you, for reasons of your own of which I know nothing, but can guess, are in league with this man and encouraging the unprecedented outbreaks of violence that have occurred ever since the arrival of the dhows. If this is true, I must ask you to use your influence to put a stop to it before more harm is done and the situation gets out of hand.'

'And if I will not?'

'So it *is* true! I had not wished to believe it – I had hoped . . .'

'Had you? Now why, may I ask.'

'Because,' said the Consul heavily, 'whatever you may have become, you were born an Englishman. And because my father was acquainted with yours.'

He saw the Captain's face change and knew that he had made a mistake and wasted his words. And his time,

Rory laughed: a laugh that was, for all its mirth, as bitter and mocking a sound as Colonel Edwards had ever heard, and he said derisively: '"*Confound their politics, frustrate their knavish tricks, on Thee our hopes we fix – God save us all!*" That, my dear sir, if it is in any way typified by my departed father, is what I think of your country. So let us dispense with appeals to sentiment. I have none.'

'Why are you doing this?'

'I thought you said you could guess.'

'I can. For a percentage of the profits and a share of the plunder. There can be no other reason. Except——' He paused, frowning, and then said slowly: 'Except revenge. And that I cannot credit.'

'Revenge for what?' asked Rory softly.

'Feruz says . . .' The Colonel did not finish the sentence, because it occurred to him that if there was any truth in that bazaar rumour that Feruz had brought him, he would do well to walk carefully. Possibly Frost had been fond of that woman, Zorah. If so, one could be sorry for him . . . It was almost a quarter of a century since a girl called Lucy Frobisher had died of a fever only ten days before her wedding to young Ensign George Edwards, but he had never forgotten her, or the blow that her death had dealt him. And although she should not, of course, be considered in the same breath with an Arab concubine, the memory of all that he had suffered then made him chary of mentioning Captain Frost's dead mistress. He said instead:

'I do not think it is a matter that we need discuss. But even if you should have grounds for – for resentment, it must surely be directed against one person only, and to visit the consequences upon the heads of all is not only unjust but vicious.'

'Supposing I did not know the identity of that one person?'

'Then you should make it your business to find out, before penalizing the innocent.'

'I have found out,' said Rory grimly.

The Colonel's eyes narrowed and his thin lips twitched and drew in at the corners. 'Indeed? Then may I hope that you will deal directly with the individual concerned, and call off your rascally friends from intimidating the town. I will give you twenty-four hours, and if by then there has been no noticeable improvement in the situation, I shall be compelled to take action. Drastic action!'

Rory laughed again, but this time in amusement only. 'Single-handed, sir? I hardly think you would achieve much with a dozen or so of the Sultan's Baluchis, whose loyalty at the best of times is apt to be in doubt. Or do you propose to bring pressure to bear on His Highness to support you with troops? I fear you are not likely to find him co-operative.'

The British Consul regarded him with cold and unemotional eyes, and said deliberately: 'I am aware of it. So I will tell you just what I propose to do. Unless you persuade this Sheikh Omar and his pirates to mend their manners, I shall send an armed party from the next British naval vessel to arrive in this port to arrest you, and I shall have you hung without trial the minute they bring you in. And if I am broken for it I shall not care – and neither will you, by that time! I hope you believe that I mean it?'

'Oh, I believe you, all right,' grinned Captain Frost. 'In fact I'm quite willing to believe that you'd do the hanging with your own hands, if necessary.'

'I should.'

'Don't worry; Danny will do it for you. He wouldn't dream of letting anyone else deprive him of the pleasure. I will wish you good afternoon, sir. It's been interesting to meet you, but I cannot honestly say that I hope to see you again.'

He bowed briefly and strolled out of the office, collected Mr Potter and Hajji Ralub who had been waiting in the hall, and went out into the wet evening, whistling 'God Save the Queen' very softly between his teeth.

28

The arrival of the dhows had put an end to any further prospect of walks on the *maidan* or shopping expeditions in the town, but Hero saw no reason why they should interfere with her morning rides on those occasions when the weather permitted such exercise.

She could not agree that a stroll in the garden provided an adequate substitute, and argued that there could be little danger in riding along un-frequented byways at an hour when almost all the unwelcome visitors were either still asleep, or too lethargic after their nightly brawls, raids and revels to be a menace to anyone. Besides, she would not be alone, since Clay and two of the grooms, armed with pistols and carbines, would accompany her, and could be trusted to protect her from any num-ber of marauding pirates – who would in any case be on foot, and quite unable to stop or pursue a party on horseback.

Uncle Nat had allowed himself to be persuaded, and the early morning rides had been continued. They had done much to mitigate the tedium of being confined behind closed doors and drawn shutters for the re-mainder of the day, and at first they had been pleasant and uneventful, for as Hero had so rightly observed, the crews of the dhows were not to be met with in the hour of dawn, and it was easy enough to keep out of the way of any group of men on foot. But the morning following the British Consul's unsatisfactory interview with Captain Emory Frost had dawned clear and bright, and the riding party had left at an early hour – to return without Hero and bringing with them an ugly and almost un-believable story.

It seemed that they had ridden out as usual, keeping to the open country, and turned back shortly before the sun rose, in order to reach the safety of the Consulate while the streets were still comparatively empty. Riding down a narrow lane they had found their way blocked by a *homali* cart that had been drawn across the road and had got wedged against the door of a house, and the two grooms had dismounted and gone forward to help the owner remove it. As they did so, half-a-dozen men who had been lying in wait behind the door leapt upon them and disarmed them, and in the same instant Clayton himself had been dragged from his horse by a loop of rope flung over his shoulders from behind and jerked tight. A moment later the lane had been full of horsemen, one of whom had thrown a blanket over Hero's head and lifting her from the saddle, blanket and all, had ridden off with her . . .

'It was Frost!' raved Clayton, his face a queer greyish-white with rage and his hands shaking as though he had the ague: 'It was that swindling slaver Frost – Goddamn his soul to Hell!'

'You're sure of that?' snapped the Consul, disregarding his wife's hysterics.

'D'you suppose I don't know him? The bastard sat there and watched while two of his filthy cut-throats pulled me up on my feet, and when I asked him what in hades he thought he was doing he said he was merely giving me a taste of my own ... Hell, I don't know what he said! The man's crazy! – I thought he was going to murder me. And now he's got Hero. What are we going to do?'

'Get her back,' said the Consul harshly. 'He can't have gone far. We'll get Edwards and Kealey and Platt and a dozen of the other Europeans, and break his house down if necessary. You'd better go get Lynch and Dubail and some of the younger ones.'

But it was already too late, for by the time they had collected shot guns and revolvers they could neither leave the Consulate nor send for assistance, because the riff-raff from the dhows were fifty deep outside the house. And when four panic-stricken house-servants escaped by the garden door they were caught and badly beaten by the mob, who imagined them to be fetching help.

Mr Hollis had gone out on to the front steps and courageously faced the rabble, protesting against their behaviour and asking to be allowed to speak to their leaders. But he had not been able to make himself heard, and in the end had been forced to retreat when the crowd rushed the house, blocking the hastily barred door and brandishing swords and knives before the ground-floor windows, yelling that they would kill him.

Clayton would have followed the servants' disastrous example and attempted to escape to one of the other consulates, carrying the news of Hero's abduction and a request for men to break into The Dolphins' House; but his mother had clung to him weeping and screaming, and his step-father had told him sharply that to commit what amounted to suicide would not only kill his mother but do his betrothed no good. His death could only serve to acerbate the situation and possibly even lead to a general massacre of all Europeans, and they would have to find some other way of sending for help. But they had found no other way; and did not know that even if they had been able to smuggle a message out of the house it would have done no good, since a similar rabble was already demonstrating before every Consulate and European-occupied house in Zanzibar city.

In the Palace the Sultan had withdrawn to his private apartments on the upper storey, where he remained in seclusion; impervious alike to the tumult that raged outside and the agitated pleas and protests that poured in from the German and French consulates, the nobles and the rich merchants of the town.

'I can do nothing,' repeated the Sultan to a frantic deputation of Arab landowners and prosperous Banyan shopkeepers who had finally been admitted to the Presence. 'These evil men greatly outnumber my guards, and it would require a very large sum of money to bribe them to go away. And this year, alas! my Treasury is empty and I have nothing with which to pay them. So what is there left for me to do but endure their insults and pray to Allah to deliver me from their knaveries? If we could but offer them sufficient money . . .'

The landowners and the shopkeepers had retired to discuss the problem, and had returned that same evening bringing with them a thousand rupees which subsequently proved to be only the first small instalment of a very substantial bribe. The money had been sent immediately to the mob seething about the consulates, with a polite request that they would accept it and return peacefully to their dhows; and the mob, considering it inadequate, pocketed it and continued to demonstrate with unabated frenzy.

The night that followed had been a nerve-racking one, not only for the foreigners beseiged in the consulates, but for all Zanzibar. More than a dozen shops and houses in the city had been broken into and looted, and several country mansions of well-to-do sheikhs and noblemen had been attacked, their slaves kidnapped and their valuables stolen.

With the morning a further deputation called upon the Sultan to discuss what sum would be considered adequate to buy off the pirates, and by the late afternoon it had been raised: though whether it ever reached Omar-bin-Omar and the masters of the dhows, or stayed to swell the Sultan's coffers, remained in doubt, since there was very little slackening of tension in the succeeding hours, and after another uneasy night dawn found the city still terrorized by the invaders. But help was at last at hand, for as the day broke greyly in a sky full of clouds, it brought with it Her Majesty's steam-sloop *Daffodil*; and half an hour later Lieutenant Daniel Larrimore and a file of armed bluejackets were marching through the streets, while the shouting men who had been besieging the consulates melted away down the lanes and side-alleys of the city and fell silent.

Dan had gone straight to the British Consulate, where he had found Colonel Edwards breakfasting frugally on an orange and a cup of black coffee (it had been impossible to obtain eggs or fresh food during the past two days) and had received a warm welcome. The Colonel had as yet received no information as to how the other consulates had fared, and giving orders that the *Daffodil*'s guns were to be trained on the anchored fleet of dhows, he set off, accompanied by the Lieutenant, to see if any of his colleagues were in need of assistance.

Every Arab on the coast knew Lieutenant Larrimore and the *Daffodil*, and the news of their arrival spread through the city with the speed of a cloud shadow on a windy day, so that by the time Colonel Edwards and his escort reached Mr Hollis's house the last of the rioters were vanishing in the direction of the bazaars or the harbour, and the few who remained stood back sullenly and made no attempt to bar their way.

The servants were still cowering in the back of the house, and it was Mr Hollis himself who admitted them. He looked as though he had aged ten years in two days and even Colonel Edwards was startled at his appearance, while Dan, whose own face had been grim with anxiety, felt his heart jerk and stop with the sudden presage of calamity, and said hoarsely: 'Is she all right?'

'She hasn't come back,' said the Consul, his voice as hoarse as Dan's, but flat from exhaustion: 'We tried every way to get out and get word to you, but they wouldn't let us through. It's been two days and we've heard nothing.'

'*God!*' said Dan in a harsh whisper, 'Cressy——!' He reached out and gripped the Consul's shoulders: 'Where is she? When did she go? ... where ...'

He heard a sound of light running footsteps on the stairs and a choking little cry, and looked up to see Cressy above him on the staircase.

They stared at each other for a frozen, incredulous moment, and as he thrust the Consul away from him, Cressy broke into a stumbling run and he leapt forward and caught her in his arms.

'Dan ... Dan ... Oh, Dan!' sobbed Cressy, and could say no more because he was kissing her: holding her so tightly that she could barely breathe, and murmuring incoherent and passionate endearments in total disregard of an audience composed of her father, Colonel Edwards, several apprehensive house-servants and two poker-faced able seamen from his escort who had followed him into the hall.

It was Clayton who put an end to the affecting scene. Clayton, as white-faced, haggard and exhausted as his step-father, who had heard the voices in the hall and come down from the room where his mother lay weeping hysterically and alternately blaming herself for ever having invited her niece out to Zanzibar, and announcing that if no one else had the courage to fight their way through that howling mob of pirates and rescue poor Hero, she would go herself and why wasn't anyone *doing* anything?

Clayton had administered another dose of hartshorn to his afflicted parent and come downstairs to find the hall full of Englishmen, and his sister being passionately embraced by a wild-eyed young man in naval uniform.

There was something in that sight – in the way that they clung to each other as though nothing and no one else in the world mattered any more – that put the last finishing touch to his rage and despair, and he strode forward and wrenched his sister away: 'What in hell-fire do you mean by making such an exhibition of yourself?' stormed Clayton. 'You ought to be looking after mother! Get on up to her room!'

He turned to glare at the Lieutenant, and said furiously: 'As for you, you certainly took your time getting here, and now that you've finally done so, it seems all you can do is stand around making a vulgar spectacle of my sister! Why don't you go after that bastard of a slaver and make yourself useful for once? Do you realize that he's had my future wife in his filthy hands for over two days, and we haven't been able to send so much as a message out of this house or find out what's happened to her, or – or——'

His step-father said sharply: 'That's enough, Clay! I guess we all know how you feel and we can make allowances for you. But the rest of us feel just about as badly as you do, and shouting insults isn't going to help any.' He looked at Dan Larrimore, who had released Cressy but was still holding one of her hands tightly, and said: 'You must forgive my step-son, Lieutenant, he is not himself. We couldn't get the news to you, so I guess you haven't heard that my niece was abducted two days ago by that man Frost and a gang of his cut-throats.'

He told them the story as briefly as he could, and said in conclusion: 'I've no doubt that you'll find, too, that he was behind the blockading of this house and laid on the whole thing to make sure that we couldn't give the alarm.'

Dan did not say anything, but watching his face Cressy shivered and tightened her grip on his hand, for there was something in it that she had seen in Clayton's for the last two days: the desire to kill. Only it was worse than Clay's, because it did not hold any of the blind fury of rage or the frenzied desire for revenge that was staring from Clay's hot eyes, but was a cold thing and therefore doubly frightening.

Colonel Edwards said in his dry, clipped voice: 'I am afraid you may be right, for it seems too pat to have occurred by chance. Unless, of course, he realized what was brewing and took advantage of it. But even if you had been able to send word to us no one could have done anything to assist you, because we have all been besieged. However, fortunately Larrimore's arrival has put an end to that, and I think we can safely promise you that Miss Hollis will be returned to you within a few hours.'

'And what about him?' demanded Clay violently. 'What about Frost? I suppose you'll let him off with a warning as usual? It's all your god-damned fault for not shooting the skunk or running him out of here years ago! You could have done it – he's a British subject. But oh no! you wouldn't lift a finger to stop him. Well, you're sure not going to let him get away with this. He's going to pay for this if I have to shoot him down myself!'

His voice cracked with rage, and his step-father said quietly but im-peratively: 'I said, that's enough, Clay.'

Colonel Edwards had listened without interruption to this tirade, and observing his colleague's step-son with a coldly speculative eye he recalled Feruz Ali's story concerning the death of Frost's Arab mistress, and several things that Frost himself had said in the course of that brief, abortive interview that had taken place in his own office . . .

So it was young Mayo who had been responsible for that! And Frost was exacting the ancient and savage reprisal of 'An eye for an eye and a tooth for a tooth'. There could be no other possible reason for the per-petration of such a senseless and ignoble act, since Frost was not a man to run his head into a noose for the sake of a temporary lust for any woman. Particularly such a woman as Miss Hero Hollis, who in the Colonel's opinion was far too tall, forthright and unfeminine to qualify as a *femme fatale*.

He held no brief for the brutal repayment that had been exacted at the expense of an innocent victim, even though he could not regard the two cases as comparable, for Mayo could perhaps be forgiven for imagin-ing that any strumpet from The Dolphins' House was fair game. But as things had turned out there was obviously something to be said for the other side, and if Frost had taken a whip or his fists to the young man, or even had him set upon and beaten up by his crew, the Colonel would not have been disposed to blame him. It was the weapon that he had chosen that was wholly inexcusable, and no offence could justify such a despicable retaliation.

Colonel Edwards looked Mr Hollis's handsome step-son up and down with cold disapproval, and said frigidly: 'You will not be put to the trouble of taking the law into your own hands, Mr Mayo. I have already had occasion to warn Frost that if there were any further anti-European demonstrations in the city I should hold him responsible, and see that he hanged for it without trial. I intend to keep my word.'

He turned on his heel, and Clayton started forward and said: 'Wait! I'm coming with you.'

The Colonel stopped. 'By all means, if you wish: though you under-stand that we shall not be able to proceed directly to the assistance of

Miss Hollis, for though I can fully appreciate your anxiety, there is a pressing and even more important matter that must be dealt with first.'

'God in glory! what can be more important than getting her out of the hands of that blackguard? Are you seriously telling me that you aim to go parading around the town and making speeches at a time like this? – when every minute may count?'

'I am very much afraid,' said Colonel Edwards in an arctic voice, 'that at this late date a few more minutes – or a few more hours for that matter – are not likely to make much difference to Miss Hollis. But since they may make a great difference to the inhabitants of this town, my first duty is to them. I intend sending Lieutenant Larrimore to issue an ultimatum to the masters of the dhows that they have until this evening in which to collect their crews and quit the Island. And as soon as that is understood and accepted, he will take a contingent of his men, and as many Baluchis as can be spared from other duties, to release Miss Hollis and arrest Frost. If this seems dilatory and callous to you I can only say that I am sorry, but the latter is a personal matter and the former a public duty. If you care to be at my Consulate in an hour's time you may accompany us to Frost's house.'

'Thank you for nothing!' blazed Clayton. 'I'm going there right now, and if you won't go with me I reckon there are plenty who will! I can get me half a dozen white men who will be only too glad to. Hell! d'you think I'd wait another *second*?'

'In your place I expect I should feel the same. But I hope you will reconsider, because half a dozen men will be able to do little against a dozen or more who are barricaded into a house that was built to withstand siege. You would not do any good and possibly a deal of harm, and Miss Hollis's position would seem to be quite bad enough without the added indignity of knowing that every European in the Island has been made aware of it, and can gossip and speculate over what has occurred. For her sake, the fewer people who know of this the better, and if we keep it among ourselves we may be able to arrange that others do not get to hear of it. All that need be known is that Larrimore and the men from the *Daffodil* have arrested Frost for his share in these disturbances. You would be well advised to wait until you can accompany us.'

'I'm with you,' agreed Nathaniel Hollis without giving his step-son time to reply. 'There is no call for us to make bad worse.'

'Exactly. It is perhaps fortunate that every other European in the place is far too alarmed and anxious on their own account to spare much interest at this moment for the affairs of others. And long before they are free to do so Miss Hollis will be back, and anything that gets out later may be dismissed as a wild rumour. I will see you later then, Mr Mayo.'

The Colonel nodded to Mr Hollis and went out into the sunlight, and Dan jerked Cressy back into his arms, kissed her with deliberation, released her, and followed him.

Two hours later a strong force of bluejackets and Baluchis, under the command of Lieutenant Larrimore and accompanied by Colonel Edwards and Mr Clayton Mayo, sealed off both ends of a quiet street in which a forgotten Portuguese graveyard made a small green oasis among the frowning Arab houses. But The Dolphins' House was empty except for a handful of servants and a small child who stamped her foot at the invaders, and when they would not go away, cried for her mother and would not be comforted.

The servants professed ignorance as to the whereabouts of the master of the house, and said that neither he nor any member of the *Virago*'s crew had been near the house for the past three days, so they presumed that the schooner had sailed for Mombasa or the Gulf. The Sidi was not in the habit of discussing his affairs with them, and they were ignorant of his movements.

Lieutenant Larrimore had left a guard on the house and returned to the harbour, where he was informed that the *Virago* had slipped her moorings over two days ago and had been seen making for the open sea, heading southward. But no one could say where she had gone.

It had been Ralub and not Rory who had carried Hero across his saddle-bow; held in an unbreakable grip and half stifled by the heavy folds of a horse-blanket that had prevented her from struggling as violently as she would otherwise have done, since the greater part of her energies had of necessity been concentrated on fighting for every breath.

She had known where they were bound for as soon as she had heard the sound of waves. And in the next moment she had been slung over someone's shoulder like a bale of carpets, and when at last she was set on her feet and able to free herself from the smothering blanket, she was once again aboard the *Virago*. Though this time not in the Captain's cabin, but locked in the dark little privy where the skylight was far too small to allow anything larger than a monkey to escape.

She had been there for hours; knowing that the schooner had put to sea, but with no idea where she was being taken, or why. She could only imagine that Rory Frost had taken leave of his senses and was belatedly attempting a trick that he had been unable to use on that earlier occasion, and holding her for ransom. Anything else did not cross her mind, and since it did not occur to her that any attack might be made on her virtue, she was incensed to find that a plate of food, a carafe of wine and a mug had been placed on the floor, which suggested that her stay in that cramped and undignified retreat was likely to be a long one.

She had not touched the food, and as there had been only one place to sit on, she had sat on it for the greater part of that day; getting angrier with every slow-passing hour, and rehearsing a variety of cutting things that she intended to say to Captain Rory Frost at the first opportunity.

The opportunity, however, had not presented itself until the late evening; and by that time she was no longer on the *Virago*, but a prisoner in The House of Shade.

Hero had heard the schooner drop anchor and had wondered where they could be. It seemed to her that they had been running before the wind all day and would by this time have reached the coast of Africa, and it was only later that she realized they must have headed away from the Island to give the impression that they were making for somewhere far to the southward, and once out of sight of land, circled back again to run in on *Kivulimi* from the north.

The splash and rattle of the anchor had been followed a few minutes later by the sound of footsteps crossing the cabin, and then the key clicked in the lock and Hero drew herself up to her full height and swept out haughtily. But the blistering words on her tongue remained unspoken, for it was Jumah who had released her, and not the *Virago*'s Captain.

'Missie going on shore now,' said Jumah, airing his English and beaming as happily as though he brought good news and there was nothing untoward in the present situation.

The sun was level with the horizon and the clouds that had reappeared in the afternoon were dispersing again in a glory of gold and rose and apricot. The garden of The House of Shade was melodious with birds piping and twittering as they prepared to settle down for the night, and the scent of flowers was as heavy as incense on the evening air. But Hero had no eyes for the beauty of the scene and no attention to spare for such things as birds and flowers. She could see no sign of either Captain Frost or Mr Potter, and did not know that for the first time in all the years that they had been together, Mr Potter had quarrelled seriously with his Captain.

'I don't 'old with it!' Batty had said. 'If you wants to whale the living daylights out of that fornicatin' scum, it'll be a pleasure to give you an 'elpin' 'and. But what 'e done ain't nowise Miss 'Ero's fault, and I don't 'old with taking it out on 'er for what 'er young man does. I ain't no plaster saint, as well you knows; but I ain't such a crawlin' low-down son-of-a-bitch as that!'

Rory had looked at him for a long moment and then shrugged and turned away, and Batty, who had hoped to provoke him into losing his temper, had stumped down below, cursing all women, and relieved his feelings by quarrelling instead with the *Virago*'s cook.

If only, thought Batty, the Captain would work off his feelings in a rousing fist-fight or get roaring drunk, he might lose that tight, frozen look he had worn ever since he had heard the news of Zorah's death, and recover his sense of proportion. But he had refused to be provoked, and though for the past week he had been drinking steadily and to excess, alcohol seemed to have lost the power to arouse any emotion in him save an intensification of that cold rage.

'Blubber-'eaded, bloody-minded, Friday-faced bung-nipper!' muttered Batty, refraining from worse words for fear that Hero might hear them, and keeping below decks and out of sight in order to avoid having to meet her eyes.

The interior of The House of Shade had been very like that of The Dolphins' House, or any other large Arab house in Zanzibar: a central courtyard open to the sky and surrounded by tiers of colonnaded verandahs. Curving staircases with low iron-work balustrades led up from the four corners of the courtyard, linking each verandah to the next, and the room into which Hero had been ushered was similar in many ways to the one she had seen at The Dolphins' House. Except that here the doorway had not been protected by a curtain, but by a stout and well-fitting door that had been closed and locked behind her.

She was still angry rather than apprehensive, for although she had heard the key turn and knew that she was still a prisoner, the three windows that faced the sea stood open, and the vast expanse of gold-framed looking-glass that occupied most of one wall reflected the sky and the tree-tops and the open sea, and made the long room seem twice as large. There was a wide divan bed hung with mosquito netting, several small inlaid tables and two carved sandalwood chairs, and in place of rugs or carpets the floor was covered by matting. A second door at one end of the room led into a stone-tiled bathroom, and although a third led out of it, that one too was locked from the outside.

Hero went to the central window and looked down on to the garden, but any idea she might have had of escaping that way was clearly useless, for the wall was smooth and sheer and provided no possible foothold, and the drop from the window-ledge to the stone-paved terrace that surrounded the house was all of thirty feet. She turned and looked meditatively at the mosquito net and the bed sheets (there were no blankets) and decided that the former were far too flimsy to hold any weight, while the latter, if tied together, would not reach nearly far enough. But with the aid of a knife she should be able to tear them in half, and then . . .

It was a possibility, and such an encouraging one that when Jumah eventually appeared with a lamp and a supper tray, she was able to eat a little food with a tolerably quiet mind, and a growing conviction that the unexplained absence of Captain Frost must be due to the fact that he had remained behind in Zanzibar city in order to negotiate the terms for her release.

Uncle Nat would presumably have no alternative but to pay whatever was asked, but she hoped that Captain Frost would find that he had over-reached himself at last and would not remain at liberty to enjoy his ill-gotten gains for very long. Even in such a lawless part of the world as this, kidnapping must surely be a punishable offence, and if the authorities had so far failed to convict him of other crimes for lack of proof, there could be no lack of it now. Uncle Nat and Colonel Edwards could be trusted to see that the least he received for this was a long prison sentence. And if he found himself shut into a cell as cramped and uncomfortable as the humiliating one he had provided for her that day, it would serve him right! That indignity still rankled disproportionately, and Hero was even ready to regret the quixotic impulse that had led her to visit his unfortunate little daughter at The Dolphins' House. She should have hardened her heart and avoided anything that had to do with him, and she would know better in future.

She had been on the point of blowing out her light and retiring to bed in her petticoat and under-bodice in lieu of a nightdress, when she heard horses' hooves and voices from somewhere outside, and then minutes later there had been footsteps on the stairs and the key grating again in the lock. And this time it had been Rory.

He shut the door behind him and stood with his back to it, looking at her for a long time and in silence: and she did not say any of the cutting things she had meant to say. She said nothing at all because she was suddenly afraid, and when he moved at last and came towards her she realized with a sharp stab of panic that he was drunk. Drunk and dangerous.

He walked with a deliberation that contained a curious suggestion of unsteadiness, as though he were walking the deck of a ship in windy weather. His voice was an equally deliberate drawl, and she did not believe a word that he said——

Clay would never have done such a thing! It was a lie. A vulgar, vindictive lie! Of *course* he did not keep rooms of his own in the city . . . he would have told her if he had . . . Uncle Nat would have known. The top floor of a house in a quiet cul-de-sac, Captain Frost said, with its own stair and its own door into the street, where he entertained a few selected friends and transacted private business. Where he met Thérèse Tissot: and other women . . .

'Who do you suppose I sold those rifles to? Who do you suppose ordered them in the first place? Your upright, high-minded future husband. That's who! And he must have been livid with fright and fury when he heard who'd fished you out of the sea and what ship you'd been on. No wonder he didn't want either his step-father or himself to be jockeyed into calling on me to say "Thank you". And I'll bet anything he did his damnedest to give me the worst character he could to make sure that *you* wouldn't try it!'

'You're lying,' said Hero. 'You're lying!'

'Am I? Ask him how much he made on that deal. He paid me a hell of a good price, but it was nothing to what he made himself out of re-selling them to Bargash and his supporters. Ask your little friends at Beit-el-Tani how much they paid him for those useless rifles. And don't imagine that your noble Clayton didn't know what they were going to be used for. He'd been Thérèse's lover for a good long time and *he* knew what she was up to all right! Thérèse was doing it for her husband's sugar interests, not to mention *La Patrie* and the prosperity of the French plantations of Bourbon and Reunion. But Clayton Mayo was doing it for money. For money and nothing else!'

Hero said breathlessly: 'Now I *know* you're lying! Or else you've been listening to some garbled rumour about someone else. One of the European clerks, or someone off a ship. A bazaar story! Clay would never dream of doing such a thing. He didn't need money. He——'

Rory gave a short and ugly laugh. 'I don't know about needing it, but he certainly liked it. That wasn't the only time I've had dealings with him. I've bought and shipped slaves for him too, and he's made a pretty penny out of it – and taken a strong dislike to his sister's slaver-chasing admirer, for fear of what Dan might find out if he were around too much!'

'You know why you're saying all this, don't you? Because you know that he hates and despises you! – and all slavers. Because you know he would like to see you run out of the Island!'

'I know he hates me all right. That was all part of the deal once: officially he was to hate my guts and make a great show of wanting to see me deported. It made him feel safer, for if his step-father had ever begun to suspect what he was up to he'd have shipped him home steerage and never spoken to him again. But it became the real thing, because he was ashamed of what he was doing. And because he knew that I knew too much about him, and he was never quite sure that I wouldn't tell. Oh, he hates me all right; that's natural enough – I'm "The one who knows". And why the hell should I care what he says or thinks as long as he pays? – and he paid! But this is different. He thought that because she was an Arab slave-girl – a "kept woman" – he could snatch Zorah in the street and use her for his own filthy pleasures for a few days, and then throw her back again with a handful of money to pay her off and buy her silence. Well now he's going to know what it feels like to have his own girl snatched in the streets and treated like a cheap strumpet, and handed back to him with a fat purse to compensate her for the experience. That's unfair, isn't it? Unfair on you. But then I don't have to be fair to you. Any more than your honourable lover was fair to my ... to Amrah's mother.'

'You're making a mistake,' said Hero in a panting whisper 'Clay wouldn't ... You're drunk! You're lying——'

She would have screamed then, except that she knew that no one who heard her would come, and that it would be a waste of time – and a waste of breath that she needed for other things. For trying to reason with him, and at the last, and equally fruitlessly, for fighting him.

29

Beyond the windows the morning sky was as clear and as serenely blue as the sky of a New England summer, and on the window-sill a fan-tailed pigeon cooed and strutted and preened its feathers in the sunshine.

There had been fan-tailed pigeons at Hollis Hill, thought Hero inconsequently. Eighteen of them. How long ago that seemed – how impossibly long ago! As long ago as yesterday, which was suddenly separated from her by an impassable gulf that yawned as deep and as wide as the one that separated her from the summer mornings of her childhood and those other white pigeons . . .

She had not cried last night, and she did not cry now. She lay still and listened to that liquid cooing; looking out at the blue sky and thinking of her father's house and the settled peace and safety of all that she had left behind – and lost . . .

'If you feel that you have to do something for your fellow-men,' cousin Josiah Crayne had said, 'you don't have to go as far afield as Africa. You'll find there's plenty needs doing right here in your own back yard. If folk would only begin by getting rid of the beam in their own eye before hurrying off to remove the one they can see in their neighbour's, we'd all be a heap better off. When there's no more room for improvement in your own country, then's the time to start in improving someone else's and telling them how they should go on. There's too much self-righteous interference in the world: every nation sure it's better than the next one and running off to set the other one to rights, leaving its own middens to look after themselves.'

'But surely,' Hero had argued, 'one should try and help one's neighbours? To work only at improving one's own yard is being plain selfish.'

'Maybe. But it's sense.'

Perhaps it was; for she had certainly done no good in Zanzibar, and helped to do much harm. Not from any lack of good will, but because these people were not her people, and she did not understand their processes of thought or the way they reasoned or felt, and so she could not guess how they would act. Yet she had insisted on coming here, and it had led her by devious routes and blind alleys to . . . *this*!

Even now she could not really believe that it had happened – and to her. Things like that might happen to other people: to slaves and concubines. To people in books and women in seraglios. But not to her, in this enlightened and progressive nineteenth century! Not to Hero Hollis, who only a short while ago had been pitying the subservient occupants of harems, and wondering what it must be like to be forced to submit to the embraces of a man who inspired no affection but only fear and repulsion. Well, she knew now; and the knowledge had left her bruised and aching, and so exhausted by shock, that even knowing also that the open windows offered her the chance of escape and a way of avoiding the appalling ignominy of having to face him again after what he had done to her, she could not rouse herself to take it. She did not want to do anything but just lie still – and not think . . .

The pigeon flew off with a noisy flutter of wings, and a warm breeze wandered in at the uncurtained windows and brought with it a scent of cloves and orange blossom and the sound of the surf. And all at once the glittering morning held nothing that spoke of home or familiar things, but only of the tropics: of strange, wild, exotic places where men were violent and lawless and took what they wanted and did what they chose, and held life and honour cheap.

Hero sat up slowly and found that it was an effort to move at all But it was an effort that had to be made, because she could not lie here for ever, staring through the mosquito net at the sky beyond the windows and thinking useless thoughts. Presumably she would be allowed to go now, for if it was not ransom money but revenge that Rory Frost had wanted, he had taken that and could have no further use for her, or any reason to keep her here.

He must, she thought, have loved that girl Zorah very deeply to have done such a thing. It would be terrible to love someone so much and lose them so tragically. She had loved her father and lost him, and had grieved for him. But that was a different form of love – and of loss. Last night she had accused Rory of lying, but now, thinking back on it in the bright daylight, she knew that he must at least have told her the truth about Zorah's death, and that it was because he had loved her and she was the mother of his child that her death, and the manner of it, had turned his brain and driven him first to drink and from there to plotting this brutal, senseless act of revenge. But he had been wrong about Clay. Clay would never have done such a thing, and it had obviously been someone else.

She had tried to tell him this last night, but he would not listen. Yet it was so easy to see how the mistake had occurred. Neither he nor his ship had been in Zanzibar when it happened, and when he returned he had been told some garbled story involving an unknown white man, retailed to him by one of his disreputable friends: probably a local slave dealer who had a grudge against her because she was known to be an active opponent of slavery, and who, knowing that she was to marry Clay, had deliberately embroidered the tale with scraps of malicious gossip and innuendo designed to point to her betrothed as the man responsible for the tragedy. (Harsh experience had already taught Hero how little conscience people had about telling lies when it suited them to do so!). As for the rest of Emory Frost's wild accusations, he had either invented them in an attempt to justify himself further, or else – which seemed highly probable – someone had been using Clay's name – possibly Madame Tissot! Clay had always distrusted Thérèse. Or perhaps the Banyan, Balu Ram, in whose cellars the rifles had been stored? It would have been an excellent cover, and she was quite sure that Clayton himself had never exchanged a word with the *Virago*'s captain!

Freeing herself from the mosquito net, Hero looked about the room, but could see no sign of her clothes, so she pulled a sheet from the bed and wrapping that around her instead, went to the table by the window. It still bore the remains of her last night's meal, but even the fruit did not tempt her, for she was not hungry: only very thirsty. She poured herself out a glass of the harsh red wine and drank it as though it had been water, and poured and drank a second that made her feel a little light-headed but considerably stronger.

Turning from the table she caught sight of her own reflection in the damp-spotted expanse of looking-glass, and crossed the room to stand in front of it; staring at herself as though at a stranger.

There had once, long weeks ago, been a grotesque stranger who had looked back at her from a mirror in the cabin of the *Virago*. But the woman who faced her now did not seem to have altered at all from the girl who only yesterday morning had combed her curls and adjusted her riding-habit before the cheval-glass in a bedroom at the American Consulate.

It seemed incredible to Hero that the past night should have made no difference to her outward appearance and left no stamp on her face. She ought to look different: aged and soiled and ugly with the knowledge and experience of ugliness. It was an affront that she should look exactly the same.

She let the sheet drop, and for the first time in her life studied her naked body, and was surprised to find that though there were bruises on the white skin, it looked smooth and innocent and astonishingly beautiful. She had not known that naked, living flesh could be so lovely a thing, and as satisfying to the eye as the pure curves of stone nymphs and marble Aphrodites. Or that her own proportions could vie with either. The girl in the looking-glass was as tall and rounded and slender as Botticelli's grave young Venus standing lightly on her sea-shell, and the damp-mottled glass lent her a curious look of unreality; as though she were indeed a picture – or a dream.

Intent upon her own reflection she did not hear the key turn or the door open, and it was a movement and not a sound that caught her attention, for there was suddenly someone else in the looking-glass, and she snatched the sheet back about her, holding it close.

Rory said: 'A very charming and virginal gesture, but in the circumstances, surely unnecessary?'

Hero turned and looked at him for a full minute: and found that she did not experience any of the emotions she expected to feel at having to face him again in the harsh daylight. Perhaps her capacity for emotion had been exhausted; or perhaps the wine she had drunk had given her a temporary armour against such futile things as shame or anger for something that had been done and could not now be revoked.

She said slowly: 'You are only talking like that because you are ashamed of yourself.'

'I suppose so. I never thought I should come down to wasting my time regretting something I've done and can't undo. But it seems I was wrong. And yet that isn't quite true either . . .'

He pushed back the mosquito netting and sat down on the divan, leaning his head against the wall and surveying her with detached interest, his hands in his pockets and his face no longer tight and strained. His rage had left him as suddenly as it had come, and he felt as though he had recovered from a bout of fever or rid himself at last of a crushing weight that had been pressing intolerably upon his shoulders.

He said thoughtfully: 'In theory, I regret having made you a whipping-boy for Clayton Mayo, because Batty was right and it was an unpardonably dirty trick. But I can't honestly say I'm sorry, because anything that turned out to be so surprisingly enjoyable cannot be a matter for regret. Which is probably why I am suffering a slight pang of conscience on your account; for to be honest with you, I hadn't expected to enjoy it much, and the fact that I did puts the whole thing on a different footing. I suppose I ought to send you back to him; though I must say it seems a pity. Like casting pearls before swine. Do you still want to marry him?'

'How can I – now?'

'Then that's one good thing to come out of this. You deserve something a deal better than that double-dealing Lothario.'

'You don't understand,' said Hero, evenly and without anger: 'Nothing that you have said or could say can alter my opinion of Mr Mayo, or make me not wish to marry him. But he will no longer wish to marry me, and I shall not blame him for it. No one could wish to, now.'

'You mean because you are now a "Fallen Woman"?' Rory's pale eyes were amused. 'I don't think you need worry. For one thing, no one in his senses could blame you for something that you could not possibly have prevented. And for another, your fortune if not your virtue is presumably still intact, so I expect he'll be magnanimous and agree to overlook this distressing incident.'

Hero said: 'Even if he were willing to do so, how could I allow it? Knowing he would always know, and remember? I could not let him make such a sacrifice.'

'I'm delighted to hear it. Don't let him talk you out of it. If it isn't too personal a question, what has this paragon done to make you believe in him in the face of all the evidence?'

'What evidence?' asked Hero in the same controlled and expressionless voice. 'You have given me no shred of evidence. Do you think I would convict a dog on the strength of wild verbal charges brought by such a person as yourself? I know Mr Mayo. I also know you; and if it is a case of his word against yours I shall know whose to accept.'

'Not even if I tell you——'

'There is nothing you can tell me that will make me believe ill of him,' said Hero, cutting him short. 'I will not argue with you, because I am prepared to give you the benefit of the doubt and believe that you think you are telling me the truth. But then you do not know him, and I do.'

'And you really love him?' enquired Rory, but without mockery.

Hero hesitated for a barely perceptible moment, and then she said quietly, and quite definitely: 'Yes.'

Rory laughed and stood up, stretching himself. 'You deceive yourself, Miss Hollis – as usual. I can see that I shall have to do something about it. Meanwhile I hope you will make yourself at home. I'm not sure how soon I can arrange to return to you to the arms of the immaculate Mayo, because it depends on how much mayhem my fellow law-breakers are creating in the city. Once they really get the bit between their teeth it may be a little difficult to stop them, so you might have to spend another night here. But this time I shall behave like a perfect gentleman and leave you the key.'

He stooped and picked up the lamp that he had overturned the previous night, and went out, and Hero did not see him again until late that evening.

It had been an odd, unreal day; and not the least curious thing about it had been the dress she had been given to wear. Her riding-habit had not been returned to her, and when she emerged from her bath she found in its place the dress and ornaments of an Arab lady neatly laid out on the divan. As she could hardly spend the day draped in a bed-sheet she had put them on; remembering as she did so the other occasions on which she had worn Arab dress. Those ill-advised visits to The Dolphins' House, and the disastrous night when she had run through the streets to

Beit-el-Tani to help smuggle the Heir-Apparent out of his house to *Marseilles* and the bitter end of his brief rebellion.

That wild night seemed almost as far away and as long ago as the days of Hollis Hill and Miss Penbury, and she felt infinitely old and tired and disillusioned – because she had imagined herself, then, to be playing a heroic part, and discovered too late that she had merely been an insignificant pawn in an ignoble game. And now once again she was being used as a pawn, and in an even more ignoble one.

The loose silk tunic and thin trousers were at least pleasantly cool, and in the matter of comfort a vast improvement on her own laced, boned and buttoned garments with their complements of petticoats and pantelettes: though for the sake of the moral support they lent her she would at that moment have greatly preferred the latter. She glanced at the ornaments and discarded them with a shiver of distaste, for they reminded her of Zorah and might even have once belonged to her and been worn by her in this house. But there was also a curious half-mask such as she had sometimes seen Cholé wear during those morning calls at Beit-el-Tani: a thing of stiffened silk elaborately embroidered in gold thread and spangles and edged with a little fringe of beads.

Hero picked it up, and trying it on before the glass found that it gave her a comfortable feeling of anonymity, because the woman she could see reflected there was no longer herself: the eyes that looked out through the embroidered slits were shadowed and unreadable, and the mouth below the dangling fringe of beads expressed nothing and gave nothing away. She drew courage from the sight, and turning from it, tried the door of her room and found that it was no longer locked.

Opening it cautiously, she saw that the key had been left in the lock, and she took it out and stood looking at it, turning it over and frowning. It was a clumsy iron thing that might have been made for a dungeon door in medieval England, and for a moment she considered locking herself in and refusing to come out again until Uncle Nat or Clayton came to fetch her. But the silence of the house and the apparent emptiness of the long, pillared verandahs that surrounded the open well of the courtyard made her decide against it, and removing a strand from the twisted silk cord that tied the trousers about her waist, she hung the key round her neck, hidden from sight by the loose tunic, and went boldly out into the verandah and down the shallow, curving stairs to the courtyard and the garden.

A solitary, white-bearded retainer, drowsing in the shade of a pillar, rose and saluted her gravely as she passed, but except for a murmur of voices from somewhere at the back of the house and an elderly negro, presumably a gardener, who was lazily smoothing the crushed shell of the garden paths with a primitive rake, there was little evidence of activity, and no one made any attempt to stop her. But the sight of her own reflection in the placid water of the lily pool made her abandon any idea of flight, for the graceful Arab dress and glittering mask, though completely obliterating the identity of Hero Hollis, were far too colourful and arresting to avoid arousing considerable attention if their wearer were to be found wandering along the road or the open shore in broad daylight.

There was obviously nothing for it but to wait until Captain Frost arranged to return her to the Consulate, since she would not get far on foot in this unsuitable attire; and if she attempted it she might well fall into the hands of the dhow Arabs and end up in a far worse situation than she was in at present – if such a thing were possible! She would have to stay, even if it meant spending another night here: and at least she now possessed the key to her room. She could feel it hanging warm and heavy under the soft silk of the tunic, and touching it, was reassured.

The garden was full of butterflies and the scent of strange flowers, and a bougainvillæa scattered its bright blossoms on to the lily pads and the quiet water as the breeze shook it. Under the orange trees the ground was still damp from the last heavy fall of rain, and the buzzing of innumerable bees made a sound as drowsy and as soothing as the warm wind stirring the leaves overhead and the lazy surf creaming on the shore beyond the sea wall. It was, thought Hero, a very peaceful spot; which surprised her, for considering its past history and present lawless associations it should not have been.

The sudden creak of a hinge disturbed the morning silence, and she turned to see a second elderly negro come through the door in the wall and go away down a path that lay parallel to the dark, creeper-hung cells that had once been guardrooms and granaries. He had not seen her, and neither had he closed the door behind him. It stood ajar, showing her a brilliant glimpse of sunlight and blue water beyond the solid stone and the dense tree shadows of the garden, and she waited for a minute or two to see if he would return, and when he did not, went quickly and cautiously to the door and out on to the rocks above the bay.

The tide was out and the shadows of the palms and pandanus that fringed the shore lay black and sharp-edged on the wet, shelving beach where the sand was alive with little scuttling ghost-crabs, industriously digging holes that the waves would obliterate within an hour or two. The surf broke dazzlingly white on the curving shore and the sea was once again sapphire and turquoise, emerald and jade. But today there were no cloud shadows – and no ships. The bay was empty and the *Virago* had gone.

Hero went swiftly down the steep path to the beach, and keeping in the shadow of the palms, reached one of the tall outcrops of wind-worn coral that formed a natural breakwater on either side of the small bay; and rounding it, found herself looking down the long stretch of coast that she had last seen on the day of Aunt Abby's picnic. Somewhere along there, beyond the green headlands and the mangrove swamps, lay Zanzibar city. But she could see no sign of any sail and not even a fishing *kyack* moved upon the blue.

Had the *Virago* returned to harbour? and if so, why had they not taken her with them? It would surely have been a simpler matter to take her back in the same way as they had brought her, land her at the water-steps and let her find her own way back to her uncle's house, instead of making arrangements to have her sent or fetched by road. Unless that last had been a lie to keep her quiet? She could believe anything of Rory Frost, and if it were not for these wretched clothes she would walk along the shore now and get home by herself: it could not be more than ten miles at most, and was probably less. But there would be villages in between, and roving bands of Gulf Arabs. It was not possible . . .

Hero sat down tiredly in the shade of the coral rocks and stared at the sea and watched the busy ghost-crabs, and she must have fallen asleep, because the shadows had shortened and the sunlight was hot on her lap when a sound that was not the surf or the breeze made her look round, and there was Jumah; salaaming politely and informing her that the midday meal was prepared and waiting for her.

It had been served on Moorish china in a cool, colonnaded apartment strewn with Persian rugs, but she had eaten very little of it, and afterwards she had gone up to the room in which she had spent the previous night, and locking herself in, stayed there all the long, hot afternoon. Listening to the waves and the warm wind and the drowsy cooing of the pigeons, and trying to think clearly – and finding that she could not do so, because her mind was a jumble of foolish, trivial and disconnected thoughts of no importance.

As the shadows lengthened the quiet garden of The House of Shade began to fill once again with chattering birds coming home to roost, and beyond the windows and far away on the horizon Hero could see the lilac-coloured hills of Africa, clear and sharp in the evening light and looking closer than she had ever seen them look before: so close that it seemed as though one might reach them in an hour. The sun plunged behind them in a blaze of glory and green twilight enfolded the Island; and suddenly it was night and there were a million stars in the sky.

The wind died with the day, but though the birds were now silent the night was full of sound. Frogs croaked in chorus from the lily pool and cicadas shrilled among the leaves, a distant drum throbbed with the soft insistent rhythm that is the heart-beat of Zanzibar, and the faint, phosphorescent line of the surf was still murmurous on the beach. In the garden the trees were full of fireflies; and the moon was rising.

Hero became aware of footsteps and voices, and leaning over the window-sill saw someone carrying a lantern along the terrace. A few minutes later Jumah came tapping at her door with the announcement that the master had returned and requested the honour of her presence below.

Hero considered replying that if the master had anything to say to her he could come up and say it through the door. But on second thoughts there seemed to be little point in that, since it could only serve to antagonize him, and if he really had made arrangements to send her back to the city she would have to open the door in order to leave. She asked instead for her own clothes, and found that Jumah had not waited for a reply, but merely delivered the message and gone away again. There was nothing for it but to unlock the door and go down; and she did so: wearing the Arab dress, and the spangled mask that hid her face and made her expression unreadable.

The moon had already topped the palm trees, and Rory was standing on the terrace, his tall shadow black on the silver-washed stone. He turned when he heard her step, and though he grinned at the sight of the mask, he did not comment on it. A table had been laid on the terrace, and the lamplight gleamed on glass and silver and the white robes of Jumah who stood beside it.

Rory said: 'I hope you will not object to dining with me. We are a little short of staff, because it became necessary to send the *Virago* on a voyage to the coast.'

He walked over to the table and drew back a chair, but Hero did not move. She said: 'When are you sending me back?'

'Tomorrow, I hope. The situation in the city is still a bit disturbed, but I have received information from a reliable source that the *Daffodil* is on the way back here and should make harbour about dawn. If I know anything about Dan he'll make the place a deal too hot for our friends from the dhows, so I imagine that peace will be reigning around mid-morning, or at latest by the afternoon, and it should be safe enough for you to ride back to the city after dusk tomorrow.'

'Why didn't you send me back on the *Virago*?'

'Because as soon as Dan drops anchor he's going to hear the whole sad story, and since I have no desire to have my ship boarded or sunk and my crew clapped in irons, I thought it best to send them out of harm's way until this has all blown over.'

'Then why didn't you go with them? Why are you still here?'

'Someone had to see that you got back safely, and Dan isn't in the least likely to catch me. And neither is your uncle!'

'They will some day.'

'I doubt it. But while there's Life, there's Hope. Sit down and have something to eat. You must be hungry, for Jumah says you've eaten almost nothing today, and you don't seem to have had much yesterday.'

'Thank you,' said Hero frigidly, 'but I am not in the least hungry, and if you have said all that you have to say I should prefer to go back to my room.'

'And I should prefer you to stay down here. So that settles the question, doesn't it?'

Hero looked at him for an appreciable time, her eyes showing still and watchful through the slits of the concealing mask. She knew that he was quite capable of fetching her back by force if she were to turn and walk away, and even if she ran he could easily catch her; which would be undignified and humiliating. It had been a tactical error to leave her room, but having done so it would be better to humour him.

She accepted the chair he offered, but found that she could not force herself to eat, though she had taken little food that day and less the day before, and only an hour ago had been feeling distinctly hungry. Jumah poured her a glass of white wine, and she sipped it and found that it was ice cold and refreshing, and having finished it, discovered that it gave her courage and enabled her to reply in a cool, disinterested voice to her host's bland flow of small-talk. But the food still seemed to stick in her throat and taste of nothing at all, and she toyed with her fork and made no more than a pretence of eating.

Rory watched Jumah refill her glass, saw her empty it and have it filled again, and presently remarked in a detached and conversational voice that wine taken on an empty stomach, and by someone unaccustomed to it, was apt to have unexpected effects, and was she not afraid of reaching a stage that he might be tempted to take advantage of?

'No,' said Hero positively.

'Don't tell me that you are trusting to my honour?'

'Naturally not – as you do not appear to possess such a thing. But you seem to forget that there is no longer anything that you could do to me that you have not already done.'

Rory laughed and said: 'My dear innocent! What a lot you have to learn! However, if that's the way you feel about it, far be it from me to discourage you. Only don't blame me if you regret it in the morning.'

He signed to Jumah to fill her glass again, and told him to take the lamp away, for the flame was attracting the attention of too many night-flying moths and insects who battered their wings against the glass and fell into the food and wine. Without it the moonlight seemed brighter and the hot night pleasantly cool, and Hero pushed her chair back from the table and looked at the star-spangled sky and the shimmering fireflies that filled the shadows with glancing points of light, and wondered why nothing seemed to matter any more.

She supposed that it was the wine she had drunk that was giving her this lofty feeling of detachment; as though she were merely an onlooker, standing somewhere outside herself and supremely uninterested in the problems and strivings and emotional agonies of Hero Hollis. The man sitting opposite her with the moonlight full on his face was equally unimportant, for he could not harm her any more. Nothing and no one could harm her any more. She need not even think about him, because tomorrow she would go away and forget him, and no one could blame her for what he had done to her; not even Clay.

Not that Clay's opinion mattered either, for she was not going to marry him. Or anyone! She had learned things about men that she had never dreamt of or imagined, and knowing them she would never again give any man the opportunity, let alone the right, to touch her. Miss Penbury had been right when she had once described them as 'Animals' and women as their 'Poor, helpless victims'; though at the time Hero had very little idea what she was talking about, and had certainly not looked upon herself as either poor or helpless.

She was helpless now. But she was not poor, and she could go back to Hollis Hill and become ... What would she become? Not a nun. One had to have a vocation to become a nun. A recluse, perhaps? But that would be selfish. No, she would do what cousin Josiah Crayne had advised her to do: devote herself and her fortune to doing good in her 'own back yard'. She might even turn Hollis Hill into a home for Fallen Women, which would horrify the Craynes but be quite understood by Aunt Abby and Uncle Nat, and by Clay ...

She must have spoken that last name aloud without knowing that she had done so, for Rory said abruptly: 'What about him? Are you still so sure he is Sir Galahad – *sans peur et sans reproche*? Or are you beginning to have your doubts about him?'

'It doesn't matter, does it? He won't want me now, so I don't have to worry any more. Not about anything.'

She finished the contents of her glass and reached out to put it back on to the table. But for some reason she misjudged the distance, and the glass fell to the stone flags of the terrace and shivered into a dozen pieces.

'Just as well,' commented Rory, removing the decanter out of her reach. 'You've had about enough, and any more'll give you a head in the morning that you won't forget in a hurry.'

Hero looked down at the shining fragments that reflected the moon-light, and pushing them away with her foot, stood up and said carefully: 'I think I shall go to bed now. Good night.'

She held on to the chair-back and frowned at the terrace which seemed to be moving up and down in a curiously unsteady manner, and Rory got to his feet, and walking round the table picked her up and carried her into the house and up the curving flights of stone stairs that led to her room.

Hero had offered no resistance, and as he set her on her feet outside the door something that had caught on a button of his shirt jerked free and fell to the floor with a sharp metallic sound, and he stooped and picked it up. It was the heavy iron door key that Hero had tied about her neck and forgotten.

She said uncertainly, looking at it: 'That's mine. Will you give it to me, please?'

He made no move to do so, but stood there holding it in his hand and looking at her. It was difficult to see his expression because the moon-light only touched the edge of the verandah. But she thought that he was smiling, and she said with a touch of impatience: 'You said that I could have it.'

'I've changed my mind,' said Rory, and put it in his pocket. 'I did warn you, didn't I?'

Hero stared at him uncomprehendingly, frowning a little in an at-tempt to see his face in the moon-thinned shadows. 'But – that's not fair.'

'I never play fair,' said Rory softly. 'You ought to know that by now.'

He pushed open the door, and picking her up in his arms, carried her through it and kicked it shut again behind them.

30

The sky that had been clear when the moon rose had clouded over before it set, and on the far horizon beyond the mountains of Africa lightning licked and flickered, and the faint reverberations of thunder came uneasily on the wind. The brief, golden break in the monsoon was over and the morning dawned grey and misty. And before midday it was raining again.

The rain fell steadily in warm, heavy torrents that transformed the unmade roads and bridle-paths into rivers and quagmires, and soaked through Hero's cloak to drench her riding habit and blind her eyes until she gave up any attempt to see where she was going, and allowed her horse to find its own way.

They had left The House of Shade a good deal earlier than Rory had intended, for tonight there would be neither moon nor starlight to guide them, so they must reach the outskirts of the city before darkness fell. And they were within less than a mile of it, at a place where the track passed through a mango grove, when two horsemen materialized out of the pouring twilight immediately ahead of them.

Hero heard Rory say sharply: '*Batty!* – what the hell are you doing here? What's happened? Who's that with you? Ibrahim?'

'Yus,' said Batty, speaking in an undertone. 'I've left Ralub in charge of the ship. He and I, we suspicioned you'd be comin' by this path. You've got to go back, Captain Rory. Young Dan's watching out for you, and this time 'e means to get you for sure.'

'He won't,' said Rory briefly. 'That is, not unless you and Ralub between you have given him the idea that I'm not on the ship after all. I told you to keep clear and keep out of sight. As long as he thinks I'm cruising somewhere away up the coast, I'm safe enough.'

'Well, 'e don't think it. Not judging by the way 'e's actin'. Or if 'e do, 'e's playing safe and taking no chances neither way. 'E ain't 'ad a sight of the *Virago*, I can promise you that, but 'e's got every road watched and the orders is "Shoot on sight and shoot to kill." S'*now!*'

'Are they, by God! That's going to make a difference.'

'So I should say! And don't say as I didn't warn you. You gone too far this time, for there was two got snuffed in them riots, and they're out to get you for that, dead or alive. And if it's alive they're for stringing you up and no questions asked. It's the truth, I tell you.'

'I know. Our respected Consul took the trouble to tell me as much when he sent for me a few days ago.'

'And I suppose you thought 'e were joking? Well 'e ain't! – not now. This time you been an gone an made the place too 'ot to 'old you, and I 'opes you're satisfied. Only thing you can do now is——'

Batty checked himself and turned to peer at the grey shadow that was Hero, and then reaching out he caught the Captain's rein and led the horse a few yards down the soggy, tree-shaded track until they were out of ear-shot, and lowered his voice to a hoarse whisper:

'Ralub 'e says the only place you'll be safe is with 'Is 'Ighness, for 'e'll 'ide you until that danged *Daffodil* clears off. Dan can't 'ang around 'ere for ever, so the quicker you gets to the Palace the better.'

'I thought you said all the roads were watched?'

'S'right. And old Edwards 'as got 'is Baluchi sharpshooters out after you too. But we got a purdah cart and a coupla gigglin' wimmin back of them bushes, and you'll 'ave to go in that. They won't dare 'old it up, and if they stops it them wimmin'll screech a bit just to satisfy them that there's bints in it.'

'What about Miss Hollis? We can't leave her wandering round alone with the place crawling with Gulf Arabs.'

'It ain't any more. Dan 'e gives them notice to quit, and they're quitting right spry. They don't fancy the look of 'is guns. Well, are you going?'

'I don't seem to have much choice. I evidently underestimated Dan. I thought he'd be so sure I was on the *Virago* and a couple of hundred miles away by now that he wouldn't keep a look-out except to seaward. What are you going to do, Batty? You can't go taking that girl into the city either, for if they get their hands on you they'll probably string you up as a substitute for me.'

'I ain't taking 'er in. I'm going to drop 'er off at old Seyyida Zuene's 'ouse, and ask them to see 'er safe back: she went there once before to meet that bint 'oo skips with young Ruete, so they know 'er. After which I'll lay low and bide me time, and when they gets tired of watching the roads and the 'ouse I'll let you know.'

Rory thought for a minute or two, and then he said: 'All right. Where's this cart of yours?'

'Ibrahim'll take you to it. I'll take Miss 'Ero. Did you know that she'd been to your 'ouse to see if young Amrah were being looked after proper? Didn't let on, I suppose – which don't surprise me. But she did. Ibrahim told me. There's a lot you don't know as you ought to.'

'I'm beginning to think so,' said Rory, and turned his horse.

They rode back to where Hero sat silent in the wet dusk, and he said curtly and without preamble: 'Batty will take you as far as old Seyyida Zuene's house and ask them to get you back to the Consulate from there. You'll be quite safe.'

Hero said nothing. Her face in the last of the misty grey daylight was no more than a pale oval against the dripping darkness of the trees; remote and enigmatic.

Rory said: 'He tells me that you went to see my daughter. That was kind of you; though hardly wise. This is coals of fire indeed!'

Hero still did not speak, and he smiled at her and said: 'It doesn't look as though I shall be seeing you again, but I should like you to know that if the Navy or the Consul catches up with me and evens the score for you, it will have been well worth it.'

'Because you have had your revenge for Zorah?' Hero's voice was as remote and unreadable as her face.

Rory laughed; lightly and without bitterness: 'No. From a purely personal point of view – as you are well aware.'

He put out a hand and touched her cool wet cheek, and said: 'The first time I ever saw you, you were soaked to the skin, so I suppose it's only appropriate that you should be in the same condition for the last. Goodbye, my lovely Galatea. It's nice to know that you are unlikely to forget me.'

He turned his horse's head, and followed by Ibrahim vanished into the rainy dusk, and Hero heard the sound of hooves on sodden ground grow fainter and fainter, until it was swallowed up at last in the sound of the falling rain.

Batty sighed and said: 'We'd best be going, miss,' and they rode out of the dripping gloom of the trees into an open stretch of ground that ended in a village street. Once past that the surface of the road improved and the horses moved at a quicker pace.

Batty made no effort to talk, and it was Hero who at last broke the long silence:

'Will they really hang him if they catch him?'

'If they don't shoot 'im first,' said Batty grimly.

'But that wouldn't be legal.'

Batty made a rude noise indicative of contempt: 'The Captain ain't never been one for keeping the law himself – not to notice. 'Sides, there's times when blokes forgets the law, and this is one of 'em. It all come of muckin' about with wimmin. Wimmin – begging your pardon, miss – is pisen. Cold pisen! Don't touch 'em, is my motter. Captain Rory, 'e's a reasonable man and 'e uses 'is brain-box; but when 'e 'ears what your young man, God damn 'is dirty 'ide, does to Zorah, 'e loses 'is 'ead and goes on the booze, and ends up behaving like 'e was only fit for Bedlam.

And now 'ere's Dan and the Colonel cutting up rough for the self-same reason. *Wimmin!*'

Hero said quietly: 'It was not Mr Mayo. He would not have done such a thing. It has all been a mistake, and you will find that it was someone else.'

Batty threw her a glance that combined scorn with a certain measure of sympathy. 'You'd 'ave to think that, I reckon. But it ain't so. I gets it out of the African barstard what rents 'im the rooms 'e keeps in a lane off Changu Bazaar – 'e knew! And it's best that you does. Better know the worst of 'im before you starts, then you knows where you are and can make do. No good findin' out once you been tied up to 'im legal, now is it?'

Hero made no answer and Batty did not appear to expect one. He brooded awhile, jogging forward in the growing darkness, and presently he said:

'I'd 'ave liked to 'ave cut 'is liver out meself – me 'aving known Zorah since she were a nipper. But I been thinking, and I reckon 'e didn't see it that way. 'Ow was 'e to know she weren't just another native trollop and 'appy to 'ave a bit of fun for an 'andful of dollars? There's plenty of that kind in this 'ere town; all colours. Daresay 'e's sorry. But Captain Rory now – 'e knows what 'e's a' doing of, and 'e done it for wickedness pure; which I don't 'old with. Lost 'is temper like. *Tch, Tch!*'

Hero was still silent and Batty turned in the saddle to peer at her, and said in a fatherly tone: 'You get that young man of yours 'ome quick, miss, and maybe 'e'll sober up. 'E might even make you a good 'usband yet, if you educates 'im right. But this ain't a good part of the world for 'is kind. Too many temptations, as y'might say. You take 'im 'ome, miss.'

A high white wall loomed up ahead of them, and ten minutes later Batty was explaining glibly to the Major-domo of the Seyyida's household that the American lady had been out riding on the morning of the disturbances, and while on her way back to the Consulate had been attacked by a band of men from the dhows and rescued by the Captain and some of the crew of the *Virago*, who had given her shelter at *Kivulimi*. Hearing that the city was now quiet again she had set out at once to return, but had been delayed by the rain. And as he, Batty, could escort her no further, owing to urgent private affairs that must be dealt with immediately, he would be more than grateful if the Seyyida would graciously provide an escort to take her back to the city. The Seyyida had graciously done so, and Batty had vanished into the rainy night without further words or any farewell, leaving Hero to cover the last lap of her journey by lantern-light and accompanied by half-a-dozen of the Seyyida's mounted retainers.

Batty had been right about the roads being watched, for as they neared the outskirts of the town they were challenged by three Baluchi sepoys under the command of a seaman from the *Daffodil*, and after a brief parley the seaman and one of the sepoys had added themselves to the party and escorted Hero to the Consulate, where they had found the Consul and his family at dinner.

Her arrival there seemed a nightmare repetition of the scene that had been enacted once before in that house, on the day she had first set foot in Zanzibar. But this time Hero herself took no part in it. She stood in the hall looking white, wet and exhausted, while her aunt indulged in a fit of hysterics, Cressy wept, Uncle Nat asked questions and Clayton held her in his arms and said a great many things that did not seem to make any sense.

Water trickled from the sodden riding cloak that was one of Rory Frost's, forming small, gleaming pools on the polished floor of the hall, while Clayton's voice and her uncle's and the incoherencies of Aunt Abby went on and on, and Hero stood motionless and unresponsive; a lay figure. Saying nothing and letting their emotions swirl around her without touching her, until at last Aunt Abby, recovering herself, pulled away the wet cloak, and seeing that the rain had soaked through it to drench the habit it covered, raised hands of horror and whisked her upstairs to bed.

Colonel Edwards and Lieutenant Larrimore, who had been sent for in haste, arrived at the Consulate half-an-hour later. But as Hero was already in bed, and according to her aunt must on no account be disturbed that night, they had had to content themselves with questioning the Seyyida's servants, who had faithfully repeated all that Batty had said.

'Pack of lies!' flared Clayton in furious contempt. 'They weren't rescuing her from anyone. It was a barefaced abduction!'

'Of course it was,' agreed the Colonel. 'Nevertheless, I think it would be wiser not to contradict that version, since as far as Miss Hollis is concerned, the truth will not do.'

'You mean we've got to let that man pose as having gallantly rescued her from a raving mob? I never heard of anything so downright crazy! Why, I thought you meant to string him up when you caught him! How in thunder do you think you're going to do that if we support this story? Or do you suggest that we thank him instead?'

'Hardly, Mr Mayo.' The Colonel's voice was aloof and reproving. 'Nor do I propose that we make any mention of what has occurred unless we hear that it is being talked of. If that should happen you would be wiser to support the version we have just been given, and I can assure you that it will make no difference at all to my dealings with Frost. I warned him of what I intended to do before there was any question of his abducting Miss Hollis, and I shall stand by it.'

'The question at the moment,' said Dan Larrimore curtly, 'is where is he now? Has Miss Hollis been on the *Virago*, and if so, where was she landed and when, and where is the *Virago*? Surely she can tell us that much?'

'She won't,' said Aunt Abby unhappily. 'I asked her myself. But she said she didn't want to talk about it tonight, and would we please leave her alone. And I'm sure I don't blame her.'

'But cannot you see, ma'am, that we need to know at once? We can't afford to give him time to get clear away. Could you not put that to her?'

'I'm afraid it wouldn't do a mite of good to ask her again. The poor child has not only been through a harrowing time, but is soaked to the skin and may well contract a fever. You can see her in the morning, but not before that.'

Aunt Abby could when she chose be quite as stubborn as her niece, and they had had to be content with that. But when the morning came Hero had refused point-blank to see either Colonel Edwards or Lieutenant Larrimore, or to answer any questions put by her aunt until she had first seen Clayton.

She had seen him an hour later in the drawing-room. But she had not answered questions. She had asked them instead, and Clayton had been deeply wounded and concluded a hurt and dignified speech by saying that although in the circumstances he could make every allowance for her, he found it astounding that she should think it necessary to ask him to deny the trumped-up charges of a venal slave trader such as Rory Frost.

'But you *haven't* denied them, Clay,' said Hero quietly.

'Nor do I intend to. If you have so little faith in me – so little trust or affection as to even ask me to do such a thing – then I cannot believe that denials will do any good. How *could* you believe such a thing of me, Hero! How could you listen while a vile libertine like Frost attempts to blacken me to you in order to excuse his own inexcusable behaviour?'

Hero had wanted to be convinced, and he had almost convinced her. And yet . . . She had expected Clay to be shocked and outraged at the recital of such appalling charges, but he had been reproachful instead, and there had been something in his manner – in the colour that patched his cheekbones, a wariness in his eyes and a certain lack of surprise – that did not quite square with his words, and suggested that he might have been prepared for some such thing and had decided in advance how to deal with it.

She remembered then, and wondered why she had not done so before, the two occasions on which she had seen Clayton in the city in a lane near the Changu Bazaar, and the fact that on the second occasion she had seen Thérèse Tissot ride out of the same cul-de-sac not two minutes afterwards . . .

She said slowly: 'Clay, you haven't got rooms in the city, have you?'

'Is that something else he told you?'

'He said you rented the top floor of a house in the city.'

'"*He said! — he said!*" Hero, I would not have believed it of you! He's probably seen me coming out of the house where Joe Lynch has a room, and used that as a basis for this pack of lies that you seem to have listened to so eagerly.'

'Joseph Lynch! I – I didn't think of that. Has Mr Lynch got rooms in a house near the Changu Bazaar?'

'Yes, he has, if you want to know. And I have occasionally been there. But not with Arab trollops!'

'I'm sorry Clay. But – but I had to ask. You do see that?'

But Clayton did not see it; or would not. He abandoned hurt reproach and became angry, and listening to him, Hero wondered why his anger should suddenly seem to her as unreal and as calculated as his initial reproach had been, and hating herself for the thought, could not dismiss it. He was accusing her now of trumping up these wild and monstrous charges in order to deflect attention from her own unhappy situation, and it was difficult not to wonder if he had only ceased being hurt and dignified – and cautious! – simply because she herself had begun to apologize, and so he felt the danger to be past and could now afford to be angry?

'Don't think I can't understand it,' said Clayton, returning at last to a more reasonable tone of voice, 'because I can. I can fully appreciate your feelings, and you have all my sympathy. And in spite of what has happened, my love. But that you should try, in order to forget your own unhappy predicament, to persuade yourself that my case is no better than yours, and to accuse me of sharp practice and immoral behaviour, is unworthy of you. I have not blamed you for what has occurred, for you could not have prevented it, and we will agree never to talk of it again but to forget that it ever happened.'

'You mean you are still prepared to marry me?'

'Of course, dear.'

'That is very noble of you Clay. Very . . . generous.'

'It would be ignoble and ungenerous of me if I were to cast you off for something that was no fault of yours. I have told you, we will forget it.'

'Even if I have his child?'

'*Hero!*' Clayton's face was suddenly scarlet with rage. 'I don't know how you can bring yourself to say such a thing, and I refuse to discuss it.'

'But if we are still to be married we shall have to discuss it.'

'We are not going to do so now! I should have thought that you would have had more delicacy than to ... But you are not yourself. You are shocked and upset and I don't wonder at it. It would be better if we did not talk of these things until you are in a calmer frame of mind. And better still if they were never mentioned again!'

Hero said tiredly: 'There are some things you cannot run away from Clay, and this is one of them. I have done a great many ill-advised things because I would not stop and think for long enough before doing them. But at least I ran towards them, and not away.'

'It is not "running away" to refuse to take part in an unprofitable and deeply distasteful discussion of a situation that may never arise,' retorted Clay angrily.

'It arose with Zorah,' said Hero.

The colour deepened in Clayton's face and his handsome mouth twitched and looked ugly, but he controlled himself with a palpable effort and said: 'There is not the least need for you to degrade yourself by mentioning such a creature, my dear. May I tell Colonel Edwards that you will see him, or would prefer me to see him on your behalf?'

'What is it that he wants to know?'

'Where he may find Frost and the *Virago*.'

'I don't know that.'

'But you must have *some* idea! Were you on the schooner all the time? And if so, where did they land you? On what part of the Island?'

'I don't know,' repeated Hero, her voice devoid of expression and her eyes looking past him as though they did not see him: 'I will think about it. But at the moment I feel as you do; that it is something I do not wish to talk about. I am sure you will understand that.'

'But this is an entirely different matter!' protested Clay. 'It is something we've got to know, and the sooner we know it the more chance we shall have of coming up with the man.'

'I'm sorry, but I do not feel well enough to discuss it at present,' said Hero.

No amount of argument or persuasion had been able to move her from that, and turning a deaf ear and a white, stubborn face to him she had gone up to her room, and shutting herself into it, unlocked her jewel-case and removed from it a small packet of letters tied with a piece of ribbon; those well-phrased but hardly passionate love-letters that she had received from Clayton, and cherished and re-read and admired so much for the nobility of their sentiments.

She glanced through them now, searching for something. And when at last she found what she was looking for she put it on one side, and locking the rest of the letters away again, sat for a long time staring at her own reflection in the glass.

She knew that what she was about to do was mean and underhand. But somehow Clay had not convinced her as she had expected to be convinced, and she had to be sure: she had to know. Not only for her own sake, but because if Clay had indeed been responsible for Zorah's death, he had invited retaliation; and the fact that she had paid the score on his behalf was immaterial, for Zorah too had been innocent of offence.

If there was any justification for the uncivilized revenge that Rory Frost had taken, then she could not be responsible for handing him over to be executed without trial. It would have been different if they had merely intended to run him out of the Island and to forbid him to enter any territory owing allegiance to the Sultan of Zanzibar. Or even sentence him to a term of imprisonment and confiscate his property and his ship. But if Clayton had lied she would not give information that might lead directly to the Captain's death, and therefore she could see no one and speak to no one until she knew. And if in order to gain the proof she needed she must stoop to spying and deceit, then she was prepared to do that too.

Hero drew a long breath and reaching resolutely for a pair of scissors, carefully cut off the last four inches of a letter written in this house over a year ago, and received less than a week before she set sail for Zanzibar on the *Norah Crayne*: a four-inch slip of paper bearing only a dozen words – the very last that Clay had ever written to her: '*Come as soon and as quickly as you can. Ever your devoted C.*'

Hero folded it carefully, and enclosing it in a blank envelope summoned Fattûma and gave her careful instructions:

'It must be given into Madame Tissot's own hand, you understand Fattûma, and when there is no one with her. And she is not to know who has sent it, so you must not take it yourself, but send one of the gardeners, or the water-boy, and tell him that I will pay him well if he sees that it is put into her hand and says nothing. Can you do that?'

Fattûma nodded, her eyes bright with the love of intrigue and the prospect of a bribe, and an hour later she reported that the letter had been safely delivered. Hero handed over a liberal sum and then sent for the groom, Rahim, to whom she talked for several minutes in the garden. After which she returned to the house and asked her aunt for camphor drops, and pleading a headache, spent the remainder of the day in her own room professing herself quite prostrated and unable to see anyone – even Dr Kealey.

Colonel Edwards had fumed and Clayton and Lieutenant Larrimore had looked tight-lipped and grim, and even Nathaniel Hollis, with all his sympathy for his niece, considered that Hero was behaving in an unhelpful and hysterical manner and should at least summon up the strength to inform them where she had been and from what point on the Island she had returned. But Hero merely locked her bedroom door, and Aunt Abby startled her husband by roundly informing all four gentlemen that if they possessed the slightest degree of sensibility – which of course they did not! – they should be able to comprehend some small proportion of what her niece must be suffering, but that in such matters all men, without exception, were insensitive brutes!

Dusk was falling by the time that Fattûma scratched at Hero's door to say that Rahim had brought Sherif from the stables, and Hero emerged at last and went downstairs; informing her uncle, whom she met in the hall, that she had asked to see the horse in order to satisfy herself that he was well. She went out to pat Sherif and give him sugar lumps, and to speak to Rahim, and when she came back into the house her face was so white and drawn that Uncle Nat was seriously disturbed, and told her with a good deal of concern that she should be in bed.

'Yes,' said Hero numbly, but not as though she were agreeing with him or had even heard what he had said, and without making any move to comply. She sat down with some suddenness in the nearest chair, and Mr Hollis, anxiously patting her lax hands, wondered if she were going to faint and was profoundly relieved at the unexpected sight of Colonel Edwards, who had called again in the hope that Miss Hollis might by now have imparted some useful information. The sight of that lady up and dressed, and therefore presumably recovered from her former prostration and in a more reasonable frame of mind raised his expectations. But all too briefly.

'You can't talk to her now!' snapped Mr Hollis, exasperated. 'Can't you see the poor girl isn't well? Fetch my wife – get a glass of water!'

He was interrupted by his niece, who straightened her back and said clearly and with composure: 'I am perfectly well, thank you Uncle Nat, and quite able to answer any questions that Colonel Edwards may wish to put to me.'

'That is indeed kind of you, Miss Hollis,' said the Colonel, studying her colourless face a little anxiously. 'I appreciate it. Can we talk somewhere where it is a little more private?'

'I have nothing to say that cannot be said here,' announced Hero, making no attempt to move.

'Oh – er – quite so. In that case, all we wish to know is if you have any idea where either Frost or his ship are now, and if you could tell us where you were taken after you were abducted.'

'I was not abducted,' said Hero.

'*What!*' both gentlemen stared at her, dumbfounded. Her uncle, the first to recover, begged her with some tartness to pull herself together and not to talk nonsense.

'It is not nonsense,' said Hero, telling a flat and deliberate lie for the first time in her life, and proceeding to embroider it: 'Captain Frost had been informed that a mob of men from the dhows were about to attack the consulates, and as he did not think it wise for me to remain here, he removed me to a place of greater safety, and sent me back with a suitable escort as soon as the danger was over. That is all.'

Uncle Nathaniel said explosively: 'I never heard such goddamned rubbish in my life, and if you think I'm going to swallow a tale like that——! Now see here, Hero——'

The Colonel lifted a deprecatory hand and said: 'Just a minute. Might I ask, Miss Hollis, why Frost should not have taken Mr Mayo and your grooms to safety also? Or have sent any message to your family?'

'I imagine that he thought that the men could look after themselves, but that a woman might have suffered worse things than a few injuries at the hands of a mob. In any case, there was little time in which to argue. Mr Mayo misunderstood the situation, which is not surprising; and owing to the trouble in the city it proved impossible to send any message.'

Mr Hollis said angrily: 'You must be plumb crazy to lie like this!'

Hero rose and shook out her skirts, and said in a remote and colourless voice: 'I am sorry; but that is all I intend to say, and I think you will find that it is confirmed by the men who brought me back here.'

'Well, yes. But——'

'Can you think of any better reason for Captain Frost's action?' enquired Hero in a constrained voice.

Her uncle stared at her in wrathful bewilderment, but the British Consul nodded and said heavily: 'I am afraid I can. And I presume that you have found out that it was true. I am sorry.'

He saw a faint flush of colour show briefly in Miss Hollis's white cheeks, but she did not speak, and he said slowly: 'Even if you think that Frost may to some extent have been justified, there can be no excuse for his other activities; or for his inciting these pirates to rioting and violence in order to further his own ends. Two men have died and others have been severely wounded as a result of it; there is that to be thought of. And even if your own abduction – your rescue if you prefer it – had never occurred, it would still make no difference at all to my decision to bring him to summary justice.'

'I know,' said Hero, in a voice that was barely more than a strained whisper: 'But you must see that the . . . the circumstances do not permit my assisting you to bring him there. I am sorry.'

'So am I,' said the Colonel gently. He took her cold hand, and with a gesture that was entirely alien to him and totally unexpected, bent and kissed it with the stiff respect of an older and more formal age, and turned and went quietly away.

Nathaniel Hollis, recovering from his surprise, began to demand explanations but was checked by an equally unexpected sight. Hero was crying. Not noisily, as his Abby cried, or with childish, gulping sobs like Cressy, but making no sound: the tears brimming from her wide-open eyes and running helplessly down her face to drip off her chin. He had never seen his niece cry before, and after the dry-eyed stubbornness she had displayed since her return on the previous night had begun to think she was incapable of it. But the sight of that silent weeping disturbed him a great deal more than any more vocal display of emotion would have done.

'Now, now, Hero,' said Uncle Nat helplessly. 'Now, now, dear——' He took her arm and propelling her upstairs, sent for his wife, who said wildly and unjustly that she would not be at all surprised if dear Hero did not go into a decline and that it was all his fault!

Hero allowed herself to be undressed and put into a nightgown and a muslin wrapper without protest, and Aunt Abby, hurrying off to prepare a soothing draught, passed her son coming up the staircase three steps at a time and with a face of thunder.

'It's those fool men worrying her,' said Aunt Abby indignantly. 'So inconsiderate! But she'll be all the better for a good night's sleep. Where are you going, Clay? No, you can't see her——! *Clay!*'

But Clayton had paid not the slightest heed to his parent's scandalized protest, and brushing past her had gone straight to Hero's door, flung it open without knocking and banged it shut behind him. Aunt Abby heard the key turn in the lock, and went downstairs to inform her perplexed and disquieted husband that she did not know what the world was coming to.

Hero turned a white, ravaged face, but there was no surprise in it. It was as though she had expected to see him and found nothing odd in the fact that he should burst into her bedroom without her leave and when she was dressed in no more than a nightdress and a thin, ruffled wrapper. Modesty had ceased to mean very much to her, and it was of no importance where and under what circumstances this interview should take place. It had to be got through and got over, and that was all that mattered.

Clayton jerked the key from the lock, and holding it clenched in his hand said furiously: 'Say, what's the meaning of this balderdash you've been telling Colonel Edwards? Have you gone out of your mind?'

Hero sat down wearily on the edge of her bed as though she found the effort to stand too great for her, and said tonelessly: 'No, Clay, I have not. Though it would not have been so strange if I had. I have just found out that part of what I was told about you was true, and now I cannot be sure that all the rest of it is not true as well. I think it must be.'

'I don't know what you're talking about, and I'm damned sure you don't! If you're still harping on that ridiculous pack of lies that Frost invented, I can only say——'

'Don't say it. Clay. Please don't! You see, I know now that you do keep a room in the town, and that Thérèse Tissot does meet you there. Perhaps you had your friend Mr Lynch take it in his name; or perhaps he uses it too. But I guess that doesn't make much difference, does it?'

'You are being nonsensical and you know it! Are you really going to lose your head and behave in an unbalanced manner on the mere word of a slanderous scoundrel who cannot supply a shred of proof?'

'But I have the proof.'

Clayton's face turned from red to white, and he said between his teeth: 'I don't believe it! You're inventing.'

'You shouldn't judge everyone by yourself, Clay.'

'You couldn't—— There was no . . .'

'No what? Do you mean that there was no written contract? No, I don't suppose there was. I expect you counted on that. And on my taking your word against anyone else's if anything of this should ever come to my ears. You were very nearly right. That's why I had to have proof.'

Clayton said harshly: 'There can be no proof of something that isn't true, and if someone else has been spinning you a tale you'll find it'll turn out to be just another lie.'

'No one has been spinning me a tale. I – I don't like to tell you this, Clay, because I am not proud of it. But . . . I had to know, and so I cut off part of the last letter you wrote me and sent it to Thérèse. It wasn't even signed with your name; only with an initial, and if she had not known your handwriting it would have meant nothing to her, because I did not send it by anyone she would know.'

Clay said scornfully: 'And you're going to pretend that she answered it? Hero, this is madness!'

'No, she did not answer it. Not in writing. But I sent Rahim to watch a house with two doors in a cul-de-sac near the Changu Bazaar, and to tell me how many people went in at the side door, and who they were. There was only one, and though she wore a heavy veil and he did not recognize her at first, he followed her back through the streets, and he says it was Madame Tissot. So you see . . .'

There was a brief moment of silence, and then Clay said angrily but with less assurance: 'And what is that supposed to prove?'

'That she knew the writing, and knew too where to go to meet the writer. For she didn't come to this house, but to the one in the city, and

I had not told Rahim who to watch for or even suggested that it might be a European. I hope you will not tell me that it was a coincidence, because I shall not be able to believe you.'

Clayton said sharply: 'Rahim must have made a mistake. He must have mistaken——' He stopped, realizing the futility of such words, and Hero said quietly and without anger, but as though it was something she must know: 'Why did you do it, Clay?'

'I didn't——' began Clay automatically. 'I . . .' He sat down suddenly on the bed beside her and put his head in his hands.

He was silent for a long time, and Hero looked at his slumped shoulders and bent head and knew that she had never loved him. That mysterious instinct possessed by all Eve's daughters and which men refer to – often derisively – as "woman's intuition", told her that had she truly done so, the fact that he had lied to her, and was not at all the sort of person she had imagined him to be, would not have been able to destroy that. It could only have caused pain and bitter disappointment, but nothing worse, for she did not believe that you could stop loving someone because they hurt or disappointed you – however much you might wish to do so. It could not be as easy as that. Your head might reject them, but surely your heart would not?

Clayton said in a muffled and uneven voice: 'I suppose it's because I like women and I can't leave them alone. Mother doesn't understand that. She must have had a hell of a life with my father; he liked them too, and maybe I get it from him. Nat – my step-father – doesn't understand it either, and I couldn't let them know. I had my own place, back home, so it was easy there. But here I had to live in the same house. So I rented those rooms in town. Somewhere where I could do what I liked . . . be myself.'

'Weren't you afraid of being found out?'

'Oh, I knew there might be talk, but I thought I could deal with that. I got Joe to do the actual renting for me. It's in his name, and I knew he wouldn't give me away. Thérèse used to meet me there. We – we had an affair. It wasn't altogether her fault; I began it. Old man Tissot's twice her age and more like her grandfather than her husband, and she – well I guess she fell in love with me . . .'

Hero said: 'Why did you want to marry me, Clay?'

'It seemed a good idea. Ma and Nat both wanted me to marry a nice, steady girl with plenty of money, who would sober me up and settle me down. You, in fact! Oh, I liked you all right. I liked you a lot, though you scared me plenty at times and I used to wonder if I could go through with it and how long I should be able to keep it up – acting noble and high-minded and prosing away like a moralizing missionary! I knew you'd find me out sooner or later, but I thought I might be able to bring you round. One of my uncles told me that Ma was every bit as high-minded when she married my father, but in spite of everything she'd always loved him and had never really gotten over him. And then I – I fancied I knew a hell of a lot about women, so I thought it might work out. That I could bring you down to earth a bit. Teach you to like the things I liked. Making love – parties – having a high time. Spending money on fun instead of using it to convert the heathen or put a stop to drinking or gambling and all the rest of it.'

'Is that why you speculated in slaves and guns? To have money for . . . for fun?'

'No. Just to have money. You've always had it, so you don't know what it means to be without it. Or not to have enough. It was so damned easy to make it in a place like this, and I'd have been a fool if I'd turned down the chance.'

'But Clay – *slaves*! How could you? If it had been anything else . . .'

'The few slaves I bought and sold didn't make a mite of difference to the wholesale traffic that's being carried on in this part of the world! If I hadn't sold them someone else would have done it. And I didn't make them slaves; they were slaves already – caught and numbered and landed here. There was nothing that could be done about that.'

'And I suppose there was nothing that could be done about the fire-arms either?'

'That was different. That was just a plain matter of business, and one can't afford to be sentimental over such things. The politics of these people are no concern of mine.'

'But they concerned Uncle Nat. If he had known——'

'If he'd known he'd have thrown me on to the next ship bound for home. And that might have been no bad thing, either! He's your kind, Hero: and I suppose that old stick Edwards' kind too. They probably couldn't do a crooked thing if they tried. Wouldn't know how. But they'll neither of them ever get anywhere, and I shall – unless I end up in jail, or with some hysterical woman's bullet through my head, like my father!'

He laughed, but with a harsh note of bitterness, and Hero said: 'And Zorah?'

Clayton looked up, his face drawn and bewildered: 'I thought she was just a – just another prostitute, and no different from the rest except that she was prettier than most of them. I didn't think she'd care a damn as long as she got her money, and I never dreamt she'd . . . I never thought . . . How could I have known? Hero, I swear I didn't mean any harm there. Not real harm; not to her. I thought it would rile Frost if she spent a few days with me for a change, but that was all. He's always gotten my goat . . .

carrying on as though there was nothing wrong in slaving and smuggling and wenching just as long as you spoke out about it and didn't give a damn who knew, but that there was something sneaky and low-down and rotten about doing it on the quiet. That isn't true! Boasting about it doesn't make it a mite better. And keeping quiet about it doesn't make it any worse.'

'Or excuse it,' said Hero.

'I'm not excusing it. I'm just telling you how I came to do it, and why. I'm not proud of it, God knows, and if I could have kept you from finding out I would. But Zorah . . . that was your fault too. You and your "touch-me-not" attitudes! You may not be my type, but you're a damned good-looker all the same, and I'm not a dried up stick or a block of ice. You don't know what it's been like . . . not being allowed to kiss you or lay a finger on you for fear of scaring you into running for cover and breaking the whole thing off . . . I tell you it's been hell! Holding myself in; playing prunes and prisms and all the while wanting to throw you down and show you what it's all about. Sometimes I used to sneak out at night, after a chaste evening with you and one kiss on your shrinking cheek, and get me a woman from the Lal Bazaar. If I hadn't, I'd have gone crazy. And if it hadn't been for the state you got me in I daresay I wouldn't have made a fool of myself over Zorah!'

Hero said in a whisper: 'Oh no, Clay! Oh no . . .' as though she were pleading with him, or with herself.

But Clay was not listening to her. He said: 'As for all the rest of it, the money was there for the making, and if I hadn't made it myself, someone else would. You can be as sentimental and self-righteous as you like about it, but I've done a sight less harm and caused a lot less misery by dealing in captured negroes than men like Dan Larrimore, who spend years of their lives trying to free them. There have been literally thousands of wretched blacks flung into the sea to drown, or landed and left to die of thirst and starvation, by captains of slave ships who were being chased by the British and didn't dare risk being caught red-handed with slaves on board. But all I've done is to buy them at one price from a rascally trader, and sell them for a higher one to rich men who will provide them with food and clothes and their keep for life – and who'll treat 'em a sight better than many a white servant-girl gets treated back home in Boston, at that! It's all in the way you look at it.'

He rose and stretched himself, straightening his shoulders as though he shrugged off a burden, and said: 'Well, now I guess you know all about me, and maybe its better that way. Maybe it'll give us a better chance of making a go of marriage.'

Hero said quietly: 'But I'm not going to marry you, Clay.'

'You haven't any choice, dear. And since what happened to you was mostly my fault, I haven't either. If we get married at once, and you should have a child, it will be thought to be mine even if it's not. That's the very least I can do for you. And it's the least you can do for—— Well, for all of us. You do see that, don't you?'

Hero was silent for so long that he thought that she had not understood him, and he said more urgently: 'We just can't afford to have a scandal. It would involve not only ourselves but my step-father, and Mama and Cressy too. And then there are the Craynes to be thought of, as well as your own father's family. Hollis Hill still stands for something, and you can't go back there to have a nameless child, or even to bear one that we must pretend is prematurely born. You can't think only of yourself. I can promise you though, that I shall do everything in my power to protect you and make it up to you.'

Hero stood up slowly and went to stand by the window, holding aside the curtain and looking out at the darkened garden and the lights of the city. She said without turning: 'I guess not ... I – I will think about it.'

'Don't think about it too long. And try not to blame me too much.'

'I'm not blaming you. I know that I am the one to blame. For being blind and self-opinionated and so sure that I must always be right about everything. For not realizing that people do things, or don't do them, because there is something in them that pushes them that way and that they are not always strong enough to fight against ... something that perhaps they cannot help; heredity, or the wrong sort of teaching. Or strong appetites that need to be satisfied, and which I – I never really understood anything about ... before. You couldn't resist women or the chance of making easy money, and I couldn't resist interfering and helping to cause a great deal of harm because I was so sure that I was right, and – and I suppose because I enjoyed feeling that I was so much better and more public-spirited and intolerant of injustice than other people. Cousin Josiah was right and we ought to start with ourselves. I thought that was selfish once, but he said it was sense, and I guess it is.'

Clayton looked relieved, if not entirely sure what she was talking about, and he went over to her with the intention of putting an arm about her and assuring her of his continued affection. But when she turned her head and looked at him there was something in her face that made him think better of it, and he contented himself with saying that he appreciated her generosity and would be grateful if she would add to it by saying nothing of all this to his step-father.

'Mama would forgive me,' said Clay, 'but Nat wouldn't, and I'd rather he kept his illusions – he and Aunt Lucy and the rest of them. It's kind of queer, when you come to think of it, that your father should have been the only one I couldn't fool. He told me he believed in "Live and Let Live", and that if you'd fallen in love with an out-and-out no-good with your eyes open, he wouldn't have raised too much dust, because it might have worked out. But he reckoned that if you took on someone you thought was as high-minded and strait-laced as yourself, and then found that you'd been tricked into marrying a rascal, it would just about destroy you, and he wasn't going to stand for you being sold a fake. Maybe I should have listened to him. But then you won't be buying a fake now. You know what I'm like and you won't expect me to behave like a plaster saint. It'll work out, dear. I know it.'

Hero did not say anything, and he lifted her hand and kissed it lightly, and went away, looking considerably less hag-ridden than he had been at any time since he had heard of Zorah's death. He was sorry about that. And about what had happened to Hero. But he could not help thinking that it had not ended as disastrously as it might have done. Or at least, not as far as he himself was concerned.

31

Mr Potter, unrecognizable in the garb of a Banyan shopkeeper, was admitted to a quiet room in the Sultan's Palace where he found Captain Emory Frost sleeping the sleep that should by rights belong only to the just, and awakened him without compunction.

'You seems to be doin' all right,' remarked Batty, gazing sourly about him. 'Comfortable little place you 'ave 'ere.'

'Very, thank you. Was that all you woke me up to tell me?'

'Not likely! I don't go running me 'ead into an 'ornets' nest just for the sake of 'aving a chat. Thought you'd like to know as I been back to The Dolphins' 'Ouse.'

'Damned silly of you,' observed Rory, yawning. 'You might have been caught.'

'No fear. I goes in with old Ram Dass as 'is assistant, selling cloth an' such. Someone 'as to find out 'ow the nipper is. Misses 'er Ma, she does, poor babby.'

Rory made no comment, but Batty saw the muscles of his jaw tighten and a corner of his mouth twitch, and recognizing those signs was partially satisfied. 'What y'going to do with 'er?' he demanded.

'She's all right where she is for the time being. All those women spoil her: and so do you!'

'Maybe I does, but now that we got to play 'Ide-and-Seek with young Danny, I ain't there to do it. And no more are you.'

'What do you expect me to do about it?'

'That's what I come to see you for. We ought to take 'er away. It ain't safe for 'er to be around in these parts just now.'

'Oh, talk sense, Batty! No one's going to harm her. If you think either Dan or old Edwards would lift a finger against her you must be losing your mind!'

'It ain't that kind of 'arm I'm talking of,' said Batty angrily. 'You been too bloody busy with your blasted self to keep your lugs open, but I been 'earing things that I don't like.'

'What sort of things?'

'Remember them yarns we 'eard on the coast, about a plague? Well, Ibrahim 'e meets a cove off a dhow from Kilwa last night, and this cove tells 'im that it's the black cholera, and that it's rampagin' all across Africa. The Masai are dying like flies, and 'ole slave caravans 'ave been lost – 'e says 'e meets a man who was the only one left alive out of one of 'em, and this cove reaches the coast on 'is own, but dies two days later. I don't like the sound of that, and I'd be a lot 'appier if young Amrah were took out of this, for if it's got to the coast there's no saying but it won't get 'ere.'

'Or anywhere else, for that matter,' said Rory, 'which means that she's safer here than she would be anywhere on the mainland. Even if these stories are not exaggerated there is a good chance that it'll miss Zanzibar, for there won't be any more slave dhows in until May.'

'I weren't thinking of the mainland,' said Batty. 'If them yarns is true there ain't no place in all Africa that would be safe. I was thinking maybe we could take the old *Virago* across to Cutch, or try our 'and at a bit of pearling off Ceylon. Wouldn't do none of us no 'arm to get outer this place for a spell – what with Danny and 'is dinky little shellbacks a'raging and a'roaring round as fierce as lions. What do you say?'

'It's a thought,' said Rory. 'When's the *Virago* likely to be back?'

'Well, you told us to light out for the Amirantes and stay clear of Zanzibar for a matter of a month or so – or until we 'ear that Dan 'as shifted 'is 'unting grounds. So I suspicions that Ralub'll carry out your orders.'

'Just as you did,' observed Rory dryly.

'*Someone* 'ad to stay and see that you didn't go bargin' about the island getting yourself 'ung,' retorted Batty defensively. ''Sides, I didn't like leaving young Amrah with just them silly women to look after 'er. 'Ajji Ralub is a sensible man 'oo can be trusted not to behave foolish, so I reckon 'e'll be back soon as it's safe. And when 'e comes I 'ope you'll 'ave the sense to pick up the nipper and light out of 'ere – which'll keep you clear of the Colonel and the cholera both. I don't like neither of 'em, and I'm for loping off quick!'

'I'll think about it,' said Rory. 'I might even see if I can get the Sultan to put a stop to any more ships from the coast putting in here for a while. Don't go getting yourself caught, Uncle.'

Mr Potter made a noise that dismissed the suggestion as one beneath contempt, and left. And that same evening, over a game of chess in the Sultan's private apartments, Rory brought up the matter of the cholera, and Majid dismissed it with a wave of the hand. He had, he said, heard similar tales – a dozen at least. And if it were true that the Masai were being decimated, it was no bad thing, since they were a savage and war-like people, unsuitable as slaves and much given to attacking the caravans of slave traders in order to train their young men in battle. They would be no loss, and the cholera was not in the least likely to reach the coast.

'It is nothing,' said Majid lightly. 'I tell you, cholera has never yet come to us from that direction, so you need not fear that it will come now. And since our treaty with the English forbids us to import any slaves from the mainland during the months of the north-east monsoon, the risk of it being brought here by sea is negligible. That is one of the advantages of living on an island. But rest assured, if we hear it has broken out in any of the coastal towns we shall see that any dhow from an infected port is forbidden to send men ashore, or to anchor too near the town. The merchants and the Customs House officials will see to that!'

His hand hovered for a moment above the ivory army: 'The Lieutenant is still here,' he remarked pensively, advancing his bishop to capture one of the Captain's pawns: 'And his ship.'

'I am aware of it,' sighed Rory, studying the chequered board. 'Very tiresome of them.'

'Are you also aware that they watch your house night and day, and this morning I receive yet another call from the British Consul, who enquires once again if I have any knowledge as to where you may be found or what you are doing?'

'What did you tell him?'

'The truth. As I did not know in which room you were at that precise moment, or if you were engaged in eating or sleeping or meditating upon your many sins, I was able to reply that I had no idea.'

'Did he believe you?'

'I don't think so. He is not a fool.'

'No, alas. How long do you suppose they'll keep this up?' Rory moved another pawn, unmasking a knight: 'Check.'

Majid clicked his tongue and frowned above the chessboard, and after due deliberation moved a second bishop to cover his queen and said: 'As far as the good Colonel is concerned, until he leaves Zanzibar: which I think will be soon, for his health is not good and he has applied to be sent on leave to his own country. But without the *Daffodil* he can do little, and it is a great pity that the Lieutenant cannot be persuaded to go and look for slave ships and slavers elsewhere. I tell the Colonel that I am sure many slaves are being illegally taken out of my territories on the coast, and he agrees with me and does nothing. It is scandalous!'

Rory laughed, and took his bishop with an innocent-looking pawn. 'Check.'

'*Bah!*' said Majid irritably. 'Why did I not see that?'

'Because I didn't mean you to.'

'You are indeed a son of Eblis; but you have not defeated me yet, and I take your pawn – so!'

'And I, alas! take your queen. Checkmate.'

Majid scowled at his cornered monarch, laughed ruefully and swept an impatient hand across the board, scattering ivory chessmen over the soft blues and reds of the Shiraz carpet. 'You defeat me too easily today, for I am thinking all the time of other things. Tomorrow I shall beat you; but tonight I am too worried.'

'Why? What have you got to worry about? Your beloved brother Bargash is safely out of the way in Bombay, and no one seems to be trying to murder you at the moment. The dhows have gone – and without your having to pay them anything out of your own pocket – and the chances are that the next time they come your disillusioned subjects will give them such a warm reception that they'll think twice about coming again. On top of that you've got your hands on enough treasure to keep you in comfort for a good many years. You shouldn't have a care in the world!'

'It is not for myself that I am anxious. It is for you, my friend. I do not like it that this English gun-ship stays in harbour and will not go.'

'I shouldn't let that worry you too much,' said Rory, gathering up the scattered chessmen and restoring them to their box. 'It's always possible that it is not staying here solely on my account.'

'That is true. I have heard that the Lieutenant is much enamoured of the young American lady, and while she is here he will not be anxious to leave. Men in love are all the same – whatever their race. But it is also true that the British Consul has vowed vengeance on you, and he is a stubborn man. And so too is the Lieutenant.'

'If it comes to that, so am I,' said Rory with a grin.

'Allah! do I not know it! But this time I think that you have provoked them too far, and that you are no longer safe here; either in the city or even here in my house. They think that I know where you are, but I do not think that they suspect yet that you are here – within a spear's throw of them. But once they learn it, as they will! I would not trust either of them not to demand you of me at the gun point, or to refrain from bombarding my Palace if I refused to deliver you up.'

'To be frank with you, neither would I,' admitted Rory. 'In fact I've been thinking for the last day or two that it's high time I moved to some less vulnerable spot. I'd hate to see the *Daffodil* dropping anchor out there one morning with her guns trained on your windows.'

'I too,' confessed Majid. 'And I have been wondering where would be the safest place for you to go. You cannot go to your house in the city or to the one on the coast, since both are now watched; and it would be unwise to try and leave by sea. But I have remembered a little house near the shore beyond Mkokotoni, that belongs to a cousin of mine who is at present in Muscat I will send word to the caretaker that he is to see that you are well looked after and that no one knows that you are there, and also to your ship to tell them where you are, so that they can arrange with you what is to be done. If you will take my advice you will remain there quietly and in hiding until the Colonel has departed for England, and the young lady who has the Lieutenant's heart has gone back to America and he has got tired of waiting for you. Then it may be safe for you to come back. But not until then.'

'I expect you are right,' conceded Rory philosophically. 'But it sounds as though I am in for a damned dull time.'

'It is better to be dull than dead! And if you do not leave the city quickly, I think you will very soon be dead. As for your servants and the child in The Dolphins' House, they will come to no harm, since it is only your blood that is required.'

'I know it. When do I leave, and how?'

'Tomorrow night, I think. Some of the women will be visiting friends in a house beyond the Malindi Bazaar, and you shall go with them as one of the guard and separate yourself from them near the creek, where there will be horses waiting and a man who will be your guide. It will be simple enough to arrange; and safer than remaining here where there are too many peeping eyes and chattering tongues – and too many takers of bribes!'

Majid had been as good as his word. He had arranged it, and Rory had left by the women's gate of the Palace after dark and by lantern light, wearing Arab dress and forming one of an escort of eunuchs and armed guards who convoyed a dozen closely veiled, chattering women through the tortuous maze of twisting, turning, intersecting streets, lanes and alleyways of the planless city. The sight of such a procession was too common a one to arouse much interest, and though they had twice been stopped by Baluchi soldiers and once by a naval patrol from the *Daffodil*, no one had cared to inconvenience a party of women from the Palace, and they had been allowed to proceed after the briefest of halts.

The bridge over the creek had been the greatest hazard, because by that time Rory had separated himself from the procession and was alone. But presumably Majid had bribed or otherwise dealt with the men who should have been watching it, for no one disputed his passage. There was no sign of any guard, and he passed safely over the malodorous creek that separated the Stone Town from the squalid shanties of the African Town, and found two men awaiting him on the open ground beyond it.

One of them was Mr Potter, with whom Rory exchanged a few whispered words before mounting the spare horse, and with the guide that Majid had provided, riding away toward the open country while Batty returned by unfrequented byways to the house of a friend in the city.

It had been a long, dark ride, taken more often than not at a foot's pace, and they had broken their journey at midnight near Chuni and slept in an empty hut on the edge of a clove plantation: awakening to eat cold food in the first grey light of dawn before riding on with more speed through the wet grass and jungle scrub, while day broadened over the palm-clad hills to their right and the north-east Trade Wind, sweeping across the island, whipped their cloaks out into billowing folds behind them.

There were few roads in this part of the island, and those few mere cart-tracks or footpaths between villages, and except for an occasional peasant glimpsed at a distance in a cane field or coconut grove, they saw no one, and the countryside seemed quiet and deserted and very tranquil. The sun had risen by the time they came within sight of Mkokotoni, and they skirted the little village, taking care to keep out of sight, and rode on up the coast with the wind-ruffled sea lying blue and foam-flecked to their left, until a branch of the wandering track took them at last through a grove of palms to a small, two-storeyed Arab house, protected by a high wall built of coral rag and shaded by orange trees and pomegranates.

The ancient caretaker who admitted them led away the tired horses to a stable at present tenanted by a single lethargic donkey, and Rory went up to the flat rooftop, and looking down on the tranquil domain that was to provide him with a safe hiding-place for the next few weeks, decided that it might have been a good deal worse. The place was certainly quiet enough, and its location so remote and secluded that few people were likely to hear that anyone other than the caretaker and his elderly, silent wife were living there. And neither Dan nor Colonel Edwards had sufficient men at their disposal to enable them to do more than watch the approaches to the city.

The house that belonged to the Sultan's cousin stood near the edge of a line of low, coral cliffs, facing the little island of Tumbatu that lies off-shore in the long curving bay above Mkokotoni. A coconut grove sheltered it from the prevailing winds and it was a peaceful spot; and though Rory Frost had never entertained any particular hankering for peace, he was surprised to find that the prospect of spending several idle weeks if not months there, with no company but his own and nothing to do but eat, sleep and swim, or lie on his back and look at the sky, was in no way unpleasant. *I must be getting old*, he thought. And was disconcerted by the reflection.

The guide whom Majid had sent with him returned to the city that night, and the days that followed were long and very quiet. Christmas came and went, and still the shore stretched white and empty below the low cliffs of coral, and sometimes a dhow would pass on the far side of Tumbatu, and sometimes the *Daffodil* – patrolling the coast to watch for the *Virago* and make sure that she was not hiding in any small bay or deep-water creek, or lurking off-shore in the lee of an islet. But the only craft that ever ventured into the narrow channel separating Tumbatu from the main Island was an occasional *kyack*; the little island-built canoes belonging to fishermen who lived in small scattered communities among the palm trees and pandanus and casuarina scrub that fringed the coral beaches.

For the first time in twenty years Rory found himself with nothing to do and unlimited leisure in which to do it, and the experience, paradoxically enough, proved both restful and disturbing.

It was pleasant to lie out naked on the lonely beach in the shade of a palm tree, watching the sandcrabs sidling to and fro among the sea-wrack, and listening to the tide lapping against the long shore and the wind-worn rocks. To swim in cool, glass-clear water above a multicoloured submarine world of trees and gardens, where shoals of brilliant fish darted through the branching coral and his own shadow followed him, three fathoms below, across the reefs and rocks and the white bars of sand. To walk through the long aisles of the coconut grove, or sit on the flat roof of the house on the cliffs and watch the sun set behind the mountains of Africa, or the lightning flicker in the belly of the far distant clouds.

There were days of steaming heat when the palm fronds drooped in the humid air and the birds perched motionless in the shade with beaks agape; when nothing moved and the sea seemed made of molten metal. Days when he would awake to the drumming of rain on the roof and find the world about him veiled in mist and hidden by slanting rods of grey and silver, and blessedly cool again. And other days when thunder rolled above the island and wind and storm swept across it, setting the palms lashing to and fro like demented broomsticks at a Witches' Sabbath while the sea raced white and roaring up the beach to crash in flying foam against the coral cliffs.

The storms would pass and the sun rise in a cloudless sky, and once again it would be hot and still, with nothing to tell of the furious hours except the scattered coconuts and shredded palm fronds, and here and there a broken tree and a dead butterfly . . .

Sitting one evening on the low parapet of the roof and watching the first star glimmer palely in a green lake of sky, Rory found himself reviewing his past life with a curious feeling of looking for the last time at the pages of a familiar book that must shortly be closed and put away for ever. As though he were an old man looking back with detachment and nostalgia on all the days that had gone: forgetting nothing, and regretting nothing – except that they would not return.

He did not know why he should feel so strongly that he had come to the end of a long road; unless it was because Batty and Majid had both been right when they had told him that this time he had gone too far and made

Zanzibar and the Sultan's territories too hot to hold him. And yet that alone did not account for it, for the *Daffodil* could not stay permanently in the harbour, and the British Consul was due to go home, from where he would be sent to some other appointment. Dan Larrimore, too, had done more than his stint of service in the tropics, so it was only a matter of keeping in hiding for a few months at most, and when Dan and the Colonel had gone it would be safe enough to return and pick up his old life once more. Only quite suddenly Rory knew he would not do it. That book was closed and the story was over.

There were other seas and other islands; and other strange and beautiful lands to explore. But once again he had the feeling that time was running out, and Authority – in the form of an acid-faced woman in black bombazine, and a heavy-jowled, cold eyed business man with mutton-chop whiskers and a gold watch-chain stretched across his stomach – was advancing with relentless swiftness to convert and exploit the wild places of the world and to drag them forward, in the sacred name of Progress, toward uniformity and a dead level of humourless hygienic money-grabbing mediocrity. Aunt Laura and Uncle Henry were on the march, and it was their seed that would inherit the earth.

Watching the stars blossom one by one in the darkening sky above the glass-still sea, Rory could hear in the silence the faint, insistent beat of a far-away drum, and the sound transformed itself to him into the feet of Progress, trampling ruthlessly forward and destroying as it came: abolishing old savageries and creating new and worse ones in their place.

The bow and arrow, the spear and the poisoned dart would go, but the sword would not be beaten into a ploughshare: it would be fashioned instead by the civilized West into weapons that would destroy by the hundred thousand – because men were covetous and the world no longer wide enough. The iron ships and iron trains would make an end of old barriers and older customs, and the harnessing of steam and gas and electricity would mean larger and larger cities and more and more factories – and a soaring birthrate. It would not be long before there were twice as many people in the world as there had been when he, Emory Frost, had been born in that quiet old manor house in Kent. And after that three times as many; and then four – and five . . .

There would be more Restrictions, more Discipline, more Laws. And more Tyranny! . . . all the things he had rebelled against. There would be no escaping them, and he wondered if the world of the next century would be the better for them or the worse, and why he should never have realized before that what he had taken to be misfortune had, in reality, been luck in disguise. Incredible luck!

He had fancied himself ill-treated, and revenged himself by cutting loose from the ties of country and acknowledging no law. But if his fickle mother had not deserted him and his stiff-necked and embittered father had not died and left him to the untender mercies of Uncle Henry and Aunt Laura, he would in all probability have seen no more of the world than the Kentish countryside and the smoke-stained, grimy city of London. He would never even have known what he was missing, or that his generation would be among the last to see the strange and far-away places before they were overtaken, altered and finally submerged by the hungry tide of industrialization and uniformity. But he had escaped – and he had seen them.

He had traded up and down the Ivory Coast and dealt in slaves and cowries and coral, pearls and muskets and elephant tusks. He had anchored in harbours unknown to Western ships and roistered in towns that were old when London was young. He knew every port from Aden to Akabah and Suez; had crossed the Arabian sea to Bombay and Goa, bartered ivory for pearls in the Persian Gulf and marched inland across deserts of burning sand to strange, hidden cities that until then no other white man had ever seen. But before the century was out there would be steam-driven ships churning a path across those seas, and one day the old cities – if they were not destroyed by war and the bigger and better engines of destruction that men were so industriously devising – would be pulled down and swept away, and in their place would arise a flavourless uniformity of brick and mortar, populated by once-colourful people aping the white man's dress and speech, so that all cities would in time become identical masses of houses and factories, shops, boulevards and hotels, linked by trains and steamships and filled with imitation Westerners imitating Western ways.

But he had escaped – and he had seen them. He had seen the squalor and the enchantment, and known that although the world was shrinking with the relentless swiftness of a sandbar when the tide has turned, it was still, for a little while longer, a vast and mysterious place full of unexplored territories, secret cities and beautiful, beckoning horizons. And he was suddenly and sincerely sorry for all those people who would come after him and never know what it had once offered, but would think, as each generation in its turn had thought, that it was the best organized and most enlightened of all.

Yes, he had been fabulously lucky! It was strange that he should not have realized that until now. Though he supposed that he must subconsciously have known it, for the roving, lawless, swashbuckling years had not constituted an aimless journey, but a means to an end: the acquiring of a sum large enough to enable him to ruin his uncle – a sum he intended to get by fair means or foul. But he had got it even before that fabulous fortune in gold had come into his hands. The figure he had aimed at had been reached on the day that Clayton Mayo paid in good coin for a consignment of temporarily worthless rifles. Yet he had made no attempt to dispose of his ship or return to the land of his fathers, and he wondered now if he would ever do so?

Uncle Henry's hated image had suddenly become a foolish rag-and-pasteboard bogey whose arms and legs jerked to strings: a thing hardly worth revenging oneself upon. And supposing he were to return and regain his patrimony? – what then? Would he really be able to settle down to the life of an English squire, walking his acres and discussing crops and cattle, local politics and the affairs of a small market town? It seemed highly unlikely and the prospect held no allure for him. Yet there was little point in regaining his family acres only to leave them empty and idle, or sell them to some stranger.

There had been Frosts at Lyndon Gables for more than a century before its title and acres had been listed in Doomsday Book. A Frost had fought for Saxon Harold at Senlac, and ten years later his manor had been restored to his sons by Norman William. The first Emory had returned to it, one-armed, from Agincourt, and a Cavalier grandson of the Tyson Frost who had built the stately rose-brick mansion in the days of Elizabeth, had held it for King Charles and seen it reduced to a shell by Cromwell's men; and lived to rebuild it in the years of the Restoration.

Father to son, the land had been held and tilled and tended by men of his name and his blood, and it was probably better to let his unamiable cousin Rodney carry on the tradition than to leave the place to go to wrack and ruin, sold piecemeal for building lots, or as a whole to some rich industrialist who would have no feeling for the land. Someone ought to care for it and keep it, and a Frost could probably be counted upon to do that better than a stranger – if only because his roots would be deep in that particular patch of earth.

As for himself, he had no roots. Unless they were here in this island, in which for the time being he had made himself an outlaw. Yet even when both Colonel Edwards and Dan Larrimore were gone and it might once again be considered safe for him to return to the city, that safety would only last as long as Majid lived – which did not look like being over-long if he continued his present mode of life! And since Majid had no son to succeed him, one day Bargash would return and inherit the throne, and then Zanzibar would cease to be a refuge and a happy hunting-ground for Captain Rory Frost and the *Virago*. He would have to find somewhere else. Go further East, to Java or Sumatra or the islands of the Coral Sea.

A year ago, even a few months ago, such a prospect would have been alluring enough. But now that strange sensation of having come to the end of the road had brought with it an unfamiliar and disconcerting feeling of uncertainty, and of being no longer free and untrammelled: a vague disinclination to set out in search of new horizons. Perhaps it was the gold lying hidden in The House of Shade that was dragging at him like an unseen anchor; chaining him to possessions and robbing him of the desire to be free. Or perhaps . . .

Rory shook himself impatiently, and coming to his feet realized that he must have been sitting idle on the parapet for a considerable length of time, for the moon had risen and his shadow lay black on the warm stone of the rooftop.

The night was hot and very quiet, and the sea so still that it lapped against the long curve of the beach in lazy ripples that barely broke into foam, and made a sound no louder than the rustle of the dead palm leaves that stirred in the soft night breeze. The cicadas that had shrilled before moonrise and the frogs that had croaked in the marshy ground beyond the coconut grove had fallen silent and only the drum still beat.

There were always drums beating in Zanzibar, and this one was so far away that the sound was barely more than a vibration in the stillness. But for some reason the faint, insistent beat seemed to hold an odd note of urgency that added to Rory's sudden feeling of restlessness and dissatisfaction, and he came down from the roof, and walking swiftly across the quiet garden, summoned the dozing caretaker who slept by night in a small brick-built cell to one side of the massive gateway in the outer wall.

Kerbalou shuffled out yawning, and lifting the heavy bar, drew the door open to allow Rory to pass out, wondering sleepily where the white man could be going at this time of night and on foot, since except for a few isolated huts belonging to fishermen there was no village of any size for several miles.

But Rory had only gone out to drown his restlessness and cool his hot body in the placid sea, and though he had not been particularly successful in the first of these objectives, a long swim out towards Tumbatu and back had both refreshed him and made him ready for sleep. The deserted beach was white in the moonlight and the sea a shimmering expanse of watered silk, and he leant against the trunk of a coconut palm that stretched low over the sand, and rested a moment in the shadow of the coral cliffs; looking out towards the steel-grey shadow of Tumbatu while the night breeze breathed coolly on his body.

Something moved in the silver stillness, and he discovered that he was not the only person abroad that night, for there was a small boat flitting down the channel; a thing as ghostly and insubstantial as a moth in the moonlight. It was a fisherman's *kyack*, a common enough sight in those waters, and he watched it idly as it tacked and ran into shore barely twenty feet from where he stood among the shadows. He heard the prow grate upon the wet sand and the slap of the sail as it swung idle in the light breeze, and then a man stepped out of it into the shallow water and turned to peer down into the bottom of the boat as though examining his catch.

The night was so still that Rory could hear the newcomer's hard breathing, and another sound from inside the boat that might have been the flapping of a dying fish. But when the man straightened up he held neither fish nor nets, but only a large tin box and a small bundle that presumably contained food or clothing which he placed on the dry sand out of reach of the tide. Returning to the *kyack* he lowered the sail, but instead of drawing it further up the beach he waded out, thrusting it strongly before him, and pushed it off into deep water where the current that ran between Tumbatu and the main island took it and drew it out gently, and carried it away from the island. It seemed to be riding low as though it were still weighed, but the man stood waist-deep in the glittering water and watched it drift away down the long moonlit coast. And when at last it vanished he turned and came slowly back to retrieve his possessions, and lifting them, passed within a yard or two of where Rory stood leaning against the palm trunk in the shadows.

The moonlight fell full upon him, and Rory saw that he was a negro, and that he was labouring under some strong emotion that might have been excitement or fear: unless it was only exhaustion, for he had been paddling to increase the *kyack*'s speed. Beads of sweat glistened on his forehead and trickled down his face and neck, and his eyes seemed to protrude unnaturally from their sockets, white-rimmed and staring. Rory concluded that he was probably a runaway slave, who had stolen the *kyack* from a fishing village further up the coast or on the mainland – and possibly filched some of his master's goods as well, for the moonlight glinted on a heavy silver thumb-ring set with a flat piece of glass or crystal the size of a Cape dollar: a bright, glittering thing that stood out with startling whiteness on the ebony hand. If this were so, he would have turned the *kyack* adrift in the hope that it would run aground far down the coast and serve to mislead any pursuit.

Good luck to him! thought Rory idly, watching the dark figure pad on down the white stretch of sand and turn in among a thicket of pandanus and casuarina scrub to be lost to sight in the shadows. He had a fellow feeling for law-breakers and hunted men, and though he had himself traded in slaves, he saw no reason why he should assist in apprehending any who had sufficient spirit to make a bid for freedom. Or any necessity for making his own presence known.

He straightened up, yawning, and became aware that the light breeze that had brought the *kyack* to land had died away, and that the far-away drum that he had heard earlier that night was still beating, but more audibly now; as though it had come nearer and been joined by a second or even a third. There were mosquitoes too, droning shrilly in the shadows, and he slapped at them with an impatient hand and rewinding the loin-cloth that was his sole garment, walked up the uneven path to the cliff-top, and through the grass and the grey casuarinas to the house.

He had expected to find its aged custodian asleep, and was surprised to find him not only awake but standing a yard or two outside the gate, facing inland with his head cocked on one side as though he were listening. The moonlight that turned his grey hairs and venerable beard to silver glinted oddly in his staring eyeballs, as it had glinted on the negro's, and there was that in his face that made Rory say sharply: 'What is it? What troubles you?'

'*The Drums!*' said Kerbalou in a whisper. 'Do you not hear the Drums?'

'What of it? They are beating for a wedding, or a feast. There are always drums by night.'

'Not these drums!' The old man shuddered and Rory heard his teeth chatter. 'It is the Sacred Drums that are beating. The hidden drums of the Mwenyi Mkuu!'

'That is foolishness,' said Rory shortly. 'Dunga is many miles to the southward and even on a night such as this the sound would not carry a tenth of the distance. It is a *nagoma* in Mkokotoni or Potoa. Or some child beating a tom-tom in one of the fishermen's huts.'

'No tom-tom makes such a sound. Those are drums – the Drums of Zanzibar! If you were not a white man you would know it too, but perhaps it is only to us of the Island that they speak. Once before, when I was young – only once in all my life – have I heard them. On the night that the curse of the Great Drought fell upon the Island because of the capture and escape of the Great Lord, the Mwenyi Mkuu. No man laid a hand upon them that night, yet all men heard them sound; for the evil spirits beat upon them, foretelling disaster, and there followed three years of drought and famine. Who knows what they speak of now?'

'Your ears deceive you, my father,' said Rory. 'That sound speaks only of dance in some nearby village.'

'Nay,' whispered Kerbalou. 'It speaks of death!'

32

A storm broke over the Island shortly after dawn, and Rory awoke fancying that he could still hear drums. But the sound that had aroused him proved to be no more than the monotonous creak and crash of a shutter that had broken loose from its fastening and was banging to and fro in the wind.

He lay and listened to it in mounting irritation, for he had passed a restless night and was feeling tired and bad-tempered. For some unaccountable reason he had been unable to dismiss Kerbalou's absurd assertion with regard to the drums, and it had stayed with him throughout the hot night, troubling his dreams and haunting his wakeful hours as insistently and urgently as the distant throbbing that had not ceased until the sky began to pale with the dawn.

Even now, lying awake in the grey wetness of the stormy morning and listening to the scream of the wind through the coconut grove and the maddening slam of the shutter, something of that unease remained with him, and he concluded impatiently that his years in the East must, after all, have infected him with superstitions that would be considered fantastic in the bustling modern world of gas-lamps, steam-driven trains and paddle-steamers.

He would not have suspected himself of any such stupidity, and it annoyed him to think that the maunderings of an ancient grey-beard, who was presumably hard of hearing, should have the power to rob him of a night's sleep and fill him with uncomfortable forebodings. Perhaps it was just as well that he could no longer live in safety in the Island and must find some other base for his operations, because if he could allow himself to be disturbed by the sort of mumbo-jumbo that Kerbalou had talked last night, he would soon be good for nothing!

He rose impatiently and went out to deal with the shutter and get drenched in the warm, flailing rain; and peering out into the liquid greyness where the unseen breakers roared upon a beach that only a few hours ago had stretched still and silent under the tranquil sky, he wondered where the *Virago* was; and whether Batty was still at large? – presumably he must be, since had he been caught Majid would have sent word. Besides, Batty had too many friends in the city for it to be any easy matter to corner him while he wished to elude pursuit. He would be in touch with Ralub, and as soon as it was safe to do so the *Virago* would appear in the Tumbatu channel to take her Captain off, and Batty himself would rejoin them with Amrah and Dahili, who had been Zorah's maid, and they would set sail for Ceylon – or the Celebes.

Batty would be sorry to leave Zanzibar, but as long as he had Amrah he would be happy. It was strange that Batty Potter, who had fathered a brood of children and abandoned them without a qualm to the chilly mercies of orphan asylums and charitable institutions, should in his reprehensible old age have developed such a deep and selfless love for this half-caste baby who was the illegitimate offspring of another man. But there was no accounting for the vagaries of the human heart, and the fact remained that he had done so.

From the day that she had first attempted to speak his name, Amrah's tiny, grasping fingers had clutched at Batty's affections and never relaxed their hold. He was her willing and devoted slave, and she ruled him with a rod of iron and gave him in return a love and trust that should by rights have been her father's. And though Batty was apt to comment caustically on the Captain's undemonstrative attitude towards his small daughter, Rory was aware that he was secretly grateful for it, in that it allowed him to usurp the lion's share of the child's affection.

It was on Amrah's account more than Hero's that Batty had protested so strongly against that vengeful kidnapping, because he had known very well where it must lead: as Rory too had known, though at the time he had been too blind with rage to care.

I've made my bed, thought Rory, *but I'm not the only one who will have to lie on it – more's the pity!* Batty and Amrah and Ralub were only three of those who would have to share it . . .

The storm blew itself out before midday, and an hour or two later the sky was clear again and the sun blazed down on the drenched earth, drinking the raindrops from the grass and the trees and bringing out the scent of tamarisk and jasmine and crushed leaves. Towards evening, as the air began to cool, Rory went out to the stables and was annoyed to find that the mare, Zafrâne, was still suffering from the effects of a strained tendon acquired through putting her hoof into a rat-hole during a morning canter the previous week.

'The swelling has almost gone,' said Kerbalou, running a gnarled and expert hand across the satiny skin; 'but it would be unwise to ride her yet.'

Rory proffered lumps of raw sugar which Zafrâne accepted gratefully, and went out to take his evening exercise on foot, turning south along the coast in the direction of Mkokotoni in preference to the bleaker northern tip of the Island. The wind had dropped, and since the tide was going out and he could see no sign of ships, he left the shelter of the trees to walk along the wet sands of the open shore: and twenty minutes later, where the long, low headlands reach out into the sea and the mangroves creep down in green, tentacled ranks to meet the salt water, he came across a solitary *kyack* stranded in a shadowed cleft between two rough outcrops of coral rock.

It lay tilted on one side where the sea had flung it; its bows caught and crushed in the vice-like grip of the coral, and a dense cloud of flies buzzing above it. But despite the noise of the flies he might still have passed it without seeing it, had it not been for the obnoxious smell: a sickly and all too familiar scent of corruption that polluted the sweet evening air and brought him over to inspect the broken piece of flotsam that lay half hidden on the reef.

He glanced down at it with a grimace of disgust, and was turning away when he stopped abruptly and stood very still, and then turned back swiftly, and pulling a handkerchief out of the bosom of the Arab robe he wore, held it over his nose and mouth and bent to examine the pitiful thing that lay huddled on the bottom of the stranded *kyack*. The thing that he had heard move in the boat last night, and that had not been a feebly flapping fish, but a dying man.

The signs were plain upon it and easy enough to read, and presently he straightened up again, and removing his clothes, folded them about the pistol that he had carried day and night for the last month or so, and having cached them in a cleft of the coral, waded out into the inlet to soak his handerchief in sea water and bind it about his face.

Returning to the *kyack* he managed by dint of considerable effort to free the prow from the rocks, and having salvaged the remains of the coir rope that had once been attached to the now vanished sail, he lashed it across the quiet occupant to ensure that he should not leave, and dragging the broken boat out into deeper water sank it where even a spring tide would not uncover it. After which he swam out to sea for a hundred yards or so, and dived again and again to clean his head.

Landing at length on the narrow headland, he walked back to where he had left his clothes, and removing only the pistol, washed the rest in the sea and spread it out on the hot sand to dry in the long rays of the evening sunlight.

The breeze no longer smelt of corruption, but only of salt water and the mud flats where the crabs scuttled and clicked as the tide drew slowly out, leaving the roots of the mangroves bare. The sky overhead had paled from ultramarine to a cool expanse of palest turquoise, and the west flamed with colour and flaunted long streamers of molten gold that reflected themselves in the pearly sea and tinged the coral reefs with splendour. But Rory sat with his hands clasped about his knees and noticed none of these things.

He had no doubt at all that the broken *kyack* that he had just sunk in fifteen feet of water was the one he had seen set adrift last night. And he knew now why it had seemed to be weighted, and also why the unknown negro had abandoned it – and been afraid. The negro would have to be found as soon as possible, which might not be easy, since he had almost a full day's start, and if he had reached a village it might already be too late. But he had been tired, and so there was just a chance that he had lain hidden among the trees and the casuarina scrub to rest for a while before moving inland.

Rory came to his feet, and finding that the loose cotton robe and waist-cloth were at least partially dry, put them on and walked quickly back along the beach towards the spot where he had seen the man turn in among the trees on the previous night.

A last ray of the setting sun pierced the thickets of casuarina, coarse grass and pandanus that choked the cliff edge below the tall ranks of palms. It glinted brightly on something made of metal, and Rory, threading his way through the undergrowth, saw that it was a cheap tin box, lying open and empty outside a dilapidated palm-thatched hut.

The hut was small and roughly constructed, and looked as though it had weathered several monsoons; but because it stood some way back from the beach and was overgrown with wild grape vine, he had not noticed it before. He approached with some caution, but it was not possible to move silently in such surroundings, and he heard a rustle from inside it and the next moment a man crept out of it on all fours and stood up uncertainly, blinking in the last blaze of the sun. It was the negro whom he had last seen by moonlight, and recognizing him, Rory was conscious of an overwhelming relief that seemed to relax every tense nerve and taut muscle in his body. He was in time!

The man's ebony skin seemed tinged with grey and had the appearance of being loose on his great body, and he spoke in a hoarse blurred voice as though he were very old, or drunk: '*Jambo . . . habari za kutwa?*' (Greetings – what news of the morning?)

'*Sijambo!* The day has gone, and it is evening,' said Rory. 'What do you do here, and what of him who came with you?'

'He died,' said the man thickly. 'They all died. Our dhow put in at Pangani, and we saw men falling in the streets and came away quickly; thirty-eight all told – or so we thought. But one had come aboard without our knowledge and hidden himself, hoping to escape the sickness, and he brought it with him and died. But the pestilence stayed and struck us down like ripe nuts in a gale, until at last only two were left alive – myself and an Arab from Sharja on the Gulf. A wind took the dhow and ran it upon the reef near the mouth of the river, and we two who were left took the gold that the dead had no use for, and the pearls and silver also, and saved ourselves. We stole a fisherman's boat, and the currents brought us across the sea to this place. But the Arab had taken the sickness and he died as we reached the shore, and I only am left of all those who ten days ago left Pangani alive. I only!'

The man straightened himself with an effort, holding on to the door-post of the makeshift hut, and began to laugh loudly and foolishly, and pointing with a wavering hand in the direction of the violet silhouette of Africa behind which the sun had dipped and vanished, he said, gasping: 'My tribe and all the tribes who live in the great country that lies behind those mountains are dead – all dead. But I, Olambo, have escaped! I am safe. And rich – and rich . . .'

He looked quickly over his shoulder as though to see if they were alone, and sinking his voice to a cracked whisper said: 'I have buried it all beneath the floor of this hut; all but two pieces of silver with which I shall buy food, and the ring which was fair payment. And when I return I shall dig it up again and buy land and slaves and become great. But first I must find a village. Where is the nearest village?'

'To the southward,' said Rory, jerking his chin in the direction of Mkokotoni. 'But you cannot go there. Have you no food here?'

'What is that to you?' said the man truculently. 'And why should I not go? I am rich and I go where I choose!'

He turned away, and Rory jerked the pistol out of the folds of his waist-cloth and shot him through the back of the head.

The crack of the explosion seemed startlingly loud in the quiet thickets under the high roof of palm fronds, but the leaves muffled the sound and there was no echo, and the man fell on his face and lay still.

Rory stood looking down at him for a minute or two, watching for any sign of life. But the bullet had entered at the base of the skull, and the man had died instantly and without even knowing that he was hit. There was no need for a second shot. Rory replaced the pistol, and retracing his steps came out upon the beach once more, and returned with all speed to the house. The gold was already beginning to fade from the sky and there were several things that must be done before it became too dark to see. Things which he preferred to do himself.

He fetched matches and lamp-oil from the house and a bundle of straw from the stables, and went back to the derelict hut and the sprawled body of the man who had died without knowing that the pestilence he had thought to escape had already laid its hand upon him.

The thickets were full of birds twittering noisily as they prepared to settle down for the night, but the shadows were green and still and the scent from a nearby bush of wild jasmine mitigated that tell-tale stench of faeces. For a moment Rory was tempted to cover the body with branches and pull down the hut above it, leaving the jungle to obliterate both. But he knew that he could not risk it. There was no telling when the owner of the hut or some wandering fisherman might not take it into his head to make use of the shelter it afforded, so he set his teeth and poured lamp-oil over the corpse and spread straw above it, and splashing more oil on the walls and roof of the hut, was thankful that the wind and the sun had between them dried out a large part of the moisture from even so sheltered a spot as this.

He did not enter the hut or make any attempt to remove the riches that the man had buried beneath it, though if it were the accumulated wealth of thirty-eight men from the Gulf it might total an impressive amount – even subtracting the probable value of the pearls. But such considerations seemed, at the moment, of no importance, and he barely spared them a thought as he emptied the last of the lamp-oil over the threshold and struck a match.

The straw burned easily enough, and he fed the fire with the dead brown debris of fallen palm fronds and the rotted husks of coconuts. The hut at first only smouldered, but presently it caught alight and burned fiercely, crackling and hissing and sending up choking clouds of smoke to be lost in the branches above it.

The glare was a beacon in the gathering twilight, and if it burned until darkness fell it would be seen for miles. But Rory did not waste time worrying over such considerations, since it was unlikely to attract the attention of anyone who would be sufficiently interested to ask questions or attempt to put it out.

The nauseous fumes from the crackling pyre fouled the twilight and caught at his throat, so that even standing up-wind of the oily smoke he could not escape it, and he coughed and choked and held a folded handkerchief over his face. But he did not turn away until he was sure that not only the hut but a circle of bushes around it were well alight, and that there was nothing left that might hold or carry the infection.

It was dark when he left the thickets and came out again on the shore and into the clean air, and once again he went down to the sea and bathed in it and washed out his clothes, and carrying the wet bundle under one arm, returned to the house. Flames still gleamed brightly among the shadows and sparks and smoke rose above the palm fronds. But the blaze was dying down and it was unlikely to spread, for the grass and the tangle of casuarina, pandanus and wild coffee were green and moist and lush from the monsoon, and beyond the radius of the fiercest heat they had shrivelled but not burned.

The night had been clear and calm and breathlessly hot, and Rory dragged a string cot up to the open roof and slept out in the white moonlight. And each time he woke he saw the orange glow among the trees near the cliff edge and a smudge of smoke against the stars, and smelt the sickly odour of smouldering greenstuff and charred flesh. But he heard no drums, and once, as he was dropping off to sleep again after an hour of tossing wakefulness, he thought that if those he had heard on the previous night had indeed been the Drums of Zanzibar, then this was the disaster they had warned of, and he had averted it. But if the cholera had reached the coast there would be other dhows and other *kyacks*, for the seas that lay between the Island and the mainland were narrow ones, and all too easy to cross with a favourable wind. Batty had been right, and when the *Virago* returned they must quit these waters and sail beyond the reach of the sickness that was ravaging all Africa.

By the morning the Trades were blowing strongly again. And all that day it rained; and all the next. Warm, steady rain that fell in noisy cataracts from the gutters at the roof edge, and sluiced off the palm fronds to whip the earth into a splashing sea of mud. Fresh droves of creeping, flying insects hatched out and found their way into every room, and the sound of falling rain made a background for the silence of the isolated house.

It was impossible to go out, and Rory wandered through the empty rooms, restless and curiously uneasy; making plans and discarding them, and wondering what had become of Batty and why he had heard no word from Majid, and whether it would be safe to return to *Kivulimi* – which would at least be preferable to this lonely, god-forsaken spot. But he knew that The House of Shade was certain to be watched, and the fact that he had had no news meant that the *Daffodil* was still in port. And in any case, it was here that the *Virago* was to call for him. He would have to stay. And it was his own fault: he had brought this upon himself by abducting and raping Hero Hollis.

Considering that episode in the long, wet, idle hours, he could not understand how he had come to do such a thing. Rage alone did not account for it. He had been enraged before, and almost as greatly as when Batty had brought him the ugly story of Zorah's death; but he had not reacted to it by losing his head and behaving with the brutal and shortsighted stupidity that he had displayed in the matter of Clayton Mayo's betrothed. Not that he could even pretend to short-sightedness, because at the back of his mind he had been perfectly well aware of the probable consequences of such an act, and he had had no desire to burn his boats and find himself outlawed from Zanzibar. Yet he had done it. Deliberately, and in a cold fury that he could not explain away by saying that it was solely on Zorah's account.

His first reaction on hearing of that tragedy had been a savage anger against all those Europeans who despised the East as uncivilized, and yet considered that when living there the colour of their own skins gave them the right to behave as they pleased, and automatically placed them in a superior – and governing – class. It had seemed an excellent thing to him to set the Gulf raiders on to knocking a portion of the contempt and superiority out of some of them, and he had promised himself, too, that when he found out the name of the man who was directly responsible, he would give him a thrashing that he would remember for life. It was only when he discovered that the man was Clayton Mayo that he had lost his head and his temper and his sense of proportion, and planned an iniquitous revenge that had ended by putting him in jeopardy of a summary trial and a swift hanging, and turned him into a fugitive – hiding in an empty, echoing house on the cliffs, watching for the sails of a ship and waiting for news.

He had jeopardized them all: Batty and little Amrah, Hajji Ralub and Ibrahim; Jumah, Daoud, Hadir and a dozen others . . . and for what? It would have been easy enough, when Colonel Edwards had issued that ultimatum, to call off Omar-bin-Omar's men and content himself with thrashing Clayton Mayo in a manner that would have damaged that handsome lady-killer's features and made him unattractive to look at for several months. And since the Colonel appeared to be aware of the circumstances of Zorah's death, it was unlikely that either he or Clayton's step-father would have raised a finger in protest. They would, on the contrary, have considered him justified and let the matter drop.

But jettisoning common sense and justice together with a hitherto outstanding talent for self-preservation, he had planned that unjust and archaic method of retaliation, and carried it out in the teeth of Ralub's warnings, Batty's angry opposition and the promptings of reason. And now he could not conceive what had made him do it. Or, in spite of its disastrous consequences, feel the least regret for having done so!

Three days of rain that seemed like the prelude to another Flood kept Rory penned up and plagued by memories, uneasiness and ill-temper in the misty, untenanted house. But on the fourth morning the sky was clear again and the day breathlessly hot, and he went back along the cliff-top through the pandanus and the coconut palms, and found that the ashes and the burnt fragments left by the fire had been washed into the earth, and the rank jungle grass was already springing up to cover what little remained of the blackened ruin, the wreck of a tin box and some charred bones that had once been a man.

But the sight brought him little satisfaction, for he could not forget the negro's story. Or that Pangani and the coastal ports were all too near, and that there would be other dhows and other stowaways trying to escape the plague that was burning its way like a slow fire across Africa. He could only hope that Majid would be as good as his word and that he and the merchants and Customs officials would see to it that no man landed in Zanzibar from an infected port, and that if the news was bad, that they would close the harbour against all coastal shipping. At least the wind had died, and from the look of the sky they were in for a period of flat calm: which was not a thing he would normally have been grateful for, since it betokened a period of grinding heat. But in the present circumstances it could prove a god-send, for though it would seriously delay the *Virago*, it would also prevent dhows and fishing boats from the coast from reaching Zanzibar.

He turned from the burned patch among the steaming green thickets and went down to bathe feeling a little easier in his mind. But though the sea levelled out until it lay as still as oiled silk, and evening brought no breath of breeze to ruffle its calm surface or sway the quiet palms, his uneasiness returned; and with it a disturbing feeling of something over-looked. Something that he should have seen – that he *had* seen, but failed to comprehend or guard against.

It tugged at the fringes of his mind with the nagging persistence of a dripping tap or a creaking shutter, but though he went back step by step over every incident from the moment he had seen the negro wade ashore to the one in which he had turned away from the crackling pyre, satisfied that he had destroyed anything that might carry the infection, he could think of nothing else that he could have done. He had carried nothing away and he had walked straight from the fire into the sea. There was no need for him to trouble about it any more. And yet somewhere in the back of his mind a tap still dripped and a shutter creaked . . .

The week that followed was the hottest that he could remember for this season of year. Even at midnight, lying on the open rooftop, he found it too hot to sleep, and the slow hours dragged by in a sweating silence that was unbroken by any of the familiar sounds that he associated with the island night. Not a leaf stirred and no drums beat in the scattered villages. Even the cicadas sang no more among the palm groves or the tangled thickets, and the tired whisper of the tide did not reach the house on the cliffs. There were times when it seemed to Rory that if he were to shout aloud from the rooftop his voice would carry to Zanzibar city, so hot and still and silent were the nights.

He saw no sails in all that interminable week. The sea lay empty and shimmering, dotted with little coral islets basking in the heat-haze like mirages in a burning waste of desert, and there was no point in looking for the *Virago*, because she, like every other sailing ship on that glassy ocean, must be lying motionless and becalmed, waiting for the wind. The *Daffodil* alone would not be affected by the failure of the Trades, but there had been no sign of her for some time past, and Rory wondered if Dan had given up and left for the coast, and why there was still no word from Batty.

He considered riding into Mkokotoni for news, but knew that it would be tempting providence to do so, and he regretted that it was so seldom necessary for old Kerbalou or his wife to go to market, since at least that way he would have heard at second-hand the gossip of the villages. But as the estate provided all they required in the way of food, Kerbalou's visits to Mkokotoni were few and far between, and only undertaken when such commodities as oil or salt ran low, or his wife required a length of cloth or some trifle that must be purchased from a bazaar.

The sense of peace and quiet that Rory had at first enjoyed had been destroyed by the arrival of the doomed negro, and the slow, sweltering hours were heavy with a discomfort that was far more mental than physical, because an intolerable feeling of urgency and foreboding weighed on him and would not be shrugged off. The thought of the negro still obsessed him. Not because he had killed the man in cold blood, for that had been necessary and he would have done it again. But because of something that was in some way connected with him, or with the broken *kyack* that now lay sunk in the channel near the reef. Something that he could not remember . . .

And then on the last day of that long week, after a night made tolerable by a refreshing breeze, he had remembered it. The thing he had seen and forgotten. The words he had overlooked.

It was Kerbalou's elderly silent wife who reminded him of it, though she was unaware of having done so. Rory had been on his way to the stables when he had seen her drawing water from the well behind the house, and had gone to her assistance, for the clumsy leather bucket was heavy. She had twitched her cotton head-veil over the lower part of her face in an automatic gesture that was more a concession to convention than any attempt to hide her lined and unalluring features, and as she did so the sun glittered on the tiny piece of looking-glass that was set in a cheap silver thumb-ring that she wore on her lifted hand. And seeing it, Rory was suddenly reminded of another ring: the one that he had seen by moonlight on the negro's hand.

But it had not been on his hand when he died, and he had said something about a ring: '*All but two pieces of silver with which I shall buy food, and the ring which was fair payment . . .*'

Payment for what?

Rory turned swiftly on Kerbalou's wife and demanded to know where she had got the ring and how long she had had it, and was inordinately relieved when the startled woman replied that it had been a wedding gift and that she had worn it for more than thirty years. He carried the bucket to the kitchen door, and leaving it there went quickly away to fetch the wooden rake with which Kerbalou cleared away fallen leaves, and having found it went once again to the little clearing where the fisherman's hut had stood.

The grass was already inches tall between the black ash and the charred fragments of wood and bone, and he raked it over carefully, sifting it between his fingers, and presently came across two discoloured disks of metal. The silver coins that the negro had mentioned, which had been kept aside to buy food in the nearest village. But though he searched meticulously, covering the ground inch by inch, there was no sign of anything that could have been a ring.

Returning to the house for a spade, he dug in the circle of fire-scarred earth, and eventually uncovered a heavy bundle wrapped in a length of cheap cotton cloth. He had no idea whether the taint of infection could still linger on such an object, but this was no time for caution, and he untied the clumsy knots and laid bare the accumulated wealth of all those dead men from the dhow that had sailed so short a time ago from Pangani. It was a rich haul, and enough, as the negro had said, to keep a man in affluence for the rest of his life. Gold and silver coins, a certain amount of jewellery, and a brocade bag that was heavy with pearls. But there was no ring there either.

Rory thrust it all back into the hole where it had lain, and having stamped the earth down hard above it, scattered debris over the disturbed ground and once again went down to the sea to strip and bathe and rid himself of any taint that the dead men might have left on their lost riches. But his actions were purely mechanical for his mind was busy filling the hours that the negro had spent on the Island, and he wondered why it had never occurred to him before that others might have visited the hut before he himself had done so, and why that mention of the ring should have passed him by. He should have questioned Kerbalou.

He did so as soon as he returned to the house, and the old man replied placidly that the derelict hut in the thickets was often used by a woman of low class from Marubati, who made a living by collecting coconut fibre and fallen palm fronds from the surrounding plantations, and selling them to be made into baskets, mats and rope. He himself had seen her gleaning a bundle of such debris on the day before the last rains fell, and no doubt she had visited the hut and rested there in the noonday heat.

The day after the kyack's arrival, thought Rory. She would have found it tenanted by the last survivor of the doomed dhow, and she had probably shared her meal with him, and granted him other favours in exchange for the thumb-ring. He would have to send Kerbalou to her village to find out: and if it were true, the old man must ride to Zanzibar city with a message to Majid, warning him that the cholera might already be loose on the Island and that the village should be isolated at once.

Kerbalou had listened to the tale with a lengthening face and agreed to make enquiries. But he would not take the mare into the village, since it was known that he did not possess such a horse, and some spy of Colonel Edwards' might remark the fact and ask awkward questions.

'He has spies everywhere,' said Kerbalou, 'and it is better to be careful. But if what you suspect is true and the woman met with this man from the dhow, I will take the mare and ride to the city by night.'

He threw a folded blanket over the donkey, and mounting it, plodded off in the hot afternoon sunlight. By nightfall he had not returned, and when Rory heard men beat upon the outer gate and went down, pistol in hand, to see who called at such an hour, it was to find Jumah and Hadir waiting for him outside the wall.

Hajji Ralub had taken advantage of the winds of the previous week to return to the island, and the *Virago* had been lying becalmed off Pemba for several days. But last night's breeze had enabled them to reach a secluded anchorage on the east coast of the Island, where they had heard news of such grave import that Ralub would have sailed on by daylight and risked being seen by the *Daffodil*, except that the breeze had failed again and he did not know how long it would take him to reach Tumbatu. Therefore he had sent Jumah and Hadir on foot, and was bringing the *Virago* as soon as he could – perhaps before sunrise if the breeze were kind – and when he came the Captain must embark at once and they would immediately sail eastward. For the black cholera had reached the Island.

'And once it has gained a foothold here,' said Jumah, 'it will spread with the speed of oil thrown upon water. I have seen it strike once before, and it was deadlier than an army with swords and spears. Where is Bwana Potter and the child?'

'In the city,' said Rory; and his face greyed as he thought of the teeming labyrinth of narrow streets that turned and twisted through the capital of Zanzibar, hemmed in by houses so high that they excluded the sunlight and fresh air and held fast the heat and the stench of ordure and garbage. He too had seen what cholera could do in an overcrowded Eastern town.

Jumah said: 'Then I will bear the news and bring them here with all speed, for once the sickness reaches the Black Town there will be little hope for any, and there is not one moment to be lost.'

'No,' said Rory, 'I will go myself.'

'And be taken prisoner by the white men? Folly!' said Hadir scornfully. 'I have heard that the Baluchis and the Bwana Colonel's spies still watch The Dolphins' House.'

'In that case, neither you nor Jumah will ever get through the gate, since they know you too.'

'Maybe,' shrugged Jumah. 'But if I cannot gain entrance myself I can get word to them. Is there a horse in these stables?'

'Yes. You had better take it.'

Jumah ate a hurried meal, and was saddling up the mare when Kerbalou returned with news that was now of little importance. Rory had been right, and the woman from Marubati had gone to the hut at the cliff edge and found it tenanted by a sleeping negro who had awakened at her entrance. She had shared her food with him and fetched water, and later had lain with him in return for a silver thumb-ring set with a lump of carved crystal. Returning that same evening to her village she had sold the ring to a shopkeeper in the bazaar: explaining how she had come by it, lest he should think that she had stolen it and on that account offer less than it was worth. With the money in her hand she had begged a lift from a carter who was going to Mkokotoni, where there was to be a *nagoma* on the following day; and according to a report in the village, it was there that she had been attacked by the sickness and died within a few hours. Those who had gathered for the *nagoma* had heard the news and fled from Mkokotoni in panic, taking the infection with them, and already it had broken out in another village:

'There is no longer any need to send word to His Highness the Sultan – whom God preserve,' said Kerbalou. 'For the pestilence is already loose on Zanzibar, and there is nothing that we can do save resign ourselves to the mercy of the All Merciful. Our fate is written, and if we die, we die. But here in this house I think we shall live, because it is only in the towns and villages, where men and houses crowd upon each other, that the sickness strikes hard. And you, my Lord, it may not affect – since it is well known that it steps aside for white men, and smites fiercest at the black.'

'Let us pray then to Allah that it has not yet reached the city!' said Jumah: and mounting Zafrâne he rode off into the starlit darkness.

Rory spent a sleepless night watching for the *Virago*'s sails, but dawn saw the channel between Tumbatu and the shore as empty and as smooth as the polished *chunam* that formed the floors of the silent house, and all that day no breath of wind came to ruffle its calm surface.

Towards evening he sent Hadir to watch the track that led southward to the city, and Kerbalou along the cliffs towards Mkokotoni in case Jumah and Batty should have elected to paddle a *kyack* along the coast in preference to taking to the roads. He himself went down to walk along the shore, though he knew that there was little hope of the *Virago* rounding the northern point of the Island in a flat calm, and that he was only filling in time in preference to sitting still and doing nothing.

By nightfall there was still no sign of *kyack*, schooner or horsemen; and no breeze. The starlight seemed almost as hot as the sunlight had been, and again there were no drums. Only the shrill monotonous whine of mosquitoes disturbed the silence as Rory lay naked on the string cot under a blaze of stars, feeling the stored heat of the day beat up from the flat roof and knowing what it must be like in the city.

He lay awake for the greater part of the night listening for the sound of footsteps and voices. But in the early hours of the morning the air cooled, and he fell asleep at last; and awoke at sunrise to the dry rustle of palm fronds singing in the morning wind. There was still no sign of Jumah or Batty and no word from the city. But the breeze held, and late afternoon brought the *Virago*, picking her way delicately down the Tumbatu channel.

Hajji Ralub's normally impassive face had fallen into harsh lines when he heard that Jumah had gone to the city and had not yet returned, but he shrugged fatalistically and busied himself by taking foodstuffs and fresh water on board, and sent a man with a telescope to keep watch on Tumbatu – a precaution that Rory noted with grim amusement, remarking that the Hajji was wasting his time, since Lieutenant Larrimore did not have to rely solely on sail, and if his ship should come upon them they would never out-distance her in these light airs.

'That is true, but we might do so in the darkness,' said Ralub.

'Perhaps. But we cannot leave until Jumah returns with the old one and the child.'

'Do you sleep on board tonight?' asked Ralub.

Rory shook his head: 'No, I will wait here for them. Leave a boat and two men on the shore so that we can come aboard at any hour, and be ready to sail at once.'

'And if they do not come?'

'If they are not here by morning I will send Hadir to the city to find out what has happened to them.'

They had not been there by morning, and Hadir had gone, with instructions to buy, borrow or steal a horse, and when he reached the city to keep away from The Dolphins' House and enquire in the bazaars for news of Batty and Jumah, the doings of Colonel Edwards and his Baluchis, and the whereabouts of Lieutenant Larrimore and the *Daffodil*.

Once again the sky had been clean of clouds and the day intolerably hot, though the breeze had strengthened and the *Virago* jerked at her anchor chain as though she were consumed with impatience to leave that beautiful, tainted island and escape to clear water and cleaner air. But they could not leave without the child and the missing members of the crew. And neither could they move the schooner down the coast to a point nearer the city, since by doing so they would only increase their own danger and probably miss Batty's party, who would make for the house on the cliffs.

They could do nothing but wait, and they had waited with what patience they could muster for two scorching and interminable days: listening to the Trade Wind crooning through the palms and sighing in the casuarinas, and watching the empty track and the emptier sea. And then at last a tired horse trotted under the arch of the gate, and Hadir slid from the saddle and wiped the sweat from his dust-grimed face.

'They cannot come,' said Hadir. 'There is a guard at the gate of The Dolphins' House and the spies of the British Consul keep watch upon it. Bwana Potter they captured three weeks ago, as he climbed over the outer wall of the garden in the darkness. But because he has friends in the city and they feared that if he were imprisoned in the Fort the guards would permit him to escape, they took him back to the house and told him he must remain there, but that should he make any attempt to escape he would be put on the English ship and taken far from the Island. None may leave or enter the house except to buy food, and even those are searched and followed. Jumah too was taken and is with them——'

Hadir hesitated, as though there was something else he meant to say, but if so he did not say it. His gaze slid away from Rory's and he turned to slap the dust of the unmade roads from his robes, making a great business of it.

Rory's eyes met Ralub's and saw in them a confirmation of his own thought, and he said quietly: 'There is something else, is there not? You had better tell us now.'

Hadir did not speak for a minute. His hands continued to fret mechanically with his dusty clothes while his dark face puckered into an expression of anxiety, and Rory said sharply: 'Is it the child?'

Hadir shook his head, still without turning: 'The child is well.'

'What then? The old one?' enquired Ralub harsh-voiced.

Hadir's hands stilled and fell idle, and he turned reluctantly to face them: 'No. But there is a tale that the sickness has already broken out in the city.'

He saw the shoulders of the two tall figures, Arab and Englishman, jerk and stiffen, and said quickly: 'It was only a tale, and I do not know if it is true. But . . .'

435

He did not complete the sentence, and Rory, finishing it for him, said curtly: 'But you think it may well be. Where did you hear this?'

'I have a cousin who has a friend in one of the houses in the Malindi quarter, and he says that his friend told him; swearing him to keep it secret, for they are afraid that if it is known they will not be permitted to move abroad to buy food. He said that cholera was brought to the house by a slave who had been sent on some errand to Mungapuani, which is on the coast ten miles beyond the city, and who returned yesterday and died within a few hours. And that now another has sickened, and two more, in terror of it, have run away and hidden themselves in the Black Town, saying nothing. If that last is true——'

'There will be a hundred dead within a week,' finished Ralub grimly. 'And within two weeks a thousand!'

The tired horse shifted its weight wearily and snuffed at the sun-dried grass, and Ralub looked again at his Captain and said quietly: 'There is nothing to be gained by waiting. Do we sail tonight?'

'No,' said Rory curtly. 'You had better stay here until I send word.'

'From where?'

'From the city.'

'*Ah!*' Ralub smiled crookedly as though he had received an expected answer. 'But you cannot go until that animal is rested, and by sea we may reach the harbour before morning.'

'They would hold the ship and imprison you all,' said Rory.

Ralub laughed and made a deprecatory gesture with one lean brown hand. 'Never! The white men speak loudly and often of justice, and it is your head only that they require. Once they have that, they will not lay a hand on us.'

Rory shrugged and said: 'Maybe. But the pestilence does not concern itself with such things as justice or the colour of a man's skin, and it may not be so selective! You will be safer here. And once they have laid me by the heels they will permit Batty and the child and the others to leave, and I will send them here with any others from The Dolphins' House who wish to go, and you may take them away until the sickness has passed.'

Ralub said pensively: 'It is in my heart that this time they will surely hang you.'

'*Inshallah!* (as God wills). "What is written is written",' quoted Rory with a wry smile.

Ralub nodded gravely and spread out his hands in a slow motion that was both assent and acceptance. 'That is indeed so. Therefore we will go with you. For are not all things according to God's wisdom?'

The two men looked at each other for a long, measuring moment; hard pale eyes meeting bland dark ones. Then the Englishman laughed and threw up a hand in a gesture of a swordsman who acknowledges defeat.

'As you will,' said Captain Rory Frost. 'Let us go.'

33

'Well, I'll be *jiggered*——!'

Able seaman Albert Weeks of Her Britannic Majesty's steam sloop *Daffodil* rubbed his eyes to make sure that he had seen aright, and noting those unmistakable portholes, swore long and profanely.

The pitiless light of another cloudless dawn illuminated the white walls and crowded rooftops of the city, the greasy, rubbish-littered harbour water, and, clearly visible on the far side of a big sea-going dhow, the familiar lines of an anchored schooner that had certainly not been there on the previous evening, but must have slipped in noiselessly at the turn of the tide and under cover of the dark hour before dawn.

Mr Weeks' disbelieving gaze changed to wrathful certainty, and turning about he pelted aft to awaken his commanding officer, who for greater coolness had taken to sleeping out on the open deck.

'Beggin' your pardon, sir,' announced Mr Weeks breathlessly, 'but it's that there schooner, sir. The *Virago*, sir. She must'a sneaked in on the tide an hour or two back, and she's a'sittin' there as bold as brass abaft that dhow.'

'I don't believe it!' said Lieutenant Larrimore, stumbling to his feet. 'You must have made a mistake.'

'It's Gawd's truth, sir. I'd know the cut of 'er jib anywhere, an'——'

Dan hitched up the loose cotton trousers that formed his sleeping attire and ran forward along the dawn-lit deck. It did not need more than a brief glance to confirm the truth of the able seaman's statement. It was the *Virago* at last, delivered into his hand. And the very fact she was there argued that her Captain could not be too far away, since Dan did not believe that Rory Frost would abandon his ship, and with it his crew and his livelihood.

He could not imagine why Frost should have come back at this juncture, but it was enough that he had, and Dan ordered out the jolly-boat and hurried down to the cabin to don his uniform, belt on his sword and see to the priming of his pistol.

The city was reluctantly awakening to another day as he went over the side, and in stifling, overcrowded houses and narrow, reeking streets, in hot courtyards and cool mosques and on the dew-wet decks of the dhows, men rose to face Mecca and recite the appointed prayers with which all True Believers have saluted the dawn since the Prophet ascended to Paradise. As the jolly-boat rounded the bulk of the dhow Dan could see the Arab seamen high above him kneeling and rising as the ritual demanded, absorbed in their devotions and apparently oblivious of anything around them. But he knew that no movement escaped those devoutly raised eyes, and that they not only marked his passing but were well aware of his errand.

On the forward deck of the *Virago* the three members of her crew who were engaged in prostrating themselves did not turn their heads or betray any sign of having observed his approach. But neither Hajji Ralub nor Hadir was among them, and there was no sign of Captain Emory Frost.

Dan did not trouble to hail the schooner, and as the jolly-boat shipped oars and came alongside he climbed aboard, and ignoring the worshippers, vanished down the companion-way; no man preventing him.

Rory put down his coffee cup and rose courteously as though to an expected guest. 'Good morning, Dan. You're late. I expected to see you alongside a good hour ago. Or didn't your look-out spot us coming in? Don't tell me your Officer-of-the-Watch was asleep! You ought to keep better discipline aboard, Danny – what with all these bad characters about. Coffee? Or would you prefer something stronger?'

'You must be well aware,' said Dan without heat, 'that I would not accept so much as a drink of water from you if I were dying of thirst in a desert. So there is no need for you to waste your time and mine in trying to make me lose my temper. If you succeeded it would only mean saving the hangman trouble. Are you coming with me, or do I have to send for a guard to take you?'

'That depends on where you intend to go. If you are thinking of taking me to pay a call on our respected Consul, I shall be only too pleased to accompany you – so you can stop fingering that pistol in such an intimidating manner. I should tell you that he will be expecting us, for Hajji Ralub went ashore well over half-an-hour ago to inform him that I should do myself the honour of calling upon him as soon as you were ready to provide a suitable escort for me. He must be wondering how much longer you're going to be about it. Shall we go?'

Dan's cold blue gaze did not waver and his smile was as chilly and unpleasant as his eyes. He said meditatively: 'I'd give a good deal to know why you think you can talk your way out of this. You must have some good reason for it, and for coming back here openly. I imagine you're counting on your friends up at the Palace to save your neck. But that nag won't run this time.'

'It's their country,' observed Rory mildly.

'But you're not a citizen of it. You're a British subject and as such can be summarily dealt with under British law.'

'By which you mean summarily hanged.'

'That's right.'

'On what grounds?'

'Murder, Kidnapping and Incitement to Violence.'

'Dear me! It sounds very damning. But I feel that both you and the Colonel are running grave risks if you intend to execute me without the formality of a trial. Aren't you afraid that some officious Member of Parliament may ask a question in the House?'

'Not in the least. The British public are hardly likely to interest themselves in the fate of a renegade rapist, and I cannot see that it will help you very much if they do, since you will already be dead. Besides, it will be pointed out that the situation prevailing here was of such delicacy that your immediate demise, as the instigator of the riots, was necessary for the safety of the community. And you needn't worry yourself over the matter of a trial, because we'll see that you have one; if it's any satisfaction to you. Colonel Edwards has already taken the signed testimony of a good many reliable witnesses, and you can be sure that he will be ready to listen to anything you have to say in your own defence before he passes sentence on you.'

'Good of him. But surely a waste of time if he has, as you suggest, already made up his mind to put an end to my existence?'

'It will look better in the report,' said Dan blandly.

The Captain's laugh held a note of genuine appreciation, and he said without mockery: 'Danny, you are a man after my own heart. Which is more than I can say for that humourless old fragment of rectitude, Edwards! But what makes you think you can persuade me to put my head into your noose?'

Dan's mouth stretched in an unsmiling grin and he made a brief gesture with the weapon he held: 'This, for one thing. And for another, I have half-a-dozen men out there, and they are all armed.'

'I know. I saw them. The gentleman who designed this ship did not have those portholes put in solely with a view to ventilation.'

For the first time a flicker of doubt showed in the Lieutenant's eyes, and Rory saw it and laughed again. 'Come, come, Dan! You must have known that I'd be expecting a reception committee. You should have given the situation a little more thought and moved your ship before you came visiting. As it is, you can't bring your guns to bear on me from where you're lying. Let me show you something, Dan. You see that dhow out there? Her crew were at their prayers when you passed, but while I have been keeping you here talking they have concluded their devotions, and by now every one of your seamen will be covered by at least three muskets – not counting those on a dhow that you will observe to starboard. You see, I still have a few friends in these waters.'

'My guns——' began Dan, and was interrupted:

'Oh, I don't deny that your guns could probably blow the dhow out of the water once your shipmates realized what had happened to you. But if you will forgive the plagiarism, I don't see that it would help you very much if they did, for you would already be dead.'

The lines that strain and responsibility had etched on Dan's sunburned skin grew deeper, and his face seemed to stiffen, but he resisted the temptation to glance towards either of the two open portholes that flanked the narrow cabin, and only his trigger finger moved, tightening ominously on the cold curve of metal. He said grimly: 'You forget that you will have predeceased me, for if any of your cut-throat friends open fire I shall shoot you on the instant. I mean that!'

'I'm sure you do,' grinned Captain Frost. 'And they won't. But that pistol of yours fails to impress me, for even you must see that it at least offers me a quicker and cleaner exit than choking to death at the end of a rope. Besides, if you use it you will only make yourself responsible for a far worse outbreak of violence than anything that has gone before, and you're supposed to be here to prevent further bloodshed; not to stir it up again. Much as you and the Colonel would enjoy seeing me swing, I'm afraid you're going to have to deny yourselves that pleasure. For the time being, anyway. So I suggest you stop fingering that trigger and go up on deck and tell your men to return peacefully to their ship, and as soon as they've gone some of my own men can row us ashore to pay a call on the Consul. Well, Dan?'

The muscles of Dan's right hand tightened and quivered, and for a fleeting moment it seemed as though he would pull the trigger and take the consequences. But five harsh years patrolling the East African coast had not failed to teach him the unwisdom of leaping before he looked, and rage had already driven him to make one serious mistake that morning. He looked now, with a cold anger that did nothing to obscure the truth, and saw only too clearly that Captain Emory Frost was right. To provoke an exchange of shots between his own men and the dhows that lay on either side of the *Virago* would almost certainly end in his own death and that of the jolly-boat's crew. And although the *Daffodil*'s guns could be counted upon to exact a terrible vengeance, the sight of a pitched battle between a British ship and a pair of Arab dhows would infallibly touch off a further explosion of violence in the city; with consequences that did not bear contemplating.

Dan let his breath out in an audible sigh and lowered the pistol, and Rory smiled and said: 'That's better. I thought you'd see reason.'

He watched the Lieutenant turn and leave the cabin, heard him speak briefly to his men, and presently saw the jolly-boat returning across the harbour to the *Daffodil*. The bluff had worked. For it had been a bluff. Amah-ben-Labadi was no fool, and though it amused him to indulge Captain Frost and bedevil the Lieutenant with a little harmless play-acting, the fact that his dhow offered a certain and sitting target for the *Daffodil*'s guns was enough to ensure that every musket handled by his volatile crew that morning had first been prudently unloaded. But Dan would not know that, and Rory calculated that even if he suspected a bluff it was one that he would not dare call, since the men who manned the dhows had an unenviable reputation, and the European community in Zanzibar was small and virtually unprotected.

Considering that he had every intention of calling on the British Consul, anyone unacquainted with Emory Frost might be excused for thinking that this hollow show of force was a singularly useless piece of trickery. But then Rory knew that the incident would be reported to Colonel Edwards, and that neither Dan nor the Colonel could have any desire, at such a time, to risk a confrontation between the dhows and the *Daffodil*. It was for this reason alone that he had staged that charade, in the hope that it might serve to impress on both gentlemen the fact that the members of his crew were not without allies. A point which had, he trusted, been taken.

Nevertheless, he was well aware that so far he had been gambling with the odds heavily in his favour. It was the next throw that was the crucial one and he was less certain of the outcome, for once ashore and out of range of the dhows the advantage would lie with Colonel Edwards, who might not be prepared to come to terms. Well, if so he, Rory, had at least taken what steps he could to improve the bargaining position of his ship and his crew.

Dan was waiting for him on deck, and as the sun lipped the horizon and washed the white rooftops of the city in a dazzle of light, they landed at the rubbish-strewn beach near the British Consulate and walked up through a hot, airless alleyway to the door where two of the Sultan's Baluchis still stood on guard and Hajji Ralub, watched by a third who held his musket at the ready, waited in the sharp-etched shadow of a gold mohur tree.

'I have told this ox that I remain here of my own will,' grunted Ralub disgustedly, 'but these fools say that if I am not watched I will run away. Tell them that there is no need to set a guard on me, and that I wait for your orders.'

'They would not believe it, Hajji,' said Rory. 'Be patient. I shall not be too long.'

The British Consul was at his desk and waiting, and if the situation surprised him he gave no sign of it. He did not return the Captain's polite greeting, but sat back in his chair to give his attention to Lieutenant Larrimore's account of the morning's proceedings, and when Dan had ceased speaking, turned his bleak gaze on Captain Frost and said coldly:

'I shall not waste my time reciting the details of the indictment against you, because you must be well aware of them. To be brief, you are charged with inciting a mob to attack the foreign consulates in Zanzibar, fomenting riots that resulted in the death of two persons and the injury of many others, and abducting with violence the citizen of a friendly power. I now hear that you have only this morning threatened to open fire on Her Majesty's forces, regardless of the fact that this would instantly lead to further anti-European demonstrations and make you directly responsible for the loss of a great many more lives. So you will understand that I have no alternative but to pronounce the capital sentence upon you and see that it is carried out immediately. Have you anything to say?'

'Certainly. Otherwise I should not be here,' said Rory equably. 'May I sit?'

He did not wait for permission, but reaching behind him drew up a chair and sat down astride it, his arms folded along the back and his chin resting upon them in an attitude that betokened considerably more confidence than he felt. He saw the frigid anger gleam in the Colonel's eyes and the swift tensing of Dan Larrimore's muscles, but neither man made any move towards him, and the Colonel said harshly and with an effort: 'I am aware – well aware – that you must have felt both grieved and angered by the outrage committed against a member of your household, and by its tragic consequences. But that cannot be held to excuse the brutal action you yourself took against an innocent and unfortunate——'

He found himself unable to complete the sentence, for there was suddenly something in the expression on the lean face that looked back at him that checked him as effectually as a blow across the mouth, and he was startled to find himself flushing as hotly as though he had been guilty of some gross breach of propriety. For the space of a full minute there was complete silence in the small white-walled office, and an oppressive sense of tension that had not been there before.

It was broken by the Colonel's dry embarrassed cough, and the rigidity went out of Rory's face: the long lines of his body were once again relaxed and at ease, and he said lightly: 'I have no intention of excusing myself. Shall we dispense with abstract questions and get down to bargaining? I have a proposition to make.'

The Colonel made an angry movement of repudiation, and Rory lifted an admonitory hand and said: 'Wait! You asked me if I had anything to say, and before you put on the black cap you had better listen to it. You

443

have something that I want: a child and an old man whom you are at present holding prisoner in my house. If you will let them go aboard the *Virago*, together with any of my servants and crew who wish to accompany them, and permit them to sail on the next tide, I will surrender myself in exchange, and you can do what you like with me. Though I think it only fair to warn you that it would be unwise to try hanging me until my friends are well out of range. Well, those are my terms. And very generous ones, if you ask me.'

'Very!' agreed Dan sarcastically, 'considering that we have you already and so the question of your surrender, voluntary or otherwise, does not arise. There are no dhows protecting you here, and by now my ship will have moved to where she can get her gun-sights on yours. You've nothing to bargain with, and if that's all you have to say——'

Colonel Edwards, who had been watching Rory's face, silenced the younger man with an authoritative gesture, and said quietly: 'I presume there is something more. May I ask what action you intend taking in the event of your terms being rejected?'

'You may. I should be loath to start any further trouble in the city, but I have several friends who for purely selfish reasons would be only too pleased to foment further disorders. My crew have their instructions; and if I surrender to you voluntarily, letting it be known that I have done so and that you have accepted my terms, they will see to it that there are no further disturbances on my account. You have my word for that.'

'The word of a blackguardly slaver!' snapped Dan, unable to contain himself. 'Why, you crooked, contemptible kidnapper, there isn't a man in his senses who would accept anything from you, let alone your word, and if you think——'

'Be quiet, Larrimore!' admonished the Consul brusquely; and turned again to Captain Frost: 'And if you do not surrender voluntarily?'

Rory grinned at him and shook his head. 'Oh no! If I told you the how and the where you might be able to take measures to prevent it. Though I doubt if they'd be successful. But you can take the word of a blackguardly slaver that if you try and hold me without my consent a lot of innocent people are going to suffer for it. Which may upset you, but will not worry me in the least.'

'You're bluffing,' said Dan angrily. 'There's nothing you or your friends could do. They won't face being shelled, and even the Sultan won't dare lift a finger to help you if we train the guns on the city and threaten to open fire at the first sign of trouble.'

'*Rule, Britannia!*' said Emory Frost. 'All right Dan: I'm bluffing. Are you going to call me?'

Dan did not answer, and Rory laughed and said: 'You know you daren't – because of what might happen if the Sultan called yours and told you to go ahead and fire.'

'We've restored order before without that,' said Dan shortly. 'And we can do it again.'

'I doubt it. You had the city on your side last time, but this time it would be the townspeople themselves whom you would be fighting, and not a piratical rabble of invaders who every right-thinking citizen fears and detests. You'd have no allies, and as I happen to know that the next British ship isn't expected here for a fortnight, you'd be taking on the whole Island. There are too few of you to do that.'

He saw that the truth of this had given the Lieutenant pause, and followed up his advantage: 'Come off your high horse and talk sense, Dan. And you too, sir. You've no quarrel with old Batty Potter or a baby. Or with my crew for that matter, who were merely obeying my orders. I'm the one you want, and if you let them go you can keep me under lock and key until the *Cormorant* arrives, and then send me off to be sentenced in some less explosive spot where no one'll give a damn whether I hang or not. What have you got to lose? Or does wholesale revenge mean more to you than the safety of – shall we say – Miss Cressida Hollis?'

'You *bastard*!' said Dan in a whisper. 'You dirty, renegade bastard!'

He took a swift stride forward and the Consul leant across the desk and caught his sleeve, jerking him back: 'Sit down, Lieutenant! . . . thank you.' He resumed his seat and turned his cold grey eyes on the Captain: 'The word, Mr Frost, is "justice", not "revenge". And I do not myself believe that you have sufficient following in Zanzibar to put your threats into effect. But unhappily you are correct in assuming that we are in no position to risk any further outbreaks of violence. We also have no quarrel with the city and no intention of provoking one, and it is for these reasons, and only these, that I am forced to accept your conditions.'

Rory removed his arms from the back of the chair and stood up. 'Thank you, sir.'

'Wait!' The Consul lifted a commanding hand. 'That is not all: I have a few conditions of my own. I am willing to remove the guard from your house and permit the occupants to leave, and I will give your men twenty-four hours in which to take on water and provisions and make any arrangements they have to make. But if they are not clear of the harbour by the end of that time I shall consider the contract void, and if I hear later that they have landed in any other part of the Island, or on Pemba, I shall have no hesitation in ordering them to be detained. Is that quite clear?'

'Perfectly, thank you. But I assure you they will not be landing anywhere on the Sultan's territory.'

'That is just as well. There is also one other matter. I cannot for the moment dispense with the services of the *Daffodil*, and as I do not intend to hamper Lieutenant Larrimore by requesting him to hold you on board, or to keep you in custody myself in this house, I shall ask the Sultan's permission for you to be imprisoned in the Fort until such time as the *Cormorant*'s arrival relieves them of your charge. But as I am only too well aware that you possess influential friends in Zanzibar who might be able to arrange your escape, I must ask you to give me your parole.'

Dan made a sharp, protesting movement but did not speak, and Rory's blond eyebrows lifted in surprise. He said with an odd note in his voice: 'You flatter me, sir. What makes you think I would honour it?'

The Colonel said dryly: 'The fact that knowing what it would mean, you returned here of your own accord for the sake of an old man and a child. I may of course be mistaken. But that is a risk I am prepared to take.'

Rory's reluctant grin dawned, and he said lightly, but with a curious note of bitter self-mockery in his drawling voice: 'You win, sir. Strange how "conscience doth make cowards of us all"! You have my word that I will not attempt to escape from the Fort.'

The Colonel did not miss the reservation, and remarked grimly that he did not think the Captain would find it any too easy to escape from the *Cormorant* either, if that was what he had in mind. He reached for the small brass bell that stood on his desk, rang it briskly and gave a curt order in the vernacular to the native clerk who answered the summons.

'I presume,' said the Colonel, 'that you will wish to speak to that man of yours who is waiting outside. You can say anything you have to say in our presence.'

The door opened again to admit Ralub, who greeted the company with grave dignity, and Rory said crisply: 'It has been agreed, Hajji. You and the others have leave to depart. Take the old one and the child, and any of the household who wish to go, and get away as quickly as you can. His Excellency here permits you a day and a night to make any arrangements that are necessary, but since it is unwise to delay so long, go at once – within the hour if possible. And if we two should not . . .' He hesitated for a moment, and then abandoning whatever else he had meant to say, gave a brief shrug and spoke instead a gracious Mohammedan form of farewell: ' "May you never be poor".'

' "May you never be tired",' murmured Ralub in reply. He looked at Rory for the space of a long minute, and then said very softly: 'No, we shall not meet again . . . Bound as we are for different paradises. *Wedâ, ya Sidi.*'

He touched his head and his heart in formal salute, turned, and was gone.

'And I hope,' said Rory, his voice suddenly harsh, 'that you have called off that oaf with the musket, because if he intends to dog Ralub's footsteps all over town there will infallibly be trouble. The Hajji is apt to be quick-tempered.'

Colonel Edwards, whose quill pen was already scratching an order for the removal of all restrictions on The Dolphins' House, ignored the remark, and it was Dan who went to the door and gave a low-toned order to the servant who stood outside it, and returning, said savagely: 'You think you've won hands down, don't you? – that once you're out of this place and can get together a few lawyers to plead your case you'll get off with a fine and a prison sentence. But if I have anything to do with it——!'

'You won't,' said Rory with the ghost of a laugh: 'Not if you intend to stay here until the *Cormorant* arrives. Don't look so disappointed, Dan. You may not be able to string me up this time, but there's a more than even chance that I won't get out of the Fort alive. In fact it looks as though we may all die before long; and a deal more unpleasantly than we should at a rope's end! Cholera is a clumsy executioner, and I may even live to regret that I didn't settle for a quick drop – and you that you didn't invite a musket ball through your head this morning.'

Colonel Edwards' quill ceased to scratch across the paper, and now it dropped a blot of ink across the last word, but he did not notice it. His beetling brows twitched together in a sudden frown, and he looked at Rory with startled attention and said sharply: 'Cholera?'

Rory stared at the abruptness of the question, and said impatiently: 'What else do you suppose brought me here? You can't have thought I was fool enough to think you might hang old Batty or any of my servants in my stead? Good God – I know you better than that! No; it was the cholera. You know as well as I do that in this weather, and with the living conditions that exist in the bazaars and the African Town, it'll spread like a forest fire. There'll be no holding it, and I couldn't let you keep Batty and the child and the rest of them under house-arrest in the city at a time like this. The sooner they get clear of the Island the better. And if you have any sense you'll cram as many of the European women and children as you can onto the *Daffodil* and send them off to Aden or the Cape: or anywhere else outside this part of Africa.'

'Nonsense!' said the Colonel angrily; the sharpness of the denial itself a betrayal of his anxiety. 'There have been one or two isolated cases in outlying villages, but the disease is endemic here. As for the epidemic form which has been ravaging Africa, it may have reached the coast, but it has not yet appeared in Zanzibar, and strict precautions are being taken against it doing so. The dhows——'

'You are behind the times, sir,' interrupted Rory brusquely. 'It reached the Island well over a week ago and has already broken out in the city. At least two persons have died of it in the Malindi quarter, and a week from now that figure will be two hundred if it is not two thousand.'

'I don't believe you. I would have heard. How did you come by this rumour?'

'From a man,' said Rory laconically. 'But you don't have to take my word for it. I imagine that the unfortunate Malindi household is in no hurry to advertise the fate that has overtaken it, but they won't be able to keep it quiet for long – as who should know better than yourself, sir? I've heard you were in Bengal in the year that thirty thousand pilgrims to some shrine died in less than six days from the cholera. And from all I've heard, the Indian epidemic was child's play to the one that's been killing off half Africa; which is why I told Ralub to get clear of this place as soon as possible, and not wait out your twenty-four hours' grace.'

The Colonel's eyes had become as blank as pebbles, and they no longer appeared to be focused on anything inside the office but to be contemplating something remote and unpleasant. Rory saw his lips move soundlessly and was able to follow his thoughts . . .

There were no hospitals in Zanzibar, and except for the British Consulate's Medical Officer, Dr Kealey, no qualified doctors. Apart from the *Daffodil* and the *Virago*, the only craft in harbour at the moment were Arab dhows, a Muscat *buggalow*, the Sultan's 'Fleet' and a few fishing boats. And the only European ship expected in the near future was HMS *Cormorant*, which was not due to arrive for at least two weeks yet, and might well be delayed even longer. It would be inadvisable to dispense with the *Daffodil* until it was certain that the raiders from the Gulf were not lurking somewhere off the African coast with the intention of returning as soon as it seemed safe to do so. And it was not, at this juncture, possible to send away the Western women and children, even supposing any of them should wish to leave; which seemed unlikely, since they must all by now be used to the fact that both cholera and smallpox were endemic on the Island. There were always a few cases of both in the city. Most of them in the Nazimodo area on the far side of the noisome creek that divided the Stone Town, where the Arabs and rich Banyans lived, from the African Town where the negroes and freed slaves existed in unbelievable squalor in huts constructed from mud, palm boughs, rusty tin or anything else that could be pressed into service to provide shelter from the heat and the night and the merciless monsoon rains. The African

Town – the 'Black Town' – was a breeding ground for cholera. But at no time during the Colonel's term of office had the disease achieved the proportion of an epidemic, and on consideration he did not see why it should do so now . . .

His eyes lost their abstraction and he spoke abruptly, breaking the long silence: 'There is no reason to suppose,' said Colonel Edwards, 'that these cases you mention are more than the normal quota of such deaths at this time of the year. We are never entirely free from cholera here and may expect a moderate seasonal outbreak.'

'This does not happen to be endemic cholera, and it will not be moderate,' said Rory dryly.

He turned on his heel and looked directly at Dan, and there was no longer either mockery or impatience on his face, but something that was oddly like diffidence. He said carefully: 'You are a friend of the Hollises, and will wish to see the ladies in safety. I know it is not what either you or they would choose, but will you tell them that there will be room for them on the *Virago* if they care to make use of it, and that Ralub will take them to any port within reasonable distance that they like to name. Possibly Mayo could go with them, if he does not mind sleeping on deck.'

This time it was Dan who laughed: a short and ugly laugh compounded of anger, scorn and relief. 'So *that's* what you had in mind! I knew there was bound to be a joker in the pack. It's a pretty plot, but I'm afraid it won't work. Did you really think you could trick us into handing over a parcel of hostages just by turning up here with some cock-and-bull story about cholera? You must take us for imbeciles!'

'I took you for a man of sense,' said Rory shortly. 'But it seems I was wrong. Don't be a fool, Larrimore! I don't have to prove what I say. You'll get all the proof you need before the week's out.'

'By which time, as she's to sail today, your ship and everyone in her would be well beyond our reach. A very useful arrangement – for you.'

Rory forebore to lose his temper and said patiently: 'Look, Dan, you may not like anything about me, and I am well aware how much you and the Hollis ladies will dislike making use of my ship. But this is no time for striking attitudes. Take what you can and be thankful it is there to take. It may be the last chance they'll get.'

'You mean the last chance *you'll* get to lay your hands on something you can use to bargain with!' scoffed Dan. 'If they were mad enough to accept, the only thing that would be in doubt would be how soon one of your ruffians would make his appearance with a demand for your release in exchange for returning one of them, and the amount of ransom money you would decide that you'd like for the others. Colonel Edwards may be prepared to believe that you returned to Zanzibar of your own accord and for the sake of an old man and a child, but I'm damned if I am! It's a touching story, and nicely designed to underline the danger of allowing these women to stay on the Island. But I'm not falling for it. And even if the plague was raging in the city, or the place was in flames, I still would not advise anyone to accept your word or put a foot on your ship!'

'Please yourself,' shrugged Rory. He turned back to Colonel Edwards and said: 'The offer, sir, is still open. But Ralub will sail on the next tide, and I look to you to see that nothing is done to delay him.'

'Nothing will be,' said the Colonel stiffly.

Rory bowed his acknowledgements, and was presently escorted out by Dan and two of the Baluchi guard to temporary imprisonment in a small room on the top floor of the Consulate, where the single narrow window was latticed with stone-work and looked out onto a blank wall, and the furniture consisted of a string bed of local manufacture. The door closed upon him and the key turned gratingly in the lock, and he heard the footsteps of two men retreating down the stone stairway.

The British Consul might have his doubts as to Emory Frost's ability to raise any further riots in the city, but he was taking no chances. To march Frost through the streets by daylight and under guard might invite an attempt at a rescue, and he considered it wiser to wait until after dark before transferring his prisoner to the Fort – always supposing that His Highness the Sultan would consent to his being held there! But although the Sultan was known to be a personal friend of the Captain's, he could hardly be expected to risk offending every white man in Zanzibar by refusing to take into custody a notorious law-breaker who had incited a mob of Gulf pirates to demonstrate against them, and had brutally abducted the niece of a Consul. A fact of which Rory himself, listening to those retreating footsteps and coldly assessing his chances, was equally well aware.

Majid would have no alternative but to hold him prisoner, and having accepted the charge, to see that he did not escape. And had Colonel Edwards known His Highness the Sultan a little better, he could have saved himself that distasteful and entirely unnecessary gesture of asking for and accepting the parole of a 'blackguardly slaver'. Majid had done what he could in secret to assist his friend to evade capture, but now that Rory had openly returned and given himself up, there would be nothing more that he could do for him. He might regret the necessity, but he would see the sense of keeping Captain Frost strictly confined until such time as arrangements could be made to remove him from the island. And once aboard the *Cormorant*, guarded by unsympathetic bluejackets and en route to Aden or the Cape, there would be no hope of escape. The only time to attempt such a thing was now, before the gates of the Fort shut behind him.

Rory had given no promise not to try to escape from this house, and his quick eye had already noted a flaw in the stone lattice-work, and the stoutness of the string that had been used in the construction of the bed. It should be perfectly possible to break the first and make use of the second, which unravelled and knotted together would reach far enough to allow him to drop to the ground. But he knew that he could not do it. He must give Ralub time to get the *Virago* well clear of the Island and out of reach of pursuit. And long before he could be confident of that he would be in the Fort.

He crossed to the window, and grasping the lattice was wryly amused to discover that his guess had been correct. The slab of sandstone from which it had been carved must always have contained a flaw, and wind and weather had worked upon it until a strong blow with one of the legs of the bed would have smashed it into fragments. The drop beneath was not more than thirty feet into a narrow alley that led directly down to the water's edge, and under any other circumstances the matter would have been simple . . .

Rory sighed and let his hand drop, and turning away from the window, disposed himself as comfortably as possible on the sagging string bed and went to sleep.

34

The Fort was a solid, castellated structure of yellow coral rag, built long ago to protect the harbour, but now housing a portion of the Sultan's guard and serving as a prison. Standing at some distance from the Palace and the homes of the rich, it faced seaward and possessed several rooms with barred and embrasured windows that looked onto the harbour. But Captain Emory Frost's was not one of these, for the British Consul was a careful man, and despite his acceptance of the Captain's parole, he had insisted that the prisoner be confined somewhere where he could neither see nor be seen by men passing in the streets or along the harbour front. Thereby avoiding any risk of undesirable elements in the city communicating with him.

His Highness the Sultan (who regarded his friend's return to the city as an act of madness) had shrugged and agreed: and two days later sent him a most welcome gift of fresh fruit and a promise that more would be forthcoming to augment the spartan prison diet. But no more had arrived and nor was there any further word from Majid, and Rory had no way of knowing that the shopkeeper who had been charged with supplying the fruit had fallen a victim to the cholera, or that Majid – also unaware of this, but learning that the plague had reached the city – had hastily retired to one of his smaller and more secluded estates in the countryside beyond Beit-el-Ras, and given orders that all contact with the city must be reduced to a minimum as a precaution against couriers or visitors picking up the infection there and bringing it back with them.

His English friend, in accordance with the British Consul's wishes, had been allotted a windowless cell on the ground floor of the Fort, facing inwards onto the verandah that surrounded the inner courtyard. Light and ventilation were inadequately provided by an iron grille let into the upper part of the door, and during the daytime the small stone cell seemed cool enough, for the massive walls were a protection against the blazing sun. But at night it was a stifling purgatory, since no breeze could blow through it and scores of mosquitoes filled the hot darkness with their whining song.

The grille provided Rory with a view of a verandah pillar and, beyond it, a glimpse of the open courtyard around which the Fort was built and where members of the garrison, jailers, servants and a few favoured prisoners would congregate in idle groups to talk, sleep and quarrel. But though he was permitted such extra amenities as the use of a razor and a scanty supply of soap and water to wash with, he was not allowed under any circumstances to leave the cell. And in case he might use the razor as a weapon, it was passed in daily through the grille after the door had been safely shut and locked again, and had to be returned the same way before any food was handed to him.

Orders had evidently been given that no one was to be allowed to approach within a range that might permit of clandestine speech, for the garrison kept its distance, and he had no contact with his fellow-men except for three people: Limbili, the surly negro who brought him his food, Bhiru, the slovenly half-witted youth who cleaned his cell, and a huge, silent Nubian who morning and evening stood by with a loaded blunderbuss whenever the door of the cell was unlocked, and by night squatted outside it, additionally armed with a scimitar and an ancient musket.

The youth, a Banyan of low caste, performed his duties under the watchful eye of Limbili and was too frightened to speak; and neither Limbili nor the Nubian could be persuaded into conversation, for the latter had lost his tongue as a result of an accident in early youth, while the former, having been sold into slavery by a Portuguese trader and escaped to Zanzibar from the French plantations of La Réunion, cherished a consuming hatred for all white men.

Limbili would dearly like to have vented that hatred on the prisoner. But he was aware that the Englishman possessed powerful friends in Zanzibar – among them, it was said, no less a person than the Sultan himself; though that at least could no longer be true, since it was by the Sultan's order that he had been imprisoned in the Fort. Still, it would be wiser to refrain from ill-treating the white man until his position became clearer, and in the meantime Limbili confined himself to such overt acts as spoiling or spilling the larger part of the food and drink that he carried to the prisoner, refusing to answer when spoken to, and permitting the Banyan youth to neglect his duties and leave unemptied (or on occasions deliberately upset) the noisome bucket that served in place of a latrine.

But to Rory the heat and the stench, the ruined food and inadequate water, the lack of exercise and the monotony of the slow, hot aimless hours, were merely discomforts that he had expected, and he accepted them philosophically. They were not new to him, for he had, in one way or another, experienced them all before, and the only thing that he had not foreseen, and that fretted him unbearably, was the lack of any news. He could get no answers to his questions, and he did not know what was happening in the city, or if the cholera had spread or been checked. Or if there was any word yet of the *Cormorant*'s arrival . . .

The *Virago* should have reached the Seychelles by now, and The

Dolphins' House would be empty except for the caretaker and a handful of elderly servants who had been there too long to wish to leave, and who would wait hopefully for his return. Perhaps some day Amrah would come back and take possession of it. Unless Batty took her to England with him, and they settled there in some grey and grimy house near the Pool of London, where the sight of ships would remind the old man of other days, and Amrah would forget Zorah and Zanzibar, and the renegade slave trader who had been her father.

A week of clear skies and fierce sunlight was succeeded by five days in which the Trade Wind drove belt after belt of rain clouds across the Island, and the courtyard of the Fort became a muddy lake in which frogs croaked and the refuse of the choked gutters drifted as flotsam. The walls and the floor of Rory's cell ran with moisture, but there was little change in the temperature, and the humidity of the rains was less bearable than the dry heat of the sun-scorched days had been. The food turned mouldy and toadstools and fungus flourished in the cracks between the stones, and the mosquitoes were reinforced by fluttering, crawling hordes of flying ants.

Two more days, thought Rory; staring out at the driving torrent that obscured what little he could see of the courtyard. If the *Cormorant* was on time she should reach the Island on the seventeenth, and this, unless he had miscalculated, was the fifteenth. But the date of her arrival was an arbitrary one and a dozen things might delay her; wind and weather, the capture or pursuit of a slaver, the necessity of embarking rescued slaves and convoying captured dhows, accidents in the engine room or sickness among the crew. The *Cormorant* might arrive a week or a month late, and unless the situation in the city was causing anxiety, Colonel Edwards could hardly expect to keep the *Daffodil* hanging about at Zanzibar and neglecting her patrolling duties for much longer. Dan would have to take himself off soon, and he would presumably take Rory with him. *Cormorant* or *Daffodil*, it could not be long now. Two days – three – four?

But the seventeenth came and went. And the nineteenth and the twentieth. And still there was no sign from Dan or Colonel Edwards.

The rain ceased and the sun blazed down from a sky temporarily free of clouds, drying out the mud and the moisture and drawing an abominable stench from the steaming city. But in the reek that filled Rory's cell the evil odours of the city went unnoticed, for the half-wit youth had not been near him for three days and no one else had taken over the boy's duties. Limbili, appealed to on this score, showed his teeth in an unpleasant grin and made an obscene and impractical suggestion, and for a moment Rory was sorely tempted to smash his fist into the grinning face

But behind Limbili stood the Nubian mute; vast, unwinking and watchful, one finger crooked about the trigger of the ugly old-fashioned blunderbuss with which, at that range, he could not have missed.

The Nubian's unnaturally small head might betoken a certain lack of intelligence, but once he had accepted an idea he would retain it; and although he had been told that the prisoner was merely serving a temporary sentence and must eventually be handed over alive and in good health to his own people, Limbili had taken pains to impress upon him that should the white man show any signs of violence or make the smallest move to escape, he was to be shot without mercy; though not through the head or the heart, for that was too good and quick a death: besides, he might miss. The stomach was a better target.

It was a pleasing prospect, but the white man had been disappointingly passive, and even Limbili's cleverest insults had so far failed to rouse him to anger. And now, yet again, it seemed that he was either too poor-spirited or too cunning to display resentment, though the present provocation should surely have been sufficient to goad any right-thinking man into hitting out blindly and without regard to the consequences.

Rory saw the man's thoughts reflected clearly on his sneering face and was glad that he had not given way to that sudden savage impulse, for he had long been aware that Limbili resented the fact that his stay in the Fort was not likely to be prolonged, and would welcome an excuse to ensure that he did not leave it alive.

He let his hands relax, and because he knew that to pretend not to understand the insult would only lead to its repetition, forced himself to smile broadly as though in appreciation of a coarse jest. It was a response that Limbili found difficult to deal with and that usually drove him to glowering silence. But today the prisoner's refusal to rise to the bait had the unexpected effect of sending him into a sudden and entirely unexpected rage, and he began to shout abuse and obscenities in a hoarse, cracked voice, his lean body shaking with fury and his yellow eyeballs starting from his head.

Rory backed away against the far wall out of reach of the clawing, threatening hands, wondering if the man was going to have a fit and what he could do if he were attacked. Even the Nubian, who had begun by grinning in appreciation of Limbili's picturesque lewdness, grew apprehensive at the spectacle of that frenzied rage, and fearing that the noise would attract the attention of the Baluchi guard, plucked at the negro's arm and made soothing croaking sounds.

Limbili turned on him and struck his hand away, and taken by surprise the Nubian took a quick step backwards, stumbled, and dropped the blunderbuss, which flew out of his hand and fell with a clatter onto the flags of the verandah. A look of ludicrous dismay contorted his ebony face, and for a moment he hesitated, torn between retrieving the weapon and leaving Limbili alone and undefended with the white man. Then he lunged forward, and gripping the raging negro about the body, dragged him out backwards in one violent heave and slammed the cell door shut behind him.

Rory heard the sound of a brief, panting struggle and a stream of invective, and when at last their footsteps retreated he sat down on the narrow bed feeling oddly unnerved. After a moment or two he reached for the mug of tepid water that Limbili had brought, and drank deeply – and unwisely, for the day had been dry and cruelly hot and the night promised to be no cooler, and he knew that he would get nothing more to drink until the morning. That meagre mug of water which he had all but drained must be made to last through the night, for the liquid in the grimy earthenware bowl that served him as a wash-basin had been foul enough when the boy had brought it three days ago, and by now evaporation had reduced it to a few inches of evil-smelling slime.

But it seemed that Limbili intended to teach him a lesson, because the next day no one came near the cell, and neither food nor drink was brought to him. By the time the last gleam of sunlight left the battlements and the courtyard began to fill with shadows, he realized that he was to be given nothing that day, and his thirst having grown to a raging torment, he assuaged it, nauseously, with the soap-slimed dregs in the wash-bowl. But the relief it brought to his parched throat was only temporary, and when night fell his thirst kept him from sleep, and he leant against the door with his face pressed to the grille in an attempt to breathe fresher air, and in the hope – only a very faint one now – of seeing Limbili approach with the water jar.

The air outside was as foul as that within, and no cooler; and for once there was no sound of voices from the courtyard or the guardrooms, and the Fort seemed strangely silent. So silent that Rory caught himself listening for the familiar asthmatic breathing of the Nubian, who should have been on guard outside his door. But tonight the man had not come and there was no one on guard: and no loiterers in the courtyard.

The starlight appeared very bright in comparison with the pitch-dark cell and the dense shadows under the arches of the verandah, and staring out into it Rory's attention was caught by a slight movement at the far edge of the small grey strip that was all he could see of the courtyard. A moment later something flitted across the strip and vanished out of his range of vision.

It had been too large for a cat, and must be some hungry pariah dog, scavenging for scraps. The city was full of masterless dogs; half-starved, cringing, flea-ridden creatures who slunk hopefully from rubbish heap to rubbish heap, feeding on refuse and quarrelling noisily over a bone or the corpse of a dead kitten. But they had learned not to approach the gates of the Fort too closely, because the garrison would often fire at them for sport or to test their marksmanship, and it was surprising to see one inside the courtyard.

Rory supposed that the sentry on duty that night must have fallen asleep at his post, and that a venturesome pariah, lured by the smell of garbage, had slunk past him in search of food: and not only one pariah, but several, for once again his eye caught a flicker of movement across the starlit strip of open ground. Listening, he could hear the light patter of paws on the hot stone of the verandahs, and a soft chorus of snuffling, panting sounds. There must, he thought, be at least a dozen dogs in the courtyard, and that meant that the gate was open and unguarded.

Somewhere on the far side of the courtyard a dog growled and was answered by a snarl and a snap, and there followed a short, savage scuffle that terminated in an anguished yelping that awoke the echoes under the dark arches. Rory waited for the crash of a musket and voices shouting curses at the dogs and calling on the sentry to turn them out. But they did not come, and in the silence that followed the brief explosion of animal sounds the furtive pattering began again: only now it was less furtive, and soon it became quicker and bolder. He could hear impatient claws scratching at closed doors and eager noses snuffling hungrily under thresholds, and presently the growling started again and the darkness at the far side of the courtyard was filled with scuffling shadows and the snarling and worrying of dogs who fought over food.

The ugly sounds went on and on, but no one heeded them and no one woke. And quite suddenly Rory knew that there was no one left to wake . . .

He should have realized it before. Long before, if heat and thirst and hunger and the foul state of his cell had not numbed him to anything but physical discomfort. And now if he needed further confirmation, he got it, for a breath of the night wind, blowing in unchecked through the open gate, swung wide the heavy iron-bound outer door and brought with it a whiff of something oily, loathsome and unmistakable. A smell that had permeated the city for over a week and would soon permeate the Fort, and that he would have noticed and recognized long ago had it not been effectively hidden from him by the stench of his own cell.

There were dead men in the city. Too many to allow for the bodies to be properly buried; and the night wind that so often carried the scent of cloves and spices to approaching ships was carrying the scent of those bodies out to sea: a warning to all humans to keep their distance, and an invitation to all eaters of carrion to gather for the feast.

So the cholera had not been checked! thought Rory: it had taken hold as he had warned Dan and the Colonel that it would. Perhaps they had even taken advantage of his offer and shipped Mrs Hollis and her niece and daughter on board the *Virago* while there was still time – though recalling Dan's scathing comments on the subject he doubted it! But then Dan was in love with Cressida Hollis, and so he might well have thought better of it once his rage had cooled and he had had time to discover the truth of that 'cock-and-bull story about cholera'. But there would have been very little time, for Ralub would not have delayed. He would have taken the *Virago* out within a matter of hours, and there was no other ship on which it would have been safe to send the women away, for the crews of the Sultan's own ships lived with their families in the town, and the chances of the cholera breaking out among them would be too great. Perhaps Dan himself had taken them off on the *Daffodil*? He might well have done so, since once the deadliness of the outbreak was realized, the men from the consulates and the European trading firms would have taken prompt measures to get their families out of the Island, and the *Daffodil* would have been the only ship in harbour that could be trusted to transport them in safety. They had probably all left long ago . . .

The thought brought a grim flicker of amusement to Rory's haggard, unshaven face. How Dan must have hated leaving without him! But there was little enough space to spare on the *Daffodil*, and they could hardly ship a dangerous prisoner along with a crowd of agitated women and squalling children, and the mounds of baggage, extra stores and personal attendants they would require to take with them. Dan would have had to deny himself the pleasure of handing Captain Emory Frost over to justice with his own hands, and content himself with the knowledge that the Commander of the *Cormorant* would do so in his stead. Unless the *Cormorant* had been warned to steer clear of Zanzibar until the epidemic had burned itself out; which might take months.

Now that the cholera had taken firm hold, there would be no way of controlling it. And no way of avoiding it: not even, at this date, by flight. It would board every dhow that put out from the Island, and travel with the panic-stricken passengers, striking them down at sea with the same speed and ferocity as it struck others in the crowded hovels of the Black Town – or in the cells and guardrooms of Zanzibar Fort! For the cholera was here too, and Rory wondered tiredly why it should have taken a pack of scavenging dogs to tell him what should have been plain to him for the last three days at least. This, of course, explained why his cell had been left uncleaned and why there had been no food or water that day. The boy whose task it was to empty that noisome bucket had probably died on the day that he first failed to appear, and now Limbili too was dead – unless he had taken fright and run away.

The night wind and the pariah dogs made it plain that there were dead men inside the Fort as well as in the city, and the silence and the unguarded gate meant that the living had abandoned their posts and fled in panic. But there would be other prisoners. They could not all be dead! Or had the frightened garrison released them before they fled, expecting that Limbili or the Nubian would do the same for him? This last was somehow more unpleasant to contemplate than the thought that they might all be dead, and Rory did not want to believe it. But an ice-cold and entirely unfamiliar shiver crawled down his spine, and he knew that for the first time in years he was afraid – coldly and terribly afraid – and gripping the bars of the grille he shouted aloud.

His voice echoed eerily round the starlit courtyard and startled the quarrelling dogs into sudden silence. But no voice answered him, and something in the quality of that echo rather than in the silence that followed it, spoke of emptiness, and confirmed his first swift conviction that there was no one in the Fort. No one but the pariah dogs and the dead – and Emory Tyson Frost, slave trader, black sheep and blackguard, who would soon be dead too: if not from the cholera, then less mercifully from thirst and starvation, for he was locked in and alone and there was neither food nor water in the narrow, stifling cell. And no one left alive to bring him either.

For a timeless interval the fear that gripped him gave place to a crippling panic that made him fling himself at the door, bruising himself against the unyielding wood with the blind frenzy of a trapped animal attacking the bars of its cage. It passed, and sanity returned to him, and he groped in the darkness for the edge of the hard plank bed, and subsiding on it, put his head in his hands and forced himself to face the situation calmly . . .

There was no reason to suppose that morning would not bring some of the garrison back to the Fort. If not to bury their dead, at least to remove such property as they might have left behind them when they fled. And even if the garrison did not return there would be looters, for death and disaster bred looters as surely as carrion bred maggots, and the deserted Fort with its gate swinging open on the wind would be an invitation to more than the pariah dogs of the city. Sooner or later someone would come: and even if they did not, it might only mean the difference between a slow death in the next day or two, and a quick one later on at the hands of a public hangman. The best he could hope for was a long term of imprisonment in some jail that could turn out to be a deal worse than this one, and after a few years of that he might well find himself regretting that he had not drawn the harsher sentence.

It was a reflection that consoled him, because even now, when his parched throat and swollen tongue were already providing an ugly foretaste of the torment that lay ahead, the immediate prospect of dying from thirst seemed preferable to spending the next twenty years, or possibly the rest of his life, locked in a cell. Given the choice he would still probably settle for the former – if there was such a thing as choice, which according to Hajji Ralub's philosophy, there was not. Ralub and the majority of the *Virago*'s crew believed implicitly that a man's fate was tied about his neck and that he could not avoid it: *'What is written, is written.'* It was in many ways a comfortable philosophy, and there were times when Rory regretted that he could not subscribe to it. But in general he regretted very little.

Against the background of the dark a score of disconnected incidents from his past life rose up before him, and it was as though, standing on the crest of a ridge, he turned to look back at a road he had travelled along. A long road that dipped into dark valleys and climbed out again on plateaus and hill crests, but that seen from this vantage point gave the appearance of being a joyous and unbroken line.

He knew that the continuity of that line was an illusion, and that the valleys were there, for he had plodded through them. But now they lay below the level of his vision and were unimportant, and it was only the mountain tops that he saw, joined together by distance and bathed in retrospective sunlight. Life might have dealt him an indifferent hand but he had played it recklessly and to his own advantage, and enjoyed every move in the game! . . . The successes and the failures, the bad times and the good . . . Excitement and danger and the sights and sounds and fights in strange ports and forgotten cities . . . The late great Sultan, and his amiable weakling son, Majid. Batty and Ralub. Dan Larrimore and Clayton Mayo. Jumah and Hadir, Zorah——

Rory lifted his head and stared into the darkness trying to picture Zorah's face, and found that he could not do so. All that he could recall was a catalogue of features and colouring, but they would not come alive. Yet she had lived in his house for years, loved him and been his mistress, and borne him a child: Amrah. He straightened his shoulders, and leaning back until his head rested against the wall, shut his eyes and thought about his daughter.

It was strange to think that the only legacy he would leave to the future – the only proof that he had ever lived – would be a half-caste child whose mother had been a slave girl bought for a yard or two of calico and a handful of coins. A child who had inherited his temper and his features and who would grow up without any recollection of him, to see a new century and witness that shrinking of the world and the mushroom growth of industrialization and conformity that he had visualized with such loathing and done his best to escape.

If he had any regrets, it should be on Amrah's behalf; – for having fathered her without thought, saddled her with the double burden of bastardy and mixed blood, and left her to fend for herself in a harsh and intolerant world. But it was too late to worry about such things now, and with any luck there might be enough of himself in her to make her accept the hazards of life as a small price to pay in return for the entertainment of living. He could at least be grateful that there had been no more children. Or not as far as he knew. Unless—— Yes, there was always that: it was a possibility at least. Perhaps more than a possibility . . .

The darkness that would not show him Zorah's face presented him now with Hero's. Hero staring at him haughtily, her grey eyes scornful and her red mouth curved with disdain. Hero with her face swollen and disfigured by cuts and bruises and her cropped hair looking like a wet scrubbing brush, sobbing over a few mosquito bites. Hero laughing at one of Batty's stories; smiling down at Amrah; frowning over the iniquities of the Sultan's regime; agonizing over the plight of slaves and the injustice of the world. Hero angry, Hero defiant. Hero asleep . . . A dozen Heros; but none of them afraid and none of them defeated.

Rory found himself hoping – fervently and selfishly – that she would have his child. A son conceived of the strange, unexpected passion and ecstasy of those nights at The House of Shade, who would carry something of them both into the future and hand it in turn to other sons: to grandsons and great-grandsons who would inherit Hero's beauty and courage and his own love of the sea and strange cities, the wild places of the world and the sound of the Trade Winds blowing. It was a pity that he would never know . . .

The cell had slowly been growing lighter, and turning his head he saw that the bars of the grille were etched sharply black where before they had been no more than shadows against shadow. The moon must have risen. Soon it would be shining into the courtyard and he would be able to see if the cell on the far side of it, facing his own, was empty.

From somewhere outside the Fort, in the purlieus of the city, a cock crew, and was answered by another further away. The snarling and growling of the dogs had ceased, and the door of the outer gate no longer creaked on its hinges, for the wind had died. The world was so still that Rory could hear the harbour water lapping against the shore, and the slow creak of a cable as the night tide fingered some anchored dhow. Then a crow began to caw, and he realized that the growing light was not moon-

461

rise, but the dawn. He must have slept after all, for the night had gone and it was morning.

Other cocks began to crow and presently the birds awoke, and the blowflies. The little coolness of the night was dissipated by the hot breath of the coming day, and on the open ground between the Fort and the harbour a lone donkey brayed raucously, a sound like a harsh yell of despair that echoed desolately against the walls of the silent houses. But the normal early morning noises of the city were lacking, and inside the Fort there was no sound but the buzzing of innumerable flies.

Once again Rory felt the black wings of panic brush against him, and he shivered as though he were cold. Could the townspeople have fled from the cholera and the city be as empty as the Fort? No, that was absurd! Some might have run away, but only to the interior of the Island, since there had been few ships in harbour and Africa was known to be in the grip of the epidemic. There must still be people in the city – a great many of them. The unusual silence of the morning only meant that at such a time men would be waking to a new day and going into the streets with frightened faces and apprehensive looks at their neighbours, and would have little heart for crying their wares in the market place.

Nevertheless, the suspicion that the city too might be deserted remained like an uneasy shadow seen out of the corner of the eye, and presently it brought Rory stiffly to his feet to stand again with his face to the grid, straining his ears for some sound from beyond the walls that would tell him that there were still men in the Stone Town. Live men.

There was at least one man in the courtyard, but he was dead. The bulk of the body lay just beyond Rory's range of vision where the pariah dogs had dragged it and quarrelled over it last night, and for that he was thankful, as the little that he could see was unpleasant enough. Even as he looked, a crow alighted beside it and hopped forward to peck at what had presumably once been a hand, and it occurred to him that if he were fated to die in this cell at least his body would not be disposed of in that manner, since neither the crows nor the pariah packs would reach him here. Though there would, he supposed, be rats . . .

Another crow flew down into the courtyard, and he looked away, sickened. But he dared not leave the window for fear that someone might enter the Fort and he would miss them. It was possible to face the prospect of death with a reasonable amount of equanimity, but Rory could see no point in giving up hope.

He could not have said how long he stood there, but at last there crept to his ears the first blessed sounds of the city awakening: a muezzin calling the Faithful to prayer, the creaking of cartwheels and a distant, indeterminate murmur of voices. Ordinary enough sounds, though disquietingly few and far between. But none the less welcome for that, because they proved that the city was neither dead nor abandoned, and listening to them some of the tension ebbed from his body and he could breathe again. But the long morning dragged away and the day grew hotter and darker, and no one entered the Fort.

Rory found that his legs could no longer support him, and subsiding onto the bed, he leaned back against the wall and closed his eyes. He had no means of knowing the time, and it seemed to him that the first cock had crowed hours ago . . . aeons ago! Or else the sun was standing still. He had drunk nothing for well over twenty-four hours, and though under normal conditions this would have been no very great hardship, it was an unbelievable torment in the oppressive, humid heat that wrung the moisture from his body and soaked him in sweat, leaving him at last feeling as dry and shrivelled as an empty seed-pod. The desire for water ceased to be an active discomfort and became instead a savage and intolerable craving, and his throat was parched and his mouth sticky, while his tongue seemed to have swelled to monstrous proportions. An odd drumming in his ears mingled with the idiot buzz of the flies that filled his cramped cell and circled about him in an aimless cloud, crawling on his face and neck and preventing him from thinking clearly – or at all.

The rhythmic throbbing grew louder, until at last it dawned on him that the drums he heard were no longer confined to his brain, but were coming from somewhere outside. They were beating in the courtyard now, faster and louder, and the air was cooler.

He opened his eyes with an enormous effort, and dragging himself to his feet, held himself upright by the rusty iron bars of the grille, and saw that it was raining.

For a brief moment the sight of those swollen drops splashing onto the parched ground and forming gleaming pools at the verandah edge seemed to him the most wonderful thing he had ever seen. And then he realized that they were of no more use to him than a mirage is to a traveller lost in a waterless desert. The rain slanted down to form lines and rods, which in turn transformed themselves into an opaque wall of water that cooled the air and made a lake in the courtyard. But it did not reach the door of the cell, and he tore at the bars of the grid, wrenching at them until his hands were raw. The iron bent a little, but did not break, and he licked the blood thirstily, and reaching for his discarded shirt, tied it about the weakest bar to give him a better purchase, and threw his full weight against it. But though rusty it proved immovable, and presently he relaxed his grip and leant against the door, panting and defeated.

The torn shirt dangled limply from the grille and he stared at it because it was a light-coloured thing against the dark wood, and because he had nothing else to look at. And then all at once he saw that it could still bring him all the water he needed.

It did not take long to tear it into strips and tie them together so that one end, knotted to give it extra weight, could be tossed out between the bars and reach to where the rain poured down from the verandah edge. He hit the pillar with the first try, and drew it back and reinforced the knot with his handkerchief, and tossed it out again. And this time it fell true.

Neither shirt nor handkerchief were anywhere near clean, while the rain was mixed with the mud and dust and filth of the baking days. But Rory sucked the drenched material with a greater appreciation than he had ever accorded to any wine, and flung it back and retrieved it again; repeating the process at least a dozen times before his thirst was even partly quenched, and at the last squeezing water into the tin mug and the empty basin, until both were filled and he was assured of a reserve supply.

He had not been conscious of hunger while his tongue and his parched throat had been crying out for water, but now that the edge was off his thirst the fact that he had eaten nothing for close on two days began to make itself felt. But hunger seemed a trivial thing and easy enough to bear when compared with the craving for water that had made a hell of the past forty hours or so. He knew that he could endure ten times as long without food before reaching the stage to which thirst had reduced him so swiftly. The dark forebodings of the night and the past hours, the dizziness and the despair, had sprung from thirst and vanished with its slaking, and he realized that he must have been mad to strip the skin off his hands wrenching at those unyielding bars of iron, for even if he had succeeded in bending them apart he still could not have squeezed his body through the narrow space. As for that lunatic assault on the door, it had been an even crazier action, since no human battering-ram could have broken it down or burst those massive hinges.

He looked at it now, painfully aware of his sore shoulders and wondering how he could have been guilty of such senseless hysteria. And as his gaze fell on the cumbersome lock something seemed to click in his brain.

He did not move for a long time, and it seemed to him that he did not breathe. He sat very still, his body rigid and his gaze fixed, while the sweat crawled coldly down his unshaven face and the flies settled unheeded on his bruised back and shoulders. The slow minutes slid away to the tune of rain splashing loudly and steadily into the courtyard outside, and at last he got carefully to his feet, moving as cautiously as though he were afraid of waking a sleeper, and reached out a hand that shook uncontrollably.

The crude iron handle felt rough and clammy to the touch, but it turned easily enough, and though the door had swelled with the damp so that he was forced to ignore the pain of his lacerated hands and push at it, it opened.

The negro, Limbili, dragged shouting and threatening from the cell, and already in the grip of the cholera, had forgotten to use the key that he carried at his belt, and Rory had bruised his shoulders and torn his hands on a door that he could have opened at any time during the past forty-two hours.

He began to laugh, and laughing, tumbled out into the courtyard and stood in the lashing rain, letting it sluice off him in a cleansing torrent that washed away the sweat and dirt and stink of the last days; the tiredness and the fear.

He stood with his face turned up to it and felt it beat against his eyelids and fill his open mouth, and strength returned to him; and with it an enormous exhilaration. He stretched his arms wide and laughed in that drenched, deserted place where even the torrential fall of the monsoon rain could not submerge the smell of death; or drown the intoxication of being out in the open again after those slow weeks of intolerable confinement in the semi-darkness of a cramped and evil-smelling cell. By contrast with that darkness even the grey daylight seemed brilliant to him, and the tainted air fresh and clean, and he breathed it in deeply: savouring it as though it were incense and careless of the fact that he stood in full view of anyone who might enter the Fort, or might still be in it.

He must have stood there for at least ten minutes before a sound that was not the splashing of the rain broke his trance, and he wiped the wet out of his eyes and stepped back quickly behind the nearest pillar. Someone was coming down the verandah, walking hesitantly and wearing shoes with iron nails, for above the insistent drumming of the rain he could hear the click of metal on stone, and a shuffling, dragging sound that drew inexorably nearer and stopped at last within a yard of him, on the far side of the pillar.

Rory stayed still, rigid and listening. The Fort was filled with the noise of rain and for the space of several minutes he could hear no other sound. Then suddenly he was startled by a sigh; long-drawn, desolate and inhuman. A sound so full of despair that it made his skin prickle and the hair lift on his scalp, and he moved involuntarily: and saw that the intruder was nothing more alarming than a tired, mud-splashed horse trailing a length of broken rope.

The sight served to bring him sharply back to reality, for it was not only proof that the main gate was still open and unguarded, but suggested that the situation in the city might be even worse than he supposed if

465

animals such as this were roaming loose and masterless on the waterfront, and in this condition. The horse was a pure-bred Arab mare, and it was bleeding from a number of wounds that were not only recent but had undoubtedly been caused by teeth. Rory regarded them thoughtfully, and recalling the pariah dogs of the previous night, lost his exhilaration and was abruptly sobered. If the pariahs, normally the most cringing and cowardly of creatures, had taken to attacking runaway horses, it meant that they were becoming bold and savage on a diet of fresh meat; and if so the sooner he got away from here, and clear of the city, the better.

He had given no thought as to where he should go, but looking at the horse it occurred to him that luck had decided the matter for him by providing him with a mount. The *Virago* had gone and it would not be possible to return to The Dolphins' House, or embarrass the Sultan by asking him for asylum. And though he had other friends in the city, they would have troubles enough of their own to contend with at such a time and he could not add to them. There remained *Kivulimi*: The House of Shade. He would be safe enough there, and it would be a deal quicker and less hazardous to make the journey on horseback than on foot.

Rory rubbed the mare's nose, and picking up the trailing rope, led the animal away under the empty, rain-loud arches, past the blind cells with their gaping doors and the silent figure of a man who had crawled into an angle of the wall and died there. The door of the guardroom immediately inside the gate stood open, and he paused, and after a brief hesitation, hitched the rope to the latch and went in – to be rewarded by the discovery of a length of dun-coloured country-made cloth that had evidently been used as a sheet. A quick search disclosed nothing else that could be used as a covering, but the sheet would serve, and he could not afford to be too particular, since at the moment his sole garment consisted of drenched and dirty trousers of unmistakably European cut.

He hoped that the late owner of the sheet had not died of cholera, but that was a risk that would have to be taken, and he did not waste time worrying about it. Setting swiftly to work he tore a long strip from the cloth and wound it about his head and across the lower part of his face, Tuareg-fashion, and having rolled his trousers to the knee, tied the remainder about his waist so that it covered him from waist to calf in the manner of the seamen from the dhows. There were a pair of heavy leather sandals in one corner of the room, and he appropriated them gratefully, and releasing the uneasy mare, went out through the deserted gate and into the grey, concealing veil of the falling rain.

The wind had not found its way into the Fort, for it was blowing from the north-east, and the high Fort walls and tall, close-crowding buildings of the city had kept it at bay. But here in the open it sent Rory's makeshift garment flapping wetly against his legs, and he could hear the boom of surf breaking along the harbour front.

Despite the rain there seemed to be a great many birds on the foreshore, and the pouring day was filled with the sound of wings and screaming gull voices and the harsh cawing of quarrelling crows. The mare snorted and shied as half a dozen mangy pariah dogs trotted past making for the beach, but there were few men to be seen and fewer ships in the harbour, and the charnel-house smell that defied the rain and penetrated the drenched fold of cloth that covered Rory's nose and mouth made him think gratefully of *Kivulimi*.

The gardens of The House of Shade would be green and full of flowers, and the bay below it clean sand and clear water. Old Daud the caretaker would still be living peacefully in his room by the gate, undisturbed by the cholera, since the nearest village was a full two miles distant, and there was little reason to visit it while the kitchen gardens provided fruit and coconuts, vegetables and maize, the sea was full of fish, and Daud kept both chickens and goats.

No one would come looking for a missing prisoner there, for there would be other and more important things to occupy the authorities than the fate of Captain Emory Frost of the *Virago*. And in a day or two it was going to be impossible to identify the bodies of those who had died in the Fort, or even tell whether one of them had been a white man. As for his parole, Rory had no qualms on that score for he had certainly not plotted an escape. He had merely found himself abandoned by his jailers and walked out, and even that stiff-necked stickler for the letter of the law, Her Britannic Majesty's Consul in Zanzibar, would hardly expect him to remain behind an unlocked door and starve himself to death in the deserted Fort! – though Rory suspected that Dan Larrimore, placed in a similar position, would have proceeded to the Consulate, explained the situation, and given himself up.

But then Dan was that sort of upright fool, thought Rory, who had no sympathy with priggishness and heroics though he had always had a certain sympathy for Dan. Chasing slave traders in these waters, where every man's hand was against you and even the slaves themselves accepted their fate as an immutable law of nature and were apt to regard their deliverer as mad, must be a thankless task – its only rewards heat, discomfort and exile, the abuse of all who owned slaves and the hatred of those who sold them, the dumb incomprehension of the freed and the loud imputations of base and selfish motives expressed by Christian nations who should have known better.

Dan's job was no sinecure, and Rory smiled a little grimly at the thought of his own frequent contributions to Lieutenant Larrimore's troubles. He hoped that Dan was enjoying a brief period of respite while conveying Miss Cressida Hollis and wives and families of the Western residents to the Cape.

The rain drove into his eyes and he cupped a hand about them and peered under it at the harbour and the few grey shapes that rocked at anchor . . . And there – unbelievably, impossibly – was the *Virago*!

Even at that range and seen through the slanting lines of rain there was no mistaking her. He would have recognized her at twice the distance and by almost any light. She had *not* gone! Dan and the Colonel had cheated him! Or else – or else . . .

He would not even frame the thought, but he drove his heels into the flanks of the shivering horse, urging it to a gallop, and rode for that part of the shore that was nearest to the anchored schooner.

He had never known a day when the waterfront was not crowded or the beach free of an ugly litter of jetsam, among which the corpse of a slave flung overboard from a dhow was no uncommon sight. But today there were no crowds, and not one corpse but twenty: victims of the cholera thrown into the creek for disposal and carried out by the tide to be stranded on the sands of the harbour. The waterfront was silent and deserted, except for the crows and the seagulls and a number of pariah dogs, who between them were disposing of the dead.

There were no boats, either. Any that had been left drawn up on the beach had been stolen long ago by panic-stricken citizens fleeing from the infection, and Rory waded into the sea and making a trumpet of his hands hailed the schooner. But no one answered him. The *Virago* rocked and swung at her moorings, wraith-like in the grey sea and the falling rain, her decks deserted and her hatches battened down, and no one on watch.

Rory hailed her again, but the wind snatched his voice away and lost it among the voices of the rain and the surf and the mewing of the gulls, and he knew that he was wasting his breath. There was no one to hear him; and if he swam out to her he would not only be wasting time, but energy as well.

He returned to the horse, and mounting again, wrenched brutally on the wet rope that served for a bridle, and turning from the harbour and the road that would have taken him to *Kivulimi*, rode back in the direction he had come from: heading for The Dolphins' House and riding with a reckless disregard for his own neck and the safety of any passing pedestrian.

35

It was on the day following Captain Frost's incarceration in the Arab Fort that Dan brought the first news of the cholera to Mr Hollis.

The citizens of Zanzibar took a casual view of a disease that was always among them, and they had not at first been unduly disturbed at its appearance in the Malindi quarter, or taken the trouble to report it. Even Colonel Edwards' normally efficient grape-vine had failed to recognize its importance and neglected to mention it: with the result that the Colonel as well as Lieutenant Larrimore was inclined to regard Rory Frost's statements on that subject as deliberately alarmist, and almost certainly made with some ulterior motive in view – probably (as Larrimore had suggested) the acquiring of hostages. Nevertheless, he had made enquiries, and elicited the information that there had indeed been two cases of cholera in the Malindi quarter, though there was no reason to suppose that they indicated the beginning of a serious epidemic.

But twenty-four hours later the two cases had become nineteen, of whom eighteen had died, and there was no longer any doubt that Rory Frost's dire predictions had been no more than the truth. This was no ordinary form of cholera, but the terrible epidemic that had made its first appearance many months ago on the shores of the Red Sea, and creeping slowly southward had already depopulated half Africa.

Dan had had little time to spare for his Love in the weeks that followed upon the abduction of Hero Hollis and the rioting and violence that had accompanied it. He had been kept fully occupied with restoring tranquillity and order to the city, patrolling the coasts to ensure that the pirate dhows did not return, and prosecuting the search for Captain Frost and the *Virago*. But Cressy had never been far from his thoughts, and word that there were eighteen dead in the Malindi quarter wiped everything else from his mind.

The fate of Rory Frost, the dhows, the slave ships, HMS *Daffodil* and the citizens of Zanzibar became of no more account than a handful of dead leaves and dry grass, and only Cressy was important. The Hollises must remove from the city immediately, and put up in some house in the country until such time as a ship could be found to take them out of danger:

'I wish it might be possible to offer my own services, sir,' said Dan, his blue gaze intent and anxious: 'But Colonel Edwards considers that in view of the late disturbances and the fact that there is no saying that the dhows may not return while the north-east Trades are blowing, it would be advisable to have at least one foreign ship in harbour. So I cannot for the moment offer to convey Mrs Hollis and – and the ladies of your family from the Island. But they would be safer outside the city, and there are a number of houses in the countryside or on the coast where they would be comfortable enough until arrangements could be made to take them out of Zanzibar.'

Mr Hollis had read of such things as cholera epidemics in the East, but he had no real conception of what they entailed or the terrible speed with which the disease could strike. Dan's information disturbed him, but he was unwilling to send his family into the country unless he could accompany them himself. And this was something that he could not agree to do, since his duty lay here, and it seemed to him that to retire precipitately from the city would convey an undignified and an unnecessary impression of panic, and might well lead to unkind comment among his fellow Consuls and the court officials He thanked Lieutenant Larrimore for his information and advice, and being under no illusion as to the reasons that had prompted the young man to offer them, promised to give the matter his serious consideration, and was kind enough to add that Cressy might be found in the morning-room . . .

Nathaniel Hollis was by no means reconciled to the prospect of seeing his beloved daughter married to an English naval officer, even though that officer's father was, it transpired, an Admiral who had deserved well enough of his country to be rewarded with a baronetcy – which meant that Dan would one day be 'Sir Daniel' and his wife Lady Larrimore. That sort of thing might serve in some small way to console Abigail, but then women – even Republican ones – were always intrigued by titles. And Abby still had Clay, her son and her first-born, but Cressy was Nathaniel's only child. Nothing could compensate him for losing her to a man who would expect her to live in his country instead of her own – and her father's. It was his own fault, for if he had not let her wheedle him into allowing her to accompany him to Zanzibar, he would not now have been forced to countenance her betrothal to this stubborn young Englishman. But after that scene in the hall on the day following Hero's abduction there had been very little he could do about it, for it had resolved all his daughter's doubts and put an end to all her hesitations.

Clinging wildly to Dan and returning his kisses with passionate intensity, Cressy was sure at last that this was love! she would never love anyone else, and if she could not marry Dan she would die! Counsels of prudence and the merest hint of parental opposition had been met with floods of tears, hysterical accusations that her parents cared nothing for her happiness, and frantic pleading. Even Hero's appalling predicament had been almost forgotten in the agitating scenes that had followed, and of course Cressy had won. Dan having been reluctantly given permission to pay his addresses to her had instantly proposed and been as instantly accepted. And even Clayton, in the light of her subsequent behaviour, was no longer able to hope that his half-sister was suffering from a temporary infatuation and would be bound to think better of it before long.

I suppose she'll be able to come home for long visits, thought Mr Hollis, consoling himself. Now that there were these new-fangled steamships, travel was becoming easier and quicker and the world was getting smaller every day. England was not so far away, and already there were men on both sides of the Atlantic who had taken to referring to that ocean with careless familiarity as 'The Duckpond'. Maybe it would not be as bad as he supposed. But it would never be the same as if she had married some nice American boy and lived in the same town – or at least the same country! – as her doting father.

Cressy had been arranging spider lilies and oleander in a tall Moorish vase when the door of the morning-room opened and Dan came in quickly and took her in his arms, flowers and all, and kissed her with a satisfactory fervour that prevented her from saying anything at all for at least five minutes.

Released at last, blushing and breathless, she looked up at him with a little shiver of pure happiness, and was suddenly sobered by the expression on his face. The blood left her cheeks and her eyes mirrored the tenderness and fear and tension that was plain in his own: 'What is it, Dan? What's happened?'

'Nothing, darling,' said Dan quickly. Too quickly. He would have given a great deal to have been able to protect her from even knowing what would happen (what was already happening!) in Zanzibar city. Yet how could he avoid it? If only he could take her away now – at once! Before the sickness spread. Before there was any real danger. It was terrible to him that he should be tied here by duty when it would have been so simple to take Cressy and her mother and her cousin out of danger. But he could not do it: and in the meantime ingorance would not serve her as well as knowledge would; for she must be careful. They must all be careful. Dr Kealey would be able to tell them what precautions they should take, and if Cressy kept indoors and had no contact with the outside world, surely—— But there were the servants . . .

A faint draught of warm air fluttered the muslin flounces of Cressy's dress and her small hands came up to grip the lapels of his uniform coat. She said urgently: 'There is something the matter. I know there is. Is it Captain Frost?'

'Frost?' He was relieved at finding something else to think about, and it was a measure of his anxiety that the thought of Rory Frost could be a relief instead of an active irritant: 'Why should you think that?'

'Because you wanted to arrest him and now you have. Papa says he has been imprisoned in the Arab Fort and that his crew were ordered to leave the Island within a day and not come back. But I know they haven't gone yet. Their ship is still in the harbour. Bofabi told me. Is that why you are worried? Do you suppose they have stayed because they mean to try and rescue him? or – or to make more trouble in the city?'

Her voice quavered on the last words, for the ugly sight and the uglier sound of that threatening mob of yelling, dark-faced men who had besieged the Consulate for two terrifying days was still all too vivid in her memory, and she could neither forget it nor prevent her nerves from leaping apprehensively at every unexplained noise from the direction of the city.

Dan felt the shiver that ran through her slight body, and he put his hands over hers, holding them tightly against him: 'They couldn't do it, my darling, even if they wanted to. For one thing there aren't enough of them, and it wasn't they who were responsible for the rioting. It was the men off the dhows.'

'Then why hasn't the *Virago* gone? What are they staying for? Why are they still here?' Once again there was a note of panic in her voice, and Dan said reassuringly: 'It's only because a child who was to have gone with them is sick and cannot be moved, and they won't go without her. That's all.'

'*What child?*' The question came from behind them, and Dan released Cressy's hands and turned quickly. He had not heard the door open, for he had closed it so hastily behind him that the latch had not caught and the draught had drawn it open: and now Hero Hollis was standing on the threshold, staring at him with wide, startled eyes.

She said again, and with an odd suggestion of urgency: 'What child? Whose child is sick?'

'Frost's,' said Dan curtly.

Hero took a step into the room. 'Are you sure? Who told you? Couldn't it just be an excuse for not leaving – for staying here?'

It almost sounded as though she were pleading with him to agree with her, and Dan was puzzled by the urgency in her voice until it occurred to him that she must have heard of the cholera and was afraid of it; as Cressy was afraid of further riots.

He said quickly: 'It's only some fever. I went to the house myself when I saw that the *Virago* had not sailed, and saw Potter and Ralub. The child is not well and Potter refuses to move her, and since neither the crew nor Ralub will leave without them, they have all stayed. I suppose we could have insisted on the rest of them going, but we'd have had to escort them out, and as soon as we were out of sight they'd only have put back and turned up in the city inside two days. So they may as well stay where we can watch them.'

'Have they sent for a doctor?' demanded Hero urgently.

'Why should they want——? Oh, you mean for the child? I imagine they will have called in some local quack, but I do not suppose——'

'A local quack! You mean a *hakim*? But all he would prescribe would be something like draughts of water in which charms have been boiled. You know that! Why did you not send at once for Dr Kealey? He would know what to do. You must send word to him immediately!'

The alarm in her voice irritated Dan, for he had not previously supposed her to be lacking in courage, and to find her losing her head because she suspected that cholera might have broken out in a quarter of the city nearer to the Consulate was profoundly disturbing. He had been counting upon her to be a support and encouragement to Cressy in the trying days ahead, for he had always considered her to be a remarkably strong-minded young woman: an opinion that had been confirmed by her extraordinary behaviour following upon her rape by Rory Frost. And although the fortitude and obstinacy that she had displayed on that occasion had seemed to him misplaced (Dan preferred women to be delicate and sensitive, and would have had far more sympathy with tears, hysteria and the vapours), it had at least encouraged him to think that she could be relied upon to keep a level head in the present crisis, and provide a rock to which his gentle, sensitive Cressy, and her over-emotional Mama, could cling. Yet here she was, going to pieces at the first mention of an epidemic and showing no consideration whatsoever for his Cressida's nerves.

Dan could only presume that disease and the fear of infection was the indomitable Miss Hollis's Achilles heel and he found it difficult to keep the irritation out of his voice. Making the effort, he said in a calm and encouraging tone:

'I assure you there is not the least necessity to call upon Dr Kealey for a diagnosis, as the symptoms of cholera are clearly recognizable and this is merely some sort of fever. Even if it were typhoid there is no reason for you to suppose that it will spread, while as for the cholera, if you keep to the house and the garden and take a few simple precautions, you should have nothing to——'

'*Typhoid!*' said Hero in a whisper. 'But that is as bad as cholera . . .' Her eyes lost their frozen intentness and became bright with anger: 'And you have done nothing! Even though you know that Batty and Ralub may not dare to go to Dr Kealey, and that Captain Frost cannot because he is in jail! Why, if they would not sail on Thursday night she must have been taken sick before then: nearly two days ago! And all you can do is to talk about cholera——!'

She whirled round in a swish of petticoats and starched poplin and they heard her running down the hall, and then the slam of the front door as it swung to behind her.

'I don't understand,' said Cressy helplessly. 'Where has she gone to? What did she mean? Is there really cholera in Malindi, Dan? Is it dangerous? She's gone out without even a hat, and she'll only get sun-stroke and if there's cholera in the city . . . Oh, Dan, we ought to fetch her back at once! Run——!'

But Dan had no intention of making a spectacle of himself chasing through the streets after Miss Hero Hollis. He felt confident that she would not go further than the Kealeys' house, which was no great distance from the Consulate, and that Dr Kealey's admirable good sense could not fail to restore her to a calmer frame of mind.

In the first of these assumptions he was correct, because Hero had indeed gone to the Kealeys' house: hurrying hatless and unattended through the streets, to the shocked horror of the Consulate porter, who had feebly attempted to prevent her departure. She had found the doctor just returned from a prolonged conference with Colonel Edwards (the subject under discussion had been what measures, if any, could be taken to prevent or control the epidemic that was threatening the city), and in the circumstances he might have been excused had he shown small sympathy with Hero's anxiety, and even less for its cause. But he was a kindly man with a fondness for children and a strong liking for Hero Hollis, whom he considered a sensible woman with very little nonsense about her, and he had listened to her attentively and agreed to accompany her at once to The Dolphins' House; having first provided her with one of his wife's sun-hats and a parasol.

Batty and Ralub, and indeed every member of the household, had been inexpressibly relieved to see her, and in some curious way it had seemed a home-coming: as though she were returning to people she was familiar with and a house she had always known. It was difficult to believe that she had only been there twice before.

She recalled the first occasion on which she had passed under those carved dolphins with Fattûma: shrouded in the stifling black street-garb of an Arab woman and convinced that she was entirely in the right. It seemed a very long time ago. Almost as if it were in some other life and had involved another woman and not Hero Hollis at all.

So much had happened since then to alter and separate her from the person she had once been, that she seemed to have no affinity with that egotistical, self-righteous girl who had intended to set Zanzibar to rights, clean up the streets, change the succession and put an end to slavery, and been entirely confident of her ability to do so. Or with the puritanical young woman who had been so inexpressibly horrified to find that a lawless ne'er-do-well, who had inadvertently rescued her from drowning, kept a coloured mistress and had fathered a bastard child. She had run from the house as though it had been infected by a far worse plague than typhoid or cholera, and scrubbed herself with carbolic soap in a foolish attempt to cleanse herself from moral contamination. Yet now she knelt by that same child's bed, holding a hot little hand in hers and careless of the fact that by doing so she exposed herself to a physical infection that might do considerably more damage to her bodily health than the other had done to her susceptibilities.

The room where Amrah lay was one that had been Zorah's, and it should have been quiet and comparatively cool, for it looked out into the garden and the sea, and faced the prevailing breeze. But the windows were shut fast and it was full of mirrors and draperies, cushioned divans and a clutter of ornamental bric-a-brac, and far too many people: the fat little negress, Ifabi, wringing her hands and making low moaning noises; Amrah's nurse, Dahili, clucking like an anxious hen in an attempt to induce the sick child to swallow a cooling drink, and at least half-a-dozen other women proffering advice or crouching by the child's bed to fan her with palmetto fans.

'I can't keep 'em out, miss,' confessed Batty, his whiskered face grey with weariness and anxiety: 'They've looked after 'er since she was born, and you can't expect 'em to leave 'er be when she's took sick.'

The women stood back reluctantly to allow Dr Kealey to approach, surveying him with wary, anxious faces and a mixture of hope and suspicion, but he was surprised to note that they accepted Hero's presence not only with relief, but with a lack of surprise that suggested she was no stranger in that house. Which was a preposterous idea, and he dismissed it instantly, concentrating his attention upon the child while Hero murmured soothing endearments and Batty and the women watched him with held breath.

'I am very much afraid that it is typhoid,' said Dr Kealey, confirming their worst fears. And he had attempted to send Hero away, saying that it was dangerous for her to stay, and that there was nothing she could do that the women of the household could not do as well.

'You know very well that isn't so,' reproved Hero, not moving. 'I'm not properly trained, but I do know something about nursing. And if it is typhoid she is going to need that. I can nurse her if you will tell me what must be done, but none of these women will be any use, because they will only cry over her and fuss her and not use the least firmness – besides being quite capable of giving her horrible brews or trying the effect of some dreadful charm.'

Dr Kealey was in entire agreement with her, but since the child was clearly too ill to be moved, there was nothing for it but to leave her in their charge and hope that Mr Potter would be able to restrain them from trying any unorthodox remedies. But he had forgotten how stubborn Miss Hollis could be.

Hero had no intention of leaving, and any suggestion of removing her by force was out of the question, for though Batty Potter might be disposed of easily enough, Ralub would not stand idly by. And neither would the rest of Rory Frost's rascally crew. Dr Kealey was compelled to accept her decision, and he knew that from the child's point of view it was the right one, for although lost in a fog of weakness and fever, Amrah had still known her, and had held out dry, burning little hands with a croak of joy, clutching at her as though afraid to let her go:

'You've *did* come back! Dahili said you wouldn't, but I knewed you would 'cos you promised, and you ain't a n'angel. Unker Batty says Mama can't never come back 'cos she's a n'angel now and God wants her. *I* want 'er too! but Unker Batty says . . . You won't go, will you?'

'No honey, of course I won't. Hush now, and if you're a good girl and lie quiet, I'll tell you a story about a mermaid: *Once upon a time . . .*'

Listening to her, Dr Kealey wondered yet again how on earth Miss Hollis had come to know of the child's existence, let alone make friends with it, and what connection she could possibly have with Frost or his house or his crew? But that was a mystery that would have to keep, for what was of more importance at the moment was the undoubted fact that Miss Hollis would be invaluable in a sickroom. She not only had some experience of nursing, but her hands were firm and cool, her voice quiet and confident, and her very presence reassuring. There was, thought Dr Kealey, something indestructible about that classic beauty of feature and the tall, lovely body that was so young and strong: an enduring quality that seemed to deny the very existence of defeat or death, and that was in itself a source of refreshment and a negation of despair.

He did not think it odd that she should trouble to interest herself in the welfare of this small half-caste child, for he was an uncomplicated man who liked to believe that all normal women dote upon children. And if he gave Rory Frost a second thought, it was only to be thankful that he was safely in jail and therefore unable to subject Miss Hollis to the indignity of meeting such a person. He imagined that some servant in her uncle's house must have told her that a child whose father was white and in jail was seriously ill, and that womanly compassion had done the rest. She was known to be charitably disposed. All the same, her relatives were not going to like this! He did not like it much himself, though it comforted him somewhat to remember that working in a Charity Hospital could not have been easy or pleasant, and she had survived that.

He left a few instructions, and promising to return within a matter of hours, departed reluctantly; faced with the unwelcome task of informing the American Consul that his niece intended to spend the next few days in the house of the Dolphins, nursing a serious case of typhoid fever . . .

The resulting uproar had been every bit as unpleasant as he had imagined it would be: the girl's betrothed asserting furiously that he had no right to let her accompany him to such a house, and Mr Hollis roundly declaring that he was out of patience with Hero! she had been nothing but a constant source of trouble since her own stubborn folly had led her to being swept overboard on the outward voyage, and the sooner they packed her back to Boston the better. It was outrageous, said Uncle Nat, that the accredited representative of a powerful Democracy should be compelled to present himself at the house of a jailed slaver in order to command the return of a spoilt, head-strong and conceited chit who not only needed her bottom smacked, but was quite capable of refusing to accompany him, and thereby putting him to the shameful necessity of removing her by force.

'I hardly like to say so,' ventured Dr Kealey with some diffidence, 'but I do not think you would be able to do that. I am very much afraid that Frost's men, and indeed the entire household, would not permit it.'

'I cannot believe——' began the Consul angrily, and stopped, because he could. He could believe anything of Rory Frost's men. And almost anything of Hero Athena Hollis!

He scowled at the luckless Dr Kealey, whom he was inclined to blame for the whole outrageous situation (Clay was quite right, the man should never have allowed Hero to accompany him), and turned to look at Dan, who was fully occupied with comforting Cressy. The sight did nothing to soothe his acerbated feelings, since it not only reminded him that this was his prospective son-in-law, but that it was Dan who had rashly informed Hero that Frost's child was sick, and then done nothing whatever to stop her rushing out of the house, or made any attempt to pursue her.

He said tartly: 'In that case I suggest the Lieutenant sends an armed detachment of his seamen to escort my niece back home. I reckon that now Frost's in jail and his crew only here on sufferance, they won't come up against any serious opposition. And it'll certainly look a heap better than either myself or my step-son being obliged to call at that house, and maybe getting handed a jugful of insolence!'

Dan hastily pocketed the handkerchief with which he had been drying Cressy's tears and said a little confusedly: 'Yes, of course, sir. I mean, it seems an excellent idea. I'm sure Miss Hollis will see reason and agree to return without putting you to any further inconvenience.'

But Miss Hollis had not agreed to return and appeared incapable of seeing reason, and it was Dan who had suffered defeat. He had gone to The Dolphins' House with Dr Kealey, feeling irritated and impatient, and accompanied by half-a-dozen armed bluejackets who had remained in the courtyard while he and the doctor had been ushered upstairs to the room that had once been Zorah's.

It had undergone a startling transformation in the last hour, for it had been stripped of all the rugs, draperies and knick-knacks that had so recently furnished it, and now contained only the child's small bed, a couch, a bedside table and a single chair. Half-closed wooden shutters excluded the harsh sunlight but allowed the sea wind to blow through the room and cool it pleasantly, and the walls and floor showed signs of being freshly scrubbed.

Dr Kealey observed these details with deep approval and once again found himself thinking that Miss Hollis, whatever her uncle might say, was really a most sensible young woman. He wondered what magic she had used to induce the disreputable Mr Potter, the two devoted negresses and the various other household retainers to retreat from the sickroom and wait patiently – and silently! – in the verandah outside, and noted with approval that she had removed her hoops and managed to turn up the skirt of her plain grey poplin dress so that it did not trail upon the floor. She looked, he thought, as clean and cool and uncluttered as the room, and refreshingly free from megrims and nonsense.

The child had fallen into an uneasy sleep, and Hero, who had been sitting beside her keeping the flies from her face with a small palm-leaf fan, rose immediately and came quietly to the door, beckoning Batty Potter to take her place. She did not look at Dan; and Dr Kealey, forgetful of their mission, said approvingly: 'You have worked wonders my dear, I congratulate you. She will do a deal better now. How long has she been sleeping?'

He spoke in the unhurried undertone of one who is accustomed to talk in the presence of sleepers, and Hero answered him in the same quiet tone, giving him details that he listened to with attention, frowning or nodding in agreement, while Batty watched in silence and Dan stood back, realizing that it was not going to be as simple as he had supposed

478

to take Miss Hollis away with him and restore her to her relatives, and that he had misjudged both her and the situation.

Earlier that day he had thought her poor-spirited and hysterical, and later, while admitting his mistake, had regarded her behaviour with an exasperation that equalled her uncle's – as if they had not got enough troubles already without that damned girl adding to them! In the heat of that moment he had very nearly refused to retrieve Mr Hollis's errant niece for him, on the grounds that it was no part of the duties of Her Majesty's Navy to invite further uproar by ordering an American citizen out of an English slaver's house, thereby risking violent opposition from the Arab and African members of that household, all of whom were well aware that he, Dan, had been largely responsible for throwing the owner into jail!

That he had not refused had been solely due to the fact that he could not bring himself to add to his Cressida's anxieties by refusing to rescue her tiresome cousin from the scrape into which her own rashness had landed her, and he had arrived at The Dolphins' House in no good humour and prepared to carry out the task with a high hand. But now, looking about him, he found himself once again, and with reluctance, being compelled to revise his views; for having had occasion to visit the place frequently of late, the fact that Hero Hollis had been able, in a mere matter of hours, to bring order out of chaos and exert her authority over Frost's polyglot household, shed an entirely new light on her character and capabilities.

He knew that she must, of necessity, be tolerably well acquainted with the *Virago*'s crew. But being unaware that she had twice visited this house, he was startled to find her so much at home in it and so completely in control. And so well aware of what she was doing, that when the doctor turned to look at his patient and she had leisure to notice Dan Larrimore's presence, she waved him back from the door, and following him into the verandah outside said: 'Please don't go in there. Dr Kealey says that she has typhoid fever, and you mustn't risk taking the infection back to Cressy.'

It was a point that had hitherto escaped Dan and could not not fail to have its effect, and Hero saw the sudden startled look in his eyes and followed up her advantage ruthlessly:

'I'm not sure that you could, but it's better to be on the safe side; because Cressy's constitution is not nearly as strong as mine. So will you please tell my aunt that I think it would be better if I did not go back to the house at all just now. And *do* see that she does not worry about me, for there is not the least necessity to do so: Dr Kealey will be calling frequently, and she knows that I never get ill! And you may tell her too that there are dozens of women to look after me, and that I shall take the greatest care to see that all the drinking water is boiled and the drains kept clean, and that they do not leave food uncovered where it can attract flies. So there is really nothing for her to worry about except to see that Cressy does not go into the town, for Batty tells me that a cholera epidemic has broken out and . . . But I suppose you know that?'

'Yes,' said Dan, speaking for the first time.

He did not add anything to that brief affirmative, and Hero said: 'Oh, and there is another thing: I shall need some clothes and my nightwear. Please tell Aunt Abby, "not too much and nothing frilly". And perhaps you would be so kind as to send one of your men with them, because I would rather Uncle Nat's people did not come here; and certainly not Aunt Abby or Cressy though I know they will wish to. We cannot risk either of them contracting the fever, and with the streets in such a deplorable state, and cholera in the city, they are safer at home.'

'Yes,' said Dan again, slowly. He looked at Hero with a new respect and was silent because all the things he had meant to say seemed trivial and unnecessary.

A weak, fretful whimper made her turn swiftly and leave him, and a moment later he heard her speaking lovingly and reassuringly in the shadowed room: 'I'm here, honey. It's all right; I'm here.'

'You make 'im . . . *please* make 'im!' sobbed a small voice, so weak from fever that it was barely audible: 'You can, can't you? 'Cos you k'n do anyfing . . .'

'Make who do what, sugar?'

'God. Make 'im let Mama come back . . . jus' for a little. Tell 'im I only want to see her. You k'n tell 'im . . .'

'I can ask Him, honey. I promise I'll ask Him – we'll both ask Him. Now be a good girl and don't cry any more. Try to go to sleep, hm?'

'I will if you sing me. Sing me 'bout Ejerlan . . .'

Dan, listening, heard Hero's warm contralto, low-pitched and soothing, singing the song of a captive people to the little daughter of a slave trader and the slave whom he had bought for a few shillings and a bolt of cheap cloth – ' "*Go down, Moses, way down in Egypt's land, and tell ole Pharaoh, to let my people go . . .*" '

Dr Kealey, joining the Lieutenant in the verandah a few minutes later, looked an enquiry and was answered by a shake of the head and a brief, negative gesture that needed no interpretation.

'I agree,' said Dr Kealey, relieved. And added uneasily: 'The Hollises are not going to like it. They will certainly object.'

'Yes,' agreed Dan; but not as though it mattered.

'There is of course always the risk that she may take the infection,' persisted the doctor, arguing with himself rather than Dan as they walked together towards the stone staircase and the courtyard: 'But apart from that I cannot believe that she will come to any harm here; and she may do much good, for that child is seriously ill, and left to those serving women would not stand a chance. They have no understanding of the value of cleanliness and quiet in such cases, and most of their remedies are worse than useless. Far worse! But Miss Hollis has a great deal of sense, and can be trusted to carry out instructions. And after all, she is of age and her own mistress.'

'Yes,' concurred Dan; aware that some answer was expected of him, and continuing to confine himself to that useful monosyllable. He collected his men from the courtyard with a curt jerk of the head, and walked back through the hot, crowded streets to face a difficult half-hour with his prospective father-in-law

It had not been a pleasant interview and he was relieved when it was over. But there had, of course been nothing anyone could do about Hero, since as Dr Kealey had already pointed out, she was of age and her own mistress; and her aunt, though deeply concerned on her behalf, was even more concerned on Cressida's. That ominous word 'typhoid', had been enough to send Abigail into a maternal panic, and she had immediately sided with Dan and agreed that it would be better if Hero kept away from the Consulate while there was any danger of her bringing the infection with her.

As for Clayton, there were several good reasons why he would have preferred to keep well clear of The Dolphins' House, but when Dan's mission proved abortive, he had gone there himself, and succeeded in gaining an interview with his betrothed. But it had proved as unsatisfactory, and quite as distasteful, as the one Dan had endured at the Consulate.

Hero had only been able to spare him a few minutes, for the child was awake and racked with fever, and though she listened to him patiently enough there was an abstracted look in her eyes and a faint frown between her brows, and he was resentfully aware that she was giving him only half her attention. His voice began to rise, and she lifted a hand quickly, hushing him:

'Please, Clay. Don't be angry! I know how you feel and that you are only anxious on my account. But this is something I have to do.'

'Why? it's nothing whatever to do with you. Why in thunder can't you think of me for a change? - of *my* feelings instead of always your own? Or if mine are of no importance to you, you might try thinking of all the anxiety you are causing Ma and Cressy and your uncle.'

481

'I have thought of it,' said Hero, distressed. 'And I am very sorry that they are worried, but there is no need for them to be, because——'

'Because it doesn't mean a blamed thing to you compared with getting your own way and interfering in matters that are no concern of yours, does it?' interrupted Clay furiously.

'That is not true. And it does concern me: and you too, Clay.'

'*Me?* Just what do you mean by that?'

'You know. Or you should know.'

'I don't know what you're talking about, unless you're going to tell me that after all that has happened, you still reckon we owe that god-damned slaver something for pulling you out of the sea——'

'I wasn't thinking of him. I was thinking of Zorah.'

She saw Clayton's flushed face pale and his eyes turn aside from hers, and said unhappily: 'You see, Clay, if she had been alive she might have prevented this. Or if she could not, she would at least have noticed it earlier and been here to nurse the child. And – and you told me that it was partly my fault that you did . . . what you did. That I helped drive you to it. I don't know if that's true or not, but you must see that I – that we . . . Clay, we *cannot* let her child die! Not without trying to do all we can to prevent it. We owe her that much.'

Clayton's wandering gaze returned to her face and his grey eyes were hard. He said harshly: 'Yes, I guess I see all right! This is your way of getting back at me. Not a generous, warm-hearted gesture at all, but a carefully-thought-out punishment. Real smart of you, my dear, and I guess I deserve it. But don't you think you might have thought up some way of paying me out that didn't involve my mother and sister in so much distress, or put my step-father to so much embarrassment? It seems a mite unfair that they should have to suffer for my misdeeds. But maybe our collective misery will serve to even your score with me.'

Hero said helplessly: 'It is not that at all. I'm only trying to – to atone a little for something that . . . Oh, what's the use of talking if you do not *wish* to understand? And it is not only that; I have become fond of the child for her own sake, too.'

'One of Frost's bastards!' said Clayton, spitting the words out as though they were acid in his mouth.

Hero's face was suddenly rigid, but she did not raise her voice and it remained low-pitched and even: 'You forget,' she said quietly, 'that I may bear one of them myself.'

She turned from him with a faint rustle of poplin, and when he would have followed her he found his way barred by Batty Potter, who stepped out of the shadows of the sickroom and stood wiry and immobile in the doorway, his eyes cold chips of granite and the set of his whiskered jaw very sobering to hot blood. Batty might be getting old, but he had learned his fighting in a hard school where there were no such things as Queensberry Rules; and he too had not forgotten Zorah.

They looked at each other for a long, measuring minute, and then Batty sighed and said softly: 'I wouldn't – not if I was you, Mister Mayo.'

He shook his grizzled head regretfully, realizing that this was neither the time nor the place for loud words and blows, and that much as he would have liked to try his hand at rearranging Mr Mayo's handsome features, there was nothing for it but to see that the unwelcome visitor left quickly – and quietly.

'Ain't no sense in getting your dander up when you're one agin a dozen,' remarked Batty reasonably, 'for that ain't nowise good odds, and you don't want to go gettin' yourself 'eaved out of the 'ouse by a lot of low deck'ands, now do you? So just you go 'ome quiet-like and tell your folks that they've no call to go worritin' themselves over Miss 'Ero, for no one ain't going to lay a finger on 'er. Juman 'ere'll show you out.'

Clayton had known the risk he had run when he had come to The Dolphins' House, and he had come armed. But he also had the sense to know when he was beaten. The old man was right, and there was nothing to be gained by a show of force except the humiliation of being ejected by a handful of grinning Africans – unless he used his revolver, which would only result in the death of several people, including himself.

His left hand ceased to be a fist, and the right, which had moved towards the holster concealed under his coat, fell to his side. Turning on his heel he left without further words, ignoring Jumah who hurried ahead of him to see that the door was opened and waited to make sure that it was barred behind him. He had not attempted a second visit, and later that day his mother had packed a valise which had been delivered to Hero by an able seaman from the *Daffodil*.

Nathaniel Hollis had made no further move to bring his niece to her senses, and had flatly refused Cressy's plea that she might call and see how Hero went on. He too had become alarmed by the thought of typhoid, and so afraid for the safety of his daughter that he was almost tempted to ask Dr Kealey not to call at the Consulate with news of Hero, for fear that he might carry the contagion with him.

But it was not long before the threat of typhoid, terrible as it had once seemed, faded into insignificance against the towering menace of the cholera, and Dr Kealey no longer had time to call on Mr Consul Hollis; and little enough to spare for Amrah, struggling feebly for life in an upper room of the house of the Dolphins. The life of one small child shrank in importance when hundreds were dying daily in the crowded hovels of the Black Town, the stifling streets, the bazaars and the tall Arab houses of Zanzibar city, and in villages among the coconut groves and the clove plantations.

It was too late now for Nathaniel Hollis to regret that he had not moved his family to a house in the country, for by this time there were none available. All he could do was confine his wife and daughter to the Consulate and pray for a ship: an American ship. Or a European one bound for some safe port that would take Abigail and Cressy out of this pest-house of an island.

But no ship came, and those dhows that had been in harbour when the cholera struck hastened to leave it, and spread the news up and down the coast that to put in to Zanzibar was to court death, so that the harbour was emptier than it had been since the coming of Seyyid Saïd the first Sultan, and save for Majid's few ships and a handful of fishing boats, only the *Daffodil* and the *Virago* remained at anchor . . .

'Surely, Colonel, there can no longer be any necessity to keep Larrimore and his men here for our protection?' argued Mr Hubert Platt, whose wife Jane was in a fever of anxiety on account of the twins, and had been pestering him night and day to arrange for their transport out of the Island: 'Would it not be possible to send some of the families away on the *Daffodil*?'

But the British Consul was still reluctant to rid himself of the only deterrent the city possessed against the return of the pirates, and he hesitated to turn the *Daffodil* into a passenger ship when she might still be needed for sterner duties. Besides, for all they knew the epidemic might burn itself out sooner than they supposed, and without affecting the better built and more open portions of the Stone Town where the white community lived. Or the *Cormorant* might arrive earlier than expected; or possibly another ship——?

But the death rate leapt, and the *Cormorant*, coming on the track of a slaver, altered course and sailed southward on a long chase that was to postpone her arrival by several weeks. And two serving-women at Beit-el-Tani, a native clerk from the French Consulate, and one of Clayton Mayo's grooms, died of the cholera. Their deaths were only four among two hundred and thirty-seven deaths in Zanzibar that day, but they proved that even the privileged dwellers in the Stone Town were not immune, and Dan, calling on his betrothed the following evening, found her mother in tears and the Consul looking haggard and grim. A young relative of Clayton's late groom, who had been serving as a dish-washer in the Consulate kitchen, had died that very afternoon and in the servants' quarters attached to the house . . .

'They say he had been to his uncle's funeral,' wept Abby, twisting her wet handkerchief until the fabric tore: 'And though he did not feel well this morning, he got up as usual and helped in the kitchen until—— Cook says he just fell down on the floor and—— and they had to carry him out to the quarters and—— I didn't know it could be so quick. It was only hours! He was alive this afternoon, and now . . . And it happened right here in the house. In our own kitchen! They didn't even tell us until an hour ago, and we've all been eating our meals off plates and cups that he must have touched, and . . .'

'Now, Abby,' interposed her husband soothingly, patting her plump shoulders with a hand that was almost as unsteady as her own.

The news had shaken Dan quite as badly as it had shaken Cressy's parents, and for the same reason. What was the good of confining her to the house and the garden when the cholera was already here, inside their own walls? He looked at Nathaniel Hollis, and for the first time the two men, father and suitor, not only understood each other but were in complete agreement. And it was at that moment that Nathaniel Hollis's liking for the younger man began; born of the conviction that here was someone who cared just as deeply for Cressy as he himself did, and could be trusted to take good care of her.

'How soon can they be ready, sir?' asked Dan as though everything had already been discussed and agreed upon – as indeed it had.

'Inside an hour, I guess,' replied the Consul promptly.

'I'm afraid it won't be quite as soon as that, sir. There will be a good many arrangements to make.'

'And your Consul's premission to get.'

'Of course, sir. But I do not think that will be difficult, because he has already received similar suggestions from other residents, and it's getting plainer every day that as far as the pirates are concerned the cholera will prove a far more effective deterrent than any force we could provide. They will not be back this year, and if they have put in at any other coastal port the chances are that a good many of them are dead by now.'

Colonel Edwards had already come round to the same opinion, and as Dan had predicted, it had been easy enough to gain his consent to embark any families of foreign residents who wished to leave, and to take them at once to the Cape, from whence they could return to their several countries or wait until it was safe to rejoin their husbands in Zanzibar.

'No one is going to raise any riots at a time like this,' agreed Colonel Edwards grimly. He had sent word to the consulates and the houses of the European merchants, and helped to see that the *Daffodil* was adequately provisioned for such a voyage and provided with such medicines as could be spared from his own and Dr Kealey's all too slender resources.

485

At no time during the busy hours that elapsed between the decision to sail and the moment when the *Daffodil*'s weed-hung anchor rose dripping from the harbour bed, did either Colonel Edwards or Daniel Larrimore spare a thought for Captain Emory Frost of the *Virago*, left a prisoner in the Arab Fort. And even if they had remembered him it would have been impossible to take him on board, since every spare foot of space was crammed to overflowing with women and children, cots, perambulators, travelling trunks and bulging valises. They had, however, quite simply forgotten him: and as the white coral town and the green trees of Zanzibar began to fade in the heat haze, it was Cressy's face that Dan looked at and not the walls of the Arab Fort, still visible beyond the rocky outline of Grave Island.

The wives and families of most of the city's white colony had gathered on deck to wave a tearful 'Goodbye' to husbands and fathers standing on the shore. But Hero Hollis had not been among them. She had refused to leave the Island as quietly and as stubbornly as she had refused to leave The Dolphins' House, and when at the urgent insistence of his wife and daughter her uncle had called at the house with the intention of ordering her obedience, he had not been admitted. The only foreigner permitted entrance was Dr Kealey, and it was he who in the end had carried letters to Hero: letters from Aunt Abby, Cressy and Clay, a brief note from Uncle Nat and a verbal message, equally brief, from Dan. He had also carried the answers, which were all substantially the same; though he too had done what he could to persuade her to change her mind.

'I have to tell you,' said Dr Kealey reluctantly, 'that in my opinion the child stands very little chance of recovery. And if she dies after the ship has sailed——'

'She won't,' said Hero.

'They cannot wait for you,' warned Dr Kealey.

'No. They must go as quickly as they can. Give Aunt Abby and Cressy my dearest love, and tell them that I am sorry, but I cannot go with them. And please thank Lieutenant Larrimore for his offer, and say he must not let Cressy worry. She gets so easily upset.'

'*He* doesn't,' said Dr Kealey dryly.

'I know. I used to think he would not do at all for Cressy, but now I am not so sure, for he will always love her and look after her, and be . . .' Hero hesitated for a moment and then said: 'dependable. Cressy needs someone like that, and maybe it'll turn out after all that she has shown a great deal of sense in falling in love with him.'

'I think so,' agreed Dr Kealey.

'Do you? I'm glad. Tell her that I—— No. You had better not tell her anything. Just say *"thank you"* to them all for troubling about me and

486

that I hope they may forgive me for not wishing to go with them, but that you will be here to see that I come to no harm.'

'I will do that,' said Dr Kealey; and added with a wry smile: 'Millicent will not go either.'

'Your wife? – is she staying?'

'She insists that she must remain to see that I take the precautions I urge upon others. But that is only an excuse. The real reason is that she is a damned obstinate woman who is as stubborn as – as——'

'Myself!' finished Hero with a faint smile.

'I was going to say "as a mule",' confessed the doctor, 'but perhaps you are right. Try and get a bit more rest, my dear. You are looking very worn.'

He had conveyed Hero's messages to her relations, and informed Dan that Miss Hollis found herself unable to accept his kind offer.

'I never thought she would,' admitted Dan. 'Is the child still too ill to be moved?'

'The child is dying,' said Dr Kealey bluntly: and saw Dan's face stiffen.

'I'm sorry, I had hoped that perhaps ... How long?'

'I don't know. A day. Two days? Three at most.'

'We can't wait that long. If we go at all it must be at once.'

'She knows that. She said to tell you not to let Miss Cressida worry.'

Dan did not say anything for several minutes but stood looking fixedly at the floor, and at last he said curtly: 'Tell her I'll try.'

He lifted his head and grinned at the doctor: 'Mr Hollis told me that it was her father who insisted on giving her that damned silly name, but it seems as though he knew what he was about when he did it!'

36

Hero did not know when the *Daffodil* sailed, but Batty had seen the smudge of smoke against the hot sky, and he had fetched Rory's brass-bound telescope and watched her go. And when she had been swallowed up at last by the heat haze he had sighed with relief – because the Captain was still in Zanzibar and so was Miss Hero, and he had been deadly afraid that one or both of them would sail with her.

At least Danny and his bluejackets had gone! And it was a long haul from Zanzibar to the Cape – and a longer one back again, with the wind against them! It would be several weeks before there was any chance of their return, and Batty was inclined to think that it would be nearer three months, and that Dan would receive orders to wait until the epidemic had passed and the end of the 'Long Rains' brought the south-east Trade Winds to aid his return to Zanzibar under sail – thereby saving a parsimonious Admiralty the expense of fuel. But now that the threat of his armed seamen and the *Daffodil*'s guns had been removed, there was every chance that the Baluchi troops in charge of the Fort would prove amenable to bribery and the Captain be permitted to escape. The *Virago* was still in harbour and ready to leave at short notice, and there was no one now to prevent them sailing or to pursue them once they had left. They could quit just as soon as Amrah——

Batty's thoughts jerked to a stop as though the child's name had been a yawning crevasse that gaped suddenly across a pleasant path he had been wandering along; for though he would not admit it, he too could see that she was getting no better (even to himself he would not put it into any stronger words).

She was small, thought Batty, but she was strong and sturdy for her age. Not like these frail little native brats who went out like a candle-flame in a puff of wind at the first touch of sickness. She would soon begin to pick up; Miss Hero would see to that. Miss Hero wouldn't let her go; she was a fighter, miss was. Look how she had stood out against them all when they'd wanted her to go back to her uncle's. And when they'd wanted to ship her off to the Cape? She wouldn't let Amrah die – not Miss Hero!

Batty shivered, remembering the slightness of the little body that had once seemed so sturdy and was now so small that it barely showed under the single thin sheet. He pushed the thought behind him with an effort of will, and putting away the telescope, closed the shutters against the burning day and lay down to get some sleep, for he had taken the last watch of the night while Hero slept, and surrendered his place to her an hour after dawn.

The morning had been hot and still, for the Trade Wind too had been sleeping; but it awoke at midday, and before the afternoon was over it was blowing strongly, sweeping swollen rain clouds before it and sending clouds of evil-smelling dust whirling down the narrow streets of the city. It slammed an unfastened shutter in The Dolphins' House, and Amrah stirred restlessly and when Hero laid a hand on hers she clutched it weakly with small, hot fingers and said in a parched whisper: 'Tell ... tell ...'

'What is it, sweetheart? – what is it you want?'

'Story. Story 'bout ... 'bout ...'

'About the mermaid?'

'No ... 'bout the – the man what planted ... apperseeds.'

'Johnnie Appleseed? All right, pet. If you'll promise to lie as quiet as a mouse while I tell it. "Once upon a time——" '

'No!' – the child's fingers tugged feebly at her hand – 'that ain't ... right. It's "This is a true story 'bout a real live ..." ' The whisper failed; but Hero's heart leapt and she thought: *She's better! She must be. She's talking sensibly, and she knows me!* (she had known no one the previous day, but babbled deliriously, in a mixture of Arabic, Kiswahili and Cockney, to Zorah). Surely this must mean that she was better? Aloud she said: 'So it does. I'd forgotten. I'm sorry, sugar,' – and began the story again; this time as it had always been told before. Amrah sighed contentedly and closed her eyes, and presently, lulled into drowsiness by the narrator's low-pitched and intentionally monotonous voice, she fell asleep.

The wind moaned under the doors and the shutter banged again, echoing hollowly through the quiet house, and Hero rose softly and went out onto the verandah; and hearing voices in the courtyard below, leaned over the rail and saw a woman in a white dress and a wide, floppy hat decorated with roses and ribbons. It was only a very brief glimpse, for the next moment the rain came down and courtyard, woman and voices were all blotted out in a cloud-burst of falling water. But Hero had recognized the hat, and motioning to Dahili to take her place at Amrah's bedside, she picked up her skirts and ran along the verandah and down the winding staircase, thinking that it was just like Olivia to wear that preposterous confection in a high wind and when it was obviously going to rain!

Mrs Credwell was clutching the hat with one hand and still arguing with the doorkeeper when Hero touched her on the arm, and she turned and said as though it was the most natural thing in the world: 'Oh, there you are, Hero. I have just been telling this silly old man that I wished to see you, and – Oh, dear, the *noise*! Can we not go somewhere where we can talk? I can hardly hear myself think!'

She had to raise her voice to be heard above the roar of the rain, but she appeared more concerned with keeping her hat straight and her flounces dry than with any other matters. So like Olivia! thought Hero again, surprised to find how glad she was to see her. It seemed an age since she had last seen or spoken to a white woman, and yet it was less than a week——!

'Come upstairs,' said Hero, clutching her visitor's arm.

The room in which months before she had removed those black, Arab wrappings was dark and gloomy and smelt strongly of mildew, and its great damp-spotted looking-glasses reflected the wild wetness of the afternoon and the ghostly palm trees that flung themselves to and fro beyond the streaming window panes. But the noise of the rain was less audible here, and the wind no more than a draught that billowed the curtains and rippled the Persian carpets that covered the floor.

'I cannot decide,' said Mrs Credwell, frowning over the problem, 'whether it is worse when it rains, or not. One is so pleased when it begins, but it does not really make it much cooler, does it? And if you stand out in it, it is actually *warm*! How is the little girl, Hero? Dr Kealey says——'

'Does he know you are here?' demanded Hero, interrupting her.

'Well, not exactly, but——'

'Olivia, what are you doing here? You shouldn't be here. Haven't the others gone yet?'

'Oh, hours ago. They went this morning and I expect they're all being dreadfully sea-sick by now. With this wind, you know.'

'Why ever didn't you go with them?'

'I didn't want to,' said Mrs Credwell simply.

'But the cholera——!'

'Well, after all, Hero, *you* were not going, so I could see no reason why I should not stay if I wished. Naturally Jane had to go, because of the twins. And she wanted Hubert to go too, but he said he could not possibly leave his work, so I decided that if he could stay I could; because after all, he *is* my brother.'

'They shouldn't have let you stay. They had no right to.'

'They didn't want me to,' admitted Olivia frankly. 'They all talked at me and talked at me, but I was quite firm. I told them that I should be far more comfortable here than being deplorably sea-sick in a tiny cabin with Jane and the twins and I don't know how many other mothers and children as well. Which is quite true. And besides it seemed like – like *deserting*, if you know what I mean.'

'Yes, I know,' said Hero.

'I knew you would.' The pink in Olivia's faded cheeks deepened into an embarrassed flush, and she said hesitantly: 'It's different for the others. They have their children to think of, or—— But I haven't anyone; only Hubert, and he has never worried very much about me. So there was really no reason why I should not stay. Someone has to – if only to show all these poor people who would wish to leave too, and cannot, that we have not *all* run away. There is nothing else, really, that one can do.'

'No,' said Hero slowly, seeing Olivia Credwell with new eyes and wondering if it took disaster to bring out the best in people who would normally be accounted merely foolish and sentimental. Olivia was both. But the foolishness that had led her to prefer the horrors of a cholera epidemic to the possibility of sea-sickness in an over-crowded cabin, and the sentimentality that had urged her to stay behind in order to bring a little reassurance to 'all those poor people' for whom she could do nothing, had become changed by the changing circumstances into courage. An addle-headed courage, since it had obviously never occurred to her that she risked infection by walking through the fetid streets or visiting a house where a child lay sick with typhoid fever. But courage all the same. Olivia was not clever, but she was generous and warm-hearted; and that, thought Hero, who had often been irritated by her gushing silliness, was enough – and more than enough!

'You must wonder why I have not called before,' said Olivia. 'But I only heard about you when I went to see Jane and the children off. Cressy told me everything. And Dr Kealey was there too, and he said you were keeping well, but that it had been considered wiser not to let Cressy leave the house – except to go on board, of course – because of the infection, and that was why she had not been able to see you. She had wished so much to do so, but they would not let her; or your aunt either. And one cannot be surprised at it, for typhoid fever is a most dangerous disease, and I believe contagious.'

'Which is why you should not have come here either,' said Hero, 'and why I must send you away at once.'

'Oh, you need not trouble about me,' Olivia assured her earnestly. 'Because I have had it, you know. Mortimer – my late husband – and I both contracted it during our honeymoon visit to Brussels. It killed him, but I recovered, and I do not *think* one can get it a second time.'

'Perhaps not; I don't know. But I do know that you should not go

491

about the town when there are so many new cases of cholera every day, because you cannot have had *that* before.'

'No, indeed. But I am told that Europeans have a greater immunity to it than Africans and Asiatics, and I am sure that is true, for I was taking coffee with Thérèse after we had seen the others off, and she told me that many of the poor creatures have taken to painting their faces with white-wash in the belief that the cholera only attacks those who are dark skinned. So you see——'

'Thérèse?' said Hero sharply. 'Did Madame Tissot not go?'

'No. I am afraid dear Thérèse is not very fond of children, and when she found that she would have to share a cabin with Frau Lessing and little Karl and Hanschen, and Lotte and the baby and Mrs Bjornson and her three little girls, and—— Well, Thérèse said that death was preferable and that she would rather stay and contract cholera. She is such an amusing creature. And most courageous, for one of her house-servants died last night and even that did not make her change her mind, though there was still time for her to pack a valise and sail with the others. She asked me to tell you that she admires your courage and quite understands the attitude you have taken.'

'Does she, indeed!' said Hero, annoyed.

'I'm sure we *all* do,' endorsed Olivia warmly. 'So truly noble of you dear – when one considers who the child's father is. Or its mother, for that matter. But as I told her, that is *hardly* the poor little thing's fault, since a child cannot be held responsible for its parents, and a sick child must always command the help and sympathy of any woman of sensibility. Thérèse says that if you should need any help you have only to command her.'

'You may tell Madame Tissot,' said Hero frigidly, 'that I do not stand in any need of her assistance.'

'I did,' confessed Olivia. 'I told her I thought you would find mine quite sufficient for the time being, but——'

'Or yours either, Livvy dear.'

'But Hero——'

'No, Olivia!' said Hero firmly. 'There is nothing you can do here, for Amrah does not know you and a strange face would only worry her. But I am very grateful to you for offering. It was really kind of you. But you must not come here again, because I am sure your brother would not approve, and it is far too dangerous – walking through the streets when the whole town is full of cholera.'

'Oh, *danger*!' said Olivia, dismissing it with an impatient wave of the hand. 'If it comes to that, I do not suppose you have ever had typhoid fever, and yet you did not stay at home or run away to the Cape. And in any case I didn't walk, I rode. Well, I will not tease you to let me stay if you would really rather I did not, but if you should need help at any time will you promise to send for me? Please, Hero?'

'I will, Livvy, I promise. And now I really must go, because I don't like leaving Amrah for too long. When she is ... when she is better I will come and see you.'

'Then she is improving?'

'Yes. I hope so. I don't know,' said Hero. 'I – I think ...'

Her throat seemed to tighten and she could not get the words out, or say what it was that she thought. She could not even say 'Goodbye', and she smiled instead, a strained shadow of a smile, and went quickly away, leaving Mrs Credwell to find her own way out.

Batty and Ralub were standing at the turn of the verandah talking earnestly, their voices almost inaudible in the sound of the falling rain, and though they could hardly have heard Hero's light footsteps on the stone flags, they turned instantly and were silent. Hero stopped. 'What is it?' she demanded, startled by the look on Batty's face.

Ralub said quietly and in Arabic: 'It is nothing.'

'Then why ... Batty, is it Amrah? Is she worse?'

'It ain't 'er,' said Batty reluctantly. 'It's 'im.'

'Him? Who are you talking about?'

'Captain Rory. If you must know, I offers that Baluchi barstard up at the Fort one 'undred o' the best to fix it so that 'e can skip. "Show us your money" 'e says, and I does, and 'e ups and grabs it and says 'e's right sorry, but the Captain 'as give 'is word to old Edwards that 'e won't sling 'is 'ook, so it ain't no manner of good trying to get 'im out.'

'I told you so,' observed Ralub without heat. 'It is a matter of his honour.'

'Bah!' snarled Batty. 'I ain't got no patience with such foolishness! I'd 'ave tried it before only I knows it ain't no manner of use while Dan's 'ere; but now 'e's gone it'd be as easy as kiss-your-'and. If I could 'ave just two words with the Captain – just two——!'

'It would do no good,' said Ralub soothingly. 'You would waste your breath and your money. But he has only given his word that he will not escape from the Fort, and they will not wish to keep him there longer than they must. Once he has left it we——' Ralub stopped on a small embarrassed cough and threw a warning look at Batty; recollecting that Hero, though now regarded as a member of the household, might possibly hold different views on the subject of Captain Frost's detention. But Batty was too anxious and too angry to pay attention to warning looks:

'I know, I know! You told me. Once 'e's out of the Fort we can nab

493

'im. That's as may be. But it'd be a sight easier to get 'im out now! – what with the old *Virago* lying there 'andy-like and no one to stop 'im sailing off in 'er any time 'e fancies.'

Hero said: 'Would you go with him, Batty?'

'Don't be daft!' said Batty, rounding on her angrily: ''Ow could I, with young Amrah sick?'

Ralub grinned, his teeth a flash of whiteness in his dark hawk face. 'And you think he would go without you? You should know better than that!'

Batty scowled at them both and expectorated angrily over the rail. 'All right, all right! But it don't bear thinking of – the Captain shut up in that there stinking 'ell 'ole!'

'He will be as safe there as anywhere,' said Ralub soberly: and saluting Hero with grave courtesy he turned away and went down the two flights of stairs and out into the wet street.

It was still raining when Dr Kealey called. The daylight had faded by then and the lamps made pools of gold in the high, hot rooms where the mist drifted in through doors and windows in warm, ghostly wreaths, blurring the outlines of familiar things so that nothing seemed substantial any more. The bed on which the child lay, and the thin sheet that covered her, felt as damp to the touch as though they had been dipped in water; and there was a faint new film of mildew, like hoar-frost, on the leather cover of the book that Hero had been reading only that morning.

The sound of the rain absorbed all other sounds and created a curious illusion of silence, for though Hero could see the moths and winged insects that fluttered about the lamp and beat their wings against the glass, she could not hear them, and even the strip of coconut matting, lifting to the draught, made no noise.

Over and over again, since the rain began, she had thought that the child had stopped breathing, and had bent above her, straining to catch the faint sound of those shallow breaths. And hearing them had relaxed again, dizzy with relief and telling herself that she was behaving stupidly, because it was surely a good sign that the child should be able to sleep so peacefully?

'I think she is better,' said Hero, rising to relinquish her place to Dr Kealey: and did not know that she had said it defiantly, as though daring him to deny it.

But Batty, standing back among the shadows by the door and watching the doctor's face, knew that there was no longer any hope. And with that knowledge something in him crumbled away and was for ever lost. The last of his middle-age; the lingering remnants of youth and strength. He was suddenly an old man, and only old age lay ahead . . .

Dr Kealey left, knowing that there was nothing more that he could do and wishing that he had, after all, persuaded Dan Larrimore to wait for just one more day. But perhaps it was as well that he had not, for the cholera was gaining ground and spreading with a speed and virulence that he had not thought possible, and the very air of the city smelt of death. He had seen epidemics before, but never one like this. And it was only beginning.

Hero had not watched the doctor's face as Batty had done, because she was afraid of what she would see there. She had listened instead to the controlled, colourless voice that told her nothing, and had answered mechanically: and when he had gone she sank down on her knees beside the bed, and prayed as Miss Penbury had taught her to pray and Barclay had not:

'*Lighten our darkness we beseech Thee. O Lord, and by Thy great mercy deliver us from all perils and dangers of this night . . .*'

No one had ever taught Batty Potter to pray, but he too was putting up his own petitions, though they were different from Hero's, because Batty did not expect miracles, or ask for them:

'Let 'er go easy,' besought Batty, 'and let 'er find 'er Ma.'

The women watching in the verandah, grey-haired Dahili and Ifabi the fat little negress, nodded and slept, and one by one the lights went out until only the door of the child's room glimmered faintly through the darkness and the falling rain, and the hands of Batty's old-fashioned turnip watch stood at midnight.

The lamp flared to a sudden gust of wind that drove the rain in under the arches of the dark verandah, and the old man moved at long last, and shuffled forward to touch Hero's bowed shoulders:

'It's time you 'ad your sleep, Miss 'Ero,' said Batty. 'I'm 'ere now, so you get to your bed, there's a good girl.'

He might have been speaking to Amrah, and Hero lifted her head and tried to smile at him; her face showing white and exhausted and very young in the yellow lamplight.

'There now,' said Batty, patting her shoulder with awkward tenderness: 'There now.'

'It isn't *fair*, Batty,' whispered Hero passionately. 'It isn't fair!'

'There, there,' crooned the old man. 'You been too long on watch; that's what it is. You'll feel better when you've 'ad your sleep.'

'I couldn't sleep. She might . . . she might wake and want me.'

'A fine 'elp you'll be tomorrow if you don't! No good never come of wearin' yourself to a ravelling, and well you knows it. Get along now, Miss 'Ero. I'll call you if you're needed.'

Hero got tiredly to her feet, unwilling to go but knowing that Batty

495

was right and that if she did not rest now she would be in no fit state to take over from him at sunrise. She said: 'You won't let Dahili forget to call me, will you Batty?'

''Ave I ever? You got no call to worry, miss.'

He watched her go, and when the curtain had fallen behind her and the flame of the lamp steadied and burned strongly once more, he sat down slowly and stiffly in the chair that Hero had placed beside the bed, and reaching for one of Amrah's small, lax hands, held it gently in his own gnarled and knotted one so that the child would know that he was there and feel safe and comforted.

He did not know at what hour she died, for he too was very tired. The drumming of the rain had lulled him into the light sleep of old age, and the child slipped away easily, as he had asked. He awoke to find the lamp burning pallidly in the wet grey light of dawn, and the small fingers cold and stiff in his clasp; and did not rouse the women or make any move to wake Hero.

No call to do that now, thought Batty. *She needs 'er sleep.*

He began to croon softly to himself, patting the quiet little hand and singing a monotonous, tuneless ditty that Hero had once heard him sing on the *Virago*, and that Amrah had been fond of:

'*... For she's more t'me than any other thing what I possess,*
And I never will be parted from me Bonnie Brown Bess——'

37

Hero returned to the Consulate on the day that Amrah died.

There was no longer any reason why she should not do so, and her uncle had sent her horse and an escort of three mounted sepoys to fetch her home, because Dr Kealey would not hear of her walking through the streets.

The house seemed very quiet now that both Cressy and Aunt Abby had gone, and though Uncle Nat had welcomed her kindly enough, he had let her see quite clearly that he disapproved of her behaviour and had not forgiven it. Clayton too had been distant and disapproving, and had greeted her with a cold correctness that had been nicely calculated to remind her of her position as his future wife, and the fact that she had failed to live up to it.

He was not to know that a single word of love or sympathy could, at that moment, have won for him all that he wanted. For Hero had returned from The Dolphins' House sad, tired and defeated, and feeling even lonelier and more forlorn than she had felt after Barclay's death.

At least when her father had died there had been the thought of Clay and the future to comfort her: the knowledge that Clay was waiting for her, her plans for the regeneration of Zanzibar, and her confidence in herself. But now there was nothing to hold onto. Her plans had come to nothing and she had been wrong about Clay. Her efforts to help had only brought death and disaster, and all her theories and care and determination had not been able to save the life of one small child. She was lost and adrift in a grey world of rain and sorrow and regret, and if Clayton had only taken her in his arms and comforted her she would have clung to him and forgiven him everything, and turning her back on the past, been content to let him decide her future, because she no longer had any confidence in her own ability to do so.

She had reached, without knowing it, a crossroads that was to decide not only her whole life, but the kind of woman she would become, and Clayton had only to indicate a path for her to have taken. Having taken it she would have held to it, and urged forward by her own self-distrust, become in time all that her class and her century, and Clayton Mayo, expected of a Victorian wife. Biddable, decorous, and well-conducted; agreeing dutifully with her husband's opinions and turning a blind eye to his failings; keeping his house, submitting to his demands and bearing his children. And confining her philanthropic activities to modest donations and a helping hand at Church Bazaars and local charities.

But Clayton was in no mood to sympathize over the tragic ending of an episode that he considered ill-judged, undignified, and personally humiliating to himself. He did not recognize either the signs or the issues involved, and so missed his opportunity.

'I am sorry that you should feel upset,' said Clayton, 'but there was no necessity for you to offer your assistance in the first place. You haven't done a mite of good and merely made yourself and us unhappy. Another time maybe you'll take the advice of those who have your best interests at heart.'

He kissed her cheek in a perfunctory manner, and Hero flinched under the casual possessiveness of that cold caress and felt something die in her. *This is how it will be for the rest of my life,* she thought; and turned and went up to her own room, where she lay on her bed for a long time, wishing that she could cry and finding that she could not. She felt nothing any more for Clay, but she would have to marry him and spend the rest of her life in his company; meekly accepting his strictures or his caresses, permitting him the management of her fortune, and feeling as she felt now – as though it was she and not the child in The Dolphins' House who was dead.

For a moment she could almost envy that child and its mother, because they were finished with all problems and at peace. To have to go on, hurt and disillusioned, schooling oneself to resignation and acceptance and becoming in time a mere automaton, seemed a harder fate than Zorah's. And there was another problem too that might soon have to be faced. It was now more than two months since she had ridden away from The House of Shade in the mist of a rain-swept evening, but she did not know enough to be sure yet; only afraid.

She wished there was someone she could talk to about that, and regretted that she had not forced herself to question Aunt Abby while she had the chance. But it was too late for that now, and there was no one else with whom it could be discussed. Certainly not with Olivia, who would be delightfully shocked and deeply sympathetic, and would talk. Or Millicent Kealey, who was Aunt Abby's friend, but who was so middle-aged and dull and so primly and chillingly British. Or even Dr Kealey, who had been so kind, but still remained a man and a stranger. If only things had been different between herself and Clay . . . If Clay had been what she had once imagined him to be she might have been able to talk to him. But that was no longer possible, and there was nothing that she could do except wait.

The days that followed her return to the Consulate were the longest in Hero's life, and looking back on them she was always to remember them as an interminable stretch of time, and to imagine that they must have covered several months rather than a mere two weeks.

Uncle Nat had decreed that she was not to put a foot outside the Consulate, and reinforced his command by placing a guard upon every exit, and extra locks, to which he had the keys, on the garden gate. He had, he said, no intention of allowing his niece to indulge in any further distasteful shenanigans, and meant to see that for the remainder of her stay she behaved herself in a seemly manner, and did not again scandalize the community and bring disgrace upon himself by getting into some new and unsavoury scrape.

Hero showed no tendency to disoblige him, but her white face and listless manner began to disturb Nathaniel, and there were times when he could almost have wished to see her show a flash of her former spirits. He could not help feeling sorry for her, because he supposed that heredity had a great deal to do with it – Harriet's tiresome passion for Reform, and his brother Barclay's eccentric views. And after all, twenty-two was no great age: she was still very young and she had of late endured enough harrowing experiences to turn the brain of many an older woman. He could only hope that her pallor and that uncharacteristic apathy were not due to something more than sorrow at the death of a half-caste child. If they were, it was a damnable situation, and one that did not bear thinking of.

Hero too avoided thinking of it. Though it was difficult not to do so in the long, aimless days when there was nothing to do but sit idle, pretending to read or sew and listening to the rain dripping from the gutters, the wet palms rustling in the wind and the surf booming endlessly on the coral beaches. She would push the thought away from her, closing her mind against it as though she were shutting one of the books that she held in her hands and did not read; but odd splinters and fragments of memory escaped to torment her——

'*By God! we've caught a mermaid!*' . . . '*You disapprove of slavers, don't you?*' . . . '*Ten leagues beyond the wide world's end. Methinks it is no journey!*' . . . '*Poor Miss Hollis! that's what you get for being innocent and credulous!*' . . . '*I never play fair.*' . . . '*Goodbye, my lovely Galatea.*' A white pigeon cooing on a window-sill. The scent of sun-warmed flowers below a balcony. Fireflies in the garden of The House of Shade, and a man's hands – thin and brown and very sure. A man's hard body—— How could you hate someone so bitterly and yet remember that with a shiver that was not hatred at all? '*It's nice to know that you are unlikely to forget me . . .*'

Neither Clayton nor her uncle discussed the course of the epidemic before Hero, and though Fattûma and the other servants went about with scared faces they rarely spoke of what was happening in the city, and Hero did not ask.

Dr Kealey had not been to see her, for he was too busy to spare any time for visits of a purely social nature, and though Mrs Kealey had fully intended to do so, she had contracted a bad head cold, which allied to a sore throat and severe prickly-heat had prevented her for the moment from doing more than send a friendly letter and a bunch of flowers. But Olivia Credwell came whenever possible, and it was she who brought Hero the news of the city and provided the only break in the heat and the rain and the crawling hours.

'Oh, Hero, the children!' cried Olivia, arriving damp and distressed on a wet afternoon. 'They are by far the worst part of it all! Not the ones who die of the cholera, though there are enough of those, poor little things, but the ones whose parents have died and who have no one to look after them, and are just left to wander about the streets eating rubbish out of the gutters, or just die because there is no one to feed them. And the dogs——! you've no *idea* how terrifying! Hubert says it is eating human flesh that's making them so fierce. They're like wolves, and they snatch children right out of the houses at night – live children! Oh, if only there was something that one could *do*. It's so terrible not to be able to do anything, but how *can* one? I send the servants out with food, but I'm beginning to think that they sell it, and Hubert refuses to let me give it out myself because he says . . . Well, I suppose he is right, but . . .'

Her tales of what was happening in the city had roused Hero into asking her uncle if it would not be possible to open a soup kitchen somewhere in the town, or take some of the abandoned children into the Consulate. But Uncle Nat told her that both projects were impossible.

'You just don't understand the extent of the crisis,' said Uncle Nat. 'A big crowd of people milling about a soup kitchen would only help to breed the cholera faster than it's breeding right now. Crowds are a danger, because it's where folk are packed together that it's hitting worst. You'd kill a mighty lot more people that way than you'd save. And as for turning this house into an orphanage, the servants would light out at once. They're scared enough as it is.'

'But – but surely one ought to do *something*, uncle Nat?'

'Now see here, just you keep right out of this, Hero!' warned Clayton peremptorily, scenting danger. 'There's nothing you or anyone can do about it – except to see that you don't fall sick yourself!'

His step-father gave him a reproving frown and said soothingly: 'Everything that can be done is being done, my dear. There are a whole heap of charitable folk in this town, and people are helping each other all they can. You can be sure of that.'

'I suppose so,' said Hero listlessly, and lapsed into silence.

She talked very little these days, confining herself to a few empty generalities and replying politely, though absently, to any direct question, as though her mind were not on what she was saying. Her uncle was profoundly relieved when she did not pursue the subject, since it was not one that he cared to discuss, for the plight of the stricken city appalled him. It harassed his waking hours and haunted his sleep, and the fact that he could do little or nothing to alleviate it gave him a suffocating feeling of helplessness; as though he were the victim of a nightmare, bound hand and foot and compelled to watch while men and women drowned before his eyes.

He could not even send for help, because there was no one to send. And in a part of the world where communications were still slow and uncertain, the worst would be over long before any reply to an appeal could be received, even had there been anyone to take it. Young Larrimore had promised to do all that he could, but Zanzibar was only one small speck on the map, and half Africa was being ravaged by this same plague. It was unlikely that any form of help would or could be sent, and the Consul gave liberally to a fund for the relief of the destitute, and was grateful that his niece refrained from discussing the appalling tragedy that was taking place within a stone's-throw of his house. He had not expected it of her.

But if it surprised him that after the to-do she had made over one sick child she should show so little concern over the death of thousands, it did not surprise his step-son. Hero's lack of interest in the fate of the city seemed to Clay a clear indication that she had at last received a salutary lesson, and been brought to realize the unwisdom of interfering in matters that were not her concern.

He was sorry that the child should have died, but if the sight of sickness and death, and a close experience of the insanitary, hugger-mugger and probably immoral existence of a native household had shocked his betrothed out of any further desire to pose as an Angel of Mercy, he could only be deeply thankful. She would in any case have had to give up these tiresome ideas once they were married, since he had no intention of permitting his wife to follow in the footsteps of her mother, Harriet, who from all accounts had been a most fatiguing woman. It was therefore just as well that Hero should have abandoned them of her own accord, instead of putting him to the trouble of seeing that she did so.

She was certainly now showing every sign of becoming quieter and more tractable, thought Clay, so perhaps even that shocking abduction would prove in the end to have had its uses, in that it would not only give him a hold over her, but provide him with an effective answer to any future criticism of his own behaviour. There could not be many men who would be willing to accept the leavings of a profligate slave trader and risk lending their name to a bastard, and Hero could not fail to be properly grateful for such magnanimity; or to repay it by studying to become an uncritical and accommodating wife!

I always figured that what she needed was a real hard shock and a bit of brutal handling to bring her down a peg and put a stop to all that goddamned self-opinionated bunkum, thought Clay. It was, of course, a pity she had to get it that way. But then no one back home would ever know, and she would never be able to run tattling to her folk and making trouble for him every time he stepped out of line. It could, in fact, have been worse. A whole heap worse.

There had been a break in the rains and for a week the skies were clear and the temperature rose steadily, and Dr Kealey sent medicated pastilles to be burned in every room as a protection against infection. Their suffocating incense-like odour made the hot rooms seem hotter, and Hero gasped for air and took to spending the greater part of the day supine on her bed dressed in nothing but a thin cotton wrapper, and only appearing downstairs after the sun had set and it was possible to walk in the garden.

But even the heavy scent of the flowers was mingled now with something less pleasant and as yet unidentifiable, and the garden seemed little cooler than the house and almost as airless and enclosed. She could not go outside it because the gate was double locked; and even if it had not been she no longer had any desire to do so, or any curiosity as to what went on behind the high wall that protected it from the city. She was conscious of only one desire, and that was to be left alone to brood over her inadequacies and readjust herself to life and the fact that the future was not going to be in the least as she had planned it, because she herself was not the clear-sighted, capable and uncompromising person she had always considered herself to be, but fallible and inadequate, and humiliatingly feminine.

It was a depressing prospect, and after a time she found that she could contemplate it no longer and that it was simpler to retreat into a hazy half-world where only the heat and her headaches were real, and yesterday and tomorrow of no importance. But though Clayton and her uncle were profoundly relieved by her lack of interest in the progress of the epidemic, and only too willing to respect her desire for solitude, Olivia was not.

Olivia conceived it her duty to prevent dear Hero from 'falling into a decline', and was sure that such a public-spirited girl could not fail to be interested in the affairs of the unhappy city and as harrowed by them as she herself was. The fact that Hero paid little or no attention to her conversation, replying, if at all, in colourless monosyllables, did not alter her opinion or deter her from calling again, and it was, in the end, a remark of Olivia's that roused Hero from her morbid apathy and once again led her to behave in a manner that both her uncle and her betrothed had optimistically believed to be a thing of the past.

'Our house-boy,' said Olivia, 'has a cousin who works in the Fort, and he says that half the prisoners have died of cholera and the guards have run off and left the rest to fend for themselves. I suppose that means they'll all escape – the ones who don't catch it too. Unless they are still locked in, of course. It's rather dreadful to think that that man Frost is still there, if he isn't dead. Or even if he is!'

Olivia shuddered uncontrollably and sniffed at the small bottle of smelling salts that she had taken to carrying of late.

It was barely twelve o'clock but the day was already dark, for once again the swollen rain clouds had rolled across the bright, brassy sky, and now the first slow drops were splashing onto the parched ground and striking against the windowpanes with the staccato rattle of pebbles.

'Oh dear,' murmured Olivia, listening to that sound, 'I'm afraid it's going to rain really hard.' And she shivered again, thinking of all those shallow graves that had been hastily scratched in every piece of open ground: inadequate mounds of loose earth that the rain would scour open in the first hour. Even the terrible blinding sunlight was better than the rain . . .

She stood up abruptly, shaking out her full skirts, and said: 'I must go. Goodbye, dear. I'll try to come tomorrow if the roads are not rivers by then or—— What's the matter, Hero? Have you the headache again?'

'No – yes. It isn't anything,' said Hero confusedly.

'Are you sure? You are not looking at all well.' Olivia regarded Hero's drawn face with some concern and said: 'Would you like me to stay? Shall I call Fattûma? or Clayton——?'

'No, really, Livvy; there's nothing the matter with me. It's —— I guess it's only the heat.'

'You ought to get Dr Kealey to give you an iron tonic. Not that it does much good: I tried it. Oh bother – now it's going to *pour*, and Jane's carriage leaks abominably. I shall get soaked. Until tomorrow, then.'

She stooped to kiss Hero's unresponsive cheek and went away, the noise of her departure lost in a sudden roar of sound as the sagging clouds emptied themselves over the island, blotting it out in a grey cataract of rain.

Hero had not accompanied her to the door or made any motion to rise from her chair. She stayed where she was, facing the streaming windows without seeing them, and presently she said aloud and as though there were still someone in the room with her: 'No! They couldn't do that!'

But she knew that they could. It was more than possible that frightened men might run away and leave others to die of disease and starvation, locked in like animals and unable to escape. But then surely someone in authority would have thought of that? Or would they not care, at a time like this, what happened to a handful of convicted criminals? – or even hear of it? With hundreds of innocent people dying daily, the fate of a few malefactors would seem of little account . . . But if Olivia knew, then her brother Mr Platt must know. Surely Hubert Platt would make enquiries? Or would he, busied with more urgent affairs, merely hope that others would see to it? It was, after all, a matter for the Sultan's officials to deal with. The Fort was their province. But according to Olivia, the Sultan and his immediate family – and probably his ministers too! – were living in virtual isolation in country estates well away from the city. So although Majid was certain to have heard of the *Daffodil*'s departure, the chances were (which was in fact the truth) that he had taken it for granted that her commanding officer would have insisted on taking Captain Frost with him to ensure that he did not escape. In which case . . .

Uncle Nat had called her in to luncheon, and Hero had made only a pretence of eating and had not answered when she was spoken to: which was not sufficiently unusual to cause comment, but allied to her strained face had made both Clayton and his step-father regard her anxiously, and afterwards sedulously avoid looking at each other. The meal seemed to take a very long time, and when it was over she went up to her own room; though not to lie down. Her mind was still on the things that Olivia had told her and she could not rest.

Someone should go down to the Fort. One of the servants should be sent to see if it were true: except that they too were terrified of the cholera, and if they knew that there were dead men in the Fort they might refuse. Uncle Nat, if appealed to, would undoubtedly see that someone eventually visited it, but he would not do so without first instituting enquiries, since it was not his province; and Hero had learned by now that the East moved slowly. It would take time, and there might be no time to spare.

Perhaps if she were to speak to Clay——? No, not Clay! He would instantly accuse her of meddling in matters that were the sole concern of the authorities, and refuse to believe that it was the very idea of anyone – anyone at all! – being left to die like a rat in a trap that she could not endure.

I must go myself, thought Hero: and shivered, as Olivia had done, because she did not want to go.

She did not want to see for herself the things that Olivia had talked

504

about, because once she did that she knew she would no longer be able to sit here with folded hands, doing nothing and telling herself that there was nothing she could do; nothing useful. Nothing that would not anger Clay and exasperate Uncle Nat. Nothing that would not end in futility or disaster as all her previous efforts had done. It was so much easier to admit defeat and retire into apathy and disinterest: to pretend that Olivia was as usual exaggerating, and accept Uncle Nat's assurance that everything that could be done was being done: and to obey Clay's commands that she keep out of it. Yet she knew that she would have to go down to the Fort. And quite suddenly she knew why.

She would have to go because she could not endure the thought of Rory Frost dying slowly in a locked cell. Or dying at all——

Hero went to the window, and leaning her forehead against the welcome coolness of the wet pane, began to plan . . .

The servants had orders not to permit her to leave the house, but because she had shown no signs of wishing to do so they had become slack, and it should be a simple matter to get the doorkeeper out of the hall for a few minutes: she would only need two at most. She still had the black Arab robes that Fattûma had procured for her, and though they would offer little protection against the drenching downpour she had proved their worth as a disguise. And in any case no one was likely to stop and question a solitary woman on a day like this. She turned from the window to fetch the black clothing, and folding it small, went downstairs.

The house was dark and full of uneasy draughts and the sound of falling rain, and the doorkeeper had not heard her footsteps on the stairs or seen her go into the deserted drawing-room. He was roused from his drowsy abstraction a few minutes later by hearing his name called, and leaping to his feet found himself being requested by the master's niece to fetch a lamp and tell someone to bring a drink of cold tea and fresh lemon juice to the drawing-room.

The man hurried away, and the moment he had gone Hero returned to the drawing-room, donned the black *schele* and the concealing fringed head-dress that she had laid ready, and emerging again walked calmly to the door, opened it, and went out into the pouring rain.

The wind swirled about her snatching at the loose folds of material and billowing them briefly out behind her, and then the driving rain drenched them into subjection so that they clung about her, limp and dripping, and she could feel the wetness soaking through to her skin and trickling down her back. The road was already a rushing torrent and the rain blotted out the tall buildings and made it difficult for her to see where she was going, but there seemed to be very few people about, and those few were nearly all children who splashed through the swirling water with happy disregard for the filth it carried, or begged from her as she passed in shrill little voices that were barely audible in the downpour.

She took a wrong turning, and realizing that she had done so, stopped in the shelter of a deep-arched doorway while she tried to re-orientate herself and recall the lie of the streets. The dangling fringe that concealed her eyes ran with water and she pushed it aside impatiently and saw with a sudden jerk of alarm that she had a companion. Someone else had also taken shelter in the same doorway and was sitting propped up against the door-jamb, gazing up at her with a dropped jaw and wide, startled eyes.

Hero hastily re-adjusted the fringe and fled back into the rain; disconcerted by the man's open-mouthed surprise and hoping that he had not recognized her. But she had gone less than twenty yards when it occurred to her that if he had indeed recognized her, he must be someone she knew; perhaps someone from The Dolphins' House or one of the Platts' servants, who could direct her to the Fort or give her news that would make it unnecessary for her to go there. She turned back quickly, afraid that he might have gone, but he was still there. He had not even moved; nor had his expression altered. The eyes that stared up at her were fixed and blank, and as she bent over him a fly settled upon one staring eyeball and another flew out of the open mouth.

Hero backed away, her throat tight with horror, and turning, began to run; splashing and stumbling through the deserted streets, taking another wrong turning and then another; losing her way, and finding it again by chance rather than by design.

She had seen the Arab Fort often enough, but only from the outside and without much interest. It was the oldest building in the city and Cressy had pronounced its castellated walls to be romantic, while Olivia had made several water-colour sketches which portrayed it as pristine white by midday and bright pink, orange or lemon-yellow in a series of improbable sunsets. But there was nothing romantic or colourful about it now. It loomed greyly through the rain with its gate gaping wide and the hunched shapes of a dozen vultures forming a ragged frieze along the battlements. And there was nobody on guard and no one inside it. No one alive.

A cold scent of corruption mingled with the stench of drains and garbage, and a crow that had been feeding on something in the courtyard flapped up with a harsh croak that sent Hero's heart racing in panic. She had to force herself to make a circuit of the deserted building and satisfy herself that no one was there, forgotten and left behind to die in a locked cell, and she had steeled herself to glance at the bodies of the unburied dead to make sure that Rory's was not among them. But the eaters of carrion had been before her, and it was hardly possible to say whether one at least of the things that defaced the courtyard had even been a man, let alone a white man.

A tuft of hair showed pale among the ugly fragments: white or yellow? It might have been either. The white hairs of advancing age or the blond, sun-bleached ones of an Anglo-Saxon. *I shall never know*, thought Hero. *I shall never know* ... And was abruptly and violently sick.

The rain appeared to have spent its initial fury and was falling less heavily as she left the Fort, and she could hear, above the boom of surf on the long stretch of the harbour beach, the mewing of innumerable gulls; and did not need to be told what had brought so many birds to the Island. She was wet through, and shivering, but with nausea rather than cold, for the rain and the wind were both warm; but both seemed as sickeningly laden with the stench of death as the closed rooms of the Consulate were with the cloying incense of Dr Kealey's pastilles.

The smell of those burning pastilles had been hateful to her, and she had persuaded herself that they were to blame for her headaches and insomnia and lack of appetite, and had declared that the risk of infection would be preferable. But she realized now that they had never been intended as specific against infection, but had been burned to disguise the terrible smell of mortality; and that if she had listened with more attention to Olivia she would have known this, and not complained.

There were so many things that she had refused to listen to: shut up in the security of Uncle Nat's comfortable Consulate, with the windows barred against the tainted air of the city and the doors locked to keep her from straying outside and seeing the things that she was seeing now. The unburied dead, the vultures and the carrion crows, the children——

Hero had barely noticed the children as she hurried through the lashing downpour on her way to the Fort. But now that she was walking slowly and with dragging feet, it was impossible not to notice them.

There were dozens of them. Starving children who were not paddling through the dirt of the rushing gutters for pleasure, but in search of food, grabbing and gobbling any floating scrap of filth. Forlorn little creatures who crouched sobbing in doorways; others who were too weak to move or cry.

She saw a gaunt pariah dog nose something in the roadway and spring back with a snarl as it uttered a feeble wail, and realized with horror that it was a half-drowned baby who had been swept along in a rush of water and caught up in a tangle of garbage.

Leaping forward, she snatched it up, and saw that there was another and even smaller one a yard away ... and another ...

Twenty minutes later Hero was standing in the hall of the Consulate, clutching not one but three infants, and accompanied by half a dozen naked, starving toddlers and a famished six-year-old who looked like a walking skeleton and carried yet another wailing baby.

Her absence had only just been discovered, for the doorkeeper had at first supposed that she had returned to her bedroom, and it was only when Fattûma knocked at her door, and finding the room empty came down to make enquiries, that he realized that the front door was no longer locked.

Hero returned to find it still on the latch and the hall ringing with loud, angry voices and full of people who turned to stare at her and did not recognize her. The frantic doorkeeper had taken her to be some desperate woman from the town and shouted at her to leave at once, but he had not approached her, while the servants had backed hastily away, retreating to the far end of the hall as though she had been the black cholera itself.

It had been a full minute before anyone realized who she was, and even then they had found it difficult to believe, for with her arms full of babies she had not been able to remove the fringed head-covering that concealed her face, and it was Uncle Nat who had torn it off and said furiously: 'Hero——! What fool trick is this?'

'How did you get out? Where the hades have you been?' stormed Clay. 'I thought I told you—— Put those goddamned children outside! What in hellfire do you think you're doing?'

'I couldn't help it, Clay,' pleaded Hero. 'I had to go! I *had* to, Uncle Nat! You see, Olivia said——'

'Go to your room,' ordered Uncle Nat, his face rigid. 'It appears to me you aren't to be trusted with the run of the house, so you'd better stay there for what's left of your visit.'

'I can't – the children . . .'

'I'll see they get something to eat, and after that they'll have to go back where you found them.'

'But they haven't got anywhere to go, Uncle Nat. Their parents are dead and they have no one to look after them. They're starving. Uncle Nat – *please*! Clay, you can't——! Fattûma! Where is Fattûma?'

She dodged past her uncle's burly form and saw Fattûma standing among the servants at the back of the hall, and said with a sob of thankfulness: 'Oh there you are! Take one of these babies before I drop it, will you, and could you warm some milk, and——'

Fattûma retreated precipitately, her eyes wide with apprehension and her voice shrill with alarm: 'No! – no, Bibi! No touch . . . their mothers die of the sickness – they die too, for sure. No bring in here! Take away – take away quick, quick!'

The servants seconded her, babbling like a flock of frightened geese and crowding towards the door that led to the kitchen quarters, their eyeballs rolling whitely in their dark, panic-stricken faces.

'The woman's right,' said Clay. 'You must be plumb crazy to bring these kids here. They may be sickening for cholera already, and yet you bring them into the house and expect the servants to look after them——'

'No. We not look,' cried Fattûma shrilly. 'No look! No touch!'

'There, you see? They'll have to go; and at once.'

'Then I shall go too,' said Hero.

'You'll do no such thing!' blared Uncle Nat. 'This is one time when you're blamed well going to do what you're told. *Put those children down and get on up to your room!*'

'I won't. You can't make me!'

'Can't we!' said Clay, and moved swiftly to cut off her retreat from the door. 'That's just where you're mistaken. I'll give you exactly one minute to make up your mind whether you'll go quietly or put on a free show for the servants. Now——!'

'Clay, we can't send them away,' pleaded Hero frantically. 'Can't you see they're starving? They'll die – we *must* do something.'

'You heard your uncle say we'd see that they're fed.'

'But that isn't enough! What's one meal? Or two – or twenty? What's the good of giving them each a bit of bread and pushing them back into the street? They need looking after, they——'

'No look. No touch. Sending away quick before making all die here,' gibbered Fattûma.

'Thirty seconds.'

'Clay please! . . . Uncle Nat, there's the summer-house in the garden. I'll look after them myself . . . I'll——'

'I'm sorry, Hero, but it's just plain impossible. I've got to think of the servants too, you know. But maybe we can get the Sultan to work out some scheme that'll take care of them, and then——'

'But it'll be too late! Too late for these ones. They're so small. Please, Uncle Nat!'

'Forty,' said Clay inexorably.

'Oh Clay, *please* – don't you see . . .'

They had all forgotten that the front door had been left open and they did not hear any sound of footsteps. But suddenly someone else was there, standing in the doorway behind Clayton and looking across his shoulder at the bedraggled girl and the bewildered, skeleton children who still held to her wet skirts.

'*Rory!*' said Hero on a sob that contained neither surprise nor thankfulness, but was purely one of relief: 'Rory, do something!'

'Certainly,' said Captain Emory Frost obligingly. 'What?'

Clayton spun round with an oath, and Hero ran past him, tripping on her wet skirts and accompanied by her frightened protégés:

'They say I can't let the children stay here, but they have to go some-where and if we send them away they'll die, because they haven't anyone and no one cares and they can't – I can't——'

'Steady,' said Rory, removing an infant from her convulsive grasp and regarding it with some disfavour.

Hero paused and drew a shuddering breath, struggling for composure, and Clayton took a swift step towards her and found his way blocked by an arm that appeared to be made of steel and whipcord.

'Mind the baby!' admonished Captain Frost without heat.

'What are you doing here?' Clayton's voice was a grating whisper and his face was no longer flushed with anger but drained of all colour. 'What do you want? Edwards said you'd given him your word—— They can't have let you out!'

'Not intentionally. They merely neglected to lock me in and then ran off and abandoned the place: which came to the same thing.'

Clayton said in the same stifled voice: 'If you've got anything to say to me, say it and get out!'

'You mean about Zorah? I haven't. I didn't come here to see you.'

'Then why——?' began Clayton, and was interrupted by his step-father who said harshly: 'I guess we're none of us interested in why you're here or how you got here or who you want to see. But unless you get out here fast I'm sending for the guard.'

'What guard?' enquired Rory blandly. 'I don't think there is one any more.'

'I wouldn't count on that! There're still enough white men in the city who'd be happy to form one, so I'd advise you to leave.'

'Certainly, sir. Are you coming with me, Hero?'

Clay's fist shot out, and Rory ducked with equal swiftness, avoiding the blow, and the next instant the Consul had gripped his step-son's arm and jerked him back: 'That's enough, Clay!' He turned his head and spoke a curt word of dismissal to the saucer-eyed servants who had re-mained gaping at the back of the hall, and when the door had closed behind them said tersely: 'I'm not having any brawling before the ser-vants – or anyone else! Now get out of here, Frost.'

'Well, Hero?' enquired Rory.

'Can I take the children?'

'Why not? there's plenty of room.'

'Hero!' cried Clay: 'You couldn't—— Don't you dare! I forbid you! I——' his voiced cracked.

The Consul said sharply: 'Be quiet, Clay! There's no question of her going.'

'Yes, there is,' said Hero. 'I'm sorry, Uncle Nat. I'm so very sorry. I wish——' She broke off and shook her head in helplessness and regret, and saw her uncle's harassed face harden into deep harsh lines.

Mr Hollis was a tolerant man, but he had endured much of late and now suddenly he reached the end of his patience. 'Very well,' said Uncle Nat quietly and coldly. 'You are of age; and as you have been at some pains to demonstrate, your own mistress. But I'm telling you, Hero, if you go with that slaver you don't come back to this house. I shall wash my hands of you and have nothing further to do with you. Is that clear?'

'Yes, Uncle Nat. I – I'm sorry.'

'So am I. I'll see you get your things. Goodbye.'

'Goodbye, Uncle Nat.'

'*Hero!*' Clay flung off his step-father's restraining hand and lunged at her, and Rory put out a foot, tripping him, and hit him as he fell.

The blow was not all it might have been, for Rory was hampered by the baby. But he had a score to settle, and it made up in viciousness what it lacked in the way of science. It seemed to lift Clayton off his feet, and sent him spinning sideways to trip and fall on his face, spread-eagled and inert across the threshold of the drawing-room door.

'I owed you that,' observed Rory dispassionately. 'Come on, Hero. Time we were going.'

He bent and picked up a weeping toddler, and they turned together and went out into the rain, the bewildered children following docilely at their heels.

38

'History seems to be repeating itself again,' observed Captain Frost, regarding his soaking guest critically. 'You'd better get out of those things as soon as possible. Dahili will have to lend you something dry until your own gear arrives.'

They were back once more in The Dolphins' House, and although the majority of the household had shown little enthusiasm at the prospect of taking in a batch of starving waifs who might well be tainted with the cholera, the Captain's orders, backed by several texts from the Koran extolling the merits of charity, had overcome their reluctance.

'All things are with Allah,' agreed Hajji Ralub. 'It is good to feed the hungry and fatherless: and if the hour and the manner of our death be already written, why should we trouble ourselves over what is ordained? God is great!'

The children had been removed to be fed, a message dispatched to Dr Kealey and Jumah sent out to see about laying in further supplies of milk; and Hero and Captain Frost were alone in the long upper room where the white cockatoo still paraded on its silver perch and the Persian kitten, now grown into a large and stately cat, slept curled up on a cushion.

Hero had been barely conscious of her wet clothing for the past hour, but now she looked down at it, grimacing at the sight of the spreading pool that darkened the carpet about her feet, and glancing at Rory's own drenched clothes, said: 'Yours are just as wet.'

'So they are. When did you last have something to eat?'

'I don't know,' said Hero, startled. 'Noon, I guess. Why?'

'You look almost as thin as those children. It doesn't suit you. You ought never to have stayed behind. Why on earth couldn't you behave sensibly for once and go along with your aunt and cousin and all the rest of them?'

Hero raised her eyes from the damp stains on the carpet and looked at him briefly, and looked away again without answering; and Rory said brusquely and as though she had spoken: 'I know. And I'm deeply grateful to you.'

'You don't have to be,' said Hero bleakly. 'It wasn't any use.'

'Don't say it like that. It may be a platitude, but it's the trying that counts.'

'Who with?' asked Hero bitterly.

'Yourself, of course. Who else? You're the one you've got to live with. If anyone had told you that all those children you've collected would die anyway inside a week, I don't suppose you'd have left them there. Or would you?'

'No. And they won't die!'

'They may. You've got to face that. And if they do——'

'They will not!' cried Hero passionately. 'They will not! They're not ill, they're only hungry. And there must be hundreds more like them – thousands. If we could only——'

Rory laughed and flung up a protesting hand: 'Don't say it! I ought to have known that worse was to come. Go and get yourself into some dry clothes before you contract pneumonia. I warn you, if you go sick on me I shall throw your protégés into the street. I don't feel capable of running an orphan asylum single-handed.'

Hero stared at him for a long moment, her eyes wide and questioning. Then colour rushed up to her white face, making it young and glowing and alive again, and she gave a gasp of relief:

'*Thank you!*' breathed Hero, and smiled at him as though he had given her some fabulous present.

The curtain swung into place behind her, and listening to the sound of her footsteps running along the verandah, Rory's own smile was twisted and more than a little wry.

It was disconcerting to find himself trapped at last by an emotion he had sedulously avoided for years and ended by fancying himself immune to. And by Hero Hollis, of all people! One of the last women in the world, he would have said, to hold any appeal for him – which was possibly why this had taken him unawares. He had not even seen it coming, for though he had thought about her a good deal during the past weeks, it was always as someone he would never see again, and he had accepted that: there was a finality about it that made her a part of the past and far out of reach, and he was not given to vain regrets and useless speculation. Besides, his own life was likely to terminate painfully in the near future, and he was confident that someone – Dan or her family – would have arranged to send her away to safety once the cholera took hold. She would be well on her way home, and that, as far as he was concerned, was the end of it. Which was just as well for both their sakes.

He had been wholly unprepared for Batty's disclosure that Hero was still in Zanzibar. And even less prepared for the violence of his own reaction to it. It was as though someone had hit him across the face without provocation or warning, and after the first blinding moment of disbelief, shock had exploded into rage and he had been seized with a fury of anger against Batty, Dan, Clayton, the Hollises and Colonel Edwards for allowing her to stay – and with Hero herself for being so exasperatingly, idiotically obstinate as to insist upon staying.

Barely pausing to change out of the rags in which he had left the Fort, he had gone to the Consulate with no very clear idea in view beyond the satisfaction of telling them all exactly what he thought of them. And it was only when he walked in through the open door and saw her standing there, wet and desperate and once again disastrously involved in benevolence, that he had realized what she meant to him. Perhaps because she could hardly have looked less physically alluring, yet it had made no difference at all to the way she looked to him; and he had known in that moment that it never would . . .

It had not been a pleasant discovery. And even less so was the belated realization that part of the blind rage that had driven him to abduct her had nothing whatever to do with Zorah, but had had its roots in jealousy. Jealousy of Clayton Mayo, who must at all costs be prevented from marrying her, and if that were not possible, should at least only take her at second hand.

I must be mad! thought Rory. He shrugged philosophically, and went off to change his own soaked garments for the second time that day, and to inform Ralub that a further influx of young visitors could be expected shortly and arrangements must be made to accommodate them.

He might have felt less philosophic about it had he known the full extent of what he had let himself in for.

One of the infants – the first that Hero had acquired – died on the following day, and another a day later. But since their deaths were due to starvation and neglect, and not to cholera, the household of the Dolphins were not unduly dismayed. And in any case, by that time there were at least a dozen other infants in the house in addition to the original number, as well as over twenty children ranging in age from two to six years old.

It was Batty who had carried the message to Dr Kealey, and the doctor had called at the earliest opportunity, and not only promised his help, but brought with him twin babies, barely a month old, whom he had found wailing in an abandoned house in which their parents lay dead.

'I've been wondering what on earth to do with them,' confessed Dr Kealey, 'for Milly is in a sad way. What with boils and prickly-heat and a sore throat, she is in no condition to look after the little things, and my servants threatened to leave if I brought them into the house. I blessed you when I heard of this.'

'Uncle Nat didn't,' said Hero ruefully. 'I'm afraid he's very angry with me.'

'I can't say I'm surprised – all things considered. But then he's not a medical man, and he is your uncle and responsible for you, which makes it difficult for him. He'll come round.'

'I wish I thought so. But I don't think he will. He doesn't understand how I can come here. Because of Rory – I mean Captain Frost.'

'I'm not sure I understand that myself,' admitted Dr Kealey candidly. 'But I'm profoundly grateful that you should have felt you could. If you can help to save even a small proportion of these unfortunate infants, it will be something. There's nothing much that we can do about their elders, and one can only hope that they'll learn a few elementary lessons in sanitation from this. Though I doubt it. They appear to look upon such visitations as a necessary evil: an affliction sent by Allah, or witchcraft. And when it's over they'll forget about it until the next time, and do nothing towards preventing it from happening again. The only thing they are doing about it now is to say their prayers and let off firecrackers to scare away the evil spirits, or paint their faces white. But they still fling all their refuse into the open street and think nothing of allowing corpses to lie about unburied. I tell you, it's hopeless!'

It did not seem so to Hero. Admittedly two of the babies had died, but the rest were responding well to food and care and already looked plumper, and within three days the original handful of children had swollen to more than fifty, with the numbers increasing hourly. Word had gone round that both food and shelter were obtainable at The Dolphins' House, and the doors were besieged by a clamorous mob begging for admittance.

Left to herself, Hero might well have admitted them all. But she was not so left. Rory had been adamant in the matter. She could take in children who were too young to fend for themselves, but not their parents or any other adults.

'If we once start that, we're lost,' said Rory. 'You've got to draw the line somewhere. Anything over the age of eight will have to fend for itself. Well, ten then! But that's the limit!'

'Couldn't we just take in a few of the women?' pleaded Hero. 'They could help with the children, and we need help so badly.'

Rory could see the sense of that, but he had not given way, and backed by Ralub and his crew had finally succeeded in persuading the crowd to disperse and to accept the fact that only young children would be admitted.

It was a measure of his authority and the esteem in which his crew and the household held him, that apart from a few murmurs not one of them had rebelled on discovering that Miss Hollis had been given permission to turn the house into a temporary orphanage. They had not forgotten Hero's valiant fight to save the life of Zorah's child; nor were they left long without outside assistance, for once again Mrs Platt's carriage edged its painful way through the rain and the narrow streets, and stopping before the door of The Dolphins' House, deposited Olivia Credwell and a large portmanteau.

'Your uncle told me where you'd gone,' explained Olivia, shaking the wet out of an absurd ribbon-trimmed bonnet. 'I'm afraid he is exceedingly angry with you, and it seems that Clay's nose is broken, which is the greatest pity as it will quite *ruin* his looks. But though it was all right before (your being here I mean, dear, not Clay's nose), now that Captain Frost is here too you really *should* have a chaperone, if only to make it look a little less . . . Well, anyway, I know that you were bound to need help, and I don't mind in the least where I sleep. The floor will do. And you need not think that you can send me away, because I'm not going to go!'

Hero had not tried very hard to make her, for she was beginning to realize the full magnitude of the task she had so impetuously undertaken, and the extent of the disaster that might result if it failed.

'You can't win, miss. Not nowise,' Batty had warned her. 'If them nippers ups and dies, the 'ole town'll blame you, and like as not try and burn the 'ouse down over our 'eads. And if they lives you'll get no word of thanks. That's the way it goes, for they don't know no better – the poor bleedin' 'eathens.'

Rory had merely laughed when she taxed him with this, and said that Batty was a croaking old pessimist and she should know better than to listen to him. But Hero could not rid herself of the conviction that Batty had told her the truth. If so, there were other reasons besides purely charitable ones why this venture must not be allowed to end in failure – as her others had done! For which reason she welcomed Olivia, who for all her feather-headedness could be trusted to see that the kitchens were kept clean, the windows open and the water boiled: matters which still seemed unimportant and quite unnecessary to the majority of the household, and that had to be constantly supervised.

Olivia had not been the only volunteer. Barely an hour after her arrival another visitor, also accompanied by luggage, knocked at the door of The Dolphins' House, and being admitted by the porter, walked unannounced into a room where Hero was laying rows of makeshift mattresses on the floor.

'*Tiens!* It is true, then,' said Thérèse Tissot, looking about her with interest. 'My servants informed me that you had established an orphanage here. *Comment allez-vous*, Hero? It is long since we last met, and I see that you have become too thin.'

Hero made no attempt to return either Thérèse's greeting or her smile. She said flatly and without emotion: 'What do you want?'

'*Eh bien!* To offer you my assistance; what else? If you should need it, which I see very plainly that you do! Me, I am not afraid of hard work or

516

the cholera, and I speak the language of these people better than you. Tell me what you wish me to do, and I will do it.'

'I don't wish you to do anything, thank you,' said Hero coldly. 'We are managing very well and are in no need of assistance.'

'Ah, *bah*!' said Thérèse. 'You mean you do not wish me to be here, which is a thing that I well understand. But will these children care who it is who feeds them? Of course they will not! Be reasonable, Mademoiselle. Now that I am here I shall not go, because I can see for myself that what the doorkeeper tells me is true. There are already a great many little ones in the house, and it is plain that there will soon be more – many, many more! You cannot afford at such a time to turn away any who will help. Is that not so?'

'Yes,' said Hero slowly. 'Yes, you are right . . .'

Thérèse had stayed. And before the day was out Hero had forgotten that she had ever disliked her, and forgiven her everything: the trickery over the rifles, the affair with Clayton, the wounds to her own pride. This was a new Thérèse; her airs and affectations forgotten, her Paris dresses laid aside and her fashionable coiffeur hidden under a cloth tied peasant-wise about her head: cheerful, tireless, indomitable. Thérèse took no interest in either children or good works; but she was a born organizer, and it was not in her character to stay idle in her own home during a time of crisis. Her command of the local languages enabled her to exert considerably more authority over the women of the household than Hero had been able to achieve, and both servants and children obeyed her in a way they did not obey the gentler and more soft-hearted Olivia. Thérèse scolded and cajoled in Arabic and Kiswahili and worked wonders in the way of procuring extra beds, mattresses, sheets and clothing from the various consulates, European firms, rich merchants and landowners in the Island.

The house of the Dolphins was one of the oldest houses in Zanzibar: a huge, rambling building of four stories and many rooms. But it was not long before every available foot of space was occupied; the verandahs turned into dormitories and the courtyard itself tented in to provide extra room. But Hero was still dissatisfied, for Dr Kealey had unwisely mentioned the terrible plight of the dwellers in the African Town across the creek: 'From what I hear,' said Dr Kealey, 'their situation is a great deal worse than it is over here, and I shudder to think how many infants and young children must be lying abandoned in empty huts or on the streets, because their parents and relatives are dead and there is no one left to feed or care for them. But there is nothing we can do about it.'

'Why couldn't we go there ourselves and bring them here?' asked Hero thoughtfully.

'Good heavens!' exclaimed the doctor in alarm, annoyed with himself for not realizing how Hero would react to such information, 'on *no* account! And don't you dare try it, young woman! I haven't even been there myself – and what's more I don't intend to. We have a deal more work than we can handle already without going hunting for more. Besides, we'd only bring back the infection with us, and put the life of every child in this house at risk.'

Hero laughed at him and said affectionately: 'Now that, dear sir, if you will forgive me saying so, is downright nonsense, and I'm surprised at you! Why, every single child in this house has been in contact with cholera, and you know it! That's why they are here – because every one of them has lost parents or relatives, and many have no one left alive to look after them. Besides, surely this cholera is the same wherever it has broken out, so if we can take in the children it has orphaned here in the Stone Town, why not those from the African Town? The risk of infection can't be greater, can it?'

'Speaking as a doctor, no; I suppose not. But the sights you would be exposed to are far worse, which is why none of you are going there. That, dear girl, is an order! – and don't you dare forget it!'

'No doctor,' said Hero with deceptive meekness. Nor did she forget it. The plight of the orphaned children in the slums across the creek, who, according to Dr Kealey would have no one to bring them to the shelter of The Dolphins' House, preyed on her mind and gave her no rest.

Someone would have to go to their help. And since Hero Athena, like Dan Larrimore, was incapable of shirking responsibility by shifting it onto others' shoulders, that someone would have to be herself – though accompanied, of necessity, by one of the serving-women to act as guide and help carry babies who were too young to walk. She dared not discuss the project with anyone else either, for Dr Kealey's reaction to it had shown her that if she did so it would certainly be vetoed. So she kept her own counsel. But despite his admission that the risks of infection could be no greater on one side of the creek than the other (and no worse, surely, than those that they all incurred daily with every new foundling they admitted!) she took the precaution of soaking two complete sets of outer clothing, including slippers, in strong disinfectant, and drying them without rinsing them out. These could be put on in the house and removed before re-entering it; while as for any children rescued from the African Town, they would be treated in the same way as all the others – their clothes, if any, taken off and burnt, and they themselves dunked in a bath containing disinfectant.

With her preparations completed, Hero wasted no time, but left un-obtrusively by a side door, accompanied by the once fat little negress,

Ifabi – stout no longer but worn with anxiety and hard work. And ever afterwards she was to remember that day, and sometimes dream of it and wake up screaming.

It had rained all the previous night. Unseasonable rain, Ralub had said, since normally at this time of year there was little rainfall. But though it had ceased at dawn, the day was grey and intolerably hot, for clouds still blanketed the sky and there was no breath of wind. The sodden earth, the gaunt Arab houses, the streets and lanes and alleyways of the city steamed with heat, and now that the rain had stopped there were more people in the streets. Life had still to be lived, and food must be bought and sold to sustain it. But many of the shops were shuttered or empty, and the crowds were no longer gay and colourful, but cowed and apprehensive and for the most part silent, save for organized processions of Koranic chanters and men who prayed aloud, invoking God to stay the pestilence and spare the living.

The streets themselves were cleaner than usual, for the heavy rain of the previous night had swept the usual accumulation of filth down to the sea in a rushing spate, and scoured the open gutters free of garbage. But the city stank of death, and the smell of it was all-pervading and inescapable.

It was a smell that Hero had become accustomed to, for no walls or windows could shut it out; though in The Dolphins' House, as in Nathaniel Hollis's, they burned pastilles and incense and joss-sticks to disguise it. But here in the open street it was sickeningly evident, and even the folded handkerchief that she had soaked in Cologne and held over her nose and mouth could not subdue it. She fought down her rising nausea and hurried resolutely forward, making for the African Town on the far side of the tidal creek that separated the stone-built town of Zanzibar from the stews where the negroes and the freed slaves lived. It was there that the cholera had taken its greatest toll, and where it still raged at white heat, and there must be hundreds of helpless children there; far more than in the better quarters of the town. But nothing that she had heard or imagined had prepared her for the sight of the creek, or the reeking abomination that lay on the far side of it.

The ground that had been set apart for burials had been soon filled, and fresh fields opened in the suburbs. But these too were already crammed with hastily buried corpses that rain and the dogs had uncovered, and now the negroes of the African Town were taking their dead by night to the Darajani Bridge that spanned the creek, and throwing them into the water below. Some of these the tide carried out to sea, but others – too many others – the ebb left behind, and a dozen terrible, putrefying bodies lay sprawled on the mud flats below the bridge. But the nightmare creek was as nothing to the open ground on the far side of it, for here the earth could no longer conceal the bodies of all those whom the denizens of the African Town had attempted to bury in it, and the red, reeking ground seemed to heave with a grisly host who appeared to be struggling to escape from their shallow graves, lifting skulls and arms and bony hands out of the mire.

It was a sight that would have given Dante material for another canto on Hell, and Hero shut her eyes, and clinging to Ifabi's arm, hurried blindly down the short stretch of muddy road that spanned it, choking and gasping with horror. She had often skirted the African Town on her early morning rides, but she had never approached it closely, and seeing it now she realized that the squalor of the Stone Town, which had once so horrified her, was a paradise of cleanliness and order when compared with this. It was incredible to her that anything human could live and work and breed in hovels that the poorest immigrant from Europe would have considered unfit for his swine. And yet each of these stinking, windowless, makeshift pigsties housed from four to a dozen people: the old, the middle-aged and the young crowded together between crumbling mud walls that crawled with lice, under leaking roofs of rotted palm leaves or rusty tin.

The floors were deep in dirt and refuse and the narrow alleys no better than middens, while rats swarmed in both; scuttling unafraid between the very feet of the passers-by and skipping aside with bared teeth when a blow was aimed at them. There were cockroaches too, and swarms of flies. And everywhere the terrible scent of death, for half the huts were tenanted by dead or dying negroes and Hero leaned on Ifabi's arm, vomiting helplessly and sobbing with shock and nausea.

They had not penetrated far into the evil mazes of the African Town, because there had been a baby crying in the mud by the threshold of a hut whose other occupants were dead, and Hero had stopped and picked it up. And instantly found herself in the centre of a menacing mob of shouting negroes who jostled and threatened, accusing her of stealing it. Black, clawing hands snatched the child from her and struck at her, battering her to and fro, ripping at her Arab robes, grabbing and tearing while Ifabi's frantic shrieks of explanation went unheeded and unheard in the ugly din of yelling voices.

Hero clasped her arms above her head to protect it from the hail of blows, and a stick crashed viciously down upon them, beating her to her knees. She crouched in the mud among a forest of trampling, kicking feet, moaning with pain: hearing Ifabi's shrill screams above the howling of the mob and thinking with terror and incredulity that they were both going to be killed. This was the end of everything, and soon she and Ifabi would lie out in that terrible red field or on the mud flats below the bridge, mangled and unrecognizable. She could feel something warm and wet running down from a cut on her shoulder to soak her dress, and then a savage kick drove the breath out of her body and she toppled sideways, to lie writhing feebly in an agonizing struggle for breath; blind, deaf and disfigured by a clotted mask of mud and blood.

She did not hear the shots that were fired above the heads of the crowd, dominating the clamour and cutting it short as abruptly as though it had been a tangible thing that had been severed by the sweep of a knife. She did not even know that the mob had broken and fled and that she was alone in the fetid alleyway, and she was barely aware of being lifted. It was only when she could breathe again that she realized that someone was wiping the mud off her face and that the furious voice that had replaced the screeching tumult of the mob was Rory's.

He seemed to be addressing someone who had incurred his displeasure, and most of the words he used were entirely unfamiliar to Hero; though even in her present state of pain-racked semi-consciousness she was in little doubt as to their meaning. It was some time before she awoke to the fact that it was she herself who was being addressed.

She attempted to lift her head and was instantly sick again, and Rory said viciously: 'Serve you damned well right! – you interfering, officious, crack-brained, bungling, bloody little tramp!'

But the fog of pain and terror was lifting a little, and neither the words nor the tone in which they were uttered deceived her, because he was still holding her and she could feel the intensity of the fear that drove him, and knew that it was not for himself that he was afraid, but for her. The knowledge brought her a strange content that she made no attempt to analyse, and she turned her head tiredly against his shoulder and relapsed into a half-coma that did not lift until she was back in the safety of The Dolphins' House.

Olivia and Thérèse had put her to bed, and Dr Kealey, hastily summoned, had bandaged the cut on her shoulder and applied salves to her bruises, scolding her angrily the while, and finally made her swallow a noxious draught that must have contained a strong sedative, for she had fallen asleep almost immediately and had not woken until late on the following day.

'Oh, Hero darling, what a fright you gave us,' quavered Olivia, appearing in the doorway with a mug of strong tea. 'We quite thought you would have been killed. And so you would, if Thérèse had not happened to ask one of the women where you were, and been told that you had gone out with Ifabi wearing those Arab clothes. Of course she didn't *dream* that you'd think of going to the African Town, but she was sure that you ought not to go out with only Ifabi, because really the streets are not at *all* safe these days. Gangs, you know, and people looting. You really *must* not do these things, Hero.'

'I know,' admitted Hero apologetically. 'It was stupid of me. Batty did tell me that some of the Africans might think we were stealing children, but when I asked Rory if that could be true, he only laughed, and I guess I forgot about it. How did he know where I'd gone?'

'One of the children had heard you talking to Ifabi, which was the *greatest* piece of luck – though of course one *cannot* encourage eavesdropping and I do think . . . Well, Thérèse sent one of the men running for Captain Frost, who had gone down to the harbour with one or two of the others, and he and Mr Potter and some of the rest went after you. And just as well!'

'How is Ifabi? – is she all right?'

'Oh yes, she was hardly touched. But Captain Frost was simply furious with her for letting you go there and not telling him that you meant to, and she's been snivelling ever since, poor thing.'

'It wasn't her fault. She didn't want to go at all, but I made her.'

'*Ciel!* that I can well believe!' observed Thérèse tartly, entering with towels and warm water. 'But why? Why must you embark upon such a mad venture? And why not tell us where you were going?'

'I – I thought that if I told anyone, they'd stop me,' confessed Hero shame-facedly. 'Or that you might insist on going instead, and I couldn't let you do that.'

'*Quelle blague!*' snapped Thérèse crudely. 'Me, I am in agreement with your poor uncle, M'sieur Hollis, who says that you are mad.'

'But Dr Kealey said that the cholera was worse in the African Town than anywhere else, and I wanted to see for myself. And I did, and it is. It's true! It's worse than anything you could ever – why there must be *hundreds* of children there who will die if we don't do something quickly. We've just *got* to do something for them, Thérèse.'

'*Mais certainement:* but we shall not fetch them ourselves. You, *ma chère*, are too impulsive. You see only the goal and run towards it without observing the hazards in the path, which causes trouble and grief to a great many people. Your heart is warm, but one also needs a a cool head; and that, plainly, you have not got!'

Despite her protests Hero had been constrained to remain in bed for the remainder of that day, though none of her hurts was serious, for the folds of coarse black cloth had protected her with more effectiveness than might have been supposed. Apart from a superficial cut on one shoulder and a good many bruises she was relatively unharmed, and had been able to rise the following morning feeling not much the worse for her adventure, and endure with equanimity a blistering denunciation of her behaviour from Rory, delivered in a tone that would once have sent her temper flaring, however well-merited the rebuke. As it was, she had merely murmured that she was sorry, with a meekness that would have surprised her relations but seemed only to acerbate Rory's ill-temper:

'So you bloody well should be! Apart from the fact that you would undoubtedly have been killed if we hadn't happened to arrive when we did, you'd have been responsible for Ifabi's death as well as your own. I suppose you didn't think of that either? Or that she might contact cholera from going into a slum where it has gained such a foothold that the deaths there are now over a hundred a day? It's the negroes who are most vulnerable to it, and she's a negress. And yet you made her go with you!'

'I'm sorry. I only took her because she knew the way and I didn't. I never thought——'

'You never do!' interrupted Rory savagely. 'Well you can start thinking now! One or both of you may well have taken the disease off that mob – they were mauling and man-handling you and spitting in your faces, and it's safe to say that several of them are dead by this time. If you have, it'll be no more than you deserve! A child of six should have known better, and I am rapidly acquiring a deep sympathy for your uncle and that double-dealing bastard you were going to marry!'

'*Someone* had to go,' protested Hero defensively. 'And I thought it had better be me. I couldn't just sit here and do nothing about it.'

Rory's face changed and some of the anger and impatience left it. He said less harshly: 'You're not sitting here and doing nothing. You're doing a deal too much. But you don't understand these people. I do; so you'll kindly leave me to deal with this sort of thing in future.'

'Would you? Could you really do something about it – explain to them so that they would understand?'

He stood looking at her, his face grim again and his mouth not quite under control. Seeing what the mob and the past weeks and he himself had done to her; she was so thin that it hurt him to look at her. The lovely, rounded body whose every line and curve and hollow he knew so intimately – that he had once possessed with such savagery and later with such astonishing, heart-stopping rapture – was wasted now to the point of emaciation. Her hands were rough from hard work and her grey eyes with their circles of dark shadows too large for her white face, and it was suddenly all he could do not to reach out and pull her into his arms and say: 'Hero, for the love of God do you have to do this?' But he knew that it was no use to say it and that he must not touch her. Not again. Yesterday

523

had been bad enough in all conscience! Worse than he had thought possible . . .

Hero said: 'Could you, Rory?'

'I suppose so,' said Rory, resigned.

39

'We shall need more mattresses and more milk and food. More *everything*!' wailed Olivia, struggling with an influx of starving infants from the slums across the creek, who threatened to put an unbearable strain upon the resources of The Dolphins' House.

'*Vraiment!* – and more soap,' said Thérèse, wrinkling her nose at the overpowering odour of unwashed and filth-encrusted babies.

'And more *room*!' sighed Hero. 'Thank goodness there is still the garden. We can put up tents. Thérèse, could you——?'

'I will arrange it,' said Thérèse. And went off to beg, borrow or otherwise acquire tents and canvas, and anything else that could be used to construct shelters, from Colonel Edwards, Monsieur Dubail, Mr Nathaniel Hollis and a dozen other sources in the city.

The majority of the newcomers from the African Town were in a shocking state of dirt and starvation, and for too many of them help had come too late. More than a dozen of them died that same night, and many others looked as though nothing could save them. But Dr Kealey, walking along the packed verandahs and through the noisy, crowded rooms was not dissatisfied and pronounced them to be doing well: a deal better than he had expected.

He enquired after Hero's injuries and she replied lightly that they were nothing and scarcely troubled her at all, but he looked at her with more attention than he had given her of late, and did not like what he saw. He knew that she had been roughly handled and that her body must by now be black and blue with bruises, but he did not think that she had received any internal injury. It was not this that worried him, but the thought of the appalling prevalence of cholera in the Black Town.

As a humanitarian Dr Kealey could understand and sympathize with the motive that had driven Hero into going there, but his views on the unwisdom of her action agreed entirely with Rory's. Besides, the girl was not looking at all well, and though he was aware that she could hardly be expected to do so after such an experience, he could not throw off his uneasiness, and he found himself praying that her extreme pallor and the black shadows that encircled her eyes were nothing more than the result of shock and superficial bruising, and not of something infinitely worse. He spoke sharply to her, ordering her to take more rest, and on departing informed Mrs Credwell that he looked to her to see that Hero lay down for at least two hours every afternoon until further notice.

Olivia had done so – fully expecting opposition. But for once Hero had been tractable, since by then she was feeling hot and ill, and in pain. It was a relief to retire to the small room on the top floor that she shared with Olivia and Thérèse and to take off her clothes and stretch out on the bed clad in only a thin shift. The cut on her shoulder was throbbing unpleasantly, while the bruises that disfigured her body ached abominably and reminded her of the days when she had lain similarly bruised in Rory's cabin on the *Virago* after her rescue from the sea. Only this time it was worse. Much worse—— The room seemed to be moving as the cabin had moved, so that for a moment she imagined that she must be back there, with the schooner dipping and lifting to the long blue swell of the Indian Ocean . . .

Olivia, tiptoeing in an hour later, found her writhing in pain, her face trickling with a cold sweat that had nothing to do with the humidity of the hot little room, and her teeth clenched hard on her knuckles to stop herself from crying out. She looked up with eyes that were dilated with agony and desperation, but did not speak because she was afraid of screaming, and Olivia gave a gasping sob and ran from the room.

She was back again almost immediately, and this time Thérèse was with her, and neither of them said anything. They lifted her up and held a cup to her mouth, and Hero drank from it with chattering teeth, and grimaced at the taste because there were drugs in it and it was not a particularly pleasant brew.

The pain slackened a little and she lay back and breathed deeply again, but the respite was brief, for it returned with renewed savagery, and she bit on her hand while the sweat broke out on her forehead and ran down her face, blinding her eyes. She was aware of Olivia's trembling hands on her wrists while Thérèse sponged her tormented body with cold water, and presently of their voices whispering urgently above her head.

Olivia seemed to be urging that they send for Dr Kealey at once, and Thérèse that they should wait. And of course Thérèse was right, thought Hero, feeling a brief diminution of the pain and letting her hand fall from her mouth. The doctor was far too busy to be worried by further calls, and there was very little that he could do for her beyond recommending a further dose of the mixture they had just given her. In any case he would be here before dark, because he always came twice a day even though his wife was still sick. And meanwhile the laudanum was taking effect, for when the next bout of pain tore at her it was more bearable.

There was more low-voiced conversation above her head, and presently Hero heard Olivia's skirts swish on the matting and the door close behind her, and she opened her eyes and looked at Thérèse who was standing beside the bed; and saw none of the panic that had been in Olivia's face and hands that had inevitably added to her own fear. Thérèse was looking oddly drawn and bitter, but not in the least frightened, and she smiled palely at Hero and said in a hard emotionless voice: 'You do not need to alarm yourself. In a little while it will be over.'

For the last hour or so, ever since the pain had started, Hero had not been able to frame the word 'Cholera' even to herself. It was as though she dared not admit it for fear that once she did so it would be true, while as long as she refused to consider it, it could not be. But now, looking at Thérèse's calm, cold face, she found that she could speak of it after all, and that to do so made it less frightening:

She said: 'I guess I – I caught it from one of those people in the Black Town. Rory said that . . . if I did . . . it would serve me right. It is cholera, isn't it?'

Thérèse shook her head. Inexplicably, there was scorn in her face as well as bitterness; and something else too: something that was very like envy. She said harshly: 'It is not so bad as that. Do you really not know what it is? No . . . no, I see that you do not!'

She turned away angrily and struck her hands together, and Hero reached out and caught her skirt and tugged at it so that she was forced to turn back.

'What is it, Thérèse?'

'It is nothing to be afraid of,' said Thérèse stonily. 'I can tell you that, because to me it has happened twice – to my great sorrow. But for you it cannot be a sadness that you lose this child. You will have others.'

She saw the slow, painful colour stain Hero's white cheeks, and watched it fade again, and presently she said with a palpable effort: 'Do you wish that I should send for him?'

'No! He mustn't know!' There was stark panic in Hero's voice. 'He must never know – never! Promise me, Thérèse?'

'But you are affianced! Surely it is only right that he should——'

'Affianced? Oh – oh, you mean Clay. But it isn't——' She caught her breath and coloured again, but this time more painfully.

'Mon Dieu!' whispered Thérèse in sudden startled comprehension. 'So that is it! Yes. I had heard some wild tale, but I did not believe . . . I did not think . . . Ma pauvre petite!'

Hero looked up at her changed face and thought fleetingly: She thought it was Clay. So she does love him! Oh, poor Thérèse! Then the pain caught her again, and she raised herself on the pillows and said in a desperate, gasping voice: 'Thérèse, do something! There must be something one can do to stop it. Don't let me lose it!'

Thérèse stared at her open-mouthed; unable for a moment to believe that she had heard aright or understood what she had heard. 'You mean——? But, *ma chère*, it is a great mercy for you that this has happened. You cannot wish to have this child!'

'Yes, I do! I didn't think I would: I thought . . . But I do! I want it. I mustn't lose it. You don't understand!'

'I think perhaps I do,' said Thérèse slowly.

'You can't. No one could! I don't even understand it myself.'

'We are both women,' said Thérèse dryly. 'Does he know?'

Hero shook her head. 'No . . . and he *must* not! This is something that I want for myself. That is why——' Her face twisted to another spasm of agony, and when she could speak again she said imploringly: 'Isn't there anything you can do? There must be something. *Please*, Thérèse!'

'It is too late to do anything. But you are young, and you will——' She pulled herself up sharply, realizing that in the circumstances this was hardly a suitable observation to make.

It was all very strange, thought Thérèse, and very surprising . . . She wondered if one ever really knew about other people. Or even about oneself . . .

After a moment she said instead: 'It will be over soon. And I think it is best that we do not speak of this to Olivia – or to anyone else. No?'

'No,' agreed Hero. And began to cry: the slow tears forcing themselves under her closed eyelids and running down her face to drip on the pillow.

Thérèse had been right when she said that it would soon be over. It was over little more than an hour later; and Hero had kept to her room for two more days, and then left it because the ever increasing number of children needed every pair of hands that could be mustered to care for them. And though the time came soon enough when she was forced to admit that the house could contain no more, by then several charitably disposed persons in the city had offered their own houses, and close on four hundred children were being sheltered and fed.

There had been no message from her uncle or Clayton, and she knew that neither of them would find it easy to forgive her for walking out of the Consulate with Rory Frost. But they had sent something a great deal better: money and food and clothing. As had Majid, from the rural seclusion to which he had retired in the hope of escaping the plague that was decimating his Island, and from where he sent all the help he could to The Dolphins' House, together with a message congratulating Rory on his escape, and another to Miss Hollis and her helpers, thanking them for the good work they were doing.

Cholé too had sent gifts of fruit, vegetables and grain; though no messages, since it was not in her nature to forgive an injury, and she would always hold the 'foreigners' responsible for the defeat of Bargash and the ruin of all her hopes. As for news, they relied largely on Dr Kealey and Thérèse, whose particular skills took them everywhere. It was from the former that Hero learned that two more members of her uncle's household had died of cholera – Fattûma and her partner in crime, Bofabi, who had both met a richly deserved end, brought down on their own heads by leaving the comparative safety of the Consulate to visit the latter's small-holding outside the city, where he overworked the slaves he had purchased with Hero's money, and where they had contracted the disease.

Millicent Kealey had at last recovered from her illness and now spent the greater part of the day working at The Dolphins' House, and Colonel Edwards not only supplied them with fresh vegetables from his own garden, but also purchased a herd of goats who were milked daily under his own eye, the milk then being personally delivered to Hero. 'Good stuff in that girl,' declared Colonel Edwards – which was generally recognized to be praise of a high order.

The Colonel had accepted without comment the fact that Captain Frost was at large again and living openly at The Dolphins' House. There would, in any event, have been little use in attempting to get him re-arrested while the cholera raged in the city, and Colonel Edwards had too much sense to consider it. He had even – and of necessity – spoken to the Captain on several occasions, and had once actually been heard to remark to Olivia Credwell that the fellow couldn't be quite as black as he was painted, and perhaps there was something to be said for him after all; though damned little.

Time enough, thought Colonel Edwards, to consider what to do about Frost when the epidemic was over: always supposing that they both survived it, for as yet it showed no signs of abating. The cholera still claimed its victims in the city and in every village throughout Zanzibar: from houses, hovels and palaces; on the anchored dhows and the ships of the Sultan's fleet. And as yet no man could see the end – certainly not the Colonel. There was nothing to do but work and hope. And pray.

There had, inevitably, been deaths among the children in The Dolphins' House. But these had not totalled anywhere near the numbers that Dr Kealey had feared, and the majority were due to previous neglect and starvation. Five only had died of the cholera; and though the house and the garden, the courtyard, verandahs and outhouses and even the roof were so crammed with children that at times there seemed barely room to move, only nine had contracted it, of whom four had recovered. And the infection had not spread . . .

'It is a miracle!' declared Olivia.

'It is the mercy of the Mother of God, who has heard our prayers and taken pity on the children,' said Thérèse.

'Surely the hand of Allah and the favour of His Prophet is upon this house!' said Ralub. 'Praise be to the Rewarder!'

The warm rain fell and the Trade Wind blew, but always there was the close, humid heat, and when there were clear days and the sun blazed in a cloudless sky the temperature leapt until the very walls of The Dolphins' House were hot to the touch. But to Hero it was the clear nights that were the worst, for at least the falling rain swallowed up other sounds, and there was a certain soothing rhythm in its steady drumming. But on the white nights when the moon rode high and the wind slept, every sound was sharp in the stillness, and above the continual noise of restless children she could hear the barking of the pariah packs as they fought over the bodies that rotted on Nazimodo – that terrible spit of land where the poor of Zanzibar had, from time immemorial, driven out their dying animals to perish in order to save themselves the trouble of destroying them, and where they now left their dead. That sound was a constant reminder that the enemy was still among them, and that it might yet invade the house and destroy them all.

Thérèse went down with a sharp attack of fever and raved through one whole night in high-pitched rapid French, and Rory had ridden through the downpour to fetch Monsieur Tissot and a covered litter, the mud having made the roads impassable for a carriage, and Thérèse had been removed to her own house for fear of the fever taking hold among the children.

She had been back within a week, looking ten years older but as brisk and efficient as ever, and neither Hero nor Olivia, nor even Milly Kealey, who had suffered a return of boils and prickly-heat but ignored them and continued to work, had even noticed her pallor or her thin cheeks and sunken eyes, for they were all too thin and too pallid these days. And too busy to pay any attention to their personal appearance.

They were harassed and overworked and always tired, but Olivia at least was happy. She looked her age at last – and more than her age. But George Edwards did not seem to mind it, and he had taken to bringing her small nosegays of flowers and worrying about her health.

No one had ever worried about Olivia before. Or, for that matter, given her flowers. As for George, he had always looked upon himself as a confirmed bachelor and thanked God for it. That silly widow, Mrs Credwell, with her brassy yellow curls, suspiciously pink cheeks and gushing manner, had frankly terrified him. But Olivia, pale and hollow-eyed, her hair scraped back and hidden under a hastily tied kerchief, her dress covered with an enveloping apron and her arms full of negro babies, earned his unqualified approval and aroused in him a strong desire to cherish and protect her.

'They have a case, those two!' said Thérèse. 'And it is most suitable, I think. They will do very well, and I am surprised that no one has arranged it before.'

She looked sideways at Hero under her bristling black lashes: a long, speculative look. But Hero's face told her nothing. Hero was very quiet these days, and Thérèse had noticed that she never looked directly at Rory even when she was speaking to him, and that he, for his part, seemed to go out of his way to avoid her.

Well, that was as it should be, thought Thérèse with a sigh. No one could possibly consider that connection suitable, and nothing could ever come of it. She wondered what would happen when the epidemic had at last burned itself out, and the ships returned to harbour and the *Daffodil* came back? Would Dan and George Edwards arrest Rory Frost again, and send him off to face trial and imprisonment, if not the gallows? They were both consistent men and held inflexible views. But somehow she did not believe that they would take any further steps in the matter – beyond seeing that Rory left the Island as soon as the cholera epidemic was over. If it were ever over!

There were times when Thérèse could see no end to it, and when she wondered if it would continue to rage until at last all of them were dead, and the Island was swept clean of men and given back to flowers and green jungle – and peace.

Men, thought Thérèse (who liked them), *are truly abominable!* And she looked at Hero again and saw that she was surreptitiously watching Rory, who was standing in the courtyard below supervising the stretching of a piece of canvas that had come adrift last night.

'Not only abominable, but devoid of understanding!' said Thérèse aloud; and shrugged and went away to see that the pans in which the milk was boiled had been properly scoured, and that the hot liquid was not then cooled by the addition of unboiled water.

But the cholera had reached its peak and was already on the wane; though it was to be a good many days before any of them realized that. It had taken the lives of over twenty thousand of the Sultan's subjects, left whole villages empty and destroyed more than two-thirds of the population of Zanzibar. But now, at last, its grip began to slacken and men began to hope again.

There came an evening, after a day of brooding heat and curious stillness, when a great storm swept down upon the Island. All through the night that followed the wind shrieked like a thousand banshees, driving torrents of rain before it and piling up gigantic waves that rushed upon the beaches and deluged the town in flying spray. It snapped the trunks of palm trees as though they were no more than rotted twigs, laying waste

531

whole acres. Stripped the fruit and flowers and leaves from orange groves and clove plantations, and drove the tide in upon the creek behind the town so that the water rose to within a foot of the Darajani Bridge and flooded the houses on either side of it.

It raged for the best part of two days, and then died as suddenly as it had arisen. And with the morning the sun rose in a clear sky, the air was cooler than it had been for months past, and the creek and the beaches had been swept clean of the bodies that had defiled them.

The monsoon had ended. And with it the cholera. For the storm that had roared across the Island, cleansing the streets of foulness and carrying the dead out to sea, seemed to have taken the sickness with it, and the long nightmare was over.

In the garden of The Dolphins' House the ground was littered with torn leaves and broken branches, but the high wall that surrounded it had protected it from the full force of the gale, and most of the tents and shelters that had been erected there still stood, and were soon made habitable again. The courtyard had been flooded to a depth of six inches, a few shutters had been broken and two children had received superficial cuts from splinters of flying glass when one of the windows blew in. But apart from the fact that those who had been under canvas had been hurriedly crammed into the already grossly overcrowded rooms, The Dolphins' House had suffered very little from the storm, and the cooler weather and bright sunshine that followed it were worth all the anxiety of those two wild days.

The land breeze still carried the smell of the dead from the burial ground beyond the creek, as it would carry it for many weeks to come, and the wild dogs who had feasted on Nazimodo, finding themselves short of food, took to roaming through the streets by night, snatching children from doorsteps and attacking any man who walked alone. But dogs could be beaten off with firearms and cudgels, and were not an invisible enemy like the cholera.

Zanzibar licked its wounds and counted its dead, and according to its several faiths gave thanks to Allah and a variety of gods and demons for deliverance. Life began to return to normal, and parents, grandparents and relatives who had brought children to The Dolphins' House claimed them again, and the rooms began to empty.

'What are we going to do with the ones who haven't anyone at all, and whom no one wants?' asked Olivia, watching Mustapha Ali close the front door on a gaunt woman who had just claimed two small children. (They were, she had said, the orphaned sons of her only sister who had died with her husband and his family in the epidemic, and she had snatched them away as though she feared they would be kept from her.)

'Keep them here,' said Hero. 'We could start a school and teach them useful crafts, so that when they grow up they will be able to support themselves.'

Thérèse looked at her scornfully, but with affection and a certain envy for that capacity to see things as simple and right when they were in reality difficult and very complicated, and often impossible to resolve. 'Myself, I do not think there will be any left,' said Thérèse.

'But there are. There must be! Lots of them lost everyone, and no one even knows who they belonged to.'

'That is true. But I think you will find that they will all be claimed.'

'I don't understand?'

Thérèse's smile was a little wry. 'No, *chérie*. That is plain. But there are now many people who have lost sons and daughters and grandchildren, and have no one to care for them and work for them when they are old. There are also others who need slaves. These will come here, as that woman has done, saying "This one is the child of my brother who is dead, and I am now his only relative and will take care of him." And who is to say that it is true – or false?'

'But that's terrible!' Hero's eyes were wide with horror. 'We can't let them do that. We must stop her!'

She turned as though she would run after the woman who had just left, and Thérèse caught her arm and pulled her back. 'No, Hero. That one at least spoke truth, for the children knew her and went with her gladly.'

'Why, yes, I'd forgotten that. Oh what a fright you gave me! But after this we must insist on proof.'

'You will not get it. How can they produce proof? Some perhaps, but only a few. And if even *one* finds that a child is withheld, they will screech that you are plotting to steal it yourself, and raise a tumult against us all. It is true what I tell you! Already there have been stories. Did you not see how that woman looked at us? and how she snatched at the children and left in great haste? They were willing to let you keep and feed all the children you could while the cholera raged, but now it is over they will behave as though it is this house that has the plague and they who must rescue the little ones from it. You will see! – *Bon gré, mal gré!*'

'I shall insist on proof,' said Hero stubbornly.

But she had not done so. Dr Kealey and Colonel Edwards, Batty, Ralub and Dahili had all advised her against it, for they too had heard the whispers in the bazaars, and they knew the East; and Zanzibar.

Rory had been her last hope, for he had supported her against Uncle Nat and Clay and allowed her to fill his house with homeless children, and but for him none of this could have happened. But he too had sided with the others: 'They're right,' said Rory, 'and you're going to have to accept it whether you like it or not. At least you know that no child will be turned out to starve. They'll have homes – of a sort – and food and a roof over their heads. And thanks to you and the others, they are alive. You'll have to be content with that.'

'I didn't think *you'd* be afraid of a lot of superstitious natives,' said Hero bitterly.

'Didn't you? Well, you were wrong. I am. I have no desire to have my house stormed by a mob of hysterical citizens who have persuaded themselves that you are murdering babies in order to melt down their fat to use in some form of Western magic, or that I am castrating small boys in order to ship them to Arabia to sell as eunuchs.'

He saw the white shock on Hero's face, and laughed.

'It astonishes me,' said Rory, 'that after all you've been through and all you've seen, you are still capable of being shocked by a plain statement of fact. Do you mean to say that in all your researches into the iniquities of the slave trade, you never came across the information that hundreds of boys are made into eunuchs every year, to be sold as such? Or that thousands of little girls are bought by jaded old men who have a taste for youth? I suppose such matters are considered too crude to be mentioned before ladies. But they're true all the same, and the sooner you realize it, the sooner you'll come around to realizing that the population of Zanzibar is not merely being superstitious when it begins to wonder what I intend to do with a profitable houseful of small children.'

Hero said in a choked voice: 'Did you . . . did you ever——?'

'No. I have my limitations, and they do not include trafficking in children. But Zanzibar wouldn't know that – or care. They know I've run slaves, and that's enough. I'm sorry, Hero, but you're going to have to disband your orphanage and that's all there is to it. Don't take it too hard. You did your best.'

'I "did what I had to do",' said Hero; but not as though she were speaking to him.

She had not thought of old Biddy Jason's prophecy for a long time, and now suddenly it came into her head again, and the familiar words repeated themselves for the hundredth time . . . or the thousandth——

'You'll have a hand in helping a power of folk to die, and a sight more to live . . . and you'll get hard words for the one and no thanks for the other . . .' It had all come true after all. And it was Rory, and not Clayton, who was the one who had helped her to do both . . .

If Rory had not sold a cargo of rifles, and she had not helped to smuggle them into Beit-el-Tani, there might never have been a battle at *Marseilles*.

And if he had not offered her asylum, she could not have saved the children. There was only the gold . . .

Rory said: 'What are you thinking of?'

Hero returned to the present with a start, flushed and said: 'Nothing,' and went away to help Dahili lay out mattresses to air in the sun.

40

Thérèse had gone back to her own home near the French Consulate.

'There is nothing more for me to do here, and my husband complains that his digestion suffers, for the cook – *est comme une vâche* unless one supervises him!' said Thérèse.

She had invited Hero to stay with her, but Hero had refused on the grounds that Olivia and Millicent Kealey had both issued similar invitations, and she had promised to accept one of those as soon as the future of the remaining children had been decided.

'It will be Millicent, then,' said Thérèse. 'For Olivia cannot take you upon her honeymoon. No bridegroom would permit it! You had better come to me, for Milly is a woman with the heart of gold and all else of a dullness insupportable. But I will not press you. The offer remains.'

She kissed Hero and left, and the house seemed a great deal emptier without her.

Olivia stayed; though more for the sake of propriety than for any other reason, for there was little to do and that little was adequately attended to by the women of the household. But there had been no word as yet from Nathaniel Hollis, and since Hero made no move to leave The Dolphins' House, she could hardly be left there unchaperoned.

'But you will have to leave some time,' said Olivia. 'Are you sure you would not rather come back with me now? Hubert says he would be only too delighted, and you could help me with my trousseau. Not that one can get much here, but George says that we can go shopping for anything we need at Cape Town, and we are going home via Paris – he is *so* good to me. Oh, Hero, I am so happy!'

'You deserve to be,' said Hero; who privately considered George Edwards to be unendurably dull and could not imagine how anyone – even a widow in her thirties! – could possibly contemplate having to live with him for the rest of her life.

But Olivia went about in a daze of rapture, while Colonel Edwards became visibly younger and less hidebound every day, and patently considered himself unbelievably lucky to have found, so late in life, both love and a woman as admirable in every way as his lost Lucy.

There were times when the sight of their happiness made Hero feel lonely and restless and acutely dissatisfied with life, and listening to Olivia's glowing plans for the future, her own future seemed to stretch in front of her like a dull road that led nowhere. It was at these times that she took refuge in feverish activity; inspecting the kitchen quarter to make sure that it was being kept clean and that Ifabi had not forgotten to boil the children's milk, or worrying Jumah to step up the campaign against flies and see to the mending of the broken shutters. But now only five little orphans remained, and as these had already been absorbed into the household there was no longer any real work for her to do: or any reason for her to stay. She knew that she must go. If not tomorrow, then the next day. Or next week. But it would have to be soon, for there were foreign ships in the harbour again, and one of them had brought mail from the Cape and another letters from Aden, and soon the women and children who had left on the *Daffodil* would be back – and so would the *Norah Crayne*. But neither Cressy nor Aunt Abby would be returning. Or Dan Larrimore either.

The mail had brought news that reached Hero through Olivia, who had heard it from George Edwards who had been told it by Nathaniel Hollis. Dan's father had died of a stroke, and a letter telling of his death, together with one granting his son a year's leave of absence to settle his affairs, had arrived at the Cape only two days after the *Daffodil* had docked there.

There had been a ship sailing for England within the week, and Dan and Cressy had pleaded to be allowed to marry immediately so that she might go with him. Aunt Abby had remained adamant for three whole days, and then finally given way to their entreaties; so Cressy was now Lady Larrimore, and if not already in England would be there shortly. And as there seemed little point in Aunt Abby making the long voyage back to Zanzibar only to leave again on the *Norah Crayne*, she had elected to stay where she was and await the arrival of Nat and Clay and dear Hero at the Cape, from where they could all take passage on an East-Indiaman or one of the new steamships of the Peninsular and Oriental Steam Navigation Company, and proceed to England for a short stay with the newly married pair before returning to Boston.

'Isn't it *wonderful*?' sighed Olivia, her eyes brimming with sentimental tears. 'Dear, *dear* Cressy! I am sure she will be truly happy. And I *must* tell you – George has heard that he is to go as District Commissioner to Lunjore, in India, and can take long leave before taking up the appointment. So we too shall be sailing on the *Norah Crayne*, because his replacement will be arriving next week. We thought at first that we might be married on board by that nice Captain Fullbright, but now we think we shall wait until we reach Cape Town and have a proper church wedding. Hubert is accompanying us so that he can escort Jane and the children back here, and he will give me away, and you of course, dearest Hero, must be my bridesmaid. Unless you are married first, and then I will be yours, for I am *sure* you will make it up with Clayton and everything will come right for you.'

Olivia was so happy that she wanted everyone else to be equally happy, and it disturbed her to think that the breach between Hero and her betrothed was still unbridged, and that Nathaniel Hollis showed no sign of relenting toward his niece. She urged George Edwards to speak to Mr Hollis on Hero's behalf, and though the Colonel was strongly averse to interfering in other people's private affairs he had, in the end, reluctantly done so: and with gratifying results.

Uncle Nat, who had never yet been known to go back on his word, swallowed his pride and sent to tell his niece that he would like to see her. Though even then he would not come himself to The Dolphins' House and he had not written, but only sent a verbal message by Colonel Edwards.

'I hope you will go, my dear,' said Colonel Edwards, who had developed a fatherly affection for this girl whom he had once considered to be both tiresome and unwomanly. And he had added, somewhat unexpectedly: 'Don't be too hard on him.'

Hero imagined that he referred to Uncle Nat, but George Edwards had been thinking of Clayton. And it was Clayton and not Uncle Nat who awaited her in the drawing-room at the Consulate.

'I was afraid you wouldn't come for me,' admitted Clay, 'and I wanted to see you alone, and not in Frost's house where there would have been a crowd of people to distract you. Besides, I thought they might not let me in.'

She had actually not recognized him for a moment and thought that it was some stranger who stood there, for his broken nose altered his Byronic good looks in a startling fashion, though the effect was not unpleasing. He was still a handsome man and always would be; but the broken nose added character to a face which had previously lacked it.

He had changed too, in other ways; for no one who had lived through the terrible holocaust of the last two and a half months had been un-affected by it. For better or worse the horror of those weeks; the sights and sounds, the sickening, inescapable stench and the fear; had changed them all.

'I've been thinking——' said Clay.

He had thought to some purpose, and now, once again, he asked Hero to marry him. Not for any of the reasons that had seemed good to him before, but only if she herself felt in need of a refuge and protection, and because he sincerely wished to offer her both.

'I reckon I'm not much of a fellow,' admitted Clay ruefully, 'and I know darned well you could do a whole heap better for yourself. I've done

538

a lot of things – and thought plenty more – that were pretty low-down and that I'm sorry for. But if you feel you could marry me after all, I'd do my damnedest to make you happy. It would be a real privilege to do so. I mean that, Hero. I truly mean it.'

'I know,' murmured Hero; because there was something in his eyes and face and his voice that had never been there before, and that she recognized as sincerity. She wondered why she should never have noticed its absence before, and supposed that she must be growing up. Which was a humbling thought, for she had prided herself on being adult from the age of fifteen.

Looking soberly at Clay she realized that he too had been young and careless, but that his youth had died in the epidemic as surely and almost as painfully as any of the victims it had claimed. Yet she did not believe that he had changed very much.

There were two people in Clay. His wild, dissolute father and his humdrum, home-loving mother. The first had had its fling, and it was always possible that the other might take over, and that one day Aunt Abby's son would become one of those men who, while liking to boast that they were gay dogs in their day, look back on their own escapades as mere boyish devilry, and conveniently forgetting that they ever strayed into forbidden territory, loudly deplore the immorality and dishonesty of the rising generation. Yet even then she doubted if he would ever be able to resist temptation, whether it came in the form of easy money or women.

Clayton said urgently, breaking the long silence: 'I'd be good to you, Hero. And if – if there is a child, his child, I swear I'll try and care for it as much as if it were my own. Because it will be yours. And because it was my fault, all of it. If I hadn't . . . But there's no sense in going over all that again. I just want you to know that I know I was responsible, and that I'll do everything I can to make up for it.'

But there was not going to be a child and now was the time to tell him so. Only all at once it was unimportant, and she said instead: 'Do you love me, Clay?'

'Why, sure. What I mean is, well I'm——'

But Hero had seen the answer to that question in his face before he spoke, and she laid a hand on his arm, checking him, and said quickly: 'You don't have to say anything, Clay. I shouldn't have asked you that, because I know that you don't; I guess I've always known. Not in the – in the way I mean it. And without that, none of the rest is enough.'

'I don't know how you mean it. But I'm very fond of you, and I'd do my best to make up to you for all you've been through. And at least you'd be safe. There won't be any talk, because as my wife . . .'

But Hero was not listening to him any more. She was discovering with amazement that she did not want to be safe: that she did not care how many people talked or did not talk——

She said hurriedly, cutting across something that Clay was saying about 'respect and devotion', 'I'm very grateful to you, Clay, and I'm sure you would be good to me. If I loved you I'd take advantage of you and say "Yes", which would be mean of me, because one day you would meet someone you could truly love, and find yourself tied to me: and never forgive me – or yourself. But I don't love you so I can't do it. And I'm not going to have a child, so you don't have to worry about me.'

'You're in love with him!' said Clay abruptly.

Hero stared at him without replying, and was suddenly very still. It was a totally unexpected statement and one that presented her with an answer to something that, curiously enough, she had never even thought of asking herself. Perhaps because it was so patently impossible. Faced with it now, her instinct was still to reject it immediately and with anger. But she did not do so. She considered it instead for a long while and in silence, and when at last she spoke there was astonishment in her voice, and an odd note of wonder:

'Yes,' said Hero slowly. 'Yes, I guess I am.'

Clay said harshly: 'You can't possibly marry him!'

'I know.'

'Well, thank God you've got that much sense! Has he asked you to?'

Hero shook her head, and Clay said: 'No, I don't imagine he would. He must have some sense of fitness! And in any case he'll be taken off to stand trial as soon as the *Cormorant* gets in, and if he doesn't swing he'll get ten years – if not twenty!'

'I don't believe it. They couldn't do that now. Not after all that's happened.'

'Why not? Old Edwards is a mighty stubborn man, and he's got a set of hard and fast ideas on the subject of justice. I guess he isn't going to pass them up just because Rory Frost let you use his house to keep a parcel of starving kids in. It'ud take a heap more than that to make him go back on his word! – you've seen enough of him to know that.'

'Yes,' said Hero slowly. 'I – I hadn't thought about it. It all seems so long ago. I'd forgotten . . .'

She thought of it now, and realized that Clay was right. The Colonel might be disposed to take a less rigidly censorious view of Rory Frost while the cholera raged and there were other and more immediately urgent matters to occupy his attention. But he was, as Clay had said, a stubborn man, and now that the epidemic was over he would not allow his personal feelings to interfere in any way with what he considered to be a straightforward question of justice. He had already passed judgement on Rory and he would not go back on that.

Clay said: 'I'm sorry, Hero. But it won't last. Once you're away from here you'll find you'll soon forget about him. You'll get over it.'

'I – guess so.'

'What do you plan to do?'

'I don't know, Clay. Go back to Boston I suppose – and forget all about it!' Hero's voice was suddenly bitter. 'I shall go to Ladies' Luncheons and Musical Evenings, and play whist and take a stall at the Church Bazaar, and behave myself. And forget about . . . about the sun and the rain and the salt water, and the "*men whose heads do grow beneath their shoulders——*"'

'What's that?' asked Clay, looking puzzled. 'What men are you talking about?'

'Nothing: just something that Papa once said to me when I was a little girl.'

'Oh, I see,' said Clay, who did not. 'Then you'll be coming back with us on the *Norah Crayne*?'

'I suppose so, if Uncle Nat doesn't mind.'

'Mind? Why should he mind? He'll be delighted. He's waiting to see you, but he let me see you first.'

'I'm glad. I was afraid he meant it; about never speaking to me again. I couldn't have borne that.'

'He was blazing angry with you for going off with Frost after what had happened. But he knows what you did during the epidemic, and he's real proud of you. He's waiting out on the terrace. I'll send him in to you.'

Uncle Nat had greeted her kindly enough, but his manner was distrait and he was looking old and worn and dispirited. The tragedy of the cholera epidemic had shaken him badly, and now there was this news that his only child was already married and gone to a strange country. Hero's behaviour was still a sore subject and one that he had no wish to discuss, and he confined himself to remarking that he guessed there were faults on both sides and least said soonest mended. He was, he said, sorry to hear that she had decided not to marry Clayton, but reckoned that in the circumstances she was probably right. They had both been through too much that they would not be able to forget, and maybe they would be happier apart. Hero must come back to the Consulate as soon as possible, and he hoped she would make arrangements to do so, because George Edwards, who had told him of the excellent work she had done during the epidemic, had also said that it was now virtually ended and there was no longer any reason why she should not return home.

'Let's you and me try and forget what's past and make a fresh start,' said Uncle Nat.

He kissed Hero's cheek, and murmuring something about files, returned to his office and did not see her leave. Two of the Consular servants escorted her back to The Dolphins' House, because she had refused to let Clay do so. Not that she thought there would be any further scenes if he should encounter Rory Frost, but it seemed better not to risk it. There was, after all, nothing left to be said, and no profit to be derived from vain repetitions and the repaying of violence with violence.

She walked in under the carved dolphins and past the beaming Mustapha Ali and thought: *This may be the last time.* Because five words of Clayton's had demolished the wall of pretence and evasion that she had so carefully constructed in order to hide from herself the fact that she had not been staying on for the sake of the remaining children, nor because Uncle Nat did not want her back and she was unwilling to impose on the kindness of Olivia or Thérèse or Millicent Kealey; nor for any of the other reasons that she had used as an excuse for not leaving The Dolphins' House. But simply and solely because of Rory.

There was good in Rory as well as bad: she knew that now. Yet neither the good nor the evil counted any longer, and it was this that was terrible to her. It frightened and humiliated her to find that a physical attraction (it could not be more than that!) was strong enough to make her hunger for the mere sight of a man whose code and conduct and way of life was detestable to her. '*Adventurer, black sheep, blackguard*' – a slave trader! It reduced her in her own estimation to the level of an animal, but though she could feel bitterly ashamed of it, she could not alter it; for he had awakened something in her that she had not known she possessed, and now it possessed her. It was like a virus in her blood – a fire and a raging thirst. She could not hear his voice without remembering it murmuring endearments, or look at his hands or his mouth without recalling the caressing touch of them: the slow delight of his kisses. '*One of Frost's women*' . . .

There was only one thing she could do, and that was to go away quickly; and now that Uncle Nat had asked her to return to the Consulate there was no longer any excuse for not doing so. '*If thy eye offend thee, pluck it out*' . . . But this was not just an eye. It was not so simple as that. A heart would be harder to pluck out. One could live without an eye: but without a heart——?

I must leave today, thought Hero. *I must leave at once* . . .

She went slowly up the winding stone stairways and along the verandahs that were empty now and echoed softly to the sound of her footsteps, and thought how beautiful the house was, and how familiar it had become. As familiar as Hollis Hill . . .

A door ahead of her opened and Batty Potter came out of a room at the turn of the verandah, his arms full of assorted garments and followed by Jumah, who was staggering under the weight of a large sea-chest. Hero stopped and enquired what they were doing.

'Packing,' said Batty dourly. ''Aven't you 'eard? We're off. The Captain's been give notice to quit.'

'To quit? You mean he's – you're going? But why? When? Where are you going, Batty?'

''Ome. So 'e says, and 'e wouldn't say it if 'e didn't mean it.'

'But I thought . . . Batty, what's happened? I don't understand——'

'S'easy enough. There's a new ship in with another barrel of mail that she picks up at the Cape, and the Colonel 'e gets word as 'is replacement is arriving in tuthree days, and 'oos a'bringing 'im but the *Cormorant*. And the *Cormorant*'s orders is to pick up Captain Rory and take 'im back to stand trial.'

'*No!* No, Batty! They mustn't – they can't——' Hero's voice was a whisper and she sat down with some suddenness on the sea-chest that Jumah had got tired of carrying. Knowing that they could, and feeling empty and helpless.

'Can't they!' said Batty and expectorated viciously. 'No knowing what them pig-'eaded barstids can't get up to! But the Colonel 'e comes round 'ere 'arf an hour back and tips Captain Rory the wink to light out quick; and stay out. Because if so be 'e ain't 'ere when the *Cormorant* puts in, then there ain't nothing they can do. And nothing more won't be said neither; 'e gives 'im 'is word on that. So they shake 'ands like gents, and there y'are.'

'You mean he's – the Colonel is going to let him get away? But why, Batty? I thought . . . It doesn't matter. Are you going with him?'

''Oo else? Yes, it's goodbye t'Zanzibar for Batty Potter. I'll miss the old place. But after what we seen 'ere lately I can't say as I'll be so sorry to leave. Not with Amrah gone. Though it's going to be 'ard to leave the 'Ajji and the rest of 'em – crool 'ard. Ah well, that's life, miss. "'Ere today and gone tomorrow!" You'll be going 'ome yourself, I fancy. If you wouldn't mind gettin' up off that ditty box, Jumah and me'll be getting these 'ere duds stowed. Thank you, miss.'

He stumped off down the verandah and Hero went slowly to her room and found Olivia there, also engaged in packing

'Oh, there you are, Hero. Is this yours, or is it one Thérèse left behind? No, it's Milly's – I remember I borrowed it. We have to leave, dear. George had another letter from the Cape this morning, and it seems that the *Cormorant*——'

'Yes,' said Hero. 'I know. Batty told me.' She sat down numbly on the bed and stared at Olivia, making no attempt to help her: 'He says they are going to leave before the *Cormorant* gets here. That Colonel Edwards told them to go and that nothing would be . . . I don't understand, Livvy. Why is George doing this?'

'Well it was really something that the Sultan said. Of course George says it is not an argument that would carry any weight in a court of law, but he thinks that there is enough on the credit side to make it balance – because he's been going over Dan's records and the official returns and things like that, and he says it adds up to quite an impressive total. In lives, I mean.'

'What lives? I don't—— Oh, you mean the children?'

'Well, I didn't, but now I come to think of it I suppose they would count too. No, George meant the slaves.'

'What slaves? What are you talking about, Olivia?'

'Captain Frost, of course. George said that he had no intention of going back on his word and meant to see that Rory Frost was taken away on the *Cormorant* – for of course he'd still have been here, because it seems that he once gave his word to George that he wouldn't escape, and you know what men are. Too ridiculous! But then the other day the Sultan said something rather odd; about other slavers doing better once he's gone even if the Navy didn't, and when George asked him what he meant, he told him the whole story, and that's how George found out.'

'Found out *what*?'

'That it was Rory Frost who was responsible. George says that a great many of the really bad slave ships that the *Daffodil* caught – the ones George calls "Hell ships" – were only caught because someone told on them. Where they were sailing from, and when, and things like that – so that Dan would know where to wait for them and be there at the right time and everything. So you see . . .'

'You mean – you mean that Rory told Dan?'

'Goodness, no! He only saw to it that he knew. Dan hadn't any idea who was behind it, and I don't think Captain Frost was at *all* pleased at being found out. In fact he was positively rude! He pretended not to know what George was talking about when he asked him straight out why he'd done it, but George had questioned Ralub and Mr Potter too, and they'd told the same story as Majid, so in the end he said any fool ought to know the answer to that: it was a plain matter of business, since it got rid of his rivals and improved his own prices. George became excessively cross and told him not to talk fustian, so then he laughed and said he had to admit it was only craven superstition. You don't happen to know where I put my straw bonnet, do you Hero? The one with the bunches of daisies on it?'

'No, I don't. What did he mean by "craven superstition"?'

'I quite thought I'd put it—— Yes, here it is! Oh, he said he "made it a practice to keep something on the credit side of the ledger, so that he'd have a sop to throw to his conscience in the unlikely event of its ever giving him any trouble"; and besides, he didn't like pointless brutality or brutal fools. Something like that. But George says that whatever his reasons were, the fact remains that he must have been responsible for freeing at *least* forty or fifty negroes – and probably far more! – for every one he sold himself, so that the balance is really in his favour. Which one can quite see – though Captain Frost said there was a flaw in that logic that was wide enough to sail the *Great Eastern* through. I can't think what he meant, but George said he was well aware of it and he still felt justified in doing his own arithmetic. And he says he can make it all right with the authorities, which I own is a great relief. I could not have *borne* to think that it was George who had done it – after all that has happened. Had him hanged, I mean – if he *was* hanged. And on our honeymoon, too! Well, I mean, a person one has come to like and have confidence in . . . It would have been too dreadful.'

'So – they are going,' said Hero numbly.

'Yes. I suppose they'll hate leaving this house; and Zanzibar. Though I should think that the others will all be able to come back one day: his crew, I mean. But George says that Rory Frost will have to keep away and that he'll be all right as long as he does, and that he's really very lucky. They're going to leave on the *Virago* tomorrow morning, so I said that you and I would stay here tonight and help with the packing. Men are *never* any good at it: they just throw things in and sit on the lid. And as they won't be coming back, or not for years, there will be a great deal to do. It's a pity they haven't got a little more time, but George says that if the *Cormorant* . . . Here's *another* of Milly's petticoats! We'd better make a separate parcel. Will you be going back to your uncle's house now?'

She had to repeat the question twice, for Hero did not seem to have heard it.

'What? Oh – oh, yes. He says I may go back whenever I wish.'

'Then you've made it up! Oh, Hero darling I'm *so* glad for you. And what about Clayton? You are going to marry him after all?'

'No. We decided that it would be better not to. I think he was relieved. I guess I'm not really his kind of woman, and he – he isn't my kind of man.'

'Why not? I should have thought . . . Well, perhaps not. No, I see what you mean.'

Olivia sighed, frowned, and presently said hopefully: 'Oh well, you are sure to find the right one some day. Like I have.'

* * *

Rory, having visited Majid, had been down to the harbour, and returning some hours later to The Dolphins' House he found Hero in the long upper room, kneeling on the floor to help Ifabi pack one of the carved camphorwood chests.

She had not heard him, because the white cockatoo was flapping its wings and screeching and Ifabi was chattering, and he stood in the doorway for a moment, watching her and wishing that he was not so acutely aware of being in love with her and that it was possible to make some other decision than the one his emotions were forcing upon him.

Half an hour ago the matter had been cruelly simple, for there had been nothing to decide. But a brief conversation on the waterfront had changed all that, and walking back from the harbour he had fought a battle with himself, and lost it. This was defeat; and if he needed proof, he had it, for although he had made no sound, Hero's head jerked round almost instantly, and he knew that she had been aware of his presence as surely as he too would always be aware of hers.

For a long moment that had no measure in time they looked at each other, steadily and with something that was almost hostility. Then Rory said abruptly: 'I've had a boat sent round to the water-steps at the bottom of the garden. Will you come out with me for an hour or so? There is something I want to show you, and this seems about the last chance I shall get.'

He came into the room and held out a hand to help her to her feet as though he were confident that she would not refuse, and Hero looked at it without making any attempt to take it or to disguise her reluctance to do so.

'What's the matter? Are you afraid?' gibed Rory. 'You needn't be; Batty's coming with us. And if you insist, we'll take Olivia. Though I'd far rather not, for she tells me she's a poor sailor and there's a reasonable breeze blowing.'

Why not? thought Hero. This time tomorrow he would be gone. It would all be over and ended. The Dolphins' House would be empty and Batty too would have gone – and Ralub and Jumah and Hadir and the *Virago* – sailing out into the wide blue wastes of the Indian Ocean and out of her life for ever. There was no reason why she should not go. It would be the last time . . .

She would not take his proffered hand because she was afraid of touching him, but she rose and said composedly: 'There is no need to trouble Olivia. If you will wait a moment, I will get a hat.'

It was mid-afternoon and the sun glittered blindingly on the dancing sea, sending nets of gold shivering down through the glass-clear water to entangle the fish and the branching coral. The wind that shrilled through the sheets and sang in the taut canvas no longer smelt of corruption, and Hero screwed up her eyes against the sun-glare and the flying spray and was silent.

She had not needed to ask where they were going, for once past the harbour, she knew. They were going to *Kivulimi*; though she did not know why Rory should wish her to see it again, unless it was to remind her of something he must know very well she would not forget. He had told her that himself – 'It's nice to know that you are unlikely to forget me.' Tomorrow he would be gone; and however long she lived and however hard she tried, she would not be able to forget him.

The tall, misshapen rocks of wind-worn coral came slowly into view, and beyond them the sheltered beach that she had first seen by starlight without knowing that this was her first sight of Zanzibar. The sun was lower now, and already there was an evening quality in the warm glow that shone on the ancient fortress wall and the tall Arab house that rose up behind it among a green foam of trees.

Behind them in the city, and in villages scattered all over the island, more than twenty thousand people had died since she had last been here. But looking at The House of Shade it was difficult to remember that, for here time appeared to have stood still. The garden was green and cool and smelled sweetly of jasmine and late roses, and once again there were pigeons cooing among the shadows. It was the same as the first time she had seen it – and the last.

Rory did not take her up to the house. He sent Batty there to speak to Daud, and led her instead along the narrow path that lay parallel to the outer wall, stopping in front of one of the stone cells that were half concealed by curtains of bougainvillæa, trumpet-flower and morning glory. He lifted aside the trails of creeper so that Hero could go in, and she obeyed him reluctantly. Mystified and a little apprehensive.

The place smelt of damp earth and mildew, and the light that filtered through the hanging curtain of leaves was green and aqueous. She felt the skin prickle on her arms and the back of her neck and was suddenly conscious of an acute feeling of disquiet: an animal awareness of evil, as though there was something dangerous lurking in the dimness of the small stone cell that she could sense but not see.

A lizard scuttled away across a drift of fallen leaves and she drew back with a sharp intake of breath, and saw for the first time that the thing Rory carried was not a stick but a short iron crowbar. She heard it clink against the stone, and said uncertainly: 'Why have you brought me here? What is it you want me to see?'

'This,' said Rory briefly, thrusting the sharpened iron into a crack that he must have known was there, since he could not have seen it under the dust and the leaf mould. The stone came out with surprising ease and he laid the crowbar aside and took a candle and a box of matches out of his pocket.

The small flame leapt and wavered in the draught, striking sparks from the gleaming pile of yellow metal, and Hero forgot her fear of spiders and scorpions, and kneeling on the dank stone, touched the cold ingots with incredulous fingers.

'What is it?'

'Gold,' said Rory.

'But ... but ... It must be worth a fortune! How did it get here? Did you find it?'

'In a way,' said Rory laconically.

He blew out the candle and returned it to his pocket, and taking Hero's arm lifted her to her feet and led her back into the sunlight:

'It belonged to Majid's father——' began Rory. And told her the tale of Sultan Saïd's hidden treasure and of how he had come by the gold.

He made no excuses and softened no details, and Hero listened and winced; watching his face as he told it and glancing from time to time at the crimson veil of bougainvillæa, as though it hid not only a fortune but the wrinkled, malevolent face of the witch-doctor from Pemba who had died because of it, and cursed it in dying.

'That's all,' said Rory at last.

Hero shivered and said in a low voice: 'Why did you tell me that?'

'I thought you ought to know.'

'Why? Why did you want me to see it?'

'You once told Batty that someone had said that you'd one day have a great fortune in gold. Well, there it is, if you want it. Shall we take it or leave it? We haven't got much time in which to decide.'

'We?' said Hero.

'Who else? You didn't think I'd leave you behind, did you?'

The sun slid down below the level of the outer wall and the garden was suddenly in shadow; and it was no longer afternoon but evening. The wind was blowing less strongly now and would die with the twilight, and already the birds were coming home to roost. Soon it would be night ...

There will be a moon tonight, thought Hero. The garden would be white with moonlight, as it had been on that other night. And on hundreds of other nights to come. Fireflies in the shadows and the scent of strange flowers; the sound of surf on a coral beach. '*Teach me to hear mermaids singing*' ... She was not thinking clearly. She must say something. She must tell him at once that it was impossible and that she had no intention of going with him. That it was an insult and an impertinence to even suggest such a thing. That oil and water ...

But life would never be dull with Rory, and the world would never seem small or parochial. There would always be wide horizons and a wind blowing. '*Sun and rain and salt water . . .*' She had thought once that if she married Clay she would be only half alive: an automaton. That the rest of her life would be flat and savourless and that she might just as well be dead. But she could not imagine anyone feeling dead in Rory's company. Or an automaton, or half alive.

'At least you will not be buying a fake' . . . Clay had said that; and he had been quoting her father who had known her as well as anyone had ever done, and who had once told Clay that if she should fall in love with an 'out-and-out no-good' with her eyes open, he would not raise much objection, but that it would destroy her to find that she had been 'tricked into marrying a rascal'. There was plenty of trickery about Rory Frost, thought Hero, remembering the rifles. But not in that way. And she would never be able to pretend that her eyes had not been open. Wide open . . .

She said: 'Where are you going?'

'To England.'

'But I thought——' Hero stopped short, and Rory gave a curt laugh.

'No, dear love, I haven't suffered a change of heart in that direction. But it's somewhere to go. Besides, I have a house there that I've always intended to take possession of one day, and now seems as good a time as any.'

'You mean you'd settle down and stay there?'

'For good? No. I like the world too much to stay anchored in one place, and I shall probably go off at frequent intervals to take another look at it.'

'And run slaves, and smuggle, and sell guns!' said Hero bitterly.

Rory's laugh held a tinge of regret. 'Not any more. Those were strictly bachelor pursuits and unsuitable for a sober married man. In future I shall try to keep on the right side of the law. Will that content you? Or must you have good works too? You'll find plenty of scope in England right on your own doorstep – the East hasn't got a monopoly of misery and squalor! And then there's myself. I don't think you'll be able to change me – or not much. But you can always try. Perhaps this is the work you have to do: making a useful and law-abiding citizen out of a no-account slave trader. It may sound a small matter compared to setting your neighbours' affairs to rights, but then charity, we are told, should begin at home. Why are you looking at me like that? What have I said?'

' "*The work that you have to do*",' said Hero. 'That was what *she* said: Biddy Jason. That I would always do the work that I had to do and – and that I would make my own bed, and lie on it.'

549

'We all do that, my dear darling.'

'I – I guess so . . . Cousin Josiah said that people ought to set their own affairs to rights before trying to settle other people's for them.'

'There you are, you see?'

'But you are not my affair and I don't have to marry you.'

'Not now,' said Rory. 'But you're going to marry me all the same – if I have to kidnap you all over again in order to see that you do! I thought once that you might have to, but when you lost the child I thought I'd lost my only chance with it, and that I might as well give up.'

'Who told you?' said Hero in a whisper. 'How did you know?'

'It was my house,' said Rory dryly.

'I – I see. Then why——?'

'Thérèse. I met her on the waterfront this morning. I'd just seen Edwards and I was feeling like cutting my throat. But when I told her that I'd got to leave at once she asked me if I was going to take you with me. I knew I shouldn't: that I ought to do the right thing – well the sensible thing anyway! – and get out and stay out. But . . . She said that you'd wanted that child and that you couldn't have done so unless you loved me. Did you want it?'

'Yes,' said Hero.

Rory put his arms about her and held her so hard against him that she did not know if it were his heart that she could feel beating or her own. But resting her head against his shoulder she knew that she had come home, because although he might never stay long in any one place, anywhere he happened to be would always be home to her. She would do the work that she had to do and lie on the bed she had made – because she no longer had the power to choose differently: and did not want it.

Rory said slowly, murmuring the words against her ear so that they seemed like an echo of her own thoughts: 'You are not in the least the sort of woman I could ever have imagined myself marrying. You are everything I didn't like and thought I couldn't endure. But somehow you've got into my blood and I can't get you out again – and I don't even want to.'

He took her chin in his hand and tilted her face up and kissed her. And knew that this was the end of a life he had loved and the beginning of a new one that was going to be very different, and probably very difficult: because he did not believe that people changed over-much in essentials, and Hero was unlikely to turn into a different person; and neither was he.

There would be times when she would remember his sins and throw them in his face, and others when he would resent her virtues and be exasperated by them – and by her. There was a part of Hero that he would never be able to possess, and part of himself that would always be beyond her reach. But for some unfathomable reason they were the right people for each other. They should not have been, but they were. Each supplied a crying lack in the other, and possibly Fate had known what it was about when it tipped Hero Hollis overboard in mid-ocean and permitted Emory Frost to rescue her . . .

'*God is a great deviser of stratagems,*' thought Rory, recalling with a smile one of Hajji Ralub's favourite quotations from the Koran. But the smile held more than a trace of wryness, for he had never intended to marry anyone. He had meant to stay free and without ties to the end of his life; and he had intended to see if he could not turn a frigid piece of Grecian marble into a warm flesh-and-blood woman, and had done so – and found that he could not live without her . . .

Batty Potter's hoarse voice addressed them from the shadows that were gathering in the garden:

'Well, are you takin' it or leavin' it? We ain't got much time.'

Hero turned her head and Rory released her without haste. She blinked at the old man as though awakening from a dream, and said:

'Taking what, Batty?'

'The gold, of course. Ain't that what 'e bring you 'ere for?'

'Oh that,' said Hero, and shuddered. 'No. We don't need it. Cover it up again.'

'*Ah!* – just what I says meself,' approved Batty. 'That yellow muck ain't 'ealthy. There's blood on it.'

Rory shrugged and said: 'All right: it's two to one. Put the stone back, Uncle, and we'll let it lie. Even if I never come back I still own this place, and maybe one day a son of mine will come here and find the stuff, and put it to better use than I would have done.'

'If 'e 'as the sense to take after 'is Ma,' observed Batty pointedly, ' 'e'll pull it out and pitch it into the sea. Best place for it!'

He ducked under the trails of bougainvillæa, and after a time re-appeared again, carrying the crowbar, and announced with relief that that was done, and good riddance. 'And now,' said Batty, 'I reckons we'd best be goin' before we loses the wind. There's a mort of work to be done before morning.'

They went out by the door in the outer wall, and the Trade Wind met them. Blowing from the south-east and smelling of cloves and the sea and strange flowers, and rustling the fronds of the coconut palms that fringe the white beaches of Zanzibar.

POSTSCRIPT

Back in the mid-fifties I was fortunate enough to be invited to Zanzibar, and as a result of my stay in that lovely island, I wrote a light-hearted 'whodunnit' entitled *The House of Shade*. Its plot hinged on certain papers left by a black-sheep ancestor of one of the characters: Emory Frost, one-time slave-trading owner of *Kivulimi*. Later on, after the publication of that book, it occurred to me that it would be interesting to try my hand at writing the story of this fictional Emory. The reason being that I had discovered a fabulous hoard of books about the slave trade, the Island and the Arabs from Oman in the little library of Zanzibar's British Club; read the lot and taken copious notes.

Trade Wind is that story. But for the benefit of readers who like the history in a historical novel to be reasonably accurate, I must confess to taking certain liberties in this one.

The attempt on Majid's life, the whole Bargash rebellion (except of course for the parts played in it by the fictional characters) and the way it ended, Salmé's elopement and the great cholera epidemic, really happened; and in that order. But over a period of years, whereas here I have compressed them into one year, for the sake of the story. The date of Hero's departure from Boston is therefore purely arbitrary, and should not be taken too seriously by students of Zanzibar's history. But the American Consulate really was besieged by the pirates from the Gulf, whose annual raids are also fact and not fiction, though my Consul and his family, and all the British, American and European characters in *Trade Wind*, with the exception of Wilhelm Ruete and Commander Adams, are pure invention and not intended to be portraits of any real persons. I have given to Dan Larrimore and H.M.S. *Daffodil* some of the parts played at that time, in real life, by Commander Adams of H.M.S. *Assaye* and Captain Oldfield of H.M.S. *Lyra*; for which piece of author's licence I hope the shades of those officers and their ships' crews will forgive me.

I am chiefly indebted to Salmé for the details of Saïd's life at Motoni, his death and the quarrels and plotting and rebellion that followed it, since she recorded it all in her autobiography, *Memoirs of an Arabian Princess*. But my thanks must also go to many more writers. Some of them modern, such as Genesta Hamilton and Christopher Lloyd; others, the authors of the old, musty volumes on a bottom shelf of the Club library, published long ago in the nineteenth century and — judging from the number of uncut pages — largely unread. These contained a treasure-trove of information on Zanzibar, and one of them gave a detailed and horrific eye-witness's account of the cholera epidemic – a far more gruesome one than I have given here. I heard later that when the Island ceased to be a British Protectorate and became independent, all the books in the library were removed and burnt; which, if true, is a tragedy, as the ones I read were all first editions and irreplaceable. Most, though not all, can be read in the British Museum. But it would have been nice to know that they were still available in Zanzibar. Maybe they are.

Any reader interested in what happened to Zanzibar's quarrelsome royal family may like to know that Bargash did, in fact, achieve his ambition. He became Sultan when Majid died, and one hopes that Cholé was still around to enjoy the fruits of his triumph. Majid's death at the early age of thirty-six was due, I regret to say, to over-indulgence in 'sensuality and stimulants' – aggravated, one suspects, by constant anxiety! But at least he was luckier than his brother Thuwani of Muscat, who was murdered three years earlier by his son Selim, who like too many of his family could not wait for a throne. As for Salmé, she did indeed see Zanzibar again (though that, as Kipling used to say, is another story). But sadly, her life with Wilhelm was all too short, for they had only been married for three years when he was killed in an accident, leaving her a widow with three small children to bring up. By then she was known as Frau Emily Ruete. When I was in Germany in 1964 – my husband, Major-General Goff Hamilton, having been posted to Bonn in the Federal Republic – I was enthralled to learn that one of her children, a daughter, was alive and living in that country. Naturally, I hoped very much that I might be allowed to meet her. But alas, she was not only too old, but too frail to have visitors; which was a great disappointment to me, as it would have been a tremendous privilege to actually meet and talk to the niece of Majid, Bargash and Cholé, and all the rest of those colourful children of the great Sultan Saïd, 'Lion of Oman'. May they rest in peace!

ABOUT THE AUTHOR

M. M. KAYE was born in India and spent much of her childhood and adult life there. She became world famous in 1978 with the publication of her monumental bestseller about India under the British Raj, *The Far Pavilions*. She is also the author of the bestselling *Shadow of the Moon*. Mollie Kaye is married to retired Major General Goff Hamilton, and it was during one of his assignments that she was first introduced to Zanzibar, the "Isle of Cloves" and the setting for *Trade Wind*. She and her husband now live in the English countryside not far from London.

THE LATEST BOOKS IN THE BANTAM BESTSELLING TRADITION

DON'T MISS
THESE CURRENT
Bantam Bestsellers

SPECIAL
MONEY SAVING
OFFER

Now you can have an up-to-date listing of Bantam's hundreds of titles plus take advantage of our unique and exciting bonus book offer. A special offer which gives you the opportunity to purchase a Bantam book for only 50¢. Here's how!

By ordering any five books at the regular price per order, you can also choose any other single book listed (up to a $4.95 value) for just 50¢. Some restrictions do apply, but for further details why not send for Bantam's listing of titles today!

Just send us your name and address plus 50¢ to defray the postage and handling costs.